KU-673-789

THE SECOND SEAL

DENNIS WHEATLEY

DENNIS WHEATLEY

THE SECOND SEAL

Frontispiece Portrait by
MARK GERSON

Original Illustrations by
ANTHONY MATTHEWS

Published by arrangement with
Hutchinson and Co. (Publishers) Ltd.

13 043 22 R1

To the memory of that fine soldier and friend,
the late:
Colonel H. N. Clarke, D.S.O., T.D.

For those good companions of my youth,
J. Albert Davis and Douglas Gregson:

and for those other Officers, N.C.O.s and Men with whom I had the honour to serve in the 2nd/1st City of London Brigade R.F.A. (T) from September 1914

"And when he had opened the second seal, I heard the second beast say, Come and see.

And there went out another horse that was red: and power was given to him that sat thereon to take peace from the earth, and that they should kill one another: and there was given unto him a great sword."

Revelation vi: 3 and 4.

CONTENTS

CHAPTER I

THE MAN IN THE TAXI

In April, 1914, the Dorchester Hotel was still unbuilt, unplanned, undreamed of. Instead, its fine triangular corner site, half-way up Park Lane, was occupied by Dorchester House, the London residence of Colonel Sir George and Lady Holford. A great, square, grey, Georgian mansion, it stood well back at the base of the triangle, its privacy secured by two low, curving wings, running outward from it, which contained stabling for forty horses and enclosed a spacious courtyard.

The London season had not yet begun, and in most of the Mayfair mansions nearby the covers that shrouded the furniture would not be removed till the first week in May; yet on this evening in mid-April every window in Dorchester House was ablaze with light. The Holfords had come up from the country early in order to entertain a Royal visitor. Her Imperial Highness the Archduchess Ilona Theresa, grand-daughter of old Franz Joseph, Emperor of Austria, was making a short stay in England, and in her honour they were giving a masked ball.

By a quarter to ten the courtyard in front of the house was a constantly moving medley of high-sprung motors and darkly gleaming private carriages. On the box of almost every vehicle a footman with folded arms sat beside the driver, and as they sprang down to fling open the doors of car or brougham the light glinted on their colourful liveries and cockaded top hats.

Inside the hall of the house a double line of flunkeys, with powdered hair, striped waistcoats and satin knee-breeches, were rapidly relieving the men of their coats, and conducting the women to the cloak-rooms, where they could put the finishing touches to their toilets and receive the black masks which would conceal their identities from all but those who knew them fairly intimately.

The men were in sober black and white, but the women rivalled the proverbial rainbow. Their gleaming necks and shoulders were set off by ropes of pearls and parures of diamonds: their many-hued dresses of silk, satin, and lace, fell smoothly to short trains. Hair was dressed high that season and crowned with sparkling tiaras, jewelled aigrets or paradise plumes. A king's ransom in gems scintillated on arms and corsage.

At a few minutes to ten a vehicle, strangely in contrast to its opulent companions in the queue, pulled up before the porch. It was one of the taxis that were rapidly replacing the hansoms and growlers on London streets, but the man who stepped from it showed no sign of embarrassment at having arrived in such a mediocre conveyance. Unhurriedly he paid off the driver, adding a generous tip: then, with the unconscious self-assurance that is the hallmark of good breeding, walked lightly up the steps.

He was in his middle thirties, somewhat above medium height, and a slim, delicate looking man; but the fragility of his appearance was deceptive. His nose was aquiline, his mouth a hard line, redeemed only by the suggestion of a humorous lift at its corners, and his aristocratic features had a slightly foreign cast. As he took off the glossy topper that he had been wearing at a somewhat rakish angle, the gesture disclosed dark hair and 'devil's' eyebrows that slanted upwards towards the temples of his broad forehead. Beneath them were grey eyes flecked with yellow: the directness of their glance indicated their mesmeric qualities, and at times they could flash with an almost piercing brilliance. He was known to both the police and crowned heads of several countries: his name was Jean Armand Duplessis, and he was the tenth Duc de Richleau.

On leaving the cloak-rooms the little parties of guests, now masked, were meeting again in the wide hall and passing slowly up one or other of the wings of the splendid horseshoe staircase, for which Dorchester House was famous, to be received by Sir George and Lady Holford on the first landing. As de Richleau joined the right hand queue he was wondering if, after all, he had not been a little foolish to go there.

He had arrived in London only the day before, and received the invitation solely because he had happened to run into Sir George, who was an old but not very intimate acquaintance of his, that morning at the Travellers' Club. It was some years since the Duke had been in England and to attend this big reception had seemed, at the time of Sir George's hospitable bidding, an excellent way to meet again a number of his old friends in London society who were almost certain to be present.

He realized now that he had paid insufficient attention to the fact that the party was to be a masked ball, and so would defeat his main object in attending it. The masking was no serious attempt to preserve the incognito of the guests, as there was no question of their wearing dominoes to conceal their clothes and figures, and they were even being announced by name as they were received at the top of the stairs: it was simply a device to dispense with formal introductions and thus add to the gaiety of the evening. But, while friends could easily recognize one another, de Richleau saw that it was going to be far from easy for him to identify people whom he had not met for several years.

Having greeted his host and hostess, he consoled himself with the thought that masks would be removed at midnight. So, reconciled to seeking such amusement as he could find till then, he passed into the ballroom. The band was playing one of the new ragtime tunes recently imported from America and, being conservative in his taste for dancing, he decided to let the number finish while he took his time in selecting a promising partner for the next.

After an interval the band swung into a waltz, and by that time the Duke had fixed upon a slender dark-haired young woman who made one of a group of three seated on a long Louis Quinze settee. She proved to be the wife of a South American diplomat recently arrived in Europe, and could speak very little English. As de Richleau spoke several languages, including Spanish, with great fluency, that proved no bar to conversation; but she had been married only a few months earlier, straight from a convent, so he found her abysmally ignorant of the great world, and almost tongue-tied.

His next venture proved even less to his taste. A somewhat Junoesque girl, with a head of flaming red hair, had caught his eye, and he invited her to polka. Polka she did, but mainly on his feet and, although he was a fine horseman himself, he found the lady's conversation—which consisted entirely of her equine exploits—boring in the extreme.

Feeling that his luck was not in, for the time being at least, he made his way downstairs to the buffet on the ground floor, where he whiled away twenty minutes eating some *foie gras* sandwiches, and washing them down with a couple of glasses of Pommery 1906. There was still well over an hour until midnight, and he had not yet seen among the masked company anyone with whom he could definitely claim acquaintance. So he then decided, rather reluctantly, to try his fortune again up in the ballroom.

Only a few belated guests were now arriving, so the great staircase was no longer crowded, and the wing that he approached had only one couple coming down it. The man was young, slim, shortish, and fair-haired. The girl upon his arm was as tall as he was, so by comparison seemed taller. She had chestnut hair, on which rested a delicate filigree ornament forming a crescent of stars, each set with a yellow diamond. It was almost too light to be termed a tiara, but the Duke was a connoisseur of jewels, and as he glanced up at her he recognized at once that it was an antique piece of considerable value. Below her mask, he saw that she had a generous mouth with a slightly pouting lower lip, fresh-complexioned cheeks, and a round but determined chin.

He was only two steps below the couple, and about to pass them, when the young man slipped. In a second he had pitched forward, unavoidably dragging the girl with him. Too late, he snatched his arm from hers: she was already off her balance and about to take a header. De Richleau swiftly side-stepped to avoid collision with the man. Then, tensing his muscles, he caught the girl as she fell. Instinctively her arms had flown out, and now closed round his neck.

She was no mean weight, but her body was soft and pliant as, following their sudden impact, he held her tightly to him for a moment. Her face was within an inch of his and slightly above it, but he saw the swift flush that had turned her cheeks bright pink at finding herself so unexpectedly in the embrace of a complete stranger. With a little gasp she freed herself, then murmured her thanks in awkward English with a strong foreign accent.

Meanwhile, the fair-haired youth had tumbled to the bottom of the stairs. As two footmen ran to help him to his feet he gave an "Ouch!" of pain, looked up, and said, "I'm terribly sorry. That was awfully clumsy of me. I—I'm afraid I've twisted my ankle."

"Not badly, I trust?" inquired the Duke.

The young man tried the injured member gingerly, and screwed up his face. "It hurts a bit—not much, but I'd rather not put my weight on it till the pain has eased a little. Would you oblige me, sir, by taking my partner back to her chaperone, while I go to the cloak-room and find out if it's swelling?"

"It will be a pleasure, sir," de Richleau replied, and bowed to the girl.

She gave a little inclination of her head, then asked her ex-partner anxiously: "Are you assured you are not gravely hurt?"

He nodded, smiling up at her. "Yes. I promise you it's nothing serious. I'm jolly glad, though, that this gentleman happened to be there to prevent your coming a cropper with me. I hope I'll be able to claim our second dance and sit it out with you. But if the ankle drives me home, you must forgive me. I'll not let it prevent my seeing you tomorrow, anyway."

As he hobbled off, the Duke turned again to the charming charge who had been thrust upon him, and said: "Allow me to introduce myself. I am——"

"But, no!" She quickly put up a hand to check him. "This night it makes for the gaiety that the guests of Lady Holford talk and dance together without knowing who is which. But my English is much muddled. You speak French perhaps?"

"*Mais, oui, Mademoiselle,*" he assured her. Then, with a quizzical smile, added in the same language, "Or should I say *Madame*?"

She laughed at that and, breaking into rapid French, declared: "Not yet, but soon, I hope; otherwise I shall be counted, as they say, upon the shelf. But your question makes it clear that you do not know who

I am. So far this evening everyone I have spoken to has recognized me. That is most dull, and an encounter like this between strangers is much more in the spirit of the party."

"True! And, as this dance has only just started, I trust that you will not insist on my escorting you back to your chaperone until it is ended."

Seeing her hesitation, he went on quickly; "You were, I suppose, going downstairs to partake of some refreshment. Shall I conduct you to the buffet, or would you prefer to dance?"

The strains of the 'Blue Danube' floated down to them.

"Do you waltz?" she asked, and added with barefaced frankness, "Really well, I mean. Except for duty dances, to which I am compelled by politeness, I waltz from choice only with the best partners."

As she stood there, her gown of shimmering blue satin moulding her graceful figure, and coppery lights glinting in her high-piled chestnut hair, de Richleau judged that even if her mask did not conceal great beauty, she was fully attractive enough to command a good choice of men. But her words and manners struck him as those of a spoiled, impertinent chit, who needed a lesson, so he replied smoothly.

"Then out of politeness you shall dance with me, and find out for yourself whether my waltzing is up to your high standard." And, taking her firmly by the arm, he turned her towards the ballroom.

For a second he glimpsed a pair of defiant dark blue eyes staring at him through the slits in her mask. Then she laughed again, allowed herself to be led up the stairs, and murmured: "This is a strange way to behave, Monsieur. Do you always treat the ladies of your acquaintance in such a cavalier fashion?"

"But certainly," he shrugged. "Have you not heard the English proverb—'The woman, the dog, and the walnut tree: the more you beat 'em, the better they be!' I have found it an admirable precept."

The blue eyes turned to stare at him again. "You are joking. You cannot possibly mean that you would really beat a woman."

The Duke's good looks alone were a sufficient passport to the initial interest of most members of the opposite sex, but experience had taught him that the swiftest way to intrigue them was to say and do the unexpected. With or without a handsome profile to back it, he was convinced that audacity almost always paid high dividends, and that there were very few women who did not secretly love to be shocked. So, having decided that this 'haughty Miss' was well worth powder and shot, he adopted his usual technique by lying glibly.

"I have often given a woman a beating. It is an ancient and admirable custom, making for peace and obedience in the home."

She looked at him in astonishment. "You are married, then How! I pity your poor wife!"

He smiled. "You may spare yourself the trouble, Mademoiselle, for I have not got one." Then he added mischievously: "But, since you have said that you hope soon to be married, you are old enough to know that men of the world sometimes contract less orthodox alliances."

"Monsieur!" she exclaimed, flushing scarlet. "How dare you mention such matters to me. Your behaviour is outrageous. Now we have reached the ballroom, I desire you to take me to the lady with the grey hair seated over there near the band. You may then relieve me of your obnoxious company."

De Richleau knew that it had been a little wicked of him even to hint at the existence of such things as mistresses to an unmarried girl, but he was surprised by the violence of her reaction, and immediately decided that he could not possibly allow her to leave him in the belief that he was an ill-bred fellow of the baser sort. So he said:

"If I did as you suggest, Mademoiselle, that would be a great pity, for I was about to give you the best waltz you are likely to get this evening."

"So, you *can* waltz well," she countered sharply, "but add to your other horrid qualities that of a boaster."

Suddenly his voice changed to a low, vibrant tone. "Try me, and see. Forget this silly nonsense I have been talking. Dance with me once round the room, and I promise you that you will not regret it."

His brilliant grey eyes were smiling straight into hers, and the anger faded from her blue ones. For a second she hesitated, while the haunting strains of the music now came clearly to her above the swish and rustle of the dancers, and in that second she was lost. His arm slid round her waist, with the hand to which her big blue ostrich feather fan was looped she automatically caught up her dress, and they glided away into the whirling throng.

For the next ten minutes they did not exchange a single word. In becoming an accomplished swordsman de Richleau had acquired an admirable sense of balance, and his slender body concealed considerable strength; so he was able to guide and control his partner with smooth, unerring steps. From the first few turns he found that she too was light, supple, and fully capable of timing her movements in perfect union with his own. Without a shadow of hesitation she followed his lead as they spun, first one way, then the other, in wide circles round the crowded floor; often missing couples only by inches, yet touching none. Soon both of them were entranced with the ease and excellence of the other's performance, and gave themselves up entirely to the intoxicating rhythm of the dance until, at the end of their most daring spin, the music ceased.

As he released her, murmuring his thanks, her fair face was flushed, her blue eyes sparkling, and she asked a trifle breathlessly, "Where did you learn to waltz like that?"

"In Vienna," he smiled. "And you, Mademoiselle? Surely, only by also learning in the home of the waltz could you have achieved such perfection?"

She shook her head. "It was in Munich that I took my first steps. I spent much of my youth in the Bavarian capital. But I am flattered, Monsieur. It is a new experience for me to receive a compliment from a cave man."

"Oh, come!" he protested, as he offered her his arm and led her out of the ballroom by an entrance opposite to that by which they had come in. "I cannot believe you really think me that."

"I admit that neither your figure nor your dancing fit such a part. But before we danced you tried to make me believe you a veritable ogre. Only drunkards, savages, and semi-barbarous people like the Russians, beat their—beat women in these days."

"I am half a Russian. My mother was a Plackoff," he announced, with secret amusement at being able to surprise her with another unexpected reply, while this time adhering to the truth.

"I intended no slur on the Russian nobility," she assured him quickly. "And the Plackoffs are allied to the Imperial family, are they not? You must then, after all, be a gentleman. Do you know, I had almost concluded that you were an adventurer who had gained admission here by false pretences, trusting in your mask to protect you from being found out?"

Unwittingly, she had given him another tempting lead, and he took it. "Being well born is no guarantee against a man becoming dissipated, unscrupulous, and cruel. Some people believe me to be all those things, and perhaps you will do so too when I admit that you were right. I *am* an adventurer."

Her smooth forehead wrinkled in perplexity. "If that were true, why should you confess it and risk my telling our host?"

"I might well do so, counting on your natural reluctance to involve yourself in the unpleasant scene which would be certain to result from such a step."

From the ballroom they had emerged on to a semi-circular balcony, from which a flight of iron steps led down into what was normally an open courtyard with a few elm trees growing in it, but was now entirely enclosed under a great marquee. As they reached the bottom of the steps she took her hand from his arm and, turning towards him, said:

"I believe you are making fun of me. If I could see your face I would be better able to judge of that. But since I cannot, and am most averse to remaining in the company of anyone who might possibly turn out to be a jewel thief, I think you had better take me back to the lady I pointed out to you before we danced."

The Duke saw that in seeking to intrigue her he had overplayed his hand; but he was now more loath than ever to let her go. His life was far too fully occupied for him to devote much of it to the pursuit of women, and on the rare occasions when he entered on an *affaire* it had usually been with some sophisticated beauty nearer his own age. He guessed his partner to be a good ten years younger than himself, but she certainly was not a debutante, as she was entirely free of the shy, awkward coquettishness usual in young girls just entering society, and appeared to be fully mature. Yet she possessed a special fresh, youthful quality that he could not quite define. It was the unusual combination in her of youth with poise that he found so refreshing, and he swiftly cast about in his mind for a means of keeping her with him without admitting for the time being that he had deliberately misled her about himself.

The marquee in which they were standing contained not a trace of the bare, cold, courtyard that it roofed over. The magic of money had, in a few hours, converted it into a semi-tropical paradise. Sir George Holford's hobby was growing orchids. A fleet of vans had brought many hundreds of rare, exotic blooms up from his hot-houses in the country. With their pots now hidden by banks of greenery, they rose in tier upon tier over concealed heaters, forming a score or more of alleys, bays and nooks, in which couples could sit and flirt unseen by anyone more than a few paces distant.

After a second's hesitation, de Richleau said: "Since you believe that you could judge my true character better if you saw my face, I will willingly unmask for you. But I cannot do so here. Let's find a quiet spot among Sir George's lovely orchids."

As he expected, curiosity got the better of her prudence. "Very well, then," she murmured with a smile. "But you must not seek to detain me further, if I decide to return to the ballroom immediately afterwards."

Taking his arm again, she allowed him to lead her down one of the colourful alleys until they came to an unoccupied settee, concealed from its neighbours by great masses of ferns and cymbidiums. Then, turning to face her, he took off his mask.

The light was pleasantly subdued, but sufficient for her to see his lean, aristocratic features. After she had regarded him in silence for a long moment, the corners of his mouth twitched mockingly and he inquired:

"Well, what do you think now, Mademoiselle? Am I a brutal beater of women, here to commit a jewel theft in order to support my immoralities, or an honourable gentleman whom your parents might consider a suitable *parti* for you if I asked your hand in marriage?"

To his surprise her blue eyes suddenly lit up, her mouth opened, showing two rows of strong white teeth, and she burst out laughing. He could not even make a guess at the cause of her mirth, but when it had subsided a little she stammered:

"My—my parents are both dead, so that question will never arise; but I would take a bet that with such features you are of noble blood. Perhaps, though, it is also true about your being a rogue. You may be illegitimate."

A swift flush rose to de Richleau's cheeks, his chin tilted, and his eyes sparkled dangerously: but, not the least dismayed, she cried, "There! I have caught you out. Since you show such resentment at the implication, it cannot be true. You are neither an ogre nor a jewel thief. You have simply been seeing how far you could lead me on for your own amusement."

"*Touché!*" he smiled, his sense of humour at once getting the better of his indignation. "I asked for that, and confess myself outwitted. The truth is that I was invited here tonight, and there are plenty of people in London who would vouch for my respectability."

She pouted. "What a horrid word. It is so often synonymous with dull."

"You are disappointed, then?"

"Just a little. I never quite believed all that nonsense; but it intrigued me to think that you might be of another world, and quite different from the polished, insincere men of good birth whom I am always meeting."

"Would it console you somewhat if I tell you that I really can claim to be an adventurer? I am a political exile, a big-game hunter, and a 'soldier of fortune'."

Her eyes brightened, and sitting down she motioned him to sit beside her. "That sounds far from respectable and very exciting. But surely you cannot be one of those horrible nihilists who meet in cellars and plot to blow people up with bombs?"

"Dear me, no!" he laughed. "I am only half Russian. My father was French, and it was from France that I was exiled. As a young officer at the military college of St. Cyr I took a leading part in an abortive conspiracy to place the Duc de Vendôme on the throne."

"So you are a royalist. That pleases me much better. The Duc de Vendôme is the last representative of the old line, is he not; and a descendant of the great *Henri Quatre* by his beautiful mistress, Gabrielle d'Estrées?"

De Richleau nodded. It struck him as rather surprising that she should know anything of a matter so far outside the skeleton of history ordinarily taught by governesses and in schools, and he wondered if it was a true sample of a wider knowledge, or just an isolated fact that she had picked up by chance. After a moment, he added: "Unfortunately the affair miscarried badly. We were betrayed, and during a mêlée caused by our resistance of arrest a number of people were killed. I hated having to go into exile, but I suppose I should consider myself lucky to have escaped with my life."

"I should like to hear the whole story," she said. "But I doubt if there's time for it now. Another dance has just started, and I ought not to stay here much longer."

"Why not? At a masked ball like this all dance engagements are only tentative. Be kind, I beg, my beautiful unknown. Forget the poor fellow to whom you promised this one, and sit it out with me."

"I may be missed. Perhaps someone will be sent to find me."

"Why should they be? In any case, they would have to search for quite a time before they found you here."

"All right, then. I will if you'll tell me more about this exciting conspiracy in which you nearly lost your life."

"Willingly! But first I would beg a favour. While you remain masked and I am not, you have me at a disadvantage. It is like talking to a person wearing dark glasses. Will you not reveal to me the lovely features that command the best partners at every dance you grace with your presence?"

She shook her head. "No. I mean to remain incognito till midnight."

"Come!" he rallied her. "If you persist in your refusal it will lead me to believe that your face does not match your figure, and that good partners seek you out only because they know you to be an excellent dancer."

"Then you must believe that, if you will."

"It would explain, too, why, as you said when we first met, that although you wish to be married you fear that you may soon be left on the shelf."

"I am not plain!" she exclaimed with a flash of anger. "I am accounted the most beautiful—I mean, very good looking. The papers are always publishing photographs of me. That is my reason for not unmasking. You would be sure to recognize me if I did."

He was amused by her youthful conceit, that her features were so widely publicized that he would be bound to know her at the sight of them: and, having deliberately nettled her into asserting that she was a beauty, he did not hold it against her. With a good-humoured shrug, he said:

"Very well, then. If you will not unmask, at least tell me something of yourself. Although you speak French very fluently, I am sure you are not French by birth. What is your nationality?"

"I probably have as much Bavarian blood as you have Russian," she replied a little cryptically. "But my mother was a Belgian."

"And where do you live?"

"In various places on the Continent. I have relatives in Munich, with whom I spend a good part of my time: but during the past two years I have been allowed to travel quite a lot in order to complete my education. Tell me more about the Vendôme conspiracy."

"We have ample time for that. Tell me first what you have made of your life so far?"

She gave him a puzzled look. "What a strange question! How can a girl like myself make anything of her life? What she does, or may not do, is dictated for her by her elders."

"That does not prevent her having her own ambitions."

"True! Mine is to make a suitable marriage, in which I may also find love—so that through my own happiness I may be the better able to bring happiness to others."

His shrewd eyes regarded her with curiosity for a moment: then he remarked, "You said that almost as though you were repeating a well-learned lesson."

"Perhaps, unconsciously, I was." She gave a cynical little laugh. "My life so far has consisted of little else than lessons. But the part about hoping for love was my own idea."

It occurred to him that she was probably a great heiress, who might later be called on to watch over the welfare of many thousands of work-people in the industries that her money controlled. Or, in view of her mixed parentage, she might be the daughter of an American millionaire and, perhaps, had been brought up in Europe with the idea of her marrying into the higher aristocracy, where she would have to spend much of her time supervising charities and performing minor public functions.

"You speak as though you have been educated to take life very seriously," he smiled, "and were already suffering from the burden of great wealth. Am I right in guessing that you inherited a fortune from your parents?"

"Yes. I am an only child, and on my mother's death I became very rich. But I have only the vaguest ideas about the size of my fortune and how it is administered. In fact, I really know very little about money at all."

"Perhaps you make up for that by knowing a lot about love?"

The yellow diamonds in her diadem of stars sparkled as she shook her head. "Only at second-hand, through books that I have read. I have been brought up very strictly. Meeting a stranger like you to-night is quite an adventure for me."

He leaned forward. "I do not mean this impertinently; but, how old are you?"

"Nearly twenty-five."

"And do you really mean to say that you have never yet had a serious love affair?"

"I was engaged when I was twenty-one, but I had met my fiancé only about half a dozen times before he fell overboard from a yacht and was drowned. He was younger than myself and proved very shy on the few occasions we were left alone together. So, although I rather liked the poor boy, I was only just getting to know him; and one certainly could not call it a love affair."

"And then?"

"A few months later I had a serious hunting accident myself, so naturally no further plans to marry me off could be considered for quite a time. I was twenty-three when my next engagement was mooted. The man proposed for me was considerably older than I was and, although I respected him, I found him rather a bore, so I was by no means keen about the match. Fortunately for me there were religious difficulties which could not be surmounted, and after months of fruitless attempts to get a dispensation from the Holy See the project had to be abandoned. Then, last year, I lost my mother, so I was sent on my travels again to occupy the period of mourning. Can you wonder that I feel it high time now to find a husband?"

"Not in the least. Yet, with your fine figure and lovely colouring, plus the beautiful face you persist in hiding from me, I marvel that both at home and on your travels a score of eligible young men have not sought to make love to you."

She hesitated. "My—my family have rather grand ideas about the term 'eligible', in connection with myself."

"Naturally! As you are an heiress, they would do their utmost to protect you from fortune hunters. But what of your own feelings? Surely, during the past few years you must have met someone who attracted you?"

Opening her fan, she began to flutter it gently, and replied with a reminiscent smile: "When I was fourteen I used to weave the most marvellous romances round a handsome gardener's boy, who tended the flower beds underneath my windows. But, of course, he never knew it. Then, for the best part of a year, I was desperately in love with my music master. He knew, I'm sure, and returned my love; but he never had the courage to declare himself. Since then, there have been several young men that I rather fancied, but immediately they showed their interest in me they were warned off. One sent me flowers secretly for a few weeks, and another poems. But I suppose both of them were found out, as the flowers and poems stopped arriving without any apparent reason. I often wish that I could change places with some little shop girl. As it is, I am the prisoner of my circumstances. If it were not for the prospect of marriage I might just as well be a nun in a convent."

De Richleau saw nothing beyond the bounds of reasonable possibility in this pathetic story. In England, at that date, unmarried girls of good family were rarely allowed to go out shopping without their mothers, and when they did were always accompanied by a maid; while on the Continent young women of position were still more carefully guarded from the possible attentions of undesirable males. Even engaged couples were allowed to be alone together only within earshot of their elders, and to conduct a clandestine affair bristled with danger and difficulties. Yet it did strike him as strange that his obviously lovely partner should have reached the age of twenty-four without having acquired a single swain with the audacity to secure a succession of rendezvous with her, however innocent and fleeting.

After a moment's consideration, he decided that he did not believe it. Her full mouth, fresh complexion, and limpid eyes all suggested that she was far from cold by temperament. On her own confession, it was ten years since she had first become conscious of the opposite sex. In all that time it seemed incredible that she had not had a single active love affair. Suddenly, it occurred to him that she, in her turn, was amusing herself at his expense. Just as he had pretended to be cruel and dissipated, so she was now acting the role of the maiden in the ivory tower.

At once he decided to scale the tower and call her bluff.

"You poor little rich girl," he said softly. "It is high time that someone opened your prison doors for you, and I am prepared to do it if you will let me."

She started, looked at him in evident surprise, then asked with a low laugh: "Am I to take that as a proposal of marriage?"

"Hardly!" he laughed back. "It is customary for a man at least to see a lady's face before he asks her to marry him. But from the very moment when you fell into my arms on the staircase, I felt greatly attracted to you; and I ask you now to accept me as your beau."

"I appreciate your offer, and would be glad to have your friendship," she said gravely. "But, unfortunately, it is most unlikely that any future occasions will arise where we could talk like this in private."

"Why? Are you, then, returning to the Continent almost immediately?"

"Oh no. I shall be staying in England for some time yet."

"Then we are certain to meet at lots of places. London society is not large, and the season will be opening shortly. You must let me know to what parties you are going, and I shall make it my business to get myself invited."

"As soon as it was noticed that you were paying marked attention to me, my people would formally request you to desist."

"From fear that I was after your millions, eh? Then we must manage matters so that they suspect nothing. We must refrain from dancing together sufficiently to make ourselves conspicuous. Sometimes it might be wise not to do so once in a whole evening; but we could sit out together, like this. Besides, Roehampton, Hurlingham, Ascot and Henley would offer us a score of opportunities to meet, get lost in the crowd, and slip away for a while together."

As she remained silent he took her hand and pressed it. A tremor of excitement ran right up her long kid-gloved arm to the elbow, and she let her hand remain in his; so he hurried on, "Even after this brief meeting I feel myself near to being in love with you already. You say you have been starved of romance. I offer it to you now. I beg you not to reject it."

Her voice came almost in a whisper. "I am sorely tempted to say yes. But I am frightened. Not for myself, but that I might become involved in a scandal, and so bring disgrace on my family."

"I swear to you that I will be the very essence of discretion."

"And—and I believe you. But I am sure that for you to see me alone will be far more difficult than you suppose."

De Richleau did not doubt that she and her money-bags were well protected from amorous assault; but he thought it certain that she was deliberately exaggerating in order to keep up the role of snow-white innocence, and test him to the utmost. Yet, even had he fully believed her, no difficulties, real or imagined, would have deterred him now. His ardour was aroused to a greater degree than it had been for a long time, by the temptation to enter on what, for him, would be an entirely new kind of love affair.

Smiling into her eyes, he said firmly, "Leave everything to me. I promise you I am no *roué*; but I would be a poor sort of beau if, at my age, I had never been in love before. And I am rich enough to bribe servants so lavishly that I have never yet known one to betray me. It would not be the first time, either, that I have scaled a garden wall to keep an assignation with a lady on its other side in the middle of the night."

She caught her breath. "I—I can believe that too. The moment you unmasked I knew you to be bold and determined. But if I consented to let you play this dangerous game, nothing—nothing could come of it."

"Do you call *love* nothing?"

"I mean it could lead nowhere, and there would be a bitter aftermath for both of us. As an honourable gentleman, which I now feel sure you are, you would not expect of me anything—anything, the memory of which would cause me shame when I come to marry. Yet, if we were found out, people would believe the worst; and that risk is too high a price to pay for a few stolen conversations."

He raised her gloved hand to his lips, and kissed it. "My beautiful unknown, I beg you not to act your part of sweet innocence too faithfully, by pretending that you would forbid me all but talk. Tender embraces and gentle kisses never ruined any girl's marriage yet, and stolen kisses are the very salt of stolen meetings. They afterwards become the sweetest memories of our lives."

As she did not reply, he felt that the time had come to call her bluff. Slipping an arm about her waist he swiftly drew her to him, and added: "That you may have a sample to think about tonight, I am about to steal one now."

"Wait!" she exclaimed, jerking herself erect and throwing back her head. "Rather than you should regret what you are about to do, I will unmask."

For a second he paused, dreading that in boasting of her beauty she had lied, and now intended to disclose some horrid scar or blemish that disfigured her face. But, as she ripped away the black satin with her free hand, he found himself gazing on features that were delicate but strong; sensuous, yet chaste; with a skin as smooth as her kid gloves. She was still a little flushed but her blue eyes, now calm and serene, met his without a quiver.

The thought flashed through his mind that she had been wrong in supposing that he would know her at sight, as he could not recall ever having seen a photograph of her in any of the weeklies that featured the doings of society people. But, as he had spent the greater part of the past two years in the Balkans, that seemed hardly surprising, and entirely irrelevant to their present situation.

He smiled at her, and murmured: "I thank you for that gracious gesture—and the sweet surprise of your dazzling beauty." Then, crushing her against his chest, he pressed his mouth firmly on her half-open lips.

Her hands swiftly gripped his shoulders, and for a moment he felt her resist him. But under the pressure of his mouth hers opened wider, her head fell back and her whole body went limp in his arms. Overjoyed at her complete surrender, he tightened his embrace and showered more kisses upon her. She made no response, and he took her lack of it for shyness. Then he asked her to tell him her name.

She did not reply. Suddenly, with a start of dismay, he realized that she had fainted.

Next moment his distress and alarm were increased a hundredfold—he had heard the sound of approaching footsteps. His right arm was caught between the basket-work back of the settee and the girl's limp body. Before he had time to pull it free, the footsteps halted and a woman's voice cried excitedly in German:

"Here she is! *Ach! Gott im Himmel!* But this is terrible!"

At a glance the Duke recognized her as the grey-haired dowager whom his partner had pointed out to him in the ballroom. Beside her was a distinguished-looking elderly man. His voice now came sharp and angry, in good English but with a heavy accent.

"What has happened? How dare you, sir! What have you done to her?"

De Richleau considered himself an adept at slipping out of awkward situations; but rarely had he been caught in quite such an embarrassing one, and for once his habitual sang-froid deserted him.

"Nothing," he stammered. "Nothing very reprehensible, I assure you. I—I would not harm her for the world. She must be a very sensitive young lady to faint just because—because I whisked her mask off. But really, she will be quite all right again in a few minutes."

Ignoring his protests, the elderly woman ran forward, pushed him aside, and took the unconscious girl in her arms. Producing a bottle of smelling salts from her bag, she administered first aid, while the man continued to stand there glaring at the Duke.

After a moment the girl's eyes flickered open. Raising a hand, she pushed the smelling salts aside, hurriedly sat up, and murmured in German:

"Oh, *Frau Grafin*, how—how do you come to be here?"

"For the past half-hour we have been looking for you everywhere," the *Grafin* replied in tones of mingled concern and reproach. "We became alarmed by your disappearance, and with good cause it seems. I cannot say how distressed——"

"Please!" the girl interrupted. "Please say no more. I was quite enjoying myself until— Oh, it was absurd of me to faint. But—but it is the first time I have ever been kissed like that."

Then, burying her face in her hands, she burst into tears.

'Now the cat is really out of the bag,' thought the Duke grimly. 'I could at least have saved her that, had she not become hysterical. How damnably annoying that her people should make such a fuss over so little. I hope they don't put the poor child on bread and water for this, but they are probably quite capable of it. Still, from all she said, they must be appalling snobs; so perhaps when they know who I am they will regard her little lapse more leniently.'

These thoughts coursed through his mind in a second as he turned his glance from the girl to the elderly man. At her words his lined face had taken on a look of consternation that almost amounted to horror. Trembling with anger, he confronted de Richleau, and burst out:

"Did you hear what she said? Your conduct is outrageous—unpardonable. Do you not realize that it is *lèse-majesté* to have forced your vile and brutal attentions on Her Imperial Highness?"

CHAPTER II

THE FIRST LORD INTERVENES

At that moment, attracted by the raised voices, two other men appeared round the corner of the banked-up mass of orchids that hid the seat from passers-by. One was a good bit over six feet tall, with greying hair: the other, of medium height, with a bulging forehead and chubby face. Both were masked, and remained standing at the bend of the alley; silent spectators of the scene.

Amazement and swift realization of the seriousness of his offence temporarily robbed de Richleau of words. When Sir George Holford had invited him to the ball that morning he had omitted to mention that he was giving it in honour of the Archduchess Ilona Theresa. The Duke had not even known that she was in England, but the revelation of her identity explained a multitude of things that had puzzled him in the past half hour.

The person of the fair-haired young man who had fallen down stairs had seemed vaguely familiar and, by association, de Richleau now realized that the Archduchess' partner must have been one of the Royal Princes. The unusual combination in her of maturity and innocence, which had attracted him so strongly, was explained by her royal upbringing. Naturally, photographs of her were always appearing in the Press, and when she had said, 'I am accounted the most beautiful...' she had stopped short of adding 'Princess in Europe', only in order to preserve her incognito. Naturally, too, as the future bride of some crowned head or heir apparent, she would have been kept with the utmost strictness, and any young nobles who began to pay her attentions at the Court of Vienna would have been promptly banished to some distant province. It was probably true that she had spent much of her youth in Munich, as the Royal Bavarian House of Wittelsbach was more closely tied by a series of marriages to the Habsburgs of Vienna than to any other family, and she had obviously refrained from telling him that she was an Austrian in the belief that he would then guess her identity. It was now clear, too, that on removing her mask she had expected him to recognize her immediately, and so desist from kissing her.

Recovering his wits after a moment, de Richleau drew himself up and said: "My attentions, sir, were neither vile nor brutal. You overstate the case. My fault arises solely from the fact that this lady happens to be a royal personage. The liberty I took was no more than any man might be tempted to take at a masked ball, where partners are not always known to one another."

"Her Imperial Highness was unmasked," snapped the elderly man. "You could not possibly have failed to recognize her. Who are you, sir?"

De Richleau took out his gold card-case, extracted a card, and handed it over with a little shrug. "I assure you that you are mistaken. I arrived in London from the Near East only yesterday. I have never seen Her Imperial Highness before, or, as far as I can recall, any portrait of her."

With a stiff bow the other took the card, glanced at it, and said: "I am Count Mensdorf, the Austrian Ambassador, and Her Imperial Highness is in my wife's care this evening."

"Then, your Excellency, I deeply regret having caused you such grave concern, and beg that you will use your good offices to induce Her Imperial Highness to accept my humblest apologies for the lack of respect which I unwittingly showed her."

The Ambassador appeared in no way mollified. He tapped the Duke's card impatiently on his fingernail. "Your Grace cannot fail to be aware that, in view of this incident, your continued presence here would prove most embarrassing to Her Imperial Highness. Therefore I must request you to leave the house at once. Moreover, it would gravely embarrass her to meet you again at any functions she may attend: so it will be my unpleasant duty to warn anyone from whom she accepts invitations that your name should not be included in the list of guests."

The young Archduchess had swiftly overcome her tears. Standing up, she resumed her mask: then she took her chaperone's arm and, without a glance at de Richleau, moved towards the exit of the alley. The two onlookers at its bend made way for her to pass, and all four men in the group gave a low bow as, with her head held high, she disappeared behind the greenery.

The Duke was just about to express his willingness to withdraw, when the shorter of the two hitherto silent spectators stepped forward and removed his mask. His big head was well set on powerful shoulders. Beneath his beetling brows, shrewd, kindly eyes twinkled with humour and vitality. In a deep, sonorous voice, he addressed the Ambassador.

"As my friend and I chanced to witness the latter part of this regrettable incident, may I be permitted to suggest that your Excellency should give further thought to the decision you have just announced before putting it into execution. Your natural indignation is fully understandable. As a Minister of the Crown I should like formally to express my deep distress that Her Imperial Highness should have been subjected to this deplorable experience while a guest of Britain. Clearly it is our duty to protect her as far as we are able from any future repercussions of it. But should your Excellency pursue your intention of having this gentleman's name struck out from lists of guests at all parties where she is appearing, that will inevitably link his name with hers, and almost certainly give rise to scandal."

The taller man had now also unmasked. He had the lean, bronzed face of a soldier, his eyes were bright blue, and a great cavalry moustache swept up towards his high cheekbones.

"First Lord's right, Mensdorf!" he boomed abruptly. "Least said, soonest mended. No great harm done by a feller kissing a gel at a dance—even if she is a Princess. No doubt he'll give you his assurance that he won't tell tales out of school, or approach her again. That's all you want. Then forget it. I'm no diplomat. Never did understand that high-falutin' sort of stuff. But that's my advice."

Count Mensdorf's face broke into a reluctant smile. "I have met many a worse diplomat than you, Sir Pellinore, and the First Lord *is* right. I thank you both for your timely intervention. This incident perturbed me so greatly that I spoke without giving the matter sufficient thought."

"That's a very handsome admission from a man of your Excellency's calling," the First Lord chuckled, "and one which I am sure you have never been called on to make in the course of official business."

De Richleau stepped forward and bowed to the Ambassador. "Sir, I willingly give you my word I will not mention this matter to anyone, and that during the remainder of Her Imperial Highness' stay in England I will do everything reasonably possible to avoid appearing in her presence."

The Ambassador returned the bow a little stiffly. "I thank your Grace. Let us consider the incident closed." Then he bowed more cordially to the other two, adding: "You will excuse me, gentlemen, if I rejoin my wife?" and hurried away.

The giant with the cavalry moustache, who had been addressed as Sir Pellinore, was staring at the Duke. "I know your face," he declared suddenly. "We've met before; I'd bet a pony on it. Where was it, eh?"

"In Constantinople, about eighteen months ago," replied de Richleau. "We were not actually introduced, but I remember you were pointed out to me, during a conference on munitions, as Sir Pellinore Gwaine-Cust. I was then on the Turkish General Staff, and I gathered that you were representing the British Government in a big armaments deal that the Turks were endeavouring to put through."

"Nonsense!" exclaimed the tall baronet. "You're all at sea, there.

I'm not capable of representing anybody at a show of that kind. I've an eye for a horse or a pretty woman, and I'm no bad judge of vintage port. But I've no brains—no brains at all. Anybody will tell you that."

It had long been a deliberate policy with Sir Pellinore to pose as an almost childishly simple person, whereas, in fact, behind the façade of his bluff, hearty manner, he concealed one of the shrewdest minds in the British Empire. As a cavalry subaltern he had earned a particularly well-merited V.C. in the South African war, but shortly afterwards an accumulation of debts had decided him to resign his commission rather than sell his ancient patrimony, Gwaine Meads; a property on the Welsh border that his forebears had enjoyed since the Wars of the Roses. Solely on account of his being distantly connected with royalty, and having from his youth upwards known everyone who mattered by their Christian name, some people in the City had then offered him a directorship. To their surprise, he had displayed a quite unexpected interest in commerce, and an even more astonishing flair for negotiating successfully extremely tricky deals. Other directorships had followed. He was now, at forty-three, very rich, and had recently acquired a great mansion in Carlton House Terrace. In spite of that, by the constant repetition which is the essence of effective propaganda, he had managed, with all but those who knew him fairly intimately, to maintain the bluff that he was only a simpleton, who had had the luck to bring off a few big financial coups.

"Perhaps I am mistaken about the part you played at that munitions conference," de Richleau rejoined tactfully, "but I am certain it was there we saw one another."

"Oh, I was there right enough;" Sir Pellinore shrugged. "Went to Turkey to buy a few brood mares from the Sultan's stable. Got roped in at the Embassy one night to say a few home truths to the Turks, which our Ambassador didn't want to say himself. By the by, what's your name?"

"Jean Armand Duplessis de Richleau."

"Then you must be the feller who shot a lot of policemen and got chivied out of France about ten years ago. Well, no harm in that! I've shot a good few men myself in my time. Glad to know you, Duke." Sir Pellinore waved a hand the size of a small leg of mutton towards his stocky companion. "D'you know—" Pulling himself up, he added after a second: "Forgot we are all supposed to be incognito here; I'd better give him a nickname—Mr. Marlborough?"

De Richleau had already recognized the statesman, and smiled. "I count the introduction a most fortunate one, in view of my reason for coming to England."

"In what way can I be of service to you?" the First Lord inquired courteously.

"As the head of the Senior British Service Ministry you could, sir, if you would be so kind, greatly facilitate my receiving a commission in the British Army."

Mr. Marlborough's eyebrows lifted. "If I may say so, Duke, that seems a somewhat strange request, particularly from a foreigner."

"On the contrary; I am a British citizen. I took out naturalization papers shortly after my expulsion from France."

"But, your age! I judge you to be over thirty; and only in very exceptional circumstances are candidates allowed to sit for Sandhurst after they are seventeen."

De Richleau laughed. "In my case such a formality would be little short of ludicrous. I received the equivalent training at St. Cyr many years ago. I have since fought in several South American wars, and in the Balkan conflict I commanded an Army Corps."

"Indeed! Then may I remark that, while you are undoubtedly too old for Sandhurst, you appear remarkably young to be a Lieutenant-General."

"And you, sir," the Duke shot back, "appear remarkably young to be First Lord of the Admiralty."

Mr. Marlborough was then only thirty-nine, and although he had already been a member of the government for several years his natural modesty had in no way suffered from his spectacular rise to high office. It was clear from his smile that he appreciated the implied compliment, as de Richleau went on:

"I will frankly confess that mine was not the best of Army Corps. Its actual strength was little more than that of a British division, and it was sadly lacking in both specialists and the auxiliary arms which count for so much in modern war. But I have hopes that my past rank and experience may at least be considered sufficient to obtain me the command of a Brigade, or an equivalent rank on the British General Staff."

The First Lord shook his head. "I am sorry to disappoint you, Duke, but I fear that is quite out of the question. I am, of course, aware that in a number of Continental armies the practice is still followed of granting immediate field-rank, or even high commands, to gifted soldiers of fortune, who have seen active service under other flags; but that custom has long since been abolished here."

"What's the idea, though?" Sir Pellinore inquired brusquely. "I've nothing against the army, mind you. Soldier once myself. But we've no war on our hands yet, thank God! It ain't natural for a young spark like you, who goes around kissin' Archduchesses, to want to spend the rest of his life kickin' his heels on the barrack squares of our garrison towns."

"No," agreed the Duke, "Britain has no war on her hands yet, but in my opinion she soon will have. It is my belief that the general conflict, which for some years has threatened to engulf Europe, cannot be postponed much longer. When that day comes, since I am debarred from fighting for the country of my birth, I wish to fight for the country of my adoption. I arrived in England yesterday, with the hope that I should be in ample time to make arrangements which would ensure my being in a post suited to my abilities when war breaks out."

"I heartily commend your attitude, sir," Mr. Marlborough commented. "But pray tell me why you believe that a general conflagration is imminent, or even inevitable. In 1908, and again in 1911, I had the gravest fears of such a catastrophe myself; but most well-informed people are of the opinion that the danger is now past, or at least considerably lessened. At no time in recent years have the great nations shown such accord as at the present."

All de Richleau knew of the statesman was that his personal daring, coupled with his distinguished parentage, had, while he was still quite a young man, brought him into national prominence as a soldier, war correspondent, and politician; and that his swift rise to office was said to be due to his amazingly clear grasp of great issues. The opinion of such a man must obviously be well grounded, and, as it was directly contrary to the Duke's own, he said with some diffidence:

"It is a considerable time, sir, since I was in any of the western capitals, and much may have happened in them of which I am not aware. But what you say surprises me greatly; and, if you can spare the time, I should be immensely interested to hear on what you base your views."

There was nothing the First Lord loved better than such discussions, so he replied at once: "By all means, Duke. Then you shall tell us why you disagree. But if we are going to unroll the map of Europe, we might as well sit down."

Sir Pellinore disappeared for a moment to fetch an odd chair from farther down the alleyway. Mr. Marlborough lit a fresh cigar and then began:

"To assess the chances of war breaking out in the near future we must go back some way. Towards the end of the last century the five great nations of Europe—Britain, France, Russia, Austria-Hungary, and Germany—stood apart. Any of them could have attacked one of the others with a fair prospect of the remaining three standing by as on-lookers. The first four had for several centuries been powers of the first rank, whereas Imperial Germany was a new creation. As long as she had remained a chequerboard of independent states, one could be played off against another, and there was naught to be feared from the loosely-knit Teutonic family. But the Napoleonic wars sowed the seeds of combination. What the Zoll-Verein began, Bismarck completed with fire and sword in the wars against Denmark, Austria and France of the 'sixties and 'seventies, culminating in the hour of final victory with the proclamation at Versailles of the German Empire.

"The ample evidence of the rise of a new great power could not be disregarded by the rest: so, henceforth, it became the practice of the others to call Germany into consultation on all questions affecting the maintenance of peace and well-being, not only in Europe but wherever her interests might be affected throughout the world."

As his cigar was not properly alight, the statesman applied another match to it before continuing: "That policy was followed when we entered into an agreement with the French that, broadly speaking, we would give them a free hand in Morocco and they would do the same for us in Egypt. Officially, Germany gave that understanding her blessing; and indeed it was in no way prejudicial to her. But in Berlin there was already a very active party who were clamouring for German expansion overseas. Temporarily, they had been overruled, but they determined to take the first opportunity to provoke an incident.

"Early in 1905 the French sent a mission to Morocco. It acted in such a high-handed manner as to indicate an intention to treat the country as a French Protectorate, which would have been contrary to international obligations entered into by the Treaty of Madrid. The German expansionists saw their chance and brought pressure to bear on the Kaiser. Wilhelm II's vanity unfortunately rendered him a pliant tool. In March of that year he was persuaded to visit Tangiers, and while there deliver a speech which amounted to an open challenge to the French. This was followed by a formal demand from the German Government for a new conference by all the powers who had signed the Madrid Treaty.

"At first, the French refused; but the French army was in poor shape and the country in no condition to go to war; while Russia, who might have backed France in other circumstances, had been rendered temporarily impotent through her recent war with Japan. Ultimately, the French climbed down and agreed to the conference of Algeciras. They could not do otherwise; and in the event, British backing enabled them to more or less save face. But for several months it was 'touch and go', and the uncompromising attitude of the Germans caused both France and Britain to see the red light.

"Out of this incident were born three trends of great significance. Firstly, the French humiliation resulted in such a popular outcry that greater funds were voted for the army. Important measures were taken for its reorganization and expansion; and, slowly but surely, France began to prepare to face another war. Secondly, at the conference Germany had not received by any means the full support she had expected from Austria-Hungary. In consequence, from then onwards, she proceeded to court her numerically powerful neighbour, and has since succeeded in binding the Dual Monarchy closely to her. Thirdly, Britain gave a fresh turn to her age-old policy. France having now clearly become the second strongest nation in Europe, we aligned ourselves with her against the strongest, Germany, in order to maintain the balance of power. Sir Henry Campbell-Bannerman was then Prime Minister. He had inherited Gladstone's mantle as the leader of the Little Englanders, so was pledged to a policy of reduction of armaments and the avoidance of embroilment in foreign wars at almost any cost. But, so strongly did he feel the danger, that he gave permission for the British General Staff to enter into conversation with the French."

Mr. Marlborough paused impressively. "That was a momentous step. And you will realize from what I have said, that from the Algeciras conference of 1906 the great nations of Europe no longer stood alone. They began to coalesce into the two groups that we now know as the Triple Alliance and the Triple Entente.

"The next European crisis arose in the autumn of 1908. By the Treaty of Berlin, which was signed in 1878, Austria-Hungary had been awarded a mandate of administration over the old Turkish provinces of Bosnia and Herzegovina. You will recall that the Young Turk revolution occurred in the summer of 1908. Presumably the Dual Monarchy feared that this might lead to a demand from Constantinople for a re-assertion of Turkish sovereignty over the two provinces, and she acted to forestall some move of that kind. In any case, without the least warning, the following autumn she formally announced the annexation of these territories."

De Richleau nodded. "I well recall that episode, sir. But please go on."

"You will remember, then, that the great democracies showed instant indignation at this flagrant violation of the law of nations. The Czar's government even took stronger exception to the act. The Turks retaliated by placing an embargo on Austrian goods, and the Serbians went to the length of mobilizing their army. As the population of the provinces contained a high percentage of Serbians, Serbia was the most closely affected; and with her big brother, Russia, behind her, it looked as if at any moment she might declare war.

"Our Foreign Secretary, Sir Edward Grey, made it clear that Britain was not prepared to go to war over a Balkan quarrel, but he gave Russia full diplomatic support, and both nations demanded a conference. Austria, supported by Germany, refused, and a bitter wrangle ensued which dragged on into the spring of 1909. At length, Austria decided to threaten the Serbs with hostilities if they persisted in their refusal to recognize the annexations. At this point Germany secretly intervened. She insisted that Russia should herself advise the Serbs to give way, and do so without first informing the British and French governments. Should she refuse, Austria would declare war on Serbia with full German support. That was tantamount to a declaration that both countries would attack Russia, and under the threat Russia collapsed. It was another triumph for the German mailed fist; but that, too, had its repercussions. Russia, in her turn, saw the red light.

"Humbled, as France had been humbled four years before, she at once began to make great increases in her armaments, and to construct a new strategic railway system on her western frontier. Moreover, the humiliation they had both suffered drew the two countries much more closely together, and from that point their alliance became firm and dependable.

"Next, it was Britain's turn. We were not called on to swallow our pride or fight on some definite issue, as the others had been. The German menace for us became apparent in another direction. The Kaiser's Naval Laws of 1908 were by then naturally increasing the strength of his High Seas Fleet. Why? Germany had no far-flung possessions of great worth that she might be called on to defend. Her fleet increases could only be aimed at us. Despite our government's policy of retrenchment, we were faced with the alternative—build more Dreadnoughts or rue the day when Britain would no longer command the seas. The latter was unthinkable: so, build we did; and the naval race began. We, too, saw the red light, awoke from our lethargy, and while still at peace poured out the millions which now could enable us to meet the German Fleet with overwhelming strength.

"The Agadir episode comes next on the list, but the crisis of 1911 is too recent for me to need to dwell upon it at any length. It is sufficient to recall that Germany sent a gunboat to Morocco for the ostensible purpose of protecting commercial interests which later proved to be non-existent, and once again threatened France with war. Whether she definitely intended to open hostilities remains in question; but there can be little doubt that Mr. Lloyd George's speech at the Mansion House averted the danger. Once he had made it plain that if France were attacked Britain would fight beside her, the Germans climbed down. Such a combination was more than they were prepared to tackle, and they in their turn had to eat humble pie.

"Since that time Germany has not made use of any incident to threaten the peace of Europe. In the disputes which led to the two Balkan wars she might easily have found a pretext to attack her neighbours, had she wished to do so; yet she refrained. I regard that as most significant. Nearly three years have now elapsed since the Agadir crisis, so we at least have some reason to hope that the rebuff she suffered then may have shown *her* the red light that she has previously displayed to the alarm of other nations."

The First Lord's cigar had gone out again, so he broke off to relight it. Thinking he had finished what he had to say, de Richleau remarked:

"I have listened to your admirable summary of events with the greatest interest, sir; but I do not find your conclusion based on anything very substantial. Germany's pacific attitude during the past three years might well be accounted for by her biding her time while she still further increases her armaments; and the fact that she did not decide to fight at the time of Agadir is no guarantee that she will not do so when she finds an occasion that suits her better. The German expansionists may be temporarily held in check, but I think it would be most rash to assume that they have abandoned their ambitions."

Mr. Marlborough shook his head. "I did not infer that they had, and I regard Agadir only as the possible turning point in the growth of a strong nation from rash youth to responsible manhood. It is much more the general pattern of the events I have just recalled which encourages me to believe that Germany is far less inclined to draw the sword now than she was formerly. As I have pointed out, at the beginning of the century she could have attacked any of the other great powers singly and had a fair chance of overwhelming them in a short, sharp war which would have cost her little. But that is no longer so. Her own blackmailing tactics have awakened her potential enemies to their danger. France has modernized her armies; Russia has enormously increased hers, while adding to their mobility; and Britain now lies secure behind the most powerful fleet she has ever possessed in her long history. More, those same sabre-rattling tactics have driven the three nations into a mighty alliance. If Germany fights one, she must now fight all. Italy's position in the Mediterranean renders her so vulnerable to sea-power that she would be crazy to join our enemies. That leaves Austria-Hungary, seething with internal race hatreds, as Germany's only certain ally. Strong as she is, how could she hope to emerge victorious from such a conflict?"

"I believe," replied the Duke, "it is generally accepted among the higher General Staff that in the event of war Germany would adopt the Schlieffen plan. If she did, there is a possibility that she might force France to capitulate in six weeks. Russia would then find herself faced with the combined forces of Germany and Austria-Hungary, and she, in her turn, might be defeated."

"I agree with your appreciation of probable German strategy, but I think the Germans would find France a harder nut to crack than they imagine. In any case, the conquest of Russia presents immense difficulties, and once Britain has entered on a war she is not inclined lightly to give it up. So, in no circumstances could Germany hope to achieve swift and inexpensive victory. At best, it could prove for her only a long and costly struggle, terminating in an agreed peace, from which she would gain little of permanent value."

"That's true enough!" boomed Sir Pellinore. "Now let's hear what this young fire-eater has to say."

"One moment!" The First Lord held up a plump hand. "I have not yet quite done. I was about to add that never, in my experience, has Europe shown a greater inclination towards maintaining a lasting peace. I disclose no vital secret when I tell you that, so marked has this become, this year I carried the full naval estimates through the Cabinet only with considerable difficulty. I stuck to my guns because I would rather be safe than sorry; but the majority of my colleagues held that such a high expenditure on armaments could no longer be justified. That the French share this opinion is clear from the strenuous efforts now being made in the Chamber of Deputies to modify the Three Years' Military Service Law. This year, for the first time since 1870, the French President dined at the German Embassy in Paris; and this year, for the first time since 1895, we have accepted an invitation for a British Squadron to visit Kiel during the regatta week. All this, of course, is entirely due to the new spirit of reason and conciliation which Germany has been showing on all international problems; and that the change of attitude is not simply a mask to cover evil intentions, she has given reasonable proof. It is now two years since she made any increase in her naval building programme. Now, Duke, tell me, if you can, what reasons you can have for believing that we are living in a fool's paradise?"

"I admit that I find myself much shaken by your arguments," de Richleau replied, "and I can speak only of possibilities in a small corner of this vast canvas that you have surveyed. It depends whether you consider it likely that all Europe might be set aflame by a fresh incident in the Balkans."

"It is a possibility, but in the present circumstances I consider it unlikely. The Great Powers succeeded in localizing the two Balkan wars of 1912 and 1913, and if the present spirit of goodwill continues there appears an even better chance that they would succeed again."

The Duke shook his head. "It was not merely a third squabble among the Balkan states that I had in mind. I was thinking of a crisis similar to that which arose in 1908, when Austria annexed Bosnia and

Herzegovina; only this time one which would culminate in Serbia actually opening hostilities against the Dual-Monarchy."

"Ah! That would be very different. Austria-Hungary is one of the great powers, and if once she became involved in a war there is no saying what the others might do."

"There's no love lost between her and Russia," put in Sir Pellinore. "What's more, Russia regards herself as the natural protector of the smaller Slav States. Odds are, she'd go to Serbia's assistance. The Germans wouldn't stand for that. If you're right, we might all find ourselves landed in a pretty kettle of fish."

"And *that* is exactly what I fear is going to happen," said the Duke. Then he added after a moment: "Tell me. Have either of you ever heard of an organization called the Black Hand?"

CHAPTER III

THE BLACK HAND

SIR PELLINORE's bright blue eyes narrowed a fraction, but he shook his head. "No. What is it? Sounds like some sort of Sicilian secret society."

"It is a secret society, but it has no connection with the Camorra. It is purely Serbian, and originated through the murder of King Alexander and Queen Draga at Belgrade in 1903. You will, of course, recall the circumstances of that particularly atrocious crime?"

The First Lord nodded. "King Alexander had behaved outrageously towards his people, and there is every reason to suppose that his wife was his evil genius; but the whole world was shocked by the exceptional brutality which accompanied their assassination. As I recollect, the officers who had plotted it broke into their bedroom with drawn swords, pulled them naked from their bed, and literally hacked them both to pieces."

"It was those officers, sir, who founded the Black Hand. They did so for their mutual protection. Many of them were highly connected, and as a united body they proved powerful enough to escape the consequences of their abominable act. Even though the great nations pressed for justice to be done, King Alexander's successor did not feel himself strong enough to punish them, or even force them into permanent retirement."

"Then, if these blackguards have long since secured the immunity which was the cause of their banding together, what object do you suggest that they have in continuing their association?"

"Patriotism—if one may fairly apply that word to a fanatical urge, driving men on to plan any violence which might raise the status of their country, regardless of the cost. All these officers are most fervent nationalists, and in 1911 they reformed their brotherhood, giving it the name of *Ujedinjenje ili Smrt*, which means 'Union or Death' and refers to their ambition to unite all the Yugoslavs under one flag. They will stick at nothing in their attempts to make Serbia a great kingdom. Recently she has proved the victor in two wars, and emerged from them the most powerful nation in the Balkans—yet not as powerful as they had hoped. Those conflicts gained her a great increase of territory in the south, but she was robbed of the spoils that she considered rightfully hers in the west, by the decision of the London conference."

"You mean the decision of the Great Powers to support Austria's suggestion that the ex-Turkish province of Albania should be turned into an independent kingdom?"

"I do! Serbia's dearest ambition was to have free access to the Adriatic. She fought a costly campaign to that end, and with the capture of Scutari won a good port for the direct shipment of Serbian products overseas. But she was not allowed to keep it, or the great hinterland that thousands of her soldiers had died to free from Turkish rule."

Mr. Marlborough's heavy brows drew together in a frown. "No doubt you know that Prince William of Wied was selected by the powers as the ruler of this new state. He landed in Albania only last month, and I gather that he is already meeting with great difficulty in imposing his authority on its turbulent inhabitants. Is it your view that the Serbs resent having been deprived of this territory so strongly that they might seize upon its troubled state as an excuse to take up arms again and reoccupy it?"

"Hot-headed as they are, I hardly think they are likely to prove as rash as that," de Richleau replied cautiously. "For to do so would be to defy an award which has been agreed upon by all the great nations. But the fact remains that they consider that award flagrantly unjust and, since it was inspired by Austria, it will have added fuel to their already burning hatred for that country. No! I regard it as much more probable that they will instigate fresh trouble in Bosnia. As you remarked earlier, when referring to its annexation in 1908, a high percentage of the inhabitants of that province are of Serbian blood, and the arbitrary manner in which Austria acquired it aroused great resentment among the other powers. So, should Serbia at any time re-open the question of its status, she could count on a certain amount of backing. The sort of thing I had in mind was that she might secretly ferment a demand in the province for Home Rule, and, on the Austrian government refusing it, make that a cause for war."

At the words 'Home Rule' the First Lord smiled a little ruefully. In recent months the Irish question had dominated all others in the Cabinet, and given its members worse headaches than any they had had in the whole of their careers.

When, after years of bitter wrangling, it had at last become apparent that no legal measure could longer prevent the Home Rule Bill becoming law, the people of Northern Ireland had begun preparations to resist its application by force of arms. The Irish Nationalists in the House of Commons dared make no concession from fear of being repudiated by their own people, and as the third largest parliamentary party they held the balance of power between the Liberals and Conservatives, so could, if driven to it, have deprived the Liberal Government of its working majority. Yet, despite this threat, the Cabinet had decided that some provision must be made that would protect Ulster from actual coercion. Barely three weeks before, the First Lord had made his own position plain by a speech at Bradford, in which he declared that, while he would do all that was necessary to prevent Ulster from stopping the rest of Ireland having the Parliament they desired, he would never be a party to measures to force her to come under a Dublin Parliament. But how this compromise could be put into practice, still remained a matter of fierce disagreement. A week later, at the Curragh, a number of senior Army officers stationed in Ireland had openly declared it their intention to refuse to obey orders should they be called on to lead their troops against the Ulstermen; and, aroused to indignation by what appeared to be a betrayal of their ideals, the bulk of the British people were now angrily demanding that the government should either guarantee the independence of Northern Ireland, or resign. On all sides tempers had risen to boiling point. In the House, hardly a sitting now passed without some exchange of acrimonious violence; and in Ireland itself it was feared that any day civil war, coupled with mutiny in the Army, might break out.

It was, therefore, no wonder that the statesman having had his mind jerked back to the urgent problem with which he and his colleagues were wrestling as in a nightmare, should momentarily look a little glum. But Sir Pellinore ignored the train of thought that the Duke had unwittingly provoked, and boomed at him:

"These Balkan states are a pack of trouble-makers. Always were. All of 'em. But for Serbia to attack Austria would be suicidal. Habsburg Empire may be pretty rotten internally, but it's still got sufficient kick in it to settle the hash of a little country like Serbia."

"Oh, Serbia *alone*, yes!"

The First Lord gave a quick nod. "We are already agreed that, if any great power became involved in war, that might swiftly precipitate a general European conflagration. But Serbia must have been greatly weakened by the losses she has sustained in her two recent wars. Should she fight again as soon as you suggest, she would run a big risk of being overwhelmed before help could reach her from Russia, France, or Britain."

"There, I agree." De Richleau spread out his slim hands in a slightly foreign gesture. "But, as I have already pointed out, these men of the Black Hand are not ordinary people. They are both ruthless and rash; and I believe that they would take pretty well any gamble that offered a fair chance of lifting Serbia to the status of a great power. Everything you have said, sir, has reinforced my own conviction—that in the event of a war between the Triple Entente and the Central Powers, the Entente would eventually emerge victorious. No doubt these Serbian plotters are of the same opinion. If we are right, it follows that in such a war Serbia would have backed the right horse. She would be entitled to claim a seat among the victors at the Peace Table, and there demand her share in the division of the spoils. Even had she been defeated, over-run, occupied, and pillaged in the meantime, unscrupulous and ambitious minds might still consider that not too great a price to pay for the ultimate gaining of such a prize. And that is what I fear. That Serbia will challenge Austria in the near future with the deliberate intention of bringing about a world war as the most likely means of gaining her own ends."

Sir Pellinore grunted. "No holes in your reasonin'. But are your premises right? This gang of bloodstained ruffians may have had enough pull to escape a shooting party, or the rope; but it doesn't follow that they've enough influence to push their country into a war."

"In the past ten years many of them have risen to comparatively high rank in the army. They have also recruited some of the best brains among the politicians and professional classes of their country. All are pledged under the most frightful penalties to observe the strictest secrecy and to obey without question all orders from their chief. The selflessness, determination and subtlety with which the movement works can be compared only with the machinations of the Jesuits at the height of their power. That may sound an exaggeration, but I assure you that it is not. You must remember that mentally the Balkan peoples are at least a century behind those of Western Europe. In those countries of dark forests and desolate gorges, witchcraft is still practised openly. Even the upper classes carry charms to protect them from the evil-eye. They live with a violence, fearlessness and poetry that we have forgotten. They talk of their national heroes as though these ancient paladins had died only yesterday. For centuries they conspired against their Turkish overlords; so mystery, plotting, and a willingness to risk death for secret causes are in their blood. That spirit still animates rich and poor alike, and it explains how the society of the Black Hand has succeeded in getting a firm grip on the direction of Serbian affairs. I have good reason to believe that both the Crown Prince Alexander and Mr. Pashitch, the Prime Minister, have sworn allegiance to the Black Hand, and that its chief actually holds a position which would enable him, at any time he chose, to provoke an incident designed to lead to war."

"That is a grave charge to make against distinguished persons, Duke," remarked Mr. Marlborough somewhat coldly. "Have you any evidence by which you can support it?"

"None, with regard to the Crown Prince or the Premier; but I repeat only what I have heard on good authority—how good you can judge if you know who I mean by Colonel Dragutin Dimitriyevitch."

As the other two shook their heads, de Richleau continued with a reminiscent smile: "I met him in somewhat unusual circumstances. His ankles were lashed firmly to the low branch of a big tree. He was hanging there upside down; and some Kurdish tribesmen were about to slit his throat, so that he would have bled to death in the same manner as a pig."

With a loud guffaw, Sir Pellinore slapped his great thigh. "Go on, young feller; this sounds good."

The Duke smiled back. "Perhaps I should have led up to this episode by giving you some idea how it came about. You will recall that in her attempt to resist the Balkan League, Turkey had to fight three widely separated campaigns: one in Thrace against the Bulgarians attacking from the north; one in the region of Salonika against the Greeks attacking from the south; and one in central Macedonia, against the Serbians and Montenegrins attacking from both the north and west. The Turkish armies of Salonika and Macedonia were doomed to defeat from the beginning, owing to the vast area they were called on to defend with forces far inferior to those of their enemies. Moreover, it was clear that if the enemy struck to the east of them, their strategic position would be rendered hopeless, as there would be no means at all by which they could be reinforced and maintained from the bases in Turkey proper. Both armies soon suffered initial defeats, and the bulk of both fell back towards Monastir, where they met, rallied, and reformed as one strategic unit. At this juncture the Turkish High Command decided to send them such help as could be spared while there was still time, and I was placed in command of a mixed force, with orders to march to their assistance.

"The railway from Constantinople to Ferejik was still open, so we were able to make use of it for some six hundred miles, as far as Demir Hisar, and it was there I assembled my so-called corps. It consisted of half a dozen battalions of regulars, eight of reservists, three brigades of fairly good artillery, and a further five thousand auxiliaries of all kinds—Syrian, Georgian and Armenian levies with Arab and Kurdish cavalry.

"As you can imagine, the country through which we had to advance was pretty hideous. The roads were no better than tracks, and the tracks led through endless valleys dominated by rocky heights on either side. I did what I could to protect my column by throwing out a strong advance guard and large numbers of vedettes on either flank, but from the beginning we were subjected to sniping all day and raids each night. We had the Greeks to the south of us, the Bulgarians to the north, and the whole country was infested with Macedonian irregulars who appeared ready to die happily if only they could first shoot a Turk.

"Johnny Turk is a brave and determined fighter; but the pace of the force had to be that of its slowest vehicles, and often guns and wagons had to be dragged one by one up steep inclines, or across boulder-strewn gullies. And the nerves of the finest troops in the world will become frayed in such circumstances, if meanwhile they are under harassing fire from a constant succession of ambushes. After a few days they began to ignore my orders about taking prisoners, and promptly butchered any of the enemy who fell into their hands. Those were the circumstances in which I made the acquaintance of Colonel Dimitriyevitch.

"I had ridden far forward one day, with a small staff, to see the lie of the land. Apparently he had done the same, having been sent on a reconnaissance by the commander of a Serbian division. His party had had a brush with a troop of my Kurdish cavalry, and had got the worst of it. His companions were dead and he was within an ace of death himself; but my opportune arrival saved him, and I made him my personal prisoner.

"Naturally, although he expressed his gratitude, he at first refused to talk on any subject connected with the war. But he was obviously a man of culture and considerable intelligence, so I had him treated well, invited him now and then to eat at my own table, and went out of my way to win his confidence.

"In view of the anxieties of my situation, and the extraordinary heavy demands made on me as the commander of a force slowly moving forward, but attacked by enemies on all sides, why I should have devoted so much time to my solitary prisoner I cannot pretend to explain. It may be that I sensed instinctively the black, evil heart that he concealed beneath an urbane manner, and realized subconsciously that it held secrets that I had been given a unique opportunity to learn. In any case, by the time my force joined the main army in the neighbourhood of Monastir, he had come to regard me as a friend.

"A few days later a general battle took place. After four days of severe fighting the Turkish army of the west was heavily defeated. I had taken the precaution to form a small reserve of about fifteen hundred picked men. To have flung them into the battle in its final stages could not possibly have influenced its outcome; so when the break-up of the army ensued I still had intact this well-disciplined body of reliable troops. All means of communication with my superior officers had been cut off, so I decided to retire through the mountains to the south-west, in the hope of finding some town having a Turkish garrison which I might reinforce: or, failing that, eventually reaching the Turkish stronghold of Yannina in the Epirus.

"By a forced march of twenty-four hours, I extricated my troops from any risk of being surrounded and captured during the aftermath of the battle. But it was now late November, so the cold and hardships that we suffered, as we continued our progress across the bleak uplands, were intense. In addition, the peasantry were bitterly hostile, which meant that to secure food enough to keep life in the bodies of my men I had to turn a blind eye to the methods they employed in forcing the wretched country people to disclose where they had hidden their cattle and secret stores of grain. It was a nightmare journey, which I would that I could forget, except for one thing—I still had my prisoner with me.

"From the day I rescued him he realized that, guarded as he was by semi-barbarous troops who hated all he represented, if he were caught attempting to escape his life would not be worth a moment's purchase. And later, when my men became desperate from privation, he knew his life to be really safe only as long as he remained within call of me: so day and night he kept in my immediate vicinity and made himself as useful to me in small ways as he could. In fact, he became my constant companion; and after the Turkish army had been so completely defeated at Monastir, there was no reason why he should longer refrain from discussing military matters with me.

"None of the Turkish officers on my small staff had more than a smattering of any language other than their own, but Dimitriyevitch spoke French fluently. During those long, dark, winter nights we often talked for hours, as we sat, a bottle of *ouzo* between us, huddled in our greatcoats in the corner of one of the burnt-out farm-houses that I used as a temporary headquarters.

"Gradually I got to know about him: partly because there was a streak of conceit in his evil nature, and at times when the *ouzo* had warmed him up the desire to boast got the better of his discretion; partly because he admired the way in which I handled difficult situations, and, seeing that the Turkish goose was as good as cooked, he hoped to induce me to enter the service of Serbia.

"Bit by bit, he let it out that he was one of the officers who, nine years earlier, had personally participated in the murder of King Alexander and Queen Draga. He had been one of the prime movers in founding the Black Hand. He spoke with pride of its growth, iron discipline, and now nation-wide ramifications. It was he who told me that several members of the Serbian royal family and government are pledged to obey its orders; and that the secret council of the society would stop at nothing—not even the plunging of the whole of Europe into war—to achieve their final purpose of winning for Serbia a great Empire in the Eastern Mediterranean."

When the Duke ceased speaking the other two continued to regard him in speculative silence. Both thought that he looked remarkably young to have held the considerable field command with which he had been dispatched from Constantinople, yet recognized the natural air of authority in his bearing. Neither could quite decide how much of his story to believe, but they were much too polite to say so; and, after a moment, Sir Pellinore exclaimed:

"Well, I'll be damned! Pity, though, you didn't leave this feller Dimibitch hanging by his heels. Still, you weren't to know that at the time. But tell us the rest of the yarn. Did you manage to evade capture till the end of the war?"

De Richleau nodded. "I lost a lot of my men through sniping, frost-bite, and some ugly skirmishes that occurred when at last we reached the vicinity of Yannina. The place was already partially invested, so I had to fight my way in; but the remnant I brought made quite a useful little reinforcement for the Governor. Having handed my troops over to him, I spent a few days assessing the local situation, and as it did not appear to me that the town could hold out for very long I decided to make my way back to Turkey. A fishing smack took me across the Adriatic to Brindisi, and from there it was easy to get an Italian freighter round to Constantinople."

"Well done! Damn good show! But what happened to your pal, Disivitch?"

"I left him in Yannina. The Turks there were taking prisoners in the orthodox manner and treating them reasonably well, so I knew that he would come to no harm."

"Tell me," put in the First Lord, "when you got back to Constantinople, did you report to anyone these extraordinary conversations that you had had with your prisoner?"

"No, sir."

"May I ask, why? You are a British citizen; and a man of your position must surely have realized that our Ambassador would have been much interested in hearing what you had to tell."

The Duke's strong teeth flashed in a smile. "Perhaps I ought to have done so; but the fact is that I did not believe the greater part of what Colonel Dimitriyevitch told me, at the time. About the Black Hand, yes. Its existence is more or less common knowledge in the Balkans; but not the extent of its power, that such highly placed persons were involved, or his own prominent position in the movement. I regarded him as a megalomaniac, obsessed with dark dreams of power. The study of his evil personality had fascinated me, but I did not consider him a danger to anyone outside his immediate circle, much less a menace to the peace of Europe."

"What, then, has caused you to change your opinion?"

"I met him again a little over a month ago in Sofia. He told me that

Serbia is now sufficiently recovered to undertake another war, and that the experience gained in her campaigns of 1912 and 1913 would enable her to put into the field the finest army for its size in Europe. He more than hinted that a pretext would be sought to attack Austria this coming summer, and he then offered me a high command in the Serbian army—which I declined on the excuse that I was still pledged to Turkey for some time to come."

"Do you really believe that he was in a position to make you such an offer?"

"Indeed I do. What point would there be in his making it, if he were unable to secure such a post for me? And the very fact that he has sufficient influence to nominate generals for high commands gives the strongest possible support to the statement he made to me on numerous occasions while he was my prisoner. Namely, that he not only was a founder member of the Black Hand, but is to-day its Grand Master."

"You said yourself that at that time you considered him a megalomaniac. May it not be that he is still suffering from illusions of grandeur, and that all that he told you recently is pure moonshine?"

De Richleau shook his head. "No. That is the terrible thing about it. And on this you can check up for yourselves. Dimitriyevitch is, in his own black way, as sane as any of us; and he is now the official chief of all the Serbian Intelligence departments. I need not stress the power that such a position gives him. He can report adversely upon highly placed officers and government officials who are not members of the Black Hand, and so secure the removal of all opposition from his path. He controls secret funds which he can use for bribery in cases where threats fail. His post entitles him to know the innermost secrets of Serbian diplomacy; and among his agents there must be men whom, under the pretext of national safety, he can order to commit assassinations. You see now how grave is the danger that I fear. What is there to stop such a man, in such a post, choosing his own moment and creating an incident that will lead to war?"

While the Duke had been speaking, bursts of hearty cheering had broken out above them in the ballroom, and now the band struck up the Austrian National Anthem. Midnight had come: the revellers had unmasked, and were openly showing their delight at the presence in their midst of the lovely Archduchess Ilona Theresa.

Mr. Marlborough stood up. "You must forgive me if I leave you now, Duke, but I must pay my formal respects to Her Imperial Highness. Our talk has been most interesting. In fact, it will give me much to think about, and you may be sure that we shall not lightly dismiss the warning you have brought us. To procure for you a commission in the British Army is, I fear, beyond my powers; but if there is any other way in which I can be of service to you, pray don't hesitate to let me know."

As de Richleau murmured his thanks, Sir Pellinore boomed:

"Bit above my head, all this international stuff; but I'd like to hear more about your soldiering. Perhaps you'll lunch with me one day? Where you staying?"

"The Coburg," replied the Duke. "And I should be delighted to lunch with you."

"Right! Drop you a line about that. Best leave you here, now, though; and spare the blushes of the lovely Archduchess, eh?"

The three of them had just emerged from among the banked-up orchids. With a nod, and a twinkle in his bright blue eyes, Sir Pellinore turned away with the First Lord and, side by side, they crossed the broad, open space, beneath the centre of the marquee. As they reached the iron staircase leading up to the ballroom, he asked:

"What d'you make of him, eh?"

Mr. Marlborough's heavy brows drew together. "It's hard to say. He must know that we can easily verify his claim to have served the Turks as a general, so it is unlikely he was lying to us about that: and he certainly is no fool. He gives the impression of being both shrewd and honest; but perhaps he has deceived himself. I pray God that it may be so; for if he is right about Dimitriyevitch we will have even worse worries on our hands than the Irish business, before we are much older."

"He's on to something, all right. I'd bet a packet on that," muttered the tall baronet. "All he said ties up with bits of stuff that have been reaching me for months past. This Black Hand thing exists, of course. Has done for years. Not a doubt about that. So does Dimititch—or whatever the damn feller's name is. Constant replacement of people holding big jobs in Serbia by comparatively unknown men has been puzzling me a bit. This amorous young Duke has provided us with a solution that's all too clear. But what's his game, eh? Has he been sent here to pull a double bluff? Is he on our side, or theirs? That's what I'd like to know."

The First Lord nodded. "Yes. The sooner you have him vetted, the better. There should be plenty of information available about a man of his rank and past political activities. Get Vernon Kell to let you have all that is known about him. Of course, his request to be given senior rank in the British Army is quite preposterous. But he says that he is of British nationality and, if his heart is really in the right place, other work can be found for him. In fact, I believe a man having the qualities of this Duke de Richleau might prove invaluable to us."

"You've hit the nail on the head as usual," boomed Sir Pellinore. "That's why I asked him to lunch."

CHAPTER IV

THE BRIEFING OF A RELUCTANT SPY

TEN days after the masked ball at Dorchester House, four men sat round a small table in a quiet corner of the smoking-room at the Carlton Club. They were Sir Pellinore Gwaine-Cust, General Sir Henry Wilson, Sir Bindon Blackers and the Duke de Richleau. They had just lunched together and were waiting to be served with the liqueur brandies which they had ordered with their coffee.

The Duke had already lunched with Sir Pellinore during the previous week, and had, moreover, spent two long evening sessions with him, at which they had talked far into the night in the library of the millionaire baronet's big mansion, a stone's throw away in Carlton House Terrace. So they now had one another's measure; but de Richleau was meeting the other two men for the first time.

As he took from his case, and lit, a long Hoyo de Monterrey cigar—a brand that he especially favoured, and he was a connoisseur of no mean order in such matters—his apparently casual glance rested on the face of first one then the other of his new acquaintances, seeking to probe the real personalities that lay behind the pleasant, carefree manner they had both displayed at the luncheon table.

The General was a tall man with quick, humorous eyes, great vitality, and a hearty laugh. De Richleau knew a little, although not much, about him. He was Director of Military Operations at the War Office. He spoke French with great fluency, and was said to be the only British officer who had succeeded in winning the complete confidence of the French General Staff. Sir Bindon Blackers was slim and round-shouldered, with a fine domed forehead from which the hair was receding, and a large, fair fluffed-out moustache. About him, de Richleau knew nothing except that he was the Foreign Office representative on the Committee of Imperial Defence.

A dark-liveried club servant of ecclesiastical mien reverently placed the brandies on the table and silently withdrew. When they had all sniffed and sipped the *fine champagne* appreciatively, de Richleau broke the brief silence by addressing the soldier and the diplomat.

"Gentlemen, I have made my position plain to Sir Pellinore, and it might be as well if I do so to you. He has asked me, on behalf of the British Government, to undertake certain work abroad. I must state frankly that the mission proposed was not of my seeking, and is not to my liking. I am by trade a soldier and, therefore, accustomed to inflict such damage as I can on the enemy in the open. Having held high rank in several foreign armies, I am well aware of the value of secret intelligence; but never before have I visualized myself going out to get it. I have always admired the courage of those who do; but I am sure you will agree that to men of our standing the thought of attempting to steal papers in a house to which one has been invited as a guest, of pandering to weak men's vices in order to blackmail or worm their secrets out of them, of seeking to win the friendship and confidence of people with the deliberate intention of betraying them, can only be repulsive."

"Oh come!" protested the General cheerfully. "You're thinking of exceptional cases, Duke. It's not usually as bad as all that, and to my mind serving one's country justifies most things."

De Richleau nodded and rejoined a trifle coldly, "If it were not for that aspect of the matter, General, I should not be here. Sir Pellinore has been at great pains to point out to me that previous circumstances in my career, coupled with my considerable knowledge of military matters, provide me with such unique equipment for undertaking this mission with a fair chance of success, that I should be little short of a traitor if I declined it."

"So you would be," growled Sir Pellinore. "It's you who told us that this feller Dissiwitch has the power to dish out life or death for half the young manhood of Europe; and you're already in his confidence. What other Briton can claim as much, and so stand a chance of heading him off—or, at least, finding out for us when he means to spring his mine?"

"Dimitriyevitch," corrected the Duke affably. "Anyhow, it suffices for the moment that I have agreed to take on this dirty work, granted one proviso. I insist on knowing the big picture."

"You hold the threads of this affair, not we," smiled Sir Bindon. "So I hardly see how we can help you."

"Oh, yes, you can!" de Richleau smiled back. "At least, I am assuming that Sir Pellinore brought General Sir Henry Wilson and yourself here to-day for that purpose. I hold only one end of this tangled skein. Or perhaps it would be a better metaphor to say that I am the man who has an opportunity to watch the hand that holds the lighted match, but can see only a little way along the powder chain. Whereas you can see where it leads, and are in a position to give a reasonable forecast of the time, size, and immediate effects of the explosion when it occurs. And it is on such matters that I require all the information you can see your way to give me."

Sir Henry shrugged. "I honestly fail to see how our views on the opening moves in a European war can have any bearing on your mission."

"Then I will tell you. My immediate task lies in Serbia, but I have no intention of confining my activities to that country should the possibility of securing valuable information prompt me to visit others. Among the numerous titles I inherited is that of an Austrian Count, and I own a castle no great distance from Vienna. My mother was a Russian, and her family are allied to the Romanoffs by marriage. So I have powerful connections in both those countries. I am also acquainted with the rulers of several minor German states, and have often shot with them in their forests. In fact, there are few countries in Europe where I do not know people of position, who could, if they would, disclose to me secrets of some importance."

"See what I meant?" grunted Sir Pellinore, with a knowing look at the General.

Ignoring the interruption, de Richleau went on: "But unless I know roughly what to expect my opportunities will be robbed of a great part of their value."

The General nodded good-humouredly. He had been recalling his host's parting broadside the night before, when he and Sir Bindon had dined in Carlton House Terrace. Sir Pellinore had boomed at him: "You've got to open up to this feller, Henry. I tell you he's a smasher. Never get another chance like it to learn how the minds of the high-ups on the continent are working. I've had him vetted, and I'm satisfied he's straight. Had the devil's own job to persuade him to work for us. But now he's agreed, he won't stick at half measures: and if we're to get the best out of him, we've got to give him the right stuff to go on. Not vital secrets, of course; but everything up the Staff College line; and on probable enemy strategy, a bit beyond it. After all, that's still only speculation and we may have cause to modify our own views before the showdown. Dimthebitch is the feller I want to know about first and foremost; but, if I'm any judge, de Richleau's capable of pulling all sorts of other rabbits out of the hat. Anyhow, since he insists on a high-level survey of the big picture, you and Bindon, here, have got to give it him. Understand?"

Sir Henry and Sir Bindon had taken their departure in a far from happy frame of mind. Both had long been accustomed to observing the strictest secrecy in all that concerned their work, and they did not at all fancy the idea of discussing future strategy and diplomacy with a foreign-born soldier of fortune. Nevertheless, they both had great faith in Sir Pellinore's judgment, and knew that he owed his unique position behind the scenes of government largely to the fact that he never even hinted at the existence of secret matters, unless he had excellent cause to do so.

In consequence they had come to to-day's lunch party still inclined to exercise great caution, but with open minds. Then, as the meeting had progressed, those quick minds of theirs had moved forward to the same conclusion. Sir Pellinore was right; de Richleau was a man who might render incalculably valuable services to Britain if he were properly briefed. It was, therefore, their duty, short of disclosing vital secrets, to take him into their confidence.

One quick glance between Sir Bindon and the General was enough to assure the diplomat that they were in agreement. Then he said:

"Very well, Duke. What do you wish to know?"

"First, the probable line-up."

"If Serbia sets the ball rolling, as you suggest, it will be Serbia, Russia, and the Empires of France and Britain against Austria-Hungary and Germany."

"What about Italy?"

"As the third partner in the Triple Alliance the Germans are no doubt counting on her; but a secret clause in her treaty with the Central Powers releases her from any obligation to enter a war against Great Britain, and we think she will invoke it. Owing to her ambitions in the Trentino and Trieste area, she may later even come in on our side, if we play our cards skilfully."

"And the smaller countries?"

"The probability is that, with the exception of Belgium, they will stay out unless the struggle is a prolonged one."

"It will be," grunted the General.

"In that case, Bulgaria, Rumania, Greece and Turkey will probably be drawn in. Each has its pro-Entente and pro-German parties; so the side each takes will be determined by the apparent prospects of victory of one or other of the great combinations at the time that circumstances decide them to enter the conflict."

"You mentioned Belgium as an exception?"

"Yes. We have reason to believe that, instead of attempting to force the great fortress system that guards the Franco-German frontier, the Germans intend to adopt the Schlieffen Plan. That involves the infringement of Belgian neutrality; and, of course, as Britain is one of the signatories of the Treaty of London, guaranteeing Belgium neutrality; such an act would commit us to sending an ultimatum to Germany, quite apart from any obligation we may have to aid France."

De Richleau turned towards the General. "How many divisions do you estimate that Germany will be able to put in the field for the opening phase?"

"When her mobilization is completed, one hundred and ten," replied Sir Henry promptly.

"And France?"

"Eighty-five."

"However, the French have only one frontier to defend, whereas Germany has two. That should even matters up as far as the Western Front is concerned."

With a quick movement, Sir Henry knocked the ash off his cigar. "Sir Bindon has just mentioned the Schlieffen Plan. As a military man, Duke, you will no doubt have heard of that plan and be aware of its broad outline?"

"Yes. Its essence is the immediate concentration of all available forces in the West; then a gigantic turning movement for the invasion of France by way of Belgium."

"Exactly! Field Marshal Count von Schlieffen was completely ruthless and entirely logical. He said that, even if Russia unexpectedly declared war and her cavalry overran the provinces of northern Germany, even if the French took the offensive and penetrated deep into Alsace-Lorraine, even if the invasion of Belgium meant Britain going to France's assistance—all these liabilities must be accepted in order to bring overwhelming force against the French Army, and put France out of the war in six weeks. However, now that Russia is definitely committed to declare war immediately France does so, Germany cannot possibly leave her northern frontier entirely undefended; but we believe she will adopt a modification of the Schlieffen plan. Our estimate is that the Germans will leave one-fifth of their forces to defend their Russian frontier and concentrate the other four-fifths against France."

"If you are right eighty-eight German divisions will be opposed to eighty-five French. That is not overwhelming force."

"The Germans may achieve it in the vital sector."

"Why?"

"According to the Schlieffen plan, less than a third of the German forces are to be disposed along the Franco-German frontier. The key Belgium fortress of Liége is to be seized by a *coup-de-main* immediately the order for mobilization is given. Immediately the five railways radiating from it are under German control, the greater part of the German Army is to debouch through Belgium and, in a scythe-like movement, descend on Paris. Therefore, should the French forces be more or less evenly distributed, they will find themselves outnumbered by about three to one at the western end of their line."

"Knowing this, surely the French will take the precaution to guard against such an eventuality, by concentrating a large part of their army in the neighbourhood of Amiens?"

The General hesitated a second, then he said: "You will appreciate that I cannot give you any definite information about the plans of the

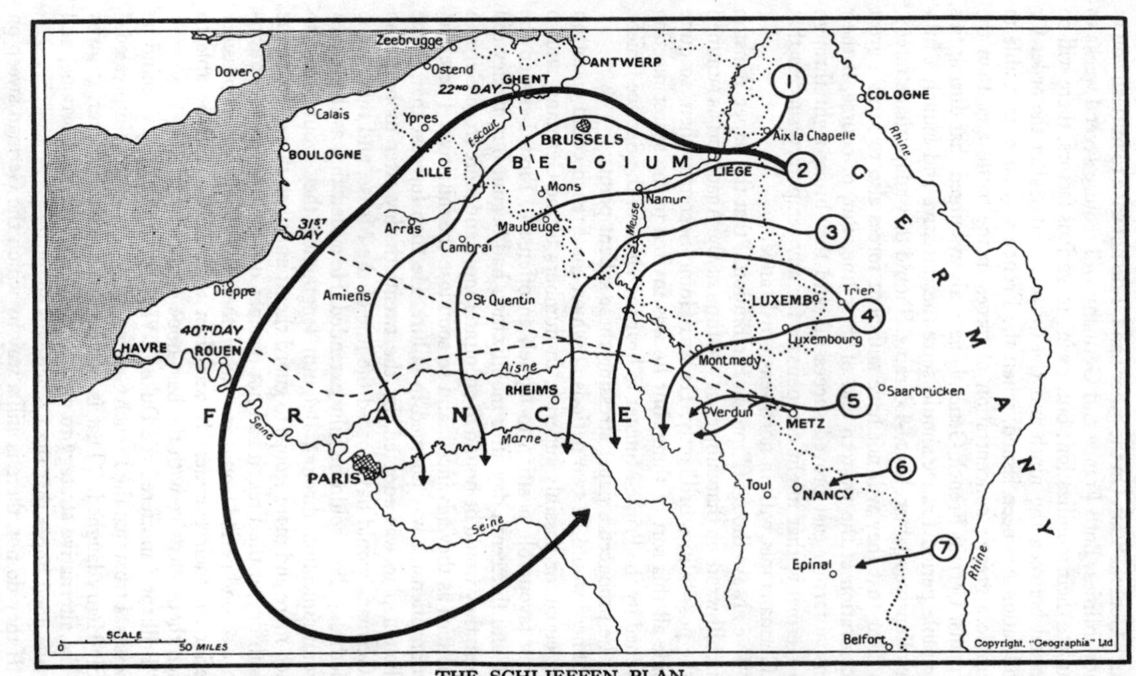

THE SCHLIEFFEN PLAN

Thick line: the original plan for enveloping the French Armies. Thin lines: routes actually taken by the German Armies. Note the full extension of the invading forces (broken line) on the 40th day

French General Staff. On the other hand, I do not wish to mislead you as to possibilities. Both France and Germany will require several weeks to complete their mobilization; but, owing to various factors, there will be a period between the ninth and the thirteenth day after the order for mobilization has been issued, when the French will have been able to assemble a greater concentration of forces in the battle area than the Germans. Certain French Generals have always urged that during this favourable period France should seize the initiative and launch a full-scale offensive against Alsace-Lorraine. Should they adopt that strategy, it is clear that they will not have sufficient forces also to form a great concentration at the western end of their line. But, of course, if their offensive farther east proved successful, and they broke right through into Germany, that might compensate for any temporary success that the Germans met with in north-eastern France."

"I've always thought," put in Sir Bindon, "that the paper Winston Churchill wrote on that subject at the time of the Agadir crisis summed up the possibilities brilliantly. He was Home Secretary then, so quite outside all this sort of thing, but he was invited to the secret meeting convened by the Prime Minister to hear the views of the Service Chiefs. Later he produced a paper stressing these salient points:

"There would be two periods at which the French could count on being equal, or possibly superior, in numbers to the Germans, and so be in a favourable position to launch an offensive. First, between the ninth and thirteenth day after mobilization had begun. But, if they did so then, they would be bound to encounter more and more fresh German formations as they advanced, and so soon lose the initiative. Therefore, such an offensive was doomed to failure. He then forecast that, if the Schlieffen plan was adopted, by the twentieth day after mobilization the Germans would have forced the line of the Meuse, and that by the fortieth day they would be fully extended. He added that as their lines of communication through Belgium lengthened they would have to detach more and more troops to guard them; and that, therefore, by the fortieth day, if the French had not dissipated their forces in the meantime, a second period would arise when they would be equal, or possibly superior, to their enemies. It was then that they should be able to launch their offensive with the best hope of success."

"Brilliant!" muttered the Duke. "What amazing clarity of mind he possesses. I trust that the French General Staff were suitably impressed."

Sir Henry laughed. "That is not for me to say. However, it gives you the alternative strategy to an attack through Alsace-Lorraine, and we have good hopes that the French will adopt it."

"If they do not, there is still a way by which the German sweep on Paris could be arrested."

"I should be most interested to hear it, Duke."

"It is to land a British Army at the French Channel ports, and deploy it to strengthen the French left."

Sir Bindon did not flicker an eyelid, and the General's laugh rang out quite naturally. They were both past masters in the art of dissimulation where Britain's vital secrets were concerned. For years Sir Henry Wilson had spent all his leaves cycling up and down the roads of Belgium and northern France, so that he might know by heart every stream and contour of the country when the time came, as he was convinced it would, to undertake that very operation. But half its value would be lost if even a hint of our intentions reached the Germans.

"No, no, Duke!" he protested. "That would be far beyond our capabilities. Think of the immense difficulties with which we should be faced in organizing and transporting such an Expeditionary Force—and the time it would take. The Germans would be half way to Paris before we could even get started. Besides, how many divisions could we put into the field? Four—six at the outside. They would be swallowed up and lost in the general mêlée, and such a force could not possibly hope to turn the tide of battle."

He was using the very arguments that the Naval Staff had used in 1911, when they had opposed the War Office plan, and had maintained that the British Army should be retained at home, as a striking force to be used later against Antwerp or the German coast, as opportunity offered.

De Richleau shrugged. "The British have a peculiar genius for organization, General, and in an emergency are capable of acting with surprising speed; so I believe the difficulties you refer to could be overcome. In such a case, too, it is not the size but the high quality of the British Army that would count; and, above all, the moral effect of such a stroke. Every French soldier would fight with redoubled determination if he knew that British troops were facing the common enemy with him."

Now it was the Duke who was using the arguments with which Sir Henry had got the better of the sailors; but Britain's leading strategist only shook his head again, and said a trifle brusquely: "Can't be done, Duke. Take it from me!"

"What use, then, do you propose to make of the Army? Surely you do not intend to keep it here indefinitely from fear of invasion?"

The General grinned. "That's a leading question, and one that I'm not prepared to answer. We shall find a use for it in due course, never fear. But it's going to take time to build it up to a size at which it would be capable of intervening with definite effect in a continental war; and to begin with great numbers of regular officers and N.C.O.s will be needed to train the new levies. As for invasion, we have little fear of that. Of course, the Navy can't guarantee us against enemy landings carried out on dark nights or during periods of fog; but such raiding parties could have no more than a nuisance value. Within a few hours they would find themselves cut off, and as soon as they ran out of ammunition would be compelled to surrender. No major force with heavy equipment would stand an earthly chance of getting ashore and establishing a permanent foothold. I don't pretend to know much about the Naval side of the picture, but it is obvious that the French and British fleets combined will give us overwhelming superiority at sea."

For a minute they were silent while again sipping their brandy. Then de Richleau asked, "What views do you take of Russia's prospects of making a deep penetration into Germany, should she leave her eastern frontier comparatively open in order to carry out the Schlieffen plan?"

"We're not counting very much on that," Sir Henry replied, setting down his empty glass. "The snag about Russia is the slowness of her mobilization. It may be several months before she can bring her great masses face to face with the enemy. In the meantime it is almost certain that a decision of sorts will have been reached in the West, and we shall be entering a new phase of the war. In the worst event, France will have shot her bolt and be on the defensive the wrong side of Paris—or even out of the war. In the best, the French will be holding the Germans on a line from Antwerp to Verdun. In either case the Germans should have ample time to reinforce their eastern front before the Russian steam-roller really gets going."

"There is, you know, a second Schlieffen plan," remarked Sir Bindon quietly. "Before he died, Count Schlieffen saw the possibility of the Franco-Russian friendship developing into a firm alliance, so that Germany might be faced with war on two fronts simultaneously. Even then he would not allocate more than one-eighth of the German forces to the Russian front; but he placed them skilfully. A glance at the map will show you the Masurian Lakes. Situated in a vast tract of impassable marshes, they form a chain sixty miles in length, having the fortress of Lotzen in its centre, and running north-to-south about thirty miles inside the East Prussian frontier. The Germans call it the Angerapp Line, and von Schlieffen directed that the German Army of the East should deploy some way behind it. He assumed, probably rightly, that the Russians would advance both to the north and south of the barrier. Should they do so, the Germans would be well placed to attack each of the invading forces in turn, and neither would be able to give assistance to the other. In that way it is possible that the Germans might defeat, or at least inflict a severe check on, forces double the number of their own. And, of course, the initial effort of Russia against Germany must be limited by the fact that she also has her Austrian front to think of."

De Richleau nodded, glanced at the General, and asked "What strategy do you think Austria is likely to adopt?"

"She has two alternatives. She can stand on the defensive against Russia and make a maximum effort against Serbia, with the object of putting her smaller enemy right out of the war before coming to grips with her great antagonist. Or, she can devote just sufficient troops to her southern front to hold Serbia in check while launching the bulk of them in an immediate offensive against Russia. Personally, I think her best course would be to adopt the second policy."

"Why?"

"In the first place, because the factor of the comparative slowness of the Russian mobilization enters into matters again. It is estimated that by M plus 18 Russia will have been able to muster on the Austrian front only thirty-one divisions plus eleven cavalry divisions, against a probable Austrian concentration of thirty-eight divisions plus ten cavalry divisions. So, you see, if Austria strikes at once, her initial superiority in numbers should give her a good prospect of gaining a victory which would paralyse Russian activities on that front for some considerable time. There is also the factor that an Austrian offensive against Serbia would be of no value as far as the great over-all battle is concerned. Whereas an offensive against Russia would almost certainly have the effect of lightening the Russian pressure on East Prussia, thus making it unnecessary for the Germans to recall divisions from France. To sum up, I think the second policy is not only to Austria's own best interests, but also the best service she could render to her ally; and it seems obvious that Germany will press her to adopt it."

"Your reasoning is excellent, General," smiled the Duke. "It seems, then, that there is little hope of the Russians drawing any appreciable pressure off the French until the first great clash is over."

There fell another pause. Sir Pellinore, who had long since learned the virtues of refraining from pointless comments when experts were talking, had remained silent for the past half an hour. He now leaned forward, stubbed out his cigar, and said:

"Any more questions, Duke?"

De Richleau shook his handsome head. "No. I am most grateful to Sir Henry and Sir Bindon for having discussed these matters so frankly with me. Except in certain minor respects, the forecast they have given is not very far from that which my own deductions would have led me to expect. But I considered it important to have confirmation of my ideas. It would be of further assistance if I could be supplied with the names of the officers who are expected to play a leading role in the enemy armies, and such data as is available about them. In certain circumstances such knowledge might prove very useful."

"I'll give you a line of introduction to Maurice Hankey," Sir Bindon offered. "He is the Secretary of the Committee of Imperial Defence, and will be able to provide you with all the information we possess on such matters."

"Many thanks, Sir Bindon. And the sooner I see him the better, as now I have agreed to undertake this work, that also applies to my setting out for Serbia."

Five minutes later the four of them were walking from the entrance of the Club, down its short garden path to the street. As they reached the pavement, and paused there to say good-bye before going their several ways, an open motor-car, coming down the hill from Carlton House Terrace, passed them.

In it were the German Ambassador, Prince Lichnowsky, who had just left his Embassy, and Herr Gustav Steinhauer, the Chief of the German Secret Service.

The Ambassador swiftly touched his companion on the arm. "Quick! You see that man standing with his back to the railings? The youngish man with the thin aristocratic face, wearing a Homburg. Do you know him?"

Herr Steinhauer shook his head. "No, Excellency. Who is he?"

"He is a French political exile and a soldier of fortune. De Richleau is his name. The Duc de Richleau. I last saw him a little over a week ago at the ball at Dorchester House. He was then in the company of the First Lord of the Admiralty and Sir Pellinore Gwaine-Cust. They were talking together for nearly half an hour in a secluded corner. From where I was sitting I saw the First Lord and Sir Pellinore go in there, and all three of them come out; so it looked like a pre-arranged rendezvous. Now we see the Duke in Sir Pellinore's company again, and behind the scenes that big bluff Englishman has a finger in every pie. You know, of course, who the other two were?"

"Yes, Excellency. Sir Henry Wilson, the British Director of Military Operations and Sir Bindon Blackers of the Committee of Imperial Defence."

"Correct. And it is obvious that the four of them had had a prolonged lunch together. Why should such important men give so much time to a dangerous adventurer like de Richleau? You must do your best to find out. In any case, have some of your people keep an eye on him. Was the sight you got of him just now good enough for you to recognize him again?"

"*Jawohl, Excellenz*. And I pride myself on never forgetting a face."

CHAPTER V

ON A NIGHT IN MAY, 1914

DE RICHLEAU was loath to leave London. In the past fortnight he had looked up several old friends and made a number of new ones. The season was just opening; the wealth, beauty, rank and fashion of all Britain was now congregating in the capital. Hardly a house in Mayfair, Belgravia, Kensington or Bayswater remained shuttered. In some, as many as forty servants had taken up their summer quarters, and in very few were there less than half a dozen ready to ensure the smooth working of the luncheons, dinners, dances and musical parties which their masters and mistresses would be giving.

The streets and squares were gay with window-boxes full of flowers, and from eleven o'clock each morning until two or three the next they were a scene of constant activity, as chauffeur-driven cars honked their way between carriages and broughams polished to a mirror-like brightness, and drawn by beautifully groomed horses.

It had been the Duke's intention to give himself up to the pleasures of this gay, idle world for the ten weeks or so before its elegant denizens dispersed to seek new distractions on the moors of Scotland, yachting at Cowes, on the vine-covered terraces that overlook the Rhine, or in the casinos of Biarritz and Deauville. He felt that he had well-earned such a holiday, but it was not to be; and with considerable reluctance he had written excusing himself from a score of invitations he had already accepted, on the plea that urgent business necessitated his return to the Continent.

To his additional annoyance a dinner party, to which he had been going on his last night, was cancelled unexpectedly. He was already dressing for it, when a telephone message came through that his hostess had suddenly been taken ill; so he found himself at a loose end. As a rich and distinguished bachelor, he was being made welcome everywhere, and had the poor lady been stricken earlier there were a dozen houses at which he could have proposed himself to dine; but it was now a little late to adopt such a measure, so, after a moment's thought, he rang down and asked the hall-porter to get him a stall at the Gaiety.

At eight-fifteen he alighted from his taxi at the far end of the Strand, his glossy topper at a slightly rakish angle; his white waistcoat, tails, and the star-shaped orchid he wore in his button-hole, hidden by a long evening cloak with a high velvet collar fastened by a gold clasp at the neck. In his left eye he wore a plain glass monocle, without gallery or ribbon, and in one kid-gloved hand he carried a fine malacca cane, at the top of which sparkled a topaz the size of a pigeon's egg, set in a circle of small diamonds.

The show was *After the Girl*, with pretty Isobel Elsom as leading lady, and the catchy music of Paul Rubens. Its plot was of the slenderest, a mere framework on which to hang sentimental duets, dialogues of rather childish humour and rollicking choruses; but its setting, costumes and crowded, colourful, stage were typical of the lavish expenditure of the period. The audience was carefree, easy to please, and added much to the gaiety of the scene for, even as far back as the front rows of the upper circle, everyone was in evening dress, and feminine fashion still dictated low neck-lines and bright colours.

De Richleau was a man who had a great appetite for life. He loved gay music and pretty faces as much as fighting, and hated to waste a single day of his youth without savouring some new experience. So, although his sight was excellent, he was soon using his opera glasses to get a close-up view of the ladies of the chorus. He had decided, almost subconsciously, that he would take one of them out to supper. But which, was now the question.

The female chorus was thirty strong, and chosen for their looks rather than their voices. The management counted on their personal charms to fill a good portion of the stalls each night with rich young men, who came several times every week to admire the graces of individual girls to whom they vowed themselves devoted.

After a careful survey the Duke settled on a slim but well-made blonde who was fifth from the left in the front row. He knew that he might prove unlucky if she was already engaged for the evening to some wealthy young spark whom she hoped to hook in marriage. But, short of that, he thought his prospects fair. Experience in a dozen capitals had shown him that the title on his card usually possessed the magic to induce such fickle beauties to wriggle out of previous engagements, rather than forgo the chance of counting a Duke among their admirers.

At the end of a rousing song by the male chorus, he slipped from his seat, went out to the foyer, and ascertained from an attendant that the lady's name was Lottie de Vaux. Then, still hatless, as the night was warm and fine, he left the theatre. The Strand was a blaze of light, and although it was just on nine o'clock most of the shops were still open. A little way along it he found a florist, where, for a sovereign, he bought a double armful of tall pink roses. On a card he gave the position of his stall, and asked the honour of Miss de Vaux's company at supper. The florist's boy gladly accepted a shilling to convey the bouquet to its destination without delay, and the Duke returned to the theatre.

In the interval an attendant brought him a message that Miss de Vaux would be delighted to sup with him, and would he please meet her at the stage door after the show. In consequence, when the time came, he secured a hansom, and sat in it until he saw the members of the company begin to emerge from the side entrance of the theatre; then he alighted and joined the group of top-hatted young amorists who had assembled there with a similar object to himself.

When Miss de Vaux appeared, her mass of fluffed-out golden hair now half-hidden under a coquettishly-draped lace scarf, he at once bowed over the plump little hand she gave him, and kissed it.

"Oh, my!" she exclaimed, with a giggle, and added as they walked towards the waiting cab: "Of course, I knew from your card you were a foreigner, but I wasn't expecting anything quite so dashing. Acting like that with all those people looking on was enough to make any girl blush. Though it's a pretty custom all the same, and I'm not saying I didn't like it."

"It was no more than a proper tribute to your beauty;" the Duke smiled, "and from your name I thought you might quite possibly be French yourself."

"Me! Oh yes, but only on my mother's side," declared Miss de Vaux hastily, illogically, and untruthfully. Her real name was Emily Stiggins, and her family had originally come from Yorkshire.

With her foot on the step of the hansom she paused, the foreignness of her new acquaintance occurring to her again, and asked a trifle suspiciously, "Where are you taking me?"

"To Romanos," replied the Duke. "Unless there is anywhere else that you prefer."

"Oh fine! I love it there." She flashed him a bright smile as she stepped in, her momentary qualms now at rest. She had feared that, being a foreign nobleman, he might have intended to take her to Claridges or the Ritz, and Emily Stiggins knew her station. Such haunts of the aristocracy were not for chorus girls, until and unless they had the luck to marry into it. On the other hand, it had been equally possible that he had planned to give her supper in a private room at Kettners. The self-styled Miss Lottie de Vaux was no prude and had more than once risked her reputation to retain a wealthy admirer, but experience had soon taught her that it never paid for a girl like herself to let a man suppose her easy game to begin with.

As she settled herself in the cab, she wondered whether the Duke was as rich as he looked, and how long she would be able to keep him dangling before she had to let him take her somewhere less public than Romanos. She decided that he looked the sort who would soon come out with a straight offer, and give her little chance to shilly-shally. She had had plenty of practice in handling men, but she already doubted her ability to make this one dance to her usual tune.

It was now just on midnight, but the pavements of the Strand were still crowded. The pubs were closing, and from them issued small knots of people, quite a number of whom were a little tipsy. Whisky was only three shillings a bottle, gin half a crown, and beer a penny a pint. Here and there groups of three and four, walking arm-in-arm, were singing lustily the catch tunes of the day, as they set off on their way home after a jolly evening of talk and laughter. From Benoists, Gows and Gattis, other more subdued groups emerged—mainly family parties who had come up to the West End for an evening out, and now, as they waited for the horse-drawn or new motor buses to take them back to the suburbs, were a little breathless from the big Dover soles and juicy steaks they had consumed, with *hors d'œuvres* and ices thrown in, all for a modest five shillings. But it would be hours yet before the great thoroughfare emptied, as the theatre crowds were pressing in to occupy the vacant tables of the fish shops and restaurants, where mountains of chips were still being fried, thousands of oysters being opened, hams and sides of smoked salmon being sliced unceasingly and torrents of stout, iced lager, and champagne flowing.

At Romanos, as soon as they had been relieved of their wraps, the Duke escorted the glamorous Lottie de Vaux down the stairs. The *maitre d'hôtel* recognized her at once and proceeded to bow them to a table; but de Richleau held up a slim hand and said quietly: "I desire a table in one of the alcoves."

The man hesitated only a second. All the alcoves were already booked, but it was his profession to know a good customer when he saw one and, with a lower bow than he had accorded Lottie, he led them to the side of the room where, on a long raised dais, a row of Moorish arches with partitions between them enabled favoured guests to dine in semi-privacy.

De Richleau fully justified the *maitre d'hôtel's* appreciation of him. "You must be tired, so I propose to suggest a supper for you," he told his companion. "But if there is anything you prefer when I have done, you have only to name it and it shall be served, even if they have to send out to get it for you."

He then proceeded to order caviare, lobster cardinal, quail in aspic and *omelette surprise*, with a magnum of Cliquot 1904 and two glasses of vodka to drink while the champagne was being iced.

Lottie's blue eyes shone. There had been no matinée that day, and her strong young body felt no fatigue from the high-kicking to which she was well accustomed. But it was nice to meet a fellow who was so considerate: she was never quite at home pronouncing the names on the menu, either. She would really have preferred steak and onions, but onions were taboo anyhow when out with a toff, and this one was certainly doing her proud. Her only comment was, "If we drink a whole magnum between us we shall both be tiddly."

The Duke shook his head. "Surely you have heard the saying: 'The only trouble with a magnum is that it's too much for one and not enough for two'? And, anyhow, champagne should never be sipped: it should be drunk like lemonade if one is to get the full flavour of it."

She smiled at him archly. "I believe you're trying to lead me astray. But you won't find that so easy. My friends tell me I've a jolly good head for wine, and things."

"You've got a jolly pretty one; and much the best figure in your show."

"D'you really think so?" Lottie preened herself at the compliment, but she was a little nervous. This quietly self-confident man with the compelling grey eyes was very different from both the gay young sparks and the middle-aged would-be seducers who made up her usual following. She had picked up a lot since she had been at the Gaiety, but anxiety not to spoil this promising evening by some social gaffe now made her avert her eyes from his and fidget with her long kid gloves.

Sensing her uneasiness, when the vodka arrived de Richleau made her join him in drinking it down straight, Russian fashion. She coughed, spluttered, and the tears came into her blue eyes; but he pulled a face of such pretended contrition that she could not help laughing, and the warm spirit coursing through her veins soon dispelled her self-consciousness, which was just what he had intended.

He had summed her up very swiftly—as pretty off the stage as on it: about twenty-three: full of healthy vigorous life: a pleasant voice which no longer betrayed her lower middle-class origin, although her turns of phrase and mannerisms did so. Beneath her mass of puffed-out fair hair her brain was conspicuous by its absence. She had, no doubt, learned in a hard school how to look after herself; but to a man who had money and experience she would surrender easily enough, and probably quite willingly. She would, therefore, provide quite a pleasant evening for anyone who did not require intellectual entertainment.

As the meal progressed he led her on to talk about herself, and listened with sympathetic understanding to the story of her struggles. Now and then she remembered to gild the lily by inferring that she was well-connected and worked only because her family had fallen on evil times. But in the main hers was the truthful account of a good-looking girl who could sing and dance a little, and, rather than spend her best years behind the counter of a shop, had defied poor but honest parents in order to earn a precarious living on the stage.

She told him of bad times in the provinces, when shows had packed up unexpectedly, leaving her to get back to London the best way she could: of having to submit, up to a point, to the unwelcome attentions of provincial managers and the wealthy patrons that they often brought round to the green-room after the shows: of the tyrannous ill-temper of leading ladies, and the jealous squabbles that took place among the girls. But, in the main, she was gay and optimistic. For just over a year she had been playing in London, and, although she never expected to rise above the chorus, that gave a girl a living wage and opportunities. The management insisted on its girls being well-dressed, so now and again she had to let herself be kissed by some 'old buffer' as the price of a new frock. But being at the Gaiety gave her a chance to meet 'real gentlemen', and maybe she would marry one, or even into the peerage, as several of her friends had done.

She would not have confessed as much had she had any illusions that the Duke bore the least resemblance to the type of vapid youth who, still half tight, had led some of her friends to the altar at St. George's, Hanover Square. But, all the same, with her fair head cocked a little on one side, she gave him her most encouraging smile.

For a while they talked of the London shows, leading actors and actresses, and the whispered scandals connected with their names. Now that she was well under way, de Richleau let her do most of the talking while he enjoyed his supper and gave only half an ear to her inconsequent chatter. From time to time he paid her some small compliment or gave her an admiring glance, as her presence contributed almost as much to his sense of well-being as did the excellent champagne. He had always felt that if he could not, while eating, discuss the subjects that interested him, the next best thing was to have a beautiful woman to look at. And Lottie at least fulfilled his requirements in that respect. Health and vitality radiated from her well-made person: her blue eyes were large, her golden hair apparently untinted, her features, if a little full, not yet even faintly blurred by the least sign of advancing age.

For her part, Lottie was enjoying herself immensely. Her pleasure was increased in no small measure by the fact that three other girls from the Gaiety were also supping in the restaurant. How she would be able to crow over them to-morrow, when they asked her who her new friend was, and she could reply with a little lift of her chin, "Oh, a Frenchman that I've known for some time. De Richleau is his name. He's a Duke, you know, and has huge estates in France. He's a distant relation of my mother's, and wants us to visit him at his castle later on this summer."

By the time they tackled the hot, fluffy *soufflé*, with its solid block of ice cream inside, she had definitely decided that, marriage being out of the question, when he asked her for a private rendezvous she would not pretend any silly scruples, but let herself go for once—even if it did mean another row with 'ma' about coming home with the milk in the morning.

But de Richleau had other views. He was much too blasé to be disappointed, because he had often done this sort of thing before when finding himself alone and bored in a great city. There had been occasions when he had had the luck to pick a winner—some girl of character and temperament who had gone on the stage because she was determined to become a star; or a gay little guttersnipe who made no pretences, but had the wit, the warmth, and the magnetism of a Nell Gwyn. Lottie de Vaux had nothing to offer but her lovely healthy body. In the first fine careless rapture of his exuberant youth that would have been enough, but now he required of a woman something more than good looks to satisfy his epicurean tastes.

When coffee was served to them by a negro in Turkish costume, in tiny porcelain bowls supported on stands of silver filigree, the Duke turned the conversation to Command Performances, then to the Royal Family, and took occasion to infer that the Prince of Wales's second title was Duke of York. She promptly declared that he was wrong, and that it was Duke of Cornwall. He offered to bet her a fiver to a shilling that he was right; but a reference to the smiling *maitre d'hôtel* quickly proved him wrong. Having pretended momentary annoyance at losing the wager, he smilingly produced a crisp banknote from his wallet and handed it across. It was his tactful way of ensuring that Miss de Vaux would be able to console herself by buying a new frock for the fact that her evening had led to no proposal for a further meeting.

A quarter of an hour later he escorted her upstairs and out into the street, where a taxi he had ordered was waiting. He had already obtained her address, and as soon as she was inside gave it to the driver. Leaning forward, he took and kissed her hand for the second time that night, then murmured blandly:

"I do hope you will forgive me, but the night air is bad for my bronchitis, so I must deny myself the pleasure of seeing you home. The driver is paid and tipped. I have greatly enjoyed this evening, and I hope that we shall renew our acquaintance when I am next in London."

Poor Emily Stiggins had drunk her share of the champagne and had a double *crème de menthe* on top of it, so her vision of the Duke as he closed the door of the cab was slightly blurred and her reactions slow. By the time the blissful smile had faded from her pretty face, to give way to an expression of petulant annoyance, the taxi was bowling along the now almost empty Strand on its way to Clapham. She never saw the Duke again, but it is pleasant to be able to record that three years later she married an ironmonger in a good way of business and made him an excellent wife.

As for de Richleau, before the taxi was even out of sight she had passed from his mind as completely as the quail he had eaten at supper. At the moment he had many more important things to think of, and the principal of them was that he believed he was being shadowed.

Just as he handed Lottie into the cab, out of the corner of his eye, he had noticed a tall, thin, shabby-looking man, wearing a pork-pie hat, who was standing half-concealed in a shop entrance a few yards along the street from the restaurant. De Richleau was prepared to swear that the same figure had been lurking near the stage-door of the Gaiety when he picked up Lottie; and after he had walked a little way towards Trafalgar Square, a casual glance over his shoulder verified his impression. The man had left cover and was following him.

The thought that instantly jumped to the Duke's mind was that the charming Miss de Vaux might be married, and the man a private detective who was endeavouring to secure evidence for divorce against her. The good wine he had drunk, and Lottie's vivacious company, had put him in a merry mood: moreover he felt that he owed her something over and above the fiver for the disappointment he had caused her. So he promptly decided to give the unfortunate detective a lesson that would make him chary about following her friends in future.

Ignoring the invitation of a prowling growler, he continued on across Trafalgar Square, now walking a little erratically, as though he had had too much to drink; his object being to nullify the steady rhythmic ring of his footfalls on the pavement.

Turning up the Haymarket, he entered Piccadilly Circus. There were still quite a number of ladies of the town about, and several of them called invitations to him. Outside Appenrodts' German restaurant he stopped, ostensibly to talk to two of them, but actually because it gave him an opportunity to turn round quite naturally and see if he was still being trailed. He was. The man in the pork-pie hat had also halted, and was buying an early edition of the morning paper from a newspaper boy on the corner.

Waving aside the inducements offered by the two girls with a merry "Good-night!" the Duke crossed the Circus to Swan and Edgar's corner and, with several pauses, during which he acted ineffectual attempts to light a cigarette, continued on his way westward. As he passed Bond Street, seeing his apparent condition, another girl was bold enough to come up beside him, take his arm, and plead in a husky voice:

"Come home with me, dearie. You'll get what for from your wife if you go home to her like this. I've got a nice place—honest I have: and it's not far from here. Come back with me and I'll make you a nice cup a' tea. That'll sober you up."

The Duke thanked her politely, but persistently declined her offers and managed to shake her off by the time he turned down Berkeley Street. Normally, he would have gone across Berkeley Square, and up Mount Street to the curve of Carlos Place, on which the Coburg Hotel was situated. Instead, he crossed the road when he reached Hay Hill and stumbled down the steps into Lansdown Passage.

The passage was some feet lower than the street; wide enough for only two people to walk abreast, and enclosed by high walls on both sides. The north wall was the boundary of the private garden that ran right up to the Duke of Devonshire's mansion in Piccadilly; the south wall bounded the slightly smaller garden of the Marquis of Lansdown's mansion overlooking Berkeley Square. At its far end the passage opened on to the dead-end of Curzon Street, and could be used as a short cut only by pedestrians either going in, or coming from, that direction. In consequence it was secure from observation, both from the windows of nearby houses and passing traffic. A bracket lamp cast a pool of light in its centre, but its two ends were in deep shadows cast by the high walls, and at this hour it was deserted.

On emerging into the cul-de-sac at the lower end of Curzon Street, de Richleau took a step to the right and flattened himself against the wall. After leaning his malacca cane up against the projection of a pillar, so as to have both his hands free, he remained absolutely motionless. He was reasonably confident that his shadow would not become suspicious at the cessation of his footsteps, owing to his erratic course and frequent halts in Piccadilly. His thin mouth now closed like a trap, he waited to spring the ambush he had so skilfully prepared.

Footfalls were now echoing hollowly from the long passage. It seemed quite a time before they grew nearer. Then all at once they were close at hand. The thin man came hurrying out of the narrow entrance, like a rabbit from a burrow; and, his eyes peering straight ahead up the ill-lighted street, he would have passed the Duke without realizing his presence.

Like a bolt from the blue, de Richleau's left hand shot out and caught him by the throat. As he clutched at it he was swung round and forced against the wall. Next second, the Duke had driven his right fist with all his force into the fellow's stomach.

With a horrid choking sound, the man's head jerked forward; his knees lifted and his heels began to beat an uneven tattoo on the pavement. He would have slumped to the ground and lain retching there, had not the Duke's grip on his throat been strong enough to keep him propped against the wall.

After giving him a moment to recover, de Richleau eased the pressure on his windpipe, and snarled, "Try any tricks and I will tear you limb from limb. You were following me, weren't you? Why?"

"*Nein!*" gasped the wretched man, spittle running down his chin. "*Nein*! I follow no ones."

"So, you're a German, eh! You lying rat! I'll make you talk. Take that!" As de Richleau spoke, he struck his victim a glancing blow downward across the face. It was an old apache trick and, as he knew would be the case, the kid of his glove taut over his knuckles caught on the man's cheek, tearing the skin open for a couple of inches.

"Ples!" whimpered the man. "Ples! I do not follow you. I am printer. I work late. I often goes home zis way."

"And you do your printing outside the stage-door of the Gaiety, I suppose?" mocked the Duke with an angry chuckle.

Then, taking a firm grip of the man's left ear, he began to shake him violently by it, as he added: "I have a prejudice against being followed. A very strong prejudice. And let me tell you that to-night you have been very lucky. Had I had a knife on me it would not have been my fist that I should have stuck into your miserable stomach. See what an escape you have had! But things will yet go ill with you should you persist in refusing to tell me what I wish to know. I shall tear off both these big ears of yours and ram them down your throat. Then you will suffer such acute indigestion that you will find it difficult to talk to anyone. Are you prepared to answer my questions, or must I proceed to make you into a cannibal?"

The man had seized de Richleau's wrist with both hands, and was desperately trying to stop the alternate tugs and shoves that were rocking him back and forth and threatened to wrench his ear from his head at any moment. But, finding the Duke's grip too firm to be broken, he suddenly moaned: "*Ja!* I talk! I talk! Only I beg let go, mister."

"Well?" said the Duke, temporarily stopping his vigorous action.

"I haf follow you. But I mean no harm. I follow only to make report on your movements."

"Why?"

"I am a poor man. I make a liddle money that way."

"Who from?"

"Der Argus agency."

"Who are they?"

"A firm for the inquiry making."

De Richleau nodded. "How long have you been trailing Miss de Vaux?"

The man looked blank. "*Die spiel-fräulein* you have given *abendessen*?

I do not follow her. I haf her name only from the porter at the restaurant."

"You're lying!" snapped the Duke, seizing the man by the lapel of his coat in preparation for another attack upon him.

With tears and blood still running down his face, the terrified wretch cowered back against the wall. "*Bitte! Bitte!*" he begged, "I tell truth. But perhaps some other agent follow her. Those who employ me tell me noddings."

After a moment de Richleau decided that the odds were he had now got as much of the truth as he was likely to get from this poor underling of some shady detective agency. The business of shadowing people, which entailed hours of hanging about on draughty street corners, often in the rain, was, he knew, a poorly paid occupation, in spite of its intense dreariness and discomfort; so, except where the police were concerned, or in important cases, only the lowest type of nark was employed upon it. Such people were rarely told to what end inquiries were being made, and if Lottie de Vaux had a husband it seemed unlikely that he would be in a position to afford having her watched by sleuths of a high calibre. What little the Duke had learned fitted in with his original assumption. But there was one more line he could try before releasing his victim.

Jerking the man forward, he thrust his free hand into the fellow's inside breast pocket. His fingers closed upon a few thin papers. Pulling them out, he gave the German a push, and said: "Stay where you are, or I'll catch you and choke the life out of you."

Then he turned, tucked his cane under his arm, and walked up the road towards the nearest street lamp.

He had hardly covered ten paces when he heard a slither of feet, followed by the sound of footsteps pelting away down the passage. Despite the blood-curdling threat he had made, he had expected that, as the fellow would have had to be a moron not to seize such an opportunity to escape from his tormentor. Having no further use for him, the Duke had thought it as good a way as any other to terminate the interview.

Under the street lamp he examined the papers. They were two letters recently delivered to Herr Heinrich Kronauer at an address in the East End of London. Both were in German. One had been posted in the same neighbourhood, and was simply a note making an appointment for a hair-cut. The other had been posted in Hanover. Its writing was uneducated, and it gave only news of a German family with a casual reference to Herr Kronauer's hair-dressing activities in Walthamstow.

It did not strike the Duke as at all strange that his shadower had proved to be a German, as there were then said to be over 100,000 Germans earning their living in England. There was a German band,

and often several, in every town of any size; every theatre orchestra in the country contained a high percentage of them. Their blond, cropped heads were to be seen among the waiters in every restaurant, and hundreds of them worked in barbers' shops. The latter fact confirmed the Duke in his impression that his victim was no more than he appeared to be—simply a poor foreigner who eked out a precarious living by occasionally taking on the job of tailing people in the evening, and a pathetic rather than a sinister figure.

Ten minutes later de Richleau had reached the Coburg, but before turning-in he took the trouble to look up the Argus Inquiry Agency in the telephone book. It was not there.

That did not surprise him. It simply showed that the man had lied about the name of his employers, and, in the circumstances, it was to be expected; for they would certainly not have employed him further if his indiscretion had led to a violent character like de Richleau appearing at their office the following day and threatening to murder everyone in it.

With a shrug, de Richleau closed the book and retired to bed. But his head had hardly touched the pillow when he sat bolt upright again. Why the point had failed to register before, he could not think, but it was only at the threat of further maltreatment that the man had admitted as a possibility that some other agent might have been detailed to follow Lottie. His job, as he had confessed from the first, had been to report upon the movements of the man he had followed down Lansdown Passage, and not merely because he had happened to be Lottie's cavalier of that evening. In his terror the poor sleuth had given it away that he had not even known Lottie's name until he had got it from the porter outside Romanos.

That put a very different complexion on the matter.

CHAPTER VI

STORMY PASSAGE

BELATEDLY, but swiftly now, de Richleau realized that he had fooled himself by allowing his theory, that Lottie had a husband who was trying to secure evidence on which to divorce her, to dominate his mind. Lottie did not even enter into the affair. The sleuth must have been put on to watch him, de Richleau, before either of them even knew of Lottie's existence.

But why?

Could it possibly be that the German Secret Service had already got wind of his projected activities in Serbia? That seemed in the highest degree improbable. Yet what other explanation was there? It recurred to him that his victim had used the word 'agent'. That might easily be an inexactitude due to a foreigner's imperfect understanding of English. On the other hand, the term was more generally applicable to persons acting under official orders than to the casual employees of a private firm. Perhaps the two visits he had paid to Major Hankey's office since lunching with Sir Bindon Blackers at the Carlton Club had aroused the interest of a spy whose job it was to watch comings and goings there. If so, to order the tailing of such casual visitors as a matter of routine, the German Secret Service in Great Britain must be both much more active and employ a far larger personnel than he had supposed.

Once made, these somewhat perturbing speculations did not rob the Duke of any sleep. But, when he recalled them immediately on waking the following morning, he decided that, even if he were barking up the wrong tree, caution counselled observance of the old tag, 'he who is forewarned is forearmed'; so he decided to take such precautions as he could to evade observation during his mission.

As his reservations on the Orient Express were already made, and his baggage already labelled 'Belgrade *Via* Dover-Ostend', short of putting himself to enormous inconvenience, there seemed nothing he could do to cover his tracks for the moment; so he pushed the matter into the back of his mind and, after a hearty breakfast, set out for Victoria.

The day was fine, and now that May had come the streets had assumed an air of summer gaiety. The more solid citizens were making their way to business in black top hats and short coats as usual, but here and there a less conventional figure was to be seen in a straw boater with a bright ribbon. In South Audley Street he passed a party making an early start for a day's racing in a coach-and-four, and all the men on its roof were sporting grey toppers. Then, in Grosvenor Place he noticed a little group of sailors wearing the wide-brimmed round straw hats still favoured by the Navy; while all along the way there were girls and women in colourful dresses, crowned with the milliners' flower-decked creations of the period, and holding ruffled parasols.

At Victoria station de Richleau kept an alert eye open for his acquaintance of the previous night; but that unfortunate personage was no doubt endeavouring to explain away his battered appearance to some customer he was shaving in Walthamstow, as he was nowhere to be seen; neither could the Duke spot any other suspicious character covertly observing him. So he took his seat on the train some moments before it was due to leave, and the journey to Dover passed without episode.

In those days, in the greater part of the world true freedom still existed. Men had not been robbed yet of their natural right to go where they would, either on business, pleasure, or, taking their families and all their worldly wealth with them, to settle in a distant land for the remainder of their days. Passports were rare and potent documents, issued only at the request of travellers going to uncivilized parts of the earth, where they might need to call upon His Majesty's Consuls to assist them in securing pack mules, guides, or native porters for a journey into little-known territory. And, such was the prodigious plenty and wealth of Britain that no Customs officer had ever dreamed the day would come when he would be called on to search outgoing passengers' baggage, as a precaution against a woman going abroad with her engagement ring, or a man taking a York ham as a present to friends with whom he was going to stay on the continent.

In consequence, the Duke walked from the train on to the Dover-Ostend boat without let or hindrance, and, proceeding at once to the first-class upper deck amidships, settled himself comfortably in a steamer chair that had its back to a roped-off part of the deck abaft the funnel.

He had been seated there only a moment when out of the crowd that was seething about him emerged a tall, youngish man of about his own age, who greeted him with surprise and pleasure. It was a Count Julien Esterházy, whom he had met, and by whom he had been most kindly entertained, a few years previously in Budapest.

When they had shaken hands, de Richleau quickly removed his dressing-case from the chair beside the one in which he had been sitting, and the two old acquaintances settled down side by side to gossip about their doings since they had last seen one another.

The crowd sorted itself out; the porters grabbed their tips and hurried down the gangways: the steamer's siren blew two long blasts, signifying that she was about to proceed to sea. Only then did the two men catch the sound of footsteps and scraping chairs behind them. At the last moment, the private party, for whom a portion of the after-deck had been roped off, had come aboard and were now being ushered to the space reserved for them.

Esterházy sat up and turned his head to take a look at the newcomers. Then, with a quick exclamation, he jumped to his feet and swept off the travelling cap he was wearing. At his sudden gesture, the Duke stood up too. Next moment he found himself gazing straight into the face of Her Imperial Highness, the Archduchess Ilona Theresa.

Only the low rope and three feet of deck separated them. She was dressed in a coat and skirt of Harris tweed that set off her figure to perfection. Her rich, dark brown hair was hidden by a big flat cap, a blue scarf of some soft material that held it in position framed her pale face and was tied in a large bow under her chin. She was looking directly into de Richleau's eyes, and her own were wide with surprise at so suddenly being confronted with him.

The Hungarian Count had noticed nothing unusual in her attitude. Brushing up his black moustache with an elegant flick of the fingers, he greeted her in German, with due deference but as an old friend.

"What a delightful surprise to come upon your Imperial Highness in such circumstances. I knew that you were due to leave England shortly, but not the actual day of your departure. May I crave the honour of forming one of your suite, and so derive great additional pleasure in my journey home?"

As he spoke, she turned towards him and extended her hand. "Certainly you may, Count. It is always a pleasure to have your gay company."

Stepping over the rope, he took her hand, bowed low over it, and kissed it. Then, with a smile and a wave towards de Richleau, he said:

"I pray your Highness, permit me to present an old and treasured friend: a distinguished soldier and traveller, who will prove far more capable of entertaining you than myself—The Duke de Richleau."

The whole episode had taken place so unexpectedly, and so suddenly, that there was nothing de Richleau could possibly have done to avoid this embarrassing denouement. He had already removed his hat, so he could now only maintain a suitably grave expression and, remaining where he stood, bow formally before her.

He expected her to acknowledge his presentation with a bare nod, then evade further conversation with him by saying that she did not wish to increase her suite further; or even to take her revenge by announcing that they had met before and she did not find his company amusing. But she did neither. Instead, she greeted him with the regal graciousness that she might have accorded to a stranger, but her words contained a subtle innuendo that was meant for him alone.

"I have heard of M. de Richleau. It is said that he is a hunter of great daring, and goes only for the most difficult game. I shall be delighted for him to join my party and entertain us with some of his more successful exploits." Again she extended her slim hand; and as de Richleau kissed it his heart suddenly began to beat faster from the vivid memory that when last they had met he had held her in his arms and kissed her lips.

She then introduced the members of her suite. There was a middle-aged couple, the Count and Countess Aulendorf, in whose charge she was obviously travelling; two ladies-in-waiting of about her own age, Baroness Paula von Wolkenstein and Fraulein Sárolta Hunyády; her equerry, Captain Count Adam Grünne; and her treasurer-secretary, Herr Rechberg.

While she was making the introductions, two sailors appeared and began to erect a canvas screen where the rope crossed the deck. It had, at first, been rigged on the leeward side of the vessel, with the object of screening the Archduchess from the stares of the passengers further forward. But it transpired that she was an excellent sailor and preferred the deck to windward, so the ladies' maids, valet, grooms and footmen of the party had been given its more sheltered side.

As the steamer nosed its way out of the harbour it became apparent that, although the day was fine, a cross-wind was making the sea distinctly choppy. So Ilona Theresa turned to the fairer and slighter of her two ladies, and said: "Paula, I know how you hate it when it's like this. Do please go and lie down in your cabin. You'll be much more comfortable there."

Bobbing a curtsy, the fair girl thanked her and left the group. Then Herr Rechberg stepped forward and asked permission to retire for the same reason. The others tucked their rugs about them and made themselves comfortable in their chairs. But Ilona had been telling Julien Esterhazy about her experiences while in England, for only ten minutes, when the Chief Steward arrived to announce that luncheon was now ready and would be served at any time Her Imperial Highness wished.

She smiled and shook her head. "I believe it is going to be really rough when we get farther out, and I don't want to miss a minute of it. I will have a cup of soup and a chicken sandwich up here. But that is no reason why any of you should be deprived of a proper meal. You will please all go below and enjoy your luncheon. I insist upon it."

It was clearly a command, so no one thought of remonstrating. Count Grünne summoned a tall footman, who took up his position behind the Archduchess' chair, in case she required anything; and, with the plump, grey-haired Countess Aulendorf leading the way, the rest of the party went below to the dining-saloon.

As the stranger in their midst, de Richleau was given the place of honour at the table, with Countess Aulendorf on his right and the dark-haired Fraulein Sárolta Hunyády on his left. While the *hors d'œuvres* were served the talk continued to be about Ilona's visit to England, and after a while the Countess remarked a trifle tartly: "In some ways it was quite enjoyable, but I shall be extremely glad to get her home."

"Why do you say that, Countess?" inquired Esterházy. "I have always understood her to be a model of propriety and tact."

"She was until quite recently," the Countess sighed. "No mistress of a princess' household could have asked to be responsible for a more docile and well-behaved girl, particularly at her age."

"Ah! There you have it, my dear," remarked the elderly Count. "She should have been married long before this, and at the first opportunity I mean to speak to the Emperor about it."

Adam Grünne was a short, dark man, with broad shoulders, and a small brown moustache. He gave a quick shrug. "The trouble with the Emperor is his great age. He hardly notices any longer as the years drift by, and probably thinks of his granddaughter as still scarcely out of the nursery."

"But tell us, Countess," Esterházy urged, "what pranks has your lovely charge been up to?"

"Oh, nothing very serious; yet enough to cause me considerable anxiety. On three occasions during the past fortnight she got up before the household was astir, ordered a horse to be saddled for her, and went riding, with only a groom in attendance, in Hyde Park. Even more perturbing, she slipped out of the house one afternoon all on her own and went shopping in Bond Street. Then, when I remonstrated with her, she only laughed and declared that she was tired of being treated like a child."

Sárolta Hunyády kept her dark eyes fixed demurely on her plate. She had abetted these escapades and knew that the Countess had more grounds for her disquietude than she chose to relate. Without consulting anyone, Ilona had sacked her elderly tiring-woman and engaged a flighty-looking French maid through someone she had met at one of the embassies. When asked for an explanation, she had replied sharply that she did not intend to be spied upon any longer. At two balls she had drunk just a little too much champagne; not enough for anyone who did not know her intimately to notice it, but enough to make her refuse to come home at the time scheduled for her departure; and, as etiquette forbade anyone leaving before she did, hundreds of people had been kept up till five in the morning. Then there had been the episode of the book. Only Sárolta knew how Ilona had got hold of it. She was a gay young minx herself and prepared to take any risk to make her charming mistress' life a little more amusing. It had been a copy of *Three Weeks* by Elinor Glyn, and when poor old Olga Aulendorf had caught her charge reading it she had nearly had a fit. None of them could imagine what particular devil had got into Ilona these past ten days or so, but Sárolta hoped that he had found a permanent home, as that would mean much more exciting times than she had been used to when they got back to Vienna.

Count Aulendorf stroked his pointed grey beard with a well-manicured hand, then quite unconsciously poured cold water on Sárolta's thoughts by saying to his wife: "Really, my dear, I don't think you have any great cause to worry. Compared with ourselves, the English are very unconventional, and no doubt it is having been so much in their company that has affected her. As soon as she gets back to the more decorous atmosphere of the Emperor's court she will soon settle down again. I am much more concerned about her health."

"Why do you say that, sir?" de Richleau asked. "She looks the very picture of healthy young womanhood to me."

"Yes, she looks strong enough, I agree. But as a young girl she was delicate. That was the main reason why the abortive arrangements for her marriage were put off longer than they would normally have been. But it is her cough that worries me, and the hectic flush that colours her cheeks every time she gets at all excited."

"Has she seen a doctor?" inquired the Duke.

"Not recently. I tried to persuade her to see one in London, but she refused. Probably because she feared he might prescribe the curtailing of her amusements."

"I think," put in Grünne, "that her cough has only been worse recently owing to the dampness of the English climate. A few weeks at Ischl should soon make it disappear."

"Or at Godolfo," added Esterházy, who naturally favoured his native country. "She loves horses, and nowhere in the world can she get better riding than we can give her on our Hungarian plains."

The talk then turned to the Duke's last visit to Budapest, and he inquired after numerous friends he had made there. Several of them were known to various members of the party, and during the rest of luncheon they gossiped cheerfully about their mutual acquaintances.

By the time they got back on deck the sky had clouded over, and a heavy sea was running. It was clear that Ilona's hopes were to be fulfilled, and that long before they reached Ostend the ship would be ploughing her way through a storm. The Archduchess looked up at her duenna and said:

"I fear the weather is going to favour me at your expense, *Frau Grafin*. Please do not attend me further if you would prefer to lie down. And I know that on such occasions you like to have the *Herr Graf* with you; so I willingly excuse him too, from further attendance."

With a murmur of thanks the Aulendorfs retired. Then, as a bigger wave than they had yet encountered lifted the ship high in the water, Sárolta asked if she might follow them. Esterházy offered to take her below, and was evidently not feeling very well himself, as he did not return. But, meanwhile, Grünne and de Richleau had seated themselves on either side of Ilona and she had asked the Duke to tell them about some of his narrow escapes while after big game.

The Duke had been on safari in the Belgian Congo, and shot tiger from the backs of Rajahs' elephants in India, but so had many other people; whereas far fewer had hunted in the jungles of South America and, having taken part in several minor wars there, he had had many opportunities to do so.

In consequence, he began to talk of the Amazon, with its hundred mile-wide mouth, turgid sheets of fast-flowing oily water, and tributaries so long that by comparison all but the largest rivers in Europe were only streams. He told of the moist, exhausting atmosphere that made one feel like a prisoner in some vast over-heated greenhouse; of the clouds of mosquitoes; of the snakes, tarantulas and leeches that swarmed on the banks of every creek; of the swamps from which one could see the fever rising like a grey mist in the evenings; and of the alligators, jaguars, and hostile natives with poison blow-pipes—all of which lurked unseen and might at any time deal death to the unwary traveller.

But he also endeavoured to convey the beauty of the scene; the unending primeval forests, in which the branches of the huge creeper-covered trees met overhead so thickly that the blazing tropical sun filtered through only as a dappled twilight; the astounding riot of colour, the vivid green of the rank vegetation caught by a patch of sunlight, and the dazzling blue of patches of sky overhead; the monstrous white fungi, bigger than a man and splotched with red; the silvery ferns; the yellow lizards; the birds and butterflies of every hue; and, above all, the fascination of the unending mysterious silence in these distant places where white men had so rarely penetrated.

He went on to relate a few episodes in which he had unexpectedly come face to face with dangerous animals, and others in which he had seen rare species that had never yet been captured for a European zoo. Then, as he paused, she said:

"You seem to have had many narrow escapes. Tell us, now, which of your experiences you found most frightful."

He smiled. "I think my most terrifying experience was being caught and nearly crushed to death by a boa-constrictor, when my rifle was out of reach, and none of my people within call. I managed to force the brute's head against the trunk of a tree and hack it off with my knife: but I was only just in time, and it took me over a fortnight to recover."

"Gracious God!" she exclaimed, her deep blue eyes widening. "That was certainly a desperate situation. In fact it is difficult to imagine one more terrifying, even in a nightmare."

"It was, indeed, just like a nightmare while it lasted, and I was very lucky to get away alive. But your Imperial Highness asked me a moment ago to relate, not my most terrifying, but my most frightful experience; and that is a very different story."

"I don't quite follow, Duke. But please go on."

"It was at a time when my rifle went off unexpectedly. Long use of firearms has formed in me the habit of being very careful with them. But on this particular evening I forgot that I had told my servant to keep a loaded rifle handy in the camp all day, in case a big black panther which had been prowling around on the previous night made its appearance. I had among my weapons a pair of rifles that were of exactly the same pattern, and had used one of them that morning. By mistake, I picked up the wrong one of the pair and was just about to see if it had been cleaned properly. To a hunter like myself, you will appreciate that every moving thing is a mark upon which to practise swift sighting, even with an unloaded weapon. At that moment the most beautiful thing I have ever seen came into my view. It was a big butterfly the colour of roses and cream, with lustrous brown edges to its wings, and on each it had a circle of rich dark blue—the very colour, if I may say so, of your Imperial Highness' eyes. For quite a time I watched it, fascinated by its beauty. Then, as it drew away from me I took a practice sight on it with my rifle and squeezed the trigger."

"Oh, dear! Did you kill it?"

"No. It was distant and high above me; but it staggered for a moment in its flight, so my bullet must have touched it, however lightly, and proved a rude, unnerving shock. I only pray that my rash and thoughtless act may not have done it any permanent injury, and made it afraid of men in future."

"Aren't you being a bit squeamish about a butterfly?" laughed Count Grünne.

"This one was an aristocrat of its species," replied the Duke seriously. "She had all the exquisite loveliness of a young princess. She was, perhaps, on her first flight. I had her quite close to me for a moment, and the colour of her wings had not been smudged by rough contact of any kind. My brutality was unintentional, but, even so, I count it a frightful thing to have deprived so wonderful a creature of even a fraction of her bloom."

They had been talking for over an hour and the ship was now pitching and rolling with considerable violence. Dark, angry clouds hung low in the sky from horizon to horizon. Big spots of rain began to splash upon the deck. Count Grünne unwrapped himself from his rug, stood up, and said:

"Would not your Highness prefer to take shelter? It's going to pour in torrents in a few minutes."

"Don't be silly, Adam," she reproved him. "You know there is nothing I enjoy more than to feel the rain lashing my cheeks. Get under cover if you want to: but give me my ulster first."

He obediently put the rainproof cloak round her shoulders, but sat down again with a smothered sigh of resignation.

De Richleau smiled at her. "It seems, Princess, that you inherit your grandmother's love of foul weather. I have heard it said that at times the Empress Elizabeth went to the length of ordering herself to be lashed to the mast so that she might enjoy the beauty of a tempest."

"That is true. People say that I have a lot of other things in common with my grandmother Elizabeth, too. Her love of horses and travel; even my face is said to resemble hers."

They sat silent for a time, while the rain came down in earnest, and the Duke recalled what he knew of the strange woman of whom they had just spoken. She had been the second daughter of Max, Duke *in* Bavaria, the curious title having been given to him as the head of a younger branch of the family, to distinguish him from the king of that name. Back in the 'fifties a marriage had been planned between his eldest daughter and the young Franz-Joseph, Emperor of Austria. But the Emperor had chanced to see the younger daughter and, captivated by her dark beauty, he had insisted on marrying her instead. His love for her had endured until her tragic assassination in 1898, but she had not made him a good Empress, mainly on account of her acute shyness, which amounted almost to a mental aberration. She abhorred public functions and even being looked at by strangers, and had seized upon her delicate health as an excuse to leave the court, often for many months at a stretch, whenever she could possibly do so. Her travels had taken her as far as Madeira, and to England and Ireland, where she had hunted with great recklessness. To secure solitude had been a mania with her, and in the latter part of her life she had had built for herself a beautiful little retreat, after the pattern of an ancient Greek palace, on the island of Corfu. She had, from her first arrival in Vienna, developed a passionate admiration for everything Hungarian, and the one service that this gifted but morbid lady had rendered to her country was the binding of the Dual Monarchy together, at a time when Hungarian discontent had risen to a pitch that everyone else believed the two kingdoms must inevitably split apart.

The ship plunged, rolled and staggered in a horrid corkscrew motion. The force of the rain made it rebound in a thousand little fountains from the deck. Thunder rolled and lightning forked from the black sky above. But Ilona sat on entranced, exclaiming with delight at every flash.

The roaring of the storm would have drowned any attempt at conversation, so they sat there in silence while the rain streamed in rivulets from their hats and shoulders. It was not until nearly four o'clock that the downpour eased a little, and by then they were due to sight Ostend harbour, ahead through the murk, at any moment.

Having glanced at his watch, Adam Grünne pushed the sopping rug from off his knees, and stood up. "We are due in at four-fifteen," he announced. "So, with your Highness' permission, I will go below, find one of my bags, and get into some dry clothes."

"Of course, Adam," she smiled. "It was thoughtless of me to have kept you here during the downpour, but I did suggest that you should take shelter just as it was starting." She turned then to the Duke.

"Perhaps you would also like to put on dry things before we land. If so, please have no scruples about leaving me here alone."

He made her a little bow. "I thank your Imperial Highness for your consideration; but I have often been soaked to the skin while on my campaigns and taken no harm from it."

As Count Grünne left them, the rain declined to a gusty splutter, and a break in the clouds showed to the east. But the sea continued to hiss angrily, occasionally slapping hard against the side of the ship.

A few minutes later Ilona disentangled herself from her coverings and rose to her feet. "I want," she said, "to see the last of these lovely waves before we get in." And she started to walk towards the rail.

De Richleau had risen with her, and as soon as they reached the ship's side, by looking round the canvas screen, they could see the piers of Ostend harbour. Both knew that the voyage was nearly over, and neither had so far made any direct reference to their previous meeting. As they leaned side by side on the rail, she suddenly turned to him and asked:

"Did you invent that story about the butterfly as a symbol for myself, and really feel like that about me?"

"Of course, Princess," he replied gravely. "I swear to you that nothing in the world could have caused me more distress than the thought that I had wantonly taken advantage of your innocence and shattered the serenity of your mind."

"It . . . it was a shock . . . a very grave one; because nothing like that has ever happened to me before. But it had to happen sometime, and it has changed me quite a lot."

"Not for the worse, I hope."

"No. It caused me to realise that, because I had not been brought up like other girls, there is no reason why I should not act like them, providing that I always bear in mind the responsibilities of my position."

"May I take it that I am forgiven, then?"

"Do you give me your word that you really had no idea who I was?'

"I swear it. I knew only that chance had thrown into my path the most lovely person I have seen in a lifetime."

She turned to look at him again, and her eyes were kind. "You said something about being on your way to Belgrade, did you not? That is only a night's journey from Vienna. If you really want my forgiveness, come and ask for it there. I promise nothing; but you may even find that the mentors of a poor, imprisoned princess have not yet quite succeeded in turning her heart into stone."

CHAPTER VII

CITY OF DELIGHT

TWO special coaches had been attached to the Orient Express to accommodate the Archduchess' party; but de Richleau did not take advantage of his temporary acceptance as one of her entourage to travel in one. He took formal leave of her and her companions immediately they landed, with the excuse that, as he was passing through Ostend, he had arranged to meet a man in the station restaurant for a brief business conference: and she did not suggest that he should rejoin them later.

He was glad of that, as on the train they would have had no further opportunity to be alone together, and he felt reluctant to blur the memory of that moment when they had leaned side by side on the rail of the ship. Moreover, he wanted to be alone. His mind was in a turmoil, and as soon as he had made himself comfortable in his sleeper he settled down to think matters out.

It was now clear that by kissing Ilona Theresa he had done much more to her than was usually conveyed by that quite ordinary act. He had changed her from a docile girl to a rebellious woman overnight. The Countess Aulendorf's remarks at luncheon had been ample evidence of that. Moreover, she had as good as invited him to Vienna, on what could be only a pretext to cover the fact that she wanted to see him again. But why? Could it really be because Her Imperial Highness was now thinking of him as her gallant—in fact, as ready to play the part he had offered to assume while still unaware of her identity. He wondered for a moment if he was flattering himself unduly, but there seemed to be no other explanation. Her last words had been a pathetic cry for just such a friendship—perhaps even for a lover.

Staring straight ahead, as the train roared through a tunnel, the Duke shifted on his seat. Nobody knew better than he the implications of such a role. If he occupied it, the affair might end for both of them in tragedy. In any case he would court the gravest danger. There was no blinking the fact that she was over-ripe for a first love, so a spring having been touched that had released her long pent-up emotions she might soon prove capable of any rashness. Should she become so, and any man be caught making love to her in her own country, it would certainly go hard with him. Initial detection in a ballroom flirtation would result in no more than an order to quit Vienna forthwith: but if the affair went further, and love letters to her were discovered, or she was surprised while keeping a secret rendezvous, however innocent, her gallant would find himself cooling his heels in a fortress. So it was certainly not the sort of amorous adventure to be undertaken lightly.

De Richleau began to review the little he knew about her. She had been telling the truth when she had told him at the masked ball that her mother was a Belgian, but she had said nothing of her father, except that he was dead: and the manner of his death was probably a subject that she never talked about. In fact, it was doubtful if she had ever heard the full details of the tragedy herself. As she had been born posthumously it would have been already half-buried in the past by the time she was old enough to be told about it, and then it had probably been thought desirable to spare her all but the bare facts.

Her father had been the ill-fated Crown Prince Rudolph, only son of the Emperor Franz Joseph and the Empress Elizabeth. All accounts agreed that he had been a handsome and intelligent young man, but much given to secretiveness and introspection. His young wife, the Archduchess Stephanie, was devoted to him, and he returned her affection, although guilty of those temporary infidelities, the temptation to indulge in which is offered to good-looking young princes far more frequently than to other men. Such a state of affairs being by no means unusual in royal circles, neither his parents nor his friends had any reason to feel particularly concerned on his account until it was too late and the tragedy had come, like a bolt from the blue, upon them.

From the letters he left for his family, and the evidence of the servants whom he had made his only confidants, it emerged that from about the age of twenty-eight he had been beset by an uncontrollable urge to indulge his passions with low-class women of evil repute. Yet, in between these lapses, so disgusted did he feel with himself at conduct so disgraceful in an Emperor's son, that he contemplated taking his own life. For a little over two years he continued alternatively to follow his secret pursuit of vice and brood morbidly on suicide; but he had a terrible fear of death and could not bring himself to face the great unknown alone.

He then met the Baroness Marie Vetsera, a beautiful and romantic young girl of seventeen, who fell passionately in love with him and became his mistress. It was supposed that he had confided his desperate thoughts to her, and out of her great love for him she had agreed to face death at his side. In any case, he had excused himself from a family dinner party on the plea of illness, in order to take her to his hunting lodge at Mayerling. On the following morning his valet could get no reply when he knocked on the bedroom door. The man called the Crown Prince's equerry and together they broke the door down. Inside, they found the girl lying dead on the bed, with a bullet through her head and a rose clasped in her folded hands. Rudolph was seated on a chair beside her, and on the floor nearby lay the revolver with which he had blown out his brains.

De Richleau wondered how much the morbid mentality of the Empress Elizabeth had contributed to the derangement of her son; and if Ilona Theresa had in turn inherited these terrible tendencies. But there seemed nothing in the least morbid about her, and perhaps she had escaped the strain of madness that had so often proved the curse of those in whose veins ran the blood of the Wittlesbachs. He fervently hoped so; for he knew already that he was in love with her.

He knew that it was absurd that, after only two brief meetings, a man of his experience should feel as he did about a girl to whom passion was still a closed book. But there it was! There was no accounting for the genesis of such emotions: like a thief in the night, they stole upon one unawares. On one day one did not even know of the existence of some person of the opposite sex, or had known them for half a lifetime without seeing any particular quality in them: and the next, one's every thought was coloured by the desire to please and be near them. Lack of serious concern for their well-being was insensibly transformed overnight into an imperative urge to protect them from all harm and bring them joy: to squander one's money and neglect one's work sooner than see them unhappy: if need be, to risk one's health, position, reputation and ties with family and friends rather than sacrifice all hope of union with this one being who, out of all the millions that swarmed upon the surface of the earth, now seemed unique.

The Duke sighed, gave a little shrug of his shoulders, then smiled. Of course he would seek a meeting with her in Vienna. He had known that from the very moment she suggested he might do so.

Now, he admitted to himself, he felt much happier in his mind. The fact that he would be entering on a difficult and dangerous game began to intrigue him. He was used to taking risks, and more serious ones than the possibility of landing in a fortress. It would be fun to pit his wits against the guardians of the gilded cage that held the beautiful Ilona. But he would have to go warily—very warily: on her account even more than on his own.

There was, too, his mission to be thought of. He must not allow a love affair to prejudice his chances of succeeding in that. Therefore, there must be no climbing of the walls of Imperial gardens in the middle of the night. In fact, no act which could result in worse than his expulsion from Vienna—at least until he had got all he could out of Dimitriyevitch.

In any case he had intended to pay a visit to Vienna as soon as he had had a chance to assess the general lie of the land in the Serbian capital. It took two to make a quarrel, and it was Austria whom the conspirators of the Black Hand planned to provoke. Therefore he thought it very important to form an appreciation of what Austrian reactions were likely to be.

Everyone agreed that the ancient Dual Monarchy, weakened as it was by the separatist aspirations of the numerous races who composed its population, would run a certain risk of disintegrating should it become involved in a major war. If the Austrians believed that Russia would support Serbian demands by force of arms, they might well hesitate before accepting a Serbian challenge. Unless they could count with absolute certainty on German backing, they might consider that it would prove cheaper in the long run to surrender Bosnia to the Serbs, and also let them have a port on the Adriatic. In that case it was probable that the Black Hand's next move would be against Greece, with the object of seizing Salonika, and thus securing a second outlet, to the East. If so, the next war would be no more than another Balkan squabble, and the hopes of preserving the general peace of Europe be good. On the other hand, Austrian pride would certainly be ruffled by the insolence of her small neighbour, and that might lead to a public demand for instant chastisement. In the event, the issue would depend on the mentalities of the few men who controlled the destinies of Austria. Were they far-sighted? And were they strong enough to resist a popular outcry? These were matters which, from the beginning, de Richleau had felt it incumbent on him to find out.

As he thought about it, he realized that his second meeting with Ilona Theresa would greatly facilitate his investigation in Vienna. He already had several acquaintances with houses there, but some of them might be abroad, or on their country estates. Anyway, it would have taken some little time before their introductions could have gained him access to Court circles, whereas now he could call upon the Count and Countess Aulendorf, who, in view of their appointment, must be *persona grata* with all the members of the Imperial family; and Count Adam Grünne who, he had learned at lunch, was the grandson of General Count Grünne, the Comptroller of the Emperor's Household in the days when Franz Joseph was still a young man.

Soon after the train crossed the German frontier, the Duke went along to the restaurant car for dinner. The attendant showed a crop-headed Prussian to the seat opposite him, and that led his thoughts back to his encounter with Herr Kronauer. The more he considered the matter, the more fantastic seemed the surmise that German espionage should have penetrated sufficiently far into British secrets to have grounds for taking an interest in his own activities. In fact, he did not believe it possible. It was, of course, on the cards that their agent, if Kronauer really was one, had mistaken him for someone else: or that Kronauer was not acting under orders from his government, and had been employed by a private firm to watch him for some reason, at which he could not even make a guess. Still, there was no getting away from it that he had been spied upon, and it was at least a possibility that someone had got on the train at Victoria with instructions to follow him to his destination.

If that were so, whatever their object in keeping him under observation, the very fact that his movements were being recorded might later prove, not merely embarrassing, but dangerous. That would certainly be the case if at any time his work made it necessary for him to break the law, as anyone who had been spying on him while he did so would be in a position to give him away to the police, or, if it suited their book better, use their knowledge in an attempt to blackmail him.

It seemed, therefore, a situation in which, by taking a little trouble now, he might save himself from the possibility of meeting with a great deal later on. Anyone who had boarded the train for the purpose of dogging him would certainly have learned by this time, from the labels on his luggage, that he was on his way to Belgrade. The Serbian capital was not a very big place and, once there, it would be almost impossible to move about its centre without proving an easy quarry for a tracker. But if he got off the train before it reached Belgrade, that would offer an excellent chance of escaping such unwelcome attention altogether.

De Richleau chuckled to himself at the thought of how his theoretical opponent's mind would almost certainly work in such circumstances. On arriving in Belgrade and finding that his man had left the train somewhere along the route, he would naturally assume that the labels on the baggage had been stuck on deliberately to fool him, and that from the first his quarry had never intended to go there. He might work back again along the line, but by then the trail would be cold; and as the express stopped at half a dozen places he would not even know at which to start his inquiries. The man he was after might have got out at Cologne, Mayence, Karlsruhe, Stuttgart, Munich, Salzburg, Linz, Vienna, Budapest or Szeged and, by the time he discovered how he had been out-witted, might have gone on to Berlin, Rome, Trieste or Prague. So, short of having the co-operation of half the police forces in Europe, to locate him again would be virtually impossible.

Accordingly, the Duke swiftly began to formulate a new plan of campaign. He knew that the train was due to reach Munich early in the morning, when the majority of its occupants would still be asleep, so to get off there offered the best chance of leaving it without being spotted. It would be pleasant to see Munich again, and after spending twenty-four hours there, he could catch the next day's express on to Belgrade.

But no! If he was being watched there was a chance that his shadow might not be put off the scent quite so easily. He might think that he had been noticed on the train, which had led to his quarry taking emergency measures to evade him. In that case he would probably remain in Belgrade for several days, in the belief that his man would turn up there before the week was out.

Another idea then came to the Duke. Why should he not make his inquiries in Vienna before, instead of after, his visit to Belgrade. If he put in a week or ten days in the Austrian capital all the odds were that his shadow would have decided by then that he was wasting his time, and have left Serbia with the conviction that, after all, his quarry had never intended to go there.

For a few minutes de Richleau did some serious heart-searching, as he wondered if he was not being influenced to adopt this new plan by his desire to see Ilona Theresa again: but he decided that, even had he never met her, his mind would have worked on the same lines, as the plan was the logical outcome of the belief that he was quite possibly being followed.

Having finished his dinner, he returned to his sleeping berth and asked the attendant there to call him half an hour before they were due to reach Munich, as he wished to hand a letter to someone who would be waiting on the platform to receive it. Then he turned in.

When he was called, as soon as he had dressed, he made his way along the train to the baggage car, found his luggage, and asked the guard how long the train would halt in Munich.

"Ten minutes, *mein Herr*," replied the man; upon which the Duke began a casual conversation with him about his duties and the way that train conductors were often carried far from their homes.

As they pulled into Munich, the early morning light showed the platform to be almost deserted, except for a few porters and a refreshment trolley. A few passengers got out, and after the guard had dealt with their luggage and the mails de Richleau beckoned up the trolley, then offered him a cup of coffee. The guard gladly accepted, and as they sipped the steaming brew they continued their friendly chat. Only when the man picked up his flag to signal the train's departure, did the Duke suddenly say that he was getting out himself, and call a porter to take his luggage. Then, as the whistle blew, he stepped down on to the platform.

No head was poked from a window as the train drew out, so he knew that by loitering he had achieved his object and made certain of leaving it unobserved. If his shadow missed him during the next few hours and made inquiries of the train personnel, he might learn that his quarry had got out at Munich; but that would do him little good, as by the time he got back there de Richleau intended to be in Vienna, so his trail would be irretrievably lost.

He took a mid-day train on, and arrived at the Austrian capital in time for dinner. From the station he drove straight to Sacher's Hotel. It was very old-fashioned, and not very large, but extremely comfortable and maintained a small restaurant of about twenty tables which was world-famous. In the rooms upstairs the sheets and towels were of the finest linen, and the furniture of a rich Victorian solidity. A valet at once appeared to unpack the Duke's belongings, as though he were in a private house, and he took his tub in a marble bath the size of a Roman sarcophagus. Spick and span in a single-breasted dinner jacket, he went down to the restaurant, where he dined on *Ecrevisses Anet* and saddle of roe-buck, washed down with a bottle of *Rupertsberger Hoheberg*. Then he went to the office and inquired for Frau Sacher.

The elderly proprietress of the hotel was an old friend of his and a great personality. She prided herself on having had as her guests at one time or another, every crowned head in Europe who, in her younger days, had visited Vienna incognito; and counted all the leading nobility of Austria among her friends. For her special guests she kept a most unusual visitors' book: they were asked to sign their names in pencil on a large table cloth, and she afterwards embroidered their signatures into it. Its centre-piece was the autograph of the Emperor, who had started it for her, and from that radiated those of Grand Dukes, Princes, Counts and Barons by the score. Among them was that of Count Königstein, de Richleau's Austrian title, which he always used when in the Dual Monarchy.

After a few minutes he was ushered into her sitting-room. It was a fitting setting for her, as she was now a woman of another age, and hated change. The furniture was of heavy carved oak, the red velvet curtains were fringed with bobbles, there were anti-macassars on the backs of the arm-chairs, pots with ferns on high, spindle-legged stools, and many photographs in silver frames, mostly of young men with flowing moustaches and side-whiskers. She was sitting bolt upright in a stiff-backed chair sideways on to the table, her left elbow resting on it. Many yards of black silk billowed out round her lower limbs, passed smoothly over her tightly corseted waist, then rose over an ample bosom to end at chin and wrists in goffered frills of white lawn. Her grey hair was parted in the centre and looped back in a number of complicated flat plaits to form a bun on the crown of her head. She was smoking, as she often did when walking about the public rooms of her hotel, a large Havana cigar. Altogether she made an impressive, almost formidable, figure; but there was in her eyes that quick, friendly look which in all ages denotes one of life's enjoyers.

As de Richleau bowed to her, she said: "It must be nearly three years since you stayed with us, Count. After such a long absence from Vienna it is most kind of you to give part of your first evening to calling on an old woman."

"You will never be old, Madame," he told her gallantly. "And how could I better attune myself again to the atmosphere of your lovely city than by coming to talk to you about it?"

"You have not changed," she smiled, "and are as much a flatterer as was your handsome father. Vienna has not changed either. The young ones grow up and are as naughty as their parents used to be. Perhaps our music is not quite up to the old standard, but maybe that is only my imagination, and just that I still prefer the airs of Liszt, Mendelssohn and the older Strauss because they remind me of my youth."

As she was speaking a white-haired waiter came in carrying a bottle in an ice-bucket and a dish, on which was a shallow basket containing little cakes: they were the delicious *Sacher torte*, light as a feather and stuffed with cream, for which the hotel was famous. When the wine was poured into the shallow champagne glasses, de Richleau immediately noticed that its froth was pink and, raising his eyebrows, said:

"Madame, this is a great compliment you pay me—to open a bottle of Cliquot Rosé."

"My memory is still good," she shrugged. "I keep it for my own drinking now, as I have not much left and one rarely sees wines in these days to compare with the old private cuvées of the Widow. But I recall how you always used to insist on having it when you entertained that pretty opera singer to supper. What was her name? Zara something?"

"You mean Zara Jókai, the little, dark Hungarian. Yes, I remember. How gay she was, and how we laughed together!"

"And I suppose you still expect me to turn a blind eye when you find another pretty Viennese to your taste, and wish to give her good advice up in your suite over oysters and champagne?"

"Madame, I promise you that I will give you no reason to complain of my discretion."

Frau Sacher chuckled and broke off a piece of the rim of the cake basket, which was made of marzipan. "No, you have never done that, Count; and I should be sad indeed if I did not feel that life and laughter were still going on around me. How long do you intend to remain with us?"

"It all depends. It is a long time since I have visited my estates at Königstein and they are overdue for a thorough inspection. I have instructed my steward to let me know when the castle is ready for my reception. When it is, I shall go there; but as soon as my business is done I hope to return to Vienna." De Richleau felt that, when the time came, this excuse would afford excellent cover for his move to Serbia, and went on almost at once to inquire after the Emperor.

"God be praised! His Majesty keeps in excellent health," Frau Sacher replied. "Of course, he now appears in public very seldom, but he is still hale and hearty."

"And the good Frau Schratt?" asked de Richleau.

"She, too, keeps very well, and continues to be a great support to His Majesty. He still maintains his custom of walking across the gardens to breakfast with her in her little house every morning. You know he never looks at a newspaper, and relies on her to give him the news of the town."

"I have never met her, and I should much like to do so. You are well known to be one of her oldest friends, and I should consider it a great kindness if you could arrange it."

Frau Sacher looked a little dubious. "I am very fond of Katharina. She is a fine and good person, and she comes to see me quite frequently. But she lives a very retired life and does not much care for meeting strangers."

"I could probably get the Aulendorfs and a few other people who she must know," suggested the Duke. "Then perhaps you could persuade her to be my guest at a private luncheon party here."

It was not idle curiosity that made him anxious to meet Katharina Schratt. No responsible person ever inferred that she was the Emperor's mistress, as her relations with him had always been open and most decorous; but she was probably more intimate with the old man than anyone else in his empire. She had made her name as an actress at the Burgtheater in 1883, and two years later had been presented to the Emperor and Empress. Both of them had taken a great liking to her, and from '88 onwards had frequently invited her to visit them. By the following year she had become such an accepted member of the family circle that it had fallen to her, more than anyone else, to attempt to console them both at the time of the tragic death of their son, the Crown Prince Rudolph. During the Empress Elizabeth's long absences abroad the Emperor had continued to delight in the actress' company, but they made frequent mention of her in the affectionate correspondence that formed a life-long bond between them, always referring to her as *die Freundin*. And after the Empress' death in 1898 Frau Schratt remained 'the friend', and the only woman, other than his wife and mother, who had ever enjoyed the Emperor's confidence. So, in view of his mission, de Richleau felt that it would be very well worth his while to go to some pains in order to make her acquaintance.

"I will see what I can do," Frau Sacher promised him, "but she was here only this morning, so it may be some days before I see her again."

They then spent an hour or more gossiping about some of the leading figures in Viennese society, and by the time the Duke went to bed he felt that, with the up-to-date information he had obtained about 'who was now who' in the Austrian capital, he had spent a very profitable evening.

Next morning he was up and out soon after the shops were open, as convention greatly circumscribed his actions until he could leave visiting cards upon his old friends and new acquaintances. Sacher's faced on to a small square, immediately behind the State Opera House, and on turning left as he came out of the hotel a few steps took him into Vienna's Bond Street, the Kerntner Strasse. Like its London equivalent every shop held a temptation for either women or men: huge hats crowned with ostrich feathers or Paradise plumes, costing up to fifty guineas; cloaks of ermine or sable; cedar cabinets holding a thousand Havana cigars apiece. Perfumeries offered genuine Attar of Roses from the Balkans at £5 an ounce; patisseries displayed confections of an unbelievable richness; jewellers; florists; haberdashers; and antique dealers: all competed for their share of the vast wealth accumulated over centuries by the upper classes in a nation of nearly sixty million people, occupying one of the most highly developed areas in the world.

Half way down the street, de Richleau turned into a stationers displaying crested and coroneted letter papers of every hue. They had there the engraved plate for his cards as Count Königstein, and as he had always stayed at Sacher's on his previous visits to Vienna, it needed no alteration. It was soon unearthed and the assistant promised to have some cards printed from it at once on the hand press at the back of the shop. They could be delivered as soon as they were dry, and were promised for not later than two o'clock that afternoon.

A little further down, the street merged into a square, from which rose the immense but graceful edifice of the Stefanskirche. As de Richleau approached the cathedral, he craned his neck to catch a glimpse of the tip of the magnificent Gothic spire which rose skywards four hundred and fifty feet above him. Then he crossed the road to admire the colossal west door, with its wealth of carving in which, every time he had seen it, he had found new beauties.

He was now in the very heart of Vienna where, over two thousand years before, a Roman fortress had protected civilization from the inroads of the barbaric tribes north of the Danube. The city had since been besieged many times, and once in the thirteenth century almost totally destroyed by fire; but through every calamity it had survived to become greater and more beautiful. In the Stefanskirche the chivalry of all Europe had gathered to give thanks to God for the breaking of the heathen Turk before its walls, and for close on a thousand years it had been the greatest centre of wealth and culture between the Baltic and the Black Sea, the Arctic Ocean and the Adriatic.

By medieval times it had grown to a warren of narrow streets, forming a rough circle based on the Danube canal, which ran some distance south-west of the main river, and extending nearly a mile in radius. But the old fortifications had long since been replaced by a splendid boulevard called The Ring, which encircled the old palaces and churches and the finest hotels and shops. Immediately outside The Ring lay the newer Government buildings, several public gardens ornamented with fine statuary, and the streets and squares of the wealthiest residential districts. Then, beyond them, lay the suburbs and the parks, of which Vienna boasted a greater number than any other city. Yet the Dual Monarchy contained so many other rich and ancient cities that its glittering metropolis had not outgrown itself with miles of slums and sprawling jerry-built dormitory districts, as had London and New York. A tram ride could still take any of its one million eight hundred thousand citizens out into the open country; to picnic in the Wienerwald, or enjoy the lovely view of the Danube from the Kobenzl. It was indeed a city of enchantment and delight.

From the Stefanskirche the Duke made his way back along the Kerntner Strasse to The Ring, and entering the Kaisergarten café ordered that beverage inseparable from life in Vienna—morning coffee. The cafés there were not few and far between and patronized only by occasional customers who felt like a drink: they were legion, and each was filled from early morning till late at night by relays of regular patrons who used them as clubs. Billiards, chess, dominoes and cards were provided for the amusement of customers: many people took a light breakfast in them, others spent hours there writing their letters; business men used them for meetings, the girls of the town for picking up casual lovers; and thousands of idlers sat in them most of the day, discussing with their neighbours every topic under the sun.

In them, almost everyone understood German, as it was the *lingua franca* of the city; but they carried on their voluble conversations in many tongues, as the Dual Monarchy numbered among its subjects millions of Hungarians, Czechs, Croats, Slovenes, Poles, Rumanians, Slovaks, Italians, and Ruthenians. It was this extraordinary mixture of races, the upper strata of which had inter-married for several generations, that gave the Viennese women a greater variety of beauty than was to be found in any other capital; and the smartness of their toilettes, mingled with the brightly-coloured uniforms of the Austrian officers, provided a scene in real life which could have been rivalled for gaiety only on a musical comedy stage.

On the marble-topped tables were scattered newspapers and journals of every type, including many English, American, French, Italian and German publications, as the Viennese prided themselves on being true cosmopolitans who took a tolerant interest in events—particularly when they were of an artistic or scientific nature—in every part of the world. That was perhaps because, since the rise of Prussia under Frederick the Great, nearly two centuries earlier, the martial power of the Holy Roman Empire had greatly declined. It seemed that since its armies had lost the secret of winning great victories, its people had formed the habit of consoling themselves by achieving intellectual triumphs. They had no colonies, and did not desire any, but they considered themselves second to none in advancing the progress of medicine and social well-being, and as the world's leading connoisseurs in the realms of music, letters and the art of living gracefully.

De Richleau sent for a few of the leading Viennese papers and began to study them. It was the Austrian political news with which he wished to bring himself up to date, but to find it he had to search for half-columns on the less important sheets of the papers, as the Viennese took little interest in politics, either domestic or international. The front pages were almost always devoted to long masterfully-written criticisms of performances at the opera, theatres, and concerts, or any outstanding event which had occurred in the lives of their leading prima donnas, ballerinas, actors, actresses, composers and muscians. For the average citizen, accounts of these matters were the only news which held any real interest, and the careers of such celebrities were followed with an eagerness displayed in no other country. The great artistes of stage and orchestra were known by sight to every schoolboy, and their appearance on any street was immediately greeted with a murmur of enthusiasm. The nobility enjoyed a respect engendered by generations of tradition, but the aristocracy of art was honoured in a hundred ways, granted special privileges by the State, and regarded as the true heroes of this cultured nation.

For lunch, the Duke moved on to Meissl and Schardan's restaurant; then he collected his visiting-cards, secured a taxi, and made a round of calls. At the Aulendorfs and Count Grünne's he left a note explaining that he had decided to break his journey for a short stay in Vienna, and that when there he used his Austrian title. With his old friends this was unnecessary.

That evening he enjoyed an excellent comedy at the Burgtheater then, instead of taking a cab back to his hotel, he strolled across the Volksgarten to the Hofburg, and right round it. The buildings of all shapes and ages, of which the Imperial Palace consisted, covered many acres, and, exclusive of its twenty-two interior courts, its frontages were well over a mile in length. As de Richleau gazed up at the seemingly endless rows of windows he wondered, like any love-struck youth, behind which of them was hidden his beautiful Ilona. But he knew that even this closely-knit town of great mansions, built at the caprices of a long line of Caesars, might not hold its loveliest daughter. She might equally well have taken up her residence at the slightly smaller, but more beautiful, Schwarzenberg Palace on the outer side of The Ring, or at Schönbrunn, the Versailles of Vienna, which lay only three miles away in the suburbs.

Next day his calls began to bring results. Invitations came in from the Laxenburgs, Batthyanzs, Metternichs and Bukovicks for luncheons, a dinner and a dance. Captain Count Adam Grünne called in person—although the Duke missed him as he happened to be out—and, besides his own card, left an invitation to a musical party at the Aulendorfs for the following night.

On receiving the last, de Richleau's heart missed a beat, as it seemed highly probable that Ilona would be there, and he had not expected to see her again so soon. But in that he was disappointed. The gathering was a small one of only thirty-odd people: the occasion to give a try-out to a young pianist of promise. Nevertheless the Duke did not consider his evening by any means wasted, as it enabled him to consolidate his pleasant relations with his host and hostess, and ask them to be present at a luncheon party he was making up when he could settle on a date mutually convenient to them and some of his other friends.

Moreover, it chanced that Count Leopold von Berchtold, the Emperor's Foreign Minister, was present, and he was one of the people whom de Richleau particularly wished to meet. He was a highly-cultured German-Austrian aristocrat with a broad forehead, heavily lidded eyes and a long, sharp nose. His demeanour was very correct and a little haughty, even when, as on this occasion, among his equals: so, much as the Duke would have liked to draw him into a political discussion he decided that it would be wiser to refrain and remain content at this first meeting with merely having made his acquaintance.

Another matter which brought de Richleau some consolation for Ilona's absence was Count Grünne's presence at the party, and an invitation from him to occupy a seat in the Imperial box at the Horse Show on the coming Friday. He apologized that it should be for the penultimate day of the Show, rather than for the finals, but on the Saturday the Heir Apparent, the Archduke Franz-Ferdinand, was to take the salute, and for that all seats had already been allotted. De Richleau accepted with pleasure all the same, both because he liked the dark, broad-shouldered Count and knew that the occasion would afford him an opportunity to meet further people connected with the Court.

Two afternoons later, the Duke, clad in a black frock-coat, a waistcoat with a narrow band of white showing above it, striped trousers, patent leather boots, grey spats and gleaming topper, made his way to the Hofburg, as under one of its many lofty roofs lay the Spanish Riding School, which was still famous throughout Europe as the home of Haute École. As the Viennese were great horse-lovers its galleries were packed with an enthusiastic crowd, and he found more than half the seats in the Imperial Box, which held about two dozen people, already taken. But Count Grünne had had a seat reserved for him in the second row, and, with a polite bow to his neighbours, he settled down to enjoy the graceful spectacle.

The majority of the competitors were officers in the brilliant uniforms of the Dual Monarchy, but among them were a few civilians, and some visiting officers from foreign countries who were somewhat less spectacularly dressed. The horses were superb, the riding excellent, and for a quarter of an hour de Richleau watched them, entirely occupied with their well-timed evolutions. But suddenly the band ceased playing in the middle of a tune, the competitors all entered the arena together and formed up into four lines, like a squadron of cavalry, facing the Imperial box. There was a rustle in the crowd, a trumpet call rang out, everyone rose, and the band struck up the national anthem. The privileged few in the spacious box drew aside in two groups, leaving its centre empty, the curtains at its back were drawn apart and, escorted by a grey-faced man in General's uniform, there entered *Ihr Kaiserlich und Koniglich Hoheit, die Erzherzogin Ilona Theresa.*

CHAPTER VIII

THE DARK ANGEL OF THE ARSENAL

De Richleau knew that it was customary for some person of importance to take the parade every day at a show of such national interest, but somehow it had never occurred to him that Ilona might do so; and her appearance was now so unlike what it had been at their previous meetings that, for a second, he failed to recognize her.

As the function was almost entirely a military one, she was wearing the uniform of Colonel-in-Chief of her own regiment of Hussars. It was sky-blue with silver facings. The train of her habit was looped up over her left arm, showing a glimpse of Hessian riding boots beneath its skirt; a half-cloak trimmed with grey astrakhan swung gallantly from her erect shoulders, and from the centre of her flat-topped busby a white plume, eighteen inches high, nodded gaily. The Duke thought that she looked ravishing, and caught his breath in admiration as she advanced to the front of the box, looking neither to right nor left. There, instead of acknowledging the plaudits of the crowd with a bow, she stood stiffly to attention and brought her hand up in a smart salute: then she sat down in a gilt arm-chair, and the show went on.

It was not until the interval that she saw de Richleau. When it arrived, she withdrew into a reception room behind the box and everyone in it followed her. As her glance fell upon him the faint pink deepened in her cheeks, but after only a second's hesitation she beckoned him to her, and said graciously:

"I did not know that you intended to honour Vienna with a visit so soon, Duke. I hope that you are enjoying yourself in our lovely city."

He bowed over her hand. "As there are no wars at the moment, your Imperial Highness, a soldier of fortune like myself is forced to take a little leisure; and nowhere in the world holds such attraction for me as Vienna."

She flushed again and quickly introduced him to the elderly General who was her official escort. He was a small man with a flowing grey moustache that seemed too big for his withered, wrinkled face; but a pair of keen, bright eyes showed that his brain was not as atrophied as his countenance. His name was Franz, Freiherr Conrad von Hötzendorf, and it was then little known outside his own country; but de Richleau knew it, for it had been given to him by Major Hankey as that of the man who had, eight years previously, been entrusted by the Archduke

Franz Ferdinand with the reorganisation of the Imperial armies. He was their present Chief, and, it was expected, would lead them in the event of war.

Ilona had turned to receive some of the competitors, whom she had desired should be presented to her during the interval, but von Hötzendorf addressed de Richleau with quick interest:

"So you are a soldier of fortune, Duke. In which wars have you fought?"

De Richleau mentioned his South American campaigns, then that the Turks had given him the command of a ramshackle Army Corps in their war with the Balkan Federation.

"Ramshackle or not, to have commanded an Army Corps in active warfare is a thing of which not many men can boast," commented the General swiftly, "and particularly at your age. My profession is a passion with me, and I am interested in every aspect of it. I should much like to hear of your experiences while with the Turks. Will you lunch with me one day at the Arsenal?"

"I should be very happy to do so, General," replied the Duke, striving to keep out of his voice the real elation he felt at receiving such an invitation.

Von Hötzendorf produced a little book with neat, angular writing in it, cast an eye over his engagements and suggested the following Tuesday, the 12th of May. For the Duke that meant putting off a lunch party at the Metternichs but, nevertheless, he promptly accepted.

There were further introductions and small talk while the party nibbled little cakes and sipped *eis-caffee Viennoise* with a three-inch layer of rich cream on top. Then they returned to the box. After the final parade Ilona spent a few minutes making the usual tactful remarks of royalty to the people round her, before leaving. To de Richleau she said:

"No doubt, Duke, I shall see you at the Czernins' ball on Monday?"

He bowed from the waist. "Your Imperial Highness is most kind, and I count it a great honour that you should command my presence."

The Czernins were not among his acquaintances, but her remark was tantamount to an order, so he knew that he would have no difficulty in securing an invitation. Adam Grünne was, of course, in attendance on her; so when thanking him for the afternoon's entertainment, de Richleau mentioned the matter. The equerry said at once that he would have the Duke's name added to the list of guests that had been submitted to the Court Chamberlain and inform the Countess Czernin, and the following afternoon he received a big gold-crested card requesting the pleasure of his company at the ball.

Now that the Duke had been six days in Vienna, he was fully re-launched in Viennese society, so the week-end passed in a pleasant round of social engagements: but the thought of Monday night was never far from his mind, and whenever he was alone he kept wondering a little anxiously what attitude Ilona would adopt towards him when they had a chance to talk alone together.

The Czernins were one of the greatest families in Austria and occupied a palace of their own in the Josefstadt district. This lay on the far side of The Ring and had once been a garden city in which many of the Austrian nobility had country houses just outside the walls. These had since mostly disappeared, to give place to some of Vienna's finest Government buildings, the spreading of the University and big blocks of luxury flats. But some of the great private mansions still remained, and the Czernins' palace lay just behind the Rathaus.

On his arrival, de Richleau found a very similar scene to that which he had witnessed on driving up to Dorchester House just a month earlier, except that this was made infinitely gayer from the continental custom of officers wearing their uniforms, instead of civilian clothes, when off duty. The Imperial Guard were resplendent in white and gold; *jägers* in green mingled with dragoons in scarlet and hussars in light blue, pearl and grey. Here and there a more sober note was struck by officers in the dark blue of the Austrian navy, the dark green of the artillery, and the grey-blue of the infantry. But most magnificent of all were the Hungarian nobility, who wore their own hereditary costumes of rich fur-trimmed velvets and brocades.

The Duke soon found several of his acquaintances and could easily have filled up his card with dance engagements; but he committed himself only for those early on his programme, from fear that he might have to cut a later one on account of Ilona. It would have been a flagrant breach of etiquette for him to ask her for a dance, but he thought it certain that she would send for him during the course of the evening, and he eagerly awaited her arrival.

At ten o'clock she appeared in the ballroom accompanied by the Count and Countess Czernin, who had left their position at the head of the stairs to escort her to a low dais, from which she could watch the dancing or join in it, as she felt inclined. To-night she was dressed in oyster satin, and looked much more regal than she had at Dorchester House, as the bright blue cordon of an order, with a great diamond star upon it, crossed her breast: a necklace of rubies, the centre piece of which was the size of a pigeon's egg, glowed round her throat, and a tiara scintillated on her high-piled chestnut hair. As she crossed the room she passed quite close to de Richleau, but she did not appear to notice him, and she was soon surrounded by a little court of mainly elderly people who hid her from his view.

Ten minutes later his thoughts were temporarily distracted from her, as the band broke off a Mazurka it was playing to blare into the National Anthem, and the Count and Countess Czernin again appeared, this time to escort across the room His Imperial Highness, the Archduke Franz-Ferdinand and his wife.

De Richleau regarded this middle-aged couple with special interest for more reasons than one. Firstly, as heir apparent to an Emperor whose age was eighty-four, the Archduke was well on the way to replacing the old man as the most important figure in the empire. It was he who, against the Emperor's wish, had ordered the reforms which von Hötzendorf had introduced into the Imperial armies; and probably it would depend upon him, more than any single individual, whether Austria accepted a challenge from Serbia and possibly precipitated a general European war. Secondly, he had shown unusual character and determination in over-riding all opposition in order to marry morganatically.

On the Crown Prince Rudolph's death, the Emperor's brother, the Archduke Charles, had become the heir apparent, but when he died in 1896 the succession passed to his son, Franz-Ferdinand. The Emperor then decided that it would be a good plan to marry his new heir to Rudolph's widow, Stephanie of Belgium, but the unforeseen exposure of a love affair in which Franz-Ferdinand was engaged, had brought swift ruin to this project.

While staying with the Archduchess Isabella, Franz-Ferdinand had fallen in love with one of her maids of honour, the Countess Sophie Chotek, a Czech who, although titled, was very far from belonging to the highest aristocracy. The Archduchess suspected the affair but the Countess, when questioned by her mistress, flatly denied it. Then, purely by chance, the Archduchess picked up a locket belonging to her maid of honour: on opening it she found that it contained a miniature of Franz-Ferdinand which had written across its back 'Thine for ever'.

The Countess was immediately dismissed, and the reason for her disgrace injudiciously noised abroad. Upon which, feeling that he had compromised the young lady and brought about her ruin, Franz-Ferdinand declared his intention of marrying her.

The Emperor, who regarded the perpetuation of his dynasty through undiluted royal blood as a sacred charge, was horrified, and did everything in his power to prevent the match. But Franz-Ferdinand announced that he meant to go through with it, even if it necessitated his renouncing the throne both for himself and his children.

After harrowing scenes, a compromise was reached, by which he sacrificed the claims of any children he might have by the Countess, and hers to recognition as his official wife, while retaining his own as heir apparent. But this did not altogether solve the problem of her position, as, although she could never become Empress of Austria, under the ancient laws of Hungary, which permitted morganatic marriages, she would, upon the old Emperor's death, automatically become Queen of that country.

Since their marriage in 1900 she had borne her husband three children, and he now made no secret of the fact that he regretted having signed away their rights of succession in favour of his nephew, the young Archduke Charles. Moreover, the Countess Sophie was a clever woman with boundless ambition, and it was said that in due course she would stop at nothing to get herself proclaimed Empress.

At present, therefore, their position was in the highest degree invidious. The Archduke was becoming more and more the real ruler of the state, and the army already regarded him as its supreme chief. But his wife, although now over forty and recently created Duchess of Hohenberg, was still not received at court. The Emperor continued to insist that no royal honours should ever be paid to her, and many members of the ancient Austrian nobility followed his lead, partly owing to their contempt for the Czechs, whom they regarded as a subject race, and partly on account of her comparatively low birth, but above all because she had brought dissent and uncertainty concerning the succession into the imperial family.

As against that, other noble families, like the Czernins, received and courted her for a variety of reasons. If they wished to be on good terms with Franz-Ferdinand it was almost impossible not to do so as, except for state functions at which her presence was barred, he took her with him wherever he went. But some of them had formed a genuine liking for her, and others openly championed her cause from the cynical belief that in course of time she would become the acknowledged mistress of the Empire, and that she would then shower rich rewards on all who had taken her side against the old Emperor.

Not least among these was the Kaiser, Wilhelm II. The German monarch was shrewd enough to appreciate her brain and the probable extent of her future influence. He had received her in Berlin only semi-officially, from fear of offending the Emperor, but had gone out of his way to treat her with special courtesy; and whenever he passed through Vienna he never failed to pay his respects to her. As Major Hankey had informed de Richleau, this policy had already borne rich fruit, as Franz-Ferdinand was devoted to his wife and nothing swayed him more than such attentions to her. In consequence, from having been anti-German as a young man he had, in the past few years, come to regard the Kaiser as a great personal friend, and now invariably took his advice on all questions regarding the Austrian army.

As the Duke unobtrusively watched the couple from some thirty paces distant, he thought of that, and wondered if in some way he might use the Duchess of Hohenberg's ambitions, or the Archduke's eagerness to see his wife publicly acclaimed, for some purpose of his own.

Several times de Richleau endeavoured to catch Ilona's eye, and as the dancing proceeded he took occasion now and then to pass within a few yards of her. But she continued to ignore him, so he began to think that she had repented of her impulse to afford him what amounted only to another meeting in public, until, at last, after the supper dance, Adam Grünne sought him out in the buffet and told him that Her Imperial Highness desired his presence.

With his heart beating a little faster, he accompanied the equerry to the dais, where Ilona gave him her hand to kiss, and said with a smile: "I have not seen you dancing very much this evening, Duke, although I am told that you are a good dancer. I have just had my wish conveyed to the band that they should play the 'Blue Danube'. I trust you are not too blasé to partner me in it."

He returned her smile. "It is watching the perfection of Your Highness' dancing that has made me disinclined to dance with less gifted ladies to-night. You see, I was once told by someone whom I much respect that it is better not to waltz at all than with someone who does not waltz really well."

As he handed her down off the dais her blue eyes sparkled. By her ordering the 'Blue Danube' and by his remark, both had deliberately recalled their dance together at Dorchester House and all that had followed it. He took a firm grip of her waist, and a moment later they swung smoothly away across the floor.

They made their first circle of the room in silence, then he whispered, "Am I forgiven?"

"Of course you are," Her eyes were turned away from him, but her breath fanned his cheek. "Otherwise I should not be dancing with you."

"I had begun to think you never meant to. May I hope for another before you leave?"

"No. For me to dance twice in one evening with a stranger would certainly be remarked. Besides, I am dancing with you now, just this once, only because you took the trouble to come to Vienna in evidence of your repentance."

"What would you say if I told you that I do not repent?"

"I forbid you to say such things."

"You cannot forbid me to think them. And I did not come to Vienna to seek forgiveness, but in search of love."

She dropped her long dark lashes and remained silent a moment.

Then she said coldly: "I am told that Vienna is a good place for a man like yourself to find it. The girls here are very pretty, and do I not recall your telling me that you often—often formed unions of—of a temporary nature?"

"I have occasionally done so in the past; but you know very well I did not mean that."

"Then—then I prefer not to be enlightened as to your meaning."

"So you are still afraid?"

Her body tautened for a second. "Of what?"

"Of love."

Again the pink of her cheeks deepened slightly as she exclaimed: "You *must* not talk to me like this. Now that you know who I am, you have no right to do so."

"I know only that you are the most lovely person in the world."

To that she did not reply, and they circled the room in silence again. Then he asked, "Will you sit out with me somewhere in the interval after this dance?"

She shook her head. "No. That is impossible. You must take me back to the dais immediately the band stops."

"Then, when may I see you again?"

"As it is my duty to appear often in public no doubt an opportunity for you to do so will soon occur."

"You are unkind," he murmured reproachfully. "I meant, to talk to you—to tell you how I treasure the memory of that kiss more than anything in my whole life."

She hesitated a second, then burst out: "I have no wish to talk to you again. That first time the things you said were excusable. You thought me then some little heiress of no account. But now you are aware of the gulf that separates us, it is an impertinence to embarrass me in this fashion, and I will not permit it."

A wave of depression surged through him. This dance, to which he had been looking forward so eagerly, had begun so well, but somehow the secret bond that seemed to have been established between them had showed signs of strain almost from the beginning, and now she had made it plain that she had no further use for him. Surely, he thought, she would not have asked him to dance solely to pronounce her formal forgiveness on a matter that they both knew was already forgiven. She must have expected him to make love to her and, granted that, he had not said anything to which she could take exception. He did not understand her attitude, but in view of their positions there was nothing he could do other than accept it. So he said with a sigh:

"A cat may look at a king, Princess, and to every man there comes at least once in a lifetime a woman for whom he would dare everything, and of whom he dreams fond dreams. It is my misfortune that I should not only have looked at, but talked to, you; and so incurred your displeasure. But after to-night I will not trouble you again with my presence, and in the meantime you may rest assured that I will treat Your Imperial Highness only with the profound respect that is your due."

Twice more they danced round the room together, both highly conscious of the horrid silence that now hung like an invisible barrier between them, but neither made any attempt to break it. Then the band stopped. After their last pirouette, he continued to hold for a second the youthful form, shimmering with rubies and diamonds, while he looked straight down into the lovely face so near his own. But she kept her glance averted, so, with a frigid bow, he led her back to the dais.

As they drew near it he noticed, almost subconsciously, that the Duchess of Hohenberg had her dark eyes fixed upon him, and when Ilona resumed her chair the Duchess spoke. By natural law she should have been the first lady in the land, but as matters stood she remained in rank far the inferior of her beautiful young cousin-by-marriage, so she addressed her with a familiarity that was tempered with deference.

"Your Highness excelled yourself in the last dance. You seem to have found a perfect partner. Will you not present him to us?"

Ilona had recovered her sang-froid and, with the social smile that habit had already accustomed her to assume spontaneously, she performed the introduction. Franz-Ferdinand gave the Duke a cold appraising look. He was a morbidly suspicious man, and had once remarked to his Chief of Staff, 'You expect that every man will prove an angel. For my part, I always assume that anyone I see for the first time is a scoundrel, and later on, if possible, I revise my opinion'. Nevertheless, the mouth below his dark moustache, which curled up at its ends, parted in a polite smile, and he offered the Duke his hand. With a much more friendly smile, the Duchess extended hers and de Richleau kissed it with the same low obeisance he would have made had she actually been a royal personage.

The Archduke inquired if he knew Vienna well, and was enjoying his visit. He made a suitable answer, and was then asked if he travelled much. He replied by speaking of his big game-hunting expeditions and the wars in which he had been involved. Franz-Ferdinand's heavy face immediately brightened, and once again the Duke had cause to bless the fact that his experience as a general in the Turkish army seemed a sure passport to arousing the curiosity of Austria's military chiefs; for the Archduke said:

"This interests me very much. I should like to hear your views on the possible performance of the Turkish army now that it has had a breathing space to recover. Be pleased to make yourself known to one of my aides-de-camp, and ask him to arrange a time when we can have a talk together."

"I shall be most happy to place myself at Your Imperial Highness' disposal," replied the Duke. Then, as the band began a two-step, the plump, well-corseted Duchess leaned towards him and said:

"If you fight as well as you dance, Duke, you must be a great general. But in Vienna we count dancing more important, and I should like to have you for my partner in this one."

Obediently he led her out, and they had been dancing scarcely a minute before she looked down at his shirt-front and asked, "How did you earn such a highly-prized decoration?"

He was wearing the Order of the Golden Fleece, to which very few people, apart from royalty, were entitled. He was a Knight of several Orders of Chivalry, but had decided to wear this most illustrious one to-night because such a distinction might make it less remarkable that Ilona should single him out for a partner. Now he was quick to realize that the ambitious Duchess had noticed it at once, and was far less interested in his dancing than in his potentialities as a man who, by his possession of that Order, had the right to address kings as 'cousin'.

"I make no claim to merit it," he said modestly, "but His Majesty of Spain presented me with it in recognition of a somewhat unusual service that I was fortunate enough to render him a few years ago."

"You know him well, then?"

"Fairly intimately. I have, too, a great admiration for King Alfonso. He is one of the few monarchs who today still embody the charm, broad-mindedness, courage and intelligence, which the best kings of the past displayed. I mean, in the days when kingship was no mere matter of inheritance, but an art that demanded great personality to win adherents and keep a throne."

She gave him a quick look. "How I agree! The stupidity and narrow-mindedness of some of the present crowned heads of Europe positively maddens me. But let us change the subject before I begin to talk treason."

He laughed. "Your Highness has good cause. And I assure you your secrets would be safe with me, for I believe a constitutional monarchy to be the best of all forms of government, but that many of those in Europe are doomed unless fresh, healthy blood can be introduced into the effete stock of some of the ruling families."

The Duchess Sophie did not accept his invitation to confide in him, nor had he expected her to do so, but a pleasant conspiritorial feeling had been engendered between them, and for the rest of the dance they got on excellently, so that when it ended she made him promise to call upon her.

Shortly afterwards he decided to go home, as he was in no mood for further dancing. His presentation to Franz-Ferdinand and his wife had been a piece of real good fortune, but that did not make up for his disappointment over Ilona. He thought that perhaps while abroad she had been like a person on a long sea voyage, which makes people peculiarly susceptible to new outlooks and emotions that are swiftly counteracted by the habits of a lifetime on their return home. Or it might be that he had flattered himself unduly, and allowed his imagination to read more into her last words to him on the boat than she had intended. But, whatever the reason, it was clear that she had no intention of entering on even a flirtation, much less a love affair, with him.

He tried to console himself with the thought that he was probably well out of trouble, and that an affair with her might have seriously hampered him in his mission. But neither idea carried conviction. He had risked his life too often to be seriously concerned at incurring the displeasure of her family, and knew that, once he was free to do so, he would willingly have gambled a term of imprisonment against the chance to feel her lips against his again. As for his mission, had it not been for her the odds were all against his having yet got to know Franz-Ferdinand and his wife, Conrad von Hötzendorf, Count Berchtold, the Aulendorfs, Adam Grünne, and a dozen other important people, through whom he now had an excellent chance of forming a sound appreciation of Austria's attitude in the event of trouble with Serbia.

His eight days in Vienna had been far from wasted, but as he went to bed he decided that better results might come from the leads he had secured if he did not appear eager to follow them up too quickly, and that in any case a change of scene would help him to banish Ilona's image from his mind: so the coming evening he would take the train to Belgrade and begin his investigations in the Serbian capital.

He had already received a note from General von Hötzendorf, confirming their luncheon date and asking him to be at the Arsenal by twelve o'clock, in order that they could have a talk before the meal: so on the following morning he set out in good time for his appointment. A taxi carried him swiftly along The Ring as far as the Schwarzenberg Palace, then south-westward for over a mile along the wall of its garden and through the Schwarzer Park to his destination.

It was the first time he had visited the Arsenal, and he was much impressed by its size. The area it covered was considerably greater than that of the Hofburg and it contained as many buildings, but all set out in accordance with a geometrical plan. The whole formed a rectangle enclosed by a colossal wall of over a mile and a half in length which, with its corner and flanking towers, was castellated in imitation of the battlements of an ancient fortress, although it was obvious that it had been built in comparatively recent times. It housed not only an armaments foundry, but also, like the Invalides in Paris, a big military museum, as well as the headquarters of the General Staff.

Von Hötzendorf received the Duke with a brisk business-like air, and led him at once to a room in which a great map of the Balkans had already been pinned up on the wall. Without preamble, he asked his visitor to give him a résumé of the campaign and his reasons for the defeats the Turkish armies had sustained. For the best part of an hour de Richleau obliged, answered a score of shrewd questions, and pointed out various instances in which, although the Turks were outnumbered, better tactics might have enabled them to stave off defeat.

The little dark, wizened-faced General was obviously impressed, not only with de Richleau's military knowledge, but also with his grasp of the ambitions and pressures which animated the Balkan States. And as they went in to lunch he turned the conversation to international affairs.

Von Hötzendorf was by nature an ascetic. For years he had worked like a demon and denied himself every comfort in order that, by subordinating all personal pleasures to duty, he might set an example to the officers under him. So the lunch was meagre and the wine poor; but, connoisseur as the Duke was, he never gave that a thought. It soon became apparent to him that his host was as much a master of foreign affairs as he was of military matters. His mind seemed to be crammed with particulars of treaties, conventions, pacts, minorities and their ambitions, personalities of courts and cabinets, and the extent of their influence on their governments. Moreover, he made no secret of the fact that he considered it part of his task to so manipulate his country's diplomacy that, should the Austrian army ever be called upon to strike, it should not be hampered in its operations by uncertainty of the intentions of other neighbouring states.

Clearly, de Richleau's Austrian title caused von Hötzendorf to regard his guest as half-Austrian, and the Duke having fought for the Turks against Austria's traditional enemies, the Serbs, led further to the belief that his sympathies were wholly so. In consequence, as they ate their cheese and biscuits, the General spoke with blunt frankness on Austria's situation as he saw it.

He said that for half a lifetime he had watched with acute anxiety the increasing peril of the Empire. The spread of education had resulted in an enormous growth of the separatist movements among her subject peoples. Influential bodies of Hungarians, Czechs, Rumanians, Yugoslavs, Italians and Croats were constantly agitating for powers of self-government which, if granted, could only lead eventually to their complete break-away from the old Imperial system. Worse, Austria was surrounded by greedy enemies who secretly encouraged these minorities, not for the sake of the people in them, but for the territories they occupied. Rumania wanted Transylvania; Serbia, Bosnia; Russia, Galicia; and Italy, the Trientino and Trieste. Therefore, unless Austrian diplomacy could at all times secure the goodwill of a majority of these potential enemies, all of them together might one day fall upon her and rend her to pieces.

De Richleau nodded his agreement and asked: "What then, General, is your solution to this menacing state of affairs?"

The reply came promptly. "An old but, I believe, sound one. We are faced with the problem of the bundle of sticks which is too strong to be broken in one movement; but if taken one by one, each stick can be broken separately. Austria does not seek war, but a war would reunite her peoples as nothing else could do, and I am a strong believer in the offensive. If any of our enemies gives us cause, we should not hesitate, but attack and smash her before the rest have time to think up pretexts for going to her assistance and combining against us."

Again the Duke nodded, and his voice was steady as he inquired: "Say, for example, that Serbia gave fresh cause for umbrage over Bosnia, would you advise your government to commence hostilities against her?"

Again the reply came without a second's hesitation. "Yes, and they would take my advice, for Count Berchtold sees eye to eye with me in this. Given sixteen days to mobilize, I would take the field with an army large enough to crush Serbia utterly, and within three weeks blot her for ever from the map."

A cold hand seemed to clutch at de Richleau's heart. As far as Austria was concerned he now had his answer. She would make no concessions, as he had hoped. There would be no chance for arbitration by a council of nations in an endeavour to keep the peace. Unless Dimitriyevitch and the Black Hand could be muzzled, there would be war.

CHAPTER IX

RURITANIA WITHOUT THE ROMANCE

BEFORE leaving Vienna de Richleau was given cause to make a slight modification in his plans. On his return from his revealing and highly perturbing luncheon with von Hötzendorf, he was informed by the desk clerk at his hotel that Frau Sacher would like to see him, so he went at once to her sitting-room.

He found the old lady enjoying her after-lunch coffee and cigar and, having had an extremely frugal meal himself, he readily accepted an invitation to join her. As soon as he was seated, she said:

"The office informed me only an hour ago that you are leaving us to-night, Count, and I am sorry about that as I had just succeeded in arranging for you to meet Frau Schratt. I had hoped to have done so before, but she has been unwell. This morning was the first time she has come to see me for over a week, but I remembered your wish and she agreed to lunch here on Monday next, the eighteenth."

De Richleau's brain worked very quickly. Von Hötzendorf was Franz-Ferdinand's right-hand man, so evidently spoke for him, and had said himself that he and Count Berchtold were of one mind on future policy. That meant that, given a *casus belli* by Serbia, all the odds were on Austria going to war. But there still remained one slender chance that these apostles of the sword might find their hands tied when the time came. They could not act without the Emperor's sanction. The old man would have to be consulted and he might prove unwilling to let them have their heads, particularly if he was pressed to do so by the heir whom he disliked and despised. If anyone knew what attitude he was likely to adopt in such a crisis, it was Frau Schratt. She might refuse to discuss it, but that was another matter. This opportunity to endeavour to obtain her views was too precious to be neglected.

He had intended to spend at least a week, or possibly a fortnight, in Belgrade, but if things went well he might get through his business more quickly. In any case, by leaving Vienna that night and returning by the night train on Sunday, he could get in five days there and, if necessary, after the luncheon on Monday another night journey would get him back to the Serbian capital by Tuesday morning.

After barely a second's hesitation, he replied: "I am most grateful to you for arranging a meeting, and anyway, I had intended to return to Vienna shortly. I will invite half a dozen people for next Monday, and leave it, if I may, in your most capable hands to order the dishes that you think Frau Schratt would like best for our luncheon."

She shook her head. "Frau Schratt is of a most retiring disposition, and I am sure she would much prefer it if just the three of us lunched in my private dining-room. If you have no objection, I will arrange it so."

"Please do, by all means," agreed the Duke. "And I thank you again, dear Frau Sacher, for taking so much trouble on my account.'

All that evening thoughts of Ilona plagued him, but at length the time came for him to catch his train, and he found that he was sharing a sleeping compartment with a talkative French impresario in search of Balkan talent, so the amusing experiences of this voluble person took his mind off his abortive love affair until it was time to turn in. The following morning he reached Belgrade.

It was a pocket capital and, apart from being a seat of government, could hardly have claimed the dignity of the term 'city'. Its population was a mere 120,000, so it was actually no larger than Southampton, and its few good buildings were concentrated in quite a small area, beyond which spread a higgledy-piggledy collection of mostly ramshackle structures, nearly all of which had been erected a generation or less ago.

Situated on rising ground, it overlooked the confluence of the Danube and the Save, but its proximity to the former mighty river was the only thing it had in common with the splendid city that de Richleau had left the night before.

In fact, few contrasts could have been greater. In Vienna, there were endless miles of shops containing every variety of article that the ingenuity of man had devised to make life easy, elegant and pleasant. Here, there were only a few streets in which a modest selection of imported goods could be obtained. All but an infinitesimal proportion of the people in the Austrian capital were well-housed, well-fed and well-clothed; whereas the majority of those in the Serbian metropolis lived in near-squalor, ate only the coarsest foods, and were clad in home-made garments. The Viennese bourgeoisie had achieved the highest culture of any middle-class in the world: in Belgrade culture was almost non-existent, and the greater part of its inhabitants could not yet even read.

Up to eighty years earlier, the Serbs had been an entirely peasant people and, apart from cottage industries, their manufactures were still negligible. For centuries, previous to 1830, Serbia had been a Turkish province, and the Sultans had seen to it that no feudal system ever developed there, so the Serbs had no nobility. When, at last, they had thrown off the Turkish yoke, it had been through a series of revolts instigated by courageous peasant leaders. The most successful of these had been Black George—or, to use his native appellation, Karageorge—a pig-dealer who had served in the Austrian army, and Milosh Obrenovitch, who invented for himself the title Prince of the Serbs. And between the descendants of these two had ensued a long and bitter feud for the domination of the country.

Milosh's son, Michael, had reigned till 1842, then been expelled by Alexander Karageorgevitch. In 1859 Michael's partisans had regained the throne for him, and his descendants had occupied it until 1903 when, after the revoltingly brutal assassination of the unprincipled King Alexander and his ex-demi-mondaine wife, Queen Draga, by the founders of the Black Hand, the present King, Peter Karageorgevitch, has assumed the reins of power. Thus, there had been no more than a few generations of Serbian independence to form even a small middle-class of professional men and officers.

Yet this uncultured people still cherished memories of the distant centuries before the Turkish hordes had invaded Europe. They had then had their own Tsars, defeated in turn the Greeks and the Bulgars, and even laid seige to mighty Byzantium. Under Stephen Nemanya, Urosh II and Tsar Dushan, Serbia had been a great kingdom. The names of these long-dead paladins were still venerated in every cottage and their spirits were still a living force which stirred the patriotism of every peasant to dreams of re-creating Serbia's past greatness.

The success of their recent wars had aroused in them a knowledge of their latent power. In 1912 they had avenged themselves for centuries of Turkish oppression. Then in 1913, when the members of the Balkan League had quarrelled over the spoils of victory, like an omen that the future might repeat the past they had, after a lapse of many centuries, once again defeated their ancient enemies, the Bulgarians.

Now, with Turkey hurled back almost into Asia, their eyes turned north towards the Austrian Empire; for they regarded the Austrians as a race of oppressors, equalled only by the Turks, and bore them a corresponding hatred. Not only did the Dual Monarchy still hold enslaved a part of Serbia's ancient territory and many thousands of her people, but the Empire had, less than ten years before, endeavoured to apply a strangle-hold to the economic life of the smaller nation. Serbia was the greatest pig-breeding country in Europe and the very existence of her people depended upon the export of swine. For generations Hungary had been her greatest and almost sole customer. Suddenly the Austrians had clamped down a ban on the import of pigs into their Empire. The Serbians had found other markets in Egypt, Greece and France; but it had been a desperate struggle, and those lean years of the 'Pig War' still rankled.

The Serbians were a virile race, inured to hardship and, in time of war, capable of fighting a long campaign with few resources. They were, too, a dour people, as was evidenced by their national costumes which, instead of being embroidered with gay-coloured silks as was customary among other middle and eastern European peasant populations, were of sober black, white and grey. They asked little of life and were most hospitable within their modest means; but they never forgot an injury and brooded bitterly over the wrongs they felt had been done them; so they were an easy prey to agitators sent out to stir their patriotism and ever ready to snatch up their rifles at the call to arms for a war of revenge.

As de Richleau was driven in a rickety open carriage from the station to the Hotel Continental, he thought of all these things, and wondered if Colonel Dragutin Dimitriyevitch was already preparing to spring his mine. He wondered, too, if in the event of an Austro-Serbian conflict, von Hötzendorf would prove right in his estimate that, once mobilized, the armies he commanded would prove capable of overrunning Serbia in three weeks—and greatly doubted it.

The hotel proved better than the Duke expected, as it was French-run and the management were endeavouring to attract the custom of travellers from the west. Nevertheless, the time-honoured custom of providing for the possible requirements of male patrons travelling alone was still maintained. He had been in his room only a few minutes when an olive-complexioned gentleman with a spiky moustache arrived, carrying under his arm a large book of photographs. They were of young ladies in various states of semi-nudity, any or all of whom would be delighted to call upon His Grace at any time. As a connoisseur of beauty in all its forms, de Richleau looked through the book, then politely declined and, after having given the man a couple of *dinars* for his trouble, firmly dismissed him.

His unpacking did not take long as he had decided to leave most of his clothes in Vienna, and when he had completed it he went out for a walk round the town. On numerous occasions he had passed through Belgrade in the Orient Express, but he had never before visited it. Now, he found that it contained little of historical or artistic interest, except for the old walled citadel on the bend of the river, which had for centuries housed a garrison of Turkish janissaries. The churches were mostly small and had the same onion-shaped spires as those in Russia, which was not surprising since, like the Russians, by far the greater part of the population belonged to the Greek Orthodox Church.

The lettering in the shops and street signs would have appeared gibberish to most Englishmen, as it was in Cyrillic script; but that, again, being used in common with the Russians was no puzzle to the

Duke. Moreover, the language of the southern Slavs so closely resembled that of their kin in the great northern Empire that anyone who spoke one found no great difficulty in understanding the other, as de Richleau was already aware from having cross-questioned Serbian prisoners taken during his Balkan campaigns.

Walking slowly, as it was now very hot, he amused himself for some time by working out the English equivalent of the prices of things in the shops, and, apart from a few imported articles, he found them incredibly cheap. He remembered a Turkish officer once telling him that in Serbia a comfortable cottage could be built for £20, and a middle-class family live reasonably well on £100 a year, which, at the time, he had thought scarcely credible. But the prices he saw now, and the manner in which fruit, vegetables and farm produce were almost given away, went to confirm the statement.

In due course he arrived opposite the Royal Palace. It was a modern building of very moderate size, and hardly more than a villa by comparison with the vast private palaces of some of the great nobles in Vienna and Budapest. The sentries outside its gate were smart and of good physique. As the Duke regarded them with professional appreciation, he began to wonder if Dimitriyevitch had been speaking the truth when he said that certain members of the Serbian royal family were sworn adherents of the Black Hand.

One thing seemed fairly certain: that King Peter had had no knowledge of the plot to assassinate his predecessor, so could not have been involved in the origin of that sinister secret society. Owing to the hatred of the Obrenovitch for his family, he had lived abroad in exile most of his life. He had been educated in France, passed through the military college of St. Cyr, and, as a young officer, fought with distinction for the country of his adoption in the Franco-Prussian war of 1870. Seven years later, on the outbreak of a revolutionary movement in Bosnia, he had gone there, organised a small army, and for many months carried on a romantic guerilla war against the Turks. But at the time of Alexander's assassination, in 1903, he was living quietly in Switzerland, and, as far as anyone knew, had been invited to ascend the vacant throne solely because he seemed to be the most suitable person to occupy it.

Against that, it had to be remembered that he had shielded the assassins from punishment, even to the extent of remaining at loggerheads with the governments of most of the Great Powers on their account, for the first three years of his reign. The Powers had refused to accord him formal recognition as King of Serbia until he saw justice done. But he had fought the issue until, at last, conscious of the stupidity of continuing to deny the obvious, they had given way on his merely agreeing to retire the officers concerned into private life. And soon afterwards he had reinstated them.

Such conduct might well be taken to indicate a strong sympathy for the secret aspirations of the Black Hand. Yet King Peter was very far from being the type of man whom one would have expected to associate himself willingly with a gang of murderers. He was not only a brave soldier, but a man of scholarly tastes and liberal views. Of that, he had given ample evidence by personally translating John Stuart Mill's *Essay on Liberty* for the benefit of his countrymen.

By and large, de Richleau was inclined to conclude that he had been, and still was, under great pressure from the Black Hand: that, had he attempted to bring its original members to trial, his own life would have been in serious jeopardy, and that his past subservience to them must be taken as evidence that he was unlikely to offer any serious opposition to their plans in future.

Returning to his hotel, the Duke lunched, then wrote a note to Colonel Dimitriyevitch, informing him that he was staying for a few days in Belgrade, and asking when it would be convenient to call upon him. On receiving a few small coins, equivalent in value to twopence, a grinning hotel messenger ran off to deliver the note at the Ministry of War, and de Richleau retired to his room to sleep through the heat of the afternoon.

When he came downstairs at six o'clock two officers, who were sitting drinking at one of the little tables in the lounge, immediately sprang to their feet, advanced towards him, and halted side by side with a sharp click of their heels, at a yard's distance. They introduced themselves as Major Olgerd Tankosić and Captain Marko Ciganović. The former was a stocky, prematurely-bald man, with a bulldog jowl: the latter a tall fellow, almost chinless, and with heavy pouches under the light eyes of an albino. Both looked as if they could be extremely tough, but they were now obviously on their best behaviour.

The Major said in French. "I much regret that Colonel Dimitriyevitch is temporarily absent from Belgrade; but I am dealing with his correspondence, and I opened your Excellency's letter. I immediately recognized your name as that of a distinguished ex-enemy commander, and also I have heard the Colonel speak of you as the gallant gentleman who saved him from being butchered by a troop of Kurdish cavalry. He will, I am sure, be delighted to see you on his return. In the meantime Captain Ciganović and myself are entirely at your Excellency's disposal, and we shall be honoured if you will allow us to show you something of Belgrade during your visit."

Dimitriyevitch's absence was annoying, but there was nothing that de Richleau could do about it, and he felt that, with a little luck, he might pick up a few pointers from the Colonel's subordinates. So he thanked the Major, shook hands with both officers with a cordiality that he was inwardly far from feeling, and accompanied them to their table.

A fresh round of drinks was ordered, and an inquiry elicited the fact that Dimitriyevitch was not expected back before the week-end, or possibly later. That seemed to make it certain that the Duke would not have any opportunity of seeing him on this first visit to Belgrade, so he settled down to cultivate his new acquaintances with all the charm that came so naturally to him.

For their part they treated him with the deference due to the rank he had held in the Turkish army, and were obviously flattered by his easy friendliness. With all the interest that different viewpoints give to the discussion of a past campaign by ex-enemies who have no personal animosity, they talked of the Balkan war. And as the rounds of drinks succeeded one another, the little group became a merry one. Later, they dined together, then the Serbians took de Richleau to a musical show, and afterwards to Belgrade's one night haunt, which was called La Can-Can.

The last was a tawdry place compared with its equivalents in Paris or Vienna, but it had a good Tzigane band, and there was an air of riotous abandon about it which no longer arose spontaneously in such places in the cities of the west. The girls danced the can-can in the fashion of the '70s, were hoisted on to the tables to make high-kicks, and sat on the men's laps. They certainly appeared to enjoy it every bit as much as the young officers who were plying them with drinks and shouting applause at every naughty act.

The Duke was quick to notice that these boisterous young men were of a very different type from the dashing subalterns he had seen in Vienna. The Austrians were gay, elegant, charming, but they wore corsets to accentuate the slimness of their figures, and mentally had become more than a little soft. Whereas, these Serbians were youngsters only one generation removed from peasant stock. They were not good-looking, but their physique was excellent, and the moment they stopped laughing their hard, chunky faces showed determination and grit.

They had hard heads for liquor too, as was proved by de Richleau's companions, but he managed to keep up with them without difficulty, despite their efforts to make him drunk; and when they saw him back to his hotel at four o'clock in the morning, opinion was unanimous that they had had a splendid evening.

At mid-day, the chinless wonder, Captain Ciganović, called upon him again and asked what he would like to do. Would he care to inspect the barracks of the Royal Guard and visit the Serbian Staff College, or would he prefer a drive in the country? In either case Major Tankosić sent his compliments and requested that His Excellency would honour the mess of the Kargujevatz Cavalry Regiment by dining there that night.

Not wishing to show any undue interest in Serbian military affairs before Dimitriyevitch put in an appearance, the Duke said he would prefer to see something of the country.

Accordingly, they set off in a Peugeot and were driven out to the National Park at Topchidere. It was a lovely spot, surrounded by dense forests, and they lunched there at a small inn off roast sucking-pig. In the afternoon, they continued their drive, making a wide circle before returning to Belgrade. Then, in the evening, a car was sent to collect de Richleau and take him to the Cavalry barracks.

The bald, heavy-jowled Major Tankosić received the Duke and presented the other officers to him. In addition to the majors, captains and subalterns of the regiment, a bearded general and several colonels were present, and it was clear that these senior officers had been specially invited to meet the distinguished visitor. Many of them had been educated in Switzerland, and the majority spoke fairly good French or German, and used one of those languages when conversing with their guest. The effect was therefore all the more telling when, after de Richleau's health had been drunk at the end of dinner, he got up and replied to the toast in a language which most of them took to be heavily accented and somewhat archaic Serbian.

To win their hearts completely he had only to stand up again and inform them that he was half-Russian. It was to Russia, the traditional enemy of Austria, and the country of their early origin, that they all looked as friend, father and protector. The applause was terrific.

All earlier restraint caused by the presence of a foreigner in their midst was now thrown off. They no longer harboured faint suspicions of him owing to his associations with their late enemy, but regarded him as one of themselves. Their flat, Slav faces flushed with the wine they had drunk, they openly toasted the downfall of the Dual Monarchy and the day when the Serbian Kingdom would once again stretch from sea to sea.

His face belying his feelings, de Richleau smilingly drank glass for glass with them. He had his answer to another question, and it was again the reverse of what he had hoped. If this was a true sample of the Serbian army, and he saw no reason to doubt that, the Serbs were very far from being exhausted by their recent conflicts, and weary of war. These hardy virile men would shout with exultation at another chance to show their mettle. He wondered gloomily how many of the beardless ones would reach old age uncrippled by wounds—or even survive the next few years.

When at length he made ready to leave, a number of the younger ones reverted to the peasant custom, always observed at weddings and other festivals, of firing off their weapons. Waving their revolvers, they cheered him to his car, then, as it moved towards the gate of the courtyard, they yelled their battle cry and let off a volley of shots.

Next day a party of officers he had met the night before came to take him hunting, as they termed it, although it was shooting that they really meant. There was no close season and abundant game in the nearby forests. The does they sighted were spared, but they bagged several buck and a number of small wild pig. Then, when his companions dropped him back at his hotel, he had a pleasant surprise. It was as yet only Friday, but Colonel Dimitriyevitch had returned several days earlier than he was expected, and was sitting in the lounge waiting to greet him.

CHAPTER X

THE DARK ANGEL OF THE FOREST

As they shook hands, de Richleau was suddenly struck by Colonel Dimitriyevitch's likeness to General von Hötzendorf. The resemblance was only superficial, and the Serbian was considerably the younger of the two: but both had a small, wiry figure, brilliant, fanatical eyes, hard, thin mouth, and short hair standing straight up off their foreheads like a thick brush.

Directly they had ordered drinks, the Colonel said, "I am delighted to see you again, my dear Duke. But tell me, what brings you to Belgrade?"

De Richleau had long since made up his mind on the policy he must pursue if he was to render any real service to those who had sent him; so he replied:

"I came here to see you. Is the offer that you made me, when we met some months ago in Sofia, still open?"

The Colonel's bright eyes showed quick interest but, instead of giving a direct answer, he put another question. "Did you come here prepared to take it?"

"I should like to know a little more about the status you could give me before I commit myself."

"All right then; dine with me to-night and we'll talk matters over As you've been out all day, I expect you would like to change your clothes, and I have some papers to sign at my office. I'll send my car for you at seven o'clock. Better pack a bag. I live some way outside the town, so it would be more convenient for you to stay the night." With an abrupt gesture Dimitriyevitch gulped down the rest of his drink, stood up, nodded to the Duke, and marched off.

At seven o'clock to the minute the Colonel's car arrived, and as de Richleau went down the steps to it, he saw that it was a brand new Rolls Royce with a limousine body. There were as yet probably no more than two hundred motor-cars in Belgrade altogether, and those in which he had been driven about during the past few days had been small Renaults and Peugeots. As there were no family fortunes to be inherited in Serbia, her really rich men could be counted on the fingers of one hand, and no Colonel drawing only the ordinary rate of pay could conceivably afford a millionaire's toy like this. If evidence were required that Dimitriyevitch was not a megalomaniac, whose boasts of possessing unlimited power in his own country were the product of a diseased imagination, his Rolls was a good start for such a case. Even a Commander-in-Chief could not have run a finer car, and the inference was that it had been paid for out of secret service funds, over the expenditure of which the Colonel enjoyed a control that no one dared question.

A quarter of an hour later the Rolls had picked up Dimitriyevitch and was running smoothly out of Belgrade. It took them some ten miles into the country, the last four of which were through dense forest, and they pulled up in a clearing before a large châlet. The outside of the building was in no way remarkable, but once inside de Richleau soon saw plenty of further evidence that his host lived in a style more suited to a Field Marshal than a Colonel.

The main room was over forty feet long, and had something of the atmosphere of a royal shooting lodge. But its walls were not decorated only with the trophies of the chase; between the antlers and animal masks hung a score of fine paintings, many of which the Duke knew at a glance must be by old masters. Across the couches were thrown, not bearskins, but rugs of silver fox, ermine and sable. On the floor there were a dozen Persian rugs woven from silk, with not less than three hundred knots to the square inch, and in front of the great open hearth, on which a wood fire smouldered, a small table was laid for two with gleaming crystal and antique silver.

One servant in leather breeches, high boots and a white, full-sleeved blouse belted at the waist had taken their coats in the hall. Another, in similar costume, now appeared carrying a tray with champagne cocktails. As de Richleau took one he thought with an inward smile, that the superficial likeness between von Hötzendorf and his host was certainly confined to their physical appearance and a fanatical streak in the mentality of both.

Dimitriyevitch had already asked him in the car if he had come direct from Constantinople, and de Richleau, much too wily to risk a lie, had said that on leaving Turkey he had gone to London; adding that he always had his clothes made there and had been badly in need of some new ones. It was as well that he had taken that line for, although the Serbian Intelligence Chief gave no indication of knowing about the Duke's visit, he showed himself remarkably well informed on affairs in England, and now began to discuss the Irish question, which was still creating such bitter feeling there. The British authorities had done their best to keep secret all particulars of the mutiny at the Curragh, but Dimitriyevitch knew the facts and discussed their implications with his guest while they drank their cocktails.

When dinner was served he turned the conversation to the months that he had spent as the Duke's prisoner two years earlier, then to a visit he had recently made to Paris; so it was evident that he did not mean to talk about his own country until they were alone. At length, the servant who was waiting on them put decanters of vintage Port and Imperial Tokay on the table, made up the fire, and asked if his master required anything else. The Colonel shook his head and dismissed him with an abrupt good-night. Then, as the door closed behind the man, he said to his guest:

"Now we can talk. I conduct too much secret business here to take any chance of being spied upon by my own people. The servants all sleep in another châlet, half a mile away, and when dinner is over leave at once. They are forbidden even to approach this place until it is time for them to come in and clear up in the morning."

"A wise precaution," commented the Duke, "if you are still engaged on those matters of which we talked together when we made that grim march through Macedonia."

"Naturally, I am." Dimitriyevitch shrugged. "It is my life work, as I told you then. I have since eliminated all but a few of those men of little vision, who would attempt to thwart me; and through my measures Serbia is every day becoming better fitted to undertake the new ordeals which will lead to her future greatness."

"You consider, then, that she has already recovered from the strain imposed upon her by the two Balkan wars?"

"She has not only recovered, but has benefited immensely from them. Our army is one of the few that has had experience of modern war, and has learned many valuable lessons from the fighting it has seen. Such losses in manpower as we sustained have been more than made up for by the increase in our territories, which now enables us to draw on new sources previously denied us. As to morale—well, Tankosić tells me that you dined last night with the Kargujevatz Regiment, so you will have had some opportunity to judge that for yourself."

De Richleau nodded. "A fine lot of fellows! No one could ask for better men to command in battle."

"And from what I hear, you were clever enough to give them the impression that you were just the sort of man they would like to command them," remarked Dimitriyevitch dryly. "We Serbians suffered so long and so much at the hands of the Turks that it is still second nature to us to hate anything even remotely connected with them. The older men would realize, of course, that Turkey means nothing to you, and that had Serbia made you a better offer before the 1912 war started you would have been fighting for us; but the youngsters must have viewed you with very mixed feelings. It was no small triumph to win them over as you did, and I was very pleased to hear about it. I felt fairly confident that you would soon succeed in becoming a popular figure here, but it is good to have had my feelings confirmed so quickly. You see, while nobody could accuse me of being a lax disciplinarian, in other respects I am not of the school of officers who think that to have wide experience of military affairs and be a martinet is enough. I believe that a commander should also be personally liked, if he is to get the best out of his troops."

"I agree. But does that mean you are prepared to make me a definite offer?"

"Subject to discussing the matter with our C. in C., the Voyvode Radomir Putnik, yes. And it is not often that he rejects my advice in such matters."

"What rank would you offer me? And would it be a staff job or a command in the field?"

"You have a far wider knowledge of international affairs than most of our senior officers, so I feel that you would be very valuable to us at Headquarters, particularly as an adviser where politico-strategical questions are concerned. And I take it you would be content with the rank of Major General—at all events to start with?"

"I commanded an Army Corps while with the Turks," de Richleau protested, "so I do not see why I should accept lesser rank than that of a Lieutenant-General. Moreover, I am not fond of fighting wars from offices, and should much prefer a field command."

Dimitriyevitch gave a thin smile. "Having seen for myself your ability to handle troops in difficult situations, I should be the last to question it. But you will forgive me if I remind you that your Corps was very far from being at full establishment."

"Nevertheless, I was given the rank of a Corps commander."

"True!" The Colonel's smile deepened. "But I think I could give a very good guess why. It was probably at your own suggestion. Anyhow, the idea was to induce us to believe that your force was very nearly twice the size that it was, in fact."

It was de Richleau's turn to smile. "I won't deny it. I did persuade the Turks to adopt that old *ruse-de-guerre*, when I learned how comparatively few for their task were the units allotted to me. But that was two years ago. May I suggest that you consider the matter on the grounds that I now regard myself as due for promotion."

"Very well, then. It shall be as you wish, and we will give you the rank of Lieutenant-General. However, your wish for a field command is one against which there are certain objections. We have already nominated men in whom we have full confidence to take command of all our first-line army corps on mobilization, and we should not care to displace any of them. You would have to wait for one of the reserve corps which will be formed much later, and that would mean our losing the best value of your services for some months—or perhaps altogether, if the war proved a short one."

"Then I offer you a compromise. I will serve at Headquarters, in accordance with your original suggestion, to begin with; but on condition that should one of your corps commanders become a casualty, or prove unsatisfactory, you will have me appointed to fill the vacancy."

"Right! I am agreeable to that. Let us drink to your success in the service of Serbia."

De Richleau had no intention of taking service with Serbia permanently, if at all, and had haggled over the opening to be afforded him only because he felt that, as a soldier of fortune selling his brains and sword, it would not have seemed in character had he failed to do so. Dimitriyevitch had refilled the glasses, but before picking up his own he suddenly looked straight at the Duke, and said:

"Perhaps I should have mentioned it to start with, but I am assuming that you would have no objection to taking an oath of devotion to the cause of Serbia."

"An oath of loyalty to the head of the state one is about to serve is customary when entering any army."

"Of course! But I had in mind something rather more than that. You will remember my telling you about the Brotherhood which secretly dictates the path that Serbia must follow, and which alone gives me, as its chief, the power to arrange such matters as we have been discussing. No senior officer can now hope for promotion, or to be given any appointment of importance, unless he has sworn allegiance to the Brotherhood of Union or Death; so naturally we should expect you to do so."

De Richleau had been well aware that almost inevitably he would be faced with this question. He meant to avoid joining the Black Hand if he possibly could; but, even if he were required to take their oath and had to break it afterwards, he felt that he must not baulk at that if it was the only way to learn their secrets. The idea of committing such a deliberate breach of faith had greatly troubled him at first, as it was entirely contrary to his principles; but after due consideration he had become fully convinced that no personal scruples must be allowed to weigh against the possible saving of the lives and happiness of millions. So he gazed back quite calmly into the Colonel's brilliant eyes, and said:

"As I am not a Serbian, do you consider that in my case that is strictly necessary, or, seeing that this Brotherhood is one so deeply bound up with politics, even desirable?"

"I do. I regard it as imperative."

"In that case, I am fully prepared to do as you wish."

"Good!" Dimitriyevitch now raised his glass. "To your future victories, General. May you be among those who will carry standards of Serbia to the Adriatic."

"Thank you." De Richleau drank his wine straight off, and inquired as he set down his glass: "Is that, then, to be our first objective?"

The little Colonel also drained his glass, then put it down more slowly. "Perhaps. We shall have ample time to go into all the possibilities later: but much will depend on the disposition of our enemy when the storm actually breaks. And now that we have disposed of Turkey, I need hardly tell you that Austria is next on our list."

"The Dual Monarchy with her sixty million people is a mighty foe for a small country like Serbia to tackle single-handed," hazarded the Duke.

"Nonsense!" exclaimed his host. "The whole unwieldy structure is rotten to the core. The Austrian ruling caste is effete, and their army has not won a major victory in generations. Its officers are soft; the older ones caring only for their home comforts and steady promotion, the younger ones only for music and women. The troops, left almost to their own devices, are lethargic and ill-trained. In addition, a high proportion of them are Czechs, Rumanians, Serbs, Croats and Italians, who feel no loyalty towards Vienna, so lack all inducements to fight with any stubbornness."

"There is much in what you say. Yet, however low you rate their fighting power, you cannot altogether ignore their great numerical superiority. Austria-Hungary could put at least a million and a half men in the field without seriously disturbing her economy, and how many could Serbia muster? Three hundred thousand, or perhaps three hundred and fifty thousand at a pinch."

"You are thinking of the last war, my friend. Since then the levies from our new territories have more than made up for our losses. Within three months we could put half a million men into the field; and, let me tell you, they would be well equipped. We have enough 7 mm. Mauser repeating rifles to arm them all, and with its quick-firing guns from the Creusot works our field-artillery will more than equal anything the Austrians now have to show."

"No doubt; but you will still be barely a third of their numbers."

"Not at all. Austria dare not leave undefended her long Russian frontier, or those with her other potential enemies, Rumania and Italy. At least half her forces will be tied down permanently in case of sudden trouble with them. I doubt if she will be able to bring more than man for man against us; and if she does manage to rake up a few extra divisions that will not save her. Our hardy, patriotic, battle-tested troops will make mincemeat of old Franz Joseph's overfed, unreliable, parade ground soldiers."

As a Corps commander designate, de Richleau did not wish to give the impression that he had any real doubts about Serbia's chances, so he laughed and said: "Of course you're right, *mon Colonel.* I fear I have been leading you on a little by painting the picture far blacker than I know it to be. Austria's commitments will unquestionably prevent her from sending more than about forty per cent of her forces against us, and I would back one Serbian fighting-man against three Austrians, any day. Besides, I take it there are good grounds for believing that Russia would take the opportunity of settling her long-outstanding differences with the Dual Monarchy at the same time. Then it would prove a walk-over."

Dimitriyevitch's burning eyes narrowed a little. "She will certainly be tempted to, and, of course, we shall do our utmost to draw her in. It would ensure our own victory being so much quicker and less costly."

"That would almost certainly bring Germany to Austria's assistance."

"What of it? Russia and France between them would take care of her, and if France showed signs of failing, England would have to go to her assistance. But we are not counting on Russia. Whether she begins hostilities or not will make no difference to the eventual outcome of our own war against Austria. We are quite capable of forcing her to sue for peace, without outside help. And now that we have grown strong enough to revenge ourselves for the many injuries she has done us, we shall not wait very much longer before settling our account with her."

"Perhaps, then," said the Duke quietly, "it would be as well if you were to let me know the approximate date by which you wish me to place myself formally at your disposal?"

"I must speak to the Voyvode Putnik about that," replied the Colonel after a moment. "Are you free to do so at any time?"

"More or less, but not absolutely," the Duke hedged cautiously. He then proceeded to tell a glib lie. "You see, I am still officially on the Turkish Army List, or, to put it more exactly, committed to them under my original contract. But it is obvious that they have no further use for me, so I have been granted indefinite leave on half-pay. I'm sure you will agree that I ought to regularize the position by obtaining my formal release from them before donning a new uniform. But that should not take long."

The Colonel nodded. "I quite understand your position, and I will see Putnik about you tomorrow morning. If you care to remain here and take a gun out, I will return to lunch and let you know then what we have arranged."

De Richleau willingly agreed, and they talked on for a further two hours, mainly about the general state of Europe. Then they doused the oil lamps which hung at intervals along the walls, and went to bed.

As the Duke got into his, he sighed heavily. The few hopes he had had when leaving England, that peace might yet be preserved, were now dimmed almost to vanishing point. On the one hand there was Conrad von Hötzendorf spoiling for a war with Serbia, in the belief that Austria's enemies must be dealt with one by one, and that he could smash her utterly in a three weeks' campaign. On the other, here was Dragutin Dimitriyevitch with his Black Hand gang of vultures, who believed that the Dual Monarchy was already half dead, so that they had only to find a suitable excuse to go in and rip the flesh off her body. Worse, Dimitriyevitch had made it plain that since his vultures would meet with less resistance should the Russian bear decide to maul the victim at the same time, however frightful the final consequences, he meant to do his damnedest to bring Russia in.

It seemed now that the only thing remaining to be done was to find out when Dimitriyevitch intended to press the detonator of his terrible mine, and from a line that de Richleau had already laid out he had good hopes of succeeding in that.

Next morning, by the time the Duke got down to breakfast he found that the little Colonel had left an hour before for Belgrade; so, after he had eaten, he followed his host's suggestion and took out a gun. But his heart was not in the business and his eye, for once, inattentive to the opportunities offered him by the game. For appearance's sake, he eventually shot a hare and returned to the châlet with it soon after mid-day. At half past one the Colonel's gleaming Rolls purred smoothly up to the door and, giving himself barely time to swallow an aperitif, he ordered lunch to be served.

Over the meal he seemed a little distrait, and again made only general conversation while the servants were present. But after coffee had been brought, and they were left alone, he quickly came to business.

"I saw the Voyvode Putnik," he said in a low voice. "And as I expected, he fully approves my ideas. You are to be given the rank of Lieutenant General with the full pay and allowances it carries. To begin with, you will be employed at Headquarters. We propose to create a special post for you of Chief Liaison Officer between the High Command of the Army and the Ministry of Foreign Affairs. That means you will work in very close collaboration with myself. Later, should suitable circumstances arise, you will be offered the reversion of an Army Corps. Does that suit you?"

De Richleau nodded. He saw that Dimitriyevitch meant to keep him near himself for as long as possible, and was glad now that he had not pressed too hard for a field-command. If circumstances made it necessary for him to go into the Serbian army for a time before war broke out, such a post would suit his secret purpose very much better. After a moment the Colonel went on:

"You had better set about securing your formal release by the Turks at once, although we do not think it would be wise to give you immediate employment. Your presence at Headquarters in Serbian uniform might arouse undesirable speculation. Nearer the time that won't matter so much, but we don't want to give anyone in the Austrian Legation here an idea that we are preparing anything, until we are ready to strike."

The Duke's face showed nothing, but inwardly he glowed with satisfaction. Dimitriyevitch had swallowed the bait he had put out the previous night about getting his release from the Turks, and was taking just the line he had hoped. He simply shrugged, and remarked:

"Just as you wish. But I sha'n't be much use to you unless I have a week or so to read myself into your plans, get some idea of your forces, and meet some of the most important people in your Foreign Office, before you begin hostilities."

Dimitriyevitch nodded. "There, I agree. But it is not as though you are to command troops in the field to start with. A week or ten days should be enough. To-day is the 16th of May. I suggest that you should leave Belgrade to-night or to-morrow and return here in a month. That should give you ample time to settle matters with the Turks; and I take it there is nothing else likely to prevent your getting back here by mid-June?"

"Nothing," replied de Richleau. He now had the final answer. If he was to report a week or ten days before the crisis was due, that meant that Serbia intended to give Austria cause for declaring war within a few days of June 25th.

After a moment he said: "I shall not bother to go down to Constantinople. Even allowing for the dilatoriness of the Turks, I am sure I can obtain a satisfactory answer from them in writing in a fortnight or three weeks, because they will naturally be anxious to get me off their pay roll. And I know a way in which I can employ my time much more profitably."

"How?" inquired the Colonel.

"Why, by spending the coming month in Vienna, of course," replied the Duke with a blandly innocent air. "I should be able to collect quite a lot of little bits of information there, which may later prove useful to us."

Dimitriyevitch gave a short, harsh laugh, and exclaimed: "Devil take me! I knew you would prove worth your weight in gold to us if only I could get hold of you."

"Thanks," said the Duke with the smile of a cat that has just tipped over the cream jug and lapped up all the cream. And silently he chuckled at the ease with which he had covered his retreat to the other centre of trouble without arousing the least suspicion.

Evidently Dimitriyevitch favoured a simple meal in the middle of the day, as only two courses were served, and when an iced sherbet was put on the table with some fruit, he said: "I hope you don't mind: as I came in I told one of my men to pack your bag. I am holding a conference here this afternoon, and the car may be needed later. I thought it had better run you into Belgrade directly we have finished lunch. Would you care for a brandy?"

Realizing that his host had simply fitted in this lunch at the châlet because he had already planned to return there for his meeting, and was now anxious to get rid of him as soon as possible, de Richleau declined the liqueur. So ten minutes later he was on his way back to the capital.

As the car left the forest and entered the agricultural belt that lay outside the straggling suburbs of the town, peasants and their children working in the fields looked up to grin and wave at this shining chariot of a new age.

Since Serbia had never known the feudal system, there were practically no large estates in the country, and the greater part of its cultivable areas was divided up into innumerable small-holdings. On many of these the poorer peasants lived in miserable round-roofed mud huts as primitive as the Eskimo igloos that they resembled. The more prosperous lived in the villages, but even there few of them owned houses. The majority still dwelt in shapeless, one-storied buildings, each occupying up to a quarter of an acre of land and often housing as many as a hundred people, which were called *zadrugas.* These had originated from the Turkish custom of taxing only the head of each household, from which it followed that the more people who could be accommodated under one roof, the lighter the taxation on them all. So, as the young men married, instead of building a cottage for themselves, they simply knocked up another lean-to against the family building, and brought the bride to live there.

Yet, if they lived in squalor they were at least well fed, warmly clothed, and appeared quite content to remain within their limited horizon. As de Richleau waved back now and then to groups with smiling, sun-bronzed faces, he was suddenly conscious of the awful burden of responsibility borne by the ruling class and their all-too-frequent neglect of it for selfish ends.

As a professional soldier, he enjoyed war, finding its problems more stimulating to the brain and its actions more exciting than those of the very best expedition after big game. But he realized that he saw war from a privileged angle, where playing a part in its planning, direction, and leadership more than compensated for its hardships. Whereas, for the vast majority it meant an uprooting from a secure and reasonably happy way of life, enforced severance from loved ones, family and friends, the indefinite postponement of all personal plans, the harsh discipline of the barrack square, gruelling forced marches, indifferent food, exposure to torrid heat and bitter cold, and finally, often mutilation or death while still in the prime of life.

It seemed intolerable that ambitious fanatics like Dimitriyevitch, or coldly calculating patriots like von Hötzendorf, should have the power to inflict such suffering on millions of innocent people; yet humanity had so far devised no way of stopping such catastrophes, and there was no reason to believe that if kings and aristocracies were abolished things would be any different. Leaders of the people had often arisen in the ancient city states, who had driven their ex-co-workers into suicidal conflicts; and the greatest wars so far recorded in the annals of the world had been launched by a small-town youth, educated on charity, who, when first commissioned, had been so poor that he could not pay his washing bills, but whose name was indelibly stamped on history as Napoleon.

On arriving at his hotel, the Duke wrote notes of thanks to Major Tankosić and Captain Ciganović for having entertained him and, there being nothing further to detain him in Belgrade, left on the night train for Vienna.

At Sacher's he found a sheaf of invitations that had arrived for him during his absence. Among them was a note from the Duchess of Hohenberg, in which she reproached him for not having called upon her, and asked him to lunch on the 20th.

After writing an acceptance of her invitation, and of most of the others, he set himself to try to forget for a few hours the terrible implications of his meeting with Dimitriyevitch, by going that afternoon to see again the unrivalled collection of Breughels in the National Picture Gallery and, in the evening, to a Beethoven concert at the Philharmonik. Nevertheless he felt gloomy and depressed.

He still had his luncheon appointment to meet Frau Schratt, but had little hope that anything he might learn from her would materially alter the final result of his mission. Now that he knew the violently belligerent intentions of the Austrian and Serbian war chiefs, he thought it very doubtful if the aged Emperor, once caught in the web of events, and under pressure from far more dynamic personalities, would be able to influence their outcome. If he were, that would be good news indeed, but the hope was as fragile as a reed.

Soon after one o'clock next day Frau Sacher introduced him to the actress who had enjoyed no foreign triumphs, and of whom most of the world had never heard: but who, for over a quarter of a century, had been the constant companion of the ruler of the second greatest empire in Europe. She was now just over sixty, but she preserved many of the indications of the fair, Germanic beauty she had once enjoyed, and all the natural, unaffected charm that had so endeared her to both the Emperor and Empress.

In spite of imperial patronage, many years had passed before she finally left the stage, and de Richleau was able to win her goodwill at once by speaking enthusiastically of her performances which he had witnessed, when, as a boy, he had first visited Vienna with his father in the early 'nineties.

During lunch he exerted all his skill to draw her out on the leading personalities of the Empire and on various international problems, but he succeeded only in catching a single reflection of the Emperor's mind through hers in one unguarded moment. Franz Joseph did not like the Kaiser: he regarded the Hohenzollerns as an upstart dynasty, and considered that William II revealed his dubious ancestry by lacking many of the qualities that go to make a true gentleman.

On the other hand, she spoke freely of the Emperor, declaring that he was still hale and vigorous in mind and body, and that there was every reason to believe that he would continue so for a long time to come. In spite of his eighty-four years, he maintained the habit of a lifetime by getting up at four o'clock every morning and taking his first coffee at his desk while he began to go through the official papers awaiting him. He walked in his gardens for an hour or more every day and was still capable of taking an occasional ride on horse-back. But those were practically the only relaxations he allowed himself. He greatly disliked public functions and entertaining, as they interfered with his routine. On the rare occasions when he did have guests, it meant his putting off dinner until five or six o'clock, whereas normally he took his evening meal between three and four in the afternoon, and liked to be in bed and asleep by eight o'clock.

She said that underneath his cold exterior he was really kind, considerate and warm-hearted; but he had suffered so many sorrows and disappointments in his life that, while still a comparatively young man, he had become chary of giving his affections freely. The only men to whom he permitted any degree of intimacy were his three personal aides-de-camp, all of whom had served him faithfully for many years and were now over seventy. They were Count Paar, who advised him on the filling of all posts that became vacant; Baron Bolfas, with whom he dicussed matters of high policy and foreign affairs; and Count Beck, a long since retired Chief of Staff, who now arranged all public functions and military reviews. Occasionally Generals von Hötzendorf or Potiorek were admitted to lengthy audiences, and the one usually got his way by sheer persistence until the other counteracted his rival's gains owing to his courtier-like manners and the support of Count Beck. But, generally, the three septuagenarian a.d.c.s. succeeded, like a living rampart, in sheltering their master from all intrusions and minor annoyances; although his sense of responsibility was so great that even they dared not hide from him any matter, internal or external, which might affect the well-being of his Empire. In consequence, the mountains of State papers he perused occupied most of his waking hours; but he devoted himself unsparingly to this duty in the firm belief that his exemplary life and conscientious labours must in the end secure for his people the blessing of God.

As de Richleau listened to this picture of a dreary, unimaginative existence, he thought of the figure made familiar by innumerable photographs, of the aged ruler with the heavily pouched eyes and white mutton-chop whiskers, dressed in his favourite Tyrolese costume, and added what he knew from other sources.

The Emperor had been very handsome as a young man, but even then his high moral rectitude had caused him to ignore the blandishments of scores of lovely women. He had been a keen student of military affairs, but had never fought a war without losing it. From the beginning of his reign the non-Germanic peoples who formed the great bulk of his subjects had plagued him with their grievances, yet he had never devised a policy that brought contentment to any of them. He had spent the greater part of his life in a city where music and the arts were esteemed more highly than in any other, yet he had remained deaf to their appeal. He reigned over a people by nature gayer and more warm-hearted than any in the world, yet he had eschewed all friendship and preferred to live as a recluse. He was abysmally ignorant in the cultural sense, hide-bound in a narrow morality, and doggedly self-opinionated upon matters about which his strong-willed mother had made up his mind for him several generations ago. His sole virtue was his conscientious adherence to his duty as he saw it, and in the doing of it he had let life pass him by, without either tasting its joys or having to his credit a single noteworthy achievement.

Such a man, the Duke decided, could certainly not be counted on, at the very end of his life, suddenly to stand forth and veto the considered opinions of his legally appointed advisers.

After the luncheon was over, he thanked Frau Sacher for her kindness in arranging it, and escorted Frau Schratt to the carriage which, as she told him with a smile, she still used at the Emperor's request, as he had ridden in a motor-car only once himself to please King Edward VII and had disliked the experience intensely. Then, having waved good-bye to her, he went in again and straight up to his room.

The luncheon with Frau Schratt had been not only his last line of investigation, but his last chance of being able to send back to Whitehall a glimmer of hope that peace might be preserved, and he now set to work on the grim task of completing his mission by writing a long report to Sir Pellinore. In it he gave a brief résumé of the state of things as he had found them in the Austrian and Serbian capitals, then a detailed account of his conversations with von Hötzendorf and Dimitriyevitch. To quote his conclusions, they ran as follows:

1. The Austrian and Serbian peoples continue to cherish an inbred hatred for one another owing to their many centuries of irascible contact:
   (*a*) The Serbians are animated by a desire for expansion and are conditioned to war by their recent conflicts. They would take the field again with readiness and, as far as their army is concerned, enthusiasm.
   (*b*) The Austrians have no territorial ambitions and are ill-prepared for war. They would regard its coming as a major calamity, and even a large part of their army would march to it unwillingly.
2. The military chiefs of both countries definitely desire war, and wield sufficient influence with their governments:
   (*a*) in the case of Serbia, to force it at any time they consider it expedient to do so;
   (*b*) in the case of Austria, given a *casus belli*, almost certainly to over-rule any attempts by peaceable elements to prevent it.
3. Serbia will deliberately take steps to provoke an armed conflict during the last week in June, or possibly a few days earlier.
4. The Serbians will make no attempt to localize the conflict but, on the contrary, use their utmost efforts to draw Russia in to their assistance, entirely regardless of the fact that her participation may lead to a general European conflagration.

He then added a final paragraph to his letter, which read:

"Having regard to the terms of reference of my mission, I trust you will consider that I have now fulfilled it satisfactorily. No one could regret its outcome more than myself, but it is some small consolation to me that I have been able to obtain for you, within approximately a week, the date that the crisis is likely to arise, and done so without having to perjure myself by joining the Black Hand. About having disclosed the personal confidences of Dimitriyevitch I have no qualms, but I have much disliked abusing the trust of my Austrian friends and am greatly relieved to feel that I need no longer play the part of a spy among them. I plan to remain here for a further ten days or so, as I fear it will be the last chance I shall have, perhaps for years to come, to enjoy the carefree, happy atmosphere of the most delightful and civilized of all cities. I shall then return to England, and take such steps as I can to secure a niche for myself in which to take my part in the coming ordeal. In this connection I should regard it as a personal kindness if you would use your influence to persuade "Mr. Marlborough" to reconsider his decision regarding my request for a commission in the British Army, or at least to endeavour to find me some post where my military knowledge may be of value."

When he had completed his dispatch, he put it in a thick envelope, wrote on the front '*Most Secret*', on the flap '*To be opened by Sir Pellinore Gwaine-Cust personally*', and sealed it with wax. He then locked it in a small brief case, of which he had left a duplicate key at Major Hankey's office in London, and went out. Crossing The Ring, he walked up the Rennweg, entered the Metternichgasse and rang the bell at the British Embassy.

A footman informed him that the Ambassador was out, but was expected back in about an hour, so he recrossed the Rennweg and went into the Belvedere Gardens behind the Schwarzenberg Palace. On this peaceful summer evening it was delightful there. The gardens formed a wide oblong rising up a gentle slope. They were adorned by many fine pieces of statuary and their central walk, flanked by lines of sphinx, connected two charming Baroque Palaces, called the Lower and Upper Belvedere. The latter had been occupied by the Heir Apparent and his morganatic wife for the past ten years, and for a while, de Richleau stood admiring the views from below its private terrace. But he was extremely glad when his hour of waiting was up.

He was highly conscious that the few sheets of his own writing that he was carrying had the awful power to separate for ever many of the pairs of lovers strolling near him, and render fatherless within a month some of the children playing on the grass. It needed only an accident to befall him, and for his letter to get into the wrong hands, to precipitate the catastrophe which he still prayed that a God-sent miracle might yet avert. If, via a hospital and the police, his letter was placed before von Hötzendorf he had no doubt at all that, with such evidence of Serbia's intentions to hand, the fiery little General would immediately secure his government's consent to secret mobilization in order that Austria might strike first and catch the Serbians off their guard. It was for that reason the Duke had taken so many precautions to protect his dispatch, and had sought the gardens rather than a café in which to pass his hour of waiting.

On his second call at the Embassy he learned that Sir Maurice de Bunsen had returned. He sent up his card and a request that the Ambassador would spare him a few minutes on an urgent matter. Five minutes later he was shown into the library. The diplomat received him courteously, offered him a glass of sherry and, when they were seated, inquired his business.

De Richleau explained that he had been making certain inquiries in Vienna and Belgrade into highly secret matters, on behalf of the British Government.

The Ambassador frowned. "So you are one of our cloak and dagger merchants. I trust that you have not got yourself into any serious trouble, nor have come to make some request which may cause me embarrassment?"

"On the contrary," smiled the Duke. "I desire only the protection of the Embassy bag to send some papers safely to London. Or rather, if you have a King's Messenger at your disposal, I should be grateful if he could make a special trip, as the matter is urgent and of the utmost importance."

"Very well." The Ambassador appeared much relieved. "I can arrange for them to leave to-morrow. I take it you are sending them in that brief case: but I see it is not addressed to anyone."

"I thought it better to wait until I got here, then ask your Excellency for a label."

Sir Maurice rummaged in a drawer of his desk and produced one. De Richleau wrote on it '*For Sir Pellinore Gwaine-Cust, Bart.*, V.C., *c/o The Office of the Committee of Imperial Defence*', and tied it on. Without another word being said regarding the transaction, they finished their sherry and talked for some time about mutual friends in Vienna. Then the Duke took his leave with a great load off his mind.

He had done a job well that he had taken on with great reluctance, and felt now that, for a week or so at least, he was free to enjoy a world of charm and gaiety that might all too soon be wiped out for ever. But he was still wondering if, with the secret knowledge he possessed, he really would be able to enjoy it, when, just as he was about to re-enter Sacher's, he suddenly found himself confronted by a young woman.

She was neatly, although inexpensively, dressed, and was regarding him with shy, almost frightened eyes. Suddenly she bobbed him a curtsy, thrust a letter at him, and said breathlessly:

"Pray pardon, *Altess*. I was told to give you this on Wednesday, but they said you'd gone away. I was to give it into your own hands, so I didn't dare to leave it. They said you'd be back some time though, and it's been burning a hole in my pocket ever since. Last night, when I inquired again, they said you had returned; and just now the porter pointed you out to me."

As the Duke took the letter she bobbed him another curtsy, exclaimed "*Kuss die hand, Altess*", and hurried away.

For a moment he stared after her, then he glanced at the envelope. The writing was unknown to him, and he was a little surprised to see that it was addressed not to Count Königstein, as were nearly all the letters he received in Vienna, but to M. le Duc de Richleau.

On tearing it open he saw that it was in German on plain paper that bore no address or date. It had no formal beginning, and was not signed. Its single paragraph read:

Can I possibly hope that you are not altogether disgusted with me? I had looked forward to Monday night so much, but my inexperience and nerves ruined everything. I was hateful to you but I did not mean one word I said. I was so furious with myself afterwards that I ran a temperature and developed one of my attacks of coughing. So today they are keeping me in bed, and on Thursday they intend to send me to Ischl. But nothing shall stop me going for a drive in the Prater on Wednesday afternoon. If you can still think kindly of me, I beg you to be there and wear a white gardenia in your buttonhole as a sign of your forgiveness.

De Richleau's slender hands trembled slightly as he re-folded the letter and put it back into its envelope. Already, it was beginning to dawn on him what a fearful struggle it must have meant before a granddaughter of the Emperor Franz Joseph could have brought herself to put such thoughts on paper. For the letter could be only from Ilona.

CHAPTER XI

THE WHITE GARDENIAS

DE RICHLEAU went straight up to his room and re-read the letter twice. Then he kissed it. For a moment he felt rather foolish, as it was a long time since he had done that to a letter from a woman. Nevertheless, he kissed it again and sat for some time dreamily making mental pictures of Ilona as he had seen her: at Dorchester House; on the boat in the storm; in her sky-blue uniform at the Horse Show; and, lastly, at the Czernins' ball.

That had been eight days ago. In the interim his mind had been so fully occupied with his mission that he had very nearly, but not quite, succeeded in keeping her image out of it. After her dismissal of him he had made a great effort to do so, and had endeavoured to persuade himself that he was well out of trouble. But that thought had been mainly engendered by anxiety lest a clandestine love affair with an Archduchess should lead to his being arrested, or ordered to leave Vienna, and so seriously jeopardize the success of his secret work.

With a slow smile he savoured the thought that he need no longer worry himself on that score. He was now a free man again. There was no reason whatever why he should not give full rein to his natural instincts, and use his ingenuity to secure secret rendezvous with the lovely Ilona if she were willing to meet him half way. But he must still be careful—very careful—for her sake now more than his own.

The thought of her illness distressed him greatly, and he prayed fervently that it would not prove of a serious nature. Yet, owing to it, things might prove easier for them. There should be far less difficulty about managing to see her alone at Bad Ischl than there would have been in Vienna.

His quick mind at once began to plan. Poor sweet, she must have been very disappointed not to see him in the Prater last Wednesday; and evidently she had left Vienna before her sewing-woman—or whoever it was she had chosen as her messenger—had been able to tell her that she had been unable to deliver her letter. He must see her as soon as possible, and let her know that he had failed to keep the appointment only because he had already left Vienna before herself. To get to Ischl he would have to change at Linz. If he left within the next two or three hours he could catch a train that would get him to the great railway junction that evening. It was unlikely that there would be a night train on, but he could stay the night in an hotel there and be in Ischl by the following mid-day.

Quickly he took out the half dozen invitations to which he had sent acceptances, meaning to write notes excusing himself after all, on the plea that an unexpected turn in his affairs made it necessary for him to leave Vienna. Then his eye fell on that of the Duchess of Hohenberg, to luncheon on Wednesday. Tapping the card thoughtfully on the table, he wondered if it would not be wise to remain for that.

No opportunity must be neglected which would help to cover his affair with Ilona, and the Duchess, he believed, could be made to serve as a very valuable stalking horse for that. In her anomalous position she was far from being as unapproachable as the officially accepted wife of an Heir Apparent would have been, yet her marriage rendered her a conspicuous figure in Viennese society. That society took no exception to its married ladies indulging in flirtations, providing they were not carried to a point that gave grounds for scandal. She was gay, intelligent, and had already shown her interest in him. The odds were that she would welcome him as a new beau; and it was unlikely that Franz Ferdinand would object to his wife receiving the gallant but harmless attentions which de Richleau had in mind. If he could create the right impression, Vienna would soon be talking of him as 'the Chotek's' latest catch, and curious eyes would be much less likely to notice his interest in Ilona.

There was another thing. It would be a bad beginning to turn up at a small place like Ischl without due preparation. He must think of some method by which he could establish himself there very discreetly, and so run the minimum risk of compromising Ilona by his presence.

These reasons for postponing his departure were both on Ilona's account rather than on his own; so he felt that they justified him in leaving her for an additional forty-eight hours in the unhappy belief that she had ruined her own budding romance. Accordingly, he wrote notes cancelling only the invitations he had accepted which were for dates later than the 20th.

Next morning he woke full of ideas about his projected visit to Ischl and, as soon as he was dressed, went out shopping. First, at a big outfitters, he bought a complete Tyrolean costume—cut-away jacket, green velveteen shorts, gay shirt, long white stockings, heavy brogues, a felt hat with a cord round it and a brush sticking up from its back, and an alpenstock. Then he went to a theatrical costumers and selected a pair of bushy grey side-whiskers similar to those of the Emperor also purchasing some fine white rice-powder for whitening his hair and eyebrows.

Bringing his purchases back with him in a cab to Sacher's, he tried on the clothes and made himself up. After studying his image carefully in the bathroom mirror, he was quite satisfied with the effect. A false moustache or beard would have given him constant trouble, but the spirit gum held the side-whiskers firmly in place without causing him the least inconvenience. He had used only enough powder on his dark hair and devil's eyebrows to turn them grey, but the general result altered his appearance sufficiently to make him look fifteen years older, and unrecognizable by anyone who did not know him fairly intimately. Having washed the powder out of his hair and changed back into his ordinary clothes, he went out to a luncheon party at the Countess Warsberg's and thoroughly enjoyed himself.

At one-fifteen on the Wednesday, he presented himself at the *Oberes Belvedere*. Compared with the other Imperial Palaces it was quite small, but its stucco work on the grand staircase was by Bussi and made it a gem of Baroque art. The party consisted of some twenty people, several of who were already known to him. So, after greeting his host and hostess, he was immediately drawn into a cheerful group of fellow guests. Then, when they went in to luncheon he found to his great satisfaction that, as the only non-Viennese present, the Duchess had given him the place of honour on her right.

He took an early opportunity of excusing himself from having failed to call on her by the glib lie that, at times, he suffered severely from migraine, which made him fit company for nobody, and had had a bout the preceding week which had caused him to take himself off to the country until the attack had passed. She then devoted herself for a while to her other neighbour. When she turned back to him later in the meal he was ready to launch out on his usual policy with women whom he wished to intrigue, of making some remark that would either shock or astound them.

It was, of course, strictly taboo to make any reference to her equivocal status before her, but, lowering his voice, he said with a bland smile: "You know, for your Highness' friends there are at least some compensations for your never having been recognized as a member of the Imperial family."

Her dark eyes flashed and she bristled perceptibly as she replied: "I can think of none, but perhaps you would enlighten me."

"Why," he murmured, "had you been, it would be impossible for your male guests to send you flowers in recognition of your hospitality. Whereas, as things are, I trust that His Imperial Highness will not object to my sending you the finest orchids I can procure in Vienna to-morrow."

Instantly she relaxed and returned his smile. "Duke, I like you very much. You have the touch of the true noblesse which does not always go with a long pedigree. You address me as Highness, to which rank

I am not strictly entitled, yet propose to pay me a courtesy which must please any woman. Of course my husband would not object. His greatest pleasure is to see men of distinction, such as yourself, pay me nice compliments, as some compensation for my difficult position."

From that point they got on like a house on fire, finding many intellectual interests in common, until luncheon was over and the ladies withdrew. While the men were having their coffee and liqueurs the Archduke drew de Richleau into the conversation, and asked him how he was enjoying his stay in Vienna. But he seemed to have forgotten his previous wish to be informed about the state of the Turkish army, and the Duke saw no point in reminding him of it.

They joined the ladies in a lofty drawing-room with walls panelled in yellow silk, Louis Seize furniture, and cabinets of Sèvres porcelain. The Duchess soon disposed of the ladies who were talking to her and beckoned de Richleau over. As he seated himself at her side on a long settee, she said:

"Duke, I have a favour to ask you."

He made a slight bow. "Your Highness has only to command me."

"It is this," she went on after a slight pause. "You are doubtless aware that, although I am at present legally debarred from sharing the Imperial throne with my husband, the law of Hungary makes me its Queen designate. But the Hungarians are a curious people: unfortunately they cherish a particular hatred for the Czechs, and I am of that nation. On Friday the 29th the Minister-President of Hungary, Count Tisza, is coming here to dine. It is the first time he has accepted an invitation to do so, and his influence with his compatriots is immense, so I am extremely anxious to strengthen my position by ensuring that he should carry away a good impression of me."

"How could he fail to do so?" murmured the Duke courteously.

"Flatterer!" she smiled.

"On the contrary; if he is even remotely human your Highness will twist him round your little finger."

"I am reasonably confident of my own ability to get on good terms with him," she said seriously. "But I need someone else—someone other than my husband—to give him cause to believe that I should make a good Queen of Hungary. What is more, I shall; if only the Hungarians will let me. Like my own people, they have suffered much under Austrian rule, so my natural sympathies are with them; and since their generous law will make me Queen, as opposed to the Austrian which prevents my becoming Empress, I already feel myself their debtor. My friends in Vienna would be embarrassed to speak to Count Tisza upon such a subject, and even if any of them did he would consider them prejudiced. But you, although you have inherited an Austrian title, are in all other respects a foreigner; yet one who is the friend of kings and so well qualified to express an independent opinion of some weight. Count Tisza is a very intelligent man, so you should get on well with him. Will you oblige me by dining here on the 29th and seeking an opportunity to say something in my favour?"

"Gladly," replied de Richleau, feeling that it was a request that he could not possibly refuse. "But I trust your Highness will forgive me if I do not call on you in the meantime, as I am committed to leave Vienna to-night to join some friends for a mountaineering holiday in the Tyrol. However, if you wish it, I will make a point of returning for your dinner."

She gave him her nicest smile. "I shall feel very guilty at having interrupted your holiday, Duke; but I know no one else at the moment who could render me a similar service, so I shall count on you. If there is any way in which I can repay your kindness you have only to let me know."

His brilliant grey eyes held hers for a moment. "The pleasure of being in your Highness' company again will be reward enough."

Ten minutes later the party broke up. De Richleau returned to Sacher's, collected the suitcases which contained his Tyrolean costume and some other clothes, then drove to the station. On his way he stopped the cab in front of one of Vienna's best florists. There, he spent ten pounds on orchids and wrote a card for delivery with them to Sophie von Hohenberg. He also bought a dozen white gardenias, which he had carefully packed between layers of cotton wool in a box with air holes, to take with him.

That night he slept at Linz. In the morning he dressed in his Tyrolese clothes and caught the train south, through winding mountain villages, for Ischl. A little time before the train reached its destination, he took his things from the rack and repaired to the lavatory. There, he gummed on the side-whiskers and powdered his hair and eyebrows. Then he waited in the corrider until the train drew into the station.

Ischl was a town with a population of 10,000. It had originally come into being owing to the salt mines in its neighbourhood, and they were still worked with considerable profit to its inhabitants; but these enjoyed additional prosperity from the fact that it was the favourite country residence of the Imperial family, and still more on account of its beautiful surroundings which now brought 20,000 holiday-makers to it every year. So the Duke knew that he would have no difficulty in finding a modest *pension* where he could stay with very little risk of running into anyone who knew him as either de Richleau or Königstein. Ignoring the offer of a porter to carry his bag, he marched off into the town. After a brief inspection of the exterior of a score of small private hotels, he entered one called *der Gasthaus* Pohl, and took a room in the name of Mr. Richwater.

His intention was to pose as a professional guide, but he knew that he would not be able to pass himself off as one in the town; so there he meant to account for his Tyrolean costume by assuming the role of an eccentric Englishman. To establish himself in the part he addressed the hotel proprietor in shocking German, pretended to be extremely pernickety about his food, asked a dozen searching questions about the hygiene of the establishment, and finally demanded that a good guide should be on the doorstep at four o'clock the following morning to take him to some of the local beauty spots.

On Herr Pohl remarking that four o'clock seemed a little early, the Duke declared that nobody could keep really fit unless they walked at least ten miles a day, and that he often did twenty. Then he carried his bag upstairs, unpacked it, put his gardenias in water and came down to lunch. Immediately the meal was over he set out on a preliminary reconnaissance of the town.

Its setting was enchanting as it lay at the conjunction of three valleys: one, to the north, down which the train had brought him that morning past the glassy waters of the Ehensee; a second running south to Laufen; and a third to the west through gentler country to St. Wolfgang, on the shore of another great lake, beyond which lay Salzburg. The Gemunden mountains ringed the town about, but they had neither the starkness nor inaccessibility of the great Alps. In most places their slopes were gentle and the belts of forest that zig-zagged across their sides contained oaks, beeches and chestnuts, as well as pines, so they offered a paradise for rambles and picnics.

At a stationer's de Richleau bought three kinds of notepaper, a guide-book, and a large map. From the last he soon found his bearings, and walked out to the Palace. It had none of the Imperial dignity of Schönbrunn, but was just a large mansion with a pleasant private garden. Not very far from its gates there was a small café, which, at this hour of the afternoon, was almost deserted. Sitting down at one of the tables outside it, he ordered a stein of beer and got into conversation with the waitress. She was a plump, pink-faced little chatter-box and after ten minutes he had as much information about the principal inmates of the Palace as she could give him. The lovely Archduchess had arrived on the preceding Thursday. As far as the girl knew, she was perfectly well. She rode for about two hours most mornings, and had driven out every afternoon in her carriage, usually returning about five o'clock.

When he had finished his beer de Richleau returned to his *pension* and, on the notepaper he had bought, using three different pens, forged three references for himself as a guide; afterwards folding and soiling them as though they had long been in use. He then made up four of the gardenias into a small posy. Into its middle he inserted a short note, leaving just a corner of it sticking out so that it should not be overlooked. He had written the note in the painful copper plate hand of a semi-educated man, and it ran:

Erzherzogin Ilona Theresa,

Noble lady, I Johann Stein am the best guide in this district. Be pleased to engage me and I will show you our loveliest beauty spots. For this I will make no charge. The honour is enough. God be with you Erzherzogin. Küss die hand.

He had not dared to write to Ilona, even anonymously. It was certain that her mail would be opened and sorted for her, and his letter would either have gone into the waste-paper basket with the mad, impertinent and unanswerable scrawls which royal personages were always receiving, or, had it reached her at all, have first aroused the most undesirable curiosity of some secretary. But he hoped that the white gardenias would prove a key to their sender, and that if she read the note she would have the wit to act upon it.

Having completed his preparations he returned to the Palace. A sentry was posted on its gate but no officers were about, so de Richleau addressed him in good German:

"Tell me, friend, how shall I set about trying to get the Archduchess to take me on as her guide?"

The soldier shook his head. "Such matters are none of my business. I have no idea."

The Duke had not supposed that he would have, and had asked the question only as a lead-in. He went on:

"I have some pretty flowers here. I thought, perhaps, that if I threw them to her Highness as she passes she might stop to thank me. Then I would have a chance to ask her if she will let me be her guide on some excursions."

"It is forbidden to throw things at the royal carriages," said the soldier.

De Richleau had expected as much. For the past half century every royal family in Europe, except that of Britain, had gone about in fear of nihilists. They were desperate and often half-crazy men, belonging to various societies which plotted the murder of royalties quite irrespective of their personal characters, and solely as a spectacular means of drawing attention to the ills of the proletariat. Ilona's grandmother, the Empress Elizabeth, had been stabbed to death by one sixteen years before, when about to board a steamer on Lake Geneva; and hardly a year passed without a bomb being hurled at one of the Russian Grand Dukes. Actually, de Richleau's one purpose in talking to the sentry was to convince him that the bouquet was not a bomb, otherwise he might have attempted to prevent its being thrown into the carriage. Exposing the flowers by turning back their tissue paper wrapping, he showed them to the man, and said:

"See: they are very special flowers and fit even for a Princess. I am a poor man but I bought them at the best shop in the town for her. I paid a lot of money for them. It will be hard on me if they are to be wasted after all."

The sentry shrugged. "All right then. But hold them behind you and stand some distance away from me when you throw them, so that they'll think I couldn't guess what you meant to do."

After thanking the soldier with suitable humility, the Duke took up his position on the far side of the entrance and waited there patiently for some twenty minutes. At length the royal carriage came down the road at a smart trot. Ilona was seated alone, facing the horses: opposite her were the dapper, broad-shouldered Count Adam Grünne and the small, dark, mischievous-eyed Sárolta Hunyády. As the carriage slowed down to turn through the gates, de Richleau took off his hat and neatly pitched his posy into Ilona's lap.

Adam Grünne's mouth dropped open and he instantly dived at it; but as he grabbed the tissue-paper covered missile he must have felt that it contained nothing solid, as he did not throw it out. By that time the carriage was well past de Richleau, so he was unable to see the final outcome of his ruse; but, although he waited hopefully near the gate for over an hour, he was not sent for.

He spent the evening making an intensive study of the map he had bought and memorizing passages from the guide-book, so that when, at four o'clock next morning, he kept his appointment with the professional guide Herr Pohl had engaged for him, he already had a good working knowledge of the district.

The Duke, although a little above medium height, was slight of frame, so that as the hours wore on the stamina he displayed was more and more astonishing to his companion. On the guide's advice, they went up the south valley, towards Laufen, and with only brief infrequent halts, except to eat lunch at a wayside inn, they kept on the move for nearly eleven hours. During that time they made many detours and short climbs to reach some of the best view-points. As a soldier, the Duke had a trained eye for country, and he could not glance out of the window of a train without instinctively thinking that some fold in the hills would make a good battery position, or a sunken road be a good site behind which to entrench infantry. So by the time they got back to Ischl he felt that he had fully mastered the country for ten miles to the south of the town.

After arranging for his guide to call for him at the same hour the next morning, he had a short rest on his bed. Then he made up four more of the gardenias into another little bouquet and inserted among them a similar note to that of the day before.

When he arrived at the Palace gate he found a different sentry on duty, so had to repeat his little act about wishing to become the Archduchess' guide. But the man proved more obdurate than his predecessor, and the Duke had to take his posy to pieces for inspection, then tip the fellow a *florin* before he would consent to it being thrown, with due precautions, so that he could not afterwards be accused of not having attempted to prevent the act.

As the carriage approached, de Richleau's heart began to beat more quickly. When it turned into the entrance he saw that Ilona was again seated alone on the back seat, but today, instead of Sárolta, the flaxen-haired Baroness Paula von Wolkenstein was seated opposite her, beside Adam Grünne. At the moment he pitched the posy Ilona turned to look at him, but there was no sign of recognition in her eyes. Yet this time Adam Grünne caught the flowers and handed them to her. Then she called to her coachman to pull up.

De Richleau could not guess if his ruse was by way of succeeding, but he ran after the carriage until it halted some thirty yards inside the gates. Then, clutching his hat to his stomach with both hands, as a peasant would have done, he bowed jerkily, and raised his eyes only when Ilona addressed him:

"Thank you, my good fellow, for the flowers. I am very fond of white gardenias. In the note you threw to me yesterday you said you were the best guide in the district. Is that true?"

"*Kuss die hand, Erzherzogin.* Only try me and I promise you will be satisfied. But here are my references." He bowed again and held them out.

Adam Grünne took the three dirty papers, glanced through them and nodded. Then Ilona said:

"Very well, then. Be at the gate here at half past two to-morrow afternoon."

At a sign from her, the coachman's whip tickled the horses, and the carriage rolled on. Ilona's eyes had remained quite expressionless while she was speaking, and as de Richleau slowly walked away he still had no means of knowing if the gardenias had told her who he was; or if their significance had escaped her, and she had simply decided to give a trial to a new guide who had adopted an original method of bringing himself to her notice. But his uncertainty on that point did little to reduce his elation at having secured a command to attend her next day, and he returned to his *pension* in a very happy frame of mind. Nevertheless he was now feeling very tired after his long tramp so, instead of waiting for dinner, he asked the cook to slice some rolls and fill them with ham for him, then ate them while drinking a pint of the local white wine in the little lounge, and afterwards went straight to bed.

By the first light of dawn he was up again and off for another long tramp with his professional guide. This time they took the westward valley towards St. Wolfgang, and returned to Ischl in time for the mid-day meal. But the eight-hour expedition had been long enough for de Richleau to acquaint himself with the best view-points in another wide area of country. Well before half past two, with his four remaining gardenias made up into another little posy, he took up his position outside the Palace gate.

As a clock in a nearby belfry struck the half-hour, the carriage appeared, and pulled up on reaching him. With an awkward bow he humbly held out the flowers. Ilona took them, gave him an impersonal smile of thanks, and asked: "Where do you propose to take us?"

"Will the *Erzherzogin* be so good as to inform me how far she is prepared to walk?"

"For about an hour. I do not wish to tire myself too much."

"Then let us go towards St. Wolfgang. There are some fine views to be had in that direction without much climbing."

As she nodded assent, de Richleau nearly made a bad blunder. Sárolta Hunyády was in attendance to-day, and he had assumed that she would move over to the back seat beside her mistress, so that he could sit with Adam Grünne. He was just about to stretch out a hand to open the carriage door, when Grünne said: "Jump up on the box, then, and we'll be off."

The footman moved closer to the coachman, and, scrambling up, the Duke squeezed himself into the vacant space. Then they drove out of the town for about four miles, until they came to a bend in the valley between two thickly-wooded slopes, where de Richleau asked the coachman to pull up.

Jumping down, he opened the carriage door and said to Ilona: "If the *Erzherzogin* pleases we will walk up through the woods over the crest, and the carriage can meet us for our return journey on the far side."

As he spoke, for the first time he looked her straight in the eyes, but they did not show even a flicker of recognition. When the occupants of the carriage got out, he waited at the roadside track for them to join him, but Count Grünne said a trifle impatiently, "What are you waiting for, my good fellow? Lead on."

With a hidden grimace of annoyance, de Richleau did as he was bid. Never having played such a part before, it had not occurred to him that he would be expected to walk some way ahead of the party, and act merely like a pilot tug, while they continued to enjoy their private conversation. Unhappily he began to wonder if he had been to all his trouble in vain, and whether another couple of hours would see him back at the Palace gates without even having had a chance to reveal his identity to Ilona.

For some twenty minutes they walked through the woods up the easy gradient until they came out into a clearing on the shoulder of the spur. He waited there for the others to catch him up, and for a few moments they stood admiring the panorama above the tree-tops, which dropped steeply to the valley then rose again to further wooded heights beyond.

Sárolta turned her dark, piquant little face to Adam Grünne and said: "It looks much steeper going down than it was coming up, and I'm awfully bad at steep descents. I wonder if you could find me a good thick stick to lean on."

"Of course I will," he replied at once, and walking off to the edge of the clearing he began to hunt about in the undergrowth.

In her remark about disliking steep places, de Richleau instantly saw at least a slender chance of getting Ilona to himself, if only for a few moments. Behind them, the spur rose steeply for a hundred feet to another little plateau. Pointing to it with his alpenstock, he said: "If the ascent is not too much for the *Erzherzogin*, there is a far better view from up there. One can see over the next crest to the lake."

Ilona smiled at Sárolta. "It will prove too much for you, my dear, but I think I'll try it. Adam can keep you company. The guide will look after me."

Things had panned out far better than de Richleau had dared to hope. He had thought that if Ilona accepted his suggestion Sárolta might be left behind, in which case he could have got a start with his lady-love before Adam Grünne had a chance to rejoin them. As it was, he was to be spared the Count's unwelcome company for the next quarter of an hour or more.

Without looking at him, Ilona said: "I had better go first; then you can catch me if I slip" and set off up the rocky path.

De Richleau followed her, watching her every step: but she made the ascent without difficulty, and a few minutes later, when they reached the top, she sat down a little breathlessly on a large slab of rock.

He wished that she had gone a little farther, so that he could have sat down beside her without being seen from below, and was just about to suggest that the view was even better from the far end of the plateau, when she turned a smiling face up to him, and said:

"I like you with grey hair."

He laughed. "So you knew me all the time?"

"Of course! From the moment I saw the first gardenias. An ordinary peasant would never have bought such flowers for me. He would have picked some in the woods. But we've got to be awfully careful."

"Do the others suspect anything?"

"Sárolta knows. I told her. And just now she sent Adam Grünne for that stick in order to get rid of him. If you hadn't suggested coming up here I'm sure she would have thought up some excuse to leave us on our own for a few minutes."

"Bless her! May the Gods reward her a hundredfold for her goodwill."

"They are doing so already," Ilona laughed. "It is not easy for her and Adam to manage to be alone together either, and they are in love."

"Then I envy him."

She looked up with a frown. "Do—do you then admire Sárolta so much?"

"I think her charming; but only a tiny star compared with the glorious planet Venus, at whose shrine I worship. I meant that I envy him in having his love returned, for that is more than I can ever dare to hope. I can only aspire to serve the object of my devotion."

"Thank you," she said seriously. Then she lowered her eyes and went on in a low voice. "After I had sent that letter to you I was terribly ashamed. I—I was afraid you might think——"

"I thought only that you had reconsidered your decision," he answered quickly, "and that you felt, after all, that you would like to have a friend outside the court circle: someone you could confide in if you wished, and who, perhaps, would be fortunate enough to fill a small place that is now empty in your life."

"I do want someone like that," she admitted after a second. "Apart from Sárolta and a few other girls of whom I am fond, I have no one to whom I can talk about all sorts of things that interest me; and at times I feel terribly lonely. But why did you not come to the Prater?"

"I left Vienna two days before you, Princess, and I did not receive your letter until my return."

"I wish I had known that. I thought you were too angry about the way I had treated you to forgive me."

"I would forgive you anything, to see you smile again as you did just now, when we reached this summit."

She looked up at him, her blue eyes shining and her lips parted in a dazzling smile. For a moment they remained gazing at one another, then she said; "There could have been another explanation, and at times I was inclined to adopt it. To become my friend in secret like this is to court grave danger. After our waltz I could hardly have blamed you, had you felt that the game was not worth the candle."

"If you thought me so poor-spirited, that was very wrong of you."

Her brows drew together; then she gave a little laugh. "Do you know, I was just on the point of rebuking you. People tactfully express the hope that I may change my opinion, or that I will give a matter further consideration, but it is years since anyone has dared to tell me to my face that I was wrong. But you are right. I should have known that you really are the sort of man who would climb over a garden wall in the middle of the night without thinking twice about it."

"You have only to describe the situation of your window, and look out at midnight to-night to find me beneath it."

"No, no!" She shook her head hurriedly, so that a little chestnut curl came free and lay tantalizingly on the back of her neck. "You must do no such thing. This masquerading as a guide is bad enough. Heaven knows what a rumpus there would be if the good *Grafin* Aulendorf got to hear of it. How clever of you, though, to devise such a plan. I laughed so much over that little bit in your note, where you said you were prepared to forgo any payment for your services."

He smiled. "I put that bit in as a precaution against anyone other than yourself reading it. But what of the future? May I hope to be taken on as your guide, permanently?"

"Yes. Providing you promise me to be terribly careful. Of course we don't really need a guide. I have spent so much of my life at Ischl that I expect I know the country round about far better than you do. But then, I don't really need eight women to look after my clothes, either. And I can say that having you will save me the trouble of making up my mind every day in which direction we shall go."

"To-morrow, then, I will be waiting for you at the same hour."

"No. To-morrow is Sunday. In addition to the trippers, the townspeople will be picnicking all over the woods for miles around: so on Sundays we always have tea in the garden instead of going for a drive. But we shall have all next week. I am not returning to Vienna until the end of the month."

"Is it wise to go back so soon?" he asked with quick concern. "I have been most worried about your health, and was overjoyed to see you looking so well. But you came here for rest, and a fortnight isn't very long in view of the many duties you will have to perform once you are back in harness."

She shrugged. "There is nothing really wrong with me, you know. It is just that I sometimes run a temperature and get these awful bouts of coughing. My grandmother, Elizabeth, suffered from the same thing, and for years everyone was afraid that she had consumption. But she hadn't. It was only nerves, coupled with an unusual sensitiveness in the muscles of the throat. She was over sixty, and still remarkably energetic, when that horrible Italian stabbed her. If I live as long as that I shall be more than satisfied."

"What you tell me is a great relief," de Richleau murmured. "I have been fearing that your illness might be of a serious nature."

"Then worry no more, dear knight. My life is so full of dreary etiquette that whenever we meet I want our companionship to be a gay one."

A tremor of pleasure ran through him as he asked "Do you really mean that you will take me for your knight?"

She rose slowly to her feet. "Yes. I am a princess, but I have never had a knight. I am sure you are chivalrous, and I want you to be faithful and true; just as knights are in the story books."

He would have given a great deal to be able to kiss her hand, but they had not moved from their original position so were still in sight of Adam Grünne, should he chance to look up; and the risk was too great. All he could do was to murmur. "No lady ever had a truer knight than I will be to you, Princess."

She smiled at him again, then said quickly. "We have been here over-long already. We must go down and rejoin the others. You go first this time, in case I slip." And in single file they clambered down to the lower plateau.

The descent to the far side of the mountain spur did not prove as steep as Sárolta had appeared to fear, and in a quarter of an hour they had regained the road where the carriage was waiting. With de Richleau on the box they returned to the Palace, but instead of halting at the gate it drove straight on up to the portico. While the Duke stood with his hat clasped to his stomach, the footman threw open the carriage door and Adam Grünne jumped down and handed the two ladies out. As they entered the Palace he took a five *schilling* piece from his pocket and held it out to the guide.

Although the Duke had said in his note that he did not ask any payment for his services, he felt that no good purpose was to be served by arguing the matter; so, with a murmur of thanks, he extended his hand and took the coin. As he did so the Count said:

"Her Imperial Highness tells me that she has ordered you to report here again on Monday. I would like a word with you about the expedition on which you then propose to take us. Have you a map on you?"

"*Jawohl, Herr Graf,*" replied the Duke, and produced one from his pocket.

The carriage had just driven off to the stables, and the Count pointed across the drive to a small arbour, with a table and chairs in it, on the far side of the lawn. "Let's go over there," he said. "Then we can spread the map out."

Side by side they walked across the lawn. When they reached the arbour, de Richleau laid his map on the table. As he looked up he found that Count Grünne was staring straight into his face. The Count's jaw was sticking out aggressively and his brown eyes were hard, as he said:

"Can you give me any reason why I should not call the guard and have you arrested?"

CHAPTER XII

OF LOVE AND INTRIGUE

De Richleau was taken completely by surprise, but the Count showed no sign of having identified him. Instantly he decided that it was worth trying a bluff. Raising his eyebrows, and letting his mouth drop open, he stammered:

"But, *Herr Graf!* I—I do not understand. What have I done?"

"You know well enough! You are not a professional guide."

"Why should you imagine that? In what way have I failed to give satisfaction?"

The Count shrugged. "Oh, you played your part all right. That's what put me off the scent. When you produced those gardenias a faint suspicion drifted across my mind that there might be something fishy about you. As your references seemed all right I thought no more about it: but just now, when you took the crown I gave you, I noticed your hand. It is not the hand of a working man. Then I trapped you rather neatly. All the professional guides were born here and know the country blindfold. They don't need to carry a map."

"The *Herr Graf* is to be congratulated on his acumen," said de Richleau. "All right, then. I will admit that I am only an enthusiastic amateur. But it is one of my ambitions to rival the professionals, and I felt that it would be a proof of my capabilities if I could succeed in being taken on as a guide by Her Imperial Highness. Surely that is no crime. And what charge would you propose to bring against me for having done so?"

"I might accept that explanation if I did not feel that your face was vaguely familiar to me. As it is, I can have you detained as a suspicious character, on a charge of having used false pretences in order to approach a member of the Imperial family. And I intend to do so unless you tell me who you are. Instead of staring at the table, look up now—straight into my eyes."

The Duke had purposely kept his eyes lowered, but he knew now that the game was up. As he lifted them, he spread out his hands and smiled. "It speaks well for my disguise, Count, that you have not recognized me before, but I can hardly think that you will fail to do so now."

For a second the Count stared at him, then he exclaimed, "*Gott im Himmel!* You are the Duke de Richleau."

"At your service, Count. And what, pray, are your intentions, having made this interesting discovery?"

Count Adam hesitated, then said slowly, "It is my duty to have you arrested for seeking Her Imperial Highness' company in such an unorthodox fashion. But I regard you as a friend, and should be most loath to embarrass either her or you. If you are prepared to leave Ischl to-morrow, you may go now, and for my part I am willing to forget this eccentricity of yours."

"I'm sorry." De Richleau shook his head. "I, too, value our friendship, Count Adam, and I am obliged to you for your kind offer. But to leave Ischl is the one thing I am not prepared to do. I cannot possibly ignore Her Imperial Highness' order to report to her here again on Monday."

"Why? I can make some excuse for you. I'll say that I've received a message saying that you have been taken ill. You have achieved this strange ambition of yours, and it is far better for you to go now, rather than take the risk that Her Imperial Highness may discover that you have imposed upon her."

"Do you force me to choose between departure and arrest?"

"Yes. I fear that is the situation."

"Then I have no alternative but to warn you that if you carry out your threat you will find yourself most unpopular with both Her Imperial Highness and your charming friend, Fraulein Sárolta Hunyády. The one guessed my identity from the beginning, and is much amused by this masquerade that I undertook to relieve her boredom, the other sent you hunting for a stick this afternoon in order to give me a chance to make merry over my disguise with Her Imperial Highness without being observed by you."

"What!" exclaimed the Count. "Do you mean to tell me that both of them know who you are?"

"Certainly! Women's eyes are far sharper then men's, my poor Count; although you certainly have my compliments on the clever way you tricked me about the map. Tell me now, do you still intend to hand me over to the guard?"

Count Grünne did not reply at once, but stood thoughtfully curling up one end of his brown moustache. In spite of his foppish appearance, he was no fool, but, all the same, he felt decidedly at a loss how to handle this present situation.

"I can understand," he said after a moment, "that the ladies would be amused by this prank of yours, but if you insist on continuing it and it comes to the ears of Her Imperial Highness' Mistress of the Household, we shall all find ourselves in the very devil of a mess."

"There, I fear you are right. Pleasant as the Countess Aulendorf has been to me personally, she could hardly be expected to approve this frolic. But you, Count, are not your mistress' duenna; and I know your attachment to her. Surely you are not so hard-hearted as to wish to wreck this harmless plan of mine for providing her with a temporary escape from a life hedged about with restrictions?"

"No. Being set on a pinnacle, as she is, debars her from all the fun normally enjoyed by most young women, and God forbid that I should be the means of spoiling her chance to talk informally for once to someone. All the same, I beg you to be extremely careful. Fraulein Sárolta is, of course, entirely to be trusted, but the Baroness Paula takes turns with her at being in attendance, and is of a mean disposition. Should she discover what is afoot I would not put it past her to sneak on you."

"Then I will be doubly on my guard whenever the Baroness is in the party. And I am most grateful to you for allowing me to continue in my rôle as guide. I take it, though, you would prefer not to show that you have recognized me?"

"Yes, for the moment, at all events. But of one thing I must warn you. During any expeditions we may make next week I cannot allow you to take Her Imperial Highness out of my sight."

De Richleau's brows drew together. "I am sufficiently old-fashioned, Count, to have used a sword or pistol on occasions when I have felt that a reflection has been made upon my honour. My personal liking for you would make me most reluctant to call you out, but I must ask you to retract the imputation which your words convey."

Adam Grünne drew himself up. "I, too, am capable of using either weapon, but trust it may not be necessary to resort to such measures. I intend no reflection on you personally. However, I am responsible for the safety of Her Imperial Highness and if I allowed her to go out of my sight, either with you or with anyone else, or even alone, I should be failing in my duty."

"My apologies," smiled the Duke. "For a moment I feared that you were casting doubt on my intentions. But I had overlooked the commitments of your appointment, and I will give you no cause for concern on that account."

On this understanding they parted; the Count not too happy at the position in which he had been placed, the Duke well pleased at having got the best of a very tricky interview which he had felt certain he would have to face sooner or later. At the *Gasthaus* Pohl he again ate sandwiches for his supper, and retired early. On the Sunday he went for a walk up towards the Ehensee, and spent most of the day in blissful contemplation of the fact that, providing the fine weather continued, he would be spending several hours daily in Ilona's company for most of the coming week.

However, things did not go altogether as smoothly as he had hoped. On Monday, Paula von Wolkenstein was in attendance, and Ilona evidently shared Adam Grünne's distrust of her flaxen-haired lady-in-waiting. Although she gave de Richleau several very sweet smiles when the others were not looking, she quietly rejected his deferential suggestion that she should undertake a similar climb to that which she had made on the previous Saturday. In consequence, they were unable to exchange a single word in private the whole afternoon, and he returned to his *pension* much disgruntled.

Tuesday brought him better luck. A quarter of an hour after they left the carriage for the woods, Sárolta suggested going down to explore a little stream which ran some forty feet below the path along which they were walking. Ilona at once agreed to her doing so and told Adam Grünne to help her down the bank, but added that she preferred to rest for a while, so would remain at the top and call to them when she felt like going on. De Richleau, who had been walking a few paces ahead, turned back, and when Ilona seated herself on a fallen tree-trunk he came and stood beside her.

As soon as they had exchanged greetings he began to reproach her mildly for having given him no opportunity at all for a word alone with him the day before; but she cut him short with a haughty little lift of her chin.

"If you feel like that, I am disappointed in you. I thought you content to remain silent in my presence when the need arose. But it seems that you would rather that I risked compromising myself."

"God forbid that you should do that, Princess."

"Well; I might have done. I did not choose Paula von Wolkenstein as one of my ladies. Her name was put before me for the appointment in such circumstances that I could hardly reject it, and I believe her to be a sly little cat. I'm sure she spies upon me."

"So Adam Grünne appears to think."

She looked up quickly and he saw the famous Habsburg underlip jut out in annoyance. "Then you have talked to him about—about us."

"Only because he discovered my identity after our return to the Palace on Saturday. But we have nothing to fear from him. I led him to believe that I had undertaken this masquerade because I pride myself upon being for an amateur, an expert guide, and thought it would amuse you."

"Then if Adam had already warned you about Paula, there is all the more reason that you should appreciate my caution."

"I did, Princess, but in my present position I am debarred from taking the initiative in any way. I had hoped that you would think of some way to get rid of her, if only for a few moments."

"I may not have wished to do so."

He sighed. "That, of course, is very different. Am I so unfortunate as to have bored you already?"

With an impulsive gesture she put out a hand, touched him on the knee, then quickly withdrew it. "No, please. I did not mean that. But you must not be too demanding."

"I promise you I will not be," he said contritely. "Or at least, that I will not complain again when for reasons of discretion you feel it best to ignore me. But will the Baroness be in attendance again tomorrow? And, if so, does that mean another day on which I cannot hope for a word alone with you?"

"Yes. She and Sárolta are on duty alternate days, and whenever Paula is in attendance we must do nothing that might arouse her suspicions."

"Could you not find a pretext to dispense with her services till the end of the week?"

Ilona looked quite shocked. "I couldn't possibly do that unless she asked me to. It would not be etiquette."

Her words brought home afresh to de Richleau how controlled she was by customs which had governed, not only her life, but also those of her predecessors for many generations. A little sadly, he said: "If that is so, it cannot be helped. But it is a great pity as it means that Thursday will then remain my last chance of enjoying your company in this disguise."

"Oh, no. I do not return to Vienna until Monday, and Sárolta will be on duty on Saturday."

"Perhaps; but most unfortunately I have to leave here first thing on Friday morning."

"Indeed!" She turned to stare at him in surprised dismay. "I—I thought you meant to take every opportunity as long as I was here of showing your devotion to me. Yet now you speak of leaving three days before I do; and without even asking my permission to do so."

"You may be sure I would not leave Ischl so soon had I any choice in the matter," he assured her quickly. "But before I arrived here I was already committed to dine in Vienna next Friday night."

"Can you not possibly cancel your engagement?"

He gave her a rueful smile. "It is now I who must plead etiquette. I have to obey a royal command. At least it amounts to that, as my host will be the Heir Apparent; although I was actually bidden to dine by the Duchess of Hohenberg."

In a second Ilona was on her feet, her arched brows lifted in angry astonishment, her blue eyes flashing.

"What!" she exclaimed. "That woman! The Chotek! You dare to

place her before me? Oh, but I see it all now. The night when we had that horrid waltz at the Czernins; you danced with her afterwards. I saw her smiling up into your face, and you were laughing down at her. I behaved like a dumb little fool; but she is a woman of the world and knows how to attract men. So you prefer her to me? Oh, I hate you! I hate you!"

Adam Grünne was seated, barely out of earshot, beside Sárolta on the bank of the stream below. Ilona's raised voice might have caused him to look up, so de Richleau did not dare to take the hand of the outraged princess who stood glaring at him, or even to stretch out both his own in a gesture of pleading. Being debarred from such a course, he swiftly decided that the best alternative was to treat her like an ordinary girl who had given way to a fit of jealous temper without good reason.

"Stop it!" he snapped. "I have never thought you a fool, but you are behaving like one now."

Her eyes opened to their fullest extent, and she gaped at him, but he went on swiftly: "Would I be here if I preferred the Duchess to you? Why should I have hurried to Ischl on receiving your letter, instead of tearing it up and remaining in Vienna to pay my court to her. Do you think I enjoy wearing these absurd clothes and being treated like a servant? Either you will apologize for your unjust suspicions or I mean to catch the first train north this evening."

"Apologize!" she gasped.

"Yes. That is usual between people of good breeding when one of them is proved to have been flagrantly at fault. And I take it none of your governesses was quite so servile as to teach you that royal blood is an excuse for bad manners."

Slowly she sat down again, turning her white face from him; and evidently she underwent a fierce silent struggle before she could bring herself to whisper: "I'm sorry. I didn't mean what I said. It—it was the thought of your associating with that woman."

His tone changed instantly. "Believe me, dear Princess, I would not dream of going did I not feel I positively had to. And your sweet wish that I should remain here till you leave yourself, makes it all the harder. The trouble is that the Duchess has asked me specially to meet someone for a definite purpose, and I feel that to back out at the last minute would be extremely tactless. All the same, if you desire me to, I will send a telegram saying that I have met with an accident."

Ilona shook her head. "No, you had better go, although it means our losing Saturday. You are so clever, I feel sure you will find ways of seeing me when I get back to Vienna."

"Wild horses shall not prevent my doing so," declared the Duke. "But that is my main reason for wishing to remain on good terms with the Duchess. She could, I feel sure, be a dangerous enemy or a good friend; and in the latter guise might later on prove very useful to us."

Again Ilona lifted her chin a little. "I should not care to be beholden to that woman."

"Why?"

"She is a Czech—a nobody—an upstart!"

"Oh, come!" laughed the Duke. "You are talking now as though your own forebears had been noble for only four or five generations. It does not become people like ourselves, who are of truly ancient lineage, to display such snobbishness."

For a second her mouth hardened. Then she too, laughed. "Perhaps you are right; but after this afternoon I shall be tempted to think that instead of a knight errant I have acquired another governess."

"I would willingly don skirts if that would enable me to be near you more frequently."

Ilona giggled. "How funny you would look in them. But seriously, I have good cause to dislike the Chotek. She is an evil woman, and has brought dissension into the Imperial family."

"Had you given your last reason first, I would not have challenged it. But about her being evil, I am not so certain. She loves her husband, and one cannot blame a mother for fighting for what she believes to be the rights of her children. I thought her not at all a bad creature, but she is as sharp as a needle. As she watched us dancing together that night at the Czernins, she is more likely than anyone else in Viennese society to guess my interest in you. That is another reason why I wish to stand well with her. Then, if she sees us together again and suspects anything, she is much more likely to refrain from starting malicious gossip."

Ilona agreed to the wisdom of that, and for a while they talked of other people in Viennese society. Then Adam Grünne got to his feet and called up: "It is nearly four o'clock. Does not your Highness think that we ought to be getting back to the carriage?"

Too late, de Richleau and Ilona realized that their precious time together had raced by almost unnoticed, and that they had spent most of it bickering. Before the others could reach them he whispered; "If I have disappointed you to-day, please forgive me. The things I said to you were clumsy only because there is so much in my heart that I may not say."

The blood mounted to her face, then she whispered back: "I know, I understand. But you must not say it."

Wednesday, apart from stolen glances, proved a blank; for the narrow-eyed, rather stupid-looking Baroness Paula took her duties very seriously. During their walk she was never more than three paces distant from her mistress—even when de Richleau led the way up as steep a pile of rocks as he thought Ilona could manage—and, apparently, either the fear of arousing suspicion, or her upbringing as an Archduchess, still so dominated Ilona that she could not bring herself to tell the girl to remain behind with Adam Grünne while she made the climb alone with their guide.

But Thursday was a day that de Richleau long remembered as one of the happiest in his life. On the previous evening, when dismissing him, Adam Grünne had said that, if the weather remained fine, Her Imperial Highness had decided to go for a picnic: so instead of reporting at two-thirty, as usual, he was to be at the Palace at eleven o'clock.

The Duke woke early, jumped out of bed and ran to the window. There was no streak of warning red in the eastern sky, and the trees in the distance had that intense early morning stillness which presages a perfect summer day. By ten to eleven, now a familiar figure at the Palace gates, he walked through them and up to the portico. At eleven o'clock, with the punctuality which marked all the Imperial arrangements, they set off.

Ilona had decided on an expedition towards Ehensee, so they drove northward for about eight miles before halting the carriage. Normally, as they were to picnic, the footman would have brought up the rear carrying the luncheon basket: but as Ilona stepped down into the road she said that their guide could quite well do so. De Richleau, realising her intention of being freed from the prying eyes of a servant, willingly abandoned his rucksack, and had the hamper strapped to his back in its place. They then entered the shady woods that rose steeply from the right hand side of the road.

As usual the Duke led the way, some twenty paces in advance of the others, but when they had been walking for some ten minutes and were well out of sight of the carriage, Ilona called to him to stop. Then, when they had caught up with him, she smiled at Sárolta and Adam Grünne, and said:

"Both of you know the real identity of our guide, so to-day we will make no silly pretences, but really enjoy ourselves for once. Come, Duke, give me your arm, and we'll lead the way together. I shouldn't be surprised if I make a better guide than you do."

When he had exchanged a pleasant greeting with the others, he replied with a laugh, "I am quite sure you will, Princess, for I will now confess that I have never before had the chance to go so far in this direction." Then he gave her his arm, and the two couples resumed their ascent of the woodland track.

Adam Grünne was quick to realize what a happy chance the arrangement gave him to make love to Sárolta so, with her arm in his, he eased his pace until they had dropped some way behind. After the party had covered a hundred yards, Ilona glanced back, and seeing that she and de Richleau were out of earshot, said:

"Do you know, although we have really seen very little of one another, I feel that in some ways I know you more intimately than any man I have ever met. Yet I still do not know your Christian name."

"It is Jean Armand Duplessis," he replied; "but most of my friends call me Armand."

"Then, as long as we are alone together to-day, I will call you that, and if you like—Armand, you may call me Ilona."

In those days Christian names were not lightly bandied about, or ever used between men and women who were not lovers, relatives or old friends; so to hear her almost whisper his name thrilled him as few things could have done. Pressing her arm very lightly, he said:

"Thank you, my beautiful Princess. The name Ilona will come easily to my lips, for it is ever in my thoughts and in my sweetest dreams."

Unlike their previous meetings, to-day no shadow of restraint or misunderstanding lay between them. As they mounted gently through the twilit woods, they talked of a dozen subjects. He told her of some of the strange places he had visited, and thrilled her with a full account of the abortive attempt in which he had participated as a young officer to place the Duc de Vendôme on the throne of France. She shyly confessed that she sometimes wrote poetry and had had some of her poems set to music, so that she could sing them; although she said her voice was very small, and that she rarely sang except in private for her own amusement, and occasionally for her old grandfather, the Emperor, who liked her to sing him to sleep in an arm-chair when he was tired out from poring over his endless State papers.

It was Ilona who led the way to a glade on the crest, which opened out to the northward with a lovely view of lower, wooded hilltops and, beyond them, the little town of Ehensee, with its long lake shimmering in the summer sun. There, the others caught up with them and helped to spread out the picnic lunch. Ilona's gaiety infected them all and her happiness lent a new radiance to her beauty. Her lips and cheeks seemed more highly coloured than usual, her eyes were pools of deepest blue, and her chestnut hair caught the sunshine in its high-piled waves. For an hour, while they ate the cold collation which had been provided and drank a refreshing light Moselle, they laughed and joked together in all the joy of youth; the dark future, which only de Richleau feared to be so close at hand, mercifully hidden from them.

When they had packed up the picnic things, the two couples walked on a little farther and, separating by unspoken agreement, sat down some distance apart to admire the view. For another hour and a half

Ilona and Armand, as they now called one another freely, talked of their lives before they had met, which now seemed an age away. Every now and then their eyes met in a long gaze and a short happy silence fell between them. When he gently took her hand in his, she did not withdraw it; and they would have sat on, unheeding of the passage of time, until nightfall, had not Count Adam come over to warn them that they were already over-late in starting back.

To make up time a little, in case the servants began to fear that an accident had befallen them, they hurried rather on the way downwards, so talked only at infrequent intervals. But when they got to within ten minutes' walk of the road, de Richleau broached the subject of future meetings.

Ilona said that, on her return to Vienna, she would ride in the Prater every morning, except Sundays, between eight and nine o'clock, so he could meet her then as though by chance, and of course she would invite him to her birthday party on the 13th of June; but that was still over a fortnight away, and they should be able to meet several times at social functions which she would attend before then.

"As a starving man I gladly snatch at every crust," he smiled. "But I dare not run into you while riding in the Prater too frequently, or dance with you more than once at any ball, otherwise tongues will begin to wag. I think I have an idea, though, by which we might spend a good part of two or three days together."

"Oh, tell me!" she exclaimed in delight.

"It is to open up my castle at Königstein. As you may know, it is on the Danube only some twenty-five miles west of Vienna. If I gave a house-warming, with a ball and other entertainments, would it not be possible for you to come to stay for a couple of nights, with the Aulendorfs and the rest of your suite, as my guest of honour?"

Sadly she shook her head. "It is a lovely idea, but I am afraid not practical. If a married couple wished to entertain me in that way, I could express my desire to the wife to pay her a visit; but I could not do that to a single man, and it would be a shocking breach of etiquette for you to invite me, even if you did so through Countess Aulendorf."

He was greatly disappointed at this douche of cold water on the plan that he had been nurturing, and quickly began to cast about in his mind for a way of getting over the difficulty. Perhaps if he could get some suitable couple to act as host and hostess for him—his thoughts had got no further when she impulsively tightened her clasp on his arm, and cried:

"I have it! The Chotek shall help us."

"How? I thought you disliked her far too much to ask any favour of her?"

Ilona laughed. "I do. But, like yourself, I am not averse to making use of her. You must ask her instead of myself to be your guest of honour at Königstein. Nothing delights my cousin, Franz, so much as to see his morganatic wife treated like an Archduchess. Act as though she were one. Tell Franz Ferdinand, when you see him to-morrow night, that you would like to fête them at your castle, but have not the temerity to invite her. Providing he is not too heavily engaged, he will certainly accept for them both. Then submit your list of guests, including the names of myself and my suite."

"And you would then be allowed to come?"

"Yes. Unless she told my cousin to strike my name out, but that is unlikely. Although we are not friends, I have always been polite to her in public. If the Heir Apparent is to be present, then there is no rule to prevent me, as his relative, from also enjoying your hospitality."

"Then, if persuasion can do the trick, it shall be done," declared the Duke happily.

A few minutes later they were approaching an opening in the wood, from which the road was visible, so she stopped and said: "I think, Armand, that you had better go on alone from here."

He turned and faced her. "Ilona, it has been a glorious day, and one I shall always treasure in my memory. May I—may I hope from it that you feel just a little towards me, as I feel towards you?"

Her eyelashes fluttered, then she looked down and whispered; "Please don't ask me. You know that I must not even allow myself to think such thoughts. But I—I like you more than anyone I've ever met."

That night was his last at the *Gasthaus* Pohl. Next morning the eccentric Englishman, dressed like a Tyrolese, who had begun his stay with incredibly long early-morning walks and eaten sandwiches instead of dinner, was driven to the station. Before reaching Linz, he carried his bag along to a lavatory, stripped off his whiskers, changed his clothes, and emerged from the train with nothing remaining of his disguise except his grey hair and eyebrows. These were a somewhat more tricky matter, as a week's application of powder was going to take some getting off: but after lunching at Linz, he went to a barbers, told the attendant that he had been to a fancy-dress dance the night before, and had a thorough shampoo. Then he caught a train on to Vienna.

Owing to his having broken his journey for three hours in Linz, it was after seven o'clock when he arrived in the capital, so he had to hurry. As he entered Sacher's, he told the porter to have a taxi waiting for him at eight o'clock, took the sheaf of letters that the man held out to him, thrust them into his pocket and strode over to the lift. At ten past eight the taxi set him down outside the *Oberes Belvedere*, and at eight-fifteen, his dark hair now shining, and immaculate in evening dress, he was kissing the hand which 'the Chotek' extended to him with a gracious smile.

The party again consisted of about two dozen people, but when they were all assembled de Richleau saw that, whereas those who had attended the luncheon at which he had been present had been mostly of the lesser nobility, many of these held important official positions. Among them were Admiral von Kailer, the chief of the Austrian Navy, Count Krobatin, the War Minister, and Count Hoyos, von Berchtold's right hand man at the Foreign Office. So it was clear that the Duchess Sophie had done her utmost to impress her principal guest, Count Tisza.

With the exception of the Hungarians, all the subject peoples of the Dual Monarchy were treated as subservient to Austria, and enjoyed only the right to send their elected representatives to the central parliament. But Hungary, under her ancient constitution, remained a separate kingdom, enjoying a considerable amount of theoretical independence, with her own parliament, which sat in Budapest. The Emperor, therefore, had two Prime Ministers or, as they were termed, Minister-Presidents; Count Stürgkh, who represented the Imperial Austrian electorate, and Count Tisza, who represented the electorate of Hungary.

As de Richleau was presented to the Hungarian Minister-President, he took an immediate liking to him. The Count had both breadth of mind and nobility of thought stamped on his fine features. His eyes were serious, yet amiable, with a steady, honest glance. His head was of magnificent proportions, broad, lofty and highly domed under dark receding hair. When he smiled, white teeth showed beneath his dark moustache, and a short, pointed beard was not sufficiently heavy to disguise the firmness of his mouth and chin.

After the Duchess had made the introduction, she smiled from one to the other, and said: "Do you know, apart from the fact that Count Königstein is clean shaven, and something about the eyebrows, you two gentlemen are very much alike."

Both proclaimed themselves flattered, as in fact they were, because while de Richleau was the handsomer of the two, he hoped that he might have as fine a presence as Count Tisza when he reached the Hungarian's age. The episode was not lost upon the Duke as confirming his impression that Sophie von Hohenberg was a very clever woman.

Soon afterwards they went in to dinner. De Richleau was seated near the middle of the long table, so it was not until after the meal that he had any opportunity for a word with his host or hostess. However, the normally morose Archduke could become quite a pleasant man when among people whom he knew and liked, so while they drank their coffee and liqueurs he twice moved round to a different position at the table in order to talk with as many as possible of his guests, and his second move placed him next to the Duke.

De Richleau then took an early opportunity of mentioning his project of opening up Königstein, and adopted the line that Ilona had suggested. Franz-Ferdinand fingered the right curl of his heavy moustache for a moment, then replied:

"When I was a youngster, I once visited Königstein as a guest of your father, Duke, and a very good shoot we had there too. If my engagements permit, I should much like to visit your castle again. Besides, it would give me a chance to talk about the Turkish army with you. As to your project of giving a fête for my wife, I am sure she will take that as a very pleasant compliment. But ask her yourself, when we join the ladies, and if she agrees you can arrange a date between you, as she knows when we are free better than I do myself."

Well pleased, de Richleau decided to bide his time before tackling the Duchess. A game of cards was begun as soon as the men entered the yellow drawing-room, but only about half the guests took part. The others, Count Tisza among them, sat talking in little groups; while from time to time the dark-haired Duchess moved from place to place, deftly changing the composition of the groups so that each of her guests should have a chance to talk to other people.

About half past ten she detached an elderly General from the Minister-President, beckoned over the Duke, and said: "Since you two have quite a physical resemblance, I am sure you would like to discover if your tastes are also in common." Then she left them, to join the elderly lady to whom de Richleau had been talking.

"Well!" smiled the Count. "Where do we begin? I have been a soldier and am now a politician; but what little leisure I now have is devoted to shooting and my books."

De Richleau was shrewd enough to guess that his campaigns in South America and the Balkans would prove only of casual interest to an intellectual such as the Count, and he knew little of the Dual Monarchy's internal politics: so he fastened at once upon the great man's hobbies.

For a while they talked of shooting; but soon turned to literature, and discovered that they were both great admirers of the Greco-Roman civilization. They enthused together over the beauties of Virgil and Horace, then laughed at passages in Petronius, Aristophanes and Ovid, agreeing how infinitely more sophisticated they were than the sixteenth and seventeenth century dramatists, and how their sense of humour possessed a timeless quality that leapt two thousand years, still to delight any cultured modern.

After a while Count Tisza said: "You must come some time and browse with me in my library. I have a few bibelots which I feel sure would interest you." Then, as an afterthought, he added: "If you are not engaged to go on anywhere to supper, why not come back with me when I leave here. I get little free time during the day. While I show you my treasures, we could drink a glass to those noble Ancients who lived on a mental plane which we have as yet failed to regain, despite the advantage that the printed word and the spread of popular education gives us."

De Richleau accepted with alacrity, and when he next spoke to the Duchess was able to tell her that, although he had not yet talked to Count Tisza about herself, he would now have an excellent opportunity of doing so without fear of interruption. She was delighted, and when he mentioned the fête that he wished to give in her honour for the reopening of Königstein, she was even more so. Having an excellent memory, she did not need to refer to any list of the Archduke's major engagements, and declared that any minor ones could be put off; so they settled for the visit to be on the 10th and 11th of the coming month.

At half past eleven, Franz Ferdinand and his wife bade their guests good-night and withdrew. Then de Richleau accompanied Count Tisza to his car, and they drove to a small but beautiful little palace which was the Minister-President's residence in Vienna.

Feeling certain that his guest would prove a connoisseur, the Count sent down to his cellar for a bottle of Tokay of the long-past but once famous vintage, 1763. The wine was in a squat, crested bottle and when poured was of a rich, bright gold. The thick, almost treacly, sweetness of such wines when young makes them scarcely drinkable until half a century old, but enables them to far outlive any port, sherry, or madeira, and this was still in its prime; the very essence of the grape, redolent of flowers, honey and sunshine, a fitting nectar with which to toast the shades of Caesar, Lucretius and Lucullus himself.

When they had sipped the glorious amber fluid with due appreciation, they began to go round the quiet library, which glowed with a gentle warmth from its rows of gilt tooled, calf, morocco, and vellum-bound books. Here and there the Count took one from a shelf and gave it to his guest to examine. In an hour or so he produced a hundred rare and beautiful volumes which de Richleau greatly envied him; among them a Black Letter copy of *Caesar's Wars* which had once belonged to that great captain, Charles V of Spain, Heine's *Catullus*, the Emperor Napoleon's *Marcus Aurelius*, Goethe's *Longinus*, the younger Pitt's *Homer* with his annotations upon it, and Madame de Pompadour's *Martial*, bound in blue silk into which was woven the royal arms of France.

It was the last which gave the Duke the opportunity to bring up the subject of the lady who had entertained them both that evening. "Do you think," he asked, "that if the Duchess of Hohenberg had remained unmarried to the Archduke, she would have been able to hold his affections and later play the rôle of a modern Pompadour?"

"I do," replied the Count gravely. "They are extremely devoted, and she is a remarkably clever woman. I am among those who wish that she had been content to play such a part, as their marriage has already caused much trouble and will lead to even graver issues on the death of our aged Emperor."

"True; but if you are right, her influence on affairs would not have been greatly lessened."

"Not behind the scenes, perhaps. But instead of remaining a *maitresse-en-titre* she must now become Queen of Hungary."

"If the question is not indiscreet, how do you think the Hungarians will view that?"

Count Tisza shrugged. "We Hungarians are not fond of Czechs, so it is most unlikely that the people will take kindly to her. As for us nobles, there are few of new creation amongst us, and the wives of our magnates will be far from willing to make their curtsy to a woman of such little birth."

"Yet I believe she may prove a good friend to Hungary, if the road is not made too difficult for her to start with," remarked de Richleau. "I do not know her at all well, but we had some conversation on the subject recently. I know she feels that if she could win the Hungarians to her, that would greatly offset the enmity with which she is regarded by many powerful Austrian families; and she certainly intends to make the attempt."

With a slight narrowing of his eyes Count Tisza asked: "Did she ask you there to-night to tell me that?"

"Yes," admitted the Duke frankly. "But I would not abuse your hospitality now, by acting as her ambassador, did I not believe it to be true."

"I willingly take your word on that. I see, too, that she is every bit as clever as I thought. It was a shrewd move to choose an intelligent and presumably unbiased man, such as yourself, to speak on her behalf. And, of course, she is right to court the support of the people over whom she cannot be prevented from becoming Queen. If she can persuade us to forget her ancestry, and shows herself another such champion of Hungarian interests as was the Empress Elizabeth, she will be more than half way to getting herself made Empress of Austria. I thank you for having conveyed her ideas to me, and I shall not forget them."

Half an hour later, they parted on the most friendly terms, the

Count urging de Richleau to come to see him again, and with true Hungarian hospitality asking him, while in Vienna, to regard his house as his own.

It was nearly three in the morning when de Richleau got back to Sacher's. Some of the lights in the lounge were still on, but most of them had been switched off. As he crossed it, a tall figure rose from an arm-chair in a dim corner. His attention caught by the movement, the Duke glanced in that direction. Suddenly his sixth sense warned him that in some way the big form emerging from the shadows menaced himself. Next second, with relief, yet a lingering uneasiness, he saw that it was Sir Pellinore Gwaine-Cust.

CHAPTER XIII

TWO MIDNIGHT INTERVIEWS

"So there you are, eh!" boomed Sir Pellinore. "Been gaddin' about the night-haunts, I suppose? Why the hell couldn't you reply to my message before going out?"

"Well, this is a surprise," exclaimed the Duke. "Whatever are you doing here?"

"Waiting to see you, of course. Been kickin' me heels in this damn place for the past three days. Haven't you had the chit I left for you at the office, sayin' I wanted to see you urgently?"

"No. I returned from Ischl only this evening, and I had to go straight out to a dinner party. I fear I neglected to open the batch of letters I was given. I am so sorry you should have been inconvenienced on my account."

"Never mind! Come and sit down. What'll you drink? I've got some Kümmel here. It's the real Russian stuff, and not too bad. Anyhow, I've polished off half a bottle of it while waitin' for you. Will you join me, or have some other tipple?"

"I'd prefer a brandy and soda," said the Duke.

Sir Pellinore pressed the bell, and when the night waiter appeared addressed him in an incredible ***bêche-de-mer***, consisting of mangled French, German and English.

As the man did not appear to understand the order clearly, de Richleau intervened and said in German. "The gentleman says he is hungry and wants some foie-gras sandwiches. Not a few, but a whole plateful. You are also to bring a bottle of brandy, a tumbler and a syphon."

When the waiter had gone, the Duke smiled across at Sir Pellinore. "You know, all these hotel servants understand English perfectly, and it might save you quite a lot of trouble if you gave your orders to them in that language."

"No! No!" growled Sir Pellinore. "When in Rome, you know! I always talk to these fellers in their own lingo. Mustn't let them get away with the idea that we don't understand 'em. Some are such fools that they don't get the hang of their own gibberish to start with; or such knaves that they pretend they don't. But I always get what I want in the long run."

"I'm sure you do," remarked the Duke mildly. "But tell me, what brings you to Vienna?"

"I've told you already. That report of yours. Damn fine work! Damn fine! How right I was that a feller like you could go sniffin' around in all sorts of places without arousin' suspicion. You may not know it, but you're a classic."

"Thanks," remarked de Richleau with an icy air. "But I disliked parts of my mission intensely, and I am happy to think that my 'sniffing' days are over."

"Oh no they're not!"

"Oh yes they are!"

"Don't be a fool. The stuff you sent us was of incalculable value. Who else have we who could have got himself invited to lunch with old von Hotzepoff, made a monkey out of Dimivitch, and danced with the wife of Franz Frederick?"

"Well, you may make up your mind to one thing—any lunching or dancing that I do in the future will be entirely for my own amusement."

"Don't you believe it. You're British, aren't you?"

At this point the waiter entered with the brandy and a plate piled high with sandwiches. Sir Pellinore produced a large note from his pocket and said to the Duke:

"I'm not staying here, but with Maurice de Bunsen; so I'll settle up now. This will cover both bottles and the rest of it, with enough over to keep this feller in beer for a month. Tell him to keep the change and go to bed, or else bury his head under the sink in his pantry, and that if I see him snooping around I'll pitch him out of the window."

De Richleau made a suitable translation, and helped himself to a brandy and soda. He was now feeling distinctly perturbed at the turn the conversation was taking, but was quite determined not to give way to Sir Pellinore's evident desire to involve him afresh in the espionage he detested. Meanwhile, the grey-haired giant opposite him had crammed a sandwich into his mouth and was chewing vigorously. As he swallowed the remains, he picked up another and remarked:

"Not bad fodder. I always have a kindly eye for geese when I see them from a train. Silly birds, but useful. Have some?"

As the Duke had had nothing to eat since dinner, he started to help diminish the pile. Then the forceful voice boomed again:

"Where were we? I know: that thunderin' fine report you sent in. War's inevitable. Can't doubt that in view of your sources. By the by, I've brought you a thousand quids' worth of shares in Vickers-Armstrong. I need hardly warn you not to sell. They'll be worth ten thousand by the autumn."

"That's very kind of you," replied the Duke. "But I am quite well off, and I did what I did for my country, so I have no wish to take money from British Government funds."

"Government, eh!" Sir Pellinore guffawed. "That's a good one! If you were on the regular list, about all you'd get is half your expenses and a bonus of a tenner. No. This is my pigeon."

"In that case I am especially grateful. But I see no reason why I should deplete your private fortune."

"Don't you worry about that. Some people spend their cash on horses; some, like old George Holford, on orchids; some, on pictures; some, on gels. Thank God I've never had to do the last. Always got plenty by slapping their bottoms. Anyhow, as our hush-hush gentry are always kept short of money, I get a lot of fun backing a winner for them when I can find one. As for depleting my fortune, that odd thousand won't stop me payin' my lemonade bill. I stand in to make half a million out of Vickers' shares as soon as we start to fight."

De Richleau stiffened slightly. "Do you infer that you have used the information I obtained for you with the intention of making a fortune out of other people?"

"Now, now! Keep the saddle between your knees and use your common sense," Sir Pellinore admonished him. "I'm not robbin' the widow and the orphan. They're being paid what they ask for their shares here and now. If war comes the shares will go up. Somebody's got to take the profit. It will be me—that's all. I'm an awful fool about most things. Everybody knows that. But I seem to be lucky where dabblin' on the Stock Exchange is concerned."

"Damn it, man!" the Duke exploded. "Have you got the face to tell me that you're gambling on war—actually hoping for it?"

"Good God, no!" exclaimed Sir Pellinore angrily. "What the hell d'you think I'm doing sitting here talking to you? I'd lose my stake gladly if only we could stop it. Not that I *can* lose. Shares won't go down in any case. But that's beside the point."

"And how do you suppose that I can stop what we both now consider to be almost inevitable?"

"By taking up the game again, and doing as well as you did before."

"I flatly refuse to spy further on my Austrian friends."

"They'll be your enemies before you're much older, my boy. Anyway, no one asked you to. You've been clever enough to get under that feller Dimibitch's skin, and I want you to stay there."

"I'm sorry. It is impossible for me to return to Serbia. I have commitments here in Austria that I cannot now escape."

Sir Pellinore raised one bushy eyebrow and gave the Duke a leery look. "So you're still chasin' the little Archduchess, eh?"

"No!" replied de Richleau stiffly. "I have an engagement to entertain the Heir Apparent and his wife at my castle of Königstein on the 10th and 11th of next month."

"There! What did I say to Bindon? 'Feller in his position could even get under the throne itself if he wanted to.' But your party need not stymie us. You're not due back in Belgrade till the 16th, so by all means amuse yourself till then."

"I am not going back to Belgrade."

"Oh yes you are." Sir Pellinore stretched out a huge hand. "What d'you want for this job? Name your own price. Winston's seen your paper and he's been polishin' up his Dreadnoughts like a maniac ever since. If you want to go fightin', he'll make you a Royal Marine. But if you stick out for bein' a soldier, the War Office isn't the last word. No, not by a long chalk. The Monarch can still hand out commissions for any rank to whomever he likes. I'll see him personally. Get him to make you a Brigadier General. How's that, eh?"

De Richleau had gradually gone whiter, and now he almost hissed, "I thought I had made it plain, both that such business is distasteful to me, and that I am not the sort of person who accepts bribes."

"Sorry!" said Sir Pellinore. "Wrong horse. All right; we'll start again."

"You are wasting your time and mine."

"Oh no I'm not. Never spent a more valuable evening in me life, Anyhow, we've got one point clear. Now tell me what you're hopin' to get out of the accursed war?"

"Hoping to get!" repeated the Duke. "You must be crazy!"

"Far from it. The one point we have got clear is that you want it to happen. Well, seein' you're a professional soldier, I suppose you can't be blamed for that."

The Duke was quivering with rage. He stood up. "How dare you impute such motives to me?"

"Can't help it, my dear feller. Only one alternative. Shouldn't have thought it myself, but all things are possible. Perhaps you're afraid to tackle Dimitich again, and I must regard you as a lily-livered rat."

His grey eyes blazing, de Richleau snatched at his half-empty tumbler. In another second he would have thrown its remaining contents in Sir Pellinore's face. But the big man had now also risen, and seized his arm just in time.

"Sorry!" he grinned. "Wrong horse again. I did say, though, that I shouldn't have thought it myself. Still, if you're not afraid to go back, it must be that you want the war to happen. That's logic, ain't it?"

"No," snarled de Richleau. "It is not. I would do anything in the world to stop this terrible catastrophe."

Sir Pellinore shrugged his mighty shoulders. "Then why d'you refuse to lend us a hand?"

"Because I have already done what I was asked, and have got for you the only information that really matters. All else can be of only minor importance: so one of your regular agents can go to Belgrade and hold a watching brief there just as well as I can. Please get it into your head once and for all that I am not a spy, either by inclination or profession."

"Who the hell said you were? But you're about the only person in the world who stands a chance of keeping the peace of Europe."

De Richleau gave a weary sigh. "You're talking the most utter nonsense. These maniacs have made up their minds. The die is as good as cast already. There is positively nothing that I can do to stop them."

"Yes there is. Go back and muscle in on this Black Hand gang. You're the only living soul who's in a position to do that; and on it rests our one hope of preventing war. Our one and only hope, d'you understand? If you can find out what sort of a mine Dimithebitch means to spring, and let us know in advance, with God's help we'll find a way to spike his guns and save humanity."

For a moment the Duke was silent. From the instant he had set eyes on Sir Pellinore in the semi-darkened lounge, his instinct had told him that he was about to be caught up in the web again. He had struggled against it vainly, seeing no reason why he should allow himself to be made use of rather than someone else. But now Sir Pellinore had produced a reason, against which there was no conceivable argument. Slowly, he drank the rest of his brandy, then said bitterly:

"All right. Since there is no alternative, I'll do as you wish."

"Thank God!" exclaimed Sir Pellinore. "Here! Give me that tumbler, will you? I'm going to knock off the rest of this Kümmel. Heaven knows, I need it."

"Not as much as I do," muttered the Duke. "Damn you, I'll change my mind unless you give me half."

At that they both laughed; the tension was relaxed and they sat down to finish the bottle between them, while they debated the situation with the mutual liking and respect they really felt for one another.

Actually, there was little more to be said. They discussed the possibility of de Richleau returning to Belgrade before the 16th of June, in order to gain additional time in which to work, but decided against it as being directly contrary to Dimitriyevitch's instructions, so too liable to arouse his suspicions. It was, therefore, simply a question of the Duke acting on the orders he already had, then discovering details of Dimitriyevitch's intentions, if he possibly could, in time for the British Foreign Office to take measures which might either forestall or render them abortive. As an example, Sir Pellinore suggested that if Serbia was about to make a formal demand that Austria should grant Home Rule to Bosnia, the British Government could pour cold water on that powder barrel by getting in first with a proposal that a conference of the nations should be called to discuss the matter: but he had neither instructions to give, nor advice to offer. He had come to Vienna only to secure a continuance of the Duke's help and, having achieved his object, now proposed to leave for home on the next express.

In the first light of the summer dawn, de Richleau saw his visitor off in a night-hawk cab, then he went thoughtfully up to bed.

When he awoke, the sun was shining through the chinks of the heavy curtains and he found that it was close on eleven o'clock. Unhappily, he recalled his midnight interview and the new commitment with which it had landed him: but he quickly decided that as there was over a fortnight still before he could take any steps in the matter, the less he thought about it the better. Moreover, he had other urgent affairs to occupy him; for to have Königstein in a fit state to entertain the Heir Apparent there in twelve days time was no light undertaking.

After sending off a telegram to his steward, to meet him at the castle on Sunday afternoon, his first requirement was to secure a suitable staff, and in this he sought Frau Sacher's help. Although it was Saturday, she enabled him to interview a butler, a chef and a housekeeper that afternoon, all of whom he engaged on her recommendation. To them he left the task of engaging underservants required in their respective departments, with instructions that they and their teams should report for duty at Königstein on the following Tuesday.

Next, he had to find a lady who would act as official hostess for him—nominally to be responsible for the comfort of his women guests and take charge of his female staff. The problem was not easy as he would normally have chosen one of several old friends, but all of them were women whom he knew would be averse from openly associating themselves with an entertainment given for Sophie von Hohenberg. But on pondering the matter, he recalled a Countess Prava who had been a friend of his father's, and whom he had met again recently. She was of good birth and at one time had been a great beauty, but had not married till comparatively late in life, and then to a Czech who, some years later, had gone bankrupt and committed suicide. Now, in greatly reduced circumstances, she was endeavouring to keep up appearances and bring out two daughters. Unforeseen objections apart, she seemed the very person for the rôle, as she was *grande dame* in her own right, but had Czech associations and should welcome a party for her girls of the sort that she could not possibly afford to give. The Duke promptly dispatched a note to her by hand, asking if he might call upon her the following morning.

At mid-day he presented himself to his father's old flame. On his explaining matters, and tactfully intimating that he would be responsible for the dressmaker's bills of the Prava ladies for the occasion, the Countess at once expressed her willingness to act for him, and they proceeded to draw up a provisional list of guests for submission to the Archduke.

De Richleau calculated that the castle would accommodate about thirty guests, in addition to themselves; but from his boyhood he had known a number of families in the neighbourhood and felt he could rely on them to put up a further fifty or so for the night of the dance. With these neighbours, the list ran to just over a hundred, and included, besides the suites of Franz-Ferdinand and Ilona Theresa, Conrad von Hötzendorf, Count Tisza, Count Hoyos, and a number of other prominent personalities.

That afternoon, the Duke left for Königstein to undertake a herculean labour. It was several years since he had even visited the castle, let alone lived in it for any length of time, and he knew that many of the rooms had not been occupied since his father's day; so he dreaded the state in which he might find them. His only comfort was that he had always allocated a reasonable amount from the revenues of the estate to the upkeep of the castle, and when he arrived there he found to his relief that his steward had not misapplied them.

The castle was picturesquely situated on a bend in the Danube. Its pointed turrets rose two hundred feet above the river, but a large part of it had been modernized, and from a terrace on its south side gardens sloped down to the water's edge.

A thorough inspection showed that the roofs of the building had been kept in good repair, and damp prevented from penetrating the walls by the occasional lighting of fires in all the principal rooms in winter. But the place was much too large for the caretaker and his family, who were its only permanent occupants, to keep properly cleaned. Coverings protected most of the best furniture, but little clouds of dust puffed up round their feet as they walked across the carpets of the upstairs rooms, and in some places mice had battened unchecked on hangings and materials.

De Richleau congratulated his people on matters being no worse after his long absence, but said that within a week every room in the castle must be spotless. He told his steward that servants would be arriving to help on Tuesday, and in the meantime at least a hundred men and women must be mustered from the estate to start next day on a thorough spring cleaning.

On the Monday morning he was up himself by six, and as soon as the emergency cleaners arrived organized them into groups for various duties. Great cauldrons of water were boiled in the laundry for washing covers and curtains; scores of carpets were carried out into the grounds, hung on ropes and beaten; twenty women were put to scrubbing floors, and another twenty to polishing furniture. The place was a bedlam, a fog of dust and a sea of soapy water; but through it all the Duke moved as quietly and efficiently as if he were directing a battle; and by Tuesday afternoon, when the professional servants arrived, although a host of matters still required attention, order was beginning to emerge out of chaos.

First thing on Wednesday, he set off in a hired car on a round of visits to his neighbours. Some were away from home, but those whom he found in residence were delighted to hear that Königstein was to be opened up again, and that the Heir Apparent was shortly to come there on a visit. Only one stuffy old lady declined to meet the Duchess of Hohenberg; the others readily accepted, and willingly agreed to put up some of de Richleau's guests.

That evening he returned to Vienna and, after dinner, called at a first-class livery stable, where he selected a handsome bay mare for the following morning. Half past seven next morning saw him mounted on her and riding out towards the Prater. Just under the railway bridge, near the main entrance to the six square miles of park and playgrounds, he pulled up, and sat waiting eagerly to see again the lovely girl, for a few hours of whose company he was putting himself to such vast labour and expense. From the bridge ran the splendid *Hauptallee* that intersected the Prater lengthways, so he felt confident that in whatever part of the park Ilona meant to ride she would enter it that way.

Soon after eight she arrived, but in a carriage and pair, with Paula von Wolkenstein beside her and Adam Grünne opposite. On seeing the sulky-faced little Baroness, de Richleau swore under his breath, looked quickly away and made no move to draw attention to himself. As he was in the shadow of the bridge he hoped that she had not noticed him loitering there. When the carriage had passed, he turned his mount and followed it at a discreet distance, praying that Ilona's horses were waiting for her a mile or so farther along the avenue, and that when she was mounted he would have a better chance of appearing to run into her by accident.

As he rode along he now had the *Wurstelprater* on his left. It was a big area devoted to a permanent fair-ground, with merry-go-rounds, marionette theatres, scenic railways, grottoes, a dozen restaurants and a score of booths, where the Viennese enjoyed themselves by the thousand on Sundays, and took their children up in the great wheel to see the panorama of their lovely city. Then, to the right and left spread the Prater gardens, with innumerable walks shaded by fine trees and gay with flower-beds set in green lawns. On one side lay a chain of lakes and on the other rose the vast *Rotunde* which periodically housed Vienna's exhibitions.

On that morning in early June there were as yet few people about, but the scene breathed the essence of happiness, security and pleasure. It seemed difficult to believe that the brutalized armies of hostile invaders had camped there more than once; yet the black thought crossed de Richleau's mind that in the dark future, which now seemed to loom so close ahead, they might soon do so again.

It was not until Ilona's carriage reached the end of the gardens opposite the stadium, that it drew up, and there, as the Duke had hoped, grooms were waiting with horses for her party. When they were mounted, he continued to follow at a distance for another half mile. As they turned off on to the open parkland that now bordered the long avenue on either side, he did likewise and, putting his mare into a canter, set off in a wide semi-circle which would presently bring him round face to face with them.

He rode straight at the group until he was within fifty yards of it; then, as though suddenly recognizing Ilona, swept off his hat and swerved his mare away in deference to her approach. But she had already been watching him for some minutes, and now called to him to come to her.

As they halted, barely a yard apart, he thought, as always on seeing her afresh, that there could be no one lovelier. The early morning air had whipped her fresh complexion into milk and roses, and her deep blue eyes were sparkling in the sunshine. But the Baroness Paula was too close at hand for them to exchange a word in private.

Ilona greeted him as though they had not met since they had danced together at the Czernins, and asked how he was enjoying his stay in Vienna. That at least gave him the opportunity of informing her of the progress of his secret plan, as he was able to say that he had been absent from the capital for some days, preparing his castle at Königstein for a party on the 10th and 11th, which His Imperial Highness the Archduke Franz Ferdinand and the Duchess of Hohenberg had consented to honour with their presence.

Having expressed her interest, she asked him if he often rode in the Prater, and when he replied that he did so every morning when in Vienna, she graciously informed him that he might join her party now if he wished, and on any future occasion that he chanced to see it. Then she rode on with the fair little Baroness beside her, while he dropped back beside Adam Grünne.

The dark, square-shouldered Count greeted him in a very friendly fashion, but as soon as the ladies were out of earshot he said, with a worried air: "You know, Duke, I have no wish to interfere in your affairs, but I beg you most earnestly to leave Vienna. Otherwise, this flirtation of yours with the Archduchess can only end in serious trouble."

De Richleau was feeling on the top of his form, and replied with a laugh: "If it were merely a flirtation, my dear Count, I would take your advice. But you are the one man to whom I can freely confess that if I had to leave Vienna, I would leave behind my heart."

"I am sorry to hear that, but it does not affect the fact that sooner or later your secret pursuit of her is bound to be remarked."

"Why should it be, if I use all possible discretion?"

Count Adam's brown eyes were full of foreboding as he answered: "Because she has an impulsive nature and lacks your experience in concealing her thoughts. If she continues to regard your attentions merely as an amusement, you may escape. But the danger is that she may fall in love with you. Should that happen, she is almost certain to commit some folly which will lead to your ruin and disgrace."

For a moment the Duke could find no reply, then he said: "Supposing that our positions were reversed—that you were in my shoes and Fraulein Sárolta was the Archduchess—would you then leave Vienna?"

"You've got me there," grinned the Count. "Of course I shouldn't."

On that the conversation ended, as Ilona had just set off at a gallop, and the rest of them were hard put to it to keep up with her, even for a few hundred yards. The little Baroness soon dropped behind and Count Adam, although better mounted than the Duke, purposely let him get a lead; so that when Ilona reined in near the *Lusthaus* right at the far end of the *Hauptallee*, he was only a length behind her.

Turning in her saddle, she said quickly: "Not to-morrow. Sárolta is indisposed. Come on Saturday." Then the thunder of hooves drowned his swift assent as the others caught up with them.

The *Lusthaus* had once been an Imperial hunting lodge, but was now a café, and at it the two ladies drank glasses of milk while still seated in their saddles. Then the party cantered back along a ride parallel with the avenue, to the place where the carriage was waiting. There, with a few polite words, Ilona dismissed the Duke, and he watched her drive away until she was out of sight.

That day and the next he spent in a fever of activity, making a hundred preparations for the party. Frau Sacher helped him with the menus, and promised that her own chefs should provide a score of special dishes; but dozens of different foods had to be ordered elsewhere; also wines, cigars and flowers. He engaged a famous dance band and cars to transport them, bought two hundred pounds worth of fireworks and dispatched half a dozen skilled men to Königstein to start erecting the set pieces; then hired a big pleasure steamer for a water picnic on the Danube, and a stable full of horses for riding. In addition, feeling that the hangings, covers and cushions in some of the rooms badly needed renewing, he bought hundreds of yards of fine materials and had them sent out with seamstresses, to be made up on the spot.

By Friday night he reckoned that at a rough estimate he had committed himself for well over £2,000 to pay for forty hours of entertainment, out of which he would be lucky if he could get Ilona to himself for forty minutes. But he was now madly in love with her, so did not grudge a penny of it.

On Saturday morning he met her with Sárolta and Adam Grünne half-way along the *Hauptallee*. As soon as they were well away from it, among the trees of the park, she beckoned him up to her and sent Sárolta back to ride with Adam. Further than that, she dared not go. Even in the less frequented parts of the Prater there were always a few people about, and everyone knew her by sight; so had she ridden off with de Richleau to any distance from the others, it might have been thought that she was riding alone with him, and started a scandal. But she gave him her most dazzling smile and lowered her voice to ask: "How is my true knight this morning?"

"My sword arm is near to dropping off from the ache in it to kill dragons for you, Princess," he smiled back.

"Alas!" she laughed. "My dragons are all nice old ladies, like the *Grafin* Aulendorf; or old gentlemen who escort me to state functions."

"There will be no state functions when you come to Königstein, and somehow we will get rid of your female dragons for a while, I promise."

She frowned. "My secretary has not yet said a word to me about your party. In fact, I had to tell him only last night to refuse an engagement which was proposed for me for the 11th. When did you submit your list?"

"I posted it from Königstein on Wednesday evening. I could not do so before as I had to find out which of my neighbours were in residence and could put up guests. But it should have reached the Duchess first thing on Thursday morning."

"Oh well, she may have been too busy to deal with it these past two days. No doubt she will ask this week-end if I wish to go. But do tell me about the lovely time you are preparing for us. I can hardly wait to get there, and I think of it not as her party but as ours."

"And so it is, Princess," he assured her with a tender smile. Then he went on to speak of the water-picnic, the fireworks, and the dance that he was planning for her delight. But all too soon the ride was over and when they parted, as he had to return to Königstein that night, it was with the knowledge that they would have no further opportunity of meeting until they did so there on the following Wednesday.

That day he completed his final preparations in Vienna, and in the late afternoon set out for the castle. A number of letters were awaiting him, and among them a big envelope bearing the Imperial arms. On opening it he saw that it was from the Comptroller of the Archduke's Household. Then the blow fell. His list of guests was approved, except that General von Hötzendorf had begged to be excused on the plea of duty, and that the names of Ilona and her suite had been struck out.

Slowly he went white with rage. Then he tore the letter violently across and damned Sophie von Hohenberg to all eternity. The one thing which had occurred neither to Ilona nor himself was that the Chotek might for once allow jealousy to get the better of her tactfulness. It was true that Ilona, being of the Imperial blood, took precedence over her; but at a private party such as this, and one announced as in her special honour, there could be no question of her being relegated to the background. Yet jealousy seemed the only reason which could be attributed to the act; and it was one of extreme rudeness. If she felt so strongly about the matter, she could at least have done her host the courtesy of having a private word with him on it, but to have simply struck out Ilona's name was not only discourteous to him, it implied that she, of all people, was not the type of woman who could be received in polite society.

De Richleau could only suppose that the Duchess was counting on Ilona never getting to hear of the flagrant insult that had been done her. He smiled grimly at the thought that here was a case of heredity coming out, and that, though she could not know it, through her ill-breeding the Chotek had made an enemy for life. But that was no consolation whatever to him.

Seething with anger and disgust, he made a moody tour of inspection round the castle. Much had been done in his three days' absence, but innumerable things still remained to be done if the place was to be in apple-pie order by Wednesday. The thought of the money he had wasted aggravated his fury, but even that was a bagatelle compared with the bitter, searing disappointment which tore his heart at the realization that he was not, after all, to have his beautiful Ilona under his own roof for two days and nights.

He spent a long time in the bedroom that was being made ready for her. The hangings he had bought for it were nearly finished: they were of blue satin to match her eyes, and had gold cupids and true lover's-knots embroidered on them. The mattress of the bed he had chosen and tested himself as the softest in the castle. The sheets were of the finest lawn, and the pillows of finest swansdown. With his slim fingers he caressed them for a moment, and tears dimmed his bright grey eyes. Turning hastily away, he caught sight of his reflection in the long gilt cheval glass. She would have gazed into that, perhaps to put a last chestnut curl into place and admire her own perfection, before coming down to dine at his side. Then his glance fell upon a shallow alcove, in which stood a high-backed elbow chair. Behind it a panel, painted the same colour as the rest of the wall, could be slid back to reveal a low oak door. Beyond the door was a little stone balcony, from one side of which a narrow spiral of steps led down to the main terrace twenty feet below. The previous Sunday night he had oiled the lock, bolts and hinges of the door, so that it could be opened without a sound. After the dance, when everyone had gone to bed, he had hoped—Shutting his eyes, he clenched his teeth, and stood rigid in an agony of frustration. At length his breath escaped in a gasp and, wheeling round, he flung himself out of the room.

Eventually he went to bed, but proper sleep refused to come to him, and when he fell into a doze he was beset by horrid visions of Ilona in tears and the Chotek leering at him. At five o'clock he got up and, after a bath, into which he poured a quarter of a bottle of Lubin's fragrant essence, he felt a little more rational-minded, though no less bitter.

At six, he summoned his head servants and gave them fresh instructions as, although the thought of the party was now as ashes in his mouth, there could be no question of cancelling it, and the preparations must go on. Then, after toying with his breakfast, in spite of the fact that he was now needed there to supervise many arrangements in person, he left for Vienna.

De Richleau was not the man to 'say die' lightly, and he had determined to see the Duchess on the chance that he could persuade her to alter her mind. But when he arrived at the Belvedere Palace he found, to his renewed fury, that his luck had completely deserted him. The Chotek had gone away the previous morning for the week-end, and was not expected back until Monday afternoon.

He had eaten little and drunk next to nothing for the past twenty-four hours, yet he felt as sick and ill as if he had been participating in a drunken orgy for a week. Instinctively he walked back across The Ring to Sacher's. There he went up to his room, sat on his bed for a while, then rang for the waiter and ordered a double Absinthe. When it arrived, he added sugar and water and slowly drank the opal fluid. It had no more perceptible kick in it than lime juice, or a diluted paregoric cough mixture which it resembled in flavour, but he knew it held hidden properties which would act like a drug in clearing and accelerating his brain.

A quarter of an hour later, he moved over to the window table and began to write a letter to the Chotek. It was no more than a last hope, for he dared not even hint in it, as he could have done to her personally, his own desire that Ilona should be asked to Königstein: moreover, he dare not presume too far on the idea that the Duchess regarded him as her adviser. But after three drafts, he produced the following:

Your Highness,

I trust you will pardon my temerity, but I note with some disquiet that you have thought fit to delete the name of H.I.H. the Archduchess Ilona Theresa from the list of guests for your Highness' party at Königstein.

Your reasons for so doing are beyond my knowledge and, no doubt, most excellent. But, after much hesitation, I bring myself to point out to your Highness that the Archduchess' presence at your party could redound only to your own prestige—particularly with Count Tisza, who is to be among your guests.

I was fortunate enough to have a long and very friendly conversation with the Count after making my adieus to your Highness on Friday, the 29th, and it was mainly on account of my earlier talk with you that I included both him and H.I.H. in the proposed list.

I must add that my uneasiness is made the greater from having chanced to meet H.I.H. in the Prater while riding there on Saturday morning and, I pray that you will forgive me, as I was indiscreet enough to mention the fête to her; upon which she was so gracious as to say that she hoped to hear further from your Highness regarding it.

I need hardly add that I would not presume to offer these points for your consideration were I not emboldened to do so by a heartfelt desire to further your Highness' interests.

I have the honour to be, etc. etc."

Having concluded with this flat lie, he damned the woman to perdition again, sealed up the envelope, and took it across to the Belvedere himself. Then he returned to Königstein.

Monday and Tuesday the endless bustle at the castle continued. A stream of vans and wagons arrived from the surrounding district and from Vienna. Endless boxes and hampers were unpacked. Innumerable people did innumerable jobs above and below stairs, in the stables, on the river front, and in the grounds. Through this human ants' nest the Duke moved ceaselessly, like an uneasy but all-seeing ghost. He had no idea what the Chotek's reactions would be to his letter. In any case she could not have had it till Monday afternoon and by then, even if she changed her mind, Ilona might have become committed to other engagements. He knew that she would keep herself free till the last possible moment if she could, but it would not be easy for anyone in her position to refuse all duties for two days without any suitable excuse to offer.

On Tuesday evening the Countess Prava arrived with her two daughters. At dinner that night the Duke endeavoured to be a cheerful host, but excused himself soon afterwards on the plea that he still had things to see to.

On Wednesday at mid-day, accompanied by the Countess, he made a final inspection. The pandemonium of the preceding days had subsided as though it had never occurred. Except for the powdered and breeched footmen on duty in the hall, not a servant was to be seen. The June sunshine shone through the open mullioned windows on speckless rooms, kept at a comfortable temperature by small log fires, and gay with flowers. Afterwards, they went out on to the terrace. It ran along the south wall of the castle, which had been rebuilt late in the eighteenth century and contained rooms of fine proportions. From it, there was a splendid view along the Danube, which flowed a hundred feet below them. Anchored near the far shores of the river were the boats and barges from which the display of fireworks was to be given that night. It seemed that nothing had been left unthought of, and the Duke sent for his principal servants to thank them for their labours. Now, it only remained to be seen if the lady of his heart, for whom all this had been done, would ever set eyes upon it.

At four o'clock the guests began to arrive, and for the next hour or two de Richleau was kept busy with their reception. By six they were all mustered in the great hall, awaiting the appearance of the Imperial party. Punctually, almost to the moment, the line of cars rolled into the courtyard and disgorged their occupants in front of the great double doors. Outside them stood the Duke, holding a blue velvet cushion on which reposed the keys of the castle. In accordance with ancient custom, he offered them to Franz Ferdinand, who touched them lightly, then, with a friendly smile, bade him keep them.

Swiftly de Richleau's glance took in the dozen people who had arrived with the Archduke. He suppressed a sigh that was like a pain piercing his middle. The absence of the lovely face of Ilona Theresa among them made the sun go dim for him. Up to the very last minute he had been hoping against hope that she would arrive with her cousin, although reason had told him plainly that had she been coming at all he would have been notified of it officially, at latest by that morning. Only now that his last hope was gone did he taste to the full the bitterness of his disappointment and realize how desperately he loved her.

Yet with him it was one of the principles of a lifetime that a host should not mar the enjoyment of his guests by allowing them even to suspect that he was a prey to personal troubles, and years of self-discipline now stood him in good stead. As though he had not a care in the world, he smilingly welcomed the rest of the Imperial party, and ushered them in to partake of the refreshments set out in the great hall.

Soon after seven the two dozen people who now made up the house-party went to their rooms to change. At eight-thirty they assembled in the hall again, and at a quarter to nine went in to dinner. According to the custom of the day, on such occasions, the meal was a long one: fifteen courses were served and a different wine with each, so it was half past ten before they rose from the table. Other guests who were staying in the neighbourhood now began to arrive, and at eleven o'clock they all went out on to the terrace to see the fireworks.

The night was fine; the display brilliant and unmarred by accidents. Between intervals of darkness Greek fire lit a long stretch of the Danube, turning it to red, green and blue; big catherine wheels spun upon the barges moored in the river; rockets sent showers of stars higher than the topmost turrets of the castle; and the finale was a set-piece consisting of an outline portrait of the Duchess, having underneath it the words 'Long live the future Queen of Hungary'.

The Chotek was enchanted, and as the last sparks spluttered out she thanked her host effusively. Then, rising from her chair, she laid her plump hand on his arm and led him a little apart from the others towards the end of the terrace. When they were out of earshot she said:

"This is the first chance I have had for a word with you alone, Duke, and I have been wanting to talk to you about your letter."

He could cheerfully have picked her up and thrown her over the battlements, but his smile lost none of its urbanity as he murmured, "I beg you not to give it another thought. It was an impertinence on my part to even question your judgment on such a matter."

"On the contrary," she replied quickly. "You were quite right, and I was a fool not to see in the first place that Ilona Theresa's presence here would strengthen my position with Count Tisza. It was stupid of me to allow the slights which the Imperial family have put upon me to influence me in a case like this."

De Richleau looked down at her in surprise. "May I ask, then, why you did not take the advice contained in my letter?"

"I did, and covered my *faux pas* in a note that I wrote her on Monday night. In it I said I had only just learned that my secretary had been guilty of mislaying the original notification of the party, which should have reached her the previous week. But on the Tuesday I received a reply to the effect that she is committed to appear to-night at a charity ball, and to-morrow at a public luncheon; and that, much as she would have liked to come with us to Königstein, it was now too late to alter her arrangements."

Silently but fluently the Duke cursed in seven languages, both the woman beside him and Ilona's ingrained sense of duty. Then his heart gave such a jump that it seemed to hit him under the throat; for, after a little pause, the Duchess added: "However, she is going to join us here in time for the dance, and that is better than nothing."

Her last words could not have better expressed de Richleau's feelings. An evil fate had denied him the joy of having Ilona there for much the greater part of what was secretly to have been their own party, but at least he had been reprieved to the extent that she would be present at its finale, and by comparison with 'nothing' that now seemed 'everything'. His step was no more buoyant, but his heart was high as he led the Chotek back through the french windows into the drawing-room.

As some of the guests had driven a considerable distance, a buffet supper was now being served, and for an hour or more the Duke moved about, having a few words with everyone in turn. Then Franz Ferdinand went up to bed and the party gradually broke up.

Next morning de Richleau woke to find to his annoyance that it was raining. The change in the weather threatened to spoil his water-party, and might make it impossible for couples to stroll on the terrace, or in the grounds, during the dance. But the knowledge that, wet or fine, he would see Ilona that evening did far more than console him for this minor worry.

In those days breakfast was taken in bed only by women and invalids, so all the men of the party assembled downstairs for it fully dressed. Normally they would have gone shooting, fishing or riding, according to the season; but as the weather was inclement they decided to stay indoors. Four made up a table for bridge, two sat down to write letters, and the rest—Franz Ferdinand, Count Hoyos and the Duke among them—congregated in the library.

The Archduke took the opportunity of asking de Richleau his opinion of the Turkish Army, and after they had talked of it for some time the conversation turned to the amazing war machine that Germany had built up during the reign of Wilhelm II. It was clear to the Duke that the Austrians greatly envied their powerful neighbour the possession of this mighty weapon with which, had they controlled it, they obviously believed that they could have settled their long-standing differences with Russia, Italy, Serbia and Rumania at one stroke. It emerged that in the coming week Franz Ferdinand was going to his country estate of Konopischt, where he would be entertaining the Kaiser for a three-days' visit, and Count Hoyos took occasion to remark on the high hopes his chief, von Berchtold, held that this meeting would further strengthen the Austro-German alliance.

About eleven the rain stopped and the ladies began to appear, so several small parties drifted off for a walk in the grounds. As the Duchess had not come down, and Franz Ferdinand intimated that he wished to have a private talk with his aide-de-camp, Count Harrach, de Richleau found himself free to show his books to Count Tisza; who, up till then, had been writing letters. The Duke's library was very fine, having been mainly inherited through many generations of ancestors and removed from France after his exile from that country; but in individual items having historical associations with famous people it did not rival that of the Count. Nevertheless, they spent a happy hour there and cemented their strong liking for one another.

On her belated appearance the Duchess found them poring over a rare hand-coloured sixteenth-century Atlas together, and once more both men had to admire her tact. Instead of turning the conversation to other matters, she at once displayed an intelligent interest in old books and asked to be shown some more of de Richleau's rare editions. Bitter as he had secretly felt towards her on the preceding day, now that he was in a more normal frame of mind, he freely admitted to himself that her disruption of his plans had been in no way deliberate, and that she was really a kind and charming woman. So he no longer harboured any malice towards her, and the three of them remained talking together happily until it was time to go in for luncheon.

After the meal they all walked down through the terraced garden leading to the river and boarded a small flag-bedecked steamer that was waiting there. Turning up-stream, the steamer carried them to the nearest village, where the population for some miles around, which was lining the banks, gave the Imperial party a rousing reception. De Richleau had arranged an aquatic carnival, and during the afternoon they watched a variety of events—swimming, diving, life-saving, boat races, wrestling on rafts and climbing a greasy pole for a live sucking pig. After a tea with strawberries and cream, the Duchess gave away the prizes which de Richleau had provided, and 'Father Danube' came aboard attended by twelve Danube Maidens who laid at her feet a large copy of St. Stephen's crown with the leaning cross of Hungary, which had been woven in basket-work and covered with flowers.

When, to a thunder of renewed cheers, the steamer turned down-stream on her way back to the castle landing stage, de Richleau was happy to think that he had given his tenants and their neighbours, as well as his guests, a happy afternoon. All the same, he wished that it had been possible to terminate the water-party earlier, as it was now a quarter to six, and he feared that Ilona would arrive before he could get back to welcome her.

As a precaution against such a possibility the Countess Prava had remained behind to do the honours of the castle, and when they got back the Duke learned that Ilona was already upstairs in her suite; so he did not see her until the party assembled to go in to dinner.

But, before that, he had more than verbal assurance of her presence. On going up to change he found a large wooden box on his dressing-table. When he opened it he saw at once that the size of the package was designed only to deceive whoever had placed it there about its contents, as buried in a mass of tissue paper it held a single white gardenia for his buttonhole.

On this night Ilona wore white chiffon spangled with gold stars. From her tightly corseted waist it curved outward in layer after layer of filmy material like a ballet dancer's skirts which had been lengthened to sweep the floor. For jewels she wore only white diamonds so her sole colouring lay in her eyes, skin and hair. De Richleau caught his breath when he saw her. She looked light as a fairy from the top of a Christmas tree, yet pulsing with warm life.

The inevitable formal courtesies were exchanged, then her cousin took her into dinner: de Richleau followed with the Chotek, but at table had Ilona on his other side. Without ever allowing their eyes to meet they exchanged inconsequent small talk while the long procession of courses was served to them. At length Ilona caught the Duchess's eye; they rose together and the ladies left the table. Soon after, the Duke excused himself to receive his guests who were driving over from houses in the neighbourhood. At half past ten the band struck up and the dance began.

Franz Ferdinand opened it with Ilona, then de Richleau led out the Duchess, and the rest joined in. By right of his position as host the Duke had the next dance with Ilona, and he had arranged for it to be the 'Blue Danube' waltz.

As she melted into his arms and they whirled gracefully away, he whispered. "At last! At last! Until I heard last night that you were coming after all, I near died of misery."

"And I," she whispered back. "Just think what it meant, having to perform public duties yesterday and to-day instead of being here for our party. I could kill that woman."

"Forget her," he smiled. "You are here now, and that is all that matters. For the flower you sent me, I kiss your hands; and when it is dead I mean to keep it in a jewelled casket as long as I live."

The high notes of the waltz seemed to lift them with every turn, as though they were revolving above a sea of fleecy clouds. Now that he held her again, he was so intoxicated by her nearness that he could think of nothing more to say. She, too, remained silent, her eyes wide and brilliant as she swayed to the lilt of the music. In perfect accord they spun as though one being in circle after circle round the floor; and it was only at the end of the dance that he got back his wits sufficiently to mutter:

"May I, to-night, dance with you again?"

"Yes," she breathed. "As my host, you may."

"And now," he said quickly, "can we go out on to the terrace, or must we remain here?"

"You may take me out for a minute—just for a breath of air."

With her hand on his arm he led her to the open french windows, but there they halted in dismay: it had begun to rain again and was coming down quite heavily.

For five minutes they stood there, but other couples were so near them that they could only exchange platitudes. Then, when the band struck up again, she gave him a pathetic little smile and beckoned to Adam Grünne to come and dance with her.

De Richleau took advantage of his position to dance twice more with the Chotek, so that comment should not be aroused when he danced with Ilona a second time. But it was after supper before she asked him to have the band play the 'Count of Luxembourg' waltz and dance it with her.

This time he had all his wits about him. When they were well out on the floor he told her about the alcove in her bedroom, and how to slide the partition back so that the door it concealed would be revealed and could be opened.

She stiffened in his arms and turned her blue eyes up to his in a frightened glance.

"You do not mean—" she whispered. "You—you cannot mean——"

He smiled down at her. "Princess, I am de Richleau, Duke and Hereditary Peer of France, Lieutenant-General, Count von Königstein, and Knight of the Golden Fleece. Unless tradition lies, it would not be the first time that one of my line has been received by a beautiful Habsburg in her bedroom. But you are unmarried, and I love you too much to ask more than that you should leave your room to meet me for a few minutes on the balcony that lies outside the hidden door."

Ilona closed her eyes and her breath came in a little gasp as she murmured: "I am feeling faint. Take me somewhere where I can sit down."

Obediently he led her out of the ballroom, to the almost deserted buffet and, having settled her in an elbow chair, brought her a glass of champagne.

After a few sips she looked up at him. Her face was very white but her voice steady as she said: "Very well. We have missed so much to-day and yesterday, and our opportunities of being together are so few that I will grant what you ask. At what hour do you wish me to meet you?"

His grey eyes held hers. "It is after two already. I shall stop the band at three o'clock. Give me half an hour to get rid of our guests. I will be outside the door at half past three."

She nodded. The band had stopped. When she had finished her champagne, he took her back to the ballroom. For a few minutes they talked to Count Harrach, then as the music began again she asked the Count to dance with her.

At a quarter to three de Richleau prepared to end the party with ruthless efficiency. He had the band play a gallop as a prelude to the finale and ordered them to play the National Anthem at three o'clock precisely. Then he sent servants out to warn the coachmen and chauffeurs to be ready to take the departing guests home, told others to have their wraps ready in the great hall, and his steward to have half the candles put out as soon as the Archduke had retired.

No one except Ilona guessed how well affairs had been stage-managed, as the dance seemed to end perfectly naturally. But by twenty past three no one, except the servants who were clearing up, remained downstairs. When de Richleau had seen off his last guests he gave a quick look round and slipped out on to the terrace.

To his acute distress he found that the spatter of rain had now increased to a steady downpour. Up on that little balcony outside Ilona's room there was not an inch of cover for them; yet it was his fixed determination in no circumstances to enter her apartments. He had hoped for half an hour with her. That was to have been for him the high spot of all that had gone before. He had parted with £2,400, and been to infinite pains to achieve this stolen meeting; yet now the accursed weather must reduce it to a few moments and a mere good-night.

With quick light steps he ran through the sheeting rain, along the terrace and up the spiral steps that led to the balcony. He felt certain that she would not disappoint him, but all the joyous anticipation he would normally have felt was turned by the wet to bitter frustration. With his back against the stone wall he waited.

He had been there no more than five minutes when a crack of light appeared and the door swung open revealing Ilona. She was still in her ball dress of filmy white, but now wore over it a long cloak with a hood which almost concealed it. Stepping quickly out into the rain, she pulled the door to behind her.

"Princess," he murmured sadly. "We have had the most devilish luck. Even the weather is against us. I dare not detain you for more than a moment or you will be soaked to the skin."

She smiled at him. "Have you forgotten that I like the rain. I don't mind a bit about getting wet."

Trembling a little, he took a step forward and held out his hands; but she did not take them. Instead, she raised her arms and flung them round his neck.

Her soft lips were warm, moist and passionate, as she pressed them against his and clung to him with all her strength. Then, throwing back her head and gazing up into his eyes, she cried:

"Oh, Armand! Armand! I love you! I love you terribly. So much that I could die of it."

CHAPTER XIV

AN ILL-TIMED HONOUR

It was the afternoon following the dance. All the guests had left that morning, so de Richleau was now alone in the castle except for his servants. The sun was shining again and he stood once more on the little balcony where, twelve hours before, he had held Ilona in his arms. Like some poor couple in the back streets of a city, who had nowhere else to go, they had remained there, clinging together in an angle of the wall, while the rain trickled down their faces on to their sodden garments until they had gradually become soaked through. It now seemed to the Duke as if hardly twenty minutes had elapsed between his going up to the balcony in a sad state of dejection and coming down from it as though he were treading on air: but, in fact, nearly two hours had passed, for Ilona had not left him until the full light of the summer dawn had made it dangerous for her to linger there any longer.

He could remember practically nothing that either of them had said. Oblivious of their bedraggled state, they had not once relaxed their embrace, but gone on kissing, and kissing and kissing; with breath enough left between whiles only to murmur those sweet endearments that lovers have used through all the ages. He realized now that Ilona's sudden surrender must have been brought about by the same feelings that had harassed him so terribly during the past few days. Her disappointment had equalled his at the Chotek's unintentional ruining of their plan for spending two days together, and she had been through the additional ordeal of having to appear happy at public functions when she had hoped to be at Königstein. No doubt she had not even visualized what might occur between them there, but frustration had so preyed upon her mind that when, after all, fate had permitted the longed-for meeting the strength of her emotions had broken down all barriers.

They had made no plans: there were none they could make. He would see her the following night, at her birthday ball; but after that when, if ever, they would meet again lay on the knees of the gods. To-day was Friday, June the 12th, and on Monday night he must leave Vienna for Belgrade. He had meant to break the news of his coming departure to her during her visit to Königstein, but that had been so curtailed that he had not had the heart to do so during dinner or the dance, and later it had been out of the question. Now it was going to be harder than ever. He could not possibly tell her the truth and, within a few days of her having declared her love for him, to say that any matter of business necessitated his leaving her would appear unbelievably callous. Trained as she was to put duty before all else, he felt that he could best soften the blow by saying that he had been summoned to Constantinople to clear up certain questions in connection with the Turkish military appointment he had held, and promise to be back as soon as he possibly could.

But would he be able to get back once he had taken up his duties as a Lieutenant-General in the Serbian Army? If he could succeed in foiling Dimitriyevitch's plans for provoking a war, all might yet be well. If not, the probability was that he would be caught in Serbia when the war opened. He could, of course, desert and, since he was entering the Serbian Army only as the secret agent of Britain, he felt no scruples at the thought of doing so. But by that time, if he made his way back to Vienna, what would be his position there? The odds were that all Europe would by then be in flames and he, as an Englishman, be ranged among Austria's enemies.

It was difficult, almost impossible, to realize that perhaps in as little as ten days, if Dimitriyevitch's evil coup succeeded, the fighting would have started and he, de Richleau, be an enemy of the country which meant so much to him. When he was exiled from France it had been a toss-up whether he became an Austrian or an Englishman. He had a title and this fine estate in Austria, and not even a permanent home in England. He loved the Austrians, too, for their gaiety, culture and graceful way of life. Yet he had become an Englishman because he believed that on the British had fallen the spiritual mantle of Imperial Rome. The two Empires had been built on the same traditions of justice, tolerance, and freedom for all their peoples, irrespective of race or creed; and he believed in these things.

Only a dozen years earlier France had expelled the Chartreuse Fathers and seized their property. In Russia politicals were still sent without trial to Siberia and Jews knouted to death. Germany regimented her whole people. Italy was a sink of corruption. Austria repressed her Serbs and Croats; Hungary her Rumanians. The British alone seemed to possess the secret of gaining strength through liberty, and by a steady, ordered progress uniting the 500,000,000 people over whom they ruled by common interests that made for the prosperity and security of them all. Their example had already done an incalculable amount to influence other nations in the same direction, so it had seemed a sane and reasonable hope that within a few more generations tyranny and oppression would be expurgated from the world. De Richleau had thought that he might live to see that, but now, if Britain were to be drawn into a conflict against the Central Empires, and her championship of individual liberty jeopardized, then, for the very reason he had become a British citizen he must, if need be, spill Austrian blood.

With a sigh he descended to the terrace and began to make his own preparations for returning to Vienna. He cast a last look round the gracious rooms, wondering how they would look if, and when, he saw them again. It did not even enter his mind that the castle might be sequestered and his property stolen or damaged by the Austrians. They were much too civilized and chivalrous to indulge in petty spite against an individual because he happened to be fighting on the other side; but if the Russians invaded they were quite capable of looting it; or it might be partially destroyed through some hazard of war. He made a mental note to write later on to his second cousin, the Grand Duke Nicholas, and request that, in the event of the Russian armies approaching Königstein, special steps should be taken to protect the people on his estate from brutal treatment, and his property from pilfering. Then having once more thanked his steward and left a considerable sum of money to be distributed among the servants, he set off for the capital.

Next morning, when he awoke in his bedroom at Sacher's, his mind began to revolve round the sort of present he could give Ilona for her birthday. It had to be something small, which could be pressed into her hand when they danced together that night, as it was contrary to etiquette for royalty to accept personal presents from anyone outside their own families. On the contrary, it was their practice to give presents to others in the form of honours, decorations and pensions. Of this de Richleau was soon to have embarrassing evidence.

The whistle in the stopper of the speaking tube beside his bed piped gently and, when he answered it, the hall porter informed him that Captain Count Adam Grünne was below, asking to see him urgently.

It was not yet half past seven, but de Richleau asked that his visitor should be sent up. Then, getting out of bed, he put on a dressing-gown and went into the sitting-room to receive him.

The dapper Count Adam was as spick and span as ever, but he did not return the Duke's cheerful greeting. Instead, he bowed formally and, holding out a thick envelope eighteen inches wide by a foot deep, said:

"I pray your Excellency to excuse the unusual hour of my visit, but I was commanded by Her Imperial Highness to give you this without delay."

Returning his formal bow, de Richleau broke the seals of the huge crested envelope and took out the parchment it contained. Under the Imperial arms the following was set out in copperplate:

"*By these presents I, Ilona Theresa*" etc. etc., "*do hereby commission and appoint my good and loyal servant Count Königstein,*" etc. etc., "*to hold the honorary rank of Colonel in my own Regiment of Hussars.*"

"Good God!" exclaimed the Duke.

"There is more to it," said Count Adam grimly. "I am further commanded by Her Imperial Highness to order you to have the dress uniform of this rank in her regiment made to-day, and to appear in it to-night at her birthday ball."

"But this is absolute madness! It must be stopped at once."

Adam Grünne abandoned his formal attitude and made a grimace as he sat himself down on the arm of the sofa. "My friend, I wish to Heaven it could be; but it is too late. The appointment was made yesterday and will appear in this morning's *Gazette*. All Vienna that has an interest in such matters will read of it over their coffee and rolls within the next few hours."

"Could you not prevent her committing this folly?"

"I knew nothing of it till half an hour ago, when I reported for duty and Sárolta brought me out the commission and message for you."

De Richleau stared at the document and, seeing Ilona's rounded scrawl against the red, beribboned seal at its foot, said quickly; "Surely all commissions in the Imperial Army must be signed by the Emperor and the *Gazette* will not publish anything that has not first received his approval?"

"In this case it is unnecessary. The Archduchess has an absolute right to give anyone she likes a commission in her own regiment."

"Then we are in the very devil of a mess."

"I fear you are. To-night all eyes will be riveted on you and her; and I shall be surprised if you do not receive an order to quit Vienna as soon as it can be conveyed to you without giving additional point to this excellent basis for starting a scandal."

The Duke gave a rather twisted smile. He had to leave Vienna in any case on Monday. It seemed mean to take advantage of Ilona's generosity as an excuse for doing so; yet it would make her less unhappy to think that he had left in order to protect her from the results of her own rashness, rather than for any other reason: so he said:

"Then I shall forestall any such unpleasantness by leaving of my own free will."

"You could hardly do better as far as saving her name is concerned," Adam Grünne agreed with a friendly smile of appreciation. "But not until to-morrow or Monday. You must appear to-night to kiss hands on your appointment and ask leave of absence; otherwise your going will look like an insult and cause more tongues to wag than ever."

De Richleau was very glad that the stalwart little Count viewed matters so. Only to save Ilona from open disgrace could he have brought himself to leave Vienna without saying good-bye to her; and Grünne's opinion tallied with his own. Refolding the parchment that she had so impetuously ordered to be made out in a natural but ill-considered wish to do public honour to her lover, he observed:

"Your prediction has come true only too soon, Count. But I trust you do not think too ill of me for not having taken your advice to leave Vienna ten days ago."

"In the circumstances you would hardly have been human if you had. Still, it is to be regretted for both your sakes that the affair should have gone so far. What occurred between you at the dance on Thursday night is no business of mine: but she was in the deuce of a state all yesterday. She couldn't sit still for two minutes, and coughed herself sick with excitement. Last night she was running a temperature again, and Sárolta says that if her doctor saw her he would not allow her to get up to-day. But, of course, she has forbidden anyone to send for him, and wild horses won't prevent her appearing at the ball to-night."

"What you say makes me feel very guilty," said the Duke with grave concern.

Count Adam shrugged his broad shoulders. "If it had not been you, my friend, it would have been someone else. I only marvel that she has not fallen a victim to this universal complaint before. But about your uniform; how soon can you be ready to accompany me to the regimental tailors? They will do the job somehow, of course; but it is going to be the very devil of a rush, and you will have to hold yourself at their disposal for a couple of fittings this afternoon."

Walking over to the speaking tube, the Duke blew down it and ordered coffee, rolls and fruit for two. Then he said, "I'll go and bath at once. Please help yourself when breakfast arrives, and I'll join you as soon as I can. I shall be ready to leave in three quarters of an hour."

De Richleau spent most of the day at the tailors. They almost made the uniform on him; but in an interval between fittings he managed to find a heart-shaped ruby. It was quite small, but that was immaterial as Ilona had finer jewels than Rockefeller could have bought her, and its appropriateness as a gift lay in its unusual shape.

At half past eight he left Sacher's, resplendent in sky-blue and silver, with the loose sleeve of the astrakhan-trimmed half cloak swaying gallantly behind him as he walked, and his chest glittering with his orders and decorations. A quarter of an hour later a taxi, which had carried him along the *Link Wienzeile* into Vienna's south-western suburbs, set him down before the Schönbrunn Palace.

Its great courtyard was full of equipages and running footmen. Inside, its marble halls, staircases and salons were crowded with hundreds of guests: officers in an immense variety of uniforms; diplomats wearing black silk breeches, white stockings and cordons of every colour; Hungarian magnates whose costumes were trimmed with sea otter, ermine and sable; and bare-shouldered women of all ages, whose tiaras, necklaces, pendants, rings, ear-rings, brooches and bracelets would together have stocked for twenty years every jeweller's shop in the Rue de la Paix. For the last time, although they could not know it, the noblest blood, the finest brains, with all the wealth, gallantry and beauty of an ancient Empire, had gathered there in their splendour to do honour to a daughter of the Imperial House of Habsburg.

Slowly, through a sea of nodding plumes, rustling satin, and glittering epaulets, the Duke made his way across the long range of lofty salons at the back of the palace to the Throne room. At the far end of it, on a low dais, Ilona was seated in a great gilt chair, the back of which rose to frame her face with the spreading wings of the double-headed Habsburg eagle. To her right, on a similar chair, sat her cousin, Franz Ferdinand; and on her left, another cousin, the young Archduke Charles. De Richleau solemnly made his three bows to them; then, as the line moved on, passed into the next salon. He could not but be a little awed at the thought that the very apex of all this power and glory was a young and beautiful woman who had declared her love for him. But he was much concerned by her appearance as the light dusting of powder, which was all the make-up considered permissible at that date, did not disguise the fact that she was far from well.

Already a number of people had congratulated him on the birthday honour he had received, and now he ran into Sophie von Hohenberg. As a morganatic wife she had no special precedence at official functions, so had to appear as an ordinary guest.

"Well, well, my dear *Colonel*!" she greeted him with a cynical little smile. "How handsome you look in your new uniform."

"I thank your Highness," he smiled back, offering her his arm as she dismissed her previous cavalier.

"And now, of course," she went on in a low voice, "the real reason for your anxiety to have Ilona Theresa at Königstein is revealed. I must confess that you tricked me very cleverly."

He raised his dark 'devil's' eyebrows. "I fear I fail to understand."

"Oh come! You cannot pull the wool over my eyes. That little minx is in love with you, and you with her. I had a suspicion that she was more than ordinarily interested in you when I saw you waltzing together at the Czernins' dance but, knowing her reputation for frigidity, dismissed it as unlikely."

"Then I pray your Highness to dismiss the idea again, for it has not one atom of foundation."

"Why this appointment, then? It can only be so that, as a Colonel of her regiment, you can gain ready access to her without the usual formalities."

That aspect of the matter had not even occurred to the Duke, and he said so. Then he went on, "You are right, though, in assuming that it was her visit to Königstein which led to my appointment; although I had no thought of it before that. It chanced that during the two dances we had together there we talked of my campaign in the Balkans. She remarked then that the Austrian army was second to none in appearance, but had no experience of war: and that as far as her own regiment was concerned she thought it would be a good thing if they had someone like myself who could advise on modern training. She was right, of course, and I naturally agreed with her. Without consulting me further, it seems that she took my agreement for consent to undertake the work. But no one could have been more surprised that I was when I received her commission this morning."

The explanation was a good one; although the Duchess murmured a little doubtfully, "I had no idea that Ilona interested herself in military matters," he felt that he had shaken her; so he added casually:

"As a matter of fact, though, she has picked on the wrong man at the moment; as I have to leave Vienna to-morrow, and shall be detained for some time in Constantinople on important business."

The Duchess shrugged. "Ah well, perhaps I was wrong. In your case it certainly seems so. All the same, I suspect she is going to be a very disappointed young woman when she hears that her handsome new Colonel is not remaining here to dance attendance on her."

The ball was now opening with a quadrille. Franz Ferdinand led out Ilona and other couples followed in order of precedence, while the great bulk of the brilliant throng lined the walls to watch the formal measure. A waltz came next and de Richleau danced it with the Duchess; then he took up a position not far from the dais, where Ilona could easily send for him when she wished. Half an hour later she sent her equerry to him, and in another waltz they took the floor together.

Now that he was close to her, he was more alarmed than ever by the hectic flush of her cheeks and unnatural glitter of her eyes. They had hardly completed their first graceful whirl, when she said unhappily:

"Oh Armand! I have acted like a fool again."

"My dear," he murmured, "please do not blame yourself for your generous impulse. I was touched to the heart by it."

She was almost crying. "I did it because the temptation to give you some honour was too strong for me; and I chose this, thinking myself so clever, because it would also give you an excuse to be able to visit me at any time. But now Sárolta and Adam tell me that all Vienna will be talking about us, and this afternoon I received a request from the Emperor for my reasons for making such an appointment."

"Have you given one?" he asked quickly.

"Not yet. I can think of nothing to say, except that I have formed a liking for you; and that will lead him to suspect the truth."

"That, we must prevent at all costs: and I fear it is going to cost us very dear," he sighed. Then he told her of the explanation that he had given the Chotek, which would also serve for the Emperor, and of his intention to kill rumour by leaving Vienna next day.

She faltered in her step, clutched at him, and exclaimed: "No, Armand! No!"

Before he could reply she was seized with a violent fit of coughing. As they were near the side of the room, he led her from among the dancers without difficulty, and by raising her big ostrich feather fan she concealed her convulsed face from all but the people who were standing nearest to them. When the bout had subsided, she said: "Take me to one of the windows for some air."

The night was hot and down one side of the great room a line of French windows stood open, giving access to a hundred-feet long balcony that was as wide as a normal terrace. A few couples were drifting in and out and strolling along it, but he did not dare to take her outside as he knew that scores of people must be watching them, and that their disappearance for even a few moments would now be certain to set malicious tongues wagging. On their approaching the nearest window, the people about it had respectfully drawn back, and as he halted with her in its entrance no one was within earshot.

"Armand," she said in a low voice. "You must not go away. I could not bear it."

Fearing that if he even looked at her their expressions might disclose the intensity of their emotions, he stared straight in front of him across the balustrade into the gardens. Beyond the great open space below them with its eight lawns patterned by flower beds, the pleached alleys, laid out with such skill by a famous eighteenth century gardener, were gay with chains of fairy lamps. In the star-lit distance beyond the Neptune fountain rose the graceful colonnade of the Gloriette and the tall trees of the park. The strains of the 'Merry Widow' waltz came to them from within, mellowed by the gliding footsteps and the rustling dresses of five hundred dancers.

No lovers could have craved a more perfect setting for romance, but these two, watched as they were by a score of curious eyes, were blind to the beauty of the scene, deaf to the lilt of the waltz, and thinking only of striving to prevent the misery that they felt from showing in their faces.

"Darling, I *must* go," he said dully.

"No, please!" she murmured. "You cannot be so cruel. Everything will be all right if only we are very careful."

"Not now that all Vienna suspects us, my sweet."

"Oh, Armand; you don't understand. You—you have loved lots of other women. But with me it's different. I've never loved anyone before. And I love you so that it hurts. I'll die if I must lose you."

His heart felt as though it were being crushed between two revolving mill-stones, but he could only say: "My sweet Princess, I swear that I have never loved anyone as I love you; and that I would cut off my right hand, if by doing so I could spare you a moment's pain. But the only way now in which I can protect you from scandal is to leave Vienna."

She nodded, but her voice was very near to tears as she pleaded: "But not yet. Not for a few days, at least."

Deceiving her, even partially, about the reason for his departure was hateful to him; but he knew that even had Dimitriyevitch and Sir Pellinore been no more than a part of some awful dream, it would still have been incumbent on him to leave Vienna for her sake, and the sooner the better. So he said:

"I beg you to be brave and face the facts, beloved. If I stayed on we dare not risk a meeting. Even if we were seen riding together in the Prater, a story would now be made of it. And to linger for even twenty-four hours is to risk receiving an order to go. If once that happened, I should be debarred from returning; whereas if I go at once——"

Like a drowning woman she clutched at the straw. "You'll come back, then? Oh, when? When?"

"We must allow time for the air to clear—time enough for it to sink into people's minds that the honour you have done me was not for the reason they thought."

"Be more precise, I beg you."

He considered the matter for a moment without regard to any others, and replied: "If we are not to defeat our own purpose, I ought not to reappear here in less than eight weeks."

"Oh, Armand, no! I cannot wait a whole two months before I see you again. I cannot! Besides, at any time now fresh plans may be started for marrying me off. Go now if you must: but surely you can return to Vienna in secret. You were so bold and clever at Ischl, when you acted the part of a guide. If you really love me, you will think of some other plan like that by which we can at least see one another."

Her words found a ready echo in the Duke's own heart. He had every reason to suppose that within ten days of his arrival in Belgrade he would either have found out Dimitriyevitch's plans and initiated plans to foil them, or, if he had failed, that the mine would have been sprung, leaving him free to get out of Serbia as best he could. He nodded.

"If it is humanly possible, I will do as you suggest. But I beg you, dear love, to be patient for a fortnight."

Ilona's face brightened. "You promise me faithfully then, to be back here by the end of the month?"

The band stopped playing. The dance was over, and he knew that he must take her back to the dais in a few moments. Lowering his voice still further, he said: "I promise. Now hold out your hand as though a button of your glove had come undone, and you wished me to do it up for you."

She did as he asked, and he deftly slipped the little ruby through the opening of the glove into her palm. "That," he whispered with a smile, "is my birthday present to you. It represents my own heart, and I give it to you for ever."

"Thank you, dear Armand," she breathed. "You have mine already."

Five minutes later he had bowed his way backwards from her and once again mingled with the glittering throng. Perturbed as he was about her health, he had had no chance to ask her about it, or urge her again to see her doctor; but her hectic flush and coughing fits were so obviously abnormal that he hoped her family would insist on her doing so while he was away.

That led him to speculate unhappily on what he could say to her on his return, if war had broken out in the meantime and forced them into hostile camps. He was determined to keep his promise to her, even at the risk of being put into an aliens' detention camp until he could escape. But, having kept it, in the worst event, he must somehow get back to England to take his part in the fight. The whole dark future seemed to bristle with so many difficulties and dangers that he tried to force it from his mind, but its awful possibilities insisted on contrasting themselves with this magnificent assembly, in which he was but one of a thousand colourful bubbles that seemed to float and mingle so gracefully to the airs of Schubert, Liszt and Strauss. Soon after he had left Ilona he saw Sophie von Hohenberg again, and she gave him an arch smile. Had he been able to foresee the future he would have shuddered, for in fifteen days she was to die.

He would have left early if he could, but etiquette demanded that he should remain until the Imperial party withdrew. Moreover, having danced with Ilona, prudence demanded that he should also be seen dancing with other ladies, and another three hours elapsed before those walls, that had known so many generations of glory, echoed for the very last time to the Austrian National Anthem played in the presence of the Habsburgs.

He had already given notice in the office at Sacher's that he would be vacating his rooms next day. In the morning he bade good-bye to Frau Sacher, and asked her to have the bulk of his luggage sent to Königstein, as it might be a considerable time before he visited Vienna again. At the station he left one large portmanteau in the cloak-room, against the possibility of his returning in secret; then, with his two remaining suitcases, he boarded the train for Budapest.

The gay and beautiful Hungarian capital had always been a favourite spot with him so, since he had had to leave the city that held his beloved Ilona, he was by no means averse to putting in a night and a day there. He went to the Vaderskürt, where he had previously stayed, and they made him very comfortable. But he did not call upon Count Esterházy, or any of his other Hungarian friends, as to have done so would have necessitated awkward explanations regarding the shortness of his stay. The weather was heavenly, so he spent most of the Monday swimming and sun-bathing then, that night, he caught the train on to Belgrade.

The French manager of the Cosmopolitan was most pleased to see him again and installed him in the same room. Soon afterwards the moustached gentleman with the lemon-coloured boots and the photograph album of local ladies in the near-nude appeared, but was swiftly dismissed. The Duke then wrote a note to Colonel Dimitriyevitch, reporting his arrival, and sent it by hand to the War Office.

Lunch in the hotel was served at mid-day and the main course proved to be goat steaks stewed with olives. De Richleau had often eaten goat in the Balkans and thought it not unpleasant, providing it was tender; but the dish was certainly a change from the food in Vienna. By the time he had finished his meal the town had become very hot, so, no reply having so far come from Dimitriyevitch, he adopted the local summer custom of the siesta, and spent the afternoon in his underclothes, drowsing on his bed.

At four o'clock a porter came up to say that Major Tankosić was below, and would like to see him; so, as soon as he was dressed, de Richleau went down and greeted his old acquaintance of the bald head and bulldog jowl. Tankosić had been sent to welcome him and take him out to the châlet, at which, it transpired, Dimitriyevitch wished them both to dine and stay the night. So, directly the Duke had repacked a bag, they set off together in Tankosić's noisy Renault.

On their arrival, Tankosić said that it might be an hour or so before the Chief was able to join them, and proposed that they should while away the time by a little shooting. De Richleau demurred that it was hardly worth while going out after game just for an hour, but it turned out that Tankosić had in mind potting empty bottles with pistols in the yard at the back of the house. On the Duke agreeing, the bulky Serbian opened an oak chest in the hall, in which lay, besides three rifles, half a dozen automatics and some two dozen spare clips already loaded. Taking a pistol and a handful of clips each, they went outside, and one of the servants was called to set up a row of bottles on the roof of a hen house.

Tankosić then bet de Richleau a hundred *dinars* that out of fifty shots each at fifty feet he would smash the most bottles. The Duke took the bet and lost; not because he was the worse shot, but because on this particular occasion he had a sudden premonition that later it might prove to his advantage to be thought a poor one. All the same, he would have had his work cut out to beat Tankosić, as that worthy was an extremely able performer. As he took the Duke's money, he grinned cheerfully and said:

"Ah well, Excellency, it is not so necessary for a General to be a crack shot. Still, when I become a General myself in a few weeks' time, situations may yet arise in which I shall find it useful."

De Richleau raised his dark eyebrows. "I congratulate you, Major, on your prospects of such rapid promotion."

"The Chief tells me that you are to be one of us," declared the Serbian, with a shrug of his bull-like shoulders, "so there is no point in concealing the matter. Marko Ciganović, who you met with me when you were here before, and I are content with lowly ranks for the moment. So is the Chief himself. But all that will be changed in a fortnight or so. The Voyvode Putnik is to be retained as Commander-in-Chief, because he is a great soldier. But all other matters will be directed by Dimitriyevitch openly, with myself and Ciganović as his right hand and his left."

"Good luck to you then, General," said the Duke amiably, with a mock salute, as he thought to himself: 'So once a state of war has been declared, and what little liberty there is in Serbia has been suppressed by emergency decrees, these three thugs mean to run the country between them. I wonder how King Peter will like that idea?'

Returning the salute with a wink, Tankosić led the way back into the house and called for drinks. Then they sat chatting over them in the big lounge, which held the hunting trophies, old masters and Persian rugs, until Dimitriyevitch arrived in his Rolls, accompanied by the chinless, pale-eyed Captain Ciganović.

Over dinner no mention whatever was made of the future, but the little Colonel questioned de Richleau closely about his stay in Austria and, having good grounds for supposing Dimitriyevitch's espionage system there to be excellent, the Duke was much too wily to tell any lies. He confirmed the Serbian opinion that the Austrian officers were a happy-go-lucky lot, who thought much more about amusing themselves than training their troops, and spoke of having made the acquaintance of a number of important people, including the Heir Apparent; although he refrained from mentioning that he had actually entertained the Archduke, as he did not wish to stress the fact unnecessarily that his relations with the Austrians were as cordial as was actually the case. When asked his opinion of Franz Ferdinand, he replied:

"He is no fool and takes a keen interest in his duties, particularly where army matters are concerned; but he is inclined to be morose by nature and his marriage has added greatly to his unpopularity with the Austrian aristocracy. His wife has great influence with him, and having been courted herself by Wilhelm II she has used it to make him strongly pro-German. They are to entertain the Kaiser at Konopischt for three days this week."

"I know it," nodded the Colonel. "And afterwards, he is to be present at the army manœuvres which this year are to take place in Bosnia in considerable strength. Tell me, now, your impressions of von Hötzendorf, Count Tisza, Count Hoyos, and the others whom you met."

For over an hour de Richleau discoursed on these personalities, and conditions as he had found them in Austria. Then, when the servants had gone for the night, Dimitriyevitch stroked back his brush of hair, and said:

"I asked you here to-night so that I could take you with me straight to the office in the morning. Later Ciganović will take you to his tailor, so that you can be measured for your uniform, but the man is not to be told what badges of rank to put on it yet. For the time being you can quite well do all that is required of you in civilian clothes. Belgrade is a small place, and I don't want it to get about that you are to serve in a high position on our General Staff. It is lots of little pointers like that, taken together, which make a picture; and we must be careful not to set the Austrians at the Legation thinking. I will arrange for your initiation into our Brotherhood towards the end of the week, and also for you to be presented to His Majesty. In the meantime you can get a general view of our plans and resources, and meet various people with whom your duties are likely to bring you into frequent contact."

Nothing was said that night of the Black Hand's secret intentions, and de Richleau felt that it would be indiscreet to lead the conversation in that direction, so he confined his questions to matters concerning the state of things in Serbia generally, and they talked mainly about the country until they went to bed.

Next day the Duke was installed in a small but pleasant room at the War Office, in the same corridor as that occupied by Dimitriyevitch, and provided with an aide-de-camp whose name was Basil Militchevitch. He was a tall young man with a sad expression and large, sloe-black eyes, but he seemed intelligent and anxious to please his new master. The Colonel then unlocked a safe in de Richleau's room, gave him the key, and showed him a row of files inside it, the contents of which he was asked to master as soon as possible.

Nothing loath, he at once set to work upon them but, to his disappointment, a quick run through showed that they contained nothing that was not of a purely military nature.

That afternoon he was introduced to the Commander-in-Chief, Radomir Putnik, who received him very affably and conversed with him for over an hour on the Balkan campaigns, during which they had been in opposite camps. Putnik was a stalwart grey-bearded man, and the Duke already had a high respect for him as a shrewd and able soldier. Now that he met him personally, he formed the impression that he was by nature a straightforward upright character who, normally, would have had nothing to do with the Black Hand. No mention of it was made between them, but the C.-in-C. made it clear that de Richleau should look to Dimitriyevitch for his orders, so he could only assume that the gang either had General Putnik in its toils, or his patriotism was such that he preferred to continue to serve his country by remaining at the head of the army, to opposing them and risking being ousted through their intrigues.

De Richleau formed a very similar impression of the Serbian Prime Minister, M. Nikola Pastich, when Dimitriyevitch took him to lunch with the statesman on the following day. Pastich made no secret of his desire to see the Serbian population of Bosnia freed from the Austrian yoke, but he was broadminded, tolerant, and cultured, and it was clear that he hoped that a betterment of their state might be brought about by diplomatic measures.

The Foreign Minister, with whom de Richleau was to work in close collaboration, was also there; and of him the Duke took by no means such a good view. He was obviously hand in glove with Dimitriyevitch and almost fawned upon the powerful Chief of the secret society which had such a strangle-hold on Serbian affairs.

During the Wednesday, Thursday and Friday, the Duke met a number of other key men in the Serbian Government and Army, and, between whiles, devoted himself to going through the papers he had been asked to study. That which he found by far the most interesting was a copy of the Austrian war plans, or an appreciation of their probable plans drafted by the Serbian General Staff. On reading it, he could not determine which, as none of the papers was an original—they were all translations that had been made for his benefit into French before his arrival—but on asking Dimitriyevitch about it, he learned that it had been compiled from stolen documents and other reliable information, so could be graded as A.1 material.

It disclosed that Austria could put six armies into the field, and the dispositions they would take in two different eventualities.

Plan A was in the event of war with Serbia alone. In this case the 5th and 6th Austrian armies, which were based on Bosnia and Herzegovina, would invade Serbia from the west, while their 2nd army, which was based on Hungary, would do so from the north, and the remaining 1st, 3rd and 4th armies would move to precautionary positions in Galicia to guard against possible Russian intervention. The intention here, as von Hötzendorf had himself told the Duke, was to fling every man that could be spared with safety against Serbia as swiftly as possible, with the object of overwhelming her completely before any other power made up its mind to intervene on her behalf. It was further appreciated that a swift, decisive victory over Serbia offered the best chance of preventing the war spreading. If it could be achieved, even should Russia decide to come belatedly to the aid of her stricken protégé, by that time, the Serbian armies having been broken, Austria would be able to withdraw the bulk of her forces in the south to reinforce her armies in the north, and thus have a good hope of also defeating Russia.

Plan B envisaged war with Serbia and Russia simultaneously. In this case, it was argued, in view of the great weight of the Russian armies, it would be most unwise to risk any serious embroilment which would detract from the number of Austrian troops that could be brought against the bigger enemy. Moreover, as it was known that the Russian armies would take considerably longer to mobilize than the Austrian, it was hoped that by concentrating all available forces in the north to start with, Austria might obtain an initial victory which would cripple Russia for some months to come. That would later enable a strong offensive to be launched against Serbia, who, up till then, was merely to be held at bay. In pursuance of these ideas, the 5th and 6th Austrian armies were, as before, to operate against Serbia from the west, but the 2nd army was to join the 1st, 3rd and 4th on the Russian front.

The disposal of the Austrian 2nd army was, therefore, the only apparent difference between the two plans, but a glance at the composition of the armies soon showed de Richleau that there was much more to it than that. They were not all of the same strength; the 5th and 6th being considerably weaker than any of the others, with only three corps

THE ALTERNATIVE PLANS FOR AUSTRIAN MOBILIZATION
(Each square represents an army)

between them, and the 2nd having four corps, which made it stronger than the other two together. As the total number of corps available was fifteen, this meant that if Plan A was put into operation eight corps would be retained to guard the Russian frontier, while seven corps attacked Serbia on two fronts; whereas, should Austria be forced to adopt Plan B, she would send twelve corps against Russia and only three corps would be allocated to operations against Serbia on a single front.

From other papers the Duke learned that General Putnik, with commendable caution, intended to concentrate the whole of the Serbian army in a central position until it became clear which of the two plans Austria was putting into operation. If it proved to be Plan B he would then be well justified in launching a strong offensive into Bosnia: but if it proved to be Plan A he would find himself attacked from the west and north simultaneously by two forces, both roughly equal in numbers to his own. The difference in these prospects was little less than a good hope of the swift conquest of Bosnia and facing annihilation between two fires.

It had been obvious from the beginning that it would be enormously to Serbia's advantage if she could draw Russia in; but now it was clear to de Richleau that it was positively imperative to the success of Dimitriyevitch's plans that he should do so. Everything hung upon it: and with that conclusion was gone one of the last hopes that the machinations of the Black Hand would not result in plunging the whole of Europe into war.

Terribly conscious that the fateful days were passing, the Duke lost no opportunity of probing for information about that sinister secret society, whenever he could do so without appearing unjustifiably curious; but all his tentative inquiries drew a blank until Saturday, the 20th. On that morning Dimitriyevitch told him that a car would call at his hotel at ten o'clock that evening to take him out to the châlet, and that he would then be initiated there.

Striving to suppress his impatience, de Richleau got through the rest of the day wondering what the night would bring.

CHAPTER XV

THE SECRET OF THE BLACK HAND

THE car arrived punctually with his own A.D.C., Militchevitch, as its driver. As it was nearly the longest day of the year, when they left the town a gentle after-glow still lit the fields. But there was no moon and when they reached the châlet the dark forest surrounded it with a belt of blackness.

In the hallway Militchevitch asked the Duke to wait for a few minutes and went into a room at the back of the house. When he came out he was wearing a long white woollen cloak and hood, which completely hid his uniform and concealed the shape of his head, and black kid gloves. A black mask covered his features and on the right breast of the cloak a fist holding a dagger was embroidered in black silk. After he had given five quick knocks at irregular intervals on the door of the main room, a voice called 'Enter' and he led de Richleau inside.

There were about twenty people present. They were seated in a long line behind a trestle table which had been covered with a green baize cloth. All identity was concealed by cloaks, hoods and masks similar to those worn by Militchevitch. In front of them, on the table, lay a dagger pointing outwards. Militchevitch signed to the Duke to stand at the middle of the table and sat down himself at a small one in a far corner.

The room was lit only by two candles, the dim light adding to its atmosphere of sinister mystery and making it even more difficult to identify any of those present; but when the central figure in the line spoke, de Richleau had no doubt at all that he was being addressed by Dimitriyevitch.

The Colonel put to him a number of questions. They were obviously a ritual formula and began with inquiries as to his name, age, place of birth, etc.; then as to his willingness to devote himself to the cause of Serbia to the exclusion of all else, and without thought of self, to the point of sacrificing rank, fortune, wife and family, culminating in life itself. It was not until they were half-way through that de Richleau noticed that Militchevitch was taking down his answers in a big vellum-bound book: but he answered every question firmly and in the sense expected.

When the interrogation was completed the book was brought for him to sign. Then a bible was produced and he was told to place one hand on it and the other on the book, and to swear by his hope of salvation to the truth of the answers he had made. He had felt certain that he would be faced with some such demand, and had he not already made up his mind to accede to it he would not have come there: so, praying God to forgive him his perjury, he took the oath.

Next, Dimitriyevitch laid on the table something that looked like a thick piece of yellow, shrivelled leather. It was roughly circular, about four inches in diameter, and perforated with scores of small holes. Handing de Richleau the dagger he said slowly: "This was one of the breasts of the infamous Queen Draga, which I cut off while she was still living, on the night that justice was done upon her. Plunge the dagger into it as a symbolical act that you would do the same to anyone who dishonoured Serbia."

Repressing a motion of repulsion, the Duke did as he was bid.

One of the brotherhood then appeared with a chalice three parts filled with wine. Dimitriyevitch took the dagger, pricked his left thumb with it and pressed until a drop of blood splashed into the liquor. Returning the dagger to the Duke he bade him do likewise, then the chalice was passed up and down the table until each of the masked and hooded company had done the same. When this grim loving cup was returned to Dimitriyevitch he offered it with a bow to de Richleau and invited him to drink to the damnation of all enemies of Serbia. Again repressing any sign of disgust, the Duke lifted the horrid brew to his lips and sipped it. The Chief of the Brotherhood of Union or Death took a mouthful of it, and it was then passed from hand to hand until everyone present had followed suit.

Finally, Dimitriyevitch addressed the neophyte in the following terms: "By your spiritual oath and the temporal bond of blood you are now one of our brotherhood. I welcome you to it; but at the same time I warn you that should you ever betray us in the least degree the worst of fates will be your portion. Any act of treachery will invoke our united curse, which will so prey upon your mind that, in due course, you will inevitably commit suicide and go unshriven to the grave."

While Dimitriyevitch had been speaking two others, whom he felt certain were Tankosić and Ciganović, had moved up with a mask, white hooded cloak, black kid gloves and dagger. With these they now ritually equipped the Duke as an accepted member of their order.

He was much relieved to think that this unpleasant business was over. The mumbo-jumbo of it had struck him as extremely schoolboyish and had entirely failed to impress him, except with a slight nausea. But he could imagine it having a profound effect upon the undeveloped mind of the average Serbian officer, who was only one generation removed from superstitious peasant stock. In particular, he considered that the final warning, that suicide would be the inevitable sequel to treachery, was a very clever piece of psychology. The suggestion of it was well calculated to beget the desired result among such semi-primitive men, and much more likely to deter them from betraying the society than any straightforward threat to seek out and kill them.

These thoughts had hardly passed through his mind before Militchevitch appeared at his side again and indicated that he should leave the room. As he had expected to be offered a seat at the long table and allowed to take part in the further business of the gathering, he was most disagreeably surprised. He could only hope that his withdrawal was required merely temporarily, while the meeting discussed some question connected with himself. But, when he reached the hall, to his intense annoyance, Militchevitch began to relieve him of his cloak and other regalia.

Hiding his disappointment as well as he could, he asked: "Are these things common property, or are they marked in some way so that I can identify them when I need them for the next meeting?"

The tall, sloe-eyed young man smiled his sad smile, and replied: "You have been using one of the spare sets kept for such purposes, Excellency; and it is unlikely that you will need the loan of a set again. There are many hundreds of members of our brotherhood, but once they have been initiated very few of them are ever called upon to make a second appearance before the Grand Council. Excuse me, please, for a few moments now, as I must put these things away and I wish to go to the toilet before we start back."

The second Militchevitch disappeared, de Richleau tip-toed over to the door of the big room. He dared not stoop down and put his ear to the key-hole in case he was caught in that position, so he leant his back against the door-jamb and stood with a nonchalant air, his hands in his pockets, staring at the ceiling as though deep in thought; but actually he was straining his ears to catch every sound that came through the crack of the door.

He could hear the voices inside quite plainly but, unfortunately for him, they were talking in Serbian and, although he was making rapid strides in mastering that language, they were speaking too fast for him to catch much of what they said. But, in the three or four minutes which elapsed while Militchevitch was absent, he did get one thing. Sunday and the date of the 28th were mentioned several times, and it was clear that they were discussing some definite action that was to take place on that day.

The sound of footsteps gave him sufficient time to step away from the door before Militchevitch reappeared, and two minutes later they were in the car on their way back to Belgrade. On the way he learnt only one thing of minor interest. Militchevitch had not been selected to act as *cicerone* to him on this occasion because he was his A.D.C. The young man carried out the same duties for each neophyte who was initiated, and kept the register of the Brotherhood.

As de Richleau undressed that night he felt deep concern about the time he had already lost without making any appreciable advance towards the object of his mission. He had exercised considerable restraint while waiting to be initiated, counting it as certain that once he had taken the oath to the Black Hand the secret intentions of the brotherhood would be disclosed to him at once. But as things were he had not even had a chance to find out the names of the men who made up the Grand Council, much less learn their plans while they sat in session. He could only trust that now he was an initiate, Dimitriyevitch would take an early opportunity to reveal their intentions to him.

Ten hours later, outside the cathedral in Belgrade after a Sunday Church Parade, de Richleau was presented by Dimitriyevitch to King Peter. Every schoolboy in the world who collected stamps at that time was familiar with the physiognomy of the Serbian monarch. His portrait, even more than that of his royal Montenegrin neighbour and ally, typified the idea of a Ruritanian Prince. On seeing him the Duke had to repress a smile, as the King was so exactly like the decorative image that made the stamps of his country so much more intriguing than those of most other nations. Crowning the lined face, with its cavalry moustache and small tuft of beard on the chin, reposed the flat-topped white fur papenka and erect aigrette. He wore a brilliant uniform with a half-cloak, modelled on the Austrian pattern, gold striped breeches and tasselled Hessian boots.

The Duke knew that under these theatrical trappings the King possessed a liberal and cultured mind; but on this occasion he gave no evidence of it. On the contrary, he remarked on how much he owed to Dimitriyevitch's good advice, adding courteously that he was now further indebted to the Colonel for having secured a soldier of de Richleau's abilities for the Serbian army.

King Peter was known to be a sick man, and there was a rumour that he shortly intended to appoint his son, Prince Alexander, as Regent. Moreover, as the King had protected his predecessor's murderers, there seemed good reason to suppose that he was too deeply in the toils of the Black Hand for any outside influence to succeed in a last-moment attempt to persuade him to gamble his life in a coup to suppress it. So when he praised its Chief, de Richleau tactfully followed suit by saying that never, in his experience, had he met with such an efficient Intelligence Service as that run by the Colonel.

The elderly monarch then got into his carriage, the troops presented arms, the band played, and he was driven back to the Palace. De Richleau watched him go with a cynical little smile, for the time and place chosen by Dimitriyevitch for this informal presentation had not been lost upon him. Evidently the Colonel did not wish him to have a prolonged conversation with the King; and, since his appointment as a Lieutenant-General made his presentation essential, had selected the parade as an opportunity which from its nature would curtail the meeting.

In an unusually good humour at the compliments just paid him, Dimitriyevitch invited the Duke to lunch at the Senior Officers' Club. He accepted with alacrity, hoping at last to be told something of the Colonel's secret schemes. But in this he was disappointed. Three times during the meal he led the conversation with considerable skill round to the previous night's meeting, expressing the hope that it had gone satisfactorily; but each time his host evaded the issue, and at length remarked a trifle sharply:

"For the moment I think it would be best if you concerned yourself solely with our military preparations. Later, of course, I shall value your views on diplomatic issues, but until the curtain goes up I need no assistance in setting the stage."

De Richleau was perturbed at coming up against this unexpected brick wall. He had, perhaps too optimistically, counted on receiving Dimitriyevitch's full confidence after his initiation into the Black Hand, and time was growing short. As its Chief had no intention of telling him anything, his only hope of succeeding in his mission lay in getting the information he needed so urgently out of one of the other members of the Grand Council. Tankosić, Ciganović and Militchevitch were the only three he had been able to identify at the previous night's meeting, and he temporarily ruled out the last as the young A.D.C. apparently held only the position of a trusted henchman so was probably not fully in the secrets of the Council.

On Monday evening he took Tankosić out to dinner and on to *Le Can-Can*, the dance haunt that they had visited together the night of his first arrival in Belgrade. Both of them got very drunk, although de Richleau was not quite so far gone as he appeared, but he got very little for his pains. The only remark that the bull-shouldered thug made which might have had reference to the plot was shortly before they staggered arm in arm out into the street. They had been talking of their shooting match in the back yard of the châlet and with a drunken leer, he said:

"Wish to God those crazy boys could shoot as well as I do. Anyhow their weapons are all right—saw to them myself."

As, at that moment, a scantily clad cabaret girl came up and perched herself on his lap, the Duke had no chance to follow up this cryptic utterance and discover to what boys he was alluding. And, soon afterwards, Tankosić became too drunk to talk with any sense at all. Half an hour later, anxious and frustrated, de Richleau tumbled into bed.

On Tuesday he followed the same procedure with Ciganović. But the tall, chinless albino held his liquor better, and had evidently been warned not to talk. He abruptly cut short all attempts to make him do so, and, seeing that he was on his guard, de Richleau dared not show more than a natural curiosity, from fear of arousing his suspicions. Again he went to bed far from sober, and more worried than ever by his ill-success.

In desperation, on Wednesday, he asked Basil Militchevitch to dine with him. The young man was obviously flattered and much upset at having to refuse, but he said that it was his mother's name day and he could not possibly absent himself from her party. Secretly cursing the waste of a whole twenty-four hours, the Duke suggested Thursday night instead; to which Militchevitch replied that he would be greatly honoured.

Nevertheless, de Richleau was not the man to let Wednesday go by without attempting something; so he arranged a party for that evening of officers whom he suspected might be members of the Grand Council, and entertained them all to dinner in a private room at his hotel. They were a hard-drinking lot, and after the meal most of them gathered round a piano to bellow rousing choruses while they drank. As their host did not know any of their Serbian drinking songs he had a good excuse for not joining in, and was able to join the older men who were not so boisterously inclined. Yet his luck seemed completely out. They were all actively engaged in secret preparations for war but either they did not know, or would not talk about, how it was to be started. The only thing he picked up which might have been a remote clue was a scrap of conversation between two of them, to the effect that 'It was a pity that it could not be the old man instead, as that would have made even more certain of getting the desired result.'

By Thursday morning all he had to go on was this reference to 'the old man', Tankosić's to 'crazy boys who were poor shots', and the date Sunday the 28th. Puzzle his wits as he would he could make nothing of these scraps, except a possibility that someone was to be shot. But if that were so, why get children to do it? Who and where remained a mystery: moreover, he did not see how shooting any individual was likely to provoke a war. And time was now getting desperately short to take counter-measures, even if he could find out enough to suggest any.

That night Militchevitch came to dinner. During the meal it emerged that the sloe-eyed, sad-faced youth was Dimitriyevitch's nephew, and that he owed his position as keeper of the Black Hand membership roll and general factotum to the Grand Council to that relationship. He both feared and admired his uncle and, like him, was fervidly patriotic. After a while he confessed rather shyly that he spent his leisure transcribing ancient heroic Serbian legends into modern verse. When the Duke asked him if he would like to go on to the cabaret show, he replied:

"I hope you will not think me unmanly, but I don't really enjoy the company of cabaret sort of girls. And it is such a pleasure to talk to anyone like your Excellency, that I would much prefer to stay here for a while if I may."

The Duke at once agreed, although with secret reluctance, as 'wine, women and song' form a natural trinity, and he felt that his prospects of loosening his guest's tongue by frequent application of strong liquor would be very much reduced if they remained where they were. However, he poured the young man a handsome ration of cognac and, as the small dining-room was now almost deserted, told the waiter that they intended to sit on at the table instead of moving out to one in the draughty lounge.

Actually, he did not think it likely that Militchevitch knew anything worth knowing but, all the same, he set to work to lull him into that sense of ease and well-being in which confidences are made. During the next hour he learned quite a lot about his A.D.C.'s private life and ambitions. Then he gradually brought the conversation round to the future of Serbia and, having done so, proceeded to adopt a completely different technique from that which he had employed with Tankosić and Ciganović. He spoke of the coming coup as though he knew all about it, and took it for granted that his guest did too.

The result was electrifying. Militchevitch *did* know the whole plot, and evidently nobody had thought to tell him that de Richleau was to be kept in the dark until the mine was sprung. In a moment the cat was out of the bag. Heaving a deep sigh, he said:

"It saddens me greatly to think that it should have been decided to do the thing in this way. The whole idea of playing on the patriotism of those students—drugging them and hypnotizing them, and all the rest of it—to make them murder the Archduke is revolting. Of course, it's clever in a way, as the Austrians are certain to put it down to the Bosnian Serbs and take reprisals on them, which will give us just the excuse we need to champion them by force of arms. Still, although I dare not say so to my uncle, I consider that to open our campaign with an assassination is to rob it at the outset of much of the glory we hope to gain. When the facts leak out, as they are bound to do sooner or later, I fear that the events of Sunday the 28th of June in Sarajevo are going to bring dishonour on Serbia in the eyes of the whole world."

So there it was! The 'boys' were fanatical students to whom Tankosić had supplied arms. The 'old man' was the Emperor and, in view of Franz Ferdinand's unpopularity in Vienna, Austrian reactions would have been much more spontaneous and furious if their time-honoured sovereign had been murdered instead. But the assassination of the Heir Apparent would be quite enough. On principle, Austria could not ignore it; so thousands of Bosnian political suspects would be thrown into gaol and all sorts of new reprisive measures against the Bosnian Serbs would be initiated. As long as Dimitriyevitch could keep the fact concealed that Serbia had instigated the murder, Russia and the democracies would support Serbian demands that Austria should cease her persecution of the innocent Bosnian masses; and he obviously counted on being able to do that long enough for his purpose.

Once war had started, if the truth then became known it could make no difference. When the great powers had got to death-grips the rights and wrongs of the initial quarrel would be smothered in the smoke of a hundred thousand cannon, and the flash of fifteen million rifles. To emerge victorious would be the only thing that counted. It had been publicly announced that at the conclusion of the Austrian manœuvres Franz Ferdinand would pay a state visit to the provincial capital of Bosnia and, despite Militchevitch's repugnance to the plot, de Richleau saw in a flash that no more perfect opportunity could have been offered to Dimitriyevitch for the initiation of his terrible design.

The Duke was now more than anxious to get rid of his young guest; but, having fully agreed with what Militchevitch had said, he forced himself to continue talking normally and pleasantly for another quarter of an hour, before indicating by a smothered yawn that he would be glad to get to bed. His A.D.C. promptly took the hint and, having thanked him effusively for a most pleasant evening, set off on his way home.

Immediately he had gone, de Richleau borrowed a railway time-table from the office, took it upstairs, got out a map, and, his brain working at a furious speed, began to plan.

He could not do anything by telephone as, at that date, the only telephones in Belgrade were in Government offices and the palace, connecting them on a slender network with the military headquarters in the various provinces and the outside world. He would have given ten years of his life to be able to walk round to the British Legation and see the Minister, Mr. Charles Des Graz, but he knew him to be on leave, and greatly doubted if his subordinates would have sufficient authority to take any drastic action in his absence. Moreover, Dimitriyevitch had informed him quite casually only a few days before that all the Serbian servants in the foreign Legations were in his employ. A midnight visit would be certain to be reported, and might arouse such acute suspicion as to lead to arrest in the morning. And, as the only unauthorized possessor of this terrible secret, de Richleau felt that he must on no account risk his freedom.

But he could write to the Chargé d'affaires, and this he did, giving full particulars of the plot, with the request that they should be sent to London by most secret cypher on the highest priority. Next, he wrote a similar letter to Sir Maurice de Bunsen in Vienna, adding the almost superfluous line that the Austrian Government should be warned without a moment's delay. Then he set about drafting a telegram for Sir Pellinore, which would give him the gist of the matter without conveying anything to the Serbian telegraphists when they came to transmit it.

This was no easy matter, but after considerable thought he composed the following:

Wightfoot's company arriving in Sarajevo on Sunday 28th stop He will open season by putting on own play quote the Ides of March unquote with François Aragon in leading rôle.

As an English name, Wightfoot sounded quite plausible, yet Sir Pellinore could hardly fail to interpret it as Black Hand. The *Ides of March* could be connected only with the assassination of Julius Caesar, and Franz Ferdinand was virtually one of the two Caesars of Austria. Finally the name François Aragon definitely identified the victim. François was simply French for *Franz*, and no educated man could think of Aragon without Castille and the uniting of these two great Spanish kingdoms by the marriage of Isabella of Castille with *Ferdinand* of Aragon.

The Duke's only qualm about it was that it might be too clear, and that somebody in the Belgrade post office, who knew what was planned to take place on Sunday the 28th in Sarajevo, might spot its meaning and suppress it. But the text had all the appearance of a straightforward business wire from a theatrical producer to his associates in London, and it seemed unlikely that any telegraph clerk would be in Dimitriyevitch's confidence. Anyhow, the date and place could not possibly be left out and any attempt to disguise them might lead to a fatal misunderstanding, so he decided that he must send it as it stood.

It was now half an hour after midnight. Going downstairs, he walked to the main post office and posted his two letters, but found that he could not send the telegram as there was no night service. On getting back to his room, he spread out his map and consulted the time-table.

There was no point in his going to Vienna as his letter to Sir Maurice de Bunsen would now get there sooner than he could, and there was nothing he could do there that the British Ambassador was not in a position to do better. It was now very early on Friday, and it seemed a fair assumption that, if he sent the telegram to Sir Pellinore as soon as the post office opened it would arrive by Saturday morning. By that time the Chargé d'affaires in Belgrade should also have communicated with London, and Sir Maurice have received his letter in Vienna. Both London and Vienna, should, therefore, have twenty-four hours or so to work in, and, at first sight, that appeared to be ample to stop the Archduke from going to Sarajevo. But no one knew better than the cautious Duke that there could be many a slip betwixt the cup and the lip, and such a matter of life and death was not one on which to take chances.

As Franz Ferdinand was on manœuvres with the Austrian army, he would probably be moving almost hourly from place to place in the desolate Bosnian hill country, where telegraph offices were few and far between. Unless he could be located and warned on Saturday night, there was still a horrible possibility that he would turn up in Sarajevo on Sunday; so de Richleau considered it imperative that he should go to Sarajevo himself, in order to take measures to prevent the outrage should other means have failed.

A glance at the map showed that Sarajevo lay some 120 miles to the south-west of Belgrade, as the crow flies. That was no great distance but, unfortunately, no railway connected the two. The main Vienna-Orient line ran south-east from Belgrade, through Nish to Salonika and Constantinople. From it, branch lines twisted through the hill country in a westerly direction, but they ended some distance from the Drina river or Tara mountains, and only on the far side of these other branch lines wound down to Sarajevo. Užice on the east, and Yardiste on the west of the divide, were the terminal stations of the two branches, and about thirty miles lay between them. via Mladenovac, on the main line, to Užice was about 150 miles, and from Yardiste to Sarajevo about 70. So altogether it meant a journey of 250 miles, mainly in slow local trains and with 30 miles of it on horseback.

He wondered for a moment if it would not be quicker to save a hundred miles by going by road; but automobiles were very liable to break down, particularly on the rough going he would be certain to encounter, while a ride of 150 miles or more would be a gruelling experience and, with essential halts for rest and sleep, could hardly be accomplished under thirty-six hours. Having consulted the time-tables, he found that was just about the time it would take him by rail, and if he could catch a train that left Mladenovac at mid-day he should be in Sarajevo by Saturday night. So he decided on the less exhausting method of travel, then went to bed.

Owing to the long break in the middle of the day for siesta, the Serbian War Office opened early, and work began at half past eight. De Richleau was quick to realize that if he did not appear in his office at the usual hour Militchevitch would come round to the hotel to find out what had happened to him, and his disappearance would be discovered almost at once; so he decided to go there as usual and make some excuse to leave again, which would give him a longer start.

He thought it wise to abandon most of his belongings, but made up a parcel of his shaving tackle and night things, went downstairs, ordered a dinner for four that night, then went out. The parcel he left at a tobacco kiosk round the corner, where he usually bought his cigarettes, and on the way to the War Office sent off his telegram to Sir Pellinore. In his office he spent half an hour with Militchevitch going through some papers; then he said that he had arranged to spend the morning going over the Arsenal, so he would not be back until after the siesta.

That morning it had occurred to him that in a small place like Belgrade he might quite possibly be recognized at the station by some officer of his acquaintance. If he were seen leaving by train the hue and cry after him might be raised precipitately; so, on leaving his office, he went to the better of the only two garages in the town. He told the proprietor that he wanted to hire a car to drive himself for the day, and after a little haggling, was fixed up with a Renault. While the man prepared it for the road, the Duke collected his parcel from the kiosk, then went into a clothing store, where he bought a cheap ready-made suit, flashy tie, celluloid collar, and a flat, round hat like a toque, of the type most frequently worn by the Balkan trading classes. At the same store he also bought a portmanteau made of basket work. Into it he packed all his purchases and the parcel, then he returned to the garage and drove off in the car.

By twenty past eleven he had covered thirty miles and was approaching Mladenovac. Half a mile outside the market town he drove the car off the road in among a group of trees, got out and changed into the clothes he had bought. Having packed his own in the basket, he abandoned the car and walked into the town. As Mladenovac was the junction from which the branch line train started, it was already in the station. He had decided against the more complete disguise that would have been afforded by a peasant costume, because he would then have had to travel with real peasants. They would at once have tumbled to it that he was not what he appeared to be, and, suspecting him to be an escaped criminal, might have drawn the attention of the railway officials to him. But dressed as he was, he could pass himself off among second class passengers as a Greek travelling salesman, The train consisted of only four coaches, one of which was divided into an equal number of first and second class compartments. Having bought some food at the buffet, he made himself comfortable in one of the latter, which had in it only an elderly couple.

They proved to be a retired pig merchant and his wife. The old man had become almost stone deaf, and the old woman was not of a garrulous type: so, after exchanging the few remarks required by courtesy on first meeting, they fell into silence. No one else entered their carriage, and a quarter of an hour later the train moved out.

It was very hot, and as the little train chugged its way across the Serbian plain its speed was barely sufficient for any appreciable breeze to be felt through the window. Every quarter of an hour or so it halted at wayside stations for at least ten minutes, while livestock and farm produce were unhurriedly unloaded and loaded into it. During these halts the heat was positively grilling, and de Richleau, who had been attempting to doze, was kept wakeful and irritated by hordes of flies.

By half past three they had covered about forty miles, and pulled up at the little town of Lazarevac. As it was a somewhat larger place than any they had so far passed, it did not surprise the Duke that the halt was longer than usual; but when nearly half an hour had elapsed some of the other passengers began to get a little restless. When they asked the guard, he could give no reason for the delay, but said that perhaps there was a blockage on the line further on. Sticky with the heat and pestered by the flies, de Richleau got out and began to walk up and down the platform. Another half-hour passed, and still there were no signs of the train moving on. Being accustomed to the unforeseen delays of Balkan travel, de Richleau knew that another hour or so might quite well elapse before they were on their way again. But, feeling that he had stretched his legs for long enough, he turned to re-enter his carriage.

Suddenly a commotion at the barrier attracted his attention. A second later he saw Tankosić and Ciganović hurrying through it. They were within twenty yards of where he was standing, and saw him at the same instant as he saw them. With a shout they drew their pistols and ran straight at him.

He knew Tankosić's ability as a marksman too well to ask for death by making a dive for the carriage. He knew too, now, why the train had been held up. With grim foreboding, he raised his hands in a gesture of surrender.

CHAPTER XVI

THE WINGS OF THE ANGEL OF DEATH

TEN minutes later, seated between his two captors, de Richleau was in Dimitriyevitch's Rolls speeding back to Belgrade. He had refused all explanations of his conduct, saying that he was prepared to give his reasons for quitting his post without leave only to their Chief. By that move he managed to win a little time in which to decide on the least dangerous line to take. But, as he thought about it now, it seemed that whatever line he took, his danger would be acute when he was brought face to face with the fanatical Chief of the Black Hand.

He was further intensely worried at having been prevented from getting to Sarajevo. Should anything prevent his letter reaching Sir Maurice de Bunsen the following morning, the Austrian Government would know nothing of the plot until they were informed of it by London, and it was unlikely that would occur until Saturday evening. A whole day would have been lost and only one night left in which to locate the Archduke in the Bosnian wilds and warn him. The Duke tried to comfort himself with the thought that if the Charge d'Affaires in Belgrade had any sense he would not only communicate with London, as he had been asked to do, but also repeat to Sir Maurice in Vienna, as the matter so urgently concerned his colleague in Austria. All things considered, he felt that by one means or another warning would be got to Franz Ferdinand in time, and that he would still be alive on Monday. But, with a nasty qualm in the pit of the stomach, de Richleau realized that should Dimitriyevitch discover that he had sent a warning to the Archduke, he would not be alive on Monday himself.

In their delight at having caught him, his captors made no secret of the circumstances which had enabled them to do so. Owing to his pre-occupation with the plot, he had completely forgotten that he had an appointment that morning at ten o'clock to meet the Montenegrin military attaché, and Militchevitch had failed to remind him of it.

Montenegro meant very little to de Richleau—hence his lapse of memory—but it meant a great deal to the Serbian General Staff. This small, mountainous territory on the shores of the Adriatic had originally been a part of the old Serbian Kingdom. Alone among the Balkan peoples, the Montenegrins had managed to resist the Ottoman invasion; and although, through the centuries, their country had on numerous occasions been over-run during fresh efforts to conquer them, they had always succeeded in expelling the Turks and regaining their independence. When Serbia proper had thrown off the Turkish yoke, the two territories had still remained separated, until quite recently, by the Sanjak of Novibazar but, in 1912, Montenegro had been the first member of the Balkan League to declare war on Turkey and, after the victory, she and Serbia had divided the Sanjak between them, so they were now neighbours.

King Peter of Serbia had married the daughter of King Nicholas of Montenegro, which further strengthened the tie of these already consanguineous peoples; and since the beginning of the present year discussion had been going forward between the two countries for a customs union and a fusion of their armies. But the Montenegrins were an arrogant and difficult lot, so nothing had been definitely settled yet, and Dimitriyevitch had the best possible reasons for wishing to hurry the agreement through. He needed the Montenegrins to attack the Austrian armies in Bosnia from the south, and so outflank them; and had asked de Richleau to do his utmost to further matters with their military attaché.

It so happened that this Montenegrin officer was a nephew of King Nicholas, so regarded himself as a person of considerable importance. Had anyone else had an appointment with de Richleau that morning doubtless Militchevitch would have apologized for the Duke's absence and arranged another for the following day. But, overawed by the indignant visitor, and knowing the importance of placating him, the A.D.C. had immediately tried to get in touch with his master. Inquiries at the Arsenal disclosed that de Richleau was not there and, stranger still, had never been expected; nor had he gone back to his hotel, been seen in the Senior Officers' Club, or received at the hospital as a result of a street accident. Much perturbed, Militchevitch had then reported his disappearance to Dimitriyevitch, and the hue and cry had begun.

No one answering the Duke's description had been seen at the railway station, so the proprietors of the two garages were questioned, and his hiring of the Renault brought to light. Motor cyclist scouts had been sent out along all the roads from Belgrade and his trail picked up on that leading to Mladenovac. As motors were then few and far between, and still objects of interest to rural populations, it was soon ascertained beyond dispute that the car had not passed through the town; so his pursuers were convinced that he was either somewhere in the neighbourhood, or had left it by rail. The latter field was narrowed by the fact that no main line train going south halted at Mladenovac between ten in the morning and six in the evening, so a wire had been sent to hold the branch line train at Lazarevac while Tankosić and Ciganović drove on to search it.

As Mladenovac lay south-east of Belgrade and Lazarevac to the south-west of it, there was no great difference in the distance between the two towns and the capital. So in well under an hour from the time of his capture de Richleau was being handed over to the Chief Warder of the State Prison. At this, gloomy about his prospect as he was, he felt considerable relief; since he believed Dimitriyevitch's thugs to be quite capable of murder, whereas by becoming an official prisoner it seemed much more likely that he would at least be given a proper trial.

In a bare room he was searched. His money and a small automatic, which he was carrying in a webbing holster under his arm-pit and had hoped to have a chance to use later, were taken from him. Then he was conducted to a cell and its iron door was slammed upon him.

Sitting down on the truckle bed he continued his anxious speculations. One small comfort was that neither among the things that had just been taken from him, nor among the belongings he had left at the hotel, was there anything in the least incriminating. All the same, it would be futile to deny that he had left Belgrade clandestinely, as the clothes he was wearing gave that away beyond any shadow of doubt. As he had left the capital only that morning, no charge more serious than being absent without leave could be legally brought against him. But the devil of it was that the Black Hand might consider that he had broken his oath, and it was a hundred to one that they had little mercy on defaulters.

After a while, since no amount of worrying could improve his situation, he began to think about Ilona. He had promised her that he would be back in Vienna and let her hear from him before the end of the month. He had made that promise in good faith, believing that either he would have nipped Dimitriyevitch's plot in the bud, or it would have come to a head by the 25th. As things had turned out, his estimate had been three days short of the actual schedule, but even with the 28th as the fatal day, had he not belatedly discovered the Black Hand's intentions, he could still have been back in Vienna by the morning of the 30th and sent her a message through Adam Grünne.

Now his poor darling would look forward to hearing from him in vain, for it was quite certain that Dimitriyevitch would keep him under lock and key for a considerable time to come, even if no more than suspicion suggested that his flight had been inspired by his finding out the truth. He wished desperately that he could send her some ray of comfort, and at least let her know that his failure to return to her was through no fault of his own. As things were, he could only hope that she would not think too hardly of him. His firm mouth broke into a tender smile as he recalled her sweet face, all wet with rain but starry eyed, as he had held her in his arms on the balcony at Königstein. Then his mouth hardened as he thought of almost her last words to him during their tragically difficult talk during the ball at Schönbrunn. Her words had been to the effect that they must make the utmost of the little time they had, as new plans to marry her off might soon be initiated. Although he knew that he could never possess her himself, the idea of her being possessed by another, and, above all, against her will by some stranger arbitrarily selected for her, filled him with horror and despair. And now she was not even to have the solace of anything but the opening phase of her only romance to look back upon. In desperation he forced himself to stop thinking of her—it hurt too much.

He had not been in the cell much more than an hour when a warder brought him his evening meal. The man was a rough but decent fellow, who spoke kindly and said that if money had been taken from the Duke, or some could be sent by friends, he would be pleased to buy him any little comforts he required. De Richleau thanked him and replied that he would be glad if to-morrow he could be supplied with cigarettes, a few bottles of drinkable wine, paper and writing materials. The warder agreed and left him. As he slowly ate the vegetable stew and coarse bread which had been brought to him, he again thanked his stars that he at least had the protection of a proper and not ill-run prison, instead of having been carried off to some private dungeon run by the Black Hand.

But he had counted his chickens too soon. Shortly after seven o'clock the warder appeared again and beckoned him out of his cell. He was taken upstairs and, to his consternation, handed over to Tankosić. With a sinking heart, de Richleau realized that he had been put into the State Prison only as a temporary measure, until it was convenient for the plotters of assassination to take him elsewhere.

The burly Major tapped his gun significantly, and said, "No tricks, now!" as he led him outside. A Peugeot was waiting there with Ciganović in the driver's seat. As soon as de Richleau and Tankosić were inside, the car drove off, taking the road towards the châlet.

When they pulled up in the clearing, the Rolls could be seen through the open doors of the garage beside the house. Its presence indicated that Dimitriyevitch had already arrived; so, as the Duke got out of the Peugeot he braced himself, feeling that he would soon know his fate. With some uneasiness he noticed that, although it was only about eight o'clock, there was no servant in the hall, as usual, to take their hats. Ciganović opened the door of the big room and motioned him to go in. As he stepped over the threshold, he saw that the Colonel was seated at a small desk, going through some papers.

Dimitriyevitch looked up and gave the prisoner a cold, penetrating glance; then, without a word, went on with what he was doing. Tankosić and Ciganović came in, closed the door, and stood just behind de Richleau. For nearly ten minutes there was no sound except the occasional rustle of the Colonel's papers. The long silence was calculated to be most unnerving; but the Duke was rather glad of it, as it gave him an opportunity to look round the room for possible weapons that he might snatch at if, later, a situation arose which would give him a sporting chance of fighting his way out. On a nearby table there was a nine inch statuette of Napoleon in bronze, with a three inch square marble base. Used as a club it was easily heavy enough to kill a man at a blow; but he would have much preferred one of the Turkish scimitars which were arranged in a decorative fan against the wall over the mantelpiece.

At length Dimitriyevitch, finished with his papers, fixed his piercing eyes on de Richleau, and said:

"Well! What have you to say?"

"Very little," replied the Duke quietly. "I must apologize for the trouble and inconvenience to which I have put you. It was stupid of me to go off like that. I ought to have come to see you, and asked for a week's leave of absence. The trouble was I feared you might refuse to grant it."

"Why should you wish to leave Belgrade?"

De Richleau had had ample time to think things out. They had found his railway ticket to Užice on him. That did not definitely give it away that he had been heading for Sarajevo, but it was on the Bosnian frontier. He had thought for a moment of saying that he had gone there with a view to making a personal reconnaissance of the country, over which it was expected that they would be fighting in the next few weeks. But to have undertaken such a trip, without making any previous arrangements, or notifying anyone of his intention would, he decided, never be accepted as a plausible excuse. The only course was to disclose his knowledge of the plot and put all his hope in their taking his word for it that he had not intended to betray them.

He shrugged his shoulders. "I should have thought you would have guessed that. In the past week I have naturally picked up quite a lot of information about your intentions. I could hardly do otherwise, while constantly mixing, as I have been, with officers 'in the know', who thought I was 'in the know', too."

"You're lying!" cut in Ciganović. "You've been doing your damnedest to ferret things out. The night you took me out to dinner, you did your utmost to pump me."

"Oh, come!" protested de Richleau mildly, as he turned to look at the tall, light-eyed, albino. "In my position as Chief Military Liaison Officer with your Foreign Office, it was natural enough that I should want to get some idea of how you intended to rupture relations with Austria. I expected some diplomatic démarche over Bosnia, and saw no reason then why you should wish to conceal your opening move from me."

"I told you to mind your own business!" snapped Dimitriyevitch.

"Whether I had or hadn't would have made little difference. I received unsolicited hints of your intentions from several people; then, through just one more, all the rest fell into place. I am a professional soldier, and I was perfectly willing to kill as many Austrians as I possibly could for you in an orthodox manner. But it was no part of my contract to participate in an assassination."

"No one asked you to."

"Perhaps. But if it leaks out afterwards that the murder of the Archduke was plotted by officers of the Serbian General Staff, every member of it will be suspected of having known something of the plot."

"*If* it leaks out: but it will not—unless there are traitors among us."

De Richleau knew that his life might hang upon his tact, so he put the matter as inoffensively as he could. "Such things have a habit of doing so, sooner or later. And while you, Colonel, in your devotion to Serbia may be prepared to accept such obloquy for your country's sake, I have no similar inducement."

"You forget your oath to the Brotherhood of Union or Death."

This was dangerous ground. The Duke was very far from having forgotten it, and again he honeyed his reply: "On the contrary, I considered it most carefully before I acted; and I came to the conclusion that by absenting myself from Belgrade for the next few days I could protect my reputation without in any way breaking my oath."

Suddenly Dimitriyevitch sprang to his feet, and pointed an accusing finger. "You lie! You intended to make your way to Sarajevo and betray us."

The Duke's eyebrows shot up and his mouth fell open, as though in blank amazement; then he exclaimed angrily: "How dare you accuse me of such perfidy! Such a thought never entered my head."

"Explain then why you left Belgrade in disguise, and took so many precautions against your departure being discovered."

"Put yourself in my place. Had you held an appointment on the Turkish General Staff, and discovered that the Turks intended to do something with which you did not wish to be associated, would you have walked out openly? Of course not. You would have assumed, as I did, that if your associates learned of your departure they would have feared you meant to betray their secret, and immediately have taken steps to have you brought back."

"The argument is plausible," Dimitriyevitch admitted with a grim smile, "but it does not explain why you took a ticket to Užice—the nearest point on the railway to Sarajevo."

"I selected it as the point which will become our most important railhead in the event of operations against Bosnia. I felt that, instead of wasting my time lying up in some market town, by putting in a week there I should be able to carry out a valuable reconnaissance of the frontier in person, before returning to Belgrade."

"Do you expect me to believe that you meant to return?" the Colonel asked acidly.

De Richleau stiffened. "I regard the doubt you appear to entertain about that as in the highest degree offensive. The fact that you have planned a cold-blooded murder lies between you and your conscience. I consider I had every right to take such steps as I could to prevent my name being associated with it, by absenting myself from Headquarters during its final preparation and execution. But that does not affect the oath that I have taken, or my obligation to place my military ability at the disposal of Serbia. Naturally, I intended to return. Why, otherwise, should I have been on my way to a Serbian town, when instead, had I wished, I could have taken a main-line train and by now have been in Sofia or Budapest?"

"There is something in that," admitted the Colonel, "unless you really meant to go to Sarajevo. If I become convinced that was your intention, I shall have you shot out of hand. As things are, I must consider the matter further. At the moment my police are working on the case and may bring something fresh to light. In the meantime, I shall naturally continue to keep you under close arrest."

Dimitriyevitch signed to the other two, and added: "Take him down to the cellar. We'll keep him there for the night."

Ciganović stepped forward and opened a narrow door in the wainscoting of the wall, which de Richleau had not previously noticed. Tankosić prodded him in the back with his pistol, and he walked through the opening. The light from the room was sufficient to show him, to his left, a short flight of steps and, dimly, as he went down them, stone flags that stretched away to bin-lined walls. When he was half-way down, the door slammed behind him, plunging him in darkness.

Having reached the bottom, he paused there a moment. His matches had been taken from him at the prison, so he had no means of creating even a glimmer in the Stygian blackness. But, after a moment, he saw a faint, misty radiance to one side of him. Cautiously, with hands outstretched, he went forward. As he advanced, the radiance increased to the degree of pale moonlight, and took shape as an oblong about shoulder high. Then he saw that it came from an opening in the wall, and beyond that there was a small, square pit, the top of which was covered with a grille on a level with the ground outside. It was evidently the means by which the cellar was ventilated, but he soon found that it offered no prospect of escape. Across the oblong were thick iron bars concreted into the wall, and exerting all his strength on one failed to make the least impression on it. So he could not even get out into the little pit.

The light was the last glow of evening and, now that his eyes were getting accustomed to the darkness, it was enough to illuminate faintly the cellar for a few feet round the opening, but no more. However, it at least gave him a fixed point to which he could glance back, and so keep his direction as he set out to explore the rest of the cellar.

He felt certain that there must be a door somewhere, other than the one by which he had entered, as it would hardly be convenient to have the servants always going through the main room to bin away, or bring up, the wine. So he struck out along it lengthwise, hoping to find a door at the far end, under the hall. When he had gone a few yards he tripped against a scantling, barked his shin badly, and swore. Moving crabwise a few paces, his hands felt a row of three casks, but beyond them nothing, so he cautiously moved forward again. Another half dozen shuffling steps brought him right up against the door he had expected.

But five minutes' fumbling over its surface convinced him that he could not get out that way. It was of heavy oak, with a stout lock, and was quite immovable.

Shuffling sideways again, he felt his way right round the cellar. It was a large place and evidently the same size as the big room above it. Apart from the door, the ventilation aperture, and the flight of steps, its walls were solid tiers of bins from floor to ceiling, and there was no other exit. Making his way back to the scantling, he sat down upon it. He felt he might have known that Dimitriyevitch was not the sort of man to put a prisoner in a place from which there was much likelihood of his being able to escape.

For a few moments his heart beat so fast that he felt quite suffocated with apprehension. Dimitriyevitch had said plainly that if he became convinced that his prisoner had intended to go to Sarajevo, he would have him shot out of hand. As that had been the Duke's intention, he could not help a nightmare foreboding that some little thing he had overlooked would reveal it to his captors. And he had no doubt at all that, if ordered to, Tankosić and Ciganović would not hesitate about emptying the contents of their pistols into him. He wondered if they would take him outside to do it, or murder him down there in the cellar. He shivered at the thought of the bullets crashing their way through his flesh and bone. If they were content to fire at his body, that would not be quite so bad; but the idea of his face and head being smashed and rent to a hideous pulp horrified him. His mouth went dry and his hands became clammy.

De Richleau was very far from being a coward. He had been shot at many times in battles and skirmishes and had, on occasion, deliberately exposed himself in order to encourage his men. He had been wounded too, and knew that the first effect was generally no more than a burning sensation, followed by numbness—the pain came later.

After a bit he got a grip on himself and tried to regard his position objectively, as though he were entirely outside it and looking on at a situation in a thriller play. So far he had played his cards well. He had told a great many lies with all the conviction he could muster, and none of them had contradicted another. As he looked back, he was a little surprised to find how easily he had slipped into habitually lying since he had taken up this unpleasant game of espionage. But this evening, of course, he had had a special impetus to distort the truth with complete unscrupulousness. His life had hung, and still hung, on his ability to deceive his captors. No doubt that had lent an extra keenness to his wits and glibness of his tongue.

Anyhow, black as the case had looked against him, he felt sure that he had succeeded in shaking Dimitriyevitch's well-founded assumption of his guilt. So, unless some fresh and damning piece of evidence did turn up, why should the Colonel have him murdered? The scruples he had urged, about later having his name associated with the Sarajevo plot, were far from unreasonable. A temporary absence from Belgrade could not entirely have saved him from that, but would have gone a long way towards it, particularly as he was a foreigner in the service of Serbia. People would be inclined to give him the benefit of the doubt, or even think that the Serbians had deliberately got rid of him, so that he should not be aware of their complicity and they would be able to give free rein to their elation when the news of their abominable coup came through. Dimitriyevitch was no fool, and would realize all that. Besides, he was no use to the Serbians dead; whereas he could be of very considerable value to them alive.

In a slightly more cheerful frame of mind, he decided that the odds were that Dimitriyevitch would send him back to the State Prison next morning, keep him there as a precaution until the blow had been struck, then let him out and expect him to resume his duties. But what of the Archduke?

Well, there again, perhaps the picture was not so black. Full particulars of the plot had been sent out in three directions. The only real danger was that it might be found impossible to locate him while on manœuvres. But surely, with the wires buzzing from three directions, someone would be certain to find and warn him in time. The urge to set out for Sarajevo had seized the Duke owing to his realization that such an infinity of woe, destruction, misery and death, might follow the assassination that, quite apart from any desire to save Franz Ferdinand's life, no possible chance must be neglected which might add to the certainty of preventing the crime. But he saw, now that he had more time to think over the matter, that the warnings he had sent out must prove sufficient; that his attempt to supplement them had been quite redundant, and had, quite needlessly, landed him in this grim personal mess.

The faint light filtering down the ventilating shaft had now almost entirely disappeared, and he could not even see the outline of his hand, when he held it up in front of him. He supposed that the three men upstairs were now having dinner, but did not think it likely that they would bring him any, so he was glad now that he had not turned up his nose at the prison stew. However, he hoped that, before they went to bed, they would throw him down some cushions and rugs to sleep on, as otherwise he was in for an extremely uncomfortable night. It then occurred to him that, even if they were so ungracious as to forget that he might not have dined, they could not prevent his consoling himself with a good bottle of wine.

Going over to a row of bins he felt about among them till he found one containing champagne. As he opened a bottle, he wondered if it would be the sort of muck the French sent to the Balkans, of which during the past week he had had to drink far more than was good for his head or his stomach at *Le Can-Can.* At first, drinking out of the bottle, it was difficult to get the flavour, but after a moment he knew that it was a *premiere cuvée* that had been prepared either for England or Russia.

As the dry, yet full bodied, wine tickled his palate, he was reminded of the last time he had drunk champagne of that quality. It had been at Ilona's birthday ball. That had been thirteen nights ago, but it now seemed so remote that it might have been thirteen months. In fact, seen in restrospect and by contrast with the present, it might have been in a different lifetime.

In his mental vision he saw again the constant quiet movement and blending of the innumerable colours that had made up that living kaleidoscope. No one dress or uniform stood out from the others, but in a shimmering, iridescent sea, sable and yellow satin, black lace and pastel coloured silks, patent leather and paradise plumes, blue, green and scarlet cloth, gold braid and silver trimmings—the whole twinkling and winking with a hundred thousand gems—mingled like the million water globules of some vast fountain seen against the summer sun. Yet it had been composed of human beings; the flower of an ancient Empire gathered at the most brilliant court in Europe—gathered there to do honour to the woman he loved, and who loved him.

Seated there, a prisoner in that now pitch-black cellar, while three assassins, who held his fate in their hands, dined in the room above, it seemed utterly impossible that he could be the same man who, less than a fortnight before, had worn that dashing sky-blue uniform trimmed with silver braid and grey astrakhan, and had seen an Archduchess fight back her tears because he must leave her.

Slowly, he finished the bottle of champagne. He had only just drained it of the last mouthful, when he heard a car drive up outside. He wondered, vaguely at first, what that portended. Judging by the total disappearance of the light from the ventilating shaft, he knew that it must be after ten o'clock. But perhaps some of the other conspirators had driven out from Belgrade for an after-dinner conference with their Chief.

A few minutes later the noise of the engine reached him again, and he heard the car drive off. That seemed to invalidate his first explanation of its arrival. The odds were, then, that it had brought a dispatch out to Dimitriyevitch. If so, it must contain news of some urgency, to have been sent out so late at night. Uneasily, he began to wonder whether it had been a messenger who had brought some fresh information about himself.

Again, he swiftly reviewed his position, but could think of nothing that might have given him away. All the same, his sixth sense gave him an uneasy feeling that the arrival of the car spelt danger for him. Instinctively, he began to visualize being called up to the room above, re-questioned, found guilty: then being taken out into the woods and shot. He did not mean to die tamely. He would seize the first chance to break away if he possibly could, or, in the worst case, fight to the last gasp. But he knew that he would stand little chance without a weapon.

The champagne bottle he was holding would make an excellent club; but it was too big to hide under his jacket, and the moment they saw it they would take it away from him at the pistol point. Perhaps, though, if he pretended to be drunk——

Quickly, he shuffled through the darkness, found the bin again, opened another bottle, and poured about a third of its contents into the back of the bin. Returning with it to the scantling, he sat down once more, holding the bottle upright on his knee.

It was less than five minutes since the car had driven off, but it seemed longer. He was just beginning to think that his nerves had panicked him into a false alarm, when the door at the top of the steps opened and Tankosić called to him to come up.

He caught his breath and his heart began to hammer. His instinct had been right, then. Unless they had received some fresh information, why should they wish to question him again that night? Dimitriyevitch had said that his police were working on the case. They must have unearthed something and sent it out to him. Tankosić's voice had been harsh. His bulky form loomed threateningly against the lighted doorway at the top of the steps. This was it! The summons was that of the Angel of Death. In all probability he now had no more than a few minutes to live.

Instead of getting to his feet, he lurched round and called back drunkenly: "Don't wanna come up. Very happy here. You come down and have a drink."

"Come up, damn you!" shouted Tankosić.

"Don't wanna come up," the Duke repeated. "Darn good wine—an' lots of it. Very happy here."

"Come up, you bastard," bawled the Serbian. "Come up, or I'll shoot that bottle out of your hands."

The unsavoury epithet, and the threat to shoot, were ample confirmation of the Duke's fears. They did not want him up there to question him again on some minor matter. Somehow, they had found him out, and now meant to exact vengeance on him for attempting to betray them. But still he did not get to his feet. Now that he was up against it, his nerve was back. His mind was clear as a bell, his brain assessing chances as quickly as an actuary working with a life insurance table spread before him. He had gambled with death before, and now he did so again.

"Oh, go to hell!" he called thickly. "Can't you see—see I'm enjoyin' myself?" And, raising the bottle to his lips, he took a pull at it.

With an oath, Tankosić came stumping down the stairs. Marching over to de Richleau, he seized him by the arm and jerked him to his feet.

"Wait a minute! Wait a minute!" mumbled the Duke. "Wanna finish the bottle. Why you so impatient?"

"Get up those bloody stairs," snarled Tankosić, and gave him a rough push towards them with his left hand. In his right he held his pistol. He waved it with a threatening gesture.

Clutching his bottle under his left arm, de Richleau stumbled forward, muttering, "Oh, all right! All right!" On the first stair he tripped intentionally, recovered himself, and began to stagger up the flight.

Tankosić followed a yard behind him, impatiently urging him on. The Duke could no longer see the Serbian's pistol and, for all he knew, it might be pointed at his back. If so, he did know that within another moment his number would be up. But once again he gambled with death. When they were two thirds of the way up the stairs, he grasped the neck of the bottle in his right hand. He dared not give his enemy an instant's warning by turning to aim the blow. Only the Timeless

Ones could help him now, by directing the arm that he must use blindly. Pretending to stumble again, he suddenly swung the bottle round in a terrific back-hander at the spot where he judged Tankosić's head to be.

It swished through the air and landed with a dull thud, nearly dislocating de Richleau's wrist. The bottle caught the Major flat on the side of the head, smashing his right ear to pulp, and cracking his skull low down. Without a moan, he twisted sideways, fell, and rolled bumping down the stairs. The pistol he had been holding clattered noisily beside him.

De Richleau would have given ten years of his life to have been able to get that pistol. But he dared not attempt to. Down there in the heavy shadow it might be two, three, five, minutes before he could find it. Even one would be too big a price to pay. In less, Ciganović and Dimitriyevitch, having heard Tankosić fall, would be coming through the door with drawn weapons, to find out what had happened. If they caught their prisoner groping there at the bottom of the steps, they would have him completely at their mercy.

Without losing an instant, de Richleau thrust the now nearly empty bottle under his left arm again, took the remaining three stairs at a bound, and lurched into the room. Swaying drunkenly, he fell against the door-post and leaned there blocking the doorway for Ciganović, who had been just about to go through it. Thrusting out his free hand sideways, so that it pointed to the cellar, he roared with laughter, and stuttered hilariously:

"Ole Tankosić—ole Tankosić's fallen down the stairs."

Ciganović took a pace forward, seized him by the collar and tie, and gave him a violent shake. He let his eyes goggle, and his head roll from side to side on his shoulders, as though he was hopelessly drunk. But the shaking was brief. As Ciganović swung him round, away from the door, Dimitriyevitch's voice came sharply from behind him.

"Leave that drunken swine, and see what's happened to Tankosić."

Flinging him hard against the wall, Ciganović loosed his grip, turned, and stepped through the doorway. It was the very thing that de Richleau had been praying for. It should now be the work of only a second to slip through after him and, as he started down the stairs, brain him with the bottle by one mighty blow from behind.

But, for that manœuvre the Duke had counted on Dimitriyevitch still being off his guard, and he was not. His prisoner might or might not be drunk; but he was not taking any chances. Whipping out his pistol, he aimed it at de Richleau's stomach and snapped:

"Stay where you are, you perjured traitor!"

Dimitriyevitch was eight feet away, and standing on the far side of the small dinner table. It would have been suicide to attempt to rush him. De Richleau's hopes had been high a moment before. If he could have brained Ciganović, he could have got his gun, and having settled two of them, shot it out man for man with the Colonel. Now, terror gripped him for a second. He was still one against two, and both of them were armed, while he had only a bottle with which to attack them or defend himself.

Hatred blazing from his fanatical eyes, Dimitriyevitch pointed at the table and went on, almost spitting with venom:

"Here's the evidence of your treachery. You didn't know, did you, that my postal police open all letters to or from the Embassies and Legations? But for a hitch, for which someone is going to pay, these should have reached me by mid-day, and you would be dead now. There's enough here for the Brotherhood to condemn you ten times over. But I need no court to confirm my actions. Your attempt to get a warning to the Archduke has failed. Despite your perfidy, we'll blow that Austrian pig to bits on Sunday. And I mean to send you to hell two nights and a day ahead of him."

The Duke's glance fell to the table. But he knew what he would see before his look confirmed his thought. Among the half-empty glasses upon it, lay two open letters. The writing on them was his own. They were the all-important details of the plot that he had posted the previous night to the British Chargé d'affaires in Belgrade and Sir Maurice de Bunsen in Vienna. It was beyond Dimitriyevitch's powers to interfere with the Diplomatic Bags, but, as de Richleau stared at the damning letters, he felt he ought to have foreseen that such an adept at espionage would be certain to have the ordinary mails watched, and any letters which might appear of interest submitted to him before being carefully re-sealed for delivery.

Appalled at the thought that two out of the three channels he had used to warn Franz Ferdinand had been blocked, de Richleau stood slouched against the wall, where Ciganović had flung him. One ray of comfort flashed into his agonized mind. His telegram to Sir Pellinore was not with the letters and, its message having been disguised, it might yet get through. But in a second he forced the Archduke from his mind. He had done his utmost to save him, and could do no more. In this instant of time, no further fraction of thought could be spared for past or future. He was standing on the razor edge of life and death. Another moment, and Ciganović would come running up the stairs, back into the room. No man could hope to dodge the shots from two automatics, so with his reappearance the last faint chance would be gone. De Richleau knew that he must act *now*, or admit defeat and face eternity.

"You've forgotten something," he said with a drunken leer.

"What!" Dimitriyevitch shot the word out like a bullet from a gun, but his eyes narrowed cunningly.

"Le' me have a drink an' I'll tell you!" The Duke knew that he was now safe for a moment. His enemy had been led to suppose that he had slipped up somewhere, and he would not shoot until he had found out where. There was not much wine in the bottle. De Richleau put it to his lips and tipped it up. Some of the wine trickled down his chin as he tilted his head back, but under half-closed lids he kept his eyes fixed on Dimitriyevitch.

Suddenly his head and shoulders shot forward. It was as though the upper half of his body was a great spring that had been coiled and released—or the tongue of a catapult flicking out after the missile had just been discharged from it. And the missile was the bottle. As he jerked forward, the hand by which he was holding its neck pitched it punt first, like a blunt-ended javelin, at Dimitriyevitch's head.

The movement was so swift and unexpected that it caught the Serbian napping. With the bottle hurtling straight at his face, he attempted both to dodge it and shoot de Richleau at the same time. But the bottle was coming in too low for his sideways swerve to save him entirely. Instead of striking him on the chin, it thumped into his right shoulder at the very instant he squeezed the trigger of his automatic.

The pistol flashed twice. In the comparatively confined space of the room, the reports sounding like the bangs of a small cannon. A wisp of acrid smoke curled up from its barrel. But the blow on the shoulder had deflected his aim. The bullets sang past de Richleau's head, to thud into the wainscoting.

Dimitriyevitch had no time to fire a third shot. The instant the bottle had left the Duke's hand, he sprang forward. Seizing the table, he forced it violently against his enemy. Its further edge took the Colonel in the lower part of his stomach, and threw him off his balance. As he pitched backwards, de Richleau overturned the table on him. He fell heavily in a smother of china, fruit, silver and glass.

Swerving away, the Duke dashed for the cellar door. Ciganović had already started up the steps when the shots were fired. At the sound of them, he bounded up the rest. He was on the top step, and turning to rush into the room, as de Richleau reached the open doorway. For the flicker of an eyelid they stood glaring at one another. Ciganović was carrying his gun in his hand.

At the same second they acted. The pistol jerked up. The Duke's foot shot out in a savage kick. Again there came a flash and a deafening bang. Ciganović had had no time to take proper aim, but de Richleau was almost thrown off his feet. The bullet got him in the left shoulder, just below the collar bone, half twisting him round by the force of its impact. But his vicious kick had landed squarely just below Ciganović's left knee-cap. With a howl, the Serbian staggered back, lifting his injured leg a little, his face contorted by an agony of pain.

De Richleau was the first to recover. The bullet felt like the kick of a mule, followed by a red hot iron piercing his shoulder; but almost at once he realized that the wound had not seriously crippled him. Grabbing the door, he flung it shut while Ciganović was still striving to regain his balance. But before he could get it properly latched, the Serbian threw himself against it. The door was forced open a couple of inches. Sweating with renewed terror, de Richleau struggled to overcome the pressure so that he could turn the key in the lock. He knew that Dimitriyevitch must be staggering up from among the debris of the table behind him. At any second he expected to be shot in the back.

A glance over his shoulder showed him that his fears were only too well-founded. The half minute that he had spent in dashing at the door and tackling Ciganović had been sufficient for the Colonel to struggle out from under the table. He was now on his feet. But when he pitched backwards his gun had been knocked from his hand, and he was frantically searching for it among the debris.

In vain, the Duke strove with all his might to close the door. Ciganović was as strong as he was. That awful two-inch gap remained, a narrow but fatal chasm, wide enough to plunge him from life to death. Suddenly he saw it like that, and realized that he would die there, with his good shoulder pressed against the door, if he remained where he was a moment longer.

His brain was working so furiously that to think was to act. In a single movement, he flung himself back and sideways. The door flew open. As the pressure was released, Ciganović came flying through it. Losing his balance, he crashed to the floor. His pistol exploded as it hit the parquet, then jerked from his hand, and slithered away under a sofa. De Richleau ran forward and kicked him on the head. He gave a loud groan, twitched, and lay still.

Swivelling round, the Duke faced Dimitriyevitch. Another twenty seconds had sped since he last had a chance to look at the Colonel, but he was still hunting for his gun. They saw it at the same instant. It was just behind him, lying in the fireplace. As he stooped to grab it, de Richleau ran in and kicked it from beneath his fingers. Instead, Dimitriyevitch grasped the poker, sprang back a pace, and lifted it to strike. The Duke leapt forward and seized his upraised wrist. The Serbian brought up his foot and kicked him on the shin. Next moment they had closed, and were locked in a fierce embrace.

Dimitriyevitch was the smaller and, by a few years, the older of the two; but he had a wiry frame and the toughness of a peasant. By exerting himself to the full, de Richleau could have got the best of the tussle had they both started from scratch: but he was already sweating with his exertions and losing blood from his wound. Like a pair of evenly matched wrestlers, they staggered and swayed together, with the poker upthrust and jerking above their heads.

Finding that he could not break de Richleau's hold on his wrist to strike him with the poker, Dimitriyevitch suddenly kneed him in the groin. With a gasp, de Richleau released his grip. White-faced, his eyes starting from their sockets with pain, he staggered back. The poker descended with a swish. Only just in time, he jerked his head aside. The blow caught him on his wounded shoulder. It was already aching fiercely from the strain he had put upon it in grasping his adversary's wrist. He moaned and stepped back another pace. Following up his advantage, the Serbian struck at him again. He took the second blow on his left forearm. Then, still half doubled up, he lurched forward and drove his right fist into Dimitriyevitch's face.

Owing to the punishment the Duke had received, the blow was not a heavy one; but, temporarily, it was enough. Dimitriyevitch took it full on the mouth. His head shot back, his eyes glared wildly for a moment. Then he lost his balance and fell backwards on to the hearth.

De Richleau flung himself on top of him, grasped him by the throat, and forced his head back among the still-smouldering logs of the fire. As the red hot wood-ash scorched the back of his neck, Dimitriyevitch let out a scream, jerked his head up, and kicked furiously with both legs. The violence of his movement threw the Duke over on his side. With a frantic wriggle, the Serbian rolled over and on to his enemy's chest. He still grasped the poker in his right hand, and with his left now grabbed de Richleau's throat. For a full minute they put all their strength into their fingers, each trying to throttle the other, and both with their chins pressed down, endeavouring to protect their necks. Gradually Dimitriyevitch felt the Duke weaken beneath him. Heaving himself upright, he raised the poker to administer the *coup de grâce.*

But it was a trap. The poker was no more than shoulder high when de Richleau served his adversary as he had been served himself. Bringing his knee up sharply, he jabbed it in the Colonel's groin. The poker clattered on the hearth, the Serbian's eyes started and boggled horribly. In a second the Duke had turned the tables. Wriggling from under, he grabbed Dimitriyevitch again and flung him down a foot to the right of where they had been struggling, so that the back of his head was once more among the smouldering logs. He screamed again, but now de Richleau had both hands on his throat and, for good measure, kneed him again in the pit of the stomach. The screaming ceased abruptly,

but a frightful sweat broke out on the Serbian's face, and rolled from it to fall hissing into the red-hot ashes.

"Now!" gasped the Duke. "Let me tell you something. You managed to stop my letters, but not the telegram I sent to London. It was worded too cunningly for your post office spies to detect its meaning. But my friends in London will know what it means, and it will be in their hands by now. They will telegraph to Vienna and, after all, the Archduke will be warned in time. I want the knowledge that your abominable plans have been wrecked to be the last thought that you carry with you into unconsciousness. It is not Franz Ferdinand who is going to die—but you."

Dimitriyevitch understood. His eyes showed it, and the last futile effort he made to break free from the murderous grip on his wind-pipe. The glowing ash was biting like an army of ants into the back of his head, and he tried to scream again. But the Duke's strangle-hold prevented more than awful animal noises issuing from his throat. His lips drew back, showing his gums in a nightmare grin. His face turned red, then purple. A foam of bubbles began to froth up from his mouth. His tongue protruded, becoming thick and leathery. It swelled until it filled the whole cavity between his wide-stretched upper and lower teeth. His eyes protruded like marbles. They looked as though they were about to burst. Tears of blood appeared in their corners, forced their way out, and trickled down into his ears. His face became black and bloated, horrible, unrecognizable. And all the time, his body twitched spasmodically. At last the twitching ceased and he was dead.

With a sigh, de Richleau relaxed his grip. He felt not the least scruple about what he had done. It had had to be Dimitriyevitch or himself. Had he left the arch-plotter living, he would have had little chance of escaping with his life. If he had left his victim bound and gagged, within an hour of the servants arriving in the morning, the whole police force of Serbia would have been turned on to hunt him down. But none of the servants had seen him there that night, so the odds were they would have no idea who had murdered their master, and he would at least get a good run for his money. And, if that were not reason enough, the corpse that still lay warm beneath him was that of a man who, for his own aggrandizement, had plotted to plunge the whole world in fire and blood.

Although no faintest atom of remorse troubled the Duke's mind, he felt sick, ill, and exhausted. Levering himself off the body, he half rolled, half crawled, towards the nearest arm-chair, pillowed his head upon its seat, shut his eyes, and lay there, striving to calm his nerves and get back his strength.

Gradually his breathing grew normal, the sweat dried on his face, and the searing pain of the bullet wound, which he had stretched by his exertions, eased to a dull ache. How long he lay there, he did not know; but he suddenly caught the faint sound of movement behind him. It was followed almost instantly by a sharp 'ping', like the noise made by the snapping of a wire. Rolling over in swift alarm, he sat up. To his horror, he saw Ciganović glaring down at him.

CHAPTER XVII

THE ANGEL OF DEATH STRIKES AGAIN

THE kick on the head that de Richleau had given the tall albino had rendered him unconscious for nearly a quarter of an hour. But on coming to, from where he was lying he had seen Dimitriyevitch sprawled on his back in the fireplace and the Duke crouching, half asleep, against the chair. He had realized that the one was dead and the other only comatose. Having lost his pistol, he had got stealthily to his feet, crept towards the hearth and, stretching out his long arm above the overturned table, wrenched one of the Turkish scimitars from its place on the wall.

Galvanized into instant action by renewed fear for his life, the Duke sprang to his feet. Only the table and its debris of dessert lay between them, and the chinless Captain Ciganović's pinkish eyes glared murder into his. He knew that he could expect no mercy. Like a glimpse of one of the new motion pictures, he saw himself being chased, with the big chopper-like sword flashing within an inch of his back. Cursing himself for having failed to secure one of the pistols while he had the chance, he saw that he must seize some weapon in the next second or die yet in that room, slashed to pieces within a few feet of where he stood. His glance flickered to the chimney-piece. He was three feet nearer to it than his enemy. In one bound he reached it and grabbed the hilt of another of the scimitars. At the same instant Ciganović struck.

De Richleau had underestimated the tall man's reach. Only the body of Dimitriyevitch saved him from being cleft from skull to chin. As he leapt, his eyes were riveted on the weapon he meant to seize. He had no chance to watch his step. His right foot landed on the dead man's thigh, slipped, and precipitated him violently forward. But for his grasp on the hilt of the scimitar he would have pitched head down between the legs of the table. As it was, his head and shoulders curved in a dive below the level of the mantel. Above them Ciganović's blade bit into the wood of the mantel-shelf. He had to exert all his strength to wrench it free. In that moment of grace, the Duke ducked back from under the blade and pulled the one he held from its fastening.

As though by mutual consent, they both withdrew a pace and skirted the legs of the table to get out into the open. Like duellists, as they had now become, they took one another's measure and cautiously began to manœuvre for the best ground.

Had they been armed with rapiers de Richleau would have felt reasonably confident about the outcome, as he was one of the finest swordsmen in Europe; but the weapons chance had forced upon them filled him with misgiving. The nearest thing to them he had ever handled was a sabre; and, since he regarded sabre-play as uncouth compared with the finesse of the straight blade, he had given little time to it. And even the sabre had comparatively little in common with these terrible weapons. They were barely two feet long, but from the hilt they widened out in a graceful curve to nearly six inches in width towards their ends. Their blades graduated from razor-sharp edges to backs half an inch in thickness, so that their weight gave them a far greater cutting power than that of a long flat-bladed sword. On both sides they were beautifully damascened with an inlay of arabesques in gold; and it was with just such a weapon that Haroun al Raschid's executioner, the negro Mansour, had struck off the heads of standing men at a single blow.

There was little to choose between the physical state of the combatants. De Richleau had a bullet wound in his left shoulder, from which he had lost some blood, and his right shin ached badly where Dimitriyevitch had kicked him. Ciganović had a bump the size of a duck's egg above the left ear, where the Duke's boot had landed, and blood was still oozing from it; while water was already gathering painfully under his right knee-cap from the first kick he had received. Both felt groggy and uncertain of themselves; and both were aware that one slip of the treacherous mats on which they stood would lead to a swift death. Yet neither thought of attempting flight.

Suddenly Ciganović sprang forward, aiming a blow at the Duke's head. He parried it easily, but failed to get in under the other's guard. The thickness and awkwardness of the weapon prevented him from turning the Serbian's blade and seizing the advantage which he would have gained had they been fighting with swords. Moreover, to his renewed apprehension, de Richleau discovered that his opponent's height and length of arm gave him an even greater advantage in reach than he had at first supposed.

The scimitars clashed again, and again, Ciganović attacking all the time and the Duke on the defensive. He had observed one thing that heartened him a little. The Serbian was suffering great pain from his right knee every time he moved. So, by treading warily in a circle, and giving back a little each time he was attacked, de Richleau forced him to keep shifting his position.

Their eyes never left one another, each knowing that his life depended on anticipating the other's next stroke. As they fought, the room was deadly still. Even the sound of the trees outside rustling in the night breeze seemed to have died away. The tense silence was broken only by the rasp of their breathing and the slither of steel on steel.

Sweat was streaming from them both. De Richleau's arm was tiring from wielding the heavy weapon; but he could now detect a look of fear in the albino's eyes, and believed him to be nearer to exhaustion than himself. Hoping to end it before his arm had become too weak to deal a mortal stroke, he suddenly stepped in and slashed at the Serbian's neck. Ciganović succeeded in partially parrying the sideways cut, but the Duke's scimitar slid along his and its razor edge nicked an inch deep cut in the ugly dewlap that sloped back where his chin should have been.

Blood welled from the wound and poured down on to his prominent Adam's apple. He let out an oath and slashed again at de Richleau's head. To avoid the flailing scimitar, the Duke sprang back. The silk rug on which he landed slid from under him as though he had jumped in smooth-soled shoes on to a skating rink. His feet flew forward, his head flew back, and in a second he was full length on the floor.

With a yell of triumph Ciganović ran in. Using all his remaining strength, he slashed down at his prostrate enemy. The flashing blade missed the Duke by only a fraction of an inch. Just in time he heaved himself aside and rolled over and over towards the door. Again he was given a moment of grace. The power of Ciganović's stroke had driven the sharp steel he wielded through the mat and into the floor. By the time he had freed it, de Richleau was stumbling to his feet.

As he scrambled to his knees he found himself near the little table on which stood the bronze statuette of Napoleon. The second his glance fell on it, he snatched it up in his left hand. At a limping run, Ciganović came charging in again. The Duke hurled the bronze figure at his head. It took him between the eyes, halting him in his tracks. His arms flew wide and he nearly overbalanced backwards from the force with which the statuette had hit him. De Richleau took one step forward, raised his terrible weapon, and brought it down with a sickening crunch in the side of the tall Serbian's neck. Blood spouted from the jugular vein as from a fountain. For a moment he stood swaying there. Then his knees folded under him and he crashed to the floor, the blade fast in the ghastly wound dragging de Richleau down on top of him.

Letting go the hilt of the scimitar, the Duke rose slowly to his feet and stood for a moment, panting beside the still-twitching body. Then he began to look round the floor for one of the pistols. Tankosić had given no sign of life from the cellar, but he might not be dead, and de Richleau did not mean to be caught napping twice.

After a short search he found Dimitriyevitch's gun. The kick had sent it from the hearth into a dark corner behind the log basket. The Duke picked it up gingerly, knowing that its safety catch must be off. He found that it had one bullet in the chamber and five left in the magazine. Now that he was properly armed, he could allow fatigue to have its way with him, at least for a short spell. Holding the pistol on his knee, he sat down in the arm-chair on which he had previously rested his head.

A glance at the grandfather clock on the far side of the room showed it to be twenty-five past ten, and the pendulum of the clock was still swinging. It seemed incredible that so short a time should have elapsed since the arrival of the messenger with the letters that had betrayed him; but the only pause of more than seconds during the frightful scene of violence which had just taken place, had been after he had choked the life out of Dimitriyevitch.

As his muscles relaxed and his breathing came more regularly, his brain became capable again of considering matters beyond the immediate present. He had told Dimitriyevitch that his plot had failed and that the Archduke would be warned in time. Such an incarnation of Satan on earth had deserved that, and even had de Richleau not sent a telegram to Sir Pellinore he would have made up some such story for his victim to carry down to hell. But, unfortunately, the statement as a whole was probably very far from the truth.

The Duke had counted on Sir Maurice de Bunsen doing the trick in Vienna, or, failing that, the Chargé d'affaires in Belgrade sending a cipher telegram to the Foreign Office, the contents of which would immediately be relayed to the Austrian capital. But both those lines had been blocked, and Sir Pellinore was a private individual. As de Richleau knew, telegrams from the Balkans often took twenty-four hours or more to reach London. His had been sent first thing that morning, not overnight at the same time as the letters, as he had led Dimitriyevitch to suppose. So it was unlikely that it would be delivered at Carlton House Terrace until to-morrow, Saturday morning. What if Sir Pellinore were away for the week-end, as well he might be? It might be sent on to him in the country. If not, it would lie on a silver salver in his front hall till Monday, by which time the Archduke would be dead. If it were sent on to him in the country, the odds were that it would not reach him till the afternoon. Telephones were still unreliable things for discussing such matters at long distance, and it was pretty certain that only junior officials would be available at the Foreign Office over a week-end. Sir Pellinore would have to hurry back to London, and further time would be lost while he ran to earth anyone of sufficient standing to cope with such a situation. If they failed to get a message off before the evening, by the time it reached Vienna it would almost certainly be too late to find and warn Franz Ferdinand. And even at best, if Sir Pellinore did get the wire on Saturday morning, the margin was going to be extremely narrow.

It took little thought for de Richleau to see that, where his first attempt to get to Sarajevo had been no more than a proper precaution, it was now absolutely imperative that he should succeed in doing so.

Although his wound was bound to hamper him badly, and the cross-country journey would be a hideous one, he still had two nights and a day in which to make it; and now that he could get away with a clear start in Dimitriyevitch's Rolls, he felt that he ought to be able to reach the Bosnian capital by his deadline of Sunday morning.

The thought of getting a clear start reminded him about Tankosić. After that mighty swipe with the bottle, it seemed probable that the third member of the unholy triumvirate was lying at the bottom of the cellar steps with a cracked skull, and so badly concussed that he would not recover consciousness for some days. But if he did prove capable of talking when the servants found him in the morning, the Duke would be a hunted man long before he could get out of Serbia. In view of the now vital importance of his reaching Sarajevo, de Richleau felt that he ought to go down to the cellar and finish the Serbian off.

But he did not at all relish the idea. He had always loathed the business of having to shoot horses when they were wounded in action, and the thought of blowing out the brains of a helpless but still living man, however brutal his character, was much more horrible. The only alternative seemed to be to take Tankosić with him. If he did not die from a haemorrhage brought on by the bumping of the car over rough roads, he could be put out at some village just over the frontier and the peasants there told that his head wound was the result of his having been run over.

Getting up, de Richleau walked over to the cellar door and listened. There was not a sound, so he took it that he had nothing to fear from that direction. Slipping the safety catch of the pistol on, he put it in his pocket, then took from its bracket on the wall, one of the six oil lamps that lit the big room, and crossed the hall to a small pantry on its far side, where he knew that the drinks were kept. There, he mixed himself a stiff brandy and soda and drank it slowly.

By the time he had finished it his head was much clearer and he felt altogether better. Going upstairs to the only bathroom in the house, he eased himself painfully out of his jacket and shirt, and examined his wound in the mirror. It was a small, neat hole not far from his arm-pit and just below the collar bone. The wound had stopped bleeding, but was slightly inflamed round its edges, and the bullet had not come out at the back, which meant that later it must be probed for and extracted. Still, he felt he had been very lucky that it had not either penetrated his lung or smashed his shoulder joint; and he knew the latter was all right as, although it pained him to lift his arm, he could still do so without the agony he would have suffered had the bone been splintered.

After washing the wound thoroughly with soap and water, he found an antiseptic ointment among the pots in the bathroom cupboard, also cotton wool and sticking plaster, so he was able to make a rough dressing for it. He would have given a lot to lie soaking for a while in a hot bath but, apart from the fact that time was precious, there was always the risk that some unforeseen circumstance might bring another messenger out to the châlet: so he decided not to risk it.

When he had finished dressing his wound, he went into Dimitriyevitch's bedroom and opened the wardrobe. In it, in addition to several sets of uniform, there was a variety of civilian clothes for use when the Colonel travelled abroad. Selecting an undress uniform, de Richleau took off the rest of his blood-stained clothes and got into it. The tunic did not fit him at all badly, but the breeches were a good bit too short, so he had to put up with the waist-line making a thick flap round his hips and leaving their two top buttons undone. Then, to his great annoyance, when he came to try the Colonel's riding boots, he found that he could not possibly get into them. However, he decided to get over that by using Ciganović's, as they would certainly be large enough. Taking a suitcase from on top of the wardrobe, he packed some of Dimitriyevitch's civilian clothes into it, then went downstairs in his stockinged feet.

Leaving the suitcase in the hall, he stepped over to the door of the big room. His approach had been noiseless and, as he reached the door, which was standing ajar, he heard a sound inside. Getting out his gun, he slipped off the catch, and peered cautiously through the narrow opening. There, at the far end of the room, his head and face all bloody, stood Tankosić.

Evidently he had just recovered consciousness, made his way unaided up the cellar steps, and was now taking stock of the situation. He was leaning with one hand against the wall, but his bloody head moved swiftly from side to side as he took in the details of the awful scene, showing that he was fully *compos mentis*.

As de Richleau watched him his glance fell, and remained fixed for a moment on something on the floor at the far end of the sofa. Following his glance, the Duke saw it too: a dark object that was under the sofa end, but protruding a few inches from it. Next second he realized that it was the butt of the pistol which Ciganović had dropped as he pitched head foremost through the cellar door.

Tankosić left the wall and took two firm steps towards it. The Duke pushed the door open, levelled his pistol, and cried: "Hands up!"

The Serbian halted in his tracks, let out an oath, and turned to stare at de Richleau. But he made no move to surrender.

They were thirty-five feet apart, and the Duke could guess the thoughts that were racing through Tankosić's mind. He was thinking of their shooting match and what a much better shot he was than the man who was trying to hold him up. He had only to duck to get the full cover of the sofa; then, by thrusting his arm under it, he could reach the pistol. Once he had that, he would back himself any day to exact vengeance for his dead Chief and comrade. For him, the all-important question was, in the one second it would take him to duck behind the sofa, could the Duke shoot him at thirty-five feet?

De Richleau waited patiently, a grim little smile twitching the corners of his mouth. Suddenly Tankosić decided to chance it, and dived for the floor. The Duke's gun cracked and spurted flame. Its bullet smacked through the Serbian's skull while he still had a foot to drop to reach cover.

A faint wisp of smoke still trailing from his pistol, de Richleau walked the length of the room to make quite certain that he had killed the last of his three enemies. He had. There was no doubt about that. From a rent in Tankosić's skull, the grey matter that had been his brains was seeping. The Duke stared down at the body for a moment, admiring its depth of chest and splendid width of shoulder. It occurred to him that had he been compelled to grapple with that torso, instead of with the less powerful one of Dimitriyevitch, he would be dead by now. He was far from sorry that Tankosić had regained consciousness and, out of insolent self-confidence, invited a bullet. His death was going to save a lot of trouble. Turning away, de Richleau secured the two letters that had betrayed him, then set about his grim task of robbing the dead.

First, with some difficulty he got off Ciganović's boots. They were a bit large, but served their purpose. Next, he deprived Dimitriyevitch of his wrist watch. Lastly, he went through the pockets of all three and took all the money they had on them. It was more than enough to get him to Sarajevo.

The room now reeked with the sickly-sweet stench of human blood, tinged faintly with the forge-like smell of Dimitriyevitch's singed hair; and the Duke was extremely glad when he had finished his ghoulish operations. In the hall he took a torch from the table and another automatic and several spare clips of bullets from the armoury chest. Then, from the pantry he collected the ullaged bottle of brandy and another of Slivowitz, which he packed in the suitcase. The grandfather clock was chiming eleven when he left the house.

Out in the garage he tried the engine of the Rolls to make certain that she was in perfect running order. Then he looked to her tyres, oil and petrol. The tank was nearly full, but there were a number of spare cans stacked in a corner, so he filled her up from two and wedged the others in on the floor at the back. To his great satisfaction he found in one of her pockets a set of large scale military maps, and he was just about to drive off when he remembered the Peugeot in which he had been brought out to the châlet that evening.

In the morning every hour that the police could be delayed in learning of the murders would make a difference as, although the servants who reported it might be in ignorance of the murderer's identity, they would know that he had got away in the Rolls. So he got out, found a heavy spanner, and walked over to the smaller car. Lifting the bonnet, he bashed at both the carburettor and magneto until they were wrecked beyond repair. Then he returned to the Rolls. At twenty past eleven she purred out of the garage on her way to Sarajevo.

The châlet lay to the south-east of Belgrade, so it was unnecessary for him to go through the capital. By taking a left-hand turn at a cross-roads about half way to it he could head south to Ayala. His recent military studies had sufficiently acquainted him with Serbia to know the situation of her principal market towns, and the roads that connected them, without reference to the map. From Ayala he meant to continue south to Soplot. There, he would have to turn off his course, inclining south-east through Medjulužje to Topola. Thence he could swing south-west to Rudnik, and south again to Cacak. Then, at this quite considerable place, he would be able to head almost due west along the valley of the upper Morava for Užice and the frontier.

For the first forty-five miles, as far as Topola, he thought that the going would be fairly good, as it was the main road to the south. But after that he feared that it was bound to be pretty grim. As an offset against that he had the Rolls and, while it would not do her any good, he felt confident that she would stand up to practically anything without breaking down. From Topola to the frontier was roughly a further eighty-five miles, and the last twenty up into the mountains might well prove impracticable for any car. But with luck he felt that he should be able to cover a hundred miles before the death of Dimitriyevitch and his companions was discovered, so be out of danger in the mountain region by the time the police got on his track.

The night was fine and the summer sky alight with stars, so he was able to drive at a good pace. The main street of Ayala was deserted and the hum of his engine echoed back to him from the shuttered houses. The inhabitants of Soplot too were all abed, except for a pair of belated lovers who witnessed his swift progress. But five miles beyond the town he became uneasy. The watch that he was keeping on the stars suggested to him with increasing insistence that somehow he had taken a wrong turning. A mile or two farther on he pulled up, got out and looked at the road surface. Its poorness confirmed his impression. Convinced now that he was off his course, he angrily turned the car round and drove back to the town.

There were no signposts to help him, but, fortunately, the lovers were still lingering by the well in the main square. They showed him an awkward, unexpected twist out of it, which put him on the right road again; but he had covered some fourteen unnecessary miles and wasted twenty-five minutes.

Shortly after one in the morning he ran through Topola. Allowing for his ill-luck in having taken the wrong turning in Soplot, he felt that he had not done at all badly. But from there on his real troubles began. Except for short stretches here and there, the roads were little better than tracks. Whenever he attempted to put on any speed the Rolls bounded and skidded dangerously over stony humps and into deep ruts of hard-baked mud. To rest his wounded shoulder as much as possible he had made a loose sling for his left arm, and had been taking his hand from it only when it was necessary to change gears; but now he needed both hands on the wheel constantly to keep the car on the road. And, even then, he was compelled to slow down to a maximum speed of twenty miles an hour.

It took him an hour and a quarter to cover the eighteen miles to Rudnik. As he turned south there matters worsened still further; for at that point he left the plain and entered hilly country, through which the road twisted abominably. It was after four o'clock when he entered Cacak, and the results of the fight for life that he had been through, followed by five hours of exceptionally wearing driving, found him about at the end of his tether.

Yet, somehow, he had to do another thirty miles to Užice and get clear of that town before he dared pull up for the sort of rest that would be any real good to him. As Užice was the terminal of the branch railway line, it was certain to be also the last telegraph post this side of the mountains. If he did not pass through it before about nine o'clock the odds were that the police would be on the look-out for him. The Rolls was such a complete give-away that he could not possibly hope to slip through without being pulled up, and there was no way round the town. On the other hand, if he could get through before the warning to hold him was telegraphed all over the country, he would be clear of the police net and stand a good chance of getting away altogether.

Outside Cacak he pulled up for a few minutes and had a stiff tot of brandy; then he drove on. The road now wound up the Morava valley with steep hills to either side. It was wide enough to take only a single wagon. Sometimes its course ran two hundred feet above the swirling river, and the passage of a car was still so exceptional in those parts that none of the hideously dangerous bends, skirting precipices, had yet had stone walls built to prevent fast vehicles going over. It was still night, so at least he had the road to himself; but as he advanced, the mountain crags closed in about him, and every moment's driving became an appalling strain.

The stars dimmed and the first light of day began to outline the desolate skyline. His wound was now aching intolerably, and he felt so tired that only the acute danger of one false move sending the car hurtling over a precipice kept him from falling asleep at the wheel. At last, through strained and bleary eyes, he saw the first houses of Užice, now lit by the golden dawn of the sky behind him. The rural population was already beginning to go about its daily business in the streets of the little town, and a church clock showed him that it was nearly seven. Rallying his fast failing strength, he drove through the place and a few miles beyond it. Then, coming upon a wooded hill-side, he turned the car in among the trees until it was out of sight from the road, shut off the engine and, slumping where he sat, fell into a sleep of exhaustion.

When he awoke, for a moment he could not think where he was. But as he moved, an acute stab of pain from his wound, which had stiffened while he slept, brought everything rushing back to him. A glance at the wrist watch that he had taken from Dimitriyevitch showed that it was twenty past two. Horrified, he realized that he had slept for seven hours. He had hoped to be in Sarajevo that night: now, he would never do it. But he might still get there early on Sunday morning.

His eyes were gummy and his mouth tasted foul, but his sleep had renewed his strength. Quickly he got the car going, backed it out of the wood on to the road, and turned its bonnet westward. He had not gone far before it struck him that he was still on the north side of the river, when he should now have been on its south. But possibly the narrow swirling torrent he could see below him on his left was a tributary of the Morava. Pulling up as soon as he reached the top of the next rise, from which he could get a good view of the surrounding country, he got out the pack of maps, found the one delineating that district, and studied it carefully.

After a moment he swore, and put the map back. There was no doubt that he was on the road to Bisoka, and not that to Kremna as he ought to be. When he had reached Užice early that morning his brain had been so numbed by fatigue after his hundred and thirty miles' night drive that it had rejected all thought, except the imperative one that he must get through the town and out of it, so that he could find a place to pull up and sleep. He had forgotten that he should have turned left in its centre and crossed the bridge.

He dared not go back, as by now the police in every town in Serbia would be on the look-out for the Rolls. The only thing for it was to go on until he could find a bridge by which he could cross the river further up. But in that he was disappointed, as the road soon turned away from the river, winding north-west between some low hills.

Three quarters of an hour's driving over the most vile track he had yet struck brought him to within sight of Bisoka. It was the last market town that side of the frontier, and not much further from it than Kremna. But the latter was considerably nearer to Yardiste, the railhead on the Bosnian side. From either, the roads up into the mountains would be little better than goat tracks and quite impassable for a car. So the time had come to abandon the Rolls.

On his right a pine wood sloped down towards the town. Bumping the car across a shallow ditch, he drove it in among the trees as far as he could. Then, getting out the suitcase, he set off at a brisk walk down the road.

A quarter of a mile outside the main cluster of buildings he came to the first *Zadruga*. It was a huddle of hutments and lean-tos in which fifty or sixty peasants were living, apparently all mixed up with their individual live-stock. A group of women was pounding maize in front of it, and a patriarchal figure, with a long grey beard, sat nearby on a rickety chair watching them.

The old man was well dressed for his class, so de Richleau put him down as the headman of the community and saluted him politely. Even if the news of the murders had got this far in the course of the morning, the Duke thought it unlikely that anyone in the uniform of a Serbian officer would be connected with them, and it was in order not to give the impression that he might be a fugitive that he had chosen the clothes he was wearing. He told the headman that his carriage had broken an axle two miles back in the hills, and that as his duties demanded his presence in Kremna that afternoon, he wished to buy a riding horse on which to get there.

As the old man spoke only a local patois, the Duke had great difficulty in making himself understood, but with the help of some of the women, who stood round giggling, he eventually succeeded. A younger man was sent for and a string of horses led out. De Richleau chose a strong-looking chestnut and produced some of the gold and silver he had taken from his victims. The price asked was fantastic and he knew that had he cared to spend the afternoon there, haggling over innumerable cups of coffee, he could have got the beast for a quarter of what they asked. But time was more precious to him than gold. He knocked off a third, indicated that they must throw in saddlery, and told them that if they would not accept he would try the next farm.

That closed the deal to their satisfaction as well as his own. Smiling and bowing they then offered him refreshment. Soon after he had woken he had begun to feel hungry, so he gladly accepted and made a hearty meal off cold pork, goose-liver, fruit and coffee. By four o'clock, with his suitcase strapped to the back of his saddle and the cheerful good-byes of half the big peasant family ringing in his ears, he was on his way again.

While eating, he had thought of hiring one of the men to act as his guide, but a casual inquiry about the roads to the west showed that they were farmers and knew little more of the mountain country along the frontier than he did; so he decided to put off looking for a guide until he got to Kremna. Although he had found it difficult to understand their speech, he felt confident that from what they had told him, and with the aid of his map, he could find his way there. After riding through the town, he kept straight on in accordance with their information that he would come to the river again in a twenty minutes' ride, and be able to cross it then.

In due course he reached the ford they had described but, half an hour after crossing it, he came to another that they had not mentioned. His map now proved of little help as this wild frontier region had never been properly surveyed, and the only thing that seemed clear about it was that the whole countryside was intersected by winding tributaries of the Morava. Assuming the second stream to be one of these, he pressed on, hoping to come in sight of Kremna in the next quarter of an hour or so.

But now, to his concern, the track left the plain and wound up into the hills, which was contrary to what he had expected. However, in the next five miles no other track intersected it, so he had no option but to go forward. For all he knew, Kremna might be a hill town, or lie in some valley that he had not yet entered, but he felt that by this time he should have reached it.

At half past five he came upon a goat-herd, but the man spoke only some mountain dialect which was quite incomprehensible. Nevertheless, he kept grinning, nodding his head, and pointing up the road; so de Richleau endeavoured to comfort himself with the belief that the fellow meant that Kremna was in that direction, Actually, the man had meant that was the way to the nearest village, and two miles farther on the Duke came to it. But it was no more than a miserable collection of huts, and he could not make head nor tail of anything its few primitive inhabitants said.

For several miles now the road had been gradually mounting, and soon after leaving the village he came out on to a wild desolate heath. It was the first time for over an hour that he had not been shut in by low hills and belts of forest, so he was at last again able to get a wider view of the surrounding country and attempt to orient its major features with his map.

The position of the sun had already filled him with foreboding that his general direction was carrying him too far to the west, and now his fears were confirmed. A rugged peak rising well above its neighbours, some five miles distant, could be only Mount Zhoriste. He was some way past and to the north of it, whereas he should have skirted its southern flank. A quick check up with the other features of the landscape showed him that he was now up on the Tara plateau and farther from Kremna than when he had set out from Bisoka. Evidently he had taken the wrong track somewhere between the two fords. The Morava must have formed a wide loop there, and crossing the second had brought him back on to its north bank.

Cursing and fuming, he wondered what the devil to do. The fact that he was considerably nearer to the frontier than he would have been at Kremna was little consolation, as he was nearly double the distance from the Bosnian railhead, and the mountain now lay between him and it.

It was nearly two hours since he had left Bisoka, so to go back to the first ford, where he must have taken the wrong track, would mean a total loss of over three, and he would still have ten miles or more to cover before he reached Kremna. That meant he could not now get there much before half past eight. Only an hour and a half of twilight would be left, and he doubted if he would be able to find a guide willing to take him across the mountain barrier in darkness. While, if he set off on his own, he would certainly lose his way again, even if he were lucky enough to escape a broken neck.

On the other hand, up there on the Tara plateau he was already half way through the mountains, and there were still nearly four hours of daylight to go. The frontier could not be far ahead of him. If he could work his way round to the west of Mount Zhoriste and down to the Drina river, he might yet reach the rail-head by nightfall. In these wild regions travellers unaccompanied by guides were still quite frequently set upon and held to ransom by bandits; but he was well mounted and well armed, so he felt that as long as daylight lasted he need have no great fear of being captured should he come upon a band of outlaws.

In consequence he decided on the latter course and rode on. For a mile on either side of him, and two miles ahead, the heath spread unbroken; a tangle of gorse, heather and rocky outcrop. It looked beautiful in the evening light, but was so full of snags and rabbit holes that he dared not ride his horse across it. As it was unbroken by any cross track, he had to wait until he entered the next belt of pine woods before veering left.

For some time he rode southward through the trees, over ground made springy from countless generations of fallen pine needles. Then he was brought up short by the plateau ending in a deep gorge. Turning west, he followed the fringe of the wood until the gorge became less precipitous and he could head south once more. But now the ground became more broken and treacherous so, coming on a goat-track that led south-eastward, he felt that he had better take it. The track led to higher ground, then down into another wood, and there it curved again until he had the sinking sun behind him. Leaving it, he tried a new cast to the south, but gradually the trees thickened so that he had difficulty in finding a way for his horse between them. Exasperated by the slowness of his pace, he turned back a little way, then headed west again; only to find a mile farther on that in that direction the wood ended against a cliff face of unbroken rock.

It was now nearly nine o'clock and almost dark in the forest. He had left Bisoka at four so, with only infrequent pauses to rest and water his mount, he had been in the saddle for five hours. As a soldier he had often ridden for double that length of time, and normally would not have thought anything of it; but the exertions of the previous night and the constant nagging of his wound had taken a lot out of him. He was very tired and terribly dispirited. Yet he still hoped that he might strike the Drina before night had fallen, so he turned back yet again, then struck out in a new direction.

This time, when he reached the fringe of the wood, he came out on to coarse grassland which sloped away into a shallow valley. His depression lifting, he put his horse into a canter and followed the valley bottom for a mile. It then merged into further hills, the depression rising to form a pass between two rounded summits. As he rode between them he stared anxiously ahead, but even in the open the light was fast fading, and he could see no more than the faint silhouette of a distant line of hills against the faint after-glow of the long-past sunset.

Beyond the pass the ground shelved away to another belt of forest. Once in it, he had to ride with renewed caution, as the darkness there made it difficult to see the trunks of the trees. For a further twenty minutes he proceeded cautiously, then came out of the forest to find himself faced by another impassable gorge.

Wearily, he dismounted, tethered his horse to the nearest tree, and sat down with his back against it. He could have wept at his inability to go farther and the bitterness of his frustration. From Bisoka he had estimated that a three and a half hour ride would carry him across the frontier to Yardiste; so he should have been there by half past seven and, with luck, caught the last train to Sarajevo. Even had he missed it, he could have hired a carriage and, with relays of horses, easily covered the sixty miles to the Bosnian capital before morning. Yet here he was at ten o'clock at night, utterly and completely lost, without even an idea any longer in which direction Yardiste lay, and hemmed in by darkness that menaced himself and his horse with death if they attempted to continue their erratic journey.

The peasants from whom he had bought his horse had pressed some raisin cake and fruit upon him so, getting them and the bottle of Slivowatz out of the suitcase, he made a picnic meal, sharing the food with his tired mount. Then he scooped a hole among the pine needles for his hip, covered himself with the civilian clothes he had taken from Dimitriyevitch's wardrobe, and tried to sleep.

It seemed a long time before he dozed off, owing to his intense worry about the Archduke and his anxiety that he should not sleep too long. That morning he had been too exhausted to impress his brain before sleeping with the necessity to be on the road again by mid-day; but, normally, his soldier's training enabled him more or less to fix his hour of waking, and it worked on this occasion. At five o'clock he woke to find it a lovely summer morning: and, there, in the gorge below him, lay a swirling river that could only be the Drina.

He waited only to take off his uniform, throw it under a bush, and put on the civilian riding clothes that he had used for cover during the night. Then he was off. He considered it unlikely that the Archduke would make his official entry into Sarajevo before ten o'clock and, if that were so, he still had five hours to work in. He could no longer hope to get to Sarajevo in time, but by hard riding he ought to be able to reach the railway, and from there he could send a telegram of warning.

Now that daylight had come he soon found a steep but possible way down into the gorge, and it consoled him a little to think that losing his way had enabled him to cross the frontier without difficulty. To prevent smuggling, guards were, he knew, stationed along it at intervals, and he had feared that if he ran into a patrol they might hold him up. But that risk of further delay had now been averted.

On reaching the river, he watered his horse, knelt down to drink himself, and, remounting, took the track southward along its bank. When he had decided to attempt crossing the mountains to the Drina on the previous evening, his map had shown him that its course would not lead him to Yardiste, but to Visegrad, a small junction one station down the line which also served another short branch to a place called Uvac. That was all to the good, as he would now strike the railway almost ten miles nearer to Sarajevo. But the river twisted most maddeningly and he dared not attempt short cuts across its bends in case he lost his way again, or found it blocked by unforeseen obstacles.

Soon after six o'clock, he entered a village, but as it was Sunday few people were yet astir, and those he saw had the same flat Slav faces as their brethren on the other side of the frontier. They waved to him and shouted greetings in the same incomprehensible tongue, so he waved back to them but did not pause to ask them if he was on the right road. He felt certain they would not be able to understand him, and was now obsessed with the necessity of not wasting a moment.

By seven o'clock he reckoned that he had covered over twenty miles and began to be worried by the thought that, after all, he might be following the course of some river that was not the Drina. The nightmare idea came to him that during the previous evening he might have doubled on his tracks, and now be cantering along the bank of the Morava, back to Užice. But a quarter of an hour later he came in sight of a single track railway line and a small town which was certainly not the one he had driven through in the Rolls just twenty-four hours earlier.

A glance at the map and the surrounding heights confirmed his belief that it must be Visegrad, so he pushed on into it and made straight for the station. It was shut, but a name-board above the entrance to the building showed him to be right, and a few minutes later, to his ineffable relief, he saw a man dressed in the uniform of an Austrian postman.

All Austrian civil servants, whatever their race and however lowly their degree, had to possess at least a rudimentary knowledge of German. With a sigh of thankfulness, de Richleau found that he could once more make himself understood. The postman proved both friendly and intelligent. He said that on Sundays the telegraph office did not open, and that there was only one train from Visegrad to Sarajevo. It left at eleven-thirty, so that after church people could set off to whichever village up the line happened to be celebrating its summer Saint's day, and dance there in its beer gardens during the afternoon. At the same hour a train left Sarajevo for Visegrad to convey people coming in the opposite direction. Then at eight in the evening the two trains left their termini to pick up people who had gone to these village fêtes, and convey them home.

A pleasant manner and a handsome tip swiftly secured the postman as a guide to the postmaster's house. That official was just getting up but, unshaven and bedraggled as the Duke was, he had not lost his natural air of authority. Within ten minutes he had the man at his office. A telegram was promptly written out and dispatched to the Mayor of Sarajevo. It ran:

Have positive information that attempt will be made to assassinate Archduke on his arrival in Sarajevo this morning stop Imperative that you should prevent his entering city stop Am proceeding there by first train stop

Königstein Count and Colonel Archduchess Ilona Theresa's regiment Imperial Hussars.

At the thought that he had, after all, succeeded in getting a warning through in time, de Richleau felt a warm glow of elation. But his night in the woods had been far from the type of rest he needed. His twenty-three miles' ride had taxed him severely and his wound was now making him a little feverish, so he gladly accepted the postmaster's offer to look after him.

His kindly host, greatly excited by the alarming tidings he had brought, took him back to his house, sent for a doctor to dress his wound, provided him with shaving things and a good breakfast, changed some of his Serbian pieces into Austrian coin, and finally saw him into the train at eleven-thirty.

It was a *tinkel-bahn* affair which stopped at every station to collect country girls and their bucolic swains who were going to the fête which, as this Sunday was St. Vitus' day, and St. Vitus the patron saint of Sarajevo, was in the Bosnian capital itself. Normally the distance would have deterred some of the pleasure seekers, but the visit of the Archduke was an added attraction, so the train soon filled up with young people. Their healthy pink faces, gaily embroidered local costumes and shy tittering would, normally, have aroused in the Duke a sympathetic feeling of happiness and well-being; but he was much too concerned with the thought of what might be happening, or have already happened, in Sarajevo, to pay any attention to them.

With maddening slowness the little train chugged its way along the valley of the Praca. The journey seemed interminable, but at last it completed its fifty miles' trip and, at half past two, puffed into Sarajevo.

Although the town was not much more than half the size of Belgrade, it was far more beautiful. It had for many centuries been an outpost of the Turkish Empire and had not yet lost the oriental imprint through cheap and shoddy modernization. The river, which was broad enough here to be navigable, ran through it, and from the valley bottom in which it lay rose the minarets and domes of its hundred mosques, many of which were set in groves of tall cypress trees.

As soon as de Richleau reached the barrier of the station platform he asked the ticket collector if the Archduke had arrived that morning. To his relief the man answered, "No sir. I do not think he is expected till about three o'clock."[1]

[1]Note: Some accounts of these events in Sarajevo suggest that Franz Ferdinand entered the town about 10 a.m. and lunched at the Town Hall. I have preferred to follow the Rt. Hon. Winston S. Churchill, who states (Vol. 1, p.51, The Great War. Illustrated edition. George Newnes 1933) "On the *afternoon* of June 28 the Archduke and his wife entered Sarajevo". (my italics) D.W.

The Duke, having expected Franz Ferdinand either to enter the town before mid-day, or, if his telegram had had the desired result, not enter it at all, thought the reply cryptic but at all events it was clear that no tragedy had yet occurred.

Hurrying outside, he got a cab and told the driver to take him as quickly as possible to the Town Hall. The way lay through streets decorated with flags and gaily coloured rugs hung from balconies and windows; and de Richleau was considerably perturbed to see that along the side walks there were crowds of waiting people. Evidently, if the Archduke's visit had been cancelled, the fact had not yet been made public.

At the Town Hall he inquired for the Mayor and was informed that His Worship had gone out with the Military Governor, General Potiorek, to welcome the Archduke at the limits of the city. That could only mean that the warning telegram had either not been delivered, or had been ignored in the belief that it had been sent by some irresponsible practical joker. Now, frantic with anxiety, de Richleau ordered his jehu to drive him at full speed to the spot where the city officials were waiting to receive the Archduke.

As the carriage moved at a fast trot through the main streets the Duke noticed that among the banners hanging at intervals across them were some bearing the words '*Welkommen zu unser Erzherzog und die Herzogin von Hohenberg*'; which informed him for the first time that the Chotek was expected as well as her husband. He also noticed that the streets were not lined with troops and that there were very few police about. Many of the men in the crowd wore the turban or fez of Mohammedans, but the majority had on the flat round hats of Serbs or cheap caps manufactured in western Europe. As they stood lining the route in the bright sunshine they appeared cheerful and well-behaved, but in view of the known political hostility of the Bosnian population to the Austrian regime it seemed that the authorities had been extremely lax in not taking even reasonable precautions to keep order.

After a moment de Richleau guessed the explanation. Potiorek was von Hötzendorf's rival and the Emperor's favourite soldier. Naturally he would do anything he could to curry favour with his aged master. As the military Governor of Bosnia he would be responsible for all arrangements, and he must have taken deliberate steps to put a slight upon the Chotek. In accordance with the Emperor's expressed wishes no function to which she accompanied her husband need be regarded as an official one, so that was an ample excuse for the General to have refrained from ordering any troops to be paraded.

A few minutes' drive brought the Duke to within two hundred yards of the bridge across the river, over which the procession was expected to enter the centre of the town. There was a policeman there who halted the cab, told the driver that he could go no farther, and diverted him into a side street. Realizing that it was useless to waste time arguing with an underling, or attempting to explain matters, de Richleau jumped out, thrust a coin into the cabby's hand and hurried forward on foot. When he was half way to the bridge a cheer broke out beyond it.

Thrusting his way through the bystanders, he got into the open road and broke into a run. The bridge was lined with spectators on both sides. Between them he could now see some cars approaching. A policeman tried to stop him, but he dodged the man and ran on. The first car was an open six-seater yellow and black Mercedes with a low flat bonnet. To the left of its windscreen was tied the Imperial flag, a square of bright yellow with a black eagle and a border of black triangles. In its back seat were sitting Franz Ferdinand and his wife. He was wearing the cocked hat crowned with black cock's feathers of an Austrian Field-Marshal, and she a wide-brimmed, floppy straw decorated with pink roses. The car was moving at little more than walking pace. Waving wildly, de Richleau shouted to its driver to halt, but the man took no notice. Another policeman ran at the Duke, but he dodged again. Next moment he was level with the car bonnet. At that instant he glimpsed a movement in the crowd lining the side of the bridge. A shabbily dressed youth had raised his arm. In his hand he held a black object the size of a cricket ball. He was just about to throw it.

Swerving violently, de Richleau leapt at him. As he grasped the young man's upraised arm the bomb shot from his hand. But his aim had been deflected. Instead of landing in the car, it bounced off the hood at its back, fell into the road, and exploded with a loud bang.

The Duke felt a violent pain in his right leg, and, almost at the same instant, a sharp blow in the side of the head. For a second he heard the screams, shouts and roaring of the crowd about him. Then he fell unconscious among it.

When he came to he found himself in hospital. Through a mist of pain he wondered how he had got there. But after a few moments the pains localized themselves. There were three: his old wound in the shoulder, a new one in his right leg, and his head bandaged and aching. The scene on the bridge flashed back into his mind. He had succeeded in diverting the bomb from the Archduke's car, but as it had exploded two fragments of it must have hit him.

As he struggled up into a sitting position a pretty young nurse came over to his bedside.

"The Archduke!" he gasped.

"You needn't worry," she replied in German. "The bomb rolled off the back of his car and exploded in the road. Two of the officers of his suite were wounded by splinters, and yourself: but he was not even scratched. Lie down now, or you will increase the bleeding of your leg."

De Richleau's brain was now working quite clearly, so he knew that his head wound was not serious. It could have been only a glancing blow from a piece of flying metal that had temporarily knocked him out. Tankosić had spoken of 'those crazy boys' and 'pistols'. He had said nothing of bombs. That meant that there must be more than one assassin, and that the other, or others, were armed with automatics. The Archduke had not been shot at but, as long as he remained in Sarajevo, he might be at any moment. Pushing back the sheets, the Duke began to get out of bed.

The young nurse tried to stop him. Thrusting her aside, he insisted that he must get up to warn the Archduke that another attempt might be made upon him. Thinking him delirious, she abandoned her efforts to prevent his getting out of bed, and ran from the ward to fetch the doctor.

The Duke's clothes had been neatly folded and temporarily laid on a chair beside his bed. The chairs of the two beds next to his had uniforms similarly folded on them; so he knew that the occupants of the beds must be the wounded officers. One was watching him from dull eyes and moaning a little, the other was unconscious: so it seemed they had fared worse than he had.

When he put the foot of his wounded leg to the floor and tried his weight on it, the stab of pain made him break out into a cold sweat. But he knew that mind was the master of matter and that, providing the bone was not completely severed, even fractured limbs could be made to fulfil their function in an emergency.

Breathing heavily, he began to struggle into his clothes. When the nurse came hurrying back with a rather wooden-faced man of about his own age, he was already half dressed.

"You can't do this! I forbid it!" cried the doctor.

"Do you think I am doing it for fun?" the Duke grimaced with pain. "As I told your nurse, a second attempt may be made at any moment to kill the Archduke. He must be warned immediately."

"My poor fellow, you are delirious."

"I am nothing of the kind."

"I fear you are. If you refuse to return to bed at once I shall have to send for assistance to make you."

"On the contrary, you are going to get your hypodermic and give me an injection in the leg to numb this damn pain. Then you'll find me a crutch and get hold of an automobile to take me to the Archduke. If you refuse I shall charge you with having obstructed me in my duty as a Colonel of the Austrian Army. What is more, should the Archduke be assassinated through your preventing me from reaching him, I shall hold you publicly responsible for his death."

De Richleau's grey eyes were feverish and his face chalk-white; yet his cold, level voice was not that of a man suffering from delirium. The doctor did not know what to make of him, but blanched at the idea of assuming such a terrible responsibility.

"You—you really have reason to think——?" he hazarded.

"Damn it, man! I *know!* Don't stand there gaping, but do something. You must have a telephone here. Where is the Archduke?"

"He drove on to the Town Hall. He is still there, I expect."

"Then for God's sake telephone! Send a message that in no circumstances must he leave the building. Use my name. Say you are telephoning for Count Königstein, and that I'll get round there as soon as I can to inform him of this plot."

The doctor was convinced now that his patient was in his right mind. With a nod he turned to the nurse and said, "Help him to get his clothes on." Then he ran from the room.

Six minutes later he came hurrying back. Except for his right boot, the Duke was now fully dressed, and the nurse was preparing a syringe for the injection.

"I'm sorry, Count," said the doctor quickly. "The Town Hall number is engaged. With His Highness there I expect it's extra busy. But I've left a colleague to give your message as soon as he can get through. Don't worry, though. I've got an automobile outside. It's no distance, and we'll be round there in five minutes."

Swift and efficient now, he gave the injection. The nurse found a slipper for the patient's foot and a crutch to go under his arm. The alarming news had already spread and the doorway of the ward was now filled with an excited group of nurses and students; but they promptly made way and some of the men helped the doctor get de Richleau downstairs.

With a bang and a jerk the auto started. The side streets were almost clear of people, but the doctor hooted his horn without ceasing, and took the corners regardless of the rules of the road. Good as his word, he had the Duke at the Town Hall in less than five minutes.

Among the crowd a solitary policeman was standing outside it. Bracing himself to leave the car, de Richleau shouted, "Is the Archduke still in the building?"

The man shook his head. "No. You've just missed him."

"Which way did he go?"

"To the hospital, to visit the two officers who were wounded."

"He couldn't have," cried the doctor. "We've just come from there."

"As you came round from the back of the Town Hall you must have taken a short cut through the town," replied the policeman laconically. "He's gone to it along the quay."

"Drive on!" the Duke urged his companion. "Quickly! Quickly! He can't have gone far. We may catch him."

The street was full of the gaily clad crowd which had left the pavements after the passing of the procession, and was now milling about in it; so it was impossible to see far ahead. But the auto banged again and jerked forward, scattering the people.

De Richleau sat rigid, his face drained of blood, sweating with pain, and gripped by the fear that now Franz Ferdinand had left the Town Hall he might yet fall a victim to Dimitriyevitch's plot. Every attempt made to warn him had either been blocked or gone unheeded. But if they could only overtake him, his staff and such police as were close at hand could form a rampart round his body, then get him into a building where he would be safe until troops could be brought to escort him out of the town. It was not his own life only, but the peace of Europe, that still hung in the balance.

As they reached the first bridge, they saw the end of the short procession. It consisted of four cars and the last three had halted. They were slightly zig-zagged where they had stopped just opposite the second bridge. The first car, which should have gone straight on for the hospital, was half way round a corner leading to the centre of the town. Its driver had evidently taken the wrong turning and was now backing it out. The quay ahead was almost clear of people, the side turning that the car had entered full of them, showing it to be the route the Archduke had been expected to take.

The doctor honked his horn and put his foot on the accelerator. The little auto spurted for a moment at thirty miles an hour, with cursing people jumping from its path. He braked violently, and it skidded to a standstill just behind the last car in the line. The squeal it made in pulling up was followed almost instantly by the sound of two shots.

De Richleau grabbed the windscreen and hauled himself to his feet. From his elevation in the car he could see over the others and the heads of the swirling crowd. In the open yellow and black Mercedes, Franz Ferdinand and Sophie von Hohenberg were still seated upright, side by side.

For an instant the Duke's heart leapt with hope. It seemed that the second assassin had made his attempt and failed: that once again a Divine Providence had enabled someone in the crowd to deflect the killer's aim. If either of them had been hit, surely they could not remain sitting there unmoved.

Suddenly the Duchess lurched sideways. Her head fell on her husband's shoulder. The Archduke raised a hand as if to clap it to his neck. The gesture was never completed. Slowly, as though he were bowing to the crowd, his head sagged on to his chest. Then, together they slumped forward, disappearing from de Richleau's sight into the bottom of the car.

There was a mist before the Duke's eyes. The pain in his leg had become intolerable, unbearable. Desperately he fought against it, hanging on to his consciousness with every ounce of his resolution. He did not faint until fourteen minutes later—just after he had learned that both of them were dead.

CHAPTER XVIII

THE MAN WHO KNEW TOO MUCH

ON the evening of Tuesday, 30th of June, de Richleau found himself back in Vienna. That was not due to any determined last moment effort on his part to keep his promise to Ilona. He was certainly in no condition to have made the journey by himself, and had he shown any intention of attempting it the hospital authorities would have forcibly restrained him. The fact was that he had suddenly become a person of great interest to the Austrian Government. It had not been remotely suggested that he was under arrest but, all the same, his own wishes were not even consulted. They required his presence in Vienna urgently. Several telegrams about him had sped back and forth between Vienna and Sarajevo on the Monday; and, when it was reported that he was in no danger of death, an order sent that he should be brought to the capital with minimum delay and maximum precautions against worsening his condition. A military ambulance car had been attached to the train, his doctor and nurse had accompanied him, and he was now installed in one of the best rooms of a private nursing home that overlooked the Prater.

After his collapse, following the double assassination, he had become delirious and continued so for a good part of Sunday evening. Only by inference and the somewhat garbled statements of the nurse and doctor had he since been able to get some idea of what he had said in his ravings; but it had certainly been far more than he ever would have, had he remained in control of his faculties.

Later that night, during a lucid interval, he had found Franz Ferdinand's A.D.C., Count Harrach, at his bedside. The Count was still overwrought himself, and could hardly restrain his tears as he gave a rather disjointed account of the day's terrible events.

The assassin was a nineteen year old student named Gavrilo Prinzip. The two shots he had fired had hit the Archduke in the neck and Sophie von Hohenberg in the stomach. Although the shots had been fired at only three yards range, for a moment no one had realized that either of them had been hit; but after murmuring a few words to one another they had fallen forward in a faint. Neither had recovered consciousness and in less than a quarter of an hour both of them were dead.

The man who had thrown the bomb was a young printer named Nedjedliko Cabrinovitch. He had been caught and taken off to Police

Headquarters. On learning of his arrest the Archduke had exclaimed cynically, "Hang him as quickly as possible, or Vienna will give him a decoration."

At the Town Hall an address of welcome had been read. Not unnaturally, Franz Ferdinand had replied to it with some terseness. Rumours, then untraceable owing to the excitement of the moment, were running round that other attempts would be made on his life. Alarmed by the total lack of troops and few police in the streets, Count Harrach had said to General Potiorek, "Has not Your Excellency arranged for a military guard to protect His Imperial Highness?"

The Governor, evidently furious at the event having shown up his lack of precautions and wishing to justify that lack, had replied impatiently: "Do you think Sarajevo is full of assassins?"

Nevertheless, the Archduke's suite had persuaded him to take a different route from that originally intended on leaving the Town Hall. As he had expressed concern for the officers who had been wounded, it was decided to drive first to the hospital, so that he could visit them. When the little procession was about to set off, Count Harrach had attempted to ride on the left foot-board of the car, so as to protect his master with his body. But Franz Ferdinand had exclaimed, "Don't make a fool of yourself," and pushed him off.

Along the quay from the Town Hall, owing to lack of police supervision, the crowd had been all over the road; but it had parted at the entrance of Franz Joseph street to allow the car to take the route expected. The chauffeur, not knowing the way to the hospital, had turned into it. General Potiorek shouted to him that he should have gone straight on. Then, as he slowed down to back out, the car had come within three feet of the pavement. As the engine was put into reverse, the fatal shots had been fired.

Count Harrach had, however, come to the hospital not to impart, but to seek, information. At the preliminary police inquiry held that evening, a minor official had mentioned a telegram of warning sent in the morning by a Count Königstein from Visegrad. The Mayor, who had evidently meant to conceal the fact that he had received it, had hurriedly excused himself by saying that he thought it had come from a lunatic and, later, in the excitement, forgotten all about it. Someone had then said that Königstein was the name of the man who had diverted the aim of the bomb thrower, been wounded with the two officers when it exploded, and was now in the hospital. When a copy of the telegram was produced, Count Harrach had realized that the Königstein concerned must be the one who had entertained the Archduke and himself at the castle of that name just over a fortnight before. So, immediately the inquiry was adjourned, he had postponed his departure by the special train that was waiting to take him to Vienna, and gone round to the hospital to see what more he could learn about the plot, before leaving for the capital.

The doctor had reported his patient as raving about pistols being lost, crazy boys, scimitars, a black hand, and other matters, through which ran the refrain that he must reach Sarajevo in time to save the Archduke and the peace of Europe. On learning that he was temporarily in his right mind, Count Harrach had insisted on seeing him, told him what had happened, and plied him with a score of questions.

Weak from loss of blood, exhausted by strain, and still feverish as he was, the Duke had sufficient wits left to realize that he had landed himself in a fine mess. To tell the truth—that he had uncovered the plot while working to that end as a secret agent of the British Government—was out of the question: but somehow he had to account for his knowledge of it. Taking refuge in his parlous state, he declared that he had found the whole thing out by accident, then feigned a return to his delirium.

The following day he had been visited and questioned by General Potiorek and the Sarajevo Chief of Police, but they had got little more out of him. He said that on leaving Vienna he had gone down to Constantinople on business, and that having completed it he had decided to break his return journey for a few days in Belgrade. There, in a night-haunt called *Le Can-Can*, he had learned of the plot, and at once taken such steps as he could to thwart it. Then, to give himself further time to think matters out, he had insisted that talking tired him too much for him to say any more at the moment. Next morning he had been transferred from his bed to a stretcher and spent most of the day travelling to Vienna.

As he lay, in a bed that seemed absurdly small for the fine square room, and gazed at the tree-tops of the park out of the broad bay-window, for the fiftieth time he reviewed his difficult situation. Somehow he had to give a satisfactory explanation of not only how he had obtained foreknowledge of the plot, but of the bullet—since extracted—which had been in his shoulder on his first arrival at the hospital in Sarajevo; and why he had, apparently, sent no warning of the plot to Vienna, or attempted to go there, but, instead, relied entirely on his own ability to make the frightful cross-country journey to the Bosnian capital in time to stop the outrage.

On the previous day he had seen no alternative but to admit that he had learned of the plot in Belgrade; and he now doubted his ability to persuade the Austrians that it had not been hatched there. If he substantiated that, it would cut the ground from under the Serbians' feet. They were counting on gaining the sympathy of Europe for the

Bosnian Serbs in connection with such repressive measures as the Austrians might take against them as a result of the assassination. But if it became known that members of the Serbian General Staff had plotted the murders, Serbia would get no sympathy from anybody. On the other hand, if the Austrians were given the true story bout the Black Hand they might make demands for reparation from Serbia that she would refuse; in which case the outcome would still be war.

It was a horrible dilemma, and to his great distress de Richleau realized that he was in the unhappy position of a man who knew too much. Whichever course he took now might tip the scales and result in helping to ferment a lesser or greater war. But on three counts he finally decided that he would refrain from attempting to shield the Serbs.

Firstly, he had been in the State prison in Belgrade on Friday night and Tankosić and Ciganović had taken him from it. Therefore, the Serbian police could hardly fail to associate their deaths and that of their Chief with him. The Serbian secret service would almost certainly have learned and reported his activities on arriving in Sarajevo, so it would be known that he was in Austria. Therefore, although it seemed unlikely, it was, nevertheless, possible that the Serbian government would demand his extradition to face a charge of murder. If they did, his only protection would lie in having told the Austrians at least a part of the truth about the killings.

Secondly, given that the chances of war resulting from the assassinations were more or less even whatever he said, justice demanded that the Serbians should not escape responsibility for the initial cause that led to it.

Thirdly, the odium attaching to this foul deed should go a long way to deprive Serbia of the support of Russia and the great democracies, thus rendering it much less likely that they would take up the cudgels on her behalf and a general war result.

On Wednesday morning a small committee of the highest importance came to see him. It consisted of the Foreign Minister, Count von Berchtold, his right-hand man, Count Hoyos, the Emperor's aged aide-de-camp, Count Paar, General Conrad von Hötzendorf, Count Harrach and General Urbanski von Ostromiecz, the Director of the Imperial Secret Service.

Evidently the meagre report received from General Potiorek had already given them the impression that de Richleau was reluctant to tell all he knew: so to encourage him to speak frankly they opened the proceedings by disclosing what they had so far found out for themselves.

The examination of the two assassins, and other inquiries, had elicited the information that on the fatal Sunday there had been at least seven young fanatics in Sarajevo, all armed and all prepared to make an attempt on the Archduke's life. All except one were of Serbian blood and had been living in Belgrade for some time. They had recently re-crossed the frontier in secret and the weapons they carried bore the marks of the Serbian State Arsenal. It was, therefore, clear beyond dispute that the murders were not nihilistic in character, but had been deliberately planned and stage-managed by Belgrade. The existence of the Black Hand had long been known to the Austrian Government, and they had no doubt that responsibility for the crime lay with it.

Further, de Richleau's visitors admitted that numerous warnings had been received, including one from a Serbian diplomat to a minor official in the Austrian Foreign Office. But all of them had been so obscure or seemingly ill-founded that no steps had been taken about them. On the other hand, the Duke's telegram from Visegrad had been so positive and categorical that he must obviously have been aware of the true facts.

Count Berchtold, who had so far done most of the talking, looked down his long, sharp nose and added, "I need hardly stress the immense importance we attach to getting to the bottom of this terrible matter; and it is for that reason my friends and myself have come to request you to give us a personal account of the events which led up to your sending that telegram."

"I am only too willing to aid you in any way I can, Count," replied de Richleau amiably. "This, then, is the bald outline of the most unpleasant adventure into which I was quite unexpectedly precipitated owing to my having paid a short visit to Belgrade. On Friday night I went to a night-haunt there called *Le Can-Can.* The male patrons of the place were mostly young officers, and a party of them invited me to join their table. The liquor was flowing freely and as the hour advanced we all got a little drunk. They then began to toast an event that was to take place on Sunday, which would lead to war with Austria. Through my mother I am half Russian, and I was making myself understood by them in that language, so they undoubtedly took me for one. Naturally I was much alarmed, so to lead them on I pretended hatred of Austria myself. One youngster, drunker than the rest, then gave away the plot in a single sentence before his companions had time to stop him. I could see that a middle-aged Colonel who had joined us was much annoyed, but I gave a drunken grin as though I had not fully taken in the sense of what the young man had said. Some of the officers, including the Colonel, left shortly afterwards, but the party continued for another hour. I did not dare to leave before them, but avoided drinking any more, and had determined at once that as soon as I could get away I would take the first train for Vienna.

"But no sooner did I get outside in the dark street than I was set upon, bundled into a big car, and had a pistol pushed into my ribs. Three of the officers who had attacked me, one of who was the Colonel, took me in the car some miles out of Belgrade to a châlet in the forest. There," the Duke repressed a cynical smile, "I found myself in the unenviable position of 'the man who knew too much'. They informed me that they meant to keep me a prisoner in the cellar, and would have to do so for an unspecified period; or at least until their vile plot had brought about the opening of hostilities against Austria that they desired.

"I saw at once that the only chance of saving the situation lay in gambling my life in an attempt to escape. Fortunately they had not searched me, and I was carrying a loaded pistol in my hip pocket. As they led me to the cellar, I rounded on them and drew it. Having taken them by surprise gave me an initial advantage. A frightful mêlée ensued. I was shot in the shoulder, but I succeeded in leaving all three of them either dead or severely wounded, and getting away.

"The car in which they had brought me there was still outside, and it was a Rolls. I jumped into it and drove off. While I was at the châlet I had seen no servants, but I feared that the sound of the shots would bring them on the scene at any moment, and the police would soon be warned to hold me up. So I did not dare to drive back through Belgrade and attempt to cross the frontier into Hungary. Neither could I send any warning by telegraph or telephone as long as I was in Serbia. I decided that my best chance lay in heading across country for Sarajevo.

"With luck I should have got there late on Saturday night, but unfortunately I twice lost my way; and the second time I was benighted in the mountains near the frontier. As soon as I got to Visegrad, on Sunday morning, I sent the telegram of which you know, and I reached Sarajevo myself at two-thirty in the afternoon. That is the whole story."

As de Richleau ceased, his little group of visitors looked at him in unfeigned admiration, and von Hötzendorf grunted: "To have taken on three of those swine single-handed, and afterward made such a journey, although wounded, was a magnificent piece of work. I've never heard of one that better deserved a decoration."

Old Count Paar nodded. "When I inform the Emperor of your gallantry in the service of the Monarchy, I feel confident that His Imperial Majesty will wish to confer one on you."

"Your account confirms everything we already know," said Count Berchtold. "I now feel that we are amply justified in taking immediate steps against Serbia."

Von Hötzendorf turned swiftly to him. "I have already told you, Count, that I need sixteen days for mobilization."

"Surely, gentlemen," protested the Duke, "terrible as this crime is, you will not allow it to lead to war."

"No, no!" Count Paar shook his white head. "There is no question of war. But we must have satisfaction. The whole nation is seething with righteous indignation. We cannot permit the vile act to go unpunished."

"I agree." Count Berchtold gave the old man a sideways glance. "The insolence of the Serbs has long needed humbling, and this is our opportunity. But it should not be necessary to resort to war."

"I tell you it is futile to make threats unless they can be backed by force," declared the General.

"We have force enough for our purpose while the Army remains on a peace-time footing. It should not be difficult to seize some Serbian town or district, and declare our intentions of holding it until the Serbian Government surrenders the officers concerned in the conspiracy, and agrees to such other demands as we may make."

"And what if the Serbians attacked such a force?" cried von Hötzendorf, almost hopping with rage. "At the moment Potiorek has only 25,000 troops under him, and they are scattered all over Bosnia. Once we are mobilized he will have 80,000 infantry, which makes a very different picture. It would be positive madness to start anything until we are properly prepared."

Count Hoyos came to his Chief's rescue. "But, General, surely you realize the danger in allowing the sixteen days you require for mobilization to elapse before we act. All sorts of diplomatic complications may arise. As matters stand we are fully justified in seizing guarantees that will ensure Serbia punishing these criminals. If the Great Powers are presented with a *fait accompli* they will admire our resolution; but if we wait they may believe us too weak to protect our honour. That would discourage Germany from giving us her backing, and encourage Russia to threaten intervention if we belatedly show signs of taking up the Serbian challenge."

Had they not accepted de Richleau as one of themselves they would never have discussed the question in front of him at all: but, even so, the strength of their feelings had carried them further than they intended. With a warning glance at the others, Count Berchtold drew attention to the Duke's presence, and said:

"In any case, gentlemen, the two Minister-Presidents will have to be consulted further before any new step can be taken, and we must not tire our invalid by involving him in our discussions."

Taking the hint, von Hötzendorf turned back to the Duke, and asked, "During this adventure of yours, did you hear any mention of the Brotherhood of Union or Death?"

Seeing a chance to pour oil on troubled waters, de Richleau replied at once, "Yes. The officers with whom I spent the evening at *Le Can-Can* referred to it several times. They were all members of it, and spoke of the society as a patriotic fraternity pledged to advance Serbian interests by peace or war. But quite obviously the Serbian Government knows nothing of its activities."

"Why should you suppose that?"

"Because, were it so, the Colonel who kidnapped me would have had no difficulty in getting me locked up in the State Prison. As it was he intended to go to the considerable inconvenience of keeping me a prisoner in his own house. That proves that the Brotherhood are a private body, acting without the authority or approval of the State. And for that reason I beg you to resort to threats against the Serbian Government only as a last resource. If you menace them they may feel in honour bound to fight. But if you confine yourselves to demanding the punishment of the conspirators, the probability is that they will at once admit the justice of your demand and carry out your wishes."

"There's sound sense in that," Count Paar agreed. "Nothing we have yet heard has indicated the complicity of the Serbian Government; and God forbid that we should wantonly force them into a position which might lead to war."

Von Hötzendorf gave a snort of disapproval. The others remained silent, but de Richleau could see from their faces that they were not in agreement with the old man's pacific ideas.

General von Ostromiecz stepped into the breach by saying that he would be dictating a report for his police of the information supplied by the Duke, and it might assist them further if he could give particulars which would lead to the identity of his attackers.

To this de Richleau replied by describing Tankosić and Ciganović and adding that he thought the colonel's name had been Dimitrivitch, or something like it.

At that, nearly everyone in the room showed quickened interest; and when Dimitriyevitch had been identified by his description, von Ostromiecz exclaimed: "If you left that scoundrel for dead you've rendered us a greater service than ever. He was the Chief of the Brotherhood, a very able devil, and our most inveterate enemy."

Shortly afterwards de Richleau's visitors took leave of him. But before they left he extracted a promise from them that the part he had played in the affair should in no circumstances be made public. They put his request down to modesty, but actually he was acutely concerned that no account of the evidence he had given against the Black Hand should reach Serbia. The Serbs had plenty to hide themselves, and presumably they had no idea how deeply he was involved with the enemy camp, so their natural instinct would be to let sleeping dogs lie.

They had probably put his abortive attempt to save the Archduke down to a purely personal prejudice against assassination, but if they once learned that he had followed it up by breaking his oath and laying information with the Austrian Government against the Black Hand, they might seek to retaliate in a variety of ways. One would be to demand his extradition for murder and at the same time seek to discredit him with the Austrians. They could assert that his motive for the murders had been a personal one, and had a good case for making him appear a double-dyed traitor by disclosing the fact that he had both taken the oath to the Black Hand himself and been a Lieutenant-General designate of the Serbian Army.

If that came out—and ample genuine evidence could be produced to substantiate it, together with the fact that he had never been in Constantinople—he would find himself in the very devil of a mess.

After they had gone, as he lay watching the Great Wheel slowly revolve above the trees of the Prater and half listening to the plaintive notes of a zither, on which a haunting melody was being strummed in a café somewhere along the street below, he knew that never in his life had he skated on thinner ice.

For the moment he was out of the clutches of the Serbians and had satisfied the Austrians, but within the next few days a dozen matters might come to light which would show him up as a liar. Much as he liked Sir Pellinore personally, he damned him roundly for having got him into this dangerous and dishonourable game of espionage. But, weakened as he was by loss of blood, and with the muscles of his right leg badly torn, it was impossible for him to escape further complications by cutting clear of the whole business. He was in no state to get on the next train for England, even if he had wanted to: but he didn't want to because of still further complications. There was Ilona.

That afternoon he had news of her but, far from acting as a palliative to his agitated state of mind, it increased it by a new worry. Adam Grünne came to see him. That morning Ilona had learned through the Court grape-vine of his attempt to save her cousin and that he had been brought back to Vienna. She sent her equerry to say, unofficially, how proud she felt to have a dear friend who had behaved with such gallantry and, officially, to inquire after his wounds.

The message was balm to the wounds concerned, but Count Adam went on to tell him that Ilona's suite were now more than ever concerned about their mistress' health. After her birthday ball on the 13th, she had collapsed and been too ill to leave her bed for nearly a fortnight. The elderly Court doctor who attended her continued to maintain that she was suffering from an hereditary weakness, which might go on causing her trouble periodically but need not be regarded seriously.

As rest and quiet after a bout always had the effect of restoring her to glowing health quite quickly, the Aulendorfs had faith in the old physician: but Adam, Sárolta and others in immediate attendance on Ilona had not. They were alarmed by the fact that after each bout she took longer to recover, and that her coughing fits had increased to such violence that she now at times strained her lungs and spat up blood.

She had got up for the first time two days previously and hoped to be allowed soon to go out again. Count Adam felt certain that, when she was, wild horses would not prevent her coming to see the invalid, and he urged most strongly that de Richleau should then use his influence with her to persuade her to call in a lung specialist.

Greatly concerned, the Duke promised to do so; and, after he had talked on other matters with Adam Grünne for an hour, sent her messages by him urging her to take the utmost care of her health, as well as expressing his devotion.

During the next few days he lived in an emotional limbo. No act of his could any longer make for peace or war, or even better or worsen his own situation. Temporarily his mind seemed suspended in time and space; incapable of directing any useful action, yet subject to innumerable hopes, fears and sensations both pleasant and unpleasant.

The flying bomb-splinter that had knocked him out had done no more than break the skin on his temple, and his shoulder wound was healing nicely; but the torn muscles of his leg nagged at him unremittingly. He was looked after admirably and given the best of food. But night and morning the dressing of his leg wound was an ordeal that he dreaded hours in advance. He had ample distraction, as the Court grape-vine had informed all his friends in Vienna about him, and he had many visitors, who showered him with gifts of fruit, flowers, books and puzzles; but he could settle to nothing because he was all the time worried about Ilona. His visitors had all heard some garbled account of his attempt to save the Archduke, and acclaimed him as a hero, but every moment of the day he expected some new revelation to brand him as a liar, cheat and spy.

He sent for all the Serbian newspapers, including those back to the previous Saturday, and scanned every edition with feverish anxiety. But he could find no mention of the killings at the châlet, or even a bald announcement of Dimitriyevitch's death. As the Colonel had been such a prominent personality in Belgrade the latter omission seemed extraordinary. The only theory de Richleau could formulate to account for it was that, whoever had succeeded Dimitriyevitch as Chief of the Black Hand had his own reasons for not wishing the Colonel's death to be made public, so had taken deliberate steps to suppress all reference to it.

In a way, that tied up with the general tone of the Serbian papers as, although no actual mention was made of the Black Hand, it was clear from them that the Brotherhood was temporarily under a cloud. Far from adopting the gratified attitude to the Archduke's murder that might have been expected had Dimitriyevitch still been behind them, they appeared to regret it, and a few leading articles even condemned "the wicked activities of certain societies which, with misguided patriotism, encourage discontent among the Bosnian Serbs and so worsen our relations with the Dual Monarchy".

As the week advanced the Duke began to wonder if, by killing Dimitriyevitch and his two principal lieutenants, he had not, after all, made a major contribution to keeping the peace of Europe. It was highly probable that the fanatical Colonel's successor lacked both his dynamic personality and immense personal influence on Serbian affairs. The killings at the châlet might have enabled Prince Alexander—who, owing to his father's ill-health, had been appointed Regent a few days before the assassinations—his Prime Minister, M. Pastich and the C. in C., General Putnik, all of whom de Richleau believed to be decent, honourable men, to have regained control of their country's destiny. The Serbian attitude was, in the main, one of indifference, and it certainly lacked all trace of belligerence. It was in the righteous anger of Austria-Hungary that the danger now lay.

The whole world had been shocked and horrified by the crime at Sarajevo, and, although it was natural that the Austrians should feel more bitterly about it than any other race, their reaction had been of an intensity surprising in such a mild and peace-loving people. Musical festivals, favourite ballerinas and first nights at the opera, had all been pushed into small paragraphs on the back pages of the papers. Their headlines and leaders now screamed with rage and hatred against Serbia. And their fury was not confined to the Austrian press; every race that owed allegiance to the Empire displayed equal anger at the assassination of the Heir Apparent. In Budapest, Prague and Trieste, as well as in Vienna, mobs had attacked Serbian consulates and institutions, and paraded the streets nightly howling for vengeance against the despised and hated nation that they believed to have sponsored the crime. As de Richleau read these accounts he trembled for the outcome. It was clear beyond a shadow of doubt that von Hötzendorf and the other war-mongers now had the people of the whole Empire united solidly behind them.

On Saturday afternoon the matron of the nursing home suddenly appeared with three nurses, and they hurriedly began to tidy the Duke's room quite unnecessarily. A message had been received that Her Imperial Highness the Archduchess Ilona Theresa was on her way to see him. And a quarter of an hour later Ilona arrived, accompanied by Adam Grünne and Sárolta Hunyády.

To de Richleau's surprise and joy, apart from a flush that made her look lovelier than ever, she appeared perfectly well, and she was overflowing with high spirits. Immediately they had exchanged greetings, she sent Sárolta and Adam to sit on two chairs in the bay window, and gaily ordered them to keep their eyes fixed on the Great Wheel that was slowly revolving a quarter of a mile away with its load of summer trippers; or, if they preferred, on one another. Then she perched herself on the side of de Richleau's bed and gave him a long, breathless kiss.

As their lips parted, she whispered, "Oh, Armand! How lovely it is to see you again! And what a hero you have become! Do you know that even I am basking in your reflected glory?"

"I am overjoyed to hear it, my sweet Princess," he smiled, "but I cannot imagine why."

She laughed. "My grandfather sent for me yesterday and congratulated me on having acquired you as an honorary Colonel of my regiment. Before, when I sent him the explanation you suggested, I am told he expressed great surprise that it should enter the head of a girl to have her soldiers trained for war; but he has always been so keen on anything to do with the army that he was pleased to learn that I took an interest in it. Now he has heard more about you, he thinks my idea such a good one that he wants you to give a series of lectures on modern warfare to the officers at the Staff College. But shut your eyes—quickly. I have a lovely surprise for you."

"Nothing could be lovelier than another kiss," murmured the Duke as he obeyed her.

From her bag she took a bright scarlet ribbon, to which was attached a star set with brilliants. Having passed the ribbon round his neck, she said solemnly, "It is His Imperial Majesty's pleasure that for distinguished service to the Empire you should be received as a Knight into the Order of Leopold. By his command, and on his behalf, I, Ilona Theresa, hereby invest you, Jean Armand Duplessis von Königstein, with the Military Cordon of the Order."

As he opened his eyes she gave him another joyous kiss, and exclaimed: "There! Wasn't it lucky that my grandfather spoke of you when I saw him yesterday? He told me he meant to give you the decoration, but I asked that, as you were my officer, he should let me deputize for him; and he agreed at once."

Taking her hand, he carried it to his lips. "Princess, no Knight of this illustrious Order ever had my good fortune to be invested with your kiss. That will make it more precious to me than any other decoration I possess. I am most touched, too, that in his grief the Emperor should have found time to think of honouring me."

She gave him a queer look. "I don't think he is really sorry about my cousin Franz's death. He was shocked, of course, and horrified at the brutality of the act. But I am told that when Count Paar broke the news to him his first thought was that by the succession passing to my cousin Charles, it has once more been secured from risk of taint to the Imperial blood. They say he exclaimed, 'How horrible! But the Almighty does not allow himself to be challenged with impunity. A higher Power has restored the old order, which I unfortunately was unable to uphold'."

De Richleau shook his head. "How sad that anyone could possibly believe that God would exact vengeance on a man because he married for love, instead of according to the dictates of an entirely artificial convention. In point of fact, his own blood is no bluer than the poor Chotek's—or, for that matter, any street-sweeper's."

"That may be true. Yet one cannot altogether rule out heredity. Generations of nobility beget a sense of duty and responsibility to others that is not found as an instinct among common people. They may acquire it later, but are not born with it; and to come by such a sense naturally is of great importance for all who are destined to rule." Ilona sighed suddenly, and added: "All the same, I would to God I were a man."

"Why should you wish that, when God has made you the most beautiful of women?"

She smiled at him. "Because, if I were a man and you were a woman, I would follow Franz Ferdinand's example."

His hand trembled as he took hers. "Do you really mean——?"

"Yes. Even if it broke my grandfather's heart, I would marry you."

"My sweet!" he murmured. "My sweet!" Then he swallowed hard, now utterly at a loss for further words. But his mind was racing with wild thoughts which he had never before permitted it to entertain. To have her for his wife! To wake with her beside him! To spend long carefree days with her in the sunshine of the Riviera! The opposition would be terrific. He would be branded as a fortune hunter. It would never be permitted, and some charge would be faked up against him as an excuse for shutting him up in a fortress. But they could elope. That would mean that she would have to live in exile for the rest of her life. How much would she mind that? He felt certain that his love for her would endure. But by the time she was forty, would she curse the day she had met him? She was born to be a queen or empress. Would she later bitterly regret all she had given up for his sake? No! Why should she? Thrones held no glamour for those who occupied or stood near them. To her, a throne would mean only a loveless marriage and condemnation to a life-long round of official duties.

Slavery had been abolished in the modern world; except for those of royal blood, who were forced daily to leave their palaces in invisible chains, to posture and smirk before their peoples. How infinitely more fortunate were those even of modest means, but born free to live where and how they would. Ilona would be giving up nothing that could bring her real happiness. On the contrary, she was beating on the bars of her gilded cage and asking him to rescue her. And she was quite old enough to know her own mind. Then he would do it, and be damned to the consequences.

At length he said, "Ilona, if you will entrust yourself to me, I swear to you that I will never give you cause to regret it."

With a start, she drew back. "Oh Armand, no! I did not mean that."

"From what you said, I thought——"

Sadly she shook her head. "I said only that were our sexes reversed I would marry you. God, or whoever made the rules for us, has been hard on women in many ways, and my case is an example of that. If a man chooses to marry beneath him, he can, at worst, only be accused of having displayed ill-taste. And if the girl be beautiful, he escapes severe criticism on the grounds that physical desire is natural in man, so a legitimate excuse for becoming bewitched into almost any folly. But women are supposed to be made differently. If a girl runs away with an attractive man of lower station than herself, she is immediately stigmatized as unchaste. For the rest of her life people whisper about her behind her back and point at her. She soon becomes a woman with a past and fair game for every unprincipled man she may meet: and she has brought indelible dishonour on her family. That, I could not support. Marriage, alas, can never be for us; and I beg you, my love, to forget the stupid thing I said just now."

He kissed her hand again. "I understand. It was foolish of me to dream such dreams, even for a moment.

Then, in order to break the awkward pause that followed, he fingered the ribbon about his neck, and said: "This favour that the Emperor has shown me: does it mean that I may be able to see more of you without giving rise to scandal? If so, I shall prize it even more highly, as a magic talisman to Heaven."

Ilona brightened again. "It will certainly help. Greatly as it distressed me at the time, your immediate departure from Vienna, after my birthday ball, nipped scandal about us in the bud. And Adam tells me that now I am simply accounted cleverer than people thought, in having secured a paladin for my regiment. Unfortunately, as the Court is in full mourning, there will be no entertainments of any kind at which we can meet. But as soon as you are well enough, you can take up your duties, and that will enable you to come to see me at the Palace at least once a week without exciting undesirable comment."

"And in the meantime?"

"That will be even easier," Her blue eyes sparkled. "One of the heaviest crosses that we poor royal women have to bear is the convention that we should spend half our lives posing as angels of mercy, visiting the wards of hospitals. Heaven knows how weary I am at pretending interest at the sick beds of people I have never seen before, and shall never see again. But now the dreary custom will stand us in good stead. Owing to the manner in which you received your wounds, it will be thought only proper that a member of the Imperial Family should regard you as her special invalid. I'll come to see you every other day. I would make it every day, were it not that my visits could be only an unhappy farce on the days that Paula is on duty."

"Then I shall never recover," he laughed up at her. "The temptation to remain here and be sure of an hour with you in every forty-eight will prove too great. But you have not told me yet about your own health, my sweet, and I have been intensely worried about you."

"Do I not look well?"

"You look more beautiful than any houri the dreams of man could fabricate."

"Then let it rest at that."

"No. I am told you had to keep to your bed for the best part of a fortnight. That seriously alarmed me. I have no confidence in a physician who maintains that there is nothing really wrong with you, when these attacks not only keep recurring, but are of increasing severity. I beg you to call in a lung specialist—someone really first class, like that Swiss, Dr. Bruckner, who spends a good part of the year here as a consultant—and submit to a thorough examination by him."

She shrugged. "It is quite unnecessary. But I like you being so concerned for me, dear Knight; so to please you, I will consider seeing Bruckner. Tell me now of your extraordinary adventure."

He told her, a little sheepishly, the same story that he had told Count Berchtold and the others earlier in the week. Her eyes widened with excitement when he spoke of his fight for life in the châlet and, when he had done, she said:

"How fortunate I am to have the love of such a courageous and resourceful man. You can have no idea how proud of you this makes me. But do you know the amusing story that is going round the town? They say now that I was requested by our secret service to appoint you as a Colonel of my regiment as a blind—simply to throw dust in the eyes of those horrid Serbians, and lead them to suppose that you were a stupid court dandy whom I favoured for your good looks; while all the time you were a great nobleman, who had consented to demean himself by becoming a spy in the service of Austria from patriotic reasons."

De Richleau squirmed. The guess was so horribly near the truth, yet in fact poles apart from it. He wondered miserably what Ilona would think of him if she knew that he was indeed a spy, and one who had deliberately set about penetrating the secrets of Austria as well as Serbia. He took refuge in a half-truth, and said:

"How utterly absurd! People of my standing have never been known to dabble in such matters, and personally I should find work of that kind most uncongenial."

"'Naturally," she rejoined quickly. "The very idea is fantastic. And on your behalf I resented the suggestion as an insult."

In the pause that followed Adam Grünne said without turning his head, "May it please Your Highness, since I have been sitting here I have not once looked at the Great Wheel. But my watch suggests that it must have gone round at least ten times, as each revolution takes a good ten minutes."

"Oh, Adam! How horridly right you are," Ilona exclaimed. "We must be off. Please go on saying nice things to Sárolta for just another two minutes, then I'll let you drag me away."

Again she put her arms round de Richleau's neck, and he held her to him in a sweet embrace; while between more kisses she murmured, "Till Monday, Armand! Till Monday! I'll hardly live till then."

Five minutes later they had gone, and he was left to his whirling thoughts. She loved him! She loved him! And he loved her most desperately. But what could come of it? And if she learned the truth about him, what then? She would regard him as beyond words despicable.

On the following Monday and Wednesday Ilona paid him further visits. As before, Sárolta and Adam accompanied her and occupied chairs in the big bay window, while she sat perched on the invalid's bed so that they could hold hands, gaze fondly into one another's eyes and exchange caresses easily.

She appeared to be glowing with health and happiness on both occasions; but from time to time she could not repress a fit of coughing, and on the Wednesday de Richleau caught her trying to conceal from him a handkerchief that was tinged with the brilliance of blood. Attempting to laugh it off, she declared that it came from a strained muscle in her throat that had bled a little now and then for a long time past, and that she had been too busy to do anything yet about consulting a specialist. But now he insisted that she must, and extracted a firm promise from her that she would see Dr. Bruckner during the coming week.

The Duke was now well enough to be allowed visitors in the evenings as well as in the afternoons, and it was after dinner on this night, July the 8th, that Count Tisza came to see him. The Hungarian Minister-President had already sent the invalid kind messages with a present of books and wine, and he said at once that he would have come in person before this, had not the crisis of the past week kept him desperately busy.

Ilona and some of de Richleau's other highly placed visitors had told him a certain amount about what was going on behind the scenes and although the popular fury against Serbia remained unabated, he had gained the impression that the likelihood of any drastic step being taken had materially decreased in the last few days. But Count Tisza soon disabused him of that comforting belief.

The Hungarian statesman made no secret of the fact that he was at loggerheads with all his colleagues, and desperately worried by their attitude. It was, he explained, his unhappy sense of isolation that had given him the idea of talking matters over with the Duke, as a man with wide knowledge of international affairs who was unprejudiced by any official connections and entirely to be trusted.

Mentally, de Richleau squirmed at the last portion of this statement, and he would far rather not have been made the recipient of his friend's confidences. But, short of giving himself away, there was no means of avoiding that; so he listened with the most sympathetic attention while the Count went on to disclose the cause of his terrible anxieties.

On 1st July Count Berchtold had informed him that he meant to make 'the horrible deed at Sarajevo the occasion for a reckoning with Serbia'. Tisza had objected, warning the Foreign Minister of the measureless consequences that might follow such a fatal mistake. He had also written to the Emperor, pointing out that the participation of the Serbian Government had not been proved, and that if they could furnish satisfactory explanations the Dual Monarchy would be exposed before the world as a war-monger, and possibly have to enter on a great war with everybody's sympathies against her. He had insisted on a proper inquiry being made, stressed the possibility of Rumania joining Serbia, and advocated the taking of immediate steps for entering into an alliance with Bulgaria as a vital precaution against the Rumanians coming in. Finally, he had dwelt upon the appalling danger that Russia might seize the chance to attack them, and Germany leave them in the lurch.

The only satisfaction he had got was the Emperor's decision to await the result of the inquiry before agreeing to any drastic step. But in the meantime Berchtold was pressing for immediate punitive action against Serbia, and von Hötzendorf for permission to mobilize so that he could launch a full-scale war. That day Count Hoyos had given an interview to a German publicist who was in close touch with Herr von Jagow, the German Foreign Minister, and had received unofficial but weighty assurances that Austria could count on German support on the following grounds:

Over a long period of years the German army had been built up to a marvellous pitch of perfection, but its sword was rusting in its scabbard, and the Generals feared that if it were not used soon it might show signs of serious deterioration. The German Foreign Office was satisfied that England was not in a mood to fight, so considered the moment for war propitious, and that if Austria-Hungary failed to assert herself in this dispute with a small nation, she would be finished as a great power. However, the last word remained with the Kaiser. Ambitious as he was by nature, in previous crises he had shown a reluctance to go to extremes. But this case was exceptional. Not only was he boiling with rage at the murder of his personal friends, Franz Ferdinand and his wife, but he regarded the attack as one calling for prompt chastisement as a deterrent to similar ones being made on other royalties. Therefore, if he was approached without delay, there were excellent grounds for believing that, on this occasion, he would back Austria to the point of war.

Tschirschky, the German Ambassador at Vienna, had, at first, appeared much more pacific minded, and had counselled moderation; but he had later received a reprimand from Berlin for interfering in what was not his business, and had then been instructed officially to inform the Emperor that the Kaiser would stand behind every firm decision made by his ally.

Nothing could have been better calculated to encourage the Austrian war-mongers; but it was still considered imperative to secure a categorical declaration that Germany would support Austria by force of arms; so on the 4th Count Hoyos had been sent to Berlin. With him he had taken a document proposing steps to be taken for the inclusion of Bulgaria in the Triple Alliance and a letter from the Emperor to the Kaiser urging the necessity for chastising Serbia, and asking for German approval of such an act, whatever its consequences might be.

On the 5th, Hoyos had handed his letter to Count Szögyény, the Austro-Hungarian Ambassador, for delivery to the Kaiser. When William II was informed of the dispatch, he invited the Ambassador to lunch at Potsdam. After the meal he at first said he must consult his Chancellor, Herr von Bethmann-Hollweg; but later he impulsively disclosed his own views. He did not think that an Austrian attack on Serbia would precipitate a European conflict. His information led him to believe that neither France nor Russia were prepared for war and he felt certain that the Czar would not associate himself with the murderers of princes. If the Dual Monarchy felt impelled to march into Serbia he advised that such action should not be long delayed. She would have his blessing, and whatever might follow he was fully prepared to stand by her.

Count Hoyos had come hurrying back from Berlin in triumph, and a Cabinet meeting had been called for noon on the 7th. At it had been Count Stürgkh, the Minister-President of Austria, Counts Tisza, Berchtold and Hoyos, Krobatin and Bilinski, the War and Finance Ministers, Admiral von Kailer and General Conrad von Hötzendorf.

When Berchtold announced the news that Hoyos had brought, with the one exception of Count Tisza the others could hardly contain themselves for excitement and delight. For years they had watched internal dissension weaken the Empire, and the potential enemies who ringed it in on every border, except that with Germany, become stronger and more menacing. Now they had something for which they had never really dared to hope—a blank cheque on the whole might of Imperial Germany with only one condition attached—that they should use it soon.

As Count Tisza described to the Duke this Cabinet meeting of the previous day his strong face was harrowed with distress. He had protested that he would never consent to a surprise attack on Serbia without previous diplomatic action, and that such a project should never have been discussed in Berlin. He had argued that such an attack would lead to their being branded as aggressors by the whole of Europe and would bring every Balkan country, with the possible exception of Bulgaria, in against them. And that, although Serbia must make suitable reparation, the idea of attempting to destroy her, or seize a large part of her territories, was suicidal, as it would inevitably lead to a life and death struggle with Russia.

But the others no longer cared if Rumania and Russia came in or not. The mailed fist of the Kaiser was now theirs to wield as they would. They had only to press the button and the mightiest army in the world would instantly march to their assistance. But it was now or never! If they showed weakness now, this God-given opportunity to crush their enemies once and for all might never occur again.

All that Count Tisza's most determined opposition had been able to secure was the postponement of any attack until an ultimatum had been sent and the Serbians given time to consider it. But he now feared that the terms of the ultimatum would be made so deliberately harsh as to ensure that Serbia would reject it, in which case war must inevitably follow.

For over an hour de Richleau and his visitor discussed the horrible implications of the course upon which the Dual Monarchy was being driven by Count Berchtold, von Hötzendorf and their adherents. As a man of fine brain, forceful character and known integrity, as a great noble and a beloved figure in his own country, Count Tisza possessed a personal influence far beyond even that bestowed upon him by his high political office. Yet his was now a voice crying in the wilderness. He alone in the Austro-Hungarian Cabinet stood for peace, and had the far-sightedness to foresee the unutterable calamity that war must bring to the civilization of Europe and its peoples, whichever nations might prove to be the victims.

He had sent a further memorandum to the Emperor, and done everything within his power to counteract the blind and evil counsels of his colleagues. He still did not despair and was determined to fight on for peace till the very last moment. But he could think of nothing more that he could do for the present, and, with all the will and sympathy in the world, the Duke could suggest nothing that his friend had not already attempted.

The Count left with a brighter air, declaring that it had at least done him good to talk things over, and promised to come to see the invalid again when he could find another opportunity.

When he had gone, de Richleau lay back and stared at the ceiling, wondering if there were anything he could possibly do which might aid the noble Hungarian's efforts. The very idea of betraying the Count's confidence filled him with repulsion. Nevertheless, he asked himself if he could do any good by requesting Sir Maurice de Bunsen to come to see him, and revealing to the British Ambassador all that had occurred at the previous day's Cabinet meeting. But he decided against it. There could be no possible justification for such treachery when by a majority of seven to one, plus the deliberate encouragement of Germany, the Emperor's advisers were advocating a policy of war. No outside influence could hope to overcome such solidarity of purpose. Nothing could now be done until the ultimatum was issued. Then, if its terms proved as brutal as Count Tisza feared they would be, Britain and other great powers could, if they chose, protest that Austria's demands exceeded anything she had the right to expect, and propose some form of mediation. Convinced that he could do no more than pray for a break in the dark clouds that threatened to engulf the manhood of three generations, the Duke fell into an uneasy sleep.

Next day the tension that he felt was considerably lightened by the news that the Kaiser had not postponed his summer cruise to Norway, but sailed upon it the very morning that the fateful Austro-Hungarian Cabinet meeting had been held. It seemed, to say the least of it, unlikely that if the Supreme War Lord of Europe really thought there was the least chance of being called on to loose his legions within a matter of days or weeks he would calmly have gone off on a holiday. This hopeful indication that saner counsels were prevailing was strengthened by the announcement that the Emperor had left Vienna for Ischl, and von Hötzendorf gone on leave. Evidently no further move was to be made for the moment, and in the past a war postponed had often proved a war averted. So de Richleau began to think that Count Tisza's apprehensions had so played upon his mind that he had exaggerated the danger of the situation.

Ilona paid her invalid another visit on the Friday, and brought him a photograph of herself in a beautiful frame set with semi-precious stones. She looked as well as ever but, for once, seemed distrait and worried. Tactfully, he endeavoured to discover the reason, but she refused to admit that she had anything on her mind; so he could only put it down to the fact that she had made a definite appointment to be overhauled by Dr. Bruckner on Monday, and must be dreading the possible verdict on her condition more than she cared to let him know.

Delighted as he was to have her photograph, caution counselled him to hide it as soon as she had gone. But he regarded it lovingly in secret many times during the next two days, and put it out again on his bed-side table just before she was due to arrive for her Sunday visit.

To his surprise and annoyance, Paula von Wolkenstein was in attendance on her instead of Sárolta. He guessed at once that some accident or indisposition must have prevented Sárolta from accompanying her royal mistress at the last moment and, it being too late to cancel the visit, she had had no choice but to bring the little blonde baroness instead. His guess proved correct, as Ilona said, after they had been talking for a few minutes, that she was sure he would be sorry to hear that Fraulein Hunyády had ricked her ankle that afternoon when coming down stairs.

Adam Grünne did his best for the lovers by taking Paula over to the window, but Ilona had to remain seated sedately in an arm-chair; and kisses, sweet whispers and tender sighs, were all entirely out of the question. After the freedom they had enjoyed during her previous visits, they found the situation extremely trying. They were now so used to talking intimately that there seemed nothing at all they could find to say while unwelcome ears were listening. In addition, Ilona's cough was worse and she seemed in even lower spirits than she had been on Friday; so de Richleau was neither surprised nor dismayed when, instead of staying for her usual hour, she stood up after twenty minutes of stilted conversation and took her departure.

His three visitors had not been gone more than two minutes when

Paula came back into the room alone. "Excuse me, please," she said demurely, "but I forgot my bag." And she walked over to the window to get it.

As she re-crossed the room she paused near de Richleau's bed and, for a moment, stood regarding Ilona's photograph with a faint sneer on her small, pursed up mouth. Then, with calm insolence, she remarked:

"You know, she thinks she can keep her secrets from me. But she can't. I wonder how Prince Boris would like it if he knew that she had given you her photograph to keep beside your bed?"

"What the devil do you mean?" exclaimed the Duke angrily.

The little vixenish face beneath the pile of flaxen hair broke into a cruel smile: then she laughed. "Oh, didn't you know? To cement the new treaty we are making with Bulgaria it has been arranged that she shall marry him."

CHAPTER XIX

THE TRUTH WILL OUT

THAT night the Duke suffered the torments of the damned. He felt certain that Paula had deliberately left her bag behind as an excuse to return and launch her poisoned shaft, and was convinced that, however malicious her nature, she would never have invented such a story. Before he had had time to collect his wits and question her further, she had walked quickly from the room. But her statement fitted in, both with what Count Tisza had said of the urgent necessity of securing Bulgaria to the Triple Alliance, and with Ilona's inexplicable depression during her last two visits.

In vain de Richleau chid himself for a fool. He told himself that he had always known that his affair with Ilona could never be more than a summer idyll, and that at any time arrangements might be made for her to marry suitably. But now that the blow had fallen, such thoughts brought him not an iota of comfort, neither did the knowledge that it was himself she loved, and not the twenty-year-old Prince Boris. He was experienced enough to realize that jealousy was a selfish, senseless, futile emotion, out of which no good could ever come; yet he was harrowed by it as he had not been since its pangs had gnawed at him when he learned in his 'teens that his first mistress was deceiving him.

Next day, the doctor pronounced his leg sufficiently mended for him to get up and take a few steps on it; so when Ilona came on Tuesday she found him sitting in an arm-chair. Sárolta had not twisted her ankle badly and two days' rest had enabled her to resume her duties. As soon as she was settled in the window with Adam Grünne, Ilona kissed the invalid and he drew her down beside him. By then he had had time enough to absorb the shock and appreciate that she must be feeling as badly about it as himself, so he took her hand and said gently:

"Why did you not tell me?"

Her blue eyes clouded with distress. "So you know—about Boris?"

"Yes. Paula told me when she came back for her bag, after your visit on Sunday."

"The little beast!" Ilona exclaimed. "I'll dismiss her for this!"

"Get rid of her by all means, dearest; but I suggest that you should find some other reason for doing so, otherwise she may cause trouble. She noticed your photograph at my bed-side, and inferred that she knew about us."

Ilona shrugged. "The photograph does not prove anything. Royalty often give photographs of themselves to their personal friends. She can know nothing, and is only guessing."

"Still, if you dismiss her for this, it will confirm her impression."

"That is true. Then I'll do as you suggest."

"But why, my sweet, why didn't you tell me about your engagement?"

"It is not an engagement—yet."

"The project then. You must have known of it some days ago."

"I did." Ilona sighed. "But I knew it would make you miserable, and I thought that if I kept it to myself for as long as possible we might continue to snatch a little happiness while we may."

"Is it—is it as good as settled?" he asked with a tremor in his voice.

She nodded. "There seems no likelihood of a hitch; and I'll have no alternative but to go through with it. Had some German or Italian Prince been proposed for me, I might have declared my personal inclination so averse to him that they would have dropped it. But I cannot do that in this case. A swift conclusion of the alliance with Bulgaria is considered of such importance that my feelings are of no account whatever. It is my duty to accept the situation with apparent pleasure. You see that, Armand, don't you? So please, please don't make it harder for me."

"I understand," he murmured. Then, after a moment, he said: "But if there can be no escape from this wretched blow of fate, would it not make it easier for you to do your duty if—if we end things now?"

Her arm was round his shoulder and she quickly put her hand over his mouth. "No, please! My private life remains my own, to do as I will with; at least until I am married."

He kissed her hand and drew it away. "As you will then, my sweet Princess. We'll do our best to forget this sword of Damocles that is suspended over our heads. But you have not told me yet what Dr. Bruckner said about you yesterday."

"Oh, Armand!" she stooped and brushed his forehead with her lips. "I must ask your forgiveness about that. I felt certain that any doctor would tell me that I ought to go back to Ischl and rest again. In view of this other business nothing would now induce me to leave Vienna, because that would mean leaving you. It seemed senseless to consult Dr. Bruckner and then ignore his advice. So I sent to tell him that I had changed my mind, and did not wish to see him."

"But, Ilona dearest, that was very wicked of you. Even if you refuse to take his advice for the time being, you must see him. You must at least find out if there is anything seriously wrong with you."

"There is not. I've told you so a score of times."

"I wish to God I were as certain of that as you seem to be. But I am far from it. If you will, count it only as a stupid whim of mine. Just to please me, and set my mind at rest, I beg you to see Bruckner before the end of the week."

She shrugged. "Very well then. I will. I promise."

By Thursday de Richleau was able to hobble about enough for him to be allowed out for the first time. So, that afternoon, Ilona took him for a drive in the Prater, and she told him that Dr. Bruckner was coming to examine her next day.

As the time was fast approaching when the Duke would be fit to leave the nursing home, the problem of how they could meet with any frequency in future was causing the lovers considerable anxiety. There would no longer be any excuse for Ilona to play ministering angel; it would be indiscreet for him to wait on her at the Palace more than about once a week; and Court mourning continued to veto her appearance at even small private entertainments.

It was dark-eyed, wicked little Sárolta who solved their difficulty for them. A relative of hers, named de Lazalo, had already achieved a considerable reputation as a painter. His studio was in a private house that he occupied, just off the Schotten Ring, and she was prepared to vouch for his discretion. She suggested that if Ilona commissioned him to paint her portrait, she could arrange for sittings two or three times a week, and the Duke could meet her there without anyone who might make trouble being the wiser. Both of them were delighted, and she was asked to arrange the matter so that the first sitting could take place early the following week.

On Saturday Ilona called for the Duke in her carriage again. Rather to his surprise, but to his immense joy and relief, she told him at once that after Dr. Bruckner had examined her on the previous day, he had confirmed the opinion of the Court physician. He had, of course, prescribed country air and rest, but declared her malady similar to that with which her grandmother had been inflicted. The symptoms of intermittent fever and the exceptional delicacy of the throat muscles were the same, and a quieter life was all that was needed to keep the attacks in check.

Dr Bruckner's view was certainly confirmed by the fact that since Court mourning had relieved Ilona of her public functions she appeared very much better. But this afternoon she was wearing an unusually heavy veil, and, after saying how glad he was to hear her good news, the Duke asked her why she had suddenly chosen to conceal her lovely features.

Leaning across the carriage towards him, she lowered her voice: "I thought we would celebrate by playing truant from the watching eyes of the servants for an hour or two. Adam has arranged it all, and we are going out to Grinzing."

Ten minutes later the carriage pulled up in a shady avenue of the Park. On the opposite side of the road another was waiting; but instead of having the Imperial Arms emblazoned on its panels and liveried servants on its box, it was a shabby old Victoria driven by a bottle-nosed cabby.

When the four of them had transferred to the meaner vehicle, it set off north-west, out of the park and along the south bank of the Danube for about three miles, then, leaving the river, carried them up the hill through the vineyards to the old village that had become an outer suburb of Vienna.

It was a very favourite spot with the Viennese, who came by the hundreds on Sundays to spend the afternoon and evening in its *Heuringer*, as the wine-gardens there were called. Each autumn, nearly every Viennese went there at least once, to try the new vintage; but all through the summer the gardens were open for pleasure seekers to drink the previous year's wine at long, wooden tables, where they could picnic if they wished, dance and listen to the band.

Adam Grünne told the cabby to pull up at an archway, over which a bunch of green fir branches hung from a pole—indicating that a fresh cask of wine had been broached there that day—and they went inside. To most people it would have been just a pleasant little outing, but to Ilona it was a terrific adventure, as she had never been informally to such a place before or sat at a bare wooden table drinking out of a thick tumbler. In the hot sunshine the fresh, slightly sharp wine tasted delicious and the merriment of the ordinary patrons of the place was infectious. Sárolta and Adam danced several times and, although de Richleau's leg made it impossible for him to dance with Ilona, he was amply compensated by having her with him in such carefree surroundings.

For a Saturday afternoon the place was fairly full, as it was the 18th of July and the summer holiday season was just beginning. During the past ten days the crisis had died down. The Austrian people were still angry, but it was now nearly three weeks since the assassinations and their Government had taken no action, so the drum-banging that had followed the terrible event at Sarajevo now looked like one more war scare that might be relegated to the history books with Agadir.

All over the world people were making their preparations to go to the beaches, the rivers and the mountains on pleasure bent. The Isle of Wight would soon be full of Germans, the Rhine of British trippers, the Belgian and Dutch *plages* of French families, and the German Baltic resorts of Russians. Every capital would have its thousands of foreign sightseers and an advance guard of them had already reached Vienna.

In the wine-garden de Richleau could easily pick out Englishmen in Norfolk jackets, crop-headed Germans and olive-skinned Italians, and a glance at any of them was enough to show that war was the very last thing they were thinking about.

On the table at which Ilona's party were sitting a previous occupant had left a copy of the morning's paper and a head-line in it caught the Duke's eye. It ran, 'King George V Reviews British Fleet', and, drawing the paper towards him he remarked to Ilona that it must have been a sight worth seeing.

Apparently Mr. Churchill had not been content to parade only the ships of biggest and latest design in honour of the Monarch. He had taken advantage of the summer training period of the Naval Reserve, which had enabled all three fleets to be assembled. Thus, on the one summer day he had concentrated incomparably the greatest assemblage of naval power ever witnessed in the history of the world. The three fleets were easily capable of destroying the navies of any other two powers together, and so numerous was this armada that, steaming in close formation, line ahead, at 15 knots, it had taken more than six hours to pass in review before the Royal yacht.

Recalling what Count Tisza had said about the Kaiser's rash encouragement of the Austrian war-mongers, the Duke thought the gesture admirably timed and worthy of the peace-loving but resolute Englishman who had planned it. The review had been scheduled to take place long before Franz Ferdinand had been murdered, so it was a purely domestic peace-time affair and a threat to no one: but if any measure could give the hot-headed Kaiser pause, this tremendous demonstration of naval might should do so.

All too soon Ilona's clandestine visit to Grinzing was over. They drove down the hill and transferred to the Imperial carriage in the Heiligenstadt wood, where Adam had arranged for it to meet them. It was, too, the last drive that de Richleau was to take with her, as on the Sunday he was leaving the nursing home to return to his old quarters at Sacher's.

On arriving there, however, he found a note from Adam, giving de Lazalo's address and the pleasing information that Sárolta had arranged with the painter for Ilona to sit for him the first time on Tuesday.

De Richleau set off in good time for the new rendezvous and, having paid off his cab, took up a position on the opposite side of the street, from which unobserved he could watch Ilona drive up. As soon as her carriage had set her down, he crossed the road, so that as it drove off he was able to hobble up to the door of the house just after it had closed behind her, and give the servant who admitted him the impression that he was a member of the Archduchess' suite who had been shut out by mistake.

The house was a comfortable modern one with a big studio at the back, which had lofty windows in its north wall and a door that led on to a small paved garden to its west. Some time passed in looking at the painter's work and discussing how Ilona should be posed, so he made only a few preliminary sketches of her that afternoon, then offered them iced coffee in the garden.

After they had been out there for a few minutes, Ilona said to de Lazalo, "Would you think me very rude if I take Count Königstein in to have another look at your sketches?" Then she added with a friendly smile, "He is quite an art critic, you know, but I would not like to embarrass either of you by asking him to criticize work in front of its creator."

The painter was a polished and charming man; moreover Sárolta had already told him to what he owed the present commission and sworn him to secrecy; so he returned Ilona's smile and only expressed the hope that they would not be too hard on his first efforts to catch her likeness.

Thus, the lovers were able to snatch a quarter of an hour alone together. Then, as Ilona was about to leave, de Lazalo, prompted by Sárolta, tactfully asked de Richleau to stay behind and give him his opinion of some more of his work, so saving him from being seen by her coachman and footman leaving the house with her.

The next sitting was on Thursday, the 23rd, and the Duke was spared the necessity of taking special measures on his arrival by de Lazalo, who had asked him to lunch beforehand. When Ilona appeared it was obvious to de Richleau that she was doing a poor best to suppress great excitement; so he was not at all surprised when, after twenty minutes, she declared that she had sat long enough for that day. Then, no sooner had they adjourned to the garden than she made the same excuse as before to take him inside again.

As soon as they were alone, he said, "What is it, dearest? Don't tell me that they are hastening on your marriage?"

"No, no!" She shook her head and her eyes were wide. "There is nothing fresh about that. But they've sent the ultimatum."

"The ultimatum!" he exclaimed.

"Yes. To Serbia. It is to be delivered by our Ambassador in Belgrade at six o'clock this evening."

He stared at her. "But this is terrible! After—after we all thought that things would be smoothed over. If they meant to send one, why ever didn't they do so before? Or is this the result of some fresh outrage that we have not yet heard about?"

"I gather now that they always meant to, but have held it up for some reason that is still being kept a close secret."

"Do you know anything of its terms?"

"Only that they are extremely harsh. Count Aulendorf told me that they were such that no nation could be expected to accept them. And the Serbians have been given only forty-eight hours in which to reply."

"Then this means war."

"I fear so. The thought is horrible. Still, those swinish Serbians have asked for it, and we shall soon give them the hiding they deserve."

"But, Ilona, there is a great danger that the war will spread. Should Russia make the least move in Serbia's favour, Germany will march against her. The Germans will take no risk of Russia striking first. And, although you may not know it, the Kaiser has guaranteed to support Austria to the limit."

"Well, so he should. He is a vulgar little man, but the least he can do for his ally is to see that Russia does not stab us in the back."

"I don't contest that from Austria's point of view. But don't you see, darling, that if Russia and Germany begin hostilities France will come in as Russia's ally, and England. Italy too, perhaps, and Rumania, Bulgaria, Turkey, Greece. It will be an immeasurable catastrophe, with the armies of every nation in Europe spreading death and desolation in their path."

A shudder ran through her. "You paint a terrible picture, Armand; but there can be no drawing back now. We can only pray that Serbia will agree to our demands, however harsh they may be; or that your fears of the conflict spreading will not be realized. If they are, Austria will need every soldier she can raise to fight her battles. When I made you an honorary Colonel of my regiment I little thought that you would be called upon to fight. But if you have to go with the rest, I know that your conduct will make me prouder than ever of you."

He looked at her aghast; then seized her hands and cried "My sweet! My sweet! How can you have forgotten that I am British?"

"British!" she gasped. "But you were born the heir to both French and Austrian titles. Since you were expelled from France, how can your nationality be anything now but Austrian?"

"Ilona, my own!" His grip on her hands tightened while he fought for words. "Our love—our love has been so different from that of an ordinary couple. We've had so little time together—never enough to do more than say we love one another. Perhaps I never told you; but I thought you knew. When I was exiled from France I considered becoming an Austrian officially. But I didn't. For reasons into which there is no point in going now, I took out British naturalization papers. So—so you see, if the worst happens we—we shall be on opposite sides."

Her eyes grew rounder, but she did not speak; so after a moment he went on: "For us, I fear this sending of an ultimatum is the end. You are the last woman in the world who needs to be told that personal interests must be sacrificed to duty. Mine, if war comes, is to serve England to the best of my ability. Ilona, to part with you is to tear my heart from my body. But it has to be. Now that hostilities against Serbia have actually been threatened, I must at once return to London."

Pulling her hands from his, she threw her arms round his neck. "Not yet, Armand! Not yet. What you tell me is a shock. It's not that I mind your being British, but that we may find our countries fighting against one another. For us to be utterly cut off from each other like that would be terrible."

"My love, even had I been Austrian our separation must have come soon."

"You mean by my marriage? I know. But at least we should still have been able to get news of one another. Besides, my engagement has not yet been announced, so it will be several weeks before they—they pack me off to Bulgaria. I was counting on those weeks to store up a further treasure of loving memories of you."

"And I of you, beloved. But we must now make shift with those we have already."

"No, no! There is still a little time for us to snatch others. I beg you not to rob me of it. Why are you in such a desperate hurry to get back to England? Your duty does not require that you should leave Vienna yet."

"By implication it does. In forty-eight hours Austria and Serbia will be at war. It will take me that long to get home, and, knowing what I do, it would not be right for me to take any risk of being stranded abroad with the possibility of a general war breaking out."

"But nothing is certain yet. Serbia may decide to grovel rather than fight."

"You forget that I have been in Belgrade recently. I know the temper of the Serbs. Their army believes yours to be effete. Despite the odds, they will accept the challenge without hesitation."

"Even then the war may not spread: And if it does—if Russia, Germany and France all come in—England may still keep out."

"If France is attacked, Britain will come to her aid. I am certain of it."

"How can you be?"

He hesitated for a moment. Distressed beyond measure as he was, at the thought of leaving her, he felt that he must get home. He was convinced that nothing could now avert war on the grand scale, and if he were to take his proper part in it, the sooner he got back to London the better. To remain a few days longer could make their parting no less painful; yet it seemed unnecessarily brutal to deprive her of them without any apparent reason. If he gave a truthful answer to her question, that would provide it.

Looking down into her eyes, he said gravely, "From conversations that I had with several highly placed men before I left London, I am convinced that Britain will honour her alliance with France."

Ilona was not impressed. She shook her head impatiently. "The awful deed at Sarajevo did not take place till the end of June—a full two months after we left London. If the conversations you speak of occurred in April they can have been only the vaguest speculations, and had no relation whatever to this quarrel between Austria and Serbia. It is absurd to attach any weight to an unofficial pronouncement on a situation which could not possibly have been foreseen."

"The possibility of such a situation arising was foreseen."

"What! They knew in England of the plot to murder my cousin?"

"No! No! But it was feared that during the summer a breach would occur between Austria and Serbia. That was the subject of those discussions, and I was informed officially that in such a case Britain would stand no nonsense from Germany."

She frowned. "You say you were informed officially. Why was that? What had such a matter to do with you?"

Too late de Richleau realized that in his anxiety to convince her of the desperateness of the situation he had gone much further than he intended. He could only reply, "I am in the service of the British Government."

Her face had lost its colour as she asked: "What do you mean by that? You have never said anything to me of being connected with the British Embassy here."

"I am not," he admitted, now seeking frantically in his mind for the best course to adopt. He could refuse to answer further questions from her. But he could not bear to have her tortured by doubts about himself. It would be better to tell her the whole truth and trust to her appreciating his motives for what he had done. That seemed to offer the only chance of preserving her faith in him and not soiling her memories of her love with miserable uncertainties.

"Listen, Ilona," he said firmly. "It is best that I should tell you now that I have deceived you in certain matters; not deliberately, but through force of circumstances. For example, I never went to Constantinople, as I told you; but during my absence from Vienna I was all the time in Belgrade. That apart, in the main, I have not lied to you about myself, but simply refrained from informing you about the work to which I was committed before we crossed the Channel together, and the secret activities that it entailed. I am not a British diplomat, but it would be fair to say that I have been acting on instructions from the British Foreign Office. Even before I met you, there was some reason to suppose that Serbia intended to give Austria provocation for war. I was sent out to inquire into that and, if I could, suggest measures to prevent it. That was how I learned of the Black Hand's plot to assassinate your cousin."

Slowly she withdrew her arms from round his neck and let them fall to her sides. "Do you——? Surely you cannot mean that you are a spy?"

"That is an unpleasant word, Ilona. Use it if you must, but at least remember my motive and who——"

Her face suddenly became distorted by horror. Drawing back from him, she cried: "What does it matter why, or on whom, you spied? You! A man of gentle birth! A nobleman! Oh, how could you demean yourself by undertaking such vile work?"

It was a question that in May and early June he had asked himself a hundred times, but he had since become so fully convinced that in this case the end justified the means, that his voice hardened as he replied:

"If it be demeaning oneself to strive to avert untold misery overtaking countless innocent people, then I am guilty of it. What is more, I would demean myself again if by ferreting out Austria's secrets I could yet prevent a war."

"Perhaps——" Her voice broke and she went on in a whisper: "Perhaps you have already endeavoured to do so. Since you left England you have spent far more time in Vienna than in Belgrade."

He shook his head miserably. "Ilona, what of your love for me? Have you not sufficient faith in me as a man to believe that I have acted only from good motives?"

"Yes, I love you," she murmured. "I cannot help myself in that. For the rest, I don't know what to think."

For a moment they stared at one another in unhappy silence. Then she drew herself up and said: "In view of what you have told me, I realize the necessity for your immediate departure. You have my permission to go."

She was near to tears, but pride held them back. Her voice held no quaver of sentiment, and her attitude was entirely regal. To him there seemed no alternative but to accept this formal dismissal. Overwhelmed with sorrow at this tragic ending to their love affair, he bowed to her, turned on his heel, and limped slowly towards the door.

He had barely reached it when he heard a choking sob behind him, and her low cry: "Armand!"

Turning, he saw that tears were now streaming down her face. She held out her arms. "Oh, Armand! We must not part like this. Not—not without one last kiss."

His game leg forgotten, he re-crossed the studio in a few strides. Trembling with emotion, he caught her to him.

"I—I simply can't understand why—why you should have done such a thing," she sobbed. "Surely only the most awful people are employed as spies? Ex-officers who have been dismissed from the army in disgrace and can find no other way to earn a living; petty criminals who are induced to do it by reduction of their sentences; and—and prostitutes in garrison towns."

He pressed her wet cheek against his. "Darling, you are right about peace-time spies being mainly recruited from the dregs of humanity; though in war many of them are honourable and courageous people who risk their lives from entirely patriotic motives. As far as I am concerned, I agreed to undertake this mission only with the greatest reluctance. But once I had done so I realized its immense importance. Surely you can see that had I been only a little more fortunate I might have been in time to prevent the assassination of your cousin? Had I been able to do that, this terrible crisis would never have arisen."

She nodded, and smiled up at him through her tears. "Yes, yes. That's true. I hadn't looked at it like that."

"Oh, thank God!" he kissed her again. "Thank God you realize what I have been trying to do. I would have eaten out my heart with misery had I been forced to leave you believing me to be unworthy of your love."

Her face clouded again. "But what of Austria? While you have been here many of our leading men must have talked freely in your presence. You must have heard many of our secrets, too."

"I have; but none of any great importance. And I swear to you that I have not used any of the knowledge I have gained to Austria's detriment."

Once more her blue eyes shone with love and trust. "Then I don't care what nationality you are or what you've done. I love you, and I shall never love anyone else. Stay with me, Armand! Stay with me yet a little time. Serbia may give in. There may be no war. Remain here at least until we know the worst, and it is absolutely necessary for you to go."

He shook his head. "No, beloved. I beg you not to ask me."

"Please, Armand! Please! Remember what is in store for me. Once I am married memories of you are all I'll have to live on—the only thing I'll have to comfort me for the rest of my life."

"I cannot," he sighed. "I must go. Do you not see that if I remain and, even despite myself, learn more of Austria's intentions, should there be war between our countries it will be my duty to tell what I know."

"You tell me that you have not passed on the knowledge that you have gained so far, so why should you disclose anything more that you may learn in these next few days? Since you are so honourable as to wish to go on that account, surely your love for me is sufficient to put the seal of honour on your lips about everything you hear until you leave Vienna."

Suddenly he kissed her violently again, broke the grasp of her hands about his neck, and exclaimed: "Ilona, you are seeking to place me in an impossible position. You ask too much. I love you desperately. I'll love you till the day I die. But I've got to go. I must. Good-bye."

Swinging away from her, he limped swiftly across the room. His heart was pounding and there was a mist before his eyes. He felt as though he were leaving a part of himself behind, but he had steeled himself to it. If he stayed the odds were all against his learning anything that mattered about Austria's military preparations unless he went out of his way to do so. And if by chance he did, he considered that the services he had already rendered would justify him in keeping his mouth shut. It had never been suggested that he should attempt to ferret out Austria's secrets, so he could have stayed on for a day or two without risk of being faced with the awful question of whether it was his duty to betray Ilona's trust in him. But Austria had her blank cheque from the Kaiser, and now that she had sent out an ultimatum he felt that war was inescapable. To remain was only to court a repetition of this agony of parting a few days hence. Torture as the thought was to him that he might never see her again, he knew that he had been wise for both of them in refusing her plea to delay his departure.

As he stumped towards the door, dragging his injured leg a little, he was terribly tempted to look round and snatch one last look at her to preserve in his memory. But he dared not do so, knowing that he would weaken if he did.

Suddenly he heard her running feet. She caught him when he was still only two-thirds of the way across the room. Seizing him by the arm she swung him round, exclaiming:

"Armand! Armand! There is something that I have not yet told you."

He made a half-hearted attempt to free his arm. "No, please," he begged. "For pity's sake! Let me go now, and don't prolong this agony."

But she ignored his plea and her words came pouring out in a breathless spate:

"Oh, Armand, I have deceived you too. I have done worse! I may have harmed you. But I love you so much that I could not find the strength to give you up. I've never loved anyone before. I was never even kissed until you kissed me. Since that night at Königstein I've only lived from hour to hour on the thought that you would soon hold me in your arms again. I've been incredibly wicked. God will punish me for it, I know. But I don't mind that. I don't mind anything if only you'll stay until we know that war with England is certain. I'll be content with very little. Just to be with you whenever we can manage it. Just to hold your hand, to see you and hear your voice. Please, *please* forgive me and grant me that much."

As she paused for breath, he asked in amazement, "But what is there for me to forgive, my sweet? In what way have you deceived me?"

Her lovely face was a picture of grief and contrition as she sobbed: "I lied to you the other day. And worse—much worse—I should never have let you kiss me. I didn't see Dr. Bruckner on Friday. It wasn't necessary. I have known for months that my lungs are affected. I am suffering from consumption."

CHAPTER XX

THE ROAD TO THE ABYSS

DE RICHLEAU raised his slender hands and took Ilona's lovely, tear-stained face between them. Before she could pull back her head, he leaned forward and kissed her on the lips. Then he said:

"My poor Princess. I feared this all the time. In fact, I felt almost certain of it."

"You knew! And yet you went on kissing me." There was adoration in her eyes, but she added unhappily, "I ought never to have let you. There is a risk that you might contract my disease—may have done so already."

He smiled. "I don't think you need worry about that. Anyway, I love you far too much to refrain from making love to you whenever we are together; and now you've told me the truth our future kisses are entirely my responsibility."

"Oh darling! You mean you'll stay? You're not going to leave me after all?"

"I ought to; but now I know what I feared to be certain, I haven't the heart. This serious illness on top of the prospect of being forced into a marriage against your wish breaks down my resolution. God knows I had no desire to go, and now it would be callous of me to add to your distress by leaving before I positively must."

"My marriage," she sighed; then gave a cynical laugh. "At least I derive a little consolation for my illness when I think of that. I am counting on it to protect me from Prince Boris's attentions."

"Could you not use it then as an excuse to get the marriage called off?"

She shook her head. "When royal unions are in question, no consideration is ever given to either party's health. Princesses have often had to marry men who had the most loathsome diseases; and Princes been given wives with the taint of insanity."

"Yes; that is terrible, but true. And many people with your complaint have married and lived for years without passing it on to their marriage partner. Besides, if only you will be careful and have proper treatment, there is every hope that you may be cured."

"Short of my going to a sanatorium, all that can be done is being done already," she assured him. "It was kept a close secret, but Franz Ferdinand was afflicted with tuberculosis when he was my age, and it was feared that he would die: but he got quite well again. And I'm better—ever so much better than I was a month ago."

"My sweet, I am tremendously relieved to hear it. But all the same, you ought to go into a sanatorium and be properly cured."

"No. That I refuse to do. My doctors tell me that, although it may take a little longer, I can be cured without doing that. I should feel so depressed in such surroundings that they would do me more harm than good. I'm certain of it. I'll get well much more quickly in a happy atmosphere."

They had been alone together for over half an hour, and felt that the time had come when they must rejoin the others. So, after a last kiss, they returned to the garden. As a small acknowledgment of de Lazalo's tactful complaisance, Ilona asked him to tea at the palace on Sunday. She asked de Richleau too; but they were to see one another before that, as another sitting had been arranged for Saturday. Ten minutes later they had separated, and the Duke was left with his thoughts a chaotic whirl of Ilona—the ultimatum—espionage—mobilization and tuberculosis.

The following morning the papers carried the full text of the ultimatum. It charged Serbia with culpable tolerance of propaganda directed against the Dual Monarchy and accused Serbian officers of planning the Sarajevo murders. There followed demands for the dissolution of all nationalist societies; the arrest and trial of all officers and officials that Austria-Hungary should name; that Austro-Hungarian delegates should take part in an inquiry into the anti-Austrian movement and that Serbia should accept the collaboration of Austro-Hungarian officials in its suppression.

The terms were even harsher than de Richleau had expected. They meant that any Serbian, against whom the Austrians had a grudge, would have to stand his trial before a court including a quota of Austrian judges, and that the Austrian police must be given a free hand to carry out any investigations they chose in Serbia. In short, the acceptance of the demands would put an end to Serbian independence.

Vienna went wild with joy. At last this insolent, upstart regime in Belgrade was to be humbled and its ignorant, brutish, murdering officers made to grovel in the dust. And if Serbia dared to refuse the terms, then a million soldiers of the Empire would cram them down her throat and teach her a still more bitter lesson. Later, special editions published an earnest request from the Czar's government that the time limit of forty-eight hours given to Serbia should be extended to permit of calm discussion, and a manifesto announcing that Russia could not remain indifferent to the fate of Serbia. But the Austrian government refused the request and the crowds proved blind to the warning note of the manifesto. All day, and far into the night, bands of students and others roamed the streets of the city, singing patriotic songs and clamouring for war.

On Saturday there were perceptibly more uniforms to be seen about in the cafés and gardens. Overnight, hundreds of thousands of reservists all over the country had laid aside their civilian clothes and got out tunics, breeches and shakos that had been packed away with moth balls in tin boxes. The Duke had no doubt at all that ever since July 7th, the day on which von Hötzendorf had first demanded mobilization, every military establishment in the Empire had been making frantic secret preparations. This influx into the streets of men in creased and often shabby uniforms was the beginning of the final phase. Austria-Hungary still refrained from openly mobilizing the whole of her Army, so as not to provoke Russia deliberately; but she had mobilized eight Army corps and was now ready to set about the chastisement of her small neighbour.

That afternoon de Lazalo was allowed nearly an hour to make a real start on his portrait of Ilona. Before leaving, she complimented him on his masterful brush work, but warned him with a smile that she did not want him to finish it too quickly; then reminded him that she expected him to tea next day.

Being summer-time, she was occupying her apartments in the Schönbrunn Palace and, as on this occasion de Richleau was waiting on her officially, he again donned his sky-blue Hussars uniform to go there. In Ilona's drawing-room he found a dozen people, the Aulendorfs and Adam Grünne among them. Sárolta was not present, but Ilona introduced him to a Fraulein Nopsca who, she said with a twinkle in her eye, had consented to take Paula von Wolkenstein's place for a while, as the 'poor' Baroness had asked for leave to take the waters at Homburg on account of her health. The new lady-in-waiting was a tall, fair-haired young woman with serious expression and a Roman nose too large for her face. But on talking to her de Richleau found her intelligent and pleasant.

Everyone there was discussing the Serbian reply to the ultimatum. In spite of the brutal challenge to Serbian independence that it answered, it had been completed within the stipulated forty-eight hours and handed to Baron Giesel, the Austrian Minister in Belgrade, at six o'clock the previous evening. For any Cabinet to have agreed a reply in so short a time, when on it hung the fate of their nation, was remarkable; but more remarkable still was the pacific tone of the answer. The Serbs accepted all the demands made upon them, except one which would infringe their constitution; and even that they were willing to submit for arbitration to the Hague Tribunal.

The Aulendorfs and another elderly couple were of the opinion that once the measures stipulated had been carried out, there would be no more to fear from Serbia, and the Dual Monarchy should rest content with having won a fine bloodless victory; but the younger people were greatly disappointed at their enemy bowing the neck so humbly, and hoped that some excuse might yet be found to launch a war. De Richleau was amazed that the Serbs had turned the other cheek. He could account for it only on the theory that the Serbian Government had, although unwillingly, been to some extent privy to the murders and, having been freed from Dimitriyevitch's strangle-hold upon it, was now both able and willing to do its utmost to make amends. If he was right in his belief, since it was he who had removed that strangle-hold, his mission had, after all, paid an incalculably high dividend; but he knew only too well that its final value still hung in the balance, and that if von Hötzendorf had his way it would prove worth nothing.

By mid-day on Monday the Austro-Hungarian Government had evening he dined with the Loecjtemsteoms' After dinner another special editions informed the waiting crowds that excitement was intense in every capital in Europe. The foreign papers, which were still flowing freely into Vienna, showed from their Sunday editions that the great bulk of opinion outside the Dual Monarchy was that she now had no cause whatever to complain further; and that Serbia was considered to have made great sacrifices in a most laudable effort to keep the peace.

That afternoon de Richleau and Ilona met again in de Lazalo's studio; but she could tell him nothing of her Government's intentions. Since moving back to Sacher's he had resumed his old round of entertaining and being entertained by his many Austrian friends. On that evening he dined with the Liechtensteins. After dinner another special edition was brought in and handed round. It stated that the Kaiser had returned from his Norwegian cruise the previous night, but otherwise appeared to contain nothing fresh. However, a heading to one of the smaller paragraphs caught the Duke's eye. It read:

"British Naval Measures. No Manœuvre Leave." There followed an official Admiralty statement to the effect that the First Fleet would remain concentrated at Portland and that the vessels of the Second Fleet would remain at their home ports in close proximity to their balance crews.

Again, it was a measure which could give offence to nobody; but once more that vigilant guardian of Britain's shores, Mr. Churchill, was making it plain for all who had eyes to see that no German Fleet could hope to attack the French Channel ports without encountering overwhelming opposition.

Tuesday, the 28th, proved to be the fatal day. At eleven o'clock that morning Count Berchtold telegraphed to Belgrade that, "The Royal Serbian Government not having answered in a satisfactory manner the note of July 23rd, Austria-Hungary consequently considered herself in a state of war with Serbia".

The news was all over Vienna by mid-day. There was a rumour that Serbian troops had already fired upon an Austrian detachment the previous afternoon. Indignation at this unprovoked attack, coupled with relief that they were not to be robbed by unwelcome mediation of their longed-for revenge, drove the people of Vienna into a frenzy of excitement. Military bands paraded the streets, blaring forth martial music. The crowds waved flags and wore paper hats, as though at a carnival. Shop-girls, laundry-hands and seamstresses left their work to dance in the squares and fling their arms round any soldier they could see. Flowers rained upon every detachment of troops that marched through the streets, and smart young officers strutted about with garlands round their necks. Night came down upon a saturnalia, excusable as a demonstration of relief after a great national deliverance; but made possible now only through an utter lack of understanding of what war meant, and of the endless distress, anxiety and tragedy which must follow in its train.

On Wednesday morning the streets were as crowded as on the previous day. Business had come to a standstill and hordes of people besieged the newspaper offices for tidings of the first clash of the armies. The great Austrian siege guns firing a 19 centimetre shell, which were made at the famous Skoda works in Bohemia, were believed to be the most powerful land guns in the world and superior in performance to anything that even Krupps could produce. It was said that these monster cannon were already in operation and bombarding Belgrade across the Danube. Thoughtless of death and havoc, people who a month before had lived only to hear the new rendering of a classical sonata, howled with delight.

Meanwhile, bodies of smiling troops swung through the streets, lustily singing gay marching songs. The great majority of them were reservists, or young conscripts, on their way to training camps, where they would spend several weeks, if not months, being knocked into shape before they were called on to face an enemy. But the crowds gave them an ovation the equal of any triumph granted by a Roman Senate to a Caesar, after long years of desperate and successful struggle to keep barbarian hordes beyond the boundaries of the Empire.

De Richleau watched it all with unsmiling eyes. He was no pessimist by nature, but ever since he had reached manhood war had been his game. He had seen too many youngsters, grinning, vigorous, determined at one moment, and screaming like maniacs from shell-rent flesh or smashed bone the next; too many still, twisted corpses and pulped, messy heads. But his own effort to prevent the colossal madness had failed, and there was nothing more that he could do.

In the afternoon he went to de Lazalo's, and after Ilona's sitting had twenty minutes alone with her. So far none of the other nations had made any move to intervene in the Austro-Serbian conflict, and this made Ilona optimistic that they would continue to refrain from doing so. Eagerly, she pointed out a passage in a paper she had brought with her. It stated that the British Foreign Secretary, Sir Edward Grey, had not given up hope of inducing the two warring countries to cease hostilities and submit their differences to a conference of the Powers; and he was said to be doing his utmost to persuade Germany to agree to support this proposal. Ilona took the statement as an indication of Britain being so anxious to maintain the peace that, whatever happened, she would not allow herself to be drawn in.

Out of love for his Princess, de Richleau did not contest her arguments, but secretly he did not agree with them. He was still convinced that, reluctant as Britain might be to go to war, if France were attacked, she would fight. He realized too, better than most people, the terrible hidden forces that seethed and bubbled beneath the thin, fair crust of apparent good will. However confident any of the great nations might be in its power to achieve victory in the end, all were terrified that an enemy might move a jump ahead of them and deliver the first stunning blow. To guard against that, every Chief of Staff must now be imploring his Government to authorize him to mobilize; and, like a chain of fireworks, once one nation mobilized, the others would follow suit within a matter of hours. Then, kings and ministers might still strive to maintain the peace, but it would need only a few shots between frontier patrols for the peace-time masters to be thrust aside, like puppets who had outworn their use. Automatically, the Generals would take charge and throw their mighty machines into gear. Almost before the shots on the frontier had ceased to echo, the cannon would thunder and the nations be at death grips, which could be severed only after one or other side had become too weakened by loss of blood to continue the struggle.

So strongly did this foreboding weigh on the Duke's mind that, although he told Ilona nothing of his intention, he decided to begin that evening saying good-bye to his friends. Since leaving the nursing home he had purposely refrained from calling on Count Tisza, as he was most averse to being made the recipient of further confidences by that statesman. But, as a man, he liked him better than anyone he had met for a very long time, and he was loath to leave without expressing the hope that they would meet again in happier circumstances. So, at about half past ten, after he had seen off two couples who had dined with him at Sacher's, he ordered a cab, had himself driven round to the Minister-President's little palace, and sent up his card.

Count Tisza had been entertaining half a dozen Hungarian Deputies to dinner, but two of them left as the Duke entered the hall, and the others were just about to do so. When they had gone, the Count took his visitor up to the library and reproached him in a friendly way for not having been to see him before. The Duke excused himself on the plea that he had not liked to intrude during a time of such acute anxiety, and added that he did so now only to make his farewells.

Having poured him a glass of wine, the Count nodded sadly. "Yes, it is tragic beyond words that it should have come to this, but I fear there is still worse to come; so I think you wise to return to France."

"I am going to England," replied the Duke. "Most of my friends here are aware that I was expelled from France for participation in a political conspiracy when quite a young man. I thought you would have heard that much of my history. It was one of the main reasons for my becoming a rolling stone and a soldier of fortune; but I took British nationality."

"No, I had not heard that. When poor Sophie von Hohenberg introduced us, I assumed that you were a Frenchman. But it makes little difference. If Russia, Germany and France are drawn in, as I fear they will be, I consider it as good as certain that Britain will come in too."

"I agree; although what is called 'informed opinion' in the Austro-German press appears to think otherwise."

"So, too, do most of my colleagues. Once again I am in a minority. But the British are not fools. They dare not stand by and see France defeated. To do so would be to court war single-handed against an infinitely more powerful Germany in a few years' time."

The Duke took the long cigar that his host offered him, and remarked: "I am sure that is how they view it themselves, and I should have thought that Mr. Churchill's having held the First and Second Fleets together would have made it plain to others."

"There are none so blind as those who do not wish to see, my friend. If the war spreads we shall have that mountebank, William Hohenzollern, to thank for it. His war-monger Generals are always dangling before him the picture of himself as another Frederick the Great, and he is a born wishful thinker. He is convinced that France is in no state to put up a serious resistance to his armies, and I would wager on it that he regards the continued concentration of the British Fleet merely as a bluff."

Count Tisza stroked his beard thoughtfully, then went on: "That man is of the type most dangerous and unsuited of any to be an absolute monarch—a mixture of timidity, impulsiveness and vanity. When Hoyos returned from Berlin early in the month we were given to understand that, although we could count on Germany's support to the limit, the Kaiser did not believe that there was the least danger of our quarrel with Serbia leading to a European war. He took his decision to support us without consulting his Cabinet, and we have since learned that afterwards he did not bother to summon it in order to hear its views on possible repercussions to his rash act. Instead, he seems to have suddenly changed his mind about the likelihood of war; but even then he did not ask the opinion of his principal advisers at a council. That afternoon and evening he sent for his Chancellor, his military chiefs, and his armaments' director, Krupp, one by one, and told them impulsively to be prepared for an outbreak of hostilities. Then, having set the German war machine secretly in motion, he calmly went off next morning on a holiday cruise to Norway. Naturally, with no hand left to check them, the delighted Generals took the bit between their teeth. And now, having been accused by them so often in previous crises of having shown the white feather at the last moment, his vanity will not allow him to climb down."

"What you tell me tallies with the sort of situation I have always feared," said the Duke. Then, so that his friend should not make any further disclosures that he might afterwards regret, he added as a deliberate warning, "And so, Count, it seems that you and I will soon find ourselves in enemy camps. May I say that in this frightful tragedy there are few things that I shall regret more deeply."

"And I." The Count smiled. "But at least I am happy to think that, for people like ourselves, war does not mean the breaking of a friendship. It is one of the greatest blessings granted to educated and travelled men, that they are not subject to the blind hatred of the mobs. The less fortunate know next to nothing of other nations, so regard them with either jealousy or contempt, and can be roused by any alarmist parrot-cry to howl for their blood. Whereas we who have seen many cities and walked the countryside of many lands, know that all races differ only in small, unimportant things; and that they hold in common the golden thread of charity, humour, courage and goodwill. For you and me war will mean a separation, during which each of us will do his duty to his country; but attributes of the spirit, such as love and friendship, can survive unsmirched by the dirt of man-made conflicts. Even if we met as two scouts upon a battlefield, instead of attempting to hack one another to pieces, I am sure we should sit down and have a drink; then return to our respective lines without giving away one another's position."

The Duke nodded gravely. He too had been brought up in the tradition of chivalry, and he agreed whole-heartedly with every word that the noble-minded Hungarian had said. Soldier as he was, he regarded war as an evil thing, arising always from the ambitions of unscrupulous men; and, although he had fought in many for the sake of the interest and excitement they afforded him, he had always observed the traditional courtesies of war, and counted his personal relationships with people who chanced to be on the other side, as a thing apart, concerning only his own honour.

"You have expressed exactly my own feelings, Count," he declared warmly. "And we can only pray that the conflict will be a brief one. That it should occur at all is beyond words tragic. In spite of your pessimism when you came to see me three weeks ago, I must confess I lapsed into a fool's paradise until I learned that the ultimatum to Serbia had actually been sent. To have thrown that bombshell after such a long delay seems really wanton. And, even knowing what I do of von Hötzendorf's ideas—I mean his theory about waging a series of wars against the Empire's potential enemies in turn as the best hope of holding it together—I still cannot understand how your Government could have allowed him to persuade them into opening hostilities after they had received Serbia's abject submission."

"I understand it only too well." Count Tisza rose from his chair and began to pace up and down the room with his hands behind his back. "Berchtold wanted to secure the complete elimination of Serbia as a factor in Balkan politics, and he made up his mind to use the Archduke's murder as an excuse to achieve that. The delay in sending the ultimatum is easily explained. The French President, M. Poincaré, and his Prime Minister were on an official goodwill visit to St. Petersburg. They were not due to leave until 23rd July. In order to prevent their conferring personally with the Czar and his advisers, so that Russia and France might formulate a common policy, it was decided to pigeon-hole the ultimatum till that date. In fact, Berchtold actually delayed its delivery for an additional hour in order to make quite certain that the Czar's French visitors should have started on their way home before the Russian Foreign Office learned of it."

"Then your pessimism was well-founded. But, even so, the meekness of the Serbian answer must have been quite unexpected. Surely it gave Count Berchtold all that he required? In fact, I find it inexplicable that he should have courted condemnation of Austria-Hungary as an agressor by pressing the matter further."

The Count shrugged. "For that the Kaiser is to blame. It was he who gave us the blank cheque. Its use was even urged upon us and implied that if Russia attempted to intervene, Germany would attack her. Is it not plain to you how the minds of von Hötzendorf and Berchtold must have worked? They said to themselves, 'Here is our chance to eliminate not only our little enemy, Serbia, but our big enemy, Russia, as well. But unless we force a war upon Serbia, Russia will not threaten us; so we shall have lost the God-given opportunity of involving the Germans in a war which should cripple the mighty Empire of the Czars for many years to come.' From that moment the tone of Serbia's reply became a matter of indifference to them. Nothing but war would any longer serve their full purpose; and they were determined to have it."

"I see that; yet I still marvel that either the Kaiser or the Emperor should have been willing to go to such lengths, once all grounds for aggression had been cut from beneath their feet by the humility of the Serbian reply."

"You may well do so. But I think the Kaiser is caught in the web created by his own initial impetuosity. His Chief of Staff, von Moltke, has stated that Germany could never hope to be in a more favourable condition to enter on a general conflict than she is at present. The German Foreign Office agrees to that. During the Kaiser's absence all preparations that could be made for war, short of actual mobilization, were hurried forward. He returned to find all his high officials not only ready for war, but awaiting his signal to press the trigger. It is possible that a return of his timidity might restrain him from taking the final plunge, but I fear his people have made up their minds that it should be given no opportunity to do so. I was told this morning on good authority that on one pretext or another they prevented him from seeing the Serbian reply until sixty hours after it had been delivered. When he did see it, apparently, he was astounded, and said at once how delighted he was that we had secured everything we could possibly wish for without resorting to war. But it was too late. By then we had already begun hostilities against Serbia."

Count Tisza coughed, then went on sadly: "The case of my own sovereign is even more distressing. He was tricked into acquiescence in a manner positively revolting to honourable people like ourselves. When the declaration of war was handed to Count Paar for him to obtain the Emperor's signature to it, the old man said: 'Well, this may be all right; but all I can say is that monarchs of eighty-four don't plunge their countries into war without a just cause for doing so'. On this being reported to Berchtold, he quickly formulated a statement to accompany the declaration when it was submitted to the Emperor. Having urged such reasons as he could for going to extremes, he went on to say that there was now no choice, as hostilities had already begun. And he ended with the announcement that Serbian troops had attacked Austrian detachments at Temes-Kurbin that morning."

After taking a drink of wine, the Count added quickly: "That was not true. It was a deliberate lie to induce the Emperor to sign the declaration. Today, Berchtold has had that last sentence erased from his statement, with the glib excuse that he had later learned that the report of the Serbian attack was unconfirmed."

De Richleau sighed. "How horrible! How unutterably shocking that such unscrupulous men should have the power to secure by fraud what amounts to a death warrant for Heaven knows how many innocent people. Was there nothing you could do?"

"By the time I learned of this awful deed, it was too late. And as far as the bigger picture is concerned, everything points to all attempts at mediation or restraint being similarly smothered by evil machinations. Russia has made it plain that she will not stand by and see Serbia annihilated. The Kaiser is ringed around by men who are now spoiling for a fight. Neither he nor the Czar are any longer the real masters of their countries. Neither of them can afford to risk being charged later with having betrayed their people by restraining their Generals from taking measures to guard against a surprise attack. They are now no more than cogs in a machine. It needs only a clash between frontier patrols and the great war which we have so long dreaded will have started."

"Again," said the Duke, "you have expressed my own thoughts as clearly as I could do it myself."

"I would to God there were more who thought as we do, and could see the bottomless abyss towards which the criminal few are driving the helpless many. Needless to say, these confidences I am making to you should go no further, either here in Vienna or when you reach London. But I am so surrounded by honest fools, misguided patriots, and self-seeking knaves, that it is a great relief to be able to talk freely for a while to a man of my own stature, who puts the welfare of humanity before a narrow nationalism."

"I consider myself much honoured; and you may rest assured that everything you have said, or may say, is safe with me," replied de Richleau; and, even had he not given his word on that, he would have regarded Count Tisza's confidences as sacred.

For a further half hour they talked on about the impending catastrophe. Then a knock came at the door and, on Count Tisza's calling "Come in", it opened to reveal a footman carrying a silver salver. Advancing into the room, he presented the card upon it to his master, and said:

"Excuse me, Excellency, for interrupting you, but two men have called who ask to see you urgently; and I understand that one of them is a high police official."

Count Tisza glanced at the card and murmured, "Major Maximillian

Ronge. Yes, I know him, but I am engaged. Tell him I cannot see him until to-morrow morning."

The footman's eyes flickered towards the Duke. "He asked me to tell you, Excellency, that the matter he has come upon concerns the gentleman who is with you at the moment."

With a smile the Count turned to his guest, and asked jocularly: "What trouble have you been getting yourself into?"

De Richleau returned the smile and answered, with a slight uneasiness which his voice did not betray: "None that I know of."

"With your permission, we will have them up, then; although I must apologize for their intrusion on you while you are my guest."

"Don't think of it," the Duke smiled again. "I shall be only too pleased to help them in any way I can."

As the footman left the room, the Count remarked: "Major Ronge is the head of the *Kundschafts Stelle*, our espionage and counter-espionage service. He is a very able fellow and it may be that he has ferreted out some new angle to the Sarajevo murders, on which he wants your opinion. If so, it must be something rather startling for him to bother us at this time of night."

At the Count's words de Richleau's uneasiness increased to apprehension, but his shrug conveyed that the matter hardly concerned him any more.

A moment later the two officials were shown in. Major Ronge was a jovial-looking fat man with sly eyes and a small dark moustache that was waxed into a pair of stiff sharp points. His companion, whom he introduced as Herr Höller, was a small wizened individual, with grey hair and a long, sad face. Ronge did nearly all the talking and, having bowed to the Minister-President, said deferentially:

"I thank your Excellency for receiving us at this unusual hour. We would not have dreamt of troubling you so late had we not learned that the gentleman who is with you took a cab from Sacher's to your house about an hour ago. I beg that your Excellency will excuse the apparent impertinence of the question; but what do you know about him?"

Count Tisza frowned. "I am not accustomed to being questioned about my guests."

De Richleau drew a shade more heavily on his cigar, while watching the Major from beneath half-lowered lids. He did not at all like the way in which the conversation had opened.

Quite unperturbed by the rebuff, Ronge attacked the matter from another angle. "No doubt your Excellency knows him as the Duc de Richleau; or as Count von Königstein." Then, with startling suddenness, he added:

"He is neither! He is an impostor!"

The Duke burst out laughing, and his laughter was quite genuine. But Count Tisza did not regard it as a laughing matter. Drawing himself up, he said icily:

"Major Ronge, you are making a complete fool of yourself. You have my permission to leave us."

The fat man made no move towards the door. Instead, he turned to his companion, pointed at the Duke, and said: "Now that you have seen him closer, do you confirm your identification of him?"

Herr Höller nodded lugubriously. "That's him all right. With them slant-up eyebrows and thin hooky nose, no one could mistake him."

"Then," declared Ronge, "it is my duty to acquaint your Excellency with certain facts. Herr Höller is one of our operatives normally stationed in Belgrade. He re-crossed the frontier yesterday a few hours before it was closed, in order to give us the latest information that he had gathered in the Serbian capital. When passing Sacher's Hotel this afternoon he chanced to see your Excellency's guest enter it. On inquiring from the porter he learned the names under which this individual passes in Vienna. He at once reported to Headquarters that the same person was living in Belgrade at the Hotel Continental for a short period in mid-May, and a longer one towards the end of June; and that during both he was on intimate terms with Serbian officers whom we know to have been leaders of the Black Hand."

After a brief pause to get his breath, the fat man hurried on: "Our interest was immediately aroused because we already have on our files a statement made to my chief, General von Ostromiecz, by this so-called Count Königstein. It is to the effect that during a forty-eight-hour visit to Belgrade he learned *by chance* of the plot to assassinate the Archduke, and records his efforts to prevent it. But this statement and Herr Höller's report do not tally. He is prepared to testify on oath that this individual was in close association with Colonel Dimitriyevitch, Major Tankosić and Captain Ciganović; all of whom are now known to us to have been concerned in the plot."

Count Tisza shrugged. "I do not see that it matters in the least if my friend was in Belgrade for forty-eight hours or a fortnight. It is nothing to do with us where he spent his time during his absences from Vienna. He may have paid several visits to Belgrade, and when making his statement not thought it worth while to mention any but the last. As for Herr Höller, he has obviously allowed his imagination to run away with him. The suggestion that this gentleman was mixed up with the Black Hand is the most utter nonsense."

"Your pardon, Excellency, but I must disagree. In his statement he alleges that he learned of the Sarajevo plot from a party of drunken officers at a cabaret called *Le Can-Can* on the night of Friday, the 26th of June. That is not true. There was a fire at the cabaret on the previous night, so on that of the 26th it was closed for repairs. Moreover, Herr Höller is a very reliable agent. He is positive that this individual was on most friendly terms with several prominent members of the Black Hand, and was working for them. During his last stay in Belgrade he used to go every morning to the War Office, and spend most of his day there."

"And what do you conclude from all this?"

"That he cannot possibly be, as your Excellency supposes, either the Duc de Richleau or Count Königstein."

"They are one and the same person. But what leads you to suppose that he is an impostor?"

"Excellency, is it not obvious?" The Major spread out a pair of plump hands. "Whoever he may be, it is beyond dispute that he did his utmost to prevent the tragedy at Sarajevo. But how did he obtain knowledge of the plot? Certainly not in the manner he has stated; and Herr Höller's report gives us the answer. He wormed his way into the confidence of the Black Hand leaders and obtained work in the Serbian War Office. That he should have betrayed them when he learned full details of the plot, makes it clear that he was not in sympathy with them, and there is no reason to believe him to be a Serbian. Therefore, he must be a professional secret agent. And in all my experience I have never heard of a nobleman who became a spy."

Count Tisza nodded. "Your reasoning is certainly logical. But should you be right, it is his attempt to save the Archduke that has led to this discovery; and it seems that he has spied on our behalf, not against us."

"True, Excellency. But the point is that he is not one of our people; so he is most probably a free-lance. Now that he is in Vienna, he may find out secrets which would be of great value to our enemies. For example, in conversation with highly placed persons such as your Excellency. That is why, immediately I learned from the porter at Sacher's that he had given this address to a taxi driver, I came here to place him under arrest pending further inquiries."

After a moment, Count Tisza said: "I will go into this matter personally. If you and Herr Höller will be good enough to go down into the hall, I will send for you after I have done so."

When the two officials had left the room, the Count turned to de Richleau, fixed his steady glance upon him, and asked: "What have you to say about all this?"

The Duke stood up, smiled and shrugged his shoulders. "My dear Count, I cannot sufficiently apologize for having caused you this inconvenience. They are, of course, completely at fault in supposing that the titles by which I am known are not my own. I could produce fifty people in Vienna who would vouch for that. Many of them knew my father and have known me since I was a boy. As for the rest, even were they not in a position to prove it, my honour would compel me to admit to you that they are right."

Count Tisza's eyes widened. "But, Duke, this sounds incredible. How can a man of your distinction possibly have brought himself to become a professional spy?"

"Hardly a professional," de Richleau said mildly. "Had I not been an amateur, I should probably have thought up a story with fewer holes in it when I was asked to make a statement to General von Ostromiecz and several other gentlemen who called on me at the nursing home. But the story is a long one. If you wish to hear it, have I your permission to sit down?"

"Of course." The Count motioned to him to resume his seat. Then, for the next forty minutes, de Richleau related how certain people in London had persuaded him to investigate the situation in Belgrade, and, for the first time, told the true story of his adventures there. He ended by saying:

"So, you see, I was drawn into this business much against my will. But, knowing what I do now, I am fully convinced that I was right to undertake the mission. Had I only had the good fortune to learn the intention of the conspirators a few hours earlier I might have prevented the war. And that having been my sole object throughout, I feel that I am entitled to retain your respect, if not your friendship."

With a sigh, Count Tisza said, "My dear Duke, you have both; and my whole-hearted admiration. It is an amazing story, and one of which you may well be proud."

De Richleau stood up and offered his hand with a smile. "I thank you, Count; your good opinion means a great deal to me. Now, I will not embarrass you with my presence further; although I make no promise that I will go quietly with these two policemen once I have left your house."

The Count waved him back. "Sit down a moment. Let us consider this matter a little further. I don't doubt your audacity and resource after what you have told me of that desperate affair at Dimitriyevitch's châlet. But it is unlikely that you could escape without injuring Ronge and his friend, which would be regrettable, as they are only doing their duty. What is more, I doubt if you could get very far before you were recaptured. Our police are fairly efficient; and you must remember that Austria is now in a state of war, so special precautions are being taken at all our frontiers."

"I would back myself to get over any frontier." de Richleau shrugged. "My difficulty is going to be in breaking free before they can get me to a police station. Still, I shall have to attempt it. What charge they intend to bring against me, I've no idea: but in time of war all sorts of measures can be invoked as an excuse for locking up a suspected individual, and I've no intention of allowing myself to be put behind bars for an unspecified period if I can possibly avoid it."

"Yes, I can well understand your anxiety. If they detain you for even a few days, we may be at war with England. Then they will put you in an internment camp as an enemy alien for as long as hostilities last. All the same, I do not think it is a good plan for you to attempt a break-away."

"I see no alternative."

"The alternative is simple. As one of the two Minister-Presidents of the Dual Monarchy, after the authority of the Emperor, that of my colleague and myself is the highest in the land. I have only to tell Major Ronge that I will be personally responsible for you and send him about his business."

De Richleau had been far more worried than he had shown by the turn events had taken. Although he had spoken lightly of it, he greatly doubted his ability to get away from the police in the middle of the city: and, once in prison, he foresaw great difficulties in getting out again. Smothering a sigh of relief, he said:

"Such a gesture would be in keeping with your generous nature. I should always remember it with gratitude, and I cannot think you would have mentioned it if you intended to allow me to be arrested."

Count Tisza laid a friendly hand on his shoulder. "No, I will not let the police carry you off. On the other hand, I do not think that I should be justified in allowing you to return to England; and you must not take offence at what I am about to say. I have your word that you will not repeat anything I have told you. As a person I am entirely satisfied with that; but as a responsible official it is my duty to take precautions that nothing you have recently learned in Vienna should reach London until the crisis has resolved itself. I must ask you to give me your *parole d'honneur* not to leave Vienna without my permission; although, of course, I will not withhold it in the event of any definite indication that war between Britain and the Central Powers is about to break out."

The request was a reasonable one. If things quietened down the Duke would have lost nothing by remaining, while, if the worst was fated to happen, it would be obvious in a few days and there would still be time for him to get out of Austria before he became liable to arrest as an enemy alien. So, feeling that he had escaped from a most dangerous predicament very lightly, he willingly gave the promise for which he had been asked.

Major Ronge was summoned and informed by the Minister-President of his decision. He appeared satisfied, and withdrew. The two friends then had a final drink together, after which the Duke walked back to Sacher's with a very thankful sense of his continued freedom.

He had intended to call on Ilona at the palace the following morning and break the news to her that, in view of the rising tension, he could delay his departure no longer, so meant to start for England that night. But now, his promise to Count Tisza bound him to remain until Britain either threatened or was threatened with war, and on that the worsening relations between Russia and Austria had no immediate bearing.

The morning papers of the 30th all carried scare headlines announcing that on the previous day Russia had ordered partial mobilization, which would bring the armies on her Austrian frontier up to a war footing. But the Czar had deliberately refrained from ordering mobilization in his territories adjacent to Germany, and the Kaiser had responded to this pacific gesture by doing no more than proclaiming a 'state of preparation for war', which committed him to nothing. Meanwhile, Sir Edward Grey and nearly all the Ambassadors in the great capitals were striving desperately to prevent the conflict spreading.

Although court mourning for Franz Ferdinand was still in force, small private dinner parties were now again being given, and for that evening the Duke had accepted an invitation to dine with the Aulendorfs in their suite at Schönbrunn. As he had known she would be, Ilona was present, and she was attended by her new lady-in-waiting, Fraulein Marie Nopsca, next to whom he was seated at dinner.

In spite of half-hearted attempts to keep the conversation off the crisis, it crept back to it every few moments, and the party proved anything but a gay one. As the Austrians had got just what they wanted, de Richleau was somewhat puzzled at this new atmosphere of depression, and it was not until the ladies had withdrawn that he learned the reason for it. Apparently they were now afraid that the Kaiser meant to let them down. It was true that he had rejected Sir Edward Grey's plea, that Germany should participate in a Council of the Great Powers to mediate on the Austro-Serbian dispute, with the abrupt reply that he would 'not consent to having his ally dragged before the bar of nations'; but from Austria's point of view his attitude towards Russia was far from satisfactory. Not only had he allowed the Russians to mobilize on the Austrian frontier without taking any adequate counter measures; he was known to be exchanging frantic personal telegrams with the Czar, in which both monarchs were begging one another to restrain the war-like ardour of their peoples and refrain from all measures likely to precipitate hostilities.

Now that Austria-Hungary was actually at war with a small but virile State and likely soon to be attacked by a far more powerful one, everybody had much more important things to think about than the possibility that a young Archduchess was having a love affair with one of the officers of her regiment. So, after dinner, as the party consisted of only eight people, the Duke was able to enjoy a happy hour's tête-à-tête with his beloved without likelihood of arousing unwelcome ideas in the mind of the Mistress of her Household; and, later, Ilona boldly enlisted the Countess to secure her more frequent meetings with him during these last few precious days which they now feared were all that were left to them.

Since the previous Saturday all the ladies of the Imperial circle had begun to busy themselves with war charities, so Ilona called her hostess over to the corner of the drawing-room, where she was sitting with de Richleau, and suggested to her that he might be most helpful to them if they asked him to assist them in organizing some of their new societies. The Countess thought the idea an excellent one and the Duke naturally assented; so the lovers were able to make appointments which would enable them to attend committees together, ensuring several hours in one another's company on each of the next few days.

De Richleau was overjoyed at the success of her strategem as, far from his ardour for her abating, it seemed to increase every time he saw her. He had again thrust the awful idea of their parting into the back of his mind, and was now living in the present, allowing her smiles to go to his head like wine. But, madly as he loved her and fond as he was of his Austrian and Hungarian friends, on the way home he could not help reflecting with cynical amusement that it would serve Berchtold, von Hötzendorf and Co. right if they now found themselves up against Russia as well as Serbia, without German support.

Friday the 31st proved to be the day of highest tension yet in Vienna. It was expected that at any hour the Russian advance guards would attempt to invade the northern provinces of the Dual Monarchy and the German attitude still remained uncertain. But when de Richleau met Ilona at de Lazalo's in the afternooon she had just received news that at least held out a possibility of rescuing Austria from her precarious situation. For some reason, as yet unknown, the previous evening the Czar had issued a new *ukase* ordering general mobilization. Surely, with Russian reservists flocking to the colours within a dozen miles of the Prussian frontier, the Kaiser must call his people to arms. Yet he had now made it very clear to Vienna that, in view of the Serbians' submissive reply to the Austrian ultimatum, he considered that the Dual Monarchy had not been justified in starting a war. If, too, his timidity got the better of his impulsiveness, he would still shrink from allowing his Generals to push him into any step which might place it beyond his power to influence the final outcome.

August came in with brilliant sunshine and its first day again saw Vienna's streets filled with cheering multitudes. The news for which all Austria-Hungary had been praying had come through during the night. At 3.30 the previous afternoon Berlin had sent an ultimatum to St. Petersburg declaring that, if Russia did not cease within twelve hours every war measure against Germany and Austria-Hungary and make a definite declaration to that effect, German mobilization would be ordered. The ultimatum had been delivered at midnight, and so far there was no news of any reply to it. But that did not trouble the Viennese. All that mattered to them was that their ally had at last come out openly on their side, and that the Czar must now accept the humiliation of withdrawing his troops from the frontiers, or face the onslaught of the mighty German army side by side with their own.

De Richleau, scanning every paper he could find for paragraphs which might throw light on Britain's attitude, found several that referred to Sir Edward Grey's tireless efforts to keep the peace, and one which stated that the Grand Fleet had passed the narrows of the Channel, steaming northward for the open sea, during the hours of darkness between the 29th and 30th. An official announcement followed, that the move was normal and must not be construed as having a war-like intent against any power. Basically that was true, but it gave the Duke fresh cause to admire Mr. Churchill's tremendous awareness and grasp of strategic imperatives. He had secured his great ships from any surprise attack by enemy submarines while still in coastal waters; and had got them unscathed into the North Sea, where they could dominate the Atlantic shipping routes and, at will, cut Germany off from the outer world.

Although the Duke had no means of knowing it then, the move was rightly interpreted by the German Admiralty and Foreign Office. Herr von Jagow and the Kaiser took alarm; belatedly they turned a willing ear to Sir Edward Grey's proposals. War did not offer so much glamour for them if Britain was coming in. On that fateful first day of August they strove at the eleventh hour to retrieve the situation and definitely accepted a new suggestion by Sir Edward for direct negotiations between Austria and Russia. But the sands were running out. Mid-day came: the time limit of twelve hours that Germany had given in her ultimatum to Russia had expired. Still the now harassed and frightened Kaiser hesitated. Must he now tread the slippery and terrifying path that he had so wantonly laid out for himself? Or should he yet draw back, to stand branded by his own people as a coward, and be humiliated before all the world? For six hours he remained paralysed by fear, still hesitating which of the two awful courses to take. Vanity won. The covert sneers on the faces of his Generals proved too much for him. At 6 p.m. on 1st August he declared war on Russia.

Immediately de Richleau learned the news, which was on the morning of the 2nd, he went to see Count Tisza. The Hungarian received him with every mark of kindness, but said that he could not yet release him from his parole. In Vienna it was considered extremely improbable that Britain would come in unless France did so, and France was maintaining an attitude of great caution. So far she had made no pronouncement that she intended to honour her alliance with Russia, and, until she did so, or was attacked by Germany, there was still a possibility that the conflict might not spread to Western Europe.

The Duke protested that Germany dared not throw her main forces against Russia with the possibility that later, when she was fully engaged, France might succumb to the temptation to attack her in the rear. Therefore, it was imperative to Germany to clarify her position. She must either take on France simultaneously with Russia, or get such guarantees from France as would render her unable to intervene later; and it was highly improbable that suitable guarantees would be forthcoming.

"That remains to be seen," replied the Count. "I understand that Germany has already asked for such guarantees in the form of a demand that France should proclaim her intention of remaining neutral, and surrender the fortresses of Toul and Verdun as a pledge of her neutrality."

"To that France would never agree!" exclaimed the Duke.

"I think you right," the Count nodded. "But all is not yet lost in the other theatre. In spite of the fact that hostilities have commenced between Germany and Russia, Sir Edward Grey is continuing his indefatigable labours to induce them to accept some form of arbitration before a clash between their main armies can occur. If he succeeds Germany's demands will automatically be dropped. And even should his efforts fail, and the war spread to France, there is still no certainty that Britain will come in. No, Duke; in view of the intimate terms on which you have been with so many people in Vienna, I cannot allow you to start for England yet. But I will do so at the first moment that I consider consistent with our security."

With that de Richleau had to be content, and he hurried off to a committee meeting at which Ilona had agreed to take the chair, although it was Sunday, as the matters to be discussed were of considerable urgency. During it, she managed to slip him a note. Much to his surprise, it told him that she was going to de Lazalo's that afternoon, and it was not until later he learned how she had been able to arrange a further escape from her usual sabbath routine.

Owing to her new war activities, she was now greatly pressed for time, and Countess Aulendorf had said that she ought to give up her sittings. She had refused to do so as they provided the only opportunities she had to be alone with her lover, and she knew that he might at any day have to leave Vienna. So, on the excuse of getting the portrait finished quickly, she had arranged for a sitting that afternoon and every day until it was done. But when they met there, far from allowing de Lazalo a chance to get on with the picture, she cut his work short after a restless sitting of only a quarter of an hour and sent him with Adam and Sárolta out into the garden, in order that she and de Richleau might have longer to delight in one another's caresses.

As soon as they had exchanged their first breathless kiss, she said that she had a piece of good news for him. Greatly as Bulgaria was tempted to revenge herself on Serbia for her defeat a year earlier, in the second Balkan war, she had decided against taking any action for the time being. The Russians, who had strong ties with the Bulgars, supported by the French and British ministers in Sofia, were straining every nerve to keep Bulgaria neutral. It had become evident that this weighty influence would restrain the Bulgarians, at least until they knew which of the Great Powers would become involved in the conflict. In consequence, the invitation by the Triple Alliance to Bulgaria to join it, had been politely put aside among 'matters requiring further consideration', and, with it, the project of Ilona's marriage to Prince Boris.

For the past three weeks that prospect had weighed heavily on them both, and, although Ilona had not been definitely saved from it, its postponement came as an immense relief. They recognized now that each of their meetings might be almost the last, so to have them free of this cloud which had been hanging over their joy in one another meant a great deal to them. Moreover, when they had to part, they would now at least escape the added distress of knowing that he was leaving her to be thrust, almost immediately, into the arms of a complete stranger.

Before they joined the others in the garden, she asked him to dine with her at the palace that evening, and added that they could make further discussion of the war charities an excuse for his doing so.

When he arrived, he found that the party consisted only of themselves, Adam, Sárolta and the Officer of the Guard, a pleasant young man whom de Richleau had already met on several occasions.

War charities were not even mentioned: and, after dinner, in an effort to forget for an hour or so both the world crisis and her own, Ilona suggested that they should play blind-man's-buff and other hilarious children's games. Then, when time enough had elapsed for her to give the young officer his dismissal without impoliteness, she said she felt like a stroll in the garden. With a demure expression, Sárolta fetched her a dark cloak and they all slipped down a back staircase out into the moonlit grounds.

As the two couples strolled towards the long pleached alleyways with Adam and Sárolta bringing up the rear, she whispered to him, "Adam, dear, now that our engagement is about to be announced we shall have lots of opportunities for kissing, but those two poor darlings get so few, and at any moment now he may have to leave her. When they sit down somewhere, we must separate. You take one end of the alley and I'll take the other, so that they can make love without any risk of being surprised."

Count Adam agreed at once; so with the aid of these two loyal friends Ilona and her lover spent a blissful hour; but it could be no more as the Countess Aulendorf would be coming on her official visit at half past eleven, to see her charge safely into bed.

Soon after de Richleau woke next morning he remembered that it was Bank Holiday Monday in England, and he wondered what was happening there. But he was not left to his speculations long, as a telephone message was brought to him from Count Tisza, saying that the Count wished to see him as soon as possible.

The Duke received it with anything but pleasure. He felt certain that it heralded his release. If war with Britain was imminent he felt that he had no option but to return at once to England; but he could have wept at the thought that the dreaded time had really come when he must leave Ilona. He had loved before but never, never, as he loved this beautiful Princess. If she had imperfections, he could not see them: her impulsiveness made her human: her childishness in some things made her so unspoiled: the zest with which she had embarked on love when it had so belatedly come to her, made her utterly adorable. Nevertheless, he dressed as quickly as he could and went round to the Minister-President's palace.

Count Tisza wasted no time in preambles. He said at once, "I asked you to call, Duke, because I am overwhelmed with urgent business that requires my presence in Budapest. My visits there in the past ten days have been of sufficient length only to enable me barely to fulfil my duties to the Hungarian Parliament, and now I must take up my residence there for at least a week. The last thing I wish is that you should be caught here: and the general situation shows no improvement. Most of my colleagues still feel that Britain will remain outside the conflict. On the other hand, I understand that she has warned Germany that should the German Fleet attack the French Channel ports she could not remain indifferent. I wanted to tell you that, should either country issue an ultimatum to the other during my absence, you are free to depart."

De Richleau accepted this conditional release with a sigh of thankfulness. Had it been, as he had expected, a complete one, he would have felt constrained to leave Vienna that day, after seeing Ilona only to say good-bye. As it was, he had been given the freedom to go without further consulting the Count directly the situation regarding Britain became acute. But until then he must continue as a prisoner of his bond, and so could also remain, unstricken by conscience, the willing captive of Ilona's kisses.

As the two men shook hands they had little doubt that they were taking farewell of one another for a long time to come, if not for ever. Their outlook on life was so similar, and their minds were so well attuned, that in a few short weeks a bond had been forged between them of the kind which occasionally unites two people of the same sex in a friendship that is akin to brother-love. The wish of each, that good fortune should attend the other, was not mere words but came from their hearts, and they parted with genuine sadness.

After the Duke had breakfasted he went to another of Ilona's committee meetings, and that afternoon met her again at de Lazalo's. Again she asked him to dine with her. He hesitated for only a fraction of a second, but she caught the thought that had flashed through his brain and checked his immediate acceptance. With a half hysterical laugh, she said:

"The time has gone when you need worry about compromising me by dining in my apartments on two nights running. I am living only for these moments now before I must weep my heart away. I grudge every second that I am not with you, and I no longer give a damn what people think or say. Come early, Armand. I shall expect you at a quarter to eight."

When he arrived fresh news of the crisis had just come in. Germany had declared war on France at 6.45 that evening.

The party was a larger one than that of the preceding night, as Ilona had invited several people some days before whom it was too late to put off. But she was brazen now in her determination to be alone with her lover. Within a quarter of an hour of dinner being over, she announced that she had matters concerning her charities that she wished to discuss with him; then dismissed everyone else except Adam and Sárolta.

Again the four of them slipped out into the friendly shadows of the palace gardens, but to-night poor Ilona could not keep back her tears. Now that France had become embroiled all hopes of a peaceful settlement were at an end. It remained only to see if England would come to her assistance and, if she did, Ilona knew that she could not detain her knight a moment longer. De Richleau did his utmost to comfort her, kissing her tear-stained face again and again, and vowing his eternal love for her; but when at last her weeping eased she was running a high temperature and being shaken every few moments by violent bouts of coughing.

Next morning, Tuesday the 4th of August, the headlines in the papers gave the news that the Duke had expected since the previous evening. German forces had over-run Luxemburg and were invading Belgium. The Germans were putting the Schlieffen plan into operation. He had a committee meeting with Ilona at mid-day. Just before he set out for the palace a special edition appeared. Britain had sent an ultimatum to Germany, forbidding her to violate the Belgian frontiers and requiring her to withdraw at once any troops who might have done so. An answer was required by midnight.

The ultimatum freed him from his parole, but meant that he must not remain in Vienna until another sun had set. He had already made his plans, knowing that in such circumstances, if the time limit were less than twenty-four hours, the western frontier of Germany would be closed to him before he could get through to Belgium. His quickest way out now was to go down to Trieste on the Adriatic and cross the border into Italy. The journey was about two hundred and fifty miles, so if he caught the 4.15 express he should have ample time to be over the frontier before midnight. To have taken an earlier train would have deprived him of his last chance to say farewell to Ilona in private. In anticipation of having to make a hurried departure he had already had the bulk of his packing done by the valet three days before. A quarter of an hour would be enough for him to finish it, and he could do that after lunch. Then he would only have to collect it on his way to the station after having said good-bye to Ilona at the studio.

He told the desk clerk that he would be vacating his rooms for good that afternoon, asked him to have his bill made up and, as for the past week all trains leaving Vienna had been exceptionally crowded, arranged with the head porter to send an under-porter ahead in good time to get him a seat on the 4.15 train for Trieste. Then he wrote a brief note, which he took with him, and set off for the palace.

At the meeting he slipped the note to Ilona. It simply said, "Be brave, my sweet. Our joyous hour is run. I shall go early to the studio this afternoon, and pray that you can do so too."

When she had read it, under cover of a batch of papers that was on the table in front of her, she looked at him and gave an almost imperceptible nod. Then she displayed a fine courage by briskly returning to the business in hand, and conducting it as though her only care in the world was that adequate provision should be made for the aged mothers of soldiers, whose sons were their only support and had been called up for the war. But she could not conceal the red rims round her blue eyes, her hectic flush or the cough that harassed her, and as he watched her de Richleau's heart was wrung as though it were in a mangle.

Immediately after the meeting he returned to Sacher's. A clerk met him in the hall-way and requested him to step into the office for a moment. His thoughts were still of Ilona's tragic face but, rousing himself, he assumed that Frau Sacher had learned that he was leaving and wished to say good-bye to him. He had meant to ask her to give him coffee after lunch, so that he could make his farewells to this old and treasured friend in as pleasant circumstances as possible; but he felt that to join her in an apéritif would serve as well, so he let the clerk usher him through the door behind the desk.

Suddenly he found himself confronted by Major Ronge and two uniformed policemen. He made a quick step back, but the fat, dark-moustached Major pulled an automatic from his pocket and said quietly, "Don't move!"

The Duke covered his consternation by an icy stare, and demanded, "What do you want of me?"

The Chief of the K.S. Bureau bowed slightly. "I am here to take you into custody as an enemy alien."

"You can't do that," snapped de Richleau. "I am a British subject, and Britain is not at war with Austria-Hungary."

A smile flickered into Ronge's sly eyes. "We have heard from several quarters that you are British, but have no proof of that. I am glad that you admit it. We shall be at war with Britain by midnight. I am merely anticipating matters by a few hours."

De Richleau was furious at having given himself away, although he was quick to realize that in any case he could not have concealed his nationality for long. Angrily he protested: "By midnight I can be over the frontier, and you have no conceivable right to detain me."

"In that you are wrong, *Herr Graf*. I have powers to question all suspects; and there is nothing to prevent me from prolonging my questioning until to-morrow morning if I wish. But why should we quibble about technicalities? I intend to take you in, and that is the end of the matter."

"Count Tisza assumed personal responsibility for me!" de Richleau replied quickly. "He knows everything there is to know about me, and has given me permission to leave."

The fat man shrugged. "His Excellency the Minister-President is now in Budapest. He is of so honest a disposition that he sometimes allows himself to be hoodwinked by clever people. I thought his interference in a matter about which we are so much better informed than he, was both ill-advised and regrettable. But he is absent from Vienna and a very busy man, so we will trouble him about it no more. Please to come quietly."

To put up a fight against three armed men would have been madness, and the Duke was at his wits' end how to get out of this trap that had so unexpectedly been sprung upon him. The last thing he wished to do was to involve Ilona, but she was now his only hope. The question of whether he could retain his liberty of action for the next few hours or not meant the difference between getting home safely and the possibility of incarceration for many months. In desperation he said:

"I am a Colonel in the Archduchess Ilona Theresa's regiment of Hussars. I have just come from a meeting with her at the Schönbrunn Palace. I insist that you telephone to Her Imperial Highness, or her equerry, Captain Count Adam Grünne, and inform one of them of your intention."

As the Major only shook his head in silent refusal, de Richleau made a forlorn attempt to scare him, by saying sharply:

"You'll rue it if you don't! Her Imperial Highness would never allow one of her officers to be arrested in this arbitrary manner. If you persist without informing her you will lose your job when she gets to hear of it."

Major Ronge sighed a little wearily. "Believe me, I have often been threatened with losing my job, but somehow nobody ever dismisses me. Do you know why, *Herr Graf*? It is because I am always right in matters where secret agents are concerned. I will admit that you are a most unusual one. I take off my hat to you for having imposed upon Her Imperial Highness, the Minister-President, and many other illustrious people. But that will not help you now, as I do not intend to inform any of them that I have arrested you. For me it is quite sufficient that I know you to be a free-lance secret agent. That you happen also to be of noble birth, as I have discovered to be a fact since our last meeting, is curious; but it makes not the least difference. What you were up to in Serbia is no concern of mine, except as evidence of the form of your activities. But since you have been in Vienna you must have collected a great deal of information that would be of value to Austria's enemies. How I hold you is, to me, a matter of complete indifference. I would charge you with robbing the poor box in the Stefanskirk if I could find nothing else that would serve. But these high ones of your acquaintance must be protected against their own lack of understanding in such affairs. It is I who am responsible for seeing that our secrets do not leak out. Therefore, it is my duty to prevent your leaving the country. I hope I have said enough to make the position clear. Come please, *Herr Graf*. I am anxious to be done with this business, as I have not yet had my lunch."

The Duke now saw that there was nothing that he could do—nothing whatever. So he allowed himself to be taken off in a cab, driven to a high-walled prison, and locked up.

For hours he sat miserably in his cell, considering his wretched position, but for the life of him he could not see any way out of it. Since Major Ronge had already made it clear that he would not allow any messages from the prisoner to be transmitted to Ilona, Count Tisza or any other of his friends, and had further refused to let him see a lawyer, there was positively no useful action of any kind that he could take.

When the lights were put out he partially undressed, lay down on the truckle bed and endeavoured to sleep: but sleep would not come to him.

He heard the prison clock toll midnight. It was a knell of doom, the like of which has rarely sounded throughout the ages. With the last stroke the final phase of the crisis had been resolved. The conflict was no longer confined to Europe. The British Empire was now at war with Germany, and ships were closing to give battle the world over, in every sea. Five million men under arms were now on the march. Double that number were to die before peace came again. One thousand nine hundred and fifty miles of European frontiers were aflame. From them a ghastly miasma of sorrow, misery and disease was to spread over the whole earth. But worse, the highest conceptions of freedom, decency and humanity, built up by a hundred generations of mankind, were, within half that number of months, now doomed to perish.

CHAPTER XXI

AN EXTRAORDINARY SITUATION

During his first day in prison the Duke had some hopes of a speedy release. It seemed certain that his failure to arrive at the studio would have led Ilona to have inquiries made for him at Sacher's, and that on learning of his arrest she would demand an explanation of the police. But as Wednesday and Thursday passed with no sign of outside intervention in his case, he was forced to the conclusion that Major Ronge must have succeeded in hushing up his arrest, and poor Ilona believed that some accident had prevented him from keeping their last rendezvous.

Meanwhile a series of interrogations by Ronge had led only to a stalemate. De Richleau took the firm line that his statement to General von Ostromiecz had, in all essentials, been the truth; and as Belgrade was now entirely cut off from Vienna by the war, the Austrian police were in no position to procure any evidence supporting Herr Höller's story. However, the Major obviously had complete faith in his subordinate, so regarded the Duke as a most dangerous character. He continued to refuse him permission to communicate with the outside world, or even to mix with his fellow prisoners when taken out for exercise; and evidently still hoped to unearth some evidence of his activities in Vienna which would enable a charge of espionage affecting the Dual Monarchy to be brought against him.

Fortunately for the Duke, the first great war had only just started, and the day was still far distant when its effects would have so brutalized the Teutonic peoples that thousands of educated men among them condoned or practised wholesale abominations, the like of which are recorded only as comparatively rare episodes in the Dark Ages. The torture of convicted criminals had been abolished throughout Europe, including Russia, a hundred and fifty years earlier, and it was still unthinkable that it would ever again be permitted. So de Richleau had nothing whatever to fear in the way of ill-treatment. On the contrary, he was well fed, lodged in reasonable comfort, and his belongings—after they had been brought from Sacher's and minutely searched—were handed over to him without as much as a boot-lace missing.

In consequence, although in no immediate danger of discomfort, the Duke had no alternative but to while away the first days of the war as best he could; thinking of his beloved Ilona, cursing Sir Pellinore as the original cause of his predicament, reviewing the past and pondering on the future.

He was allowed to have newspapers, so was able to follow the war news, such as it was; but the closing of frontiers and the secrecy necessary to conceal projected military operations had suddenly drawn a series of impenetrable curtains across the European scene, the like of which had never before been known. Between them could be caught only faint glimpses of isolated events, and these did not even suggest that great battles might be in progress; so to the ordinary reader it seemed impossible to believe that hostilities on a scale previously unequalled in world history had actually started.

The Austrians were continuing their bombardment of Belgrade across the Danube and, in consequence, the Serbian government had removed to Nish; but there was no news of Austro-Hungarian troops having so far invaded Serbia. When the Germans had marched into the little independent Grand Duchy of Luxemburg, the beautiful golden-haired young Grand Duchess had driven to the main bridge in her capital, had her Rolls Royce halted sideways across it, and forbidden the invaders to pass. The Germans had politely removed the car from their path and marched on into Belgium.

King Albert of Belgium had refused them permission to pass through his territories, and was resisting them by force of arms. But the ill-prepared Belgians could not stem the mighty tide, which was flowing on: the key city of Liége had been captured and its ring of forts was being hammered into submission by the giant Krupp siege guns that had been brought up.

On 4th August the German battleship *Goeben*, and her escorting cruiser *Breslau* were in the Adriatic. A powerful British squadron was within range and could have sunk them that afternoon, but had refrained as Britain's ultimatum to Germany did not expire till midnight. Under cover of darkness the fast German ships had slipped away. An exciting four day hunt had followed, but the Germans had succeeded in reaching, unharmed, the temporary safety of neutral Turkish waters.

Thus, in the first week and more of hostilities, nothing of real importance seemed to have happened. There was no news at all of the French, Russian and Serbian armies, very little of those of Germany and Austria, and not a word about the main Fleets of any of the nations that were engaged. The actions, if any, of all these major forces remained shrouded in mystery.

Yet, in a general sense, de Richleau's specialized knowledge enabled him to pierce the veil. He knew that great armies cannot be concentrated for action overnight. Such secret preparations as Germany and Austria-Hungary had made during the last three weeks of July would prove of considerable value to them; but nothing short of public mobilization could call the great mass of reservists to the colours. Then, between two and three weeks would be needed to pass them through the depots, move them up to the frontiers and dispose them in battle array; so no major clash could be expected before the third week in August. But in his mind's eye he could visualize the scenes that were now taking place over thousands of square miles of territory, much of which must soon become the fiercely contested ground of battle.

The operations at Liége were a thing apart. For the carrying out of the Schlieffen plan it was essential that the Germans should secure the fortress, and the network of railway that radiated from it across Belgium, at the earliest possible moment; so they would have attacked in that area with regular formations of shock troops which had, no doubt, been held in readiness for that purpose for several weeks. There, every latest device—scouts on motor bicycles, cyclist battalions, machine guns mounted in motor-cars, siege artillery drawn by tractors, and still larger guns on railway mountings—would be used for the swift reduction of the city's defences. But elsewhere the opening of hostilities would present a very different picture.

From the southern corner of Luxemburg down to Belfort on the Swiss frontier; from Memel on the Baltic down to the northern corner of Rumania; and from the Iron Gates of the Danube right round to Cattaro on the Adriatic; an unnatural quiet would have descended.

To a depth of twenty miles on either side of these three immensely long and fantastically irregular man-made divisions of territory all normal activities would have ceased. The trains that had crossed them regularly by a hundred different lines for as long as men remembered, crossed them no more. The roads were now empty of wagons and pedestrians. The ferries and river boats lay moored on hostile banks. The bridges had been seized by advance guards, or blown up. The villages within rifle shot of the enemy had been evacuated, and strips of territory as long as the frontiers themselves sealed off, so that no civilians without a permit could enter them. Even in the fields there was no movement, as the cattle would have been driven away. To the casual eye it would appear as if a mighty witch had waved a wand over these areas, paralysing their inhabitants, so that the countryside lay spell-bound and silent in the summer sun.

Yet that appearance of desertion and smiling sleep was an illusion. De Richleau knew that each army would have thrown out its cavalry screen to protect it from surprise and gain such information as it could about the concentrations of the enemy. Every coppice would conceal its vedette, every barn contain its picket of troops, every church tower hold its look-out; and along every hundred yards of river front a sentry with a loaded rifle would lie hidden, ready to fire at the first sign of movement on the opposite bank.

Occasionally enemy patrols would come face to face in a wood or gorge and skirmishes occur, a few shots be exchanged, a few men fall dead or wounded, and the weaker party beat a hasty retreat. By night, small bodies of Cossacks, Hussars, Uhlans or Curassiers would sally from the woods on a foray into enemy territory; but there would be no major engagements, and except for a few ranging shells to register targets the artillery would give no sign of its existence.

Further back, out of sight of the enemy, the scene would again be very different. There, the country roads would see more traffic in a week than they had done in a generation. Every route leading towards an enemy frontier would now be in use to its maximum capacity. Along a thousand roads endless, snake-like processions of men and vehicles would be crawling. Battalion after battalion of infantry; battery after battery of guns; train after train of wagons: machine gun units, siege artillery, signal sections, staff cars, field bakeries, field hospitals, and the sanitary corps that would dig the graves for the fallen. Still further back, with almost equal slowness, thousands of trains would be creeping up to railheads to disgorge tens of thousands more wagons, limbers and guns; hundreds of thousands more men and horses; and millions of tons of munitions. And every single individual in these vast ant-like swarms was moving to a destination unknown to himself, but already decided for him by one of a few directing brains that had long since worked out this intricate pattern.

Each of the countless columns winding through the forests of the Ardennes and the Vosges, over the Bosnian and Carpathian mountains, and across the plains of Prussia, Hungary and Poland, was advancing to a carefully planned time table. The heads of each would already have reached their deployment line, but more and more formations would be piling up behind them in the concentration areas, and those would be like long chains of lakes, each fed by innumerable rivers. When the lakes were full, the word would be given and the sluices opened. Heralded by fire and flashing with steel, the human tides would rush towards one another, to meet head-on for days, weeks, perhaps months, on end, in a series of such violent collisions that a slaughter must ensue, the like of which the world had never seen. But that was not to be—yet; not for another ten or twelve days.

Although the Duke spent much of his time visualizing such scenes and speculating on their outcome, he did so only as a grim recreation from trying to think of a way in which he might regain his freedom.

As he had committed no crime, he felt sure that if only he could get a message to his friends they would soon get him out of Major Ronge's clutches. Of course, now that the British Empire and the Dual-Monarchy were at war, he was liable to be detained in an internment camp, and he thought it unlikely that his friends would be able to do more than arrange for his transfer to one. But that would mean freedom to mix with other Britons caught by the war in Austria and, for a man of his resource, plenty of opportunities to escape. Whereas, as long as he remained confined in a cell and closely guarded by professional warders escape was next to impossible.

Puzzle his wits as he would, it was not until his fourth night in prison that an idea came to him which seemed to offer at least a slender hope of success. So on Saturday the 8th of August he awaited with suppressed eagerness the daily visit that Major Ronge paid him.

When the fat Secret Service Chief arrived, he sat down on the Duke's bed, offered him a cigarette, and said:

"*Herr Graf*, I do wish that I could persuade you to be a little more communicative. Naturally, I have never expected you to confess to any espionage activities in this country, but now that we are at war with Serbia it is of great importance that we should find out all we can about our enemies. If you would tell me the truth about your visits to Belgrade and all you learned in connection with the Serbian War Office, we might come to some arrangement about your future. Instead of keeping you in close confinement indefinitely, I could have you transferred to the more pleasant surroundings of an internment camp; and in a few months' time, when any information you have gathered in Vienna has become stale, it might even be arranged for you to leave the country."

De Richleau guessed that once the Major had obtained an admission from him that he *was* a spy, no matter where he had operated, that would be quite enough for the K.S. to have him legally put away in a fortress for the duration of the war; and he had no intention of falling into such a trap. So he replied:

"Alas, my dear Major. I fear I cannot take advantage of your offer. As I have said on several previous occasions, your friend Herr Höller has been the victim of hallucinations, and it is impossible for me to give you information that I do not possess."

With a frown of annoyance the fat man stood up, but the Duke went on: "Before you go, I have a small favour to ask. It concerns not myself but another, and I should be grateful if you would assist me to do a kindness to one of your compatriots."

"Which will at the same time inform him that I am holding you here, eh?" The Major's sly little eyes twinkled between their heavy folds of flesh. "No thank you."

"Not at all. It is merely that I owe some money and wish to pay it. You may perhaps have heard of the painter, Herr de Lazalo? After my return from Belgrade I commissioned him to paint a portrait for me. Few artists can afford to paint pictures without being paid for them, and I meant to send him a cheque before leaving Sacher's, but your arrival prevented that. My signature on the cheque will be sufficient to inform him from whom it comes, so there is no call for any covering letter, and you need not fear that this is a ruse to send him some cryptic message. I simply wish to send the poor chap the money he is entitled to, that is all."

The Major fingered one point of his waxed moustache thoughtfully for a moment, then he nodded. "All right. I see no objection to that. Give me the cheque and the address; then I will put it in a plain envelope and post it for you."

When the K.S. Chief had gone, de Richleau felt much the same as would a shipwrecked mariner on a desert island who has found a rocket and managed to get it off within sight of a ship passing a long way out.

De Lazalo would probably be a little surprised at receiving the cheque, as Ilona had commissioned him to paint her portrait and he would naturally be expecting her to pay for it. However, as he was aware of her relations with de Richleau, he would no doubt assume that the portrait was for him and she was allowing him to foot the bill. The odds were that the painter would then pay the cheque into his bank, and think no more about the matter.

On the other hand he might query the payment with Sárolta. Then things should start to happen. If they noticed that the date on the cheque was the 8th of August and that it had been posted locally, they would realize that, although the Duke was supposed to have left on the 4th, he was still in Vienna. Once Ilona had reason to believe that, he felt confident that she would not rest until she found him.

Having managed to send off his distress signal, de Richleau spent most of the week-end wondering if its significance would be realized soon after de Lazalo's post arrived on the Monday morning; but he feared it was much more likely that the artist would not mention the cheque to his lovely young relative until Ilona broached the subject of paying for the portrait, and that might not happen for some weeks to come. So he tried to put the matter out of his mind and think of others ways of letting his friends know of his unhappy situation.

In that, by Tuesday evening, he had met with no success. He was just on the point of going to bed when footsteps halted outside his cell, the door was unlocked and a warder told him that he was wanted in the Governor's office. Instantly his hopes were aroused and his pulses began to race with excitement. Hardly able to keep his hands steady, he followed the man down several long passages and into a spacious, well-furnished room.

Opposite the door, an elderly Colonel with grey mutton-chop whiskers was seated behind a big desk. Beside him stood Major Ronge. Sitting in an arm-chair on the right of the desk was Adam Grünne. With a sigh of relief de Richleau smiled a greeting to his dark, broad-shouldered friend; then, with a bow to the Governor, sat down in another arm-chair to which that functionary waved him.

The Governor stroked his right side-whisker for a moment, while regarding the prisoner thoughtfully from a pair of rheumy blue eyes, coughed, and said: "*Herr Graf*, I have never been called on to deal with a case similar to yours, and I hardly know what to do about it."

De Richleau was now on his mettle, and replied at once: "I am very happy at this opportunity to discuss the matter with you, sir. During the past week I asked repeatedly to do so, in vain. I have committed no crime, neither have I been charged with one, and I am being held here illegally. I demand that if you have anything against me I shall be given a fair trial with legal aid, or, alternatively, be released at once."

"In peace time your demand would be fully justified," The Governor tapped the ash of a cigar he was smoking off into a tray. "But we are now in a state of war. As an enemy alien suspected of activities prejudicial to the State, we are fully entitled by our emergency regulations to hold you without trial for as long as we consider desirable. However, a new factor has arisen which greatly complicates the situation. It is beyond dispute that you hold a commission in the Archduchess Ilona Theresa's regiment of Hussars; and on that account Her Imperial Highness has demanded that we should give you up to her."

"I protest!" put in Ronge. "It is also beyond dispute that the *Herr Graf* is of British nationality, and I consider him to be one of the most dangerous men that I have ever had on my files."

"Have you any proof of that?" asked the Governor.

"I am fully satisfied, sir, that while in Belgrade during June he was associating with members of the Serbian General Staff for the purpose of making himself acquainted with their secrets. While in Vienna during July, his association with many highly placed persons cannot have failed to place him in possession of information which would be of great value to the enemy. Therefore, I am most strongly opposed to his release."

The Governor stroked his right whisker again. "Unless you can bring a specific charge against him, I do not see how I can refuse Her Imperial Highness' demand."

Ronge shrugged his heavy shoulders. "The decision lies with you, sir. I do not think he can do us much damage providing that he is not allowed to get out of the country. By rights, quite apart from our suspicions of him, he should be interned; but if Her Imperial Highness is prepared to be responsible for him, that seems as good a protection as putting him in a camp, from which he would probably be able to escape without great difficulty."

"Very well then. I will sign the order for his release."

With a smile of satisfaction de Richleau watched the Governor sign the paper, then stood up. But the K.S. Chief still had a shot left in his locker, and now he discharged it:

"*Herr Graf*, before you go I should like to give you a warning. It is my duty to prevent information reaching the enemy, and I still intend to carry out that duty as far as you are concerned. Her Imperial Highness has no official status, and the responsibility she has assumed for you can only be accepted on the grounds that you are an officer in her regiment. To fulfil your functions in that respect you must remain in Vienna. As long as you do so my police will not molest you: but should you leave the city, we shall assume that Her Imperial Highness' responsibility has automatically lapsed. I intend to issue a description of you to all railway and frontier police, with orders that they are to keep a special look out for you. Should you attempt to get out of the country you will be re-arrested. Even should Her Imperial Highness have given you leave to go, I am prepared to risk her displeasure by stopping you; because I shall take the matter to my Minister, and I am confident that in the interests of security he will support me."

De Richleau bowed. "My dear *Herr Major*, I have always admired devotion to duty, and I congratulate you on your admirable sense of it. I find it regrettable only that you should not direct your energies into more promising channels."

Adam Grünne stood up and said to the Governor: "I have already given you Her Imperial Highness' letter requiring the release of her officer; so, if there are no further formalities, it remains only for me to ask you, sir, to be good enough to have his belongings sent to the barracks of the regiment."

"I will have that done with pleasure," the Governor agreed. Then he sent for the Duke's hat and coat, and personally escorted him to the outer door, where Adam had a cab waiting.

As soon as it drove off de Richleau said with a chuckle: "Well, my friend, I am truly grateful to you for your endeavours on my behalf. These war time emergency powers are quite reminiscent of the *lettre de cachet*, on which the Kings of France used to have people thrown into the Bastille for an unspecified period. I was beginning to fear that I might be kept in that damn prison until the war was over."

Adam grinned at him in the semi-darkness. "I think you might have been, but for a mysterious cheque that de Lazalo brought round to Sárolta this morning; and Ilona raising Cain with the Chief of Police every hour since, until he discovered your whereabouts."

"So my trick worked, eh? It was a long shot, but that fat Secret Service man refused to allow me to communicate with anyone. I wonder, though, that Ilona did not start her inquiries about me when I failed to appear at our last rendezvous. I might quite well have been in hospital as the result of an accident."

"Oh no! I learned the same afternoon that the reason you did not turn up at the studio was because you had been arrested."

"Then, if you knew that, why the devil have you waited all this time before doing something about me?"

"Because I was given to understand that the matter of your arrest had been straightened out, and that you had left after all that afternoon for England. When you did not appear at de Lazalo's Ilona got into a frightful state, and sent me off to Sacher's. I arrived there to find the detectives collecting your baggage. Ronge was with them. He told me that you had been arrested in mistake for someone else, and that your detention was likely to cause you to miss your train. You know, or perhaps you don't know, that hundreds of people were fighting to get on those last trains out of Vienna before the frontiers closed. Anyhow, he said that by way of amends he had sent you straight to the station with a police Inspector to get you a seat, and had come himself to collect your luggage for you."

"By Jove!" exclaimed the Duke. "One can't help admiring that fellow. He's as cunning as the devil."

Adam nodded. "Poor Ilona was nearly hysterical when I had to tell her that she had lost her last chance of saying good-bye to you; but the explanation Ronge gave me was so plausible that we naturally accepted it. Just now, before you were brought up from your cell, I charged him in front of the Governor with having told me a flat lie, but he seemed to think that he would have been justified in going to pretty well any lengths in order to make certain of keeping you under lock and key. What is all this nonsense about your being a dangerous enemy agent?"

De Richleau sighed. "I am, alas, now technically an enemy of your country, Count; but I assure you I am not in the least a dangerous one."

"You are prepared to give me your word, then, that there is not an atom of truth in the suggestion that you have been endeavouring to obtain our military secrets?"

"Certainly I am." The Duke glanced at his companion in surprise, and added a little sharply: "Knowing me well, as you do, I think it a little odd that you should require it."

Count Adam shifted uncomfortably in his seat. "I do so as a responsibility towards others. As you are aware, Her Imperial Highness got you out of prison on the grounds that you are an officer of her regiment. When I discussed the matter with her, we decided that your safest course would be to join it actively—anyhow for the time being."

"I see," murmured the Duke. "But is that really necessary? Major Ronge said that he would not molest me as long as I remained in Vienna."

"I know he did; but if he finds that you have resumed your old life at Sacher's, and are lunching and dining again with all sorts of influential people, he may reconsider his decision. He was quite right, you know, about Her Imperial Highness having no official status; so any time he feels that you have given him fresh grounds for suspicion he can go to von Ostromiecz, persuade him to disregard her, and get a special warrant to pop you back into prison. He will naturally expect you to report at the barracks. That's why I asked for your things to be sent round there. You see, he is counting on your being kept too busy by military duties to do any harm. To-morrow I propose to take you along to our mess and present you formally on joining. Even if you were an enemy agent, you couldn't learn much in a cavalry barracks; but, all the same, you will appreciate how I am placed. In fairness to my brother officers, I had to ask your word of honour that Ronge's suspicions are unfounded."

"My dear fellow, as far as my activities in Vienna are concerned, I give it you willingly. I think, too, that your plan for me to join the regiment until things sort themselves out a little is a very sound one. I would like to add that while I remain with it, in spite of my true nationality, I shall temporarily regard myself as a loyal soldier to the Emperor."

"That's damned handsome of you, seeing that you're really one of the enemy." Count Adam smiled again. "It's another load off my conscience, too. I didn't relish the idea at all of having to conceal the fact that you are British, but now that won't trouble me. They are a fine lot of fellows, and soldiering is good fun all the world over; but naturally we shouldn't expect you to go on active service."

"I should hope not," laughed the Duke.

"That is one snag about our plan, though," the Count rejoined seriously. "The regiment forms part of the 5th Cavalry Division, and on Saturday the Division is to do a ride past for its final inspection before leaving for the Russian front. They will not actually entrain for several days after that, of course; but when they do, and you are left behind, Ronge may start making trouble again."

"I don't see why he should. Knowing me to be British, he could hardly expect me to take part in a campaign against my Russian allies."

"That's true. The trouble is it's damned difficult to know what he does expect. But presumably, as he let you out as a soldier, he may start kicking directly he hears you have ceased to act as one."

"In my view, he let me out only because he could bring no charge against me; and, in the circumstances, did not feel that he had good enough grounds for inducing his Minister to have a first-class row with Ilona in order to keep me inside. Anyhow, if need be, I could maintain my rôle by remaining here to train recruits at the regimental depot. But tell me, if we are not going to the barracks until to-morrow, where are you taking me now?"

"To the palace, of course; and we'll be there in a minute." Adam Grünne hesitated, while he played with one curled-up end of his brown moustache, then added awkwardly; "I'm afraid the meeting's going to be a bit of a shock for you. She's ill—damned ill: and she looks it."

"Oh God!" breathed the Duke. "She's had a relapse, then?"

"Yes. The evening after you disappeared she worked herself up into a positive frenzy of grief. The result was that she had a haemorrhage. She's been in bed ever since."

"If only she would go to a clinic in the mountains, and undergo a proper cure."

"I know. She ought to have done so months ago; but she is as pig-headed as a mule. Still, she has agreed to at last, thank goodness, as soon as she is fit to be moved."

"When do you think that will be?"

"Any day now."

The cab slowed down, then pulled up with a jerk. As they got out, and Adam paid off the driver, de Richleau saw that instead of driving up to the entrance of the palace the cab had halted some distance from it on the far side of the bridge over the canal. It was now nearly a quarter to eleven and, catching his thought, the Count muttered:

"I don't want anyone to recognize you going in, if we can avoid it. That's why I waited till after dark to come for you. Turn up your coat collar and pull the brim of your hat down over your eyes."

At a quick pace they set off over the bridge and across the square in front of the palace. Count Adam was, as usual, in uniform and, recognizing his short, stalwart figure at once, the sentries let them through with a smart salute. Turning left, they walked to the eastern end of the palace, round it and along its garden front to a low door. As Adam took out a key and unlocked it, de Richleau recognized it as the one they had used on the two evenings when he had dined with Ilona at the beginning of the month. With Adam leading, they slipped quietly up the service staircase. At its top he peered cautiously to right and left along the dimly lit corridor; then, opening a door opposite, he pushed the Duke inside with a whispered injunction to wait there till he came back.

As de Richleau stepped inside there was just enough light for him to see that it was a housemaids' closet, then the door closed behind him and he was in pitch darkness. But he had not to wait long. Five minutes later Adam Grünne returned, beckoned him out, and led him on tiptoe down the corridor to Ilona's boudoir.

Sárolta was sitting there, and her dark almond eyes smiled him a greeting, but she put a finger to her lips. Then, as he kissed her hand, she said in a low voice: "Has Adam told you how ill she has been?"

He nodded. "Yes. And I am distraught with anxiety about her."

"She has lost a lot of weight," Sárolta went on, "and I'm afraid you will be shocked by her appearance. But she is quite a lot better now than she has been. Dr. Bruckner was very pleased with her progress when he was here this evening."

"That, at least, is good news. Adam tells me, too, that she has at last agreed to go into a sanatorium. I did my utmost to persuade her to before, but she wouldn't listen."

"It's that I want to talk to you about. Dr. Bruckner has arranged for her to go to Hohenembs, in the Vorarlberg, near the Swiss frontier. It's not a proper sanatorium. She jibbed at that. She says that even if she didn't see the other patients, the very idea of having people who were ill, and perhaps dying, in the same building would make her worse."

"But can she have proper treatment there?"

"Yes. A young doctor and two nurses who have trained under Dr. Bruckner are going with her; and he intends to visit her once a fortnight himself. It's a châlet on a hill-top overlooking the Upper Rhine and belongs to the Emperor. Members of the Imperial family have used it for convalescing before, so in a sense it is already a private clinic. We couldn't really have a more suitable place for her. But I wanted to speak to you about her leaving."

"Yes?"

Sárolta's small dark face looked very troubled. "This evening Dr. Bruckner said that he considered her sufficiently recovered to be moved to-morrow, and Count Aulendorf at once set about making arrangements for our journey. I haven't dared to tell her yet—and now she's got you back again I'm afraid she may refuse to go."

"She must," declared the Duke. "She's neglected her health for too long as it is; and the thing that is important above all else is to get her well again. I promise you I won't allow her to postpone her departure for a single day on my account."

"Oh, thank you!" Sárolta smiled her relief. "I know how much you love her, and I felt sure I could count on your help. Come with me now and I'll take you to her."

Ilona's bedroom was next door and as they entered it, although de Richleau's gaze was fixed on the figure in the bed, he could not help taking in the furnishings of the room and feeling some surprise at them.

The rest of her suite contained mainly period pieces in excellent taste, but this held only bare necessities, and these were of an ugly Victorian mould. The bed was of brass; a marble-topped wash-stand stood near it; the wardrobe and two chests of drawers were of bulky mahogany, with round wooden handles; and above the mantel there was a heavily framed mirror of unattractive design. But the thought that such lodging-house furniture was in keeping with the spartan tradition of the Imperial family, was gone in a flash as his glance met Ilona's.

She was propped up in bed with several pillows for support. Her chestnut hair, which he had never before seen down, was parted in the centre and descended over her shoulders in two long, thick plaits. Her face was much thinner and very white, except where two red patches, like the splashes of paint on a Dutch doll, burned above her cheek bones. Her blue eyes seemed enormous. But her dazzling smile was as joyous as ever, as she held out her arms to him with a cry of delight.

Sárolta turned and, smiling over her shoulder, closed the door behind her. Next moment Ilona's arms were round de Richleau's neck and she drew his dark head down to her fair one.

A quarter of an hour slipped by before they could bring themselves to talk coherently; then he told her of the dark machinations of Major Ronge, and she told him of her agony at the thought that he had left her without a last kiss to remember. She admitted that for some days she had been very ill, but declared that by the end of the week she would be up and about again.

"You are going to this place on the Swiss border, though, aren't you?" he asked anxiously. "Your last attack was much worse than any you've had before, and it would be sheer madness to trifle with your health any longer."

She nodded. "Yes. I've promised Sárolta and Adam and everybody that I would, so I really must. Hohenembs is a lovely spot and I shall be as happy there as I could be anywhere without you. I've an idea, too, that to go there will be lucky for me."

"I pray it will, my sweet," he smiled. "But why should you think so?"

"Do you not know its history? The châlet was built for my grandmother, the Empress Elizabeth, for her to have mountain air and treatment there when they thought she had consumption. But it turned out that she was not tubercular after all; and afterwards, whenever she went abroad incognito, she always travelled as the Countess Hohenembs to perpetuate the memory of her happy deliverance."

"That certainly is a fortunate omen; even if there is little chance of such a happy discovery being made about you."

"But I shall get well there, so what is the difference? When I am quite recovered I must ask Grandpapa to give me the title, so that when I come to England to see you after the war I can perpetuate its old associations."

"The thought you conjure up will make me redouble my prayers that the war may be a short one. But it reminds me, too, that now I am a free man again I must start making my plans to get home."

"No, Armand!" She seized his hand. "I forbid you to."

He gave her a puzzled look. "But, darling, my duty lies there. You know that. It's true that you have made yourself responsible for me; but no one would dare to even question you if you took it on yourself to let me go. And I am no more a danger to Austria now than I was the day they arrested me."

"Oh I know that! I know that!"

"Then give me leave to depart. Call it indefinite leave from the regiment if you like. Or, if you prefer, give me your private permission and say afterwards that I broke my parole to you."

"How can you think that I would ever disgrace your name to shield myself?"

"Darling, I spoke without thought. But for me to stay on in Vienna now for longer than I positively must would be as great a disgrace. Surely you did not secure my release from prison only to hold me as your personal captive? If so, such golden fetters would be chains of shame."

"Oh, Armand, how cruel you are! Of course I did not mean to do that. I meant only that now, when I thought you far away in England, a miracle has restored you to me. It seemed an abuse of Heaven's generosity to think of other things. I know only too well that I must let you go. But not just yet. That is the only reason why I forbade you to talk of your plans for getting away."

Instantly he was filled with contrition, and with his arm about her shoulders strove to comfort her. Yet he was terribly and miserably aware that he must break it to her that this was their last meeting. With an aching heart, he took the plunge:

"Ilona, I would never have raised the matter had I not felt bound to do so. Even if I sacrificed loyalty to my country to stay on here a while, that would be pointless now that you are leaving for Hohenembs."

"I am not going yet. Not till towards the end of the week."

The tears were in his eyes as he shook his head. "My adored Princess, they told me before I came in here that Dr. Bruckner thinks you fit to travel to-morrow, and that Count Aulendorf is already making all the arrangements."

"I won't go!" she exclaimed. "I won't go! And they can't make me!"

"Please, Ilona. You refuse to acknowledge it to others, but you know yourself that your life is in danger. Every day may be the one day that will make the difference. You must go! I beg you to!"

She shook her head. "Not to-morrow. Not until you are on your way out of Austria. It is going to be difficult for you to get away now that Ronge has ordered all his police to be on the look-out for you. If you disappeared at once it would be like ringing an alarm bell. You must wait here until we have lulled him into a false sense of security. And I'll not go to Hohenembs until we have devised some safe way for you to get across the frontier."

"To give the impression that I had settled down would require ten days or more. You cannot afford those days, Ilona. You are right that I should be stupid to rush my fences. To secure a better chance of getting clean away I am quite prepared to bide my time for a bit. But your life or death may hang upon your getting mountain air without delay. I implore you to leave to-morrow, just as you would have had you never learned that I was still in Vienna."

"I'll not do it."

Taking his arm from round her shoulders he stood up and looked down into her face. "I think you will, Ilona; because, much as I hate to do it, I am going to tell you now what will happen if you don't. Your life is far more precious to me than my freedom. I'll not allow any prospect of seeing me to do further injury to your health. If you persist in refusing to submit to the arrangements that have been made for you, when I leave here to-night I shall go straight back to the prison, and let Major Ronge do what the devil he likes with me."

"No, no, Armand!"

"Yes, I mean that." His grey eyes bored down into hers. "To be the cause of your refusing to obey your doctor's orders while in your present state, is too high a price for you to expect me to pay for my liberty."

She sighed and turned her head a little sideways. "How can I stand my ground when you use such threats?"

"I use them only because I love you so desperately."

"Yet you would drive me away."

"God knows I prize every moment with you, and do so only out of fear that if you stay you may kill yourself."

"Very well, then. I will go." Her voice trembled. "There! Are you satisfied?"

He stooped to kiss her. "I feel like an officer who has taken his objective only at the price of the lives of all his men. That is how barren and bitter this victory is for me."

"But what of you?" she asked, putting up a hand to stroke his cheek. "Have you thought yet of what course to take?"

"I think this idea of my joining the regiment actively an excellent one; at least as a temporary measure."

"Unfortunately it is going to the front quite soon."

A soft knock came on the door. At Ilona's call to come in, Sárolta opened it, bobbed an automatic curtsy, and said: "I came to warn your Highness that you have only a little over five more minutes; then your nurse will be coming to settle you down for the night."

"Can you not tell her to come later?" exclaimed the Duke in dismay.

Ilona smiled and squeezed his hand. "That is almost the first nice thing you have said to-night. But I have a better plan. Ask Adam to take you up to his rooms for half an hour; then come back to me when my nurse has gone."

"That's a much better idea," Sárolta agreed. "Nurse looked quite upset when I told her after dinner that you meant to sit up for an hour later than usual. Goodness knows what she would say if I had to put her off till midnight."

Adam had been sitting in the boudoir with Sárolta. When the Duke joined him they made another cautious progress through dimly lit corridors and up the back stairs to the floor above, where he had his suite. As he switched on the light in his cheerful sitting-room, he said:

"I've had a bed made up for you here. I thought you'd prefer that to going to an hotel without your kit or anything; and I can lend you things for the night."

"That's awfully good of you," the Duke said with real feeling. "I'm afraid I've caused you an immense amount of trouble in these past few months, through falling in love with Ilona."

The Count gave a gallant flick of his curly moustache. "Oh, don't think of it. I'll admit I was a bit worried at first; but with little Sárolta pushing me on I soon got to accept the situation. Royalty aren't like other people, you know. Most of them are brought up all wrong, and Ilona's no exception. One would have to have a heart of stone not to feel sorry for any girl who's had her life. But she's weathered it better than most of them do. She often behaves like a child or a fool, but there is something basically decent in her nature that makes us all love her. She deserved somebody like you, and I'm glad you came along."

"Thanks," said the Duke. "You couldn't pay me a higher compliment; particularly as I've more than once compromised you to a point that might have cost you your job."

"I'd have been a bit of a rotter if I'd let that stand in the way of her having her romance," Adam said seriously. Then he added, with a sudden grin, "Anyhow, I don't give a damn what happens now Sárolta's papa has agreed to our engagement. He can't go back on that."

"Oh, I *am* glad!" De Richleau held out his hand. "You're not only a lucky fellow, but you deserve your luck. I do congratulate you most heartily. When did this happen?"

"Russia's declaration of war did the trick. It gave us an excuse to press the old boy into agreeing, but the actual announcement wasn't published till last Saturday. More engagements have been announced in the Court circular these past ten days than usually appear in a whole season. Queer, isn't it, how many young people had to wait till they might soon be dead, before old fogies would permit them to enjoy their happiness."

"Are you off to the wars, then?"

"Not just yet, but I soon shall be. Whatever happened I wouldn't care to remain in a Court post while all my friends go to the front. As things are I shall go down to Hohenembs for a week or so with Ilona. But once she is settled in there she won't need me. Marie Nopsca will look after her while Sárolta takes some leave, and we plan to get married from her people's house in Budapest about the 25th. War or no war, we mean to take a fortnight's honeymoon, then Sárolta will return to Hohenembs and I shall go north to join the regiment."

De Richleau looked at him gravely. "You have never been on active service, have you?"

"No, but I'm looking forward to it immensely."

"Then will you permit me as an old soldier to give you a few tips?"

"I'd be delighted to have them."

"First, then, never forget that more men die of disease and gangrene in wars than from shells and bullets. Before you go to the front get a good doctor to inoculate you against tetanus and typhus. It's painful, but worth it. Take a big tin of permanganate of potash in your kit, and carry a little of it on you. Never drink still water from a well or ditch without first putting a few of the crystals in it. Take the trouble to learn how to apply bandages and tourniquets to yourself without aid. Always carry two field-dressing packs and a slab of chocolate on you. Never touch your spirit flask if you have been wounded in the head. Carry a few morphia tablets so that you can dull your pain if you are badly wounded; and some chlorodyne against attacks of dysentery. Body lice are one of the almost inevitable unpleasantnesses of war, so keep yourself well supplied with insect powder. Get some leather or fur lined garments and rubber boots and take them with you. As soon as you reach the front line sacrifice smartness of appearance for warm and comfortable clothes. Winter will soon be here, and on the northern front you will be fighting in snow. Take a pair of dark glasses: they will save your eyes. If you go out on a night patrol in snow, wear a mask to protect your face from frost bite, and give your nose and ears a rub every few minutes. On the other hand, if you are not fighting in snow, never wear anything white up in the line at night. Never be the third to light a cigarette off the same match. That is not a superstition; the sniper on the other side has time to aim while the other two are lighting up, and gets the third man. Don't rely on matches; carry a flint and tinder lighter. Take some extra sponge bags to protect your cigarettes and other things from the wet. Don't bother with a sword unless you are mounted. It is of little use against a man with a rifle and bayonet, and will only get in your way. Don't use your pistol at more than ten short paces, and aim low down at your antagonist's body; not at his head. For night work by far the best weapons are a loaded riding crop and a stiletto. Never attack an enemy behind barbed wire unless you are quite certain that it has first been cut. Don't be ashamed to fling yourself flat on the ground directly you come under fire, and make it a rule that the last man to follow your example gets a fatigue when the scrap is over. Dead soldiers are no further good to their country and every casualty is a liability. Never expose yourself unless your men look like running away: then, stand up to give them new confidence, but keep behind them and, without a moment's hesitation, shoot the first fellow you see trying to sneak off. Inspect your men's feet daily. Make them treat prisoners as they would be treated themselves. If you take more than one prisoner when alone, make them take off their boots and tie them round their necks. With bare feet there is much less chance of their trying any tricks. Buy the smallest automatic you can find and carry it concealed under your left armpit. If you are taken prisoner yourself the odds are all against your being searched before you reach the cage. Having a baby pistol on you may give you the chance to turn the tables on your captor before you get there. And take a small down pillow with you. However hard the place you have to lie on, you'll get sound sleep if you can rest your head on something soft."

"There!" de Richleau ended with a smile. "They say that old soldiers never die, and if you can remember all that you'll stand a better chance than most people of coming through."

Count Adam looked a little doubtful. "You seem to be thinking of an entirely different kind of warfare from anything we have ever been trained for; and I can see some of our Generals having an apoplectic fit if they found their cavalry lying down to fight."

"They'll learn," remarked the Duke acidly. "It will probably take a bit of time, but when the casualty lists reach the hundred thousand mark, they'll start to wake up to the fact that wars are no longer fought as they were in the 1870's."

"Anyhow," Adam grinned, "I'm immensely grateful for all your tips. As a peace time soldier I would never have thought of half of them, and I shall make a list to-night of things to take."

"Good. There's one other thing I'd like to do for you if I may have a pen and a piece of notepaper."

"Of course!" The Count motioned towards a small *escritoire*. "You will find everything in there."

Sitting down at it, de Richleau wrote a short note in Russian, blotted it, and handed it to his friend. "Put that in your pocket-book and keep it carefully. It is a line to my second cousin, the Grand Duke Nicholas, who is the Commander-in-Chief of the Russian Armies. If you have the misfortune to be taken prisoner permanently it will ensure you good treatment while in Russian hands."

"Really! You are too kind."

"Not at all. I am only too pleased to do anything I can to show the gratitude I feel for all that you and Sárolta have done for me."

For twenty minutes longer they continued to talk of soldiering, then at midnight they crept downstairs again and Sárolta re-introduced the Duke into Ilona's room. But as the pretty Hungarian was about to leave them, Ilona said:

"Sárolta, please call Adam and come in with him. I want to talk to you both about Armand getting back to England."

When they were all settled, she went on with a sad smile: "Armand tells me that you two have conspired with Dr. Bruckner to carry me off to Hohenembs to-morrow. I simply hate the idea now, but Armand has forced me to agree; so to-night is the last chance we shall have to help him plan how to get away. Have either of you any ideas how he could evade that horrid Major Ronge's police?"

"I'm afraid I haven't at the moment," Adam replied. "You see, his position is a most extraordinary one. They can't charge him with any criminal act, but they can arrest him at any time as an enemy alien; so he's a sort of ticket-of-leave man. By rights he should be in an internment camp now, but he has been let out owing to your Highness' influence, and on certain conditions. They are that he should serve with your regiment. That puts him in an even more extraordinary position, as it is an unheard-of thing for a known enemy to be allowed to fulfil the functions of an officer in our army. However, Ronge appears to think that he can do little harm there; but, at the same time, has made it plain that if the Duke attempts to leave Vienna he will pounce on him at once."

"And we can be certain that he will have me watched," added de Richleau. "So I fear I shall stand little chance of getting away until I can procure some really good disguise."

"It won't be easy to do that if you are being shadowed," put in Sárolta.

"No." Adam agreed. "And Ronge warned us that he meant to put his railway police on the job. They are pretty good at spotting people who are made up to look like someone else; and I greatly doubt if you would get as far as the frontier."

Sárolta suddenly clapped her hands. "I have it! Why shouldn't he travel with us to Hohenembs to-morrow as one of Her Highness' suite? We could dress him up as a woman. A nurse's uniform would serve the purpose splendidly, and I could easily get one. Once we get him to Hohenembs he could slip across the border into Switzerland."

"Oh darling, bless you! What a marvellous idea!" exclaimed Ilona.

But de Richleau shook his head. "I'm afraid that is quite out of the question. Apart from the risk of my disguise being penetrated on the journey, too many people would have to be in the secret. One of the servants or real nurses would be certain to talk afterwards; then the fat would be in the fire with a vengeance. Not only would there be ugly rumours about Ilona having aided an enemy spy to escape, but all Vienna would then believe that I must have been her lover. Nothing would induce me to risk that."

For half an hour they talked fruitlessly round the subject, then Adam said, "I wonder what line Ronge will take when the regiment leaves for the front?"

De Richleau shrugged. "As far as one can guess he won't take any action as long as I remain in some employment at the depot."

"I was wondering if you would care to leave with the regiment."

"What! For the Russian front?"

"Yes. Once you were within riding distance of the enemy you could say you were going out on a reconnaissance, and get yourself captured. Of course, it would mean your going the long way home, but since you are a relative of the Grand Duke Nicholas I've no doubt the Russians would give you every help to get down to Constantinople, or to a Norwegian port, as quickly as possible."

The Duke had as yet had no time to think out a plan for himself. Given a well thought out disguise and a fair start, he was far more confident than were his friends of his ability to slip past Major Ronge's police; but the disguise and the start remained major problems, and he felt that, all things considered, Count Adam's suggestion entailed less risk. So he said:

"That's an excellent idea. The only snag I see to it is that, while Ronge appears willing to let an enemy alien kick his heels on a barrack square in Vienna, he may not be at all prepared to allow one to go to the front as a serving officer."

Adam shrugged his broad shoulders. "Vienna is the headquarters of three Armies and the greatest military dispersal point in the Empire. Scores of formations are leaving every week, and it is most unlikely that

Ronge makes a daily check up on all military movements. I think the odds are all against his learning that Her Imperial Highness' Hussars have left for the front until several days after their departure."

"He will if he has me watched," disagreed the Duke.

"Yes. I suppose you are right there. But it's unlikely he will suspect that you intend to go with them; and his police won't be watching the military trains for you. As he thinks you want to get to England I doubt if it will even enter his head that you might go by way of Russia. When he learns you have disappeared he will imagine that you have made a bolt for the Swiss or Italian frontier, and concentrate his efforts on trying to head you off in that direction."

After some further discussion they all agreed that Count Adam's plan offered the best chance of the Duke getting out of the country; so it was decided to adopt it. Ilona then asked her lover:

"Are you very tired?"

He smiled. "I am not too tired to sit up with you, as I should like to do. If I may, I will sit here all night while you sleep."

"I hoped you would say that," she smiled back; "but I don't intend to sleep. Every moment of the time will be too precious. Sárolta darling, will you be an angel and doze on the settee in the boudoir, in case nurse or the old Aulendorf come to take a peep at me? If one of them do, you can say that I was restless and you have been reading to me; but that I've just dropped off and they're not to open my door, as it might wake me again."

"Of course I will." Sárolta kissed her fingers to her beautiful mistress, then she took her fiancé's arm. "Come along, Adam. You've made me quite proud of you to-night. I know Ilona Theresa's Hussars are celebrated for their gallantry, but I never thought any of them kept such a good brain as yours under his busby."

"That's nothing to what I will teach you in a fortnight's time," grinned Adam.

When they had left the room, de Richleau pulled his chair nearer to Ilona's bed and took her hand. Both of them were now resigned to their parting and they did not refer to it again. Instead, while the night hours slipped by, they talked quietly of many things. Of the ball at Dorchester House, that now seemed a lifetime away; of their Channel crossing in the storm; of his playing guide to her at Ischl; of Königstein and their meetings in Vienna. Those lovely memories at least could not be taken from them.

At length grey streaks of daylight began to appear down the edges of the heavy curtains. Soon afterwards there came a knock at the door, and Sárolta looked in.

"I'm sorry," she said, "but Adam has just come downstairs. It is nearly six o'clock, and he wanted me to warn you that the servants will soon be coming along to clean the rooms and passages."

De Richleau stood up. "Then I must be off. It would be disastrous if one of them saw me leaving the Archduchess' suite at this hour."

Sárolta re-closed the door. The lovers embraced. Ilona had already promised to do her utmost to get well quickly. De Richleau had sworn that immediately hostilities ceased he would come back to her. Both of them had vowed to keep one another in their hearts until that happy day. There was no more to be said. She was brave now and did not seek to detain him. With her chin up, dry-eyed and smiling, she sent him from her; hiding her grief until she could give way to it in Sárolta's arms after he had left her suite with Adam Grünne.

The wrench of this final parting had shaken de Richleau badly, and when they got upstairs he was very glad to accept some coffee laced with cognac that the Count had ready for him. While he drank it his host outlined plans for the immediate future.

"I should think," he said, "that you must need some sleep pretty badly; and there's no reason why you shouldn't put in five hours or so here. In any case it would be ill-advised for you to leave the palace until the usual morning callers start popping in and out, and when you do leave it would attract less attention if you were in uniform. I take it yours will be in your trunks, and they've been sent to the barracks; so I propose to go round there presently and dig it out for you. You'll want it this morning, anyhow, as I am taking you to lunch in the mess."

De Richleau was still thinking of Ilona, so had been listening with only half an ear; but he got the gist of it, and nodded. "That's very good of you. I'll sleep till you return, then. You'll have no difficulty in finding my uniform: it's all in a separate tin case."

Ten minutes later he was tucked up in bed, and with emotional exhaustion added to physical tiredness soon fell asleep. At half past eleven Adam had some difficulty in rousing him, but after a bath and a shave he felt fully refreshed; and, an hour later, spick and span in their sky-blue musical-comedy uniforms, they set off in a taxi for the cavalry barracks.

The commanding officer of Ilona's regiment, Colonel Prince Thurn und Taxis, was already known to the Duke, as were several of the others; and with the charming courtesy typical of their class they all expressed their pleasure that, although he held only an honorary commission, he should have decided to serve with them. A subaltern was told off to show him his quarters; a big bed-sitting-room with dated but solid furniture, in which all his trunks had been stacked. A soldier-servant was produced for him, and then they went in to lunch.

Nearly all the officers present were now wearing their field-service uniforms. De Richleau noted that they were olive-grey and felt that he ought to get one as soon as possible; so he asked the Prince for leave to spend the afternoon ordering service equipment.

"My dear fellow," replied the Prince, "please consider yourself free to come and go just as you wish. I am told that you held the rank of Lieutenant-General in the Turkish Army, so we shall look to you for counsel rather than routine duties. If you care to give us a few addresses on your experience in the Balkan wars, I am sure they would be most valuable. I'd be glad, too, if you would ride out with the troops in the morning and give me your candid opinion of them. But, otherwise, I shall regard you as a member of my headquarters staff with no particular responsibilities for the time being."

In consequence, the Duke paid another visit to the regimental tailors with Adam Grünne. Once again they promised special efforts to provide him with a service uniform by Saturday morning, so that he could wear it for the ride-past of the 5th Cavalry Division that afternoon. Then he reluctantly said good-bye to Adam, and proceeded on a shopping expedition to procure all the things he had recommended to his friend the night before as important items in the baggage of an old campaigner.

During Thursday and Friday he was as happy as he could be, considering that he had no hope of seeing Ilona again for a long time to come. It was now nearly seven weeks since he had received his wounds, so he was fully recovered from them. His talks on modern war were received as shockingly revolutionary, but with awe and diffident respect. He liked the gay, optimistic young gallants who were his companions, and his born love of soldiering made him enjoy being once again with troops. For him it was a real pleasure to sit a good horse each morning while watching their well-timed evolutions in the Prater, and afterwards to use his quick eye in the stables, making a useful comment here and there.

On Saturday the morning was devoted to a final polish of already gleaming bits, buckles, buttons, arms and saddlery. Then, in the afternoon, Ilona Theresa's Hussars rode out to meet the rest of the 5th Cavalry Division in the open spaces of the park. As the division was composed largely of Household Troops it had been purposely held back and was the last to leave for the front. So officers and men were doubly eager to show their fitness for service, and the ride past presented a fine spectacle of good training in perfect parade ground manœuvre.

All the regiments passed the saluting base twice: first in column at the walk; then in line of squadrons at the charge, with drawn swords or lances levelled. General Conrad von Hötzendorf was taking the parade and, as de Richleau rode by on the right of, and half a horses length behind, Prince Thurn und Taxis, out of the corner of his eye he saw the wizened-faced little General, unmoving and unwinking, scrutinizing the cavalcade with an eagle's eye for possible faults.

Having been subjected to that icy stare, everyone was glad when the ordeal was over, and as they rode off the parade de Richleau was just congratulating the Prince on the excellent show that the regiment had put up, when one of von Hötzendorf's A.D.C.s galloped up to him, drew rein, and said:

"The General's compliments, Count Königstein, and he would like a word with you."

Surprised and considerably disturbed, de Richleau saluted the Prince, turned his mount, and galloped back to the saluting base with the A.D.C. Von Hötzendorf had just mounted his horse. Returning the Duke's salute, he gave him a hard look and sniffed:

"What the devil are you doing in this turn-out?"

De Richleau strove to conceal his annoyance. He felt that it was a most appalling stroke of ill-luck that von Hötzendorf should have spotted him among the eight thousand odd men who had just ridden past. Gone now was any hope of his getting back to England via Russia. The General knew that he was not an Austrian, so would never permit him to go to the front. Instead, he would question the right of an alien to wear Austrian uniform. If he took the matter up, as it seemed certain he would, Major Ronge would be brought into the inquiry and give voice to his suspicions. Von Hötzendorf would ride rough-shod over any right that Ilona could claim to be responsible for the officers of her own regiment. He would have a fit at the very idea that anyone suspected of being a spy should continue to hold a commission, and would insist on the suspect's instant dismissal. Or, worse, as his powers over army personnel were virtually absolute, after hearing what the secret service people had to say, he would probably have the suspect clapped into a fortress.

Concealing his feelings with an effort, the Duke made the only reply he could. "Your Excellency, since Her Imperial Highness did me the honour of granting me a commission in her regiment, I felt that now war has come my proper course was to serve in it."

Von Hötzendorf continued to regard him with a chilly stare, and barked: "I thought you were by birth a Frenchman, and so half a foreigner?"

De Richleau knew that he was not up against a Count Tisza, from whom he could expect a sympathetic hearing if he attempted to explain his anomalous position: moreover the General's staff were gathered round him listening intently. So in a final effort to save himself, if only temporarily, he resorted to a thoroughly misleading statement:

"It is true that I was born a Frenchman, Excellency; but I long since repudiated that nationality. I bear an Austrian title, and in this emergency I am proud to serve with the Austrian army."

The General's reply was as unexpected as a bolt from the blue. With an impatience that was typical of him, he turned his horse preparatory to riding away, and flung over his shoulder:

"Then you are far too highly qualified to chuck yourself away as a spare sabre in a cavalry regiment. I haven't forgotten our talk on strategy when you lunched with me. I am leaving for my battle headquarters to-morrow morning. My special train will depart from the Arsenal station at six o'clock. Report there at half past five for duty with my operations staff."

As de Richleau rapped out, "*Jawohl, Excellence!*" and saluted the retreating figure of the little General, he could hardly believe that he had heard right. His situation had been extraordinary enough before, but von Hötzendorf's order had made it positively fantastic. Here he was, an enemy alien in Vienna, known to the police, suspected by them of espionage, and allowed a limited liberty only because they had not a strong enough case to contest the demands of a wilful Princess. And now, owing to von Hötzendorf's ignorance of all this, he had suddenly been appointed to the Operations Staff of Supreme Headquarters, where he was bound to learn all the secrets of the Commander-in-Chief of the Austro-Hungarian armies.

About the appointment itself there was nothing at all extraordinary. His wide experience of active warfare made him far better qualified than the great majority of von Hötzendorf's officers to fill such a post and had he been what he seemed, the C.-in-C. would have had every reason to congratulate himself on having secured his services.

But he was not, and he had deliberately misled the General about his nationality; so if the K.S. got to hear of the appointment he would be in the very devil of a mess. Ronge would have a case against him then, with a vengeance. It would be alleged that he had lied with intent to gain possession of military secrets, and whatever he might say to the contrary they would never believe him. In war time, espionage was a capital crime. The false impression he had given to escape being locked up in a fortress might now cost him his life. They might put him up against a brick wall and shoot him.

CHAPTER XXII

WHICH ROAD HOME ?

As the Duke rode slowly back to the barracks, he wondered what on earth he should do. Since he had told von Hötzendorf that he was proud to be serving with the Austrian army, he could not possibly refuse the appointment without an explanation; and neither Ilona's honorary commission nor Major Ronge's complaisance would prevent a martinet like the little General from having him locked up for wearing an Austrian uniform under false pretences. If he deliberately missed the train that would only be to postpone the issue, as von Hötzendorf would have him sent for. He could elude the C.-in-C. by disappearing but he had made no preparation for such a move, so that would be to take a big risk of being caught by Ronge's police. The only really safe way in which he could now keep clear of von Hötzendorf's unwelcome attentions seemed to be to go to the K.S. Chief, tell him what had happened, and ask to be put back into prison.

But de Richleau was not the man to adopt such a solution. The C.-in-C.'s train was leaving from the military station inside the Arsenal, so no railway police would be there to watch its departure, and if he said nothing of his appointment to his brother officers it was unlikely that Ronge would hear of it, at least for several days. His people would report the suspect's disappearance, but the situation would then be no different from what it would have been had he left Vienna with his regiment. And if he went with von Hötzendorf his prospects of getting away into Russian-held territory would be much the same. He realized that he would be taking his life in his hands from the moment he stepped aboard the C.-in-C.'s train but, as the only alternative to going back to prison, he decided it would be worth it.

That night he made his preparations. Unpacking a roll of bandage and a miniature automatic that he had bought when getting together his war equipment, he knotted the bandage into a neat shoulder sling which would enable him to carry the little weapon concealed beneath his coat, under his left armpit. From next morning on, he intended to wear it regularly until he was out of danger; as he felt that from the moment he left the barracks he must consider himself to be at war with the K.S., and he did not mean to be arrested and tried as a spy without putting up a fight. Having packed the rest of his war kit, he wrote a short note to leave for Prince Thurn und Taxis, excusing his abrupt departure on the grounds that he had been ordered without warning to proceed on a mission of a highly secret nature, and asking that his luggage should be sent to Sacher's to await further instructions. Then he set his alarm clock for four o'clock and went to bed.

When he woke in the morning, as soon as he had dressed, he carried his kit downstairs, telephoned for a taxi and, when it came to the door of the officers' quarters, ordered the driver to take him to the *Westbahnhof*, to which he would have gone had he been heading for Switzerland. There, he changed taxis, taking a second one to the *Sudbahnhof*, which was the terminus for Italy, and thence, having muddled his trail as well as he could, he took a third one round to the Arsenal.

In spite of the early hour, the headquarters block was already a hive of activity. Officers and orderlies were hurriedly loading kit, files, stationery, food, and other impedimenta on to the special train that was drawn up in a nearby siding. A corporal piloted the Duke through them to a waiting-room, and soon afterwards an A.D.C. appeared, who took him upstairs to a mess where von Hötzendorf was drinking coffee with several senior officers.

Among them was the elderly Archduke Frederick, who belonged to a cadet branch of the Imperial family. He was extremely short-sighted, wore side-whiskers in imitation of the Emperor, and had the reputation of being almost childishly simple. The Archduke Charles, now Heir Apparent, had left a week earlier for the temporary battle H.Q. at Teschen, but he was considered to be too young to be given Supreme Command of the armies; so, owing to Franz Ferdinand's assassination, this poor nit-wit, Frederick, had been entrusted with the task of maintaining the glories of the Habsburgs in the field. But for all practical purposes von Hötzendorf filled the role of Commander-in-Chief, and was referred to by his staff as 'the C.-in-C'. He greeted de Richleau with abrupt affability, presented him to the Archduke, to his Chief of Staff, General Count Bellegarde, and to the head of his Operations Section, a Colonel Pacher, under whom it had already been decided that the Duke should work.

Pacher was a squarely built man of middle height. His blue eyes were evidently weak, as he wore thick lensed pince-nez; but he had a broad brow and good features. De Richleau put him down at once as either an officer who had risen from the ranks, or one of bourgeois origin; but it did not surprise him to find such a type on the C.-in-C.'s staff. Unlike the Germans, the Austrian and Hungarian nobility felt so secure in the antiquity of their lineage that they gave themselves no airs and were always willing to mix freely with men of humbler birth; so there was no caste jealousy in the Austrian army and many middle-class men like Pacher rose in it to hold high ranks. He said at once that he was already overburdened with work, so would be delighted to have the Duke's assistance, then took him downstairs and had his kit stowed on the train.

It consisted of five coaches: a restaurant car, two sleeping cars, two fitted up as conference rooms and offices, and, in addition, a baggage wagon and horse boxes. At six o'clock precisely, with everyone who remained on the platform standing rigidly at the salute, it steamed out on its way to the C.-in-C.'s battle headquarters.

De Richleau had already learned that these were to be at Przemysl, a large fortress town in Galicia, on the far side of the Carpathians: and the train was hardly clear of Vienna before he began to learn a lot of other things, too. Pacher had at once settled down to work, and was going rapidly through a big pile of situation reports, while nearby two of his juniors were sticking coloured flags in a big map which had been fixed up at one end of the staff car. The map showed the whole of the Dual Monarchy and a considerable portion of all the states adjacent to it. The flags indicated the present location of all the major formations of the Austro-Hungarian armies, and as it was now the 16th of August the great majority of these had reached their battle positions. Before half the flags were in place de Richleau realized that the impetuous von Hötzendorf had kicked off with the wrong foot and was now in a howling mess.

The Duke still had very clearly in his mind the Serbian appreciation of Austria's plans in the event of war, which Dimitriyevitch had given him to read in Belgrade. The key to that had been the deployment of the Austrian 2nd army. If the war were to be against Serbia only, this, the biggest of all the armies, was to be hurled with the weak 5th and 6th against the Serbians: but if the war were to be against Russia and Serbia simultaneously it was to be deployed with the 1st, 3rd and 4th armies on the Russian front. Yet the flags on the map showed that this all-important force was concentrated in the south, along the rivers Save and Danube.

Such a set-up in the face of Russia's might seemed quite inexplicable. De Richleau could attribute it only to an incredibly rash impulse on von Hötzendorf's part to endeavour to crush his small and most loathed enemy even at the risk of the Dual Monarchy being invaded from the north. But the Duke was not supposed to know anything about Austria's pre-war plans so, with a bland air of innocence, he remarked to Colonel Pacher:

"I find it somewhat surprising that nearly half our forces should be employed against Serbia."

The Colonel gave him a worried look. "That is only a temporary measure and was brought about by our inability to foresee the present situation. When we ordered partial mobilization on the 25th of July there was every indication that the Great Powers would succeed in preventing the war from spreading. Naturally we wished to make the conflict with Serbia as brief as possible, so our 2nd army was included in the partial mobilization and despatched south. As it happened that was particularly unfortunate, as two of its four corps were stationed in Bohemia. Not unnaturally, perhaps, learning of our war-like preparations in Prague and on their own borders, the Russians thought we were mobilizing against them, so ordered mobilization along our own frontiers themselves. After that it was found impossible to control events any longer."

'So,' thought the Duke grimly, 'von Hötzendorf's unappeasable hatred of the Serbs had not only been the major cause of the original outbreak of hostilities, but with a criminal disregard of consequences, he had ordered military measures, resulting in the chain of events that had set all Europe ablaze.' But Colonel Pacher was going on:

"By the 31st of July, when Russia ordered general mobilization, it was too late to cancel the movement of the 2nd Army. With your experience of warfare you will know how such things work. We couldn't possibly stop the hundreds of trains full of troops and equipment halfway to their destinations. To have done so would have thrown our whole railway system out of gear and created chaos of the movements of the other Armies. The only thing to do was to let the 2nd Army go on to the Danube and deploy there; then work out an entirely new time-table for re-entraining it and bringing it north to the Russian front. But naturally, that sort of thing takes time, and it will not be ready to start on its northward journey until the 18th."

Recalling Sir Henry Wilson's statement, that the Russian armies would take several days longer to mobilize than those of the Dual Monarchy, de Richleau was delighted to think that von Hötzendorf had already lost his big opportunity and got himself into a glorious muddle. But he said with suitable gravity:

"That seems most unfortunate. I imagine sound strategy would have dictated an immediate offensive against the Russians with everything we could muster while we still had the advantage of numbers; but now it appears unlikely that we shall be able to bring up our 2nd Army in time to participate in the first great battle."

"I fear that is so," the Colonel agreed glumly. "But, of course, we are deriving some compensation from the deployment of the 2nd Army in the south. With his 5th and 6th Armies in Bosnia, General Potiorek could have menaced Serbia only from the west; whereas with the deployment of the 2nd Army to the north, he has been able to do so on two fronts; so the Serbians will be greatly weakened by having to retain forces along the Danube which might otherwise have been used to resist our offensive across the Drina."

"How is it going?"

"It has started well. Potiorek's 5th Army began its advance on the 12th and entered Shabatz almost unopposed. It is now approaching the Jadar. But I am not altogether happy about our future prospects down there. In my view General Potiorek has deployed his 6th Army too far to the south. Of course, he has to deal with the Montenegrins on his right flank and take care of a Serbian division that has moved up from Uzhite; but the trouble is that it is now right out of touch with the 5th. When the 2nd is withdrawn and the Voyvode Putnik realizes that he has nothing to fear from that direction, he will be able to oppose our 5th Army with practically the whole of his forces. As he has ten divisions in northern Serbia he will outnumber our people, and I fear we may suffer a temporary reverse."

Having regard to the relative quality of the troops engaged, de Richleau had no doubt at all that his new colleague's pessimism was fully justified. By now his professional interest was so fully engaged that he had forgotten not only the danger of his own situation, but its implications; and momentarily found himself thinking as though he were really an Austrian Staff officer. Instinctively, he said:

"In that case General Potiorek should be ordered to wheel the bulk of his 6th Army eastward while there is still time for it to come up alongside the 5th."

Colonel Pacher took off his pince-nez and blinked up at him with a shake of the head. "I see you are as yet unacquainted with one of our major difficulties. After the C.-in-C., General Potiorek is the foremost soldier in our army. In addition, through his friend Baron Bolfas, the Emperor's A.D.C., he has great influence at Court."

"I should have thought his incredibly inefficient arrangements at Sarajevo, having been largely responsible for the Archduke's murder, would have cost him that," put in the Duke.

"No. He is still in high favour, and remains a law unto himself. He will not accept advice from us, let alone orders, and frequently goes over the C.-in-C.'s head. He is doing so at the moment in a matter that is causing us the gravest concern. The 2nd Army has the most positive instructions that in no circumstances is it to cross the Save-Danube line; but he insists that it is essential to the success of his campaign that it should at least make a demonstration in force before leaving, and is doing his utmost to secure the Emperor's consent to involve it."

"I see his point of view; although it is most reprehensible conduct on the part of a junior commander. Of course, if he succeeds, it may give us a victory in the south. But what of the north?"

"It has been decided not to wait for the 2nd Army, and in the course of the next few days we are launching our first offensive."

"Do you consider that really wise?" hazarded the Duke.

"The C.-in-C. is a great believer in the offensive," replied Colonel Pacher non-committally. "Our ten cavalry divisions have already penetrated deep into Russian territory and are meeting with little opposition."

De Richleau had already decided that if he were going to be hanged at all he might as well be hanged for a sheep as a lamb, and indulge his passion for this fascinating game of war by learning all he could; so he asked without hesitation:

"In which direction are we going to strike?"

Colonel Pacher stood up and together they studied the map, which now had a line of pins, varying in thickness, running in a great 'S' bend across its upper half. From Cernowitz, on the Rumanian border, the line was thin, representing a scratch Command which had been got together under General Kövess to cover the upper reaches of the Dniester. It ended a little south of Lemberg, and from in front of that city up to the right bank of the Vistula, across which lay Polish soil, the pins were massed solidly, showing the 3rd, 4th and 1st Armies disposed over a front of a hundred and sixty miles. Then, along the Vistula and in the neighbourhood of Cracow, the line of pins thinned out again where General Kummer, with another scratch Command, was covering the frontier up to the German border. Kummer's Group lay at right angles to the 1st Army along the southern frontier of Poland, and from there the huge Polish salient bellied out westwards. Its arc had pins only at distant intervals to show German Landwehr units under General von Woyrsch which provided a dubious screen for Breslau and Posen. Then, north of the Polish salient, from Thorn across East Prussia to the Baltic, there was a group of flags about the same in number as those representing one of the three main Austrian Armies. It was labelled '8th German Army: General von Prittwitz'.

Placing a square-tipped forefinger in the middle of the gap that separated Warsaw, in the centre of the Polish salient, from the key railway junction of Brest-Litovsk, that lay a hundred miles behind it, Pacher said:

"We intend to strike due north, cut off Warsaw, and join up with the Germans advancing south to meet us from East Prussia."

"And where are the Russians?" inquired the Duke, as not a single flag indicating the enemy had yet been stuck in the map.

"We don't know for certain," the Colonel admitted rather lamely. "We have reason to suppose that there are four Armies in the Southern Group under General Ivanov, which is opposed to us, but we have no definite information regarding their whereabouts."

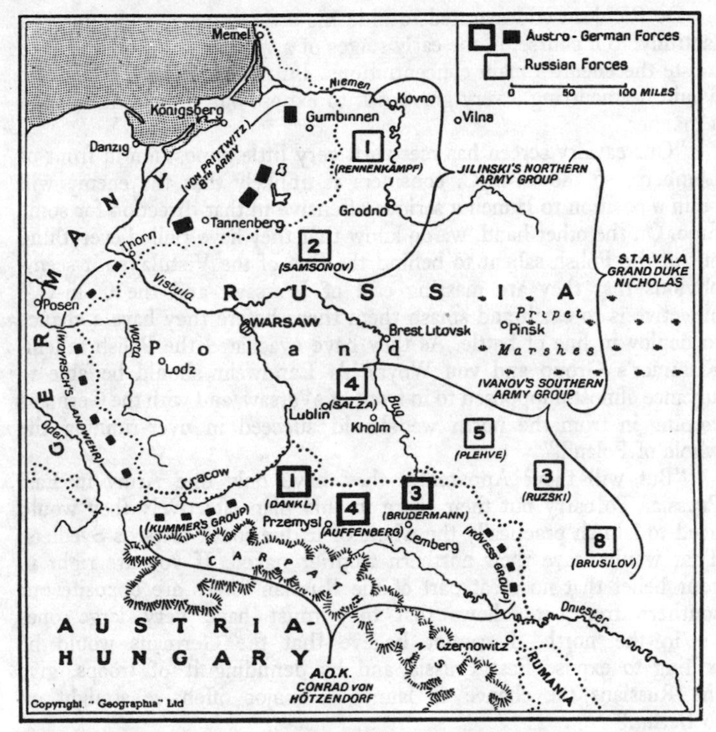

THE DEPLOYMENT OF THE ARMIES ON THE EASTERN FRONT

De Richleau endeavoured to hide his astonishment, and remarked tactfully: "Of course, in the early stages of a war it is always difficult to locate the enemy's main concentrations. But I should have thought it would be incurring a very grave risk to expose our right flank in such a manner."

"Our cavalry screen has met with very little opposition in front of Lemberg, so the C.-in-C. considers it unlikely that the enemy will be in a position to launch a serious offensive in that direction for some time. On the other hand, we do know that they have pulled everything out of the Polish salient to behind the line of the Vistula, so it seems obvious that they are massing east of Warsaw; and the C.-in-C.'s objective is to catch and smash them there before they have a chance to deploy in line of battle. As they have evacuated the Polish salient, Kummer's Group and von Woyrsch's Landwehr should be able to advance almost unopposed to in front of Warsaw, and with the Germans coming in from the north we should succeed in over-running the whole of Poland."

"But will they? Apparently they have only one Army in East Prussia. To carry out their share in this plan effectively they would need to launch practically the whole of it due south towards Syedlets. That would leave their northern frontier naked. If you are right in your belief that no great part of the Russian forces are opposite our southern front, it follows that they must have very large ones up in the north. I cannot believe that the Germans would be willing to expose East Prussia, and by denuding it of troops, give the Russians the chance to launch a major offensive straight on to Berlin."

The Colonel sighed. "I very much fear you are right about that. The Germans promised us their co-operation during peace-time talks, and for the past week the C.-in-C. has been pressing General von Prittwitz to deploy his 8th Army in the manner agreed; but we have so far got no satisfaction from him. In fact, last night a telegram came in from Captain Fleischmann, our liaison officer with the 8th Army, which was most depressing. It reported that the Russians are entering East Prussia from Kovno and Olita, and that von Prittwitz is about to strike at them; and that until he has checked the enemy advance he cannot consider committing any of his troops to a southward drive into Poland."

"Yet the C.-in-C. still intends to launch his offensive almost immediately?"

"Yes. We are hoping that by the 20th or 21st the Germans may have dealt with the Russian incursion into East Prussia, and be ready to help us. If not, the direction of our attack will probably be more to the eastward. But we shall attack all the same. The C.-in-C. is a great believer in the offensive."

With that Colonel Pacher returned to his work and left the Duke to speculate on the information he had just acquired. Since the Russians had withdrawn all their forces from western Poland, and the Austrian cavalry was meeting with little opposition further south, it seemed clear that the Grand Duke Nicholas was acting with commendable caution. It was estimated that Russia's initial mobilization in Europe would put 2,700,000 men in the field, in addition to 900,000 special reserves and fortress troops. Of this colossal force, mainly consisting of highly trained regulars, not one thousandth part could yet have been expended. Obviously the Grand Duke, whom de Richleau knew to be a very capable commander, was holding them well back, so that the bulk of them could be hurled with equal ease at any enemy offensive that developed, whether it came from the north, south or centre. Yet von Hötzendorf, minus his powerful 2nd Army, and now doubtful of the German co-operation on which he had counted, was still determined to butt his head into this Russian hornets' nest.

At lunch, when the Duke exchanged a few words with the C.-in-C., he did not wonder at finding him morose and ill-tempered, nor was he surprised to notice that several of the more capable officers, like Colonel Pacher, looked a little anxious. But the majority were delighted to be on their way to the front and talked of the coming campaign with happy optimism. Few of them had ever seen a shot fired in anger, and they displayed a contempt for the enemy that showed they knew nothing of the bravery and tenacity of the average Russian soldier.

Their attitude to their allies, the Duke found amusing. They looked down on the Germans as a people lacking in taste, refinement and sensibility; yet they were ingenuous enough to admit that they counted on them to pull Austria-Hungary's chestnuts out of the fire for her. Their admiration for the German army was unbounded, and they clearly thought of it as a miracle-machine impervious to all the hazards and human weaknesses affecting the fighting forces of other nations. They were confident that von Prittwitz's single Army in East Prussia could take on any number of Russians, defeat them in a matter of a few days; then, with unruffled precision, about turn to descend on Warsaw; and that the German armies in the west would be in Paris in a month.

There was no news yet of any serious fighting on the Franco-German frontier, although the Germans were reported to have penetrated some eighty miles deep into Belgium. But the 3,000,000 French and German troops that must soon clash head-on in the west had lesser distances to cover than the Austrians and Russians, so the great collision might now occur any day.

De Richleau recalled the paper that Winston Churchill had written at the time of the Agadir crisis in 1911. He had predicted that by the 20th day after mobilization the Germans would have forced the line of the Meuse; but had gone on to point out that by the 40th day they would be so fully extended that, providing the French husbanded their strength in the meantime, they should then have a good prospect of giving battle under favourable conditions *Would* the French husband their strength? The Duke wondered. If so, all might yet be well. If not, he feared that the optimistic prophecies of his Austrian companions, that the Germans would be in Paris by mid-September, stood a very good chance of being fulfilled.

The railway ran almost due north to Teschen on the Polish border, followed it north-east to Cracow, and only then, having rounded the corner of the Carpathian Mountains, ran eastwards through Tarnow to Przemysl. So from mid-morning the train had been right up in the operational zone; but it was not until lunch time that it entered the concentration area of the main armies. From then on every road and by-way it passed contained a slowly moving column of horse-drawn vehicles driven by troops clad in olive green; and at every railway siding stood trains, containing more men, more horses, more guns, more wagons, that had been shunted off the line to let the C.-in-C.'s train through. It seemed as if whole cities must have been denuded of their male populations and traffic so to flood this normally peaceful countryside, and it was an awe-inspiring thought that, within a week, for many thousands of this horde of healthy, cheerful human beings there would be no escape from mutilation, capture or death.

Soon after three o'clock the train arrived at Przemysl. It was a town of some size, having a population of nearly fifty thousand which, even in peace time, was considerably augmented by a large permanent garrison; as it was a major bastion in the northern defence system of the Dual Monarchy and ringed by thirty-six forts mounting between them no less than a thousand guns. On a hill above it stood the ruins of an old castle built by Casimir the Great; but the town itself offered few sights of interest. It was a dreary manufacturing and trading centre, and when a fleet of cars transported the Archduke, von Hötzendorf and their staff to the quarters assigned to them, they found these in keeping with the place.

Colonel Pacher whispered to de Richleau that the C.-in-C. had made it plain that he was most averse to conducting battles from a luxurious headquarters, so his well known asceticism had been duly catered for. They were conducted to ancient bug-ridden barracks furnished only with bare tables, a few score of wooden chairs and straw palliasses to sleep on.

That evening the C.-in-C. held a conference at which de Richleau was not present; but he learned afterwards that important news had come through from Serbia. On the previous day, the advance of the Austrian 5th Army had been held up by exceptionally heavy rain; but this did not appear to have immobilized the Serbians, as General Putnik had moved up in the night and launched a violent assault. In consequence, there had been very heavy fighting on the river Jadar all day, and General Potiorek had appealed through the Emperor for the active assistance of the 2nd Army. Its advance units were already about to entrain for the north, but von Hötzendorf, his wizened face black with rage, had felt compelled to agree to it making a demonstration in force before leaving.

However, de Richleau was far more concerned with his personal problem of getting away through the Russian lines before the K.S. should learn where he had got to; and, on the following morning, when he had a chance to examine the situation maps of the immediate front, he found that this was going to be a more difficult matter than he had supposed.

Owing to the deep penetration of the Austrian cavalry into Russia, it appeared doubtful if there were now any Russian troops within a hundred miles of Przemysl. Long before he could cover that distance on horse-back, his disappearance from H.Q. would be noticed and, fearing an accident had befallen him, his colleagues there would institute widespread inquiries, which would probably result in his being located. Then, he would be forced to return and offer some explanation, and even the outline of a satisfactory one at present exceeded the scope of his imagination. No staff car had been allotted to him, and to attempt to steal one would be a risky business. Even if he succeeded, he would have to abandon it on the edge of the battle zone, as the cavalry patrols would naturally warn any officer in a car not to proceed farther; and the sight of a staff Colonel walking towards the enemy on foot would again require an explanation of a kind that his brain refused to furnish. Anxious as he was to get away, he therefore decided that he would do better to wait, anyhow until that night, on the chance that some matter would arise during the day which would provide him with a legitimate excuse for leaving Headquarters.

Unlike von Hötzendorf, the Duke was not the type of soldier who believes that sleeping hard and eating indifferent food is necessarily good for the brain; and, to his pleasure, he discovered that the Chief of Staff, General Count Bellegarde, was of the same opinion. So he asked his senior out to lunch, and they found a good little restaurant just off the main street of the town.

The Count was a rather ponderous gentleman who owed his appointment to Imperial favour. But he was no fool, and towards the end of the meal it emerged that he was by no means happy about the prospects of the offensive. He declared that it was one thing to fling the main Austrian armies against Warsaw if the Germans were prepared to meet them there, and quite another if they were not.

Suddenly an idea germinated in the Duke's brain, and he said: "We shall certainly be taking a big risk if we go ahead without having more definite information about von Prittwitz's intentions, and in a matter of such vital importance telegrams containing half-promises are anything but satisfactory. Why not send some responsible officer to his H.Q. in East Prussia to impress upon him how essential it is that he should give us his co-operation, and find out definitely what he is prepared to do?" As an apparent afterthought, he added casually: "As I joined the C.-in-C.'s staff only yesterday morning, I could well be spared to undertake such a mission if you considered me suitable."

"That's not a bad idea," the Count nodded. "I'll think about it: and if we don't have better news by to-morrow, I may put it up to the C.-in-C. The thing that troubles me even more, though, is that the Russians probably know the composition of our forces and the broad outline of our plans."

"What on earth leads you to suppose that?" asked the Duke in surprise.

"Why, through that swine, Redl, of course."

"You must forgive my ignorance, but——"

"D'you mean to tell me that you've never heard of Alfred Redl?" The Count's eyes showed astonishment, but after a moment he went on: "Oh well, perhaps we managed to hush the scandal up better than we thought. From 1900 to 1905 Redl was head of the K.S. From then on until less than fifteen months ago he was Chief of Staff to the VIIIth Army Corps which has its H.Q. in Prague. For over ten years he was in the pay of the Russians, and during that time he sold darned near every military secret we've got."

"Good God! It sounds fantastic."

"Well, it's a fact. In the course of a few years he took hundreds of thousand of *kronen* off the Russians. Everyone thought he had private means, but he hadn't—it all came from the Czar's secret intelligence funds. He lived like a Prince: had a house in Vienna, another in Prague, four autos, and after his death they found a hundred and sixty dozen bottles of champagne in his cellar. He not only sold our plans, and every sort of information about railway capacities, weapons, methods of training and war organization, but betrayed all our best agents, many of who were his personal friends, and succeeded in protecting the Russian agents who were spying on us. You see, in his position as Chief of the K.S. everything connected with secret intelligence passed through his hands, so he could sell it if he wished, or suppress it and prevent it going any further if that suited him better."

Temporarily, de Richleau forgot that he was at the moment in the position of a spy himself, and said: "What an unmitigated scoundrel! But as you know all about his activities, I take it he was caught in the end?"

"Yes. Major Ronge got him. Clever fellow, Ronge."

At the name, de Richleau suppressed a guilty start; but the Chief of Staff tipped another dash of Kümmel into his coffee and went on reminiscently: "Some years after Ronge succeeded Redl at the K.S., he had the idea of establishing a secret censorship on suspicious-looking letters posted in frontier towns. Early in March, 1913, two envelopes came in postmarked from a place in East Prussia, and addressed *Opera Ball* 13, *Poste Restante, G.P.O. Vienna.* When opened, it was found that one contained bank-notes to the value of six thousand *kronen* and the other eight thousand, but nothing else. Ronge had a push button fitted up on the postal clerk's desk, which connected with the Police headquarters across the square and rang a bell there. Two detectives were put on to wait until someone claimed the letters; then the clerk would push the button, the bell would ring, and they would run over to see who the claimant was. For weeks those poor devils sat waiting for the bell to ring. But it didn't, and naturally they tried to get Ronge to chuck the matter up. He wouldn't though. Ronge is a very persistent fellow. Once he gets his teeth into a thing, he never lets go."

"Yes," murmured the Duke uncomfortably. "I am sure he must be."

"Anyway, on the eighty-third day—it was a Saturday afternoon towards the end of May—the bell did ring. By that time the detectives had got slack. One was out getting himself a coffee and the other was washing his hands. By the time they reached the post office '*Opera* 13' had claimed his letters and gone. But by an extraordinary stroke of luck they happened to get hold of the taxi driver who had driven him off, and they traced him to the Hotel Klosmer. Even then it might have been one of half a dozen men who had driven up to the hotel in the past half-hour. But in the taxi they had found the grey suède sheath of a pocket knife, and by that they managed to identify him. You can imagine how flabbergasted they must have been when they learned that he was Colonel Redl, the ex-Chief of the K.S."

"What happened?" asked de Richleau, his hand now steady as he lit a cigarette.

"Our C.-in-C. was informed. He nearly had a fit. They say he aged ten years in an hour. He could realize better than anyone else the colossal damage we had sustained. He was faced with the fact that all his work—

the work of a lifetime—was in the hands of the enemy. Redl knew all about his masterpiece—Plan III for our invasion of Serbia, the finest staff study he had ever done. Since the Russians had that, it was a certainty they had passed it on to the Serbs."

The Duke nodded. He knew now how Dimitriyevitch had got the information for that remarkably fine 'appreciation of Austria's intentions in the event of war' that he had been given to read in Belgrade.

"By that time," the Count went on, "the detectives had got red-hot evidence against Redl. While they were shadowing him, he had torn up some papers and thrown the bits away. When pieced together they proved his guilt conclusively. That night the C.-in-C. sent four officers to him. He was given a pistol and invited to commit suicide, which, of course, he did. But, even then, the extent of his treachery was not fully realized. That only emerged when Ronge broke open the cupboards, desks and safe at his house in Prague. They were crammed with records of the stuff he had sold to the Russians. And you know as well as I do that, if a plan falls into the hands of the enemy, it discloses the mind of the Commander who has made it. One can alter plans in detail, but not their main conception. That's what worries me: the thought that, owing to Redl's treachery, that shrewd old fox, Nicholas, must have a darned good idea what we intend to do."

De Richleau made suitable comments, expressing anxiety and distress; and he was more than ever amazed that von Hötzendorf should be proceeding with his offensive. But he felt that, in spite of its unnerving moments, the lunch might prove a very profitable one, as, if his suggestion that he should be sent on a mission to von Prittwitz was adopted, it would offer him the perfect means of getting away.

As soon as he had the opportunity to think the idea over, he saw that it possessed all sorts of possibilities. To start with, it would no longer be necessary for him to get himself captured by the Russians and have to go half round Europe to reach home. Dressed as an Austrian officer, he could travel anywhere in Germany. There would be nothing to stop him heading for the Dutch frontier. It should not be difficult to slip over it, then cross from the Hook to Harwich. And if he could get through in the course of the next week, he should be able to render a considerable service to the allied cause by bringing with him red-hot information about Austria's plans.

On the last count he had no scruples whatever. He had promised both Count Tisza and Ilona that he would not make any use of such information as he had come by in Vienna, and he had every intention of keeping those promises. Further, he had promised Adam Grünne that, while he was with Ilona Theresa's Hussars, he would regard himself as a loyal soldier of the Emperor. He had done so, but was no longer with them. He was under no moral obligation to von Hötzendorf. In fact, although unwittingly, it was the General who had placed his life in jeopardy. If he was caught now, he would undoubtedly be treated as a spy, and, since fate had once more thrust him into the position of one, he felt that it would have been disloyal to his country to refrain from making the most of the unique opportunities he was being given. Had he had the least doubt on the matter, it would have been dissipated by Major Ronge's treatment of him. The Major had first prevented him from getting home, by hitting before the bell went and imprisoning him merely on suspicion, then endeavoured to confine him to Vienna by invisible barriers. Now, his position was similar to that of a prisoner of war who has succeeded in getting himself smuggled out of a barbed wire cage. While escaping through enemy country, it is the duty of such a prisoner to bring back all the information that he can; and de Richleau fully intended to do so.

With this in mind, he spent the afternoon going through a number of Colonel Pacher's papers, ostensibly to equip himself with the knowledge necessary to become a useful assistant; but actually to gather as many facts as he could carry off in his mind. Among other things, he found that von Hötzendorf intended to employ 648 infantry battalions in his offensive. As it was to be on a front of only 150 miles, that meant a thousand men to every quarter of a mile, with forty-eight thousand to spare.

Since there seemed to the Duke every reason to suppose that, within a week, the Russians would prove capable of bringing up an equal number of battalions, it looked as if every hill, wood, field and hedge across a strip of country as long as from London to Manchester must, almost simultaneously, be the scene of charges, counter-charges and bloody encounters. By comparison, the greatest battles of Napoleonic times would be dwarfed into insignificance, and those in which he had taken part himself appear no more than skirmishes. As a trained staff officer, he estimated that the Austrian field dressing stations and hospitals should be prepared to receive not less than one hundred thousand casualties before the end of the month. And the thought appalled him.

Those figures were conservative, as they took no account of the hundreds of Sapper Companies necessary to bridge rivers and streams during the advance, of the Artillerymen required to serve the five thousand guns, or of the eighty thousand Cavalry that were already probing for the enemy. But about the latter most disturbing rumours were now percolating back to Headquarters.

It appeared that the padding in the standard Austrian service saddle had been made too thick for its prolonged use in hot weather. Forced marches under the August sun had resulted in such a high percentage of the horses getting galled backs that many units had become temporarily incapacitated. In some cases the dashing officers who had set out so gaily ten days before, as though about to participate in a glorified hunt, were now even reported to be ignominiously trudging the dirty roads as their troopers led their useless mounts back on foot.

That night more bad news came in. A major battle was now raging on the Jadar, and Potiorek's 5th Army had been so severely mauled that it looked as though it must inevitably suffer a serious reverse. A Division composed mainly of Czechs—who had no stomach for fighting Austria's wars—had stupidly been given the key position of the whole battlefield. They had been completely routed and taken to their heels, thus exposing the entire centre of the front to collapse. In this emergency Potiorek had called upon the 2nd Army to convert its demonstration into a full scale offensive against the Serbian flank. Realizing some immediate action to be the only hope of saving his superior from complete defeat, the Commander of the 2nd Army had thrown in his IVth Corps, and was now frantically wiring to know if he was to continue the action, or pull it out in order to bring it north next day and leave Potiorek to his fate. Meanwhile Potiorek was imploring the Emperor to let him engage the whole of the 2nd Army in the south.

After a spate of angry telegrams, von Hötzendorf's insistence that the 2nd Army should entrain for the north was agreed to in principle; but to his fury he was compelled to consent to its IVth Corps being left behind until Potiorek could get up his roving 6th Army and close the broken front of the 5th.

Everyone at Supreme Headquarters, except the Duke, was naturally much depressed by these tidings of the first big battle of the war, and no good news came in from von Prittwitz to offset them. To von Hötzendorf's repeated appeals that he should at least make a demonstration in force into Poland towards Syedlets, the German only replied that his intelligence reported two Russian armies to be advancing against him, so until the situation clarified he could do nothing.

On hearing this, de Richleau again broached the project of his being sent to endeavour to secure von Prittwitz's co-operation—this time to Colonel Pacher. Like General Count Bellegarde, the Colonel thought it a promising idea, but proved reluctant to approach von Hötzendorf on it that night as he was in such an evil temper.

Next morning found the Duke a very worried man. Forty-eight hours had now elapsed since he had left Vienna, and for a good part of that time it seemed certain that Major Ronge's sleuths would have been trying to locate him. He thought it unlikely that they would succeed in tracing him through their own efforts for some time to come, but his danger now increased with every hour that he remained at Supreme Headquarters.

It was his titles and connections that had given him such unrivalled opportunities for espionage; but they could also prove a menace to his safety. The greater part of three months in Vienna had made him a well known figure in society there. He realized that scores of people he had never met must know him by sight. Przemysl was already crammed with officers, and half a dozen trains had followed that of the C.-in-C., bringing the additional staffs that always congregate round a main Headquarters—vets, doctors, nurses, railway experts, paymasters, provost-marshals, padres, war-correspondents and camera men. It needed only one of them to recognize him, mention his presence there in a letter to Vienna, and for its recipient to noise the matter abroad, so that the K.S. got hold of it, for his goose to be cooked. A telegram from Ronge would arrive, as a result of which he would find himself facing a court martial on a capital charge.

For that reason he had intended to clear out the previous night at latest, and had been tempted into remaining only by the prospect of his suggestion that he should be sent as an envoy to East Prussia being accepted. The advantages of departing openly in a staff car that had been placed at his disposal, over trying to steal one, were enormous; but, when he got up that morning, he decided that if his scheme did not mature that day, it would be too big a risk to remain longer, and he must make a moonlight flitting the coming night.

The morning passed without incident; so did most of the afternoon, and he was beginning to contemplate seriously his hundred mile dash towards the Russian lines when, at five o'clock, the C.-in-C. sent for him. He had hardly saluted the grim little figure before he was told, to his great delight, that his proposal had found favour. But his elation was short lived. Two minutes later he learned that the mission was not to be given to him. He was only to accompany Colonel Baron Ungash-Wallersee upon it.

"The Baron is one of the Archduke's people," said von Hötzendorf. his grey eyes showing his annoyance, "and His Highness insists that he shall head the mission. But he's a born fool. That's why I am sending you with him."

De Richleau's brain proceeded to revolve at top speed, as he began to assess how the presence of this unwelcome companion would affect his own plans. In any case he would have had to set out for East Prussia but, at the first suitable opportunity, he had intended to give his chauffeur fresh instructions to drive him straight across Germany to Aix-la-Chapelle. He had selected his destination because it not only lay close to the Dutch border, but also happened to be the Kaiser's war headquarters, which would provide a perfect explanation for the change of direction in the mind of his military driver.

Now, that simple, direct and comfortable method of reaching neutral Holland was out of the question. Instead, he was faced with three alternatives. One, he could steal the car at the first chance that offered, and make off in it: two, he could desert the Baron *en route* and trust to other means of transport for getting away: three, he could accompany the Baron to von Prittwitz's H.Q. and produce some excuse for leaving the Baron there.

Courses one and two both presented the problem of whether he dared risk a dash across Germany as a fugitive, or had better revert to his old plan of endeavouring to reach the Russian lines. In both, the Baron would set up a hue and cry after him within an hour or two of his disappearance, and if he stole the car it would probably be identified and stopped by the military police before he had covered fifty miles. If he left without the car, he would still be in Austrian uniform, so easily identifiable in Germany, and the German police network was so efficient that his chances of getting through to Holland would be far from good. To head for Russia while still in the Austrian battle zone, therefore, seemed to offer the best prospect: but that meant taking the long road home, and for the past twenty-four hours he had become increasingly set on taking the short one, if by any possible means he could do so. Course three still offered that, although it meant going round via East Prussia, so he decided to take it.

While these swift thoughts had been passing through his mind, von Hötzendorf had been explaining the objects of the mission in detail. The Duke waited until he had finished, then, with his own secret plan still in view, said deferentially:

"Permit me to make a suggestion, Excellency. General von Prittwitz has so far proved most unresponsive to our appeals. Has not the time come when you would be fully justified in going over his head and putting the matter direct to General von Moltke?"

"I have already," replied the General. "But von Moltke's replies are equally unsatisfactory. He says that Germany's major plan demands the deployment of six-sevenths of the total German forces in France and Belgium, with the object of the swift annihilation of the French army by overwhelming odds. Until that has been achieved, he can spare nothing further for the eastern front. He is even urging me to take the weight off von Prittwitz by adhering to our original plan of launching our offensive due north, which I am reluctant to do if the Germans are unable to carry out their part of the plan by coming to meet us."

"In that case, Excellency, I feel more strongly than ever that von Prittwitz should be by-passed in favour of direct negotiations with von Moltke. Could you not propose a bargain on the lines that, if he will order von Prittwitz to deploy half his forces southward into Poland, you will strike northward to meet him. But, failing that, you must adopt a more cautious policy and strike east?"

Von Hötzendorf considered for a moment, then he said: "In any case, I do not wish to postpone the launching of the offensive after the 22nd, but I shall keep its direction open until the last possible moment. To-day is the 18th. By the 20th von Prittwitz may have dealt with the Russian threat to his northern flank, and be in a position to wheel south. Therefore, it would be best to confer with him first. But I agree that, should he still refuse us his assistance, it would be worth attempting to get von Moltke to order him to do so."

"Then your Excellency desires that, after Colonel Baron Ungash-Wallersee and I have conferred with General von Prittwitz, we should, if necessary, proceed to German Main Headquarters at Aix-la-Chapelle?"

The General's eyes narrowed. "No. I am committed only to sending the Baron to von Prittwitz. The old fool is quite incapable of dealing with those hard-headed Germans on the Kaiser's staff, and will only make a mess of things. If you can get no satisfaction from von Prittwitz, let the Baron return and report to me. Proceed on your own to German Main Headquarters and do the best you can. I'll give you a separate letter for von Moltke. But this is between ourselves. Not a word of this must reach the Archduke, or he will insist on his old crony accompanying you on the second stage of your journey."

"*Jawohl, Excellence!*" In a high good humour, de Richleau clicked his heels and saluted. Such an arrangement could not have suited him better, had he devised it himself. Moreover, if he played his cards carefully, it looked as if he stood a very good chance of so manipulating matters that von Hötzendorf could be induced to adhere to his original plan of attacking in a northerly direction, in which case the Austro-Hungarian armies would court a much greater risk of sustaining a major defeat. In any case, he felt entitled to congratulate himself on the success of the clever little intrigue, which would result in his being able to leave in safety and comfort, instead of having to take the long road home through Russia.

But he was soon to learn that the shortest road is not necessarily the safest.

CHAPTER XXIII

THE ARMIES CLASH

An hour later, while the bright light of the summer evening still lingered, the Duke was on his way out of Przemysl. He knew that he could not consider himself really safe until he had left the German headquarters in East Prussia as, if the K.S. learned that he had joined von Hötzendorf's staff, a telegram ordering his arrest could still catch him there. But as he had spent only a bare two days in Przemysl he felt that the number of people who knew that he had been in the city must still be comparatively small. One or two of them might yet mention his presence when writing to Vienna, but such a piece of social gossip was of no particular interest now that he had left, so the odds seemed against it getting as far as Major Ronge. With heart-felt thankfulness at being able to depart in easy circumstances and with such good prospects of getting safely to Holland, he decided that he must make the best of the companion fate had forced on him. And he soon found that he might have fared worse.

Colonel Baron Lanzelin Ungash-Wallersee was a final product of the once sound, but long since outworn, feudal system that was now so near dissolution. In return for certain services and rents in kind, his remote ancestors had given the people on their lands a rough justice, led them on cattle raids, defended their homes and fed them in time of famine. The present holder of the title still owned the lands, but neither he nor his predecessors in the past several hundred years had done anything very much for anybody. He was, nevertheless, a very kind and charming person. His many estates in various parts of the Empire totalled in area that of an English county. They had been accumulated through many generations by a long series of suitable matrimonial alliances, and safeguarded by a succession of entails that precluded any heir from succeeding should he be so misguided as to insist on marrying a lady whose coat of arms embodied less than sixteen quarterings. It was this principle which had resulted in nearly all the higher nobility of Central Europe being related to one another, and the Baron's veins, therefore, metaphorically contained blood of an unadulterated blue.

He was, almost needless to remark, immensely rich. He owned three castles, a palace in Vienna, another in Budapest, a villa in the south of France, a two thousand ton yacht in the Adriatic, and several hunting lodges. He also paid the rent of a number of flats for young ladies, who spent fifty weeks out of most years entertaining more sprightly, if less blue-blooded, gentlemen.

As a young subaltern in a crack cavalry regiment, he had often given parties that had gone on for several days and nights in succession, climbed the tower of the *Michaelerkirche*, and ridden his favourite charger up three flights of stairs to his mistress' bedroom. Up to the age of thirty, he had managed to keep fairly even in the number of stags he had shot and the number of young women who had succumbed to his advances. After that, the stags took a permanent lead, but he still rolled a bucolic eye whenever he saw a good-looking girl. He had not the faintest interest in either art or politics, and knew less than most corporals about warfare. He had never served his country as diplomat, jurist or statesman. On the other hand, he had drunk more champagne than would have filled the giant tun at Heidelberg, had eaten more caviare than would have served to stuff a whale, and had all his clothes made in London. In short, from his youth onward he had, within his extremely limited mental horizons, enjoyed all the fun he might have had if he had been a lesser monarch-cum-millionaire, without the necessity of devoting a single hour to business or suffering the tedious duties and anxieties inseparable from royalty.

At the present time he was just over sixty, with a square-shouldered stalwart body that he had kept in passably good shape. His skin was slightly mottled, but he was handsome in his way and, at first sight, his striking head belied its emptiness. The blue eyes had for so long had the habit of command that they gave the impression that he was not to be trifled with, and his sensual mouth was hidden by an impressive grey moustache and beard. The former curled gracefully upward, the latter was square-cut and parted in the centre, to match the parting of the hair on his head which ran right down to the nape of his neck—an eccentricity impossible to any man who lacked a valet to brush his hair every morning.

The Baron's valet was, of course, travelling with them, although temporarily disguised as a soldier, and now also filling the rôle of servant to the Duke for the duration of their mission. So was the Baron's private No. 1 chauffeur, and they were in the most recently purchased of his fifteen cars, which he had ordered up from Vienna. As he sat there, obviously thinking of nothing in particular, except possibly that it was rather a bore to have been sent to see some upstart German General, he looked and was as clean as a new pin. He smelt faintly of eau-de-Cologne mingled with the aroma of fine Havana cigars. Like most of the great Austro-Hungarian nobles, he was known by the diminutive of his first christian name—his friends called him Lanzi.

The roads to the west were still packed with columns of olive-grey troops, guns, ammunition wagons and fodder carts, all moving up towards the front; so the powerful, smooth-running car could be let out only on short infrequent stretches. In consequence, it took them six hours to cover the eighty odd miles to Tarnow, and there the Colonel Baron decreed that they should sup and sleep. As a well-stocked picnic basket had provided them with dinner, they were in no real need of food; so, using the urgency of their mission as an excuse, the Duke suggested that he should relieve the chauffeur at the wheel and that they should push on. But Lanzi Ungash-Wallersee would not hear of it.

He took occasion to point out that their mission was of no vital importance, as the Germans would make mincemeat of both the French and the Russians anyway. That, he seemed to think, was the only purpose for which an all-wise Providence had created Germany. He added that he had had it from a fellow in the *Kriegsministerum* in Vienna that the war would be over in three months, and indicated that he would have cause to feel considerable annoyance should it last longer, as he had already selected the colours and stuffs with which he planned to have some of the principal rooms in his villa at Nice re-decorated for the coming winter season.

Although it was after midnight, he had most of the staff at the best hotel roused to attend him, and after one glance they willingly ran to supply his requirements. He said little, but what he did say was quietly and pleasantly spoken. His name, and one look at his slightly protruding blue eyes above the beautifully barbered moustaches and beard, were sufficient. Lesser beings were turned out of the best rooms at a moment's notice, the chef stoked up his kitchen fires, the wine-waiter produced his best Hock, and the prettiest chambermaid was chucked under the chin, then told to get into the great man's bed and warm it.

To de Richleau he could not have been more charming. He would have behaved with easy friendliness to an ex-ranker had such an officer been sent with him, but he was obviously pleased to have a companion whom he regarded as one of his own kind. The de Richleaus were, of course, mere parvenu compared with his own House and its eight hundred years of ancestry. But he had a vague idea that they had made their mark on French history, and he recalled having once participated in a very jolly drinking bout with the Duke's father. The cigars he produced after their late supper were enormous torpedo-shaped affairs which had been specially manufactured for him in Havana and, connoisseur as de Richleau was, he had rarely smoked anything better.

They did not get to bed till two o'clock, Lanzi remarking, as they went upstairs, that he thought about half past nine would be quite early enough to start in the morning. The Duke made no protest. He understood well enough now why von Hötzendorf had no confidence in the Colonel Baron Ungash-Wallersee as an emissary, and pitied any C.-in-C. who had the services of such a man forced upon him by an idiot Prince representing an effete Imperial House. But the last thing he intended was any endeavour to persuade von Prittwitz to aid the Austro-Hungarian offensive, and the longer they delayed in getting to his headquarters the less likely it was that their mission would prove effective. So he considered any small additional risk that he might be running himself, owing to dilatoriness on the journey, amply justified.

Next morning, therefore, he did not suggest, as he would have done had his heart been in the matter, that, as all Russian troops were said to have been withdrawn from the Polish salient, they should chance a dash across it. And it did not seem to have entered Lanzi's well-groomed head that he was in any way called on to risk his life or liberty in an attempt to expedite the service of his country. Instead, they continued their leisurely, semi-royal progress for the next two days round the vast arc, by way of Cracow, Ratibor, Breslau, Posen and Thorn to von Prittwitz's headquarters at Wartenburg.

The headquarters was situated in an old manor house some way outside the town. With the usual German speed and efficiency, a number of hutments had already been erected near it, to accommodate the less important members of the staff, and a railway line laid up to within a few hundred yards of the building, so that the Army Commander could come and go in his special train with a minimum of inconvenience.

The Baron and the Duke arrived in the evening on Thursday the 20th, just in time for dinner. They were received with due deference by the Austro-Hungarian liaison officer, Captain Fleischmann, and, after a quick wash and brush up, were taken to the drawing-room of the house, which was now being used as a mess ante-room. There, they were duly presented to the fat, monocled Commander of the German 8th Army and several of his principal staff officers.

There was a great deal of clicking of heels, bowing sharply from the waist, and rapping out of surnames. Then they went in to dine. Von Prittwitz placed his distinguished guests on his left and right, but he seemed extremely ill at ease, made no effort at conversation, and ate almost nothing. Only about half the places at the long table were occupied, and most of the officers present ate rapidly in silence. After a bare, uncomfortable quarter of an hour, the General stood up, asked his guests to excuse him from discussing the situation with them that night, and said he would see them in the morning. Within another five minutes all his staff had followed him, leaving Fleischmann to look after the visitors.

On their return to the ante-room they found it empty, and settled down in arm-chairs round a wood fire that was smouldering in the grate. Fleischmann brought a bottle of brandy and some glasses over from a side table, and old Lanzi produced his enormous cigars. Then he said to the liaison officer:

"The Germans always were a set of boors, but there must be some special reason for this shocking display of ill-manners. Why are they behaving in such an extraordinary way?"

"It is the battle, *Herr Oberste Baron*," replied Fleischmann, pulling a face. "The XVIIth Corps under von Mackensen is reported to have been completely smashed and is in full retreat."

"What!" exclaimed Lanzi. "It's not possible! You cannot really mean that those Russian oafs have inflicted a defeat on the German army?"

"It's not quite as bad as that—yet. The Ist Corps under von François have done brilliantly, and von Below's Ist Reserve Corps have done pretty well too; so the position may be stabilized to-morrow. But there is certainly cause for grave anxiety."

"We know next to nothing about this front," the Duke remarked, "so it would be best if you tell us what has happened from the beginning."

"*Jawohl, Herr Oberst Graf*." The Captain bowed. "This, then, was the position. You will know that the central section of this front has a natural defence consisting of the Masurian Lakes and marshes which extend for about sixty miles, with the fortress of Lotzen in their centre. That barrier cannot be crossed, so to invade East Prussia the enemy forces must strike north of it through Gumbinnen or south through Tannenberg; or, should they do both, they must for some days be separated by the lakes, so that neither half of them could come to the assistance of the other."

De Richleau nodded. "Count Schlieffen saw that. When he made his major plan against France he made a subsidiary plan for this front. He laid it down that the remaining eighth of the Germany army should deploy centrally behind the lake screen, so that its whole weight could be thrown either north or south against the first Russian army to cross the frontier. He assumed that the Russians would split their forces, so the Germans would be equal in numbers to the first invading army and be able to defeat it. Then, with the excellent system of lateral railways they have built here for the purpose, they could switch their forces and take on the second Russian army with an equally good hope of defeating that."

"Exactly!" agreed Fleischmann. "And the Russians *have* split their forces. Their 1st Army under General Rennenkampf, is advancing against us from Kovno in the north, and their 2nd, based on Warsaw, is coming up from the south. Unfortunately, von Prittwitz lacked the courage to leave one of his flanks temporarily exposed: so, instead of following Schlieffen's plan, he spread his army out. He sent his Ist Corps, under von François, right up north; his XXth Corps, under Scholtz, down to the south; and kept von Mackensen and von Below with the XVIIth and Ist Reserve Corps in the centre behind the lake barrier."

"He must have been crazy," grunted the Duke. "Splitting his forces like that meant that whichever of his flank corps was attacked it would have to fight four times its numbers."

"That would have been the case if it had not been for General von François. He is a real tiger. I wish to God that he was C.-in-C. instead of the fat boy—that's what everyone here calls von Prittwitz. Anyhow, when Rennenkampf's army started to pour over the frontier on the 17th and 18th, von François came here and raised hell. Apparently, von Prittwitz's orders are to hold the Russians as well as he can, but not to commit himself so heavily as to risk a major defeat, which would prevent him from retiring behind the Vistula and stabilizing a front there. He wanted to retreat at once, but von François became downright insubordinate and refused to let him. I gather there was a terrific scene, and von François got the best of it. He not only bullied the C.-in-C. into ordering the XVIIth Corps north, but the Ist Reserve as well, with the intention that all three Corps should stand and fight at Gumbinnen."

"Now let's hear about the battle," put in Lanzi, helping himself to another brandy.

"It was joined at dawn to-day, *Herr Oberste Baron.* Von François's Corps was farthest north, of course, and he took the Russians by surprise. They say he gave them a terrific pasting, then succeeded in getting a cavalry division round their flank, which is playing merry hell with their transport and communications. Von Below, at the other end of the front, also did well, and drove back the Russians opposite him. It's the centre that is the trouble. Apparently, von Mackensen failed to achieve surprise and found the Russians on his front dug in. Nevertheless, he sent his troops in to attack them. They were shot down in droves. The survivors panicked and fled. He and his staff went up to the front and tried to stop the rout themselves. But it was no good. Our centre has been broken wide open."

Lanzi simply could not understand it, but de Richleau could. He knew that the bravest and best disciplined troops in the world could not stand up to machine gun fire from prepared positions, and that von Mackensen was not the only General who would learn that before he was much older.

They talked on for another hour. Occasionally one or two officers came in, had a quick drink and hurried out again. Every room in the house was ablaze with light; orderlies continually scurried up and down stairs and along the corridors. Outside, in the broad sweep of the drive, motors and motor-cycles constantly came and went. It was about a quarter past ten when the plump figure of the C.-in-C. appeared in the doorway. Only the Duke and the two Austrians were in the room at the time. They at once stood up, and de Richleau said:

"May we offer our sympathy to your Excellency on this temporary set-back. It is disappointing, but more than offset by the fine performance of your Ist Corps."

Von Prittwitz made no direct reply. He stood glowering at them for a moment, then he barked: "*Herrshaft!* It is useless for you to remain here. You are wasting your time. I have just received news that General Samsonov's army has crossed our southern frontier in force. I have no intention of allowing myself to be cut off. I have just ordered an immediate retirement to behind the Vistula."

Snapping his heels together, he made them a jerky bow, turned on his heel, and marched off.

"Behind the Vistula!" gasped Lanzi, his blue eyes popping. "But that means giving up the whole of East Prussia. He must be out of his senses."

"To order a retreat of a hundred and fifty miles after only one day of battle is certainly an extraordinary step," the Duke agreed. "Of course, with practically the whole of his army intact, he will be quite safe there. But I wonder what All Highest War Lord Willi Hohenzollern will have to say about this. I shouldn't like to be in von Prittwitz's shoes when he has to explain matters to his Kaiser."

Lanzi puffed out a cloud of blue smoke. "Well, it seems this is the end of our mission. We'd better start back tomorrow."

"I suppose you had, but I shall not have the pleasure of accompanying you," the Duke said quietly. "Our C.-in-C. asked me to go on from here with a personal letter to General von Moltke." He turned to Captain Fleischmann and added: "Perhaps you would be good enough to arrange transport for me to Aix-la-Chapelle."

"*Jawohl, Herr Oberste Graf,*" replied the Captain.

After a moment, Lanzi said: "You'll have to go via Berlin, won't you? I think I'll go with you that far. As I can't take back any German proposals for assisting our offensive, it won't make any odds if I don't turn up at Przemysl for a few days. It will be quite enough to send a wire, saying there is nothing doing. A visit to Berlin will take me only two or three hundred miles out of my way, and I'm paying the rent for a flat there for a pretty little Fraulein. It's quite a long time since I've seen her, and this seems too good a chance to be missed."

"That's just as you wish," smiled the Duke. And, although neither of them could know it, this casual decision to spend a night with a young trollop whom he had almost forgotten, was to cost Baron Lanzelin Ungash-Wallersee his life.

But they were not destined to leave for Berlin next morning. At nine o'clock Captain Fleischmann brought them a message that General Hoffmann, the Chief of the Operations Section of the 8th Army H.Q., would like to see them, and took them to a big room at the back of the house, in which the General was working.

He was a square-shouldered man with a broad forehead, dark hair and a small moustache. He looked as if he needed a wash, and his eyes were a little bleary: but he spoke with crisp decision.

"*Herrschaft!* The C.-in-C. is indisposed and has asked me to see you for him. It is most regrettable that you should have arrived here at such an unfortunate moment for us, but I can assure you that our situation is by no means as desperate as it appears. You have probably heard rumours this morning that a retirement to the Vistula has been ordered. They are entirely without foundation."

"The C.-in-C. told us himself last night that he had ordered it," put in Lanzi, with a regal disregard for tact.

"Oh, did he?" the German looked momentarily disconcerted. "Well, as a matter of fact, he did. But my colleagues and I persuaded him that it would be impossible to carry out such a movement without first fighting another battle. General Samsonov's army is eighty miles nearer to the Vistula than we are, and would cut us off before we could get there. If you will give me your attention for a moment, I will show you what we intend to do."

Standing up, General Hoffmann turned to a big map behind him, on which both German and Russian formations were marked. Pointing to a group of flags to the north of Gumbinnen, he said:

"There are our Ist Corps and a Cavalry Division, under General von François. With those forces he inflicted a severe defeat yesterday on Rennenkampf's right wing. By it he has carried out, to a degree that I consider adequate, the first move in Count Schlieffen's Plan II. General von Mackensen's XVIIth Corps in the centre was very roughly handled, but it has been rallied a few miles back, and he has succeeded in closing the gap. To the south, General von Below's Ist Reserve Corps inflicted heavy losses on the enemy. In consequence, I do not believe that Rennenkampf will be ready to strike again for some days to come."

He coughed, then went on: "Now, these are our intentions. Without a moment's delay, we shall bring the Ist Corps back by rail to Königsberg, down the Baltic to Marienburg, then south-east through Deutch

Elau. The XVIIth Corps will make a flank march behind the lakes in the same direction. The Ist Reserve Corps will follow it, and both will come up on the left of the XXth Corps, which has not yet been in action. So, with our four Corps deployed in the neighbourhood of Tannenberg, we shall meet Samsonov and smash him."

"I find your proposals most interesting, *Herr General*," murmured the Duke. "But are you quite happy that General von François will be able to extricate himself for this new move?"

"Yes!" came the unhesitating reply. "I am confident of it. He has already shown qualities of Generalship which have proved an inspiration to all who know him."

"This move of his Ist Corps, by rail, though? They will have to come nearly two hundred miles, from one end of the front to the other. With their guns and war stores that is a terrific undertaking. Most staffs would need a week to work it out before the troops could begin to entrain."

General Hoffmann smiled and stroked the dark stubble on his chin. "My assistants and I worked all through the night. It is completed."

Turning back to the map, he went on quickly, "Now, *Herrschaft*, for the broader picture. You will see that the Grand Duke has divided his forces into two Army Groups. His 1st and 2nd Armies, under General Jilinski, are opposed to us on this front. His 4th, 5th, 3rd and 8th, in that order, are massed under General Ivanov from opposite Przemysl down to the Rumanian border. But, observe, *Herrschaft*, in the Polish salient he has nothing but covering troops and the skeleton of a 9th Army which is reported to be forming behind Warsaw. If General von Hötzendorf strikes east, he will come up against the main forces of General Ivanov's southern Army Group. But if he strikes north, he will be opposed only by the flank of the 4th Army. By adopting the latter course he can be of the greatest possible assistance to us, and, I hope, by the time he reaches Warsaw, we to him. For we shall no longer be facing east ourselves, but south; and immediately we have defeated Samsonov's army we can march straight on to form a junction with your forces."

De Richleau saw at once what this brilliant staff officer was up to. Such a man would never have disclosed his plans so fully to his allies unless he thought that by doing so he could get something out of them. He wanted the Austrians to attack north so that, although distant, their line of advance would threaten Samsonov's rear, and possibly cause him to break off his battle with the re-deployed German 8th Army. What Hoffmann had deliberately refrained from pointing out was that immediately this 8th Army was relieved from Samsonov's pressure in

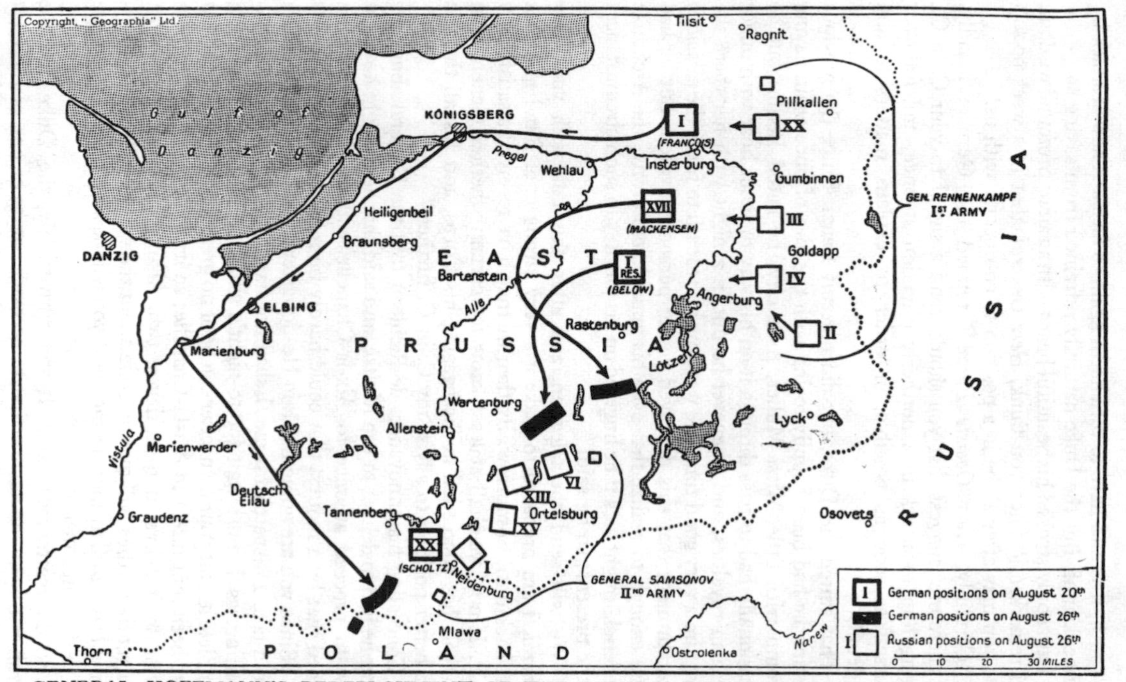

GENERAL HOFFMANN'S REDEPLOYMENT OF THE GERMAN EIGHTH ARMY AFTER GUMBINNEN

the south, it would have to turn north again to face a renewed attack by Rennenkampf. But the Duke naturally refrained from saying so.

Lanzi only stroked his beautiful beard with an air of profound wisdom, and remarked: "Then you think, *Herr General*, that in a week or so's time you may after all be in a position to co-operate with us?"

"Certainly, *Herr Oberste Baron*," replied the German blandly. "I, therefore, suggest that you should send a signal to your C.-in-C., urging him to attack in a northerly direction at once, and follow it yourself as soon as possible, in order to explain matters to him in detail."

That suited the Duke, but did not suit Lanzi. Since the previous evening he had been happily toying with the idea of once again having a romp with little Mitzi Muller. As a city, he hated Berlin; but he occasionally had to pass through it on his way to shoot boar with minor German royalties, and whenever he put in a night with her there she gave him a very good time. He was now most loath to forgo the salacious entertainment that this depraved young person provided. But he had sense enough to realize that even his amiable old crony, the Archduke Frederick, might kick if he lingered on his journey in such circumstances as the present; so he said:

"We will send the telegram, and after this talk with you, *Herr General*, I am prepared to make it a very strong one. But I shall not start back until to-morrow. By then we may have received a satisfactory reply. If not, we shall at least know for certain whether General von François has succeeded in disengaging his Corps, and I shall then be in a better position to advise my C.-in-C. further."

Concealing his annoyance, de Richleau told the General about the letter he had to deliver to von Moltke, and said that he thought he ought now to proceed at once to Aix-la-Chapelle with it. But Hoffmann vetoed that by a request that could hardly be refused.

"Since you are going to Main Headquarters, I should be glad if you would take a dispatch for me. I shall not have it ready until to-morrow morning, as I must wait for to-night's situation reports before I can complete it. But your own letter can be of no great urgency, or you would have been sent direct to Aix-la-Chapelle; so it won't matter in the least if you don't deliver it for a day or two. Also, it is certain that, when you get there, they will question you about the situation here and, if you do not leave until to-morrow morning, you will be able to give them more up to date information."

So the matter was decided; and, unwittingly, the Duke and the Baron had been among the first to be made aware of one of the most remarkable feats in military history. Overnight, General Hoffmann had taken the battle out of his C.-in-C.'s hands and, in a few hours, re-disposed the whole of the 8th Army, directing it on Tannenberg where, one week later, it was to win immortal glory.

During the remainder of the 21st, nothing of apparent importance happened, but on the morning of the 22nd a piece of news came in that electrified the Headquarters. Von Prittwitz had been sacked. In his place a combination had been appointed that was to become world famous. General Hindenburg was to be C.-in-C., with General Ludendorff as his Chief of Staff. About both, romantic and spectacular stories were soon running round.

Old Hindenburg had specialized in East Prussia. He knew every coppice and every marsh in it, but he had reached the age limit and been retired three years earlier. On the outbreak of war, he had immediately offered his services, but there were so many younger generals available that it had not been thought worth while to use him, even for training troops. For three weeks he had been sitting daily at his usual café in Hanover in a civilian suit, eating out his heart. Now, out of the blue the call had come—not to an administrative job, not to inspect new formations, or train reservists, but to be Commander-in-Chief Eastern Front and save his imperilled Fatherland from invasion.

Ludendorff was known to be one of the most brilliant officers of that talented and exclusive organization, the *Stabs Corps*. So dynamic was he, that his superiors had sent him the previous year to cool his heels for a while as a Commander of an Infantry brigade. But he had been re-posted as Deputy Quartermaster-General to the German spearhead which, after invading Belgium, had on the night of the 6th of August been given the task of capturing Liége. In the darkness the advancing columns had lost their way among the enemy forts, become mixed up, and finally halted in hopeless confusion. Out of the night, Ludendorff had appeared upon the scene, taken command of all the forces he could collect, found the right road, led the troops personally into the city and, at dawn, demanded and received the surrender of the citadel with its entire garrison.

These two were now on the way east as fast as a special train could bring them. A telegram had already been received from Ludendorff. It suspended von Prittwitz, ordered the Corps Commanders to act independently until further instructions, and required all the principal staff officers with 8th Army Headquarters to meet him and the new C.-in-C. back at Marienburg on the eastern arm of the Vistula.

It was now six days since the Duke had left Vienna and, fearing that sooner or later his presence at Przemysl must come to the ears of Major Ronge, he was extremely anxious to proceed with his plan for disappearing; so, on hearing the news, he at once went to General Hoffmann and asked for the dispatch.

The General replied that, in view of the change in command, he no longer intended to send his dispatch as it stood. He added that he felt confident that the new C.-in-C. would move up to Wartenburg as soon as he was informed of the situation, and that as de Richleau would certainly be asked about East Prussia when he reached Main Headquarters, it was essential that he should remain until he had heard General Hindenburg's views.

That left de Richleau no alternative but to make a moonlight flitting; so, reluctant as he was to remain there a moment longer than he positively had to, he decided that, rather than take such a drastic step after all had gone so well, it would be better to stay on for another day, in the hope that doing so would enable him to leave openly.

Having secured the agreement of the Corps Commanders to continue the movements he had prescribed, General Hoffmann and a number of others hurriedly set off in the train that was kept in the siding near the house, leaving only the junior officers behind to function now as an advance headquarters. But that evening a new visitor arrived, and no secret was made of the fact that he was Chief of the German Secret Intelligence Corps.

He was a tall dark man, wore Colonel's uniform and was named Walter Nicolai. He announced that all his Intelligence arrangements were working admirably in the west, so he had thought the time ripe to check up on those for the Eastern Front. During dinner he gave a glowing account of the German wheel into Belgium, and the news that the serious fighting which had been reported along the Western Front from the morning of the 20th on, had now developed into the first great battle between the French and German armies. He had innumerable figures on the tip of his tongue and said that 2,000,000 Germans were now engaged against 1,300,000 Frenchmen, so there could be no possible doubt that within a few weeks the Fatherland would destroy the French army and force its remnants to surrender.

As had been the case at Przemysl, de Richleau was known as Colonel Count Königstein, and everybody referred to him by that name, with the one exception of old Lanzi, who persisted in calling him 'Duke'. When they were sitting in the ante-room after dinner this anomaly aroused the curiosity of Colonel Nicolai, and Lanzi smilingly explained the matter. Thereupon, the Intelligence Chief gave the Duke a rather queer look, and said:

"How strange. I had an idea that the Duc de Richleau was a Frenchman who had taken British nationality. I feel sure I remember reading a report about his having been in London last spring, and our people got the idea that he was mixed up in some way with the Committee of Imperial Defence."

It was a horrid moment for the Duke, but he managed to keep his glance, and the hand that held his cigar, quite steady, as a glib lie came without effort to his lips:

"That must have been my rascally cousin, up to his tricks again. When he thinks he can get away with it, he has the impudence to use my title. For some years he has been living in the United States, and as I have never been there I have had no opportunity of showing him up as an impostor. From what you say, I suppose he must have been on a visit to London."

Colonel Nicolai seemed quite satisfied with the explanation, but de Richleau was badly shaken. He decided that night that, whatever happened, he must get away from Wartenburg the following day. But first thing next morning he learned that Hindenburg and Ludendorff were on their way up from Marienburg, so he decided not to burn his boats until the evening; by which time he hoped to have secured the sanction of one of them to his leaving.

They arrived that afternoon; Hindenburg big, square-headed, impressive; Ludendorff, plump, double-chinned and, as the Kaiser said of him, 'with a face like a sergeant'. General Hoffmann looked tired, but happy. He had feared to be made the whipping boy for von Prittwitz's blunders, and replaced. But his tremendous *tour de force* on the night of the 20th had earned him high praise from his new Chiefs. Not only were he and his staff confirmed in their appointments, but Ludendorff had not altered a single one of his brilliant re-dispositions for the coming battle of Tannenberg.

At five o'clock de Richleau and Lanzi were sent for by Ludendorff. Hoffmann was with him, and both of them were almost purring with satisfaction. A telegram had just come in from von Hötzendorf. On the previous day he had ordered his 1st Army to advance north towards Lublin and his 4th north-east towards Kholm, while his 3rd was to cover Lemberg. That morning the battle had been joined.

Thus, the main forces of all the Great Powers were now, at last, fully engaged. No less than thirty-two Armies, totalling over 7,000,000 of the best trained and equipped troops in the world, were at death grips. With every tick of the clock enough blood to fill a river was pouring from the torn arteries of the flower of Europe's youth, and hour by hour that must now continue until a decision was reached.

It was an appalling thought, but the Generals and their staffs at all the main headquarters were immersed in their plans for further slaughter, and remained impervious to it. Ludendorff expressed his great pleasure at General von Hötzendorf's most timely co-operation, and assured his visitors that the German 8th Army would reciprocate at the earliest possible moment.

The Duke again raised the matter of his departure for Aix-la-Chapelle, and the new Chief of Staff said: "I am sending one of my own officers, Major Tauber, there with dispatches by special train to-night. You can travel with him. The train will leave from the siding here about ten o'clock."

With that the interview ended, and at last the Duke's mind was partially relieved of the ever increasing strain it had been under for the past few days. If his luck now held for only another twenty-four hours, that should be sufficient to see him out of danger. When they got outside, Lanzi said with a cheerful smile:

"Well, things couldn't have worked out more satisfactorily, could they? There's no need for me to hurry back now. I shall come with you on the train as far as Berlin, and send the car down to meet me at Breslau. Come up to my room and I'll show you Mitzi's photograph. She's a delicious morsel, I promise you."

On the top floor of the house, in a small bedroom that had been allotted to him, the Colonel Baron Ungash-Wallersee produced what he jokingly called his 'Bible'. It was a small album containing the post-card size photographs of the eight girls he kept in Vienna, Budapest, Paris, and other cities. Mitzi was a blonde with slanting eyes that promised every sort of wickedness, and the collection would have done credit to any chorus.

When the Duke had expressed suitable admiration for the strategically distributed seraglio, Lanzi dug out from his kit some books of beautifully drawn and coloured erotic pictures for the amusement of his visitor, but de Richleau's mind was busy with more important matters.

He felt that General Rennenkampf had been extremely lucky to find himself opposed in his first battle by such a craven-hearted man as von Prittwitz, and that the Russians would find matters very different when they came up against the full force of the Hindenburg-Ludendorff-Hoffmann-François combination. As against that, there appeared very little likelihood of the German 8th Army being able to do much more than stave off the two armies under Jilinski. Therefore, it seemed a fair assumption that in the course of the next few weeks the opposing forces on the East Prussian front would fight themselves to a stalemate. But in France the probabilities were of a far blacker hue. Not only were the odds enormously in favour of the Germans, but their organization was better than that of the French, and their equipment more modern. If the French had the sense to conserve their strength until Churchill's 40th day, they might still have a hope of stemming the German tide; but it looked like their only one, and however carefully they husbanded their forces it would still be touch and go. At that critical hour everything would be thrown in on both sides, and even a matter of one division on

either might prove the straw that brought victory in the whole vast battle to the side that had it.

As the Duke looked over Lanzi's shoulder at the pictures of nude nymphs and agile stalwarts entwined in the more improbable positions of amorous combat, he was wondering if he could conceivably do anything to aid his sorely pressed country. That France had thrown him out on account of his dangerous political activities had in no way lessened his love for his native land, and as he thought of her fair countryside and cultured cities being over-run by the stupid, still semi-barbarous blond hordes from beyond the Rhine, he ached with the desire to bring her some assistance, however small.

In his mind's eye, ever since Colonel Nicolai had spoken the previous evening of the avalanche of fire and steel that was now descending on France, he had seen images of burning farmsteads and shattered towns, and beyond the bawdy pictures he could see them still. For an instant he visualized another Joan of Arc arising once more to lead France to victory against great odds, although he knew that even her faith would have been powerless against Krupp guns. Then, in the same vein of romantic fantasy, he saw himself on his way through Aix-la-Chapelle, planting under German Main Headquarters a bomb of such as yet undiscovered power that it would blow the Kaiser, and everyone engaged in directing the hideous battle, to hell.

The thought recalled to him General Hoffmann's remark, that when he arrived at Main Headquarters it was certain that he would be asked for all the information he could give about the situation in East Prussia. He had never had any intention of going there, but, all the same, he began to speculate on what he would have said, had circumstances similar to those which had forced him to come to Wartenburg compelled him to deliver von Hötzendorf's letter. General von Moltke would naturally have been kept informed of the main outlines of the battle, but a staff officer would certainly be in a position to colour the General's impression about future prospects on a front from which he had just arrived.

Influenced by his proximity to the Russo-German battle, his first thought was that he would paint the picture as optimistically as possible, so as to restore the General's confidence in the 8th Army; with the object that, should it meet with further reverses and appeal for help, its appeals would be less likely to receive prompt attention, and thus it would be more likely to sustain a serious defeat.

But in a second he saw the larger map, and realized that to adopt such a course would be to throw away a God-given opportunity. The picture should be painted black—black as pitch. Thus, if Hindenburg asked for reinforcements, he would be much more likely to get them.

The Russians were strong enough to look after themselves. Even if another entire German Army was sent against them, they could already match it in manpower. In another week or so, when their Asiatic formations reached the line, they would again have an enormous superiority. And, in the worst event, they could surrender territory without the least danger of collapse.

France had no reserves to draw upon. France had no territory she could afford to give. Germany was now fully mobilized and every one of her divisions fit for battle were in the field. Anything sent to East Prussia would have to be taken from the Western Front. Russia could take on another half dozen Army Corps and still maintain an unbroken line of battle. But for France the withdrawal of even a single German division might mean the difference between defeat and salvation.

Lanzi was chuckling in his beard at a picture of the devil doing curious things with the point of his tail to a lovely young witch, at the moment that de Richleau reached his decision. He knew, in one of those sudden flashes that brooks no argument, that he was not going to slip tamely over the border into Holland. He was going to deliver von Hötzendorf's letter at Main Headquarters and influence von Moltke as far as he possibly could.

At dinner he was unusually silent. He had no sooner taken his decision than a serious obstacle to his achieving his object had occurred to him. He was not going to Aix-la-Chapelle alone: he was to be accompanied by Ludendorff's staff officer, Major Tauber. The Major was much more likely than he was to be questioned about the East Prussian front. Moreover, he would give a true picture of the new confidence that the arrival of Hindenburgh and Ludendorff had inspired.

The Major, to whom de Richleau had just been introduced, was seated some way down the table. In the usual German manner, he had first cut up all the food on his plate and was now using the fork to shovel it into his mouth with an ugly greed that suggested he had had nothing to eat for a fortnight. He was a squat, corpulent man, with a thick neck, little piggy eyes and a shaven head. The Duke decided that, somehow or other, he must be got rid of *en route*.

After the meal, Lanzi and de Richleau talked for a while over coffee and brandy with their hosts in the ante-room. Soon after ten o'clock Captain Fleischmann left them to see their baggage on to the train, and they began to make their farewells. When they had exchanged stiff hand-shakes and bows with the officers present, Major Tauber said he thought it time for them to be going, and led the way across the main hall to the back of the house, as the quickest method of getting to the railway siding. Just as they were about to leave by the back door, Colonel Nicolai emerged from a side corridor and addressed the Duke:

"Ah! *Herr Oberste Graf*; I'm so glad I've managed to catch you. I've a letter for one of my colleagues at Main Headquarters, and I'd be very grateful if you would take it with you."

"Of course," replied de Richleau, holding out his hand. "Where is it?"

Nicolai jerked his head in the direction of a partly open door just down the passage from which he had come, and said, "In there. I haven't had time to address an envelope for it yet, but if you'll come with me I won't keep you a minute."

Taking de Richleau's consent for granted, the tall, dark Colonel turned on his heel. With a nod to Lanzi and Tauber, the Duke murmured: "Please don't wait for me. I can easily catch you up." Then, as they went out into the darkness, he walked down the corridor and followed Nicolai into the room.

A few weeks before it had been the gun-room of the manor, but it had since been converted into a small office. In one corner there was a porcelain stove, and near it stood a thin, sandy-haired man dressed in rather flashy civilian clothes.

As de Richleau stepped through the door, Colonel Nicolai closed it behind him and said in a sharp voice to the civilian:

"Are you sure now that this is the man on your records?"

The thin man nodded. "*Jawohl, Herr Oberste.* I never forget a face. He's the one I saw come out of the Carlton Club in London."

CHAPTER XXIV

A VERY TIGHT CORNER

FOR a moment there was dead silence in the small room. The Duke's first reaction was one of amazement. It was barely twenty-four hours since Colonel Nicolai had raised the question of the de Richleau title. That he should have remained unconvinced by the explanation given him and started inquiries was quite understandable. The staggering thing was that he should have been able, in so short a time, to produce an agent who could definitely identify the suspect as the de Richleau who had been in London.

The Duke was standing between the two Germans. He was facing the fair civilian in the flashy suit, and Colonel Nicolai was behind him. As he stared at the fair man, it flashed upon him that, even if he had been seen in London the previous April, it was no proof whatever that he was a spy. If he played his cards skilfully he might still bluff his way out of this highly dangerous situation. Showing swift indignation, he exclaimed:

"Really! I see no reason for this absurd piece of drama."

"You will soon!" The Colonel's voice came from behind him. "Stay where you are and keep facing that way."

"But I never told you that I had not been in London. I have all my clothes made there."

"Do you still maintain that it was your *cousin* who was seen coming out of the Carlton Club with General Sir Henry Wilson, Sir Pellinore Gwaine-Cust and Sir Bindon Blackers?"

"It might have been. He is very like me."

"And yet you admit that you were in London last April?"

De Richleau saw that he had blundered, and he quickly made the best of it. But he dared not tell a flat lie as he believed he had been followed from Victoria to Ostend, and they might be able to produce a man who had shadowed him on the Orient Express. He said:

"I was there for a few days; but my cousin may have been there at the same time. Anyhow, I did not visit the Carlton Club, so this gentleman is mistaken in supposing that he saw me come out of it."

The fair man shook his head. "That is quite impossible. Once I have seen a face I never forget it."

"All right then," the Duke shrugged. "Let us suppose for a minute that you are correct. Supposing that for private reasons I did not choose immediately to admit to having lunched at the Club with General Wilson and these other gentlemen. What crime do you impute to me for having done so while Europe was still at peace?"

"None," replied the Colonel. "But it goes a long way to establishing for us that it is on behalf of the British Secret Service you have been working."

"What nonsense! You have not an atom of proof to support this wild theory."

"I think you would be surprised how much we know about you."

The remark was extremely disquieting, but de Richleau met it with a determined effort to overawe his captors and gain control of the situation. With sudden biting sarcasm, he said:

"Then, if you know so much, it is a pity you did not take the trouble to find out a little more before you allowed your imagination to run away with you. To end this farce it seems that I must disclose a matter that my Government would greatly prefer should remain secret. It is quite true that I lunched in London with General Wilson last April. And I will tell you why. Not because I have the remotest connection with the British Secret Service, but because the Austrian Government asked me to see him and his friends on a highly confidential matter. Now! You have no possible right to detain me here, and as the personal representative of General von Hötzendorf I demand my immediate release."

That was a good card—a very good card—as Colonel Nicolai had already admitted that he had no proof of the reason why the Duke had lunched at the Carlton Club. But, unfortunately for de Richleau, it was not quite good enough. The Colonel held a higher card, and, with a short, harsh laugh, he played it:

"Perhaps you will explain then, why you did not mention your secret activities on behalf of the Austrian Government to Major Ronge when he had you in prison?"

De Richleau remained perfectly still; but he could feel his muscles tighten and a pulse in his throat began to hammer furiously.

They had got him, then. Nicolai had not only made inquiries of his associates in the Foreign Intelligence Department, he had also got in touch with the Austrian K.S. The cat was out of the bag. Up to a moment ago the Secret Intelligence Chief had been only playing with him, and trying to get a line on his activities in London before letting him know that they already had enough against him to have him shot whenever they wished.

A spate of regrets seethed through his brain. If he had had the strength of mind to ignore Ilona's plea to stay on in Vienna, he would have been back in England weeks ago. If he had not gone to say good-bye to Count Tisza, he would not have given his parole to remain still longer. If he had ignored von Hötzendorf's order to report at the Arsenal and, instead, disappeared, there was quite a good chance that he would have succeeded in evading Ronge's police. If he had boldly left Przemysl on the long road home through Russia, he could have been in St. Petersburg by this time. If only he had had the sense to see the red light when Nicolai had questioned him about his title, he could easily have got away last night, secured a civilian suit, and by now be safely in a train on his way to Holland.

It seemed to him in that black moment that he had let slip one golden opportunity after another through sheer weakness and stupidity. He forgot that at the time there had been sound reasons for every decision he had taken, and that had he acted otherwise he might be in an Austrian fortress, have been shot while crossing the battle-line into Russia, or already have been arrested by the German police as a deserter.

But those regrets were no more than flickers of thought that lit his mind for an instant, then were gone. Realizing their futility, he doused them in a second, and faced up to the fact that once he allowed himself to be disarmed his chance of escaping with his life would not be worth a brass farthing. He must either fight *now*—or die.

Like all officers on active service, he was wearing a pistol at his belt, but the army pattern holster was not designed for quick drawing. Its leather flap had a button-hole in it that fastened down over a mushroom-headed brass stud. Nevertheless, his movement was extraordinarily rapid. With a jerk his hand flew up, his thumb and forefinger grasped the tongue of the flap and tore it back. At the same instant he side-stepped and swung his body half round. But his next movement was forestalled by Nicolai. As the gun butt was exposed, the Colonel's hand shot out from behind him, grasped it, and dragged the weapon from its holster.

Completing his turn, de Richleau struck the Colonel a savage back-hander with his clenched fist. It caught Nicolai on the side of his face. He was thrown off his balance and fell heavily against the door. But the fair man was standing only two yards away. Launching himself forward, he flung himself at the Duke's legs in a rugby tackle.

De Richleau in turn was caught off balance. He struck downwards with his left at the man's blond head, but the force of the impact against his legs caused the upper part of his body to jerk forward. Next second he was sprawling across the German's shoulders.

Rolling over on to the floor, he jerked his knees up, then suddenly gave a violent kick with both feet. The action not only broke the German's hold on his legs; it sent him catapulting across the floor to land up with a crash against the stove. But de Richleau was left lying flat on his back.

Nicolai had recovered himself. Still standing by the door, he clicked a bullet up into the chamber of the Duke's pistol, then levelled it at him. Before de Richleau could even raise his shoulders, the Colonel snapped:

"Do you surrender? Or do you want me to save myself a lot of trouble by putting a bullet through your head?"

His cheek was a bright red from the blow he had received: his black eyes were angry. It was very clear that he was not to be trifled with, and meant what he said. De Richleau lifted his hands a little, palms outward, sat up, and slowly got to his feet.

With his left hand Nicolai turned the key in the lock, stepped away from the door, and motioned the Duke towards it. "Stand over there. Any more tricks, and you know what to expect, you dirty traitor."

The Duke did as he was bid, but he did not keep his hands up. Instead, he employed them in beating the dust from the floor off his tunic and breeches; then quite naturally lowered them as he said: "You must know by now that I am not an Austrian, so you have no right to call me a traitor."

The civilian had picked himself up with muttered curses, and moved round behind a kitchen table which was in use as an impromptu desk. Nicolai joined him there, laid down the pistol, took up a thin sheaf of papers, and replied: "Yes, we know that. You are a pig of an Englishman. I have it all on this file."

Glancing down at the top sheet, he went on quickly: "These are particulars about you, brought by Herr Steinhauer when I summoned him from Berlin to-day. You were pointed out to him in London as a dangerous adventurer. Owing to the company you were in, it was thought probable that you were being employed in some form of secret work. Agent E.7 was put on to shadow you. He reported a visit by you to the offices of the Committee of Imperial Defence. E.5 was then put on to aid him. E.7 reported a second visit to the same office, but that night he bungled matters and was roughly handled by you. Next morning E.5 followed you to Victoria Station. He telephoned that your baggage was labelled for Belgrade. A telegram was dispatched to Ostend. J.3 picked you up there and boarded the same train. But you gave him the slip at Munich. A general call was put out to locate you, but during the following week no report came in of any person answering your description having registered at an hotel in Germany. Agents in Serbia were instructed to keep a look out for you. N.2 reported on 15th May that you had, after all, gone to Belgrade. The case was not graded as a high priority, and the department then being satisfied that you were not operating in Germany, it was closed."

De Richleau was watching his captors like a lynx. Colonel Nicolai had his eyes on the papers he was holding, but Herr Steinhauer had his fixed on the prisoner in an unwinking stare. The Colonel had laid the gun down on the table, but either he or Steinhauer could grab it up before the Duke could get within a yard of it, and Nicolai had another pistol in the holster at his belt. To attempt to rush them at the moment would have been to invite a bullet.

Turning to another sheet, Nicolai continued: "Here is Major Ronge's reply to a telegram from me. Evidently he considers you of sufficient importance not to spare words. The gist of it is that you are known to have carried out espionage in Belgrade and suspected of doing so in Vienna. He says you admitted British nationality, but passed yourself off as an Austrian, imposing on many highly placed persons, including the Archduchess Ilona Theresa, the Minister-President of Hungary, and Prince Thurn und Taxis, in whose regiment you succeeded in obtaining a commission. On the 4th of August Major Ronge arrested you as an enemy alien, but not being able to charge you with any specific crime was compelled to agree to your temporary release under pressure from the Archduchess. You were released from prison on August the 12th and disappeared from Vienna on the 16th. All efforts to trace you failed, but he adds that you should be regarded as both resourceful and dangerous. He asks that you should be held in close arrest and returned under strong escort to him in Vienna."

For a moment the Duke saw a glimmer of hope on his horizon. If he were sent back to Vienna there would almost certainly occur some opportunity for him to escape during the journey. But a second later that promise of reprieve was shattered by Nicolai. His cheekbone was still aching from de Richleau's blow, and he said with vicious pleasure:

"However, that would be a quite unnecessary waste of time and troops for an escort. We are fully capable of settling your business without the assistance of Major Ronge." Then he turned to a third paper, and went on:

"Here we have Austro-Hungarian Supreme Headquarters' reply to my inquiry there. You were appointed to the Operations branch of the Commander-in-Chief's staff on August 16th, and served in that capacity until being entrusted with a special mission to this Headquarters on the evening of the 18th. Both there and here, you must have learned military secrets of the first importance. That is your death warrant. Have you anything to say?"

"Not much," replied the Duke. Standing there with his back against the door, he now looked the very picture of dejection, as he added miserably, "But I find your conclusions a little shattering to the nerves. If you permit, I will smoke a cigarette."

Without waiting for a reply, he undid the top button of his tunic and slipped his hand inside it. Next moment he drew out, not a cigarette case, but the miniature automatic that he had been carrying under his armpit ever since he had joined von Hötzendorf's staff.

"*Achtung!*" he snapped, instantly straightening himself and taking a pace forward. "One move from either of you and I shoot to kill. This little toy is as deadly at eight feet as a rifle. You know that I can't afford to take any chances now my own neck is in the noose. You'll do exactly what I tell you, unless you wish to die here in this room. Put your hands up!"

The two Germans had been taken entirely by surprise. Neither of them had even had time to thrust out a hand for the pistol lying only two feet in front of them on the table. The eyes of both flickered towards it for a second, then met the Duke's steely glance again. Glaring with hate and fury at having been caught napping, they raised their hands shoulder high.

"Higher!" snarled the Duke. "As high as you can stretch. And quick about it! I've no time to waste! Our friends on the train must be wondering what the devil has become of me. Or do they know about this?"

Colonel Nicolai's face relaxed for a moment into a malicious smile. "No. But you needn't think you're going to get away on it. I didn't want that old Austrian Baron coming back to find you, and have to waste time giving him an explanation. I told the engine driver that he would have only two officers travelling, with their servants, and that as soon as they were aboard he was to move off. The train has gone without you."

Those sneering words were a nasty blow for the Duke. He had felt certain that old Lanzi would have given the show away if he had known that anything of this sort was in the wind, and there was no reason why Nicolai should have informed Major Tauber of the trap he intended to spring. So he had counted on getting away on the train, anyhow as far as Berlin. That was now out of the question, but, all the same, he intended to ensure himself a good start.

"About turn, both of you!" he said abruptly. "Go on! Keep your hands up and walk over to the wall. Press your noses to it. Quick now! Remember I am desperate and we are at war. If you move a muscle without my orders, I shall treat you as I would prisoners on a battlefield who attempted to attack me—I'll blow your brains out!"

Cowed by the menacing light in his steely grey eyes, they did as he had ordered. When their backs were turned, he transferred the little automatic to his left hand. Then he stepped after them. As he passed the table, he picked up his pistol by the barrel. Slipping on the safety catch of the bigger weapon, he lifted it and brought its butt crashing down on the back of Nicolai's skull.

The Colonel gave a long, agonized groan, buckled at the knees, and fell senseless to the floor.

At the sound, Steinhauer started back from the wall, half lowering his hands and turning a little, a look of petrified horror on his now ashen face. But the Duke had him covered with the little automatic.

"Get back," he snapped. "It's a bullet or a rap on the head. You won't live after the one, but you will after the other. Take your choice."

With shoulders hunched and head bent, Steinhauer turned his terrified face away. A sob broke from him just before the blow fell; then he too doubled up and dropped senseless at de Richleau's feet.

Returning his weapons to their holsters, the Duke stooped down and dragged his two victims into a position where they were lying on their sides back to back. Undoing the Colonel's belt, he used it to strap their legs together. Wrenching away the cord of the window blind, he tied their wrists with it. Pulling off Steinhauer's gaudy necktie, he knotted it round both throats, so that the backs of their bleeding heads were held firmly to one another. Then he took a few sheets of foolscap from the table, crumpled them up, and forced them into the unconscious men's mouths, to prevent their crying out when they regained consciousness.

Turning back to the table, he lit a match and burnt the thin file of papers from which Nicolai had been reading. Having made certain that there were no other documents there which incriminated him, he walked to the door, unlocked it, and put out the light.

Opening the door cautiously, he peered out, and listened intently for a moment. All was quiet, so he removed the key from the lock, stepped out into the passage, re-locked the door from the outside and put the key in his pocket.

Like some great grey cat, he tiptoed down the short length of corridor to the hall. No one was about, so he slipped unobserved out of the back door. There, he paused for a moment, considering his next move. Nicolai had been telling the truth about the train leaving without him. There was a stationary train some distance down the line, but that must be the C.-in-C.'s special: the siding to the west of the house stood empty. The choice now lay between making off on foot or attempting to steal a vehicle. The latter project meant a risk of being spotted and questioned, which ultimately might lead to the most dire consequences. On the other hand, the greater distance he could put between Wartenburg and himself during the night, the better his chance of getting away altogether. He decided to risk it.

Walking as quietly as possible, but naturally now in case he should be noticed from one of the windows of the house, he went round its east end and paused on the corner of its south front. Eight or ten cars and a dozen motor-cycles were garaged in a long tin-roofed shed, which had recently been erected for that purpose on the opposite side of the drive. During the day they were constantly coming and going, but at night there were much longer intervals unbroken by their roar and clatter, and the hour was past when the drivers washed down their vehicles. There was no special guard on the long shed, as it stood in full view of the sentry who was posted on the front door of the Headquarters. Wartenburg was still fifty miles from the nearest battle zone and not even within sound of its guns, so the sentry was there only as a usual appurtenance to the presence of a senior Commander. He would challenge any civilian who approached either the house or the shed, but de Richleau thought it very unlikely that he would halt anyone in uniform, as soldiers of all ranks were moving about in the vicinity of the house at all hours of the day and night.

Nevertheless, as he stood there, he found himself trembling. If he slipped up in the next few moments, the matter might be referred to some senior officer who would want to know, not only what he had been up to, trying to make off with Headquarters' transport, but why he had not caught the train. To provide a plausible explanation would be extremely difficult, and once he fell under suspicion copies of the telegrams that had come in about him from von Hötzendorf's Headquarters and Major Ronge might be produced. Once again, he had nightmare visions of a shooting party at dawn, with himself as the target.

He knew that his shivering fit was caused by reaction from the bad ten minutes through which he had just been. Lighting a cigarette to steady his nerves, he debated whether he should take a car or a motor-cycle. Whichever he took, as soon as its loss was discovered the military police would be notified. As a car would be more easily identifiable, he decided on a bicycle.

It was a darkish night. The moon had not yet risen. Only a few stars glimmered overhead. But the area of the drive was lit both by the windows of the house and a few electric bulbs that had been left burning in the long shed. He could not possibly cross the sweep of gravel without the sentry seeing him. Checking an impulse to throw away the cigarette, he walked forward still puffing at it. His heart was hammering heavily.

When he had covered a dozen yards the sentry caught sight of him. Recognizing his uniform as that of an officer, he banged and slapped his rifle, bringing it to the salute. With a guilty start, de Richleau acknowledged the gesture. He thanked his stars that the light was insufficient for the man to have seen the expression on his face. Hoping the sentry would think that he was borrowing a motor-bike simply to run in to the town, he approached the shed with all the nonchalance he could muster.

The motor-cycles were all of the same make, so he grasped the nearest by its handlebars and pushed it off its stand. Now was the critical instant. Switching on the controls, he kicked the stand up and ran the bike forward. The engine banged twice, then began to roar. He jumped into the saddle and was off.

He knew that half a mile away, at the gate of the manor grounds, there was another sentry post. But the object of the guard there was to check up on people coming in, not stop those going out. He passed it unchallenged and a second later was out on the open road. To the left, it led north towards Königsberg and the Baltic: to the right, south towards Wartenburg. But in the town there was a cross-roads that would take him to the west. Turning right, he let out the engine, and four minutes later he was entering the little town.

It seemed hours since he had said good-bye to General Hoffmann and the other officers in the mess, so he was surprised to see many lights still on in the windows of the houses, and, here and there, little groups of soldiers flirting with the local girls in the streets. As he purred past a small café he caught sight of its clock. The hands stood at twenty minutes to eleven.

Thinking back, he realized that, hectic as every moment of his encounter with Nicolai and Steinhauer had been, it could not have occupied more than seven or eight minutes, and after leaving them he had wasted only half a minute or so standing at the corner of the house before stealing the bike, so the whole nerve-racking episode had taken place in less than a quarter of an hour.

Turning west at the cross-roads, he ran on for a further quarter of a mile, then he came to a small hump-backed bridge over a canal, which had a red light showing above and beyond it. Slowing down on the crest of the bridge, he saw the reason for the warning signal. On the far side of the bridge lay a level crossing, and its gates were closed.

Pulling up, he peered from side to side in the semi-darkness. To his left front he could make out the outline of a building that was obviously the railway station. To his right front was what appeared to be a goods yard, as several trains were standing there, and two of them were shunting.

Cursing the delay, he remained there on the crest of the bridge, waiting for the gates to open. A train coming from the direction of the station puffed slowly over the level crossing. It was a short one of only three coaches. The first and third coaches were almost in darkness. The centre one was brightly lit. It was a pullman car, and empty but for two people. At a table framed in one window sat Major Tauber and Lanzi smoking one of his big torpedo-shaped cigars.

With fury in his heart, the Duke watched it glide by. He was greatly surprised that it had got no farther. However, Wartenburg was a small junction: its station was now busier than it had ever been in all its history, with trains going to and from the front. And Nicolai had ordered the special to leave some ten minutes before it was due out, so probably it had been held up on the other side of the station until a line could be cleared for it. Or perhaps Lanzi had pulled the communication cord and insisted on waiting for him for a quarter of an hour or so. In any case, the sight of the train, and the thought that although he had caught up with it there was no hope of getting on it, was positively maddening.

When the special had passed the level crossing, the gates swung open, but it halted some sixty yards beyond them. It stood there, hissing steam, its driver evidently waiting for a further signal to proceed.

Suddenly de Richleau decided to take a wild gamble. Jumping from his motor-cycle, he gave a quick look round. There was nobody in sight. Seizing the machine, he upended it, so that its front wheel rested on the low parapet of the bridge. Grasping the saddle, he gave a terrific heave. For a moment the bike balanced on the stone coping, sideways on, both its wheels in the air. With another mighty thrust, he pushed it over. There followed a resounding splash as it struck the water in the middle of the canal. But he caught it only faintly. He was running like a madman for the train.

By his act he knew that he had burnt his boats. If he failed to get on the train there was now no hope of recovering the motor-cycle. But he had been impelled to sacrifice the bird in the hand by the thought that it would be weeks before the machine was discovered on the canal bottom. It was certain to be missed within a few hours. The sentry would report having seen him take it. But nobody would now learn where he had abandoned the stolen vehicle. Therefore, no link would be left connecting him with the special train—if he could catch it.

With flying feet he pelted down the far slope of the bridge. Swerving to the right, he turned away from the level crossing. Beside the road there was a deep ditch, but owing to the summer drought there was no water in it. The ditch was too wide to jump, so he scrambled down and up the lower bank on its far side into a field of turnips. There was now a steep embankment to his left, above which lay the railway line. The rear of the train was still forty yards farther on. His eyes were riveted on it. Every moment he expected it to move and leave him stranded. He tripped on a turnip, swore, regained his balance, and ran on. Another spurt and he was level with the end of the train. Turning, he charged the bank, but it was almost perpendicular. His initial impetus gave out when he was half-way up it. He nearly fell backwards. For a moment he hovered, his hands wildly outstretched and clutching in mid-air.

With a terrific effort he saved himself, pitched forward, and seized two tufts of coarse grass.

The train's whistle blew. In frantic haste he scrambled up the last few feet of the embankment. Hardly two minutes had elapsed since he had left the bridge, but he was panting as though his lungs would burst.

The train began to move. He hurled himself forward at the last door in it. In one spring he was on the moving foot-board, but his clutching fingers missed the handle of the door. He lost his balance and fell heavily. Lying there on the track, he saw the rear light receding. Picking himself up, he ran after it. The speed of the train increased. He knew now that he would never catch it, but he still ran on. Suddenly he tripped on a sleeper and measured his length on the ground.

Sprawled there with the remaining wind dashed from his body, he watched the light steadily moving away from him. Only now that he had failed to get on the train did he fully realize how much it would have meant for him to do so. No one at Wartenburg could possibly suspect his presence on it. Within an hour or so it would have carried him beyond all danger of pursuit. To have caught it would have meant safety and life. Having lost it meant that, long before he could reach the Dutch border, he would be hunted like a hare—and he had thrown away his only chance of getting clear of the district while darkness lasted.

Scrambling to his feet, he rubbed his bruised knees. As he looked up from doing so he could still see the rear light of the train. It was no longer moving. The train had halted again about two hundred yards down the line.

In a second he was racing after it. Gasping, panting, he leapt from sleeper to sleeper along the track. His mouth wide, his eyes staring, he forced himself forward at the utmost speed of which he was capable. His heart leaping with exaltation, he flashed past the rear buffers of the train, sprang again upon the foot-board of the last coach and, this time, seized the handle of the door. Frantically he wrenched it, first one way, then the other. It was locked.

Jumping down, he dashed along the side of the unlit rear coach, leapt on to the foot-board of the next, and seized the handle of the door there. It turned under his pressure, and swung open. Levering himself up, he lurched inside, slamming the door shut behind him. Opposite him, as he stood fighting for breath, was the door of a lavatory. Pushing it open, he staggered inside, thrust back the bolt and collapsed on the seat.

For every second of the time since he had heaved the motor-bike over the parapet of the bridge, his exertions had been of the utmost violence, but the whole episode had occupied less than two minutes, so his exhaustion was purely temporary. The moment he got his wind back he was ready for anything. His brain began to race again, exploring the possibilities of this entirely unexpected situation.

As he washed the dirt off his hands in the lavatory basin, he smiled at his reflection in the mirror. There was a good chance that Messrs. Nicolai and Steinhauer would not be found till the following morning and, even if they were, he considered it improbable that they would be in any state to tell what had happened to them for many hours to come. The sentry had seen him take the motor-cycle, but he had passed him at well over fifty yards' distance, and in the uncertain light it was unlikely that the man would have seen his features, or even noticed that he was wearing an Austrian uniform. The bike had been sunk without trace, so inquiries about it would lead nowhere. When the doctors did succeed in getting some sense out of his concussed victims the hue and cry would start with a vengeance; but even then the very last place that anyone would look for him was on the train. He recalled the saying that 'God helps those who help themselves', and, while his escape from immediate peril was due to his own wits and resolution, he gratefully acknowledged that he owed to Providence this splendid chance of getting clean away.

He began to consider if it would be better to remain hidden for the night, then drop off the train when it had carried him several hundred miles to the west, which offered the prospect of being able to disappear entirely; or face his fellow travellers and give them some plausible explanation for his sudden appearance on it.

From Wartenburg to Aix-la-Chapelle by rail was, he knew, between seven and eight hundred miles. The train was a special, but as it did not carry a C.-in-C. it was unlikely to have the highest grade of priority, and the war had caused an enormous increase in railway traffic, so he thought it probable that it would not average much more than forty-five miles an hour. If so, it should reach Berlin about seven o'clock in the morning, and Aix at about five the following afternoon.

As it was nearly empty he thought his chances of remaining hidden on it good while darkness lasted. But he could not stay in the lavatory indefinitely, and if he concealed himself in one of the empty sleeping berths there was a big risk that the train attendants might carry out a routine clean up in the morning, which would lead to his discovery. To explain his presence then would be extremely difficult, so if he hid at all he must drop off the train when it slowed up somewhere before reaching Berlin. That would mean losing many precious hours before he could hope to reach Holland.

And there was another thing. Having got on the train, he once more had the chance of carrying out his plan for attempting to influence von Moltke. That could be done only if he arrived at Aix in the special as an officer on official business from the Eastern Front. If, as he believed, he had managed to disappear from Wartenburg without leaving a single trace, the attempt he meditated entailed no more risk than it would have done had Nicolai never become suspicious of him. On the other hand, to have any considerable hope of swaying the mind of the Chief of the German General Staff, he must first somehow get rid of Major Tauber.

That was going to prove a very difficult business, and must once more involve him in the gravest dangers. But France's need was desperate. Ever since he had joined von Hötzendorf's staff, he had regarded himself as a soldier on active service in the midst of the enemy. His life had been in constant jeopardy and, if the worst came to the worst, he had been prepared to sell it as dearly as possible at any moment. If he lost it in this attempt, that would be no worse than having done so had he failed to escape from Nicolai. And the prize was tremendous. If he could succeed in getting troops withdrawn from the Western Front at this critical hour, the value of such an action might prove incalculable. Few of the ten million men now under arms would ever be given an opportunity to risk their lives for such a great result. Almost instantly he decided that he could not possibly ignore it.

The train was still at a standstill. He had been in the lavatory for about three minutes. He had not as yet the faintest idea how he was going to eliminate Major Tauber, but he realized that if he were to make his presence known at all he must not linger where he was any longer. Taking his little automatic from its hiding place under his arm, he put it in the right hand pocket of his tunic, so that he had only to slip his hand in and could fire with it through the cloth. Then, after giving himself a final brush down, he opened the door and went boldly out into the corridor.

Walking along it, he passed an empty coupé and went through the door to the main pullman. Lanzi and Major Tauber were sitting at a table half-way down it. The train was staffed by special railway troops, and an orderly stood near the table, holding a tray, from which he was in the act of putting glasses and a bottle in front of the two officers. As de Richleau appeared, the orderly showed his surprise and Lanzi sat back with a gasp.

"*Gott in Himmel*, Duke! Where have you sprung from?"

De Richleau frowned. "It is no thanks to you, Baron, that I did not miss the train altogether."

Lanzi spread out his hands. "I'm terribly sorry. It wasn't our fault. There was some silly muddle. The moment the Major and I got aboard, the darned thing started. I pulled the cord and it came to a halt. The engine driver said he had been told that only two officers were travelling, and that as soon as they were on the train he was to move off. By the time it pulled up we had covered a few hundred yards, but it didn't seem worth shunting back, as we had your baggage on board and you could easily have seen the rear lights from the siding. We waited nearly twenty minutes; then the driver said we must push on or he would be held up all along the line, and be in the devil of a mess from goods trains having got in ahead of him. That's what is hanging us up now, I expect. We thought by that time that you must have been detained by something very important, and couldn't be coming at all; so we told him he could go ahead. What the devil kept you?"

"It was that idiot, Nicolai," muttered the Duke angrily. "He kept me hanging about for nearly ten minutes while he added a postscript to the letter he wanted me to take to Main Headquarters. When I got to the siding the train had gone. I saw the rear lights, but thought they belonged to the train on the other siding that is kept in readiness for General Hindenburg."

"How did you manage to catch us then?"

"Colonel Nicolai was with me. He said that the train was almost certain to be held up for a few minutes going through the junction. So we nipped into a car, and he drove me down to the station. My luck was in, as it had only just passed, and we saw it pull up on the far side of the level crossing. I ran along the line and hopped on to it. What did you do with my baggage?"

It was Major Tauber who replied. "We thought of putting it out, *Herr Oberste*. But we were afraid that, if we did, you might not find it in the wood, there; or it might be stolen. We thought it certain that you would be coming on to Main Headquarters to-morrow, so I volunteered to take charge of it till you arrived. It is still where it was stowed, in one of the sleeping compartments."

"Thank goodness for that!" sighed de Richleau, sitting down. He noticed that the bottle on the table contained liqueur brandy but he felt like a long drink. Glancing at the orderly, who was still standing there, he said: "Bring me a large glass and some mineral water."

As the man clicked his heels and turned away, it occurred to the Duke that his having been present during the recent explanation was a piece of luck. It was certain he would repeat what he had heard to his companions, so the train staff would now have no cause to wonder at the mysterious appearance of a third officer. A few minutes later, he returned with a tumbler and a pint of Apollinaris. With a nod of thanks, de Richleau took them and mixed himself the drink of which he was much in need.

It did not take him long to realize that Lanzi and the Major had not been getting on exactly like a house on fire. They were, in fact, oil and water.

Lanzi was just a simple person who happened to have been blessed with a great name and immense riches. He considered it right and proper that anyone in the station to which God had called him should enjoy the pleasures which, all his life, had spread as a long and happy vista easily within his grasp. But he was not in the least a selfish man. He liked everybody about him to enjoy themselves, too. He even gave time and thought, as well as a great deal of money, to providing his wife and children with every material thing which might help to make their lives as enjoyable as his own.

Major Tauber, on the other hand, had had a hard life; and now that he had reached a position in which he exerted a certain authority over others, he thought it right that they too should have a hard life. He was a gross, thick-necked Prussian, with a nature that lacked both humour and generosity. But he had brains—of a kind. Although he had neither private money nor influence, he had worked his way up to that Mecca of the German Army, a *Stabs Corps* appointment. He was no puritan and indulged his lusts occasionally without a qualm of conscience, but quickly, like an animal, so that he could get back to his work and help to increase the efficiency of the Army, which was the only thing he lived for. But his fat, overworked wife trembled before him, and his sons stood rigidly to attention when he addressed them. He was tactful to the point of servility when in the presence of his superiors, but, as he held the entire Austrian army in great contempt, he did not regard an ***Austrian*** Colonel as his superior.

Evidently Lanzi had innocently disclosed his reason for going to Berlin and the Major had shown his frigid disapproval of the very idea that any officer, even an Austrian, should contemplate neglecting his duty to visit a kept woman. Lanzi did not understand this point of view, and thought it extremely bad manners on the Major's part to propound it. Being too polite himself to say so, he merely laughed the matter off, but he made no attempt to conceal his pleasure that, by joining them so unexpectedly, de Richleau had relieved him of the necessity to spend several hours in the sole company of such an uncouth companion.

The Duke came in only for the tail end of the argument, and while he agreed with the Major in principle, he felt a sneaking sympathy for Lanzi; so he thought it served the Major right when his old travelling companion, rather pointedly, engaged him in a conversation about Viennese society, of which the German knew nothing. For some moments Tauber sat looking at them in silence with a tight-lipped uncomfortable stare, then he took a quadruple set of miniature cards out of his valise and began an incredibly complicated game of patience.

As Lanzi rambled cheerfully on with stories of Archdukes, partridge drives in Hungary and the more spicy episodes in the lives of well known ballerinas, it was easy enough for the Duke to think about the private problem to which, within the next hour or so, he had to find a solution. How was he going to deal with Major Tauber?

On one thing he had already made up his mind. Major Tauber was not going to arrive at Main Headquarters next day—or any other day. He was never again going to arrive at any Headquarters. He was going to die.

CHAPTER XXV

DEATH ON THE TRAIN

YES! Major Tauber had got to die. But how? That was the question. Since he was on duty, and the type of man he was, there was no conceivable way of getting him to leave the train of his own free will. If it had been going to stop at several stations it might have been possible to trick him into doing so, then leave him behind. But it was not. Therefore the first problem was, should he be pushed off, or left to continue on it as a corpse?

In either case the deed had to be done before they reached Berlin. That was a pity, as Lanzi would still be on the train, and his presence might result in complications which could obviously not arise after he had left it. However, Lanzi was a simple soul, so it should not be difficult to pull the wool over his eyes, and the advantages of doing the job during the night, while the servants and train attendants were either asleep or dozing, were so self evident that it would have been positive madness to delay it until daylight.

As de Richleau considered the matter, he saw that, even if he could have tricked the Major into getting off the train, that would be no guarantee against his upsetting the apple cart later. He would take the next train on to Main Headquarters and undo any success that his predecessor might have had in influencing General von Moltke. Again, to entice him to a door and push him out while the train was in motion would not necessarily prove one hundred per cent effective. If he were only injured he might reach the nearest house, or be found in the morning, and telephone to Aix a report of the murderous attack that had been made upon him. That would never do. Therefore, he had to die *on* the train, and the impression be given that he had committed suicide.

But why? What reason could possibly be suggested for his having done so? De Richleau knew nothing of the Major's private life, so for a moment he was at a complete loss to provide any plausible reason why he should take his own life.

Then, in a flash, it came to him. It could be inferred that the Major had been the bearer of ill tidings from the Eastern Front; that he regarded the situation there as so grave that he believed a major defeat to be inevitable. It could be said that a few days before he had seen von Mackensen's Corps break at Gumbinnen; had actually witnessed soldiers of the invincible German Army running for their lives before the Russians. The shame of having to convey such news to his Emperor had proved too much for him. He had preferred death.

'That,' thought the Duke, 'was a really artistic touch, and it would add enormous weight to the story he meant to tell.'

He greatly disliked the horrible task that he had decided to undertake; yet he was not troubled by any moral scruples. Tauber was not only an enemy, but a dangerous enemy—a man who, if he lived, would prove very useful to the German General Staff. Such men were very necessary for the less spectacular, but absolutely essential skilled routine work of planning battles. In the final analysis their conscientious labours would cost the Allies many thousands of lives. Moreover, he carried a pistol, so was an armed combatant. If, without danger to himself, while lurking behind a bush, he could have shot dead a Frenchman, an Englishman or a Russian, he would undoubtedly have done so. In this case de Richleau proposed to be the man behind the bush. All the same, he was extremely glad that the Major had not proved to be a likable fellow.

It was close on midnight when Lanzi yawned and said: "I think I'll get to bed."

"Do," replied the Duke. "I shall follow you shortly. But I want to see, first, whether the Major manages to get out his game of patience."

"Oh well!" Lanzi shrugged good-naturedly. "In that case I'll keep you company for a bit longer."

De Richleau had the horrible business before him very much in mind, and was now anxious to get it over. Concealing his annoyance, he said with a smile: "Don't bother about me. You've got be up by six, so I should get all the sleep you can. You want to be on the top of your form for to-morrow night."

Lanzi thought for a moment, grinned and stood up. "That's true. All right; I'll be off then."

When he had ambled away, the Duke turned his attention to the table and made a pretence of being interested in the Major's game. With some disquiet he saw that it looked like ending sooner than he had expected. That was unfortunate, as he had wanted to give Lanzi time to get to bed before he acted. On the other hand, he could not afford to allow Tauber to pack up and go to his sleeping birth. It was certain that the three of them had been put in adjacent compartments. To kill him in his would entail a risk that Lanzi might hear sounds which it would be difficult to explain afterwards. The job must be done here, at the table.

When Lanzi had been gone about four minutes, the Major had only three more cards left to turn up. De Richleau decided that he dared wait no longer. Getting to his feet, he said:

"I see you are going to get out all right."

"I will if the last card is the ace," muttered Tauber.

They had taken off their belts before sitting down and put them up in the rack. Stretching over Tauber's bullet head, de Richleau took the Major's belt instead of his own. Then, just as he was about to put it on, he exclaimed: "How silly of me. I've taken your belt by mistake."

Tauber was still immersed in his game. "No matter, *Herr Oberste,*" he replied, without looking up. "Put it on the seat. I shall want it in a minute."

Instead of putting it on the seat, the Duke laid it on the end of the table, and remarked: "You use a different make of pistol from us, don't you?"

"Yes. The German pattern is the better. Its ejector is less liable to jam."

"May I look?" asked de Richleau, and without waiting for an answer he took the Mauser from its holster. By its weight he knew at once that it was loaded, and on pretence of examining it he clicked a bullet up into the chamber.

The Major gave a throaty chuckle, and made several quick moves. He knew now that the last card was the ace, so he was going to get out.

De Richleau said quietly: "How stupid it is that we staff officers, who rarely come within miles of the enemy, should have to carry loaded weapons."

"It is an order," replied the Major sententiously. "We are at war."

"Yes," murmured the Duke. "We are at war." As he spoke, he thrust the pistol to within an inch of the Major's temple and pulled the trigger.

Had the train been at a standstill, the crack of the weapon might have been heard beyond the pullman, but the special was moving at sixty miles an hour, and de Richleau was confident that its roar would have drowned the sound of the shot. For a moment he stood there contemplating his awful handiwork.

The bullet had entered the Major's head just above the ear, making only a neat little hole in the closely shaven scalp, from which a trickle of blood was issuing. But after passing through his brain it had smashed open the far side of his skull. Without a sound, he had slumped forward on to the table, scattering the patience cards in all directions, and from the horrible wound a mess of blood and brains was now seeping over them.

Suddenly the Duke heard a sound. Jerking his head round, he saw to his horror that Lanzi had re-entered the pullman.

Advancing between the tables with a smile on his face, the Baron said: "I forgot my cigar case. I——"

The sentence was never finished. At that instant he had approached near enough to see round the back of an intervening arm-chair. As he caught sight of the Major's body beyond it, the smile froze on his lips.

"*Gott im Himmel!*" he exclaimed. "What has been happening here?"

"He—he shot himself," replied de Richleau quickly. "It was—an accident. He was showing me his gun—explaining how much better the German weapon is than ours. There must have been a bullet in the chamber. It went off."

Frantically he sought in his mind for further explanations. Lanzi's damnably ill-timed arrival on the scene had ruled out the suicide story. The Major would never have taken his own life with someone looking on, and he had been contentedly immersed in his game of patience when Lanzi had left them barely five minutes earlier. But would the accident story be believed?

Lanzi's eyes fell upon the pistol that the Duke still held in his hand: then they switched to the Major's body.

De Richleau followed his glance. Even in experienced hands accidents can easily happen with loaded weapons, but when a pistol goes off by mistake the person handling the weapon is hardly likely to be holding it with the barrel pointed at the side of his own head.

Lanzi's eyes lifted. Suspicion dawned in them as they met the Duke's. Then a question issued from the moustached and bearded lips:

"How could he have shot himself with his arm doubled under him like that?"

The Duke sighed. He liked old Lanzi. He had even become quite fond of him. But he, too, was an enemy soldier. For all his self-indulgence and casual disregard of his responsibilities as an officer, he was not the man to allow himself to be made an accessory to murder. Neither threats nor promises would avail to make him hold his tongue. His life must not be allowed to weigh against the chance of being able to bring help to France in her dire need. Slowly, de Richleau said:

"You've had a wonderful life, haven't you? If I were you I should have no regrets about not living on to experience the pains and frustrations of old age."

For a second Lanzi's blue eyes bulged. There was a look of horror in them. Automatically he clasped his hand to his side, but he was not wearing his gun. Then the look faded. One of sudden comprehension replaced it, and he smiled.

"So *Monsieur le Duc de Richleau* is at heart a Frenchman after all."

"I am British by nationality," replied the Duke. "But in this I act for France. I shall always regret what I am about to do; but I am compelled to it by issues that far transcend all personal sentiment."

Suddenly he jerked up the pistol so that it pointed at the Colonel Baron Lanzelin Ungash-Wallersee's heart, and squeezed the trigger.

The Baron had his left hand on the high back of an arm-chair. For a moment he supported his weight by it. His blue eyes bulged again. Almost instantly sweat started out on his forehead. A trickle of saliva issued from his lips and ran down his carefully parted grey beard. The train roared on through the night. It rocked slightly. He coughed, blood welled from his mouth, and he fell dead at the Duke's feet.

De Richleau closed his eyes. Beads of sweat were gathering on his own forehead. His hands were trembling.

After a moment he pulled himself together. It was unlikely that one of the train staff would enter the pullman before morning. But there was no guarantee of that, so he felt that he must not waste a second. And he now had a plausible explanation for two deaths to think out.

Hastily seizing the dead Major's arm, he pulled it from beneath his chest, opened the hand and closed it round the butt of the Mauser. Taking up his belt and pistol holster from the table, he laid them on the chair beside him. Then he heaved up Lanzi's body and propped it in the arm-chair facing Tauber's corpse.

Anyone coming upon this grim charade would be certain to draw the inference that the Major had shot the Baron through the heart, then blown out his own brains. But why? Why? Why? What possible motive could be suggested to account for the Major having killed a man he hardly knew?

Money? No—out of the question. A drunken quarrel? No—middle-aged staff officers do not behave like dock-side roughs. A woman? No—the social circles in which they moved were poles apart. But yes! Why not?

As the idea struck him, the Duke snapped his fingers with excitement, then padded swiftly down the pullman and along the corridor of the next coach. The only light there came from Lanzi's sleeping compartment. It was easily identified as his soldier valet had unpacked his rich silk dressing-gown and night things for him. Slipping inside it, the Duke seized Lanzi's already open kit bag and began to rummage among its contents. In a moment he found the thing he was after. It was Lanzi's 'Bible', containing the photographs of the eight beauties who made up his scattered harem. De Richleau took out his handkerchief, and with it carefully removed the one of Mitzi Muller. To his joy he saw that it had the imprint of a Berlin photographer along its bottom edge. That was quite enough to infer that she was a German. Sliding the window back a little, he threw the album with its photographs of the other seven beauties out into the night. Then, diving his hand into the kit bag again, he fished out one of Lanzi's books of pornographic pictures. With that and the photo of Mitzi, still held in his handkerchief, he hurried back to the pullman.

Laying the book on the table in front of Lanzi, he picked up the dead man's hand and made the finger and thumb hold the upper edge of the photograph. The bottle of brandy, still two-thirds full, was standing near the window. Having poured half the remaining contents into his own tumbler, he tipped about a wine-glassful slowly on to Tauber's neck just below the ear, so that it should run down under his stiff uniform collar towards his chest. Then he replaced the bottle, now four-fifths empty, on the table.

Stepping back, he surveyed his work with the dispassionate eye of a stage-manager. Temporarily, the thought that he was responsible for this awful tableau of death and blood had entirely passed from his mind. For several moments he remained there, his glance roving over every detail of it, to make certain that he had not overlooked some little thing which might incriminate himself.

He knew that his fingerprints were scattered everywhere. But that could not be helped. No doubt a thorough examination of the scene of the crime might produce various awkward questions which he would find it difficult to answer, but he hoped to prevent such an examination from taking place, and to be out of the country before suspicion could fall on him. The one thing which might have damned him before he could get away was Mitzi's photograph, as that would be exhibit No. 1, and the first to be tested for prints. That was why he had been so careful not to touch it with his naked fingers.

Picking up the tumbler of brandy, he carried it along to the sleeping-car, found his apartment, and sat down on the bunk. He suddenly felt very cold and noticed that he was shivering, so he slowly drank about a third of the brandy, then threw the rest out of the window.

Feeling better now, as the spirit made the blood course more quickly through his veins, he carefully examined his clothing for spots of blood. But he could find none, so he undressed, got into bed, and put out the light. He did not even try to sleep, as he did not think for one moment that he would be able to. Perhaps for that very reason, sleep came to him almost immediately.

He was woken by the sliding back of his door, and a scared voice saying, "Pardon, *Herr Oberst*. Please to come at once. There is trouble on the train. A very serious matter. Murder! Suicide! I do not know. Please to come quickly."

The man in the doorway was a fat fellow in a sergeant's uniform, who was evidently acting as train conductor. De Richleau stared at him owlishly for a moment, blinked several times and muttered irritably:

"What the devil are you talking about?"

On the sergeant renewing his pleas and exclamations, the Duke got out of bed, slipped on his dressing-gown and slippers, and followed him down the corridor to the pullman. He saw at once that nothing had been altered in the grisly scene he had arranged. The soldier-servants of the two dead men were standing a few feet from the bodies, and with them was the orderly who had brought the drinks the previous night.

With an exclamation of feigned amazement and horror, the Duke halted; then stood there regarding the two dead officers. After a brief pause he asked; "When did this happen? Did any of you hear the sound of shots?"

"*Nein*, *Herr Oberst*," replied the three men in chorus, and the sergeant added: "I think it must have happened last night. The blood from the *Herr Major's* head is already thickly congealed."

De Richleau nodded. He knew very well that no officer of the German army would have dreamed of discussing such a matter with other ranks, so he proceeded to analyse the crime and talk, as though to himself, meanwhile.

The brandy he had poured over the Major's neck and collar had dried without leaving any trace except for a rich aroma, as he had known would be the case. With a loud sniff, he remarked:

"They must both have been drunk. I had only one tot out of that bottle, so they drank almost the whole of it between them."

He then flicked open the book, so that the men standing near him could catch a glimpse of one of the bawdy pictures it contained; but closed it again quickly with a frown, and said: "They were looking at that together when I left them. What the devil could have happened afterwards?"

Leaning forward, he grasped the Major's dead hand, levered back the stiffened fingers, and took the pistol from it. By so doing he neatly accounted for any of his own fingerprints that might be found on the weapon. After examining it, he laid it back on the table. "Two bullets gone. I thought as much. The Major fired both shots."

Craning his neck sideways a little, he peered down at the photograph of Mitzi, and asked: "Do any of you know this young woman? Might she by chance be the Major's daughter, or his niece?"

Lanzi's valet nodded, and said with tears in his voice: "It is the Fraulein Muller, whom the *Herr Oberst Baron* visited whenever we passed through Berlin."

Then Tauber's servant replied woodenly. "May it please the *Herr Oberst*, I was new to the *Herr Major's* service, and know nothing of his private affairs."

The Duke shrugged his shoulders and muttered: "I think it fairly clear what happened. The Baron was showing his book of pictures to us. After I left he must have produced the photograph of the young woman he was going to meet in Berlin. By an evil chance it happened that she was some relative of the Major's, or perhaps a very dear friend. In any case the sight of her photograph in connection with the pictures in the book must have proved so great a shock to him that he temporarily lost his reason. When I left he was already a little drunk. Possibly the girl is his relative, and he felt his honour to be impugned. While the victim of a brain storm, he pulled out his pistol and shot the Baron. Then, when he realized what he had done, he shot himself."

De Richleau's audience solemnly nodded acceptance of his theory, and he had no doubt at all that they would pass it on to whoever questioned them about the crime. Abruptly he asked the sergeant: "What time do we get to Berlin?"

The sergeant took out a turnip watch. "It is now nine minutes past six, *Herr Oberst*. We should arrive about twenty before seven."

"Then get me paper, pen and ink. I must write a report of this terrible occurrence for the police."

When the sergeant returned with the writing materials, de Richleau gave him a piece of paper and said: "Make a sketch of the table and mark the position clearly of everything upon it." Then he turned to the others. "Get some sheets to cover the bodies, and pails of hot water to clear up the mess."

On mobilization, the Germans followed the simple course of retaining every specially qualified man at the job he understood, but put him into uniform. In civil life, therefore, the sergeant had been a pullman car conductor, so he was well acquainted with the proper procedure when a crime had been committed on a train.

Automatically resuming his civilian outlook for a moment, he said: "Pardon, *Herr Oberst*. Nothing must be touched. When we reach Berlin this car will be shunted on to a siding for police examination."

Turning very slowly, de Richleau looked at the sergeant as though he could hardly believe his ears; then he said icily, "When I require your advice I will ask for it. I am proceeding to Kaiser's Headquarters on an urgent mission from my Emperor. That their Imperial Majesties' business should be delayed for the convenience of the police is unthinkable. I have no intention of waiting in a Berlin station while another car is found for me. We shall deposit the bodies and leave at once. Now draw that plan of the table instantly, or you will hear more of this."

The Duke knew his Germans, and the way to treat them. At his very first glance the sergeant had resumed his military outlook. He stood stiffly to attention as if he had a ramrod down his throat, and the sweat began to ooze out of his fat face.

"*Jawohl, Herr Oberst!*" he gasped, "*Jawohl!*" and set to drawing a rough plan of the table as though his life depended on it.

Sitting down at the far end of the coach, the Duke wrote a brief report, giving the bare facts as he might be presumed to know them. When he had done, and the sergeant had completed the sketch, he turned to the servants and orderlies who were standing by. On his instructions the two bodies were wrapped in sheets and carried out to the lobby of the pullman. The pistol, the photo, the book, the bottle and the cards were collected and put into a cardboard box. Then the men were set to work with their pails of water, cloths and scrubbing brushes, to obliterate all traces of the crime.

They were only just completing the job when the train ran into a suburban junction outside Berlin. Lanzi was to have alighted there, then it was scheduled to go round the outskirts of the city until it got on to the Hanover line. De Richleau had counted on the deaths of Lanzi and the Major being discovered in sufficient time for him to put the right ideas into the heads of the train staff, and to get most of the evidence done away with, before the train reached the capital. He now felt that things could hardly have fallen out better, as there had been time enough for him to do all he required, but little over for the men to discuss the tragedy among themselves.

On the platform, with the usual German efficiency, a relief engine-driver and fireman were waiting to take over, and a Railway Transport Officer, to see that the staff officers who were travelling in the special had everything they required. De Richleau, still in his silk dressing-gown, alighted and went up to the R.T.O.

With haughty abruptness he said: "I am *Oberst Herzog von Richleau* of the Imperial Austrian Army. There has been a most regrettable occurrence on this train. A drunken quarrel between two officers resulted in their deaths. I am on my way to Kaiser's Headquarters. You will understand that I must proceed on my journey without a moment's delay. Here is my report. I propose to leave the sergeant conductor of the train and the servants of the two officers to give the police such details as they can. Should it be deemed necessary, I will, of course, return here to attend the inquest as soon as my duties permit. Be good enough to take charge of the bodies and such evidence as we have managed to collect."

No people in the world have such a slavish respect for titles as the Germans. On finding that he was being addressed by a Duke, the *Oberleutnant* R.T.O., who had been a railway inspector in civil life, positively radiated deference and desire to earn a word of praise. The sheet-shrouded bodies were carried out and laid on a truck, the cardboard box containing the pistol and other items were handed to the

Oberleutnant, the kits of Lanzi and Tauber were placed in his charge, the fat sergeant and servants were turned over to him. Within five minutes of the train having pulled in, it pulled out again on its way to Aix-la-Chapelle.

For de Richleau everything had so far gone like clockwork; but he found himself unable to do more than toy with the breakfast that one of the orderlies brought him. He hoped that, by this time, some Heavenly General had detailed Major Tauber to a long spell of cleaning out latrines; but Lanzi's death lay heavily on his conscience. He had no doubts at all that he had been justified in shooting the Baron, but he admired the way in which he had stood up to death when he saw there was no escape from it; and in spite of the fact that he had never developed into more than a greedy schoolboy let loose in the tuck-shop of life, there had been nothing petty, mean or cruel about him.

To distract his thoughts, the Duke set about dealing with Tauber's dispatch case. He had feared to leave it with the Major's other kit in case some zealous official sent it on to Main Headquarters and it arrived there only a few hours after himself; so he had said that he would deliver it, and taken it to his sleeping compartment when the Major's kit had been removed from the train. As he had expected, the case was locked so, having pulled down all the blinds in the compartment, he slit open one end of it with his razor. Then he removed the dispatches and read them through.

All of them except one from Ludendorff to von Moltke were on administrative matters and of no interest to him. The latter reported on the inconclusive battle of Gumbinnen, inferring it to have been a German defeat and painting the rout of Mackensen's XVIIth Corps as even worse than it had been in fact. Only a bare mention was made of General von François, and his splendid performance was glossed over with a few words of faint praise. The writer's evident intention was to convey that on the arrival of General von Hindenburg and himself, the German 8th Army had been in a chaotic muddle and bordering on collapse. He then went on to give details of the re-deployment that was taking place, without any reference to the fact that General Hoffmann had been responsible for these brilliant moves and inferring that he had ordered them himself. The dispatch ended on a note of quiet, if rather smug, self-confidence, conveying that now the Command had been transferred to competent hands His Imperial Majesty need no longer have any fears for the safety of East Prussia.

De Richleau would have given a great deal to have been able to deliver the first part of the dispatch without the rest of it, but, that being impossible, he tore it into small pieces, did the same with the others, and at intervals of a few minutes, threw the pieces out of the window. The dispatch case carried no means of identification except the Major's initials, so when the train was passing through a tunnel he threw the case after the torn papers.

For four hours the train roared across the North German plain, reaching Hanover at ten-thirty. Then it passed through more picturesque country until it came to the outskirts of Essen at about half past one. There, it entered the black belt of Germany's vast munition works. For the next hour and a half, groups of tall, smoking chimneys, slag heaps, factory sheds and squalid slums provided a grim and seemingly endless panorama. But on the far side of Cologne it came to an end at last, and for the final hour or so of its journey the train sped through pleasantly wooded lands to Aix. After shunting in the station there, it ran out of the town for a few miles and finally came to a halt at half past four at a siding in a small wood, beyond the fringe of which could be glimpsed a big château.

The Duke sent one of the orderlies to summon the whole of the train staff, including the engine-driver and fireman. When they had collected in the pullman, he told them that the authorities would be most adverse to anything leaking out about the tragedy that had occurred the previous night. He took their names and gave them warning that, should any rumour of the scandal become current at Main Headquarters, they would be held jointly responsible for it. Having seen his baggage deposited in a shed on the siding, he then took his dispatch case in one hand, his courage, metaphorically, in the other, and walked through the wood until he came to the first sentry post.

There, he was provided with a guide, and a quarter of an hour later, an A.D.C. conducted him to a youngish-looking, clean-shaven Colonel, named Bauer. When he had stated his business, the Colonel said:

"Naturally, General von Moltke will give the letter you bring from General von Hötzendorf his earliest possible attention; but he has been out all day, accompanying His Majesty on a tour of inspection, and they are not expected back until late to-night. To-morrow morning will be the earliest he can see you. If the matter is urgent, perhaps you would prefer to discuss it with his deputy, General von Stein."

Anxious as de Richleau now was to get out of Germany, he had killed two men for an opportunity to influence the Chief of Staff, and an interview with his deputy would not amount at all to the same thing; so he replied:

"I should be very happy to have a preliminary talk with General von Stein; but I must, of course, present my letter personally."

After speaking over a telephone, Bauer announced that the General would see the Duke at a quarter past six. He then ordered the A.D.C.

to have de Richleau's baggage sent for and allot him one of the visitors' rooms at the top of the house.

At six-fifteen the Duke was received by von Stein, a handsome, monocled Prussian, with a pleasant smile; and the moment they came face to face, de Richleau realized that his luck was in. Although he had forgotten it, he had met the General some years before, when they had both been guests at a big shooting party in Hungary.

The ice having thus been happily broken, they were soon talking with complete frankness about the situation on the battle-fronts. German Main Headquarters were entirely satisfied with the progress in the West. Although, as the General remarked, his Chief had reduced the ninety-seven divisions prescribed in the original Schlieffen Plan to seventy-eight, that had not made the least difference. The line of the Meuse had been forced on the 19th–20th, the mighty wheel was swinging inexorably through Belgium, and its all-important pivot, the great fortress of Namur, had fallen on the 23rd. The quite unexpected appearance of a British Army, under General Sir John French, on the extreme left of the allied line had failed to hold the advance for more than a day, and hour by hour news of fresh victories continued to come in.

So, thought the Duke, Churchill was right about the Germans getting across the Meuse by the 20th day, and everything now hung on whether he would prove equally right about the 40th. It was good news that the Germans were employing many fewer divisions than required by the original plan. That would give the French a better chance when the attempt was made to stem the tide. But it was bad news about Namur—very bad, as that shoulder of the wheel should have been the point at which the counter-attack was launched, with the object of lopping off the extended right arm of the German armies, and the loss of the fortress would make such an operation far more difficult to launch. It was the first he had heard of the British having landed an Expeditionary Force, and he asked with much interest how it was showing.

"We came up against them at Mons yesterday at dawn," replied the General, "and they fought there very stubbornly all day; but last night they were compelled to retire. Many of their officers and men saw active service in South Africa, so if their numbers were greater they might prove quite formidable. But they have only two corps in the field. As His Majesty remarked, it is a contemptible little army. Its defeat will prove no more than a side show."

"What of the French?" inquired the Duke.

"They have been fighting with great bravery. Since the 20th they have done their utmost to turn the tide of battle, but without avail. Of course, everything was against them from the start. Their staff-work is not to be compared with ours, and most of their equipment is pitiful. They have not even field-service uniforms. The red trousers and blue coats of their infantry make them an easy mark, and the tin breast-plates of their Cuirassiers, shining in the sun, invite a bullet from a mile away. But, that apart, including the four British divisions, they have only fifty-five all told operating against our seventy-eight, so their defeat is inevitable. But tell me about the Eastern front? I fear that presents a very different picture, and we are acutely worried about it."

De Richleau gave a resumé of the situation, which might have been taken almost word for word from the first part of Ludendorff's dispatch.

As he listened, the General's face was grave, and at length he said: "It would be a great blow to our prestige if East Prussia were overrun. That might even put new heart into the French, and it is of the first importance that we should overcome their resistance quickly, so that we can about face before the bulk of the Russian hordes descends upon us. What do you think of the new Command's chances of re-forming a solid front?"

The Duke shrugged. "They were doing their utmost when I left; but, unfortunately, General von Prittwitz scattered the 8th Army over such a wide area that there is a great risk of its being defeated piecemeal."

Feeling that he had said enough for the moment, he turned the conversation to his mission from von Hötzendorf, and expressed the Austrian C.-in-C.'s disappointment that his allies had, so far, failed to give him the co-operation they had promised.

Von Stein smiled bleakly. "You know even better than I do how we are placed up there. And the fact is that the Russian attack came before we expected it. We have good reason to believe that the French begged the Russians to take the weight off them, and that the Grand Duke responded by launching his first offensive several days in advance of his original schedule. Anyhow, you can see for yourself that we are in no position to assist your army at the moment; but, of course, we'll talk the matter over with General von Moltke in the morning."

That ended their formal talk. But de Richleau met von Stein again later that evening, at dinner in the senior officers' mess. There, he had excellent opportunity of sowing further alarm and despondency about the Eastern front, both in the mind of the General and those of several other officers, to all of whom it was already a dark cloud in Germany's otherwise sunny sky.

When he went to bed, he felt he had made an excellent beginning, but he fervently hoped that he would be out of Germany within another twenty-four hours. He thought it very unlikely that anyone at Wartenburg would learn his whereabouts, or that he would be called upon to give further evidence about the tragedy on the train, for a day or two yet. But one could never tell, and it needed only one little piece of bad luck for his life not to be worth six hours' purchase.

Next morning, the 25th, at eleven o'clock, he was summoned to the presence. General Count Helmath von Moltke was the nephew of the great Field Marshal of that name, who, ably supported by the 'Iron' Chancellor Bismarck, and the extremely capable War Minister, von Roon, had directed the victorious German armies in their classic campaigns against the Danes, Austrians, and French in the late 'sixties and 'seventies. The present holder of the title was a charming elderly gentleman of sixty-six, who owed his position to a combination of the facts that his uncle's mantle had descended on him and that he was a courtier-soldier with the ability to present all army matters in a light calculated to please his difficult Monarch. His experience of military affairs was wide, but his brain only mediocre. With him were General von Stein, and Colonel Tappen, his operations expert.

Von Hötzendorf's letter consisted of only a few lines, introducing its bearer, and a strongly worded appeal that, even at this belated date, the original plan for combined Austro-German operations against the Russians should be adhered to. When the Chief of Staff had read it, he said to de Richleau:

"Believe me, all of us here feel the deepest regret that it was not possible to carry out our original intentions with regard to the Eastern Front. But the destruction of the French army as the first move in the war was, for us, a paramount necessity. However, that is well on its way to accomplishment."

"My congratulations, Excellency," said the Duke. "May I, then, carry the good news back to General von Hötzendorf that you will shortly be in a position to assist him?"

"We may be able to do so indirectly, but I do not wish to guarantee anything for the moment; and I am much comforted by the thought that his situation does not urgently demand it. His offensive is meeting with considerable success without our help. This morning the news came in that General Dankl's 1st Austrian Army inflicted a heavy defeat yesterday on the Russians, and took Krasnik."

"I am delighted to hear that, Excellency. But what of the future? Your 8th Army in East Prussia is seriously disorganized and in a most precarious position. Should it be defeated by General Samsonov, he will then be able to turn round and add his weight to the forces already opposing the Austro-Hungarian armies. How can they be expected to stand alone against the whole might of Russia?"

"Ah!" sighed von Moltke. "You have touched upon the sore point that I have just been discussing with my officers. I gather from General von Stein that you take a very pessimistic view of our prospects in East Prussia."

De Richleau gave the appearance of hesitating uncomfortably, then he said: "Excellency, how can one do otherwise with the 8th Army in such poor shape and opposed to more than double its numbers. When I left General Ludendorff, he seemed confident of being able to form some sort of front, but should his confidence prove ill-founded it may result in a major disaster. After all, one cannot forget that to the south of him the Russian frontier is only 180 miles from Berlin."

Von Moltke nodded his bald head. "That is just what we fear. His over-confidence may prove our ruin. I spoke to him on the telephone late last night and offered to send him two Army Corps. He said that he would naturally be pleased to receive reinforcements, but he could quite well do without them."

The Duke suppressed a tremor of excitement. Two Army Corps! That meant in the neighbourhood of 100,000 men. And he had been thinking only in terms of Divisions. What a magnificent relief for hard-pressed France. Quickly, he said:

"If you can spare them from the West, Excellency, I beg you to send them. That would, in broad effect, be a satisfactory answer to General von Hötzendorf's appeal; as, wherever they were employed in the East, they would take a certain amount of Russian pressure off him."

"That is what I had in mind when I said just now that we might be able to help him indirectly." Von Moltke glanced at his deputy, and added: "We talked of sending the two Corps that were earmarked for the investment of Namur, didn't we?"

Von Stein inclined his head. "Yes, Excellency. The unexpected surrender of the fortress has rendered them redundant."

Colonel Tappen had been listening attentively. Prefacing his remark with a deferential cough, he put in quickly. "As I have already had the honour to point out to your Excellency, it is bad policy to make two bites at one cherry. If we are to reinforce the Eastern Front, we should not do so in driblets. Now that the battle in the West is as good as won, we could quite well afford to detach two Corps from our left and two Corps from our right. It will take them a few days to disengage, but in any case even the two Corps held in reserve for Namur could not reach General Hindenburg in time to participate in his battle for East Prussia. I submit that our wisest course would be to create a new Army under him on the line of the Vistula. If he suffers defeat in his approaching engagement, he can then fall back upon it, and we should at least not have to fear a deep penetration by the Russians into the Fatherland.

On the other hand if he succeeds in checking the present Russian advance, he will be able to order up those six fresh Corps and deploy them on his front. Then, with an army greater than that opposed to him, he would have the means to eliminate this peril of a Russian invasion once and for all."

De Richleau held his breath.

Von Moltke looked at von Stein and said: "Tappen is right, you know. I was almost persuaded to adopt this policy when we discussed the matter yesterday, Our visitor has confirmed my worst fears about prospects in East Prussia, so I now feel we must. That's settled then. Please give orders for the entraining of the two Corps to begin at once, and for the other four to follow as soon as possible."

The Duke could hardly believe his ears. *Six Corps! Six whole Corps! Three hundred thousand men—and* 200,000 *of them to be pulled out of the fighting line.* It was beyond his wildest dreams. If the French were capable of going over to the offensive on Churchill's 40th day, they would now have the advantage of numbers. By then, owing to these huge withdrawals, the German Army in the West would be stretched to breaking point. By an all-out effort it might not only be stopped, but smashed.

But the French were now being driven back all along the line. They might not stand, and certainly would not risk attempting a counter-offensive, unless they learned how greatly the forces opposed to them had been weakened. If they did not receive intelligence of the withdrawal of the six Corps they might continue to retreat, and this God-given opportunity be lost to them for ever. Everything might still be lost if de Richleau failed to get the stupendous news swiftly to Paris or London.

Keeping the excitement out of his voice with an effort, he said: "General von Hötzendorf will be delighted to hear your Excellency's decision. Have I your leave to convey it to him?"

"Certainly," von Moltke nodded. "I will confirm it in a personal letter for you to take back with you. But at mid-day I must attend upon His Majesty, so I shall not have time to write it until to-night. It will be time enough if you leave with it to-morrow morning."

That suited the Duke perfectly. The last thing he wanted was to be put on to a special train at once, as it might carry him hundreds of miles back into the heart of Germany before he could get off it. With a bow he said:

"In that case, Excellency, if you have no objection, I will spend the rest of the day in Aix. I have some old friends living there, with whom I should like to dine to-night."

"By all means," smiled the Chief of Staff. De Richleau saluted and Colonel Tappen showed him out. The momentous interview was over.

He knew that he must abandon most of his kit, but upstairs in his room he crammed as many things as he could, including Ilona's photograph, the Austrian decoration he had been given, his pistol and his field-glasses, into a small attaché case.

As he left the building, he saw a line of powerful cars drawn up in front of its main entrance. On the bonnet of the leading one fluttered a flag bearing the Imperial Eagle. Standing aside, he waited there for a few moments then, as he had expected, the Kaiser appeared. A long grey cloak, dangling to his heels, hid his uniform except for the shining jack-boots; but with his fiercely upturned moustache and brass-pointed helmet he looked very martial. As he strutted forward to the car he was followed at six paces by a brilliant retinue of lesser German kings and princes and several generals. When within sight of troops everyone was forbidden to approach nearer to him, because he was so short, and his vanity so great, that he could not bear his lack of stature to be made obvious by the proximity of taller men. It was that same awful vanity which had tempted him to play the War Lord, and made him, after von Hötzendorf and Count Berchtold, more responsible than any other individual for plunging the civilization of his era into chaos.

When the cars had driven off, de Richleau soon secured a lift in another that was going into Aix. There, he booked a room at the ***Hôtel de la Poste*** and lunched in its restaurant. Then he went out shopping, his procedure being similar to that which he had adopted nearly two months before in Belgrade. At a leather merchant's he bought a portmanteau, then took it to an outfitter's, where he said that he wanted a good ready-made suit as a present for his manservant who was getting married, and about the same build as himself. Taking it away with him he bought a Homburg hat, six collars and two neckties at other shops. About boots he did not bother, as those he was wearing were very comfortable, and the civilian trousers would come down well, concealing their tops. He then bought ham, hard-boiled eggs, cheese, butter and rolls, enough for a good meal.

Making his purchases presented no difficulty, as in those distant days of plenty no one had even conceived the idea that the word 'ration' would ever be applied to anything except the issue of food to the fighting forces, or shared out by parties of explorers in the most distant and desolate parts of the earth.

At a garage, he hired a car, and drove it back to the hotel. Foreign currencies were still readily exchanged in every country and, Aix being so near to Holland, the cashier was able to provide him with Dutch *florins* in exchange for some of his German *marks*. Going upstairs, he changed into the civilian clothes, packed his uniform into the portmanteau and, having left enough money on the dressing-table to pay his bill, carried it, with his little attaché case, down the back stairs to the yard where he had parked the car. At a quarter to four, he was driving out of Aix.

Ahead of him to the west, lay that curious tag of Dutch territory between Germany and Belgium known as the Maastricht Appendix. The frontier was less that three miles distant, and he had only to cross it to be safe. He had received official permission to leave Headquarters and, unless something quite unforeseen connected his appearance there with his disappearance from Wartenburg, his absence would not be noticed until the following morning. And even if a telegram requiring his arrest did now come in, it would be hours before he could be traced.

But, as a result of the war, people could no longer pass freely from one country to another without official papers, and he knew that the frontier would be guarded. In every country there were still many men with strongly pacifist views. Such people saw no glamour in the war and bitterly resented the loss of their freedom when called up for it. In consequence, all the conscript armies were losing quite a considerable number of men as deserters. That was one of the main reasons why Germany had closed her frontiers. She had, moreover, insisted that the Dutch should police their frontiers as well, and return to her any deserters who were caught after managing to get across it. The Dutch were still highly nervous that if they gave offence to Germany they might suffer the same fate that had overtaken Belgium, so they had promptly agreed; which meant that there would be a double line of patrols to get through.

Two miles outside Aix, the Duke drove the car into a wood, abandoned it there, and, taking only his attaché case and the food he had bought, went forward on foot to reconnoitre.

From a piece of high ground, he saw that, extending from the frontier post, on both sides of the road a barbed wire fence had been erected. But about a mile to the south it had not yet been completed. Gangs of men were still working on it, and there was a gap of another mile or more to a distant hillside, on which tiny figures were erecting another section of the fence.

By a circuitous route, he made his way to a coppice opposite the gap and sat down there to wait for nightfall. While the light was still good, he made a prolonged study of the country in front of him through his field glasses, endeavouring to memorize every hedge and ditch within sight. At eight o'clock he ate his picnic meal, but the August evening seemed interminable, and it was not until a little before ten o'clock that he decided to make his bid for freedom.

He had a nasty open space of over a mile to cover, but the night was fairly dark and his long experience as a hunter now stood him in good stead. Once a patrol passed within twenty feet of him as he lay, holding his breath, in the long grass. When it was out of earshot he stealthily went forward again, and wriggled over the low ditch that marked the boundary. For another half-mile he squirmed along, still fearful that if he got to his hands and knees his silhouette might be seen. Then he reached a hedge and was able to move at a crouching run along it. Ten minutes later he got to a wood, so could stand up and proceed at a cautious walk without danger. A hundred yards inside the wood he sat down among some bushes and, carefully shading the spark of his lighter, lit a cigarette. While inside Germany he had striven to keep out of his mind the constant peril in which he stood. But it had never been far from his thoughts, and the knowledge that he had come safely through now filled him with ineffable relief. As soon as he had finished his cigarette he went on again.

Having studied the country so thoroughly through his field glasses in the late afternoon, he had no difficulty in finding his way back to the road about a mile and a half beyond the frontier post. The road was empty, so he advanced along it, keeping a sharp look-out. Ten minutes later he heard a motor-cycle approaching, and hid himself in a ditch until it had passed; but he met nothing further and after a two-mile tramp entered a little village that he knew to be called Gulpham.

It was not on the railway, and even if it had been he would not have attempted to take a train from a small place so near the frontier. As he could not speak Dutch it would have been too great a risk. He was heading for Maastricht, which was only ten miles farther on, knowing that in a city of its size he could ask in French or English for a ticket without arousing suspicion. It was now nearly midnight, so all the houses in the village were in darkness, save one in which a light showed through thin curtains in a pair of downstairs windows. Against its porch a bicycle was leaning. Transferring his attaché case to his left hand, he mounted the bike and rode off on it.

The country was flattish, so an hour and a quarter's hard pedalling brought him to within sight of Maastricht's spires, dimly seen against the starry sky. Only a suburb of the town lay on the east bank of the Maas, and he had to cross a bridge over the river to reach its centre. It was now too late for him to catch a train that night, but he hoped to find some small hotel where he could get a bed, then take a train north first thing in the morning.

As he approached the bridge he saw that its eastern end was brightly lit, and that two policemen were standing there on the pavement.

But as there was no barrier it did not seem likely that they would challenge him. Putting on a spurt, he pedalled past them.

Suddenly one of them gave a shout and pointed at the Duke's feet. Giving a swift glance down, he saw to his consternation that the motion of pedalling had caused his trousers to ride up, exposing his field-boots.

By the time the policemen called on him to halt, and began to run after him, he was half-way across the bridge. To his dismay, he now saw that its western end was also lit and that two more policemen were posted there. Behind him the whistles of the first two shrilled. The two in front sprang into the road to bar his passage. It was too late for him to pull up and jump over the parapet of the bridge into the river. He could only increase his pace and attempt to swerve round the men ahead of him. As he did so, one of them ran at him sideways, and was just in time to jab his truncheon into the back wheel of the bicycle.

With a metallic clang the spokes of the spinning wheel tore the truncheon from the man's hand. But the bike stopped dead, pitching de Richleau over its handlebars. He hit the road with a frightful thump. The breath was driven from his body and for a moment he lay there half stunned. By the time he got back his wits, and attempted to stagger to his feet, all four policemen were gathered round him. One of them was pointing a revolver at his head.

His attaché case had flown from his hand, burst open and scattered its contents within a few feet of him. He caught sight of Ilona's photograph, the glass of its frame now cracked across. Then his eye fell on a paper bag that contained the remains of his supper. On it was printed in large letters the name of the *chacuterie* at which he had bought the ham, and underneath the damning words *Aix La Chapelle*.

The policemen were gabbling together in Dutch, but it was like enough to German for him to catch the gist of what they were saying. One of them pointed to de Richleau's field-boots, then to the paper bag, and another said:

"Yes, yes! He is clearly a deserter. To-morrow we will send him back to Germany."

CHAPTER XXVI

THE FALSE SIR PELLINORE

Two of the Duke's captors marched him off to the police station, and there he was given first aid. He needed it. He had fallen very heavily on the right side of his body, bruising it badly, sprained his wrist and crushed his ear.

The small automatic he usually carried under his arm was found and confiscated. Then after his hurts had been attended to, he was taken in front of a police inspector who spoke German. The inspector drew a form towards him and said in a bored voice: "Give me your name, regiment, and the time and place at which you crossed the frontier."

De Richleau thought it futile to deny that he had come from Germany. There was too much evidence against him. So he replied: "I crossed near Gulpham at about half past ten. But I am not a deserter. I am a British subject, and I was caught in Germany by the outbreak of the war."

"We've heard that one before," remarked the inspector a little wearily. "Name, please?"

The Duke hesitated only a second: "Sir Pellinore Gwaine-Cust."

On receiving the reply the inspector gave a cynical laugh. The muddy bandaged figure in shoddy ready-made clothes who stood before him certainly did not give the impression of being a member of the British aristocracy; but with a shrug he said:

"All right, *Sir* Cust. Where did you pinch the bike?"

Theft is theft all the world over, and the Duke was most averse to a minor crime being added to his other difficulties, so he replied promptly:

"I did not steal it. I brought it through from Aix with me."

The inspector nodded to his men. "Put him in a cell for the night. It is a routine case and the magistrate will deal with it in the morning."

Clearly there was nothing to be gained by further argument at the moment, so de Richleau allowed himself to be led away. One of the men helped him to undress then, lying in a narrow bed, he gave free rein to his acute anxiety about the future.

It was now the early hours of August 26th, so just over two days since he had left Wartenburg. By this time Nicolai and Steinhauer should have recovered from their concussion sufficiently to make statements. The killings on the train would be having repercussions, Main Headquarters would be wondering where Count Königstein had got to, and Ludendorff would soon be wanting to know what had become of Major Tauber. It needed only a single telephone call to link all three things up. Within another day or two at most, every policeman—military, civil and secret—in Germany would be hoping to earn promotion by capturing the elusive Austrian Colonel.

That was why he had not given his own name. If an evil fate decreed that he was to be sent back to Germany, an interval must elapse before his true identity was discovered, and during it he might regain his freedom. But the interval would not be a long one, as his disappearance from Main Headquarters would soon be connected with the Austrian Colonel who had bought a civilian suit in Aix that afternoon, and the deserter who had arrived in Holland via Gulpham that night.

It was as bad a plight as de Richleau had ever been in; and it was not until near dawn that he managed to get a few hours' sleep.

At ten o'clock he was taken to the Law Courts and spent two hours seated on a hard bench in an ante-room, with a sad-faced collection of men and women charged with minor offences. Just on mid-day his turn came. He was led into the court, and put in the dock in front of an elderly magistrate with a walrus moustache.

As he had feared might prove the case, the issue was complicated by his theft of the bicycle, and he was charged with that in addition to being a German deserter who had crossed the frontier illegally. He pleaded guilty to the latter, but not guilty to the theft, and declared himself to be a British subject.

Unfortunately for him the police had found the owner of the bicycle, who was present in court; so the theft was swiftly proved, and naturally prejudiced the magistrate against him in the other matter. Having asked in a severe voice if the prisoner could name anyone in Holland who knew him to be British, and received a reply in the negative, he inquired if the police inspector could give any evidence of nationality.

The inspector drew attention to the fact that the prisoner spoke perfect German, then produced the contents of his attaché case; among them his Zeiss binoculars, service pattern pistol, the Austrian decoration and the photograph of Ilona.

The sight of these items caused a plump, crop-headed man in the well of the court to jump to his feet and point an accusing finger towards the dock. To de Richleau's alarm, he learned that this individual was the German Consul, and that it was now part of his duties to secure the repatriation to Germany of all the Germans he could run to earth who had not been granted official permits to remain in Holland.

After a scornful reference to the fact that all deserters pretended to be Belgian, French or British, the Consul insisted that the prisoner's possessions clearly showed him to be either German or Austrian, and demanded his immediate extradition.

Greatly perturbed by the way matters were going, the Duke countered by saying in English: "I may speak German well, but I speak English better, because it is my native tongue. There are any number of people in London who can identify me, and I demand that the British Minister in the Hague should at once be informed of my predicament."

On this being translated, the magistrate said gravely: "A man's possessions cannot be taken as evidence of his nationality. It is quite possible that, like the bicycle, they were stolen."

De Richleau breathed again. The sight of the decoration, particularly, had filled him with dismay, as, engraved in very small letters on its back, was the name Count Königstein. But, by the grace of God, either the police had not noticed that or, like the magistrate, believing the things to have been stolen, thought it not worth mentioning. The magistrate went on:

"The British Legation is to be informed of the prisoner's presence here. I adjourn the case till Monday, to give an opportunity for them to communicate with London and verify his statement. If they cannot do so, he will be handed over to the German authorities. In the meantime he will serve three days' imprisonment for the theft of the bicycle and pay the owner ten *gülden* compensation for damage done to the machine."

In spite of the short prison sentence, the Duke smiled with relief. In a carefully worded letter he could easily pass on to the Legation the gist of the tremendously important information he had brought out of Germany, convey the truth about himself, and bring some member of its staff to his rescue well before the five-day adjournment was up. But he had counted his chickens before they were hatched. A moment later the German Consul was on his feet again.

"I desire to draw your Worship's attention to the neutrality laws," he said quickly. "Under them it is Holland's responsibility to do her utmost to prevent leakage of information from one combatant country to another. The prisoner admits that he has come from Germany. If he is a deserter, as I maintain, it is possible that he may have intended to betray his country. His anxiety to communicate with the British Legation suggests that. If he is allowed to write to the Legation his letter might contain much information harmful to Germany. I request that he should be permitted to communicate to the British Legation, or any official from it who may visit him here, only his name and the names of such relatives or friends as he states can prove his identity."

"Granted!" said the magistrate. "Next case."

As de Richleau was led from the court he realized that he was in a frightful fix. He could prove that he was British only through the Legation. Had he given his own name, with Sir Pellinore's as a reference, a telegram to London should have brought a reply that every effort must be made to procure his release at once. But, as an insurance against his immediate extradition, he had concealed his name and given Sir Pellinore's. He had chosen that of the baronet on an inspiration of the moment; led to it by the urgency of the news he carried, and the thought that while the Legation might leave 'Tom Brown' kicking his heels in Maastricht for a week an S O S from anyone so well known as Sir Pellinore would bring a British diplomat hastening to his assistance. But what was the situation now?

He was saddled with a three-day prison sentence, and was not to be allowed to communicate with any member of the Legation staff either verbally or in writing. If he continued to maintain that he was Sir Pellinore, he could obviously not also give that name as a reference for transmission to London. On the other hand, if he recanted and gave his own, by the time he had completed his sentence the Kaiser himself would have heard of his exploits and be screaming for his blood. As Holland was neutral, whether he could prove that he was British or not, she would still observe the extradition laws in cases of murder, and so hand him over to the Germans to be tried and shot. It was, therefore, clear that, whatever else he did, his life now depended more than ever on keeping his real name secret.

In consequence, when he was asked for references by the cynical inspector in an office adjacent to the court, as he had to say something he gave the names of half a dozen of his friends in London. But the procedure was quite senseless as none of them could possibly know that he was posing as Sir Pellinore.

De Richleau was then taken in a Black Maria to the local prison. There, he did not fare too badly as the injuries he had sustained the previous night secured him admission to the sanatorium. But being excused from prison labour proved a mixed blessing, as he had all the more time to brood: and he was not only worried about himself. He had news of the utmost importance regarding the military situation, and the thought of being prevented from getting it to London made him almost crazy with frustration.

The following afternoon he was sent for, and taken down to a room that had two wire screens fixed across it with a space of six feet between them. It was the room in which prisoners were allowed to see such visitors as they were permitted. On the other side of the far screen a tall, dark young man, dressed in clothes that had obviously been cut in

Savile Row, was standing. The Duke guessed at once that his assumption of Sir Pellinore's identity had come off, and brought an attaché from the Legation post-haste to see him. But this was very far from being the private interview on which he had counted.

The young man gave him one quick glance, and said: "I'm afraid there is some mistake. This is not——"

Instantly de Richleau cut him short. "There is no mistake. Tell your Minister that six German Corps are being dispatched——"

Before he could get any further the two warders who had brought him there flung themselves upon him. One clapped a hand to his mouth and between them they hustled him from the room.

Up in the sanatorium again, he cursed his ill luck. Evidently his visitor knew Sir Pellinore, or had been given a description of him, and no one could possibly mistake the slim, dark-haired prisoner for the grizzled, six foot four inches tall baronet. But worse, although the young man had not actually denounced him as an impostor, he had got as near to it as made no difference. Anyway, he would report that to be the case to his Legation, so no help would now be forthcoming from it on Monday.

With fury in his heart, de Richleau realized that in his anxiety to procure a swift release, he had hoist himself on his own petard. Had he given his name as Tom Brown, no one at the Legation would have been in a position to say if he was or was not that person. When his case came up again the British representative would at least have given him the benefit of the doubt and asked for a further adjournment while inquiries were made. That might have provided an opportunity to tip him off about the real facts of the case. But no such heartening prospect could now be hoped for. The German Consul would meet with no opposition, and the wretched prisoner would be hauled off to Germany to meet his fate. And he had not even the consolation of knowing that he had passed on his all-important news.

The forty-eight hours that followed were black ones for the Duke, and they culminated on Friday night in a most appalling nightmare. In it he saw again Major Tauber sprawled over the table in the pullman car: but now the German would not die. He lifted his bloody head, from one side of which a horrible mess of brains and splintered bone protruded. Slowly he stood up. De Richleau fired again. His bullet had no effect. The Major stretched out a pair of claw-like hands. Again and again the Duke fired, until the pistol he held was empty. The shots passed through the living corpse without making it even quiver. The clawing hands stretched out and up, until they closed about his neck. He awoke with a groan and found himself drenched with the sweat of terror.

During the five days and nights since his killings on the train his mind had been so fully occupied with his own urgent problems that he had managed to keep it fairly free from the memory of his terrible deed, and thought of it only at odd moments with a shudder of repulsion. Now, in total darkness, and with the nightmare fresh upon him, he strove once more to reassure himself that it had been absolutely necessary. Cold logic told him that it was no worse than having shot two enemies from an ambush. In war time no soldier needed any excuse for that; and he had been impelled to it by a stupendous issue that made two human lives a bagatelle. If justification were needed, he had it a thousand times over in the French and British lives he had saved by influencing the removal of six German Corps from the Western Front. But, all the same, he knew that, should he escape, it would be months, if not years, before he could entirely free his mind of that midnight journey from Wartenburg to Berlin.

In an effort to do so now, he began to think of Ilona. It was well over a fortnight since she had left for Hohenembs. The mountain air, rest and proper treatment under Bruckner should already be having its effect. She had promised him that she would stay there until she was really well. Franz Ferdinand and other members of her family had been cured of consumption, so there was every hope that she would be, too. Now that all the main armies were locked in a death struggle, the war situation should soon clarify. They could not continue such all-out efforts for very long without exhaustion setting in. One side or the other must soon achieve major victories, and that might lead to peace negotiations. Most people were convinced that the war would be over by Christmas. If it were, in another four months or so he could be with her again, and by that time she might be cured.

He began to wonder how the war would affect them in other respects. As long as she remained in Austria her royalty would always debar them from being much together, on account of scandal; but once the war was over she might travel again. That would make things easier, although they would still have to be very circumspect. Perhaps she could use her illness as an excuse for a long convalescence in Switzerland. She would be out of the public eye there and could probably arrange for him to occupy a position in her household. That would be marvellous—as long as it lasted. But how long would it last?

There was the question of her marriage. It had been postponed so often already and could not be put off indefinitely. Again and again he had been tempted by the glorious dream of persuading her to marry him, but had refrained from any attempt to do so on account of her having told him that to marry morganatically would bring disgrace on any woman of her rank. The war would alter many things, and perhaps it would alter her views on that. But such happiness seemed too much to hope for. He must be content to consider himself blessed in her love, and with the prospect that once the war was over they could at least snatch joyous hours together from time to time.

Then, as he lay there in the darkness, the grimness of his present situation seized upon him again. By Monday death would assuredly be waiting for him on the other side of the frontier, and his sole hope now of evading being taken back there under escort lay in provoking some change of attitude in the British Legation, with which he was not allowed to communicate.

On Saturday, at mid-day, after two almost sleepless nights, his prison sentenced ended; but he was not given his liberty. Instead, he was taken in the Black Maria back to the police station, and confined there in a cell to await the hearing of his case on Monday.

However, as a prisoner awaiting trial, he was allowed certain privileges that he had not enjoyed while in prison. He was permitted to send out for better food, wine, newspapers, and to have back his belongings, minus the pistols. His warders also chatted freely with him, and he soon discovered that, from fear that at any time Holland might suffer the same fate as Belgium, they were bitterly hostile to Germany.

One elderly man who had lived for a long time in Malaya, and spoke English, proved especially sympathetic. He obviously believed the Duke's story that he was a Briton escaped from Germany and, if he could do so without risking his job, seemed prepared to help him.

De Richleau still had a considerable amount of money on him; so he made up a wad of twenty-mark notes equivalent to £25 and, when the sympathetic warder came to escort him to the lavatory in the evening, he asked him in a whisper if he would accept it as the price of carrying a letter to the Hague for him.

To his disappointment the man shook his head. "No. I tare nod. If it contained information useful to the Pridish an' it afterwards discovered was thad I act as your messenger der Shermans would never rest until they got me pud in brison for it."

On the way back to his cell de Richleau thought again. As the warder was about to lock him in, he said: "All right then. Never mind about the letter. But I have two things here which could not possibly incriminate you, and if they can be got to the British Minister at the Hague in time they may enable him to save my life. The money is beside the point. You are welcome to that anyway, for your sympathy."

After a moment's hesitation, the warder asked: "What are der dings?"

De Richleau produced the photograph of Ilona and the Austrian decoration. "Here they are," he said; "and I propose to write on a slip of paper to go with them, 'In the event of my being being sent back to Germany please deliver to Ninety-nine Carlton House Terrace'. Then, should you be caught with them, you cannot be accused of more than taking charge of some things having a sentimental value for me, that I am anxious should reach my family safely."

The warder nodded. "Very goot. If I am found out I cannod be greatly plamed for agreeing to such a request. I am off duty until to-morrow evening. I can easily travel to der Hague an' back in the early part of der day."

The Duke wrote the brief message on a piece of paper that the warder provided, thanked him from the bottom of his heart, and promised to treble the reward if the ruse procured him his liberty. When the man had put the things under his coat, locked him in and gone, he sat down on his truckle bed with a sigh of thankfulness.

It was much too early yet to count on his release, but at least he could now hope. Ninety-nine Carlton House Terrace was Sir Pellinore's address. When the Minister received the things he would surely be sufficiently intrigued to look the address up and, finding it to be Sir Pellinore's, begin to wonder who the false Sir Pellinore—who was sending a photograph and a decoration to the real Sir Pellinore—could be. Surely that would result in a telegram to London describing the prisoner and the things. Sir Pellinore knew the Duke's Austrian title to be Count Königstein, and that name was on the back of the decoration. Even if the people at the Legation missed that, any doubt about the identity of his impersonator should be removed from Sir Pellinore's mind by the portrait of the Archduchess whom the Duke had kissed at Dorchester House. The clues could hardly have been better, and if only the Minister sent Sir Pellinore a full description of them, it was a certainty that he would act. Yes, if——.

For the first time for several nights de Richleau got a fairly sound sleep; but all Sunday he was plagued by the awful suspicion that the warder might have betrayed him. In the wars in which he had fought he had often heard of cases in which the guards of prisoner-of-war camps had deliberately made up to captives, taken heavy bribes to help them to escape, and then done nothing about it. But evening brought reassurance. When the warder came on duty at eight o'clock he gave a friendly wink, and later said in a quick whisper:

"I did not tare say who I was or where I come from. But I gave them to a young Herr who seem quite pright, and told him that der barcel for der Minister was, an' most urgent."

Much heartened, but still in awful suspense as to whether the description of his clues would reach Sir Pellinore in time for the Foreign Office to instruct the Legation to come to his assistance, the Duke managed, somehow, to get through Sunday night and the early hours of Monday morning.

At ten o'clock he was again taken to the Law Courts, but this time he had not so long to wait on the hard bench with the other anxious prisoners, as his case was early on the list. At twenty-five past ten he was led into court and put in the dock. As he stepped on to the platform a stocky, red-haired young man stood up in the well of the court and came over to him. With a friendly smile, the young man said:

"Hallo! Sir Pellinore. I never expected to meet you in a place like this. You remember me, don't you—Jack McEwan?"

"Of course I do," smiled the Duke. "And I couldn't be more delighted to see you."

The rest was merely a matter of formalities, and ten minutes later de Richleau was in his rescuer's car on the way to the Hague.

The car was a brand new Rover, and a sports model that its owner drove himself with all the flair of a born motoring enthusiast: so they sped at a fine pace along the flat, sunny roads of Holland, while the Duke learned that the arrival of his parcel had caused no small stir in the accustomed quiet of a Sunday afternoon at the Legation. Sir Pellinore had been telegraphed to at once, a reply had come in from him giving the facts, that evening; and it had been followed by another, from the Foreign Office, urging that everything possible should be done to secure the release of the prisoner and expedite his safe transit to London.

They lunched at Pilburg, and over the meal discovered an affinity of interests in Gibbon and the great civilization of Rome, which added to the pleasure of the latter part of the journey. The Duke would have revelled in his freedom even if he had had to travel with a Basuto in an ox cart, but the erudite wit of his companion added just that touch needed to restore the serenity of his mind after the ordeal he had been through, and make the sunny afternoon perfection for him.

Over tea at the Legation he met the British Minister, Sir Alan Johnstone, a courtly diplomat of the old school, who congratulated him on his escape but showed a tactful restraint about inquiring into his activities while in Germany. They naturally discussed the general situation and, Holland being a neutral country into which first hand news was coming from all quarters, Sir Alan was in a position to give a very full and up-to-date picture of the whole vast conflict. It was just over a week since de Richleau had left Wartenburg and during it, although he had been aware that the most gigantic battles were raging on every front, he had been in no situation to gather anything but a rough idea how things were going. Now, to his distress, he learned that the Allies were in a far worse plight than he had thought.

The only bright spots were on the most distant Austrian fronts; and both, as the Duke's special knowledge enabled him to realize at once, were mainly due to the original blunder over the dispatch of the Austrian 2nd Army to the Danube. On its withdrawal, General Potiorek had proved quite incapable of standing up to the Voyvode Putnik and his hardy Serbians. The Austrians had been thrown back across the Drina with heavy losses, and not one of them now remained on Serbian soil. But the 2nd Army had failed to reach its proper station at the southern end of the Russian front in time to avert an Austrian disaster there. When von Hötzendorf's 3rd Army had struck eastward from Lemberg, unsupported by the 2nd, it had come up against two Russian Armies and, overwhelmed by numbers, suffered a severe defeat. The front of one Corps had completely given way, and the whole 3rd Army was now reported to be in full retreat on Lemberg.

As an offset in von Hötzendorf's favour, his 1st and 4th Armies, attacking to the north and north-east, had, respectively, captured Krasnik and Zamosc, and both had dealt heavy blows at the two remaining Russian Armies in General Ivanov's group.

But this success of von Hötzendorf's two northern Armies was of small significance compared with that of his German allies on the far side of the Polish salient. The battle of Tannenberg had been fought and won; and the Germans were so cock-a-hoop with their victory that they made no secret of the manner in which it had been achieved—except that Ludendorff had suppressed the fact that it was General Hoffmann, and not himself, who had planned it.

The battle had opened on the 26th with General Samsonov believing that he was opposed only by General Schlotz's XXth Corps, which had been in that neighbourhood from the opening of hostilities. But Below's Ist Reserve Corps was moving down to join up with it, farther east von Mackensen's XVIIth Corps was descending on his right flank and, after its long circuitous railway journey, von François' Ist Corps was just assembling on his left. For three days the battle raged. The German centre held, von Mackensen pressed in from the north and von François from the south, so that the German 8th Army took the form of a horse-shoe, almost encircling the Russians. General Samsonov attempted to pull out. But it was too late. General von François—against Ludendorff's orders as it afterwards transpired—drove his crack Ist Corps on due east to Willenberg, thus greatly lengthening the right wing of the encircling movement. On the 29th von Mackensen's troops, thrusting south, met him there and closed the circle. Two-thirds of Samsonov's Army were caught within it, and the remaining third escaped only with great losses. The following day, the bulk of the Russians, compressed into a small, thickly wooded area, which prevented them from

FINAL PHASE OF THE BATTLE OF TANNENBERG (AUGUST 29th)
The Russian XIII and XV Corps surrounded; remnants of I and VI Corps in flight

massing for a co-ordinated break-out, were shot down in droves and surrendered by the thousand. That Sunday afternoon, as Sir Alan Johnstone and the Duke sat over their tea cups, the latest German report stated that General Samsonov's Army had ceased to exist as a fighting force.

In France a similar disaster, on a far greater scale, now threatened. During the past week the right wing of the German Army had been swinging inexorably forward. Valenciennes, Cambrai, Avesnes, Hirson, Mezieres, St. Quentin, Laon, Rethel—all were gone. Only the great fortress line of Verdun-Toul-Belfort on the eastern half of the front still held. Paris was now directly menaced. The French troops had fought well but were reported to be exhausted. Under Sir Horace Smith Dorrien, the IInd Corps of the small British Army had made a splendid stand at Le Cateau, but it had then been compelled to conform to the general retirement. It was now feared that nothing short of a miracle could save the French and British from annihilation.

Greatly depressed by these awful portents of things to come, the Duke took such solace as he could from a welcome hot bath in luxurious surroundings, and later joined Sir Alan in an equally luxurious dinner. His Britannic Majesty's representative in the Netherlands held the belief that his duty lay in keeping a good and hospitable table in the country where he was stationed, and arranging for its notables to engage in golf tournaments with their British equivalents; and that if he did that, the negotiation of rather dreary affairs, such as trade pacts, would prove a simple matter for people who understood them better than he did. The success of his missions proved that there was much to be said for this policy; and it was to it that de Richleau owed the best dinner that he had eaten for a considerable time. At its end the old brandy was so superlatively good that he took occasion to compliment his host upon it. Sir Alan gracefully acknowledged his remarks, but refrained from mentioning one of his own idiosyncrasies. As his friends rarely gave him brandy half as good when he dined out, it was his habit to take some of his own with him in his overcoat pocket in a medicine bottle. Then, when coffee was served, he asked the footman who was waiting on him to fetch his 'Medicine'.

At a quarter to eleven de Richleau took leave of his admirable host and was driven by young Mr. McEwan the ten miles that separated the Hague from the Hook of Holland. With them came his wife, a lovely green-eyed girl of eighteen, to whom he had been married only a few months. She had been present at dinner and had volunteered to give her assistance should any trouble arise about the Duke leaving the country.

That morning the German Consul at Maastricht had made no protest at de Richleau's release, but, all the same, the Duke knew that he would not be really safe until he was on the ship and it had actually sailed. By this time it was certain that the Germans would be hunting high and low for him. If, during the day, he had been linked up with the deserter who had crossed into Holland six nights earlier, the German Minister in the Hague would have been instructed to apply for his extradition on a charge of murder. As neutrals, the Dutch could not ignore such a demand; so it was possible that, knowing him to be British, the police might be waiting to arrest him if he attempted to leave by the ship that was sailing for England at midnight.

Their plan was to drive the car up as close to the ship as possible. De Richleau and Jack McEwan would then get out, leaving Mrs. McEwan in it. If she saw that the police were preventing the Duke from boarding the ship, she was to scream, and later say that a wharf-rat had sneaked up to the car and tried to snatch her pearls. Her screams would provide an excuse for the two men to run back to the car. McEwan was to get in the way of anyone who attempted pursuit while de Richleau dashed straight for it. The car was technically a part of the Legation, so British soil; and, once in it, the Duke could not be arrested. They would then drive him back to the Hague and he could remain unmolested at the Legation until a new plan had been worked out for him to cross to England in disguise.

The thought that there is 'many a slip 'twixt the cup and the lip' made de Richleau rather silent during the drive, but when they reached the dock nothing occurred to alarm them. The Duke had been furnished with a diplomatic *laissez-passer*, and the officials let him through with a polite greeting. At the foot of the gangway he thanked Jack McEwan again for his help and said good-bye to him; then went on board and claimed a cabin that had been booked for him in the name of 'Rogers'. Returning to the rail, he stood there anxiously for a quarter of an hour, while his friends in the car a hundred yards away kept watch on him.

At last the mooring ropes were cast off and the ship slowly eased out from the dockside. Calls of '*bon voyage*' came from the car. In reply he waved, and blew kisses to the beautiful Mrs. McEwan. Eight hours later he landed at Harwich.

At eleven-thirty on Tuesday morning, 1st September, he was shown into the library at Ninety-nine Carlton House Terrace.

Whatever resentment he may have felt against Sir Pellinore, as the original cause of his becoming involved in so many repugnant acts, faded away at the sight of him. The tall, blue-eyed baronet received him, literally, with open arms. Clasping de Richleau's shoulders with his leg-of-mutton hands, he gave him an affectionate shake, grinned down into his face, and bellowed to his butler to bring a magnum of champagne and tankards. Then he pushed his visitor into a chair and cried:

"Gad! but I'm glad to see you again. You've no idea how the thought of you has been weighin' on my conscience. Now tell me everything."

It took the Duke an hour to cover the ground since they had last met in Vienna, and when he had done Sir Pellinore exclaimed:

"Stap me! The very moment I saw you, I knew you were a feller in a million. Six Corps eh! Six Corps! And a photograph of the little Archduchess into the bargain—not to mention an Austrian decoration."

He then fell silent for quite a minute.

At length de Richleau glanced out of the tall windows, across the Mall and the Horse Guards Parade to the stately buildings of Whitehall, and said:

"Well! Oughtn't this information to be passed on to Hankey, or the War Office, as soon as possible?"

Sir Pellinore sighed. "Yes. We'll do that. But I'm afraid—I'm afraid it won't be of much use to us. It comes too late."

CHAPTER XXVII

THE FORTIETH DAY

'Too late'. Those are the most tragic words in the English language. After all the Duke had gone through, he heard them with peculiar bitterness. For a moment he stared at Sir Pellinore; then he exclaimed:

"It can't be true! I heard from Sir Alan Johnstone yesterday that the French Army was in a bad way, and that Paris is threatened. Surely you don't mean that they've surrendered overnight?"

"No; but they're pretty well all in. Too far gone to launch a counter-offensive. Over a week ago Sir John French telegraphed that we ought to fortify our main base at Le Havre. Winston, with his usual flair, declared that the way things were going we'd be crazy to waste armaments and troops on such a half-measure; and that we'd better shift at once to St. Nazaire. Two days later the War Office agreed. The French have taken an even gloomier view. They've moved their Government to Bordeaux. There's darned little fight left in 'em."

De Richleau groaned. "But what is the reason for this catastrophe? Even the Germans admit that the French troops have been fighting magnificently."

"True. But they've been fighting in the wrong place. Those idiots at *Grand Quartier Général* are to blame. D'you know anything about the French High Command?"

"Not much. It is a long time since I was in the French Army."

"Well, this is the form. Three years ago—time of Agadir—General Michel was their top boy. Very sound feller. He believed the Germans would adopt the Schlieffen Plan. To counter it, he proposed to place his great mass—half a million strong—between Lille and Avesnes; another mass of 300,000 men between Hirson and Rethel; and to hold a further 200,000 in Paris as a general reserve. He considered the fortress line, Verdun-Toul-Belfort, strong enough to look after itself. That's what we were told the French meant to do, and we've never been notified of any change in their intentions."

Sir Pellinore took a swig of champagne, and went on: "But it's come out now that General Michel's plan didn't tally with the notions of his colleagues. They didn't believe the Germans would violate Belgium. They were not prepared to stand on the defensive. So they managed to get him sacked."

"Yes. I remember hearing he had gone. The present C.-in-C., Joffre, was appointed as his successor."

"That's right. At first Joffre wasn't in the runnin'. Galliéni was the obvious choice, but the War Minister wanted a chap called Pau. Then Pau made demands about the appointment of Generals to which the Government wouldn't agree; so they used the pretext of his age to rule him out. That ruled out Galliéni too, as he was even older. So Joffre was given the job."

"I've never understood why," remarked the Duke. "He was an engineer with a sound reputation, but no more. He is a stolid, unimaginative man. I don't think he has even commanded an Army on manœuvres, and he was only a junior member of the War Council."

"I'll tell you. He got the job because he is a bone-head who couldn't do any harm to anyone. He's never mixed himself up in politics. For three years he held his post under four Governments without upsettin' anybody. And he has no religious views, so they knew that he wouldn't favour either the Catholics or the Atheists. Naturally, an old plodder like that, with no notions of his own, was easy meat for all the young hot-heads of the French General staff. They are a powerful lot, and call themselves the Young Turks. God knows why! Anyway, they're all apostles of the offensive. They persuaded the old fool to scrap General Michel's plan. Instead, they produced a suicidal document called Plan XVII. Its object was to take advantage of the very temporary superiority in numbers that the French would have in the first stage by launching a million men in an all-out attack at the earliest possible moment."

De Richleau's face fell. "Then the French *have* frittered away their resources."

"Frittered!" repeated Sir Pellinore angrily. "Chucked, would be a better word. Twelve days ago Joffre began destroyin' his own army as surely as if he were a god with a grouse and a hatchet. Division after division was thrown in like coconuts against an iron Aunt Sally. Those lunatics chose the virtually impregnable fortress of Metz for the central point of their attack. Of course, they were influenced by all this sentimental clap-trap about liberating Alsace-Lorraine. Instead of exercisin' a reasonable patience, they've gambled their whole country against a chance to run the French flag up in Strasburg. Naturally the artillery in the Hun fortress line bowled them over as though they were nine-pins. In five days fightin' that fat imbecile they call 'papa' Joffre caused the slaughter of 300,000 French soldiers; and he hasn't even got a German town to show for them. That's why no advantage can be taken of this marvellous news you've brought about the transfer of the six Corps to East Prussia."

The Duke's head reeled under the magnitude of the blow. *Three hundred thousand men gone in five aays. It was one fifth of the whole French Army.* At that rate it must either surrender or cease to exist within a fortnight. After a moment he murmured:

"Could nothing be done to stop this madness?"

"On the sixth day it stopped itself. The four Armies on the French right were too punch-drunk to take any more punishment. So 'papa' Joffre and his Young Turks thought they would launch an offensive in another direction. The two remainin' French Armies and the British were ordered to close up and attack northward. But they were spread out wafer-thin compared with the great mass of Germans pourin' down on 'em—and already in full retreat. The only card left lay in a new Army of odds and ends that was being got together by General Maunoury in the neighbourhood of Amiens. That's the spot where Joffre *ought* to have had the 300,000 men he's squandered. He might have rolled up the German flank then. But they were dead, dyin' or prisoners. And Maunoury's lot had no chance to get going. They were pushed back with the rest."

"Is there no hope left, then?"

"Hope!" boomed Sir Pellinore suddenly. "Of course there's hope! Bags of it! War's only just started. The Ruskies have taken a nasty knock at some place called Tininberg, and the French have made a shockin' muddle. But this is only the beginning. Britain rules the waves, my boy. The world's our oyster. We've got the men, we've got the ships, we've got the money, too. The Empire's capable of putting five million men in the field, and we've got the markets of the world to buy supplies in. Britain wins the last battle in every war, and the Kaiser's a dunderheaded fool to have forgotten it."

"I meant, there is little hope now for France."

Sir Pellinore considered for a moment, then he rumbled, "There's one. Paris, with its great ring of forts, is the strongest fortress in the world. Can't possibly be taken by a straightforward assault—any more than the 800,000 men Joffre threw into his offensive could take Metz. The Huns will have to bring up their siege trains and invest the city. To subdue it will take weeks—if not months. That should give the French Army a breather. They'll be able to get their Empire troops over; and so shall we. The allies may be able to form a solid front along the Seine—if only Paris holds out."

"The Germans may decide to by-pass it. They know their business, and I'm sure their objective is the destruction of the French Army."

"True. But if they do, it will mean splittin' their forces. Von Kluck's Army, on their extreme right, and probably von Below's which is next to it, would have to pass west of the city. They'd be entirely cut off from their pals. They'd be very vulnerable to a counter-offensive then—if only the French can still find the troops to make it."

The Duke was silent for a moment in his turn, then he said glumly: "All the older people in Paris—the members of the Government and the High Command—remember the horrors of the seige in 1870. They may not be prepared to face starvation and riots again, and a far more terrible bombardment. Instead of holding Paris, they may decide to declare it an open city, and let the Germans walk through."

"Ah! That's the rub! If so, I fear the French goose is cooked. France will be forced to surrender. That will make it a darned long business; and we'll have to take our Army off. But don't worry. We'll go back again. We always do."

The butler then arrived to announce lunch, so they went downstairs. Over the meal de Richleau gave his host a more detailed account of some of his doings. Then, after the port, Sir Pellinore said:

"This afternoon I'll look in on a few people. Tell 'em about these six Corps of yours. Never say die, eh? Meantime I expect you'd like to get yourself some decent clothes. Better make your headquarters here for the time bein'. I'd be delighted to have you. I'll be back about six and let you know the form."

They went out together and separated in Pall Mall. The Duke walked up to his tailor's, where he always kept a trunkful of clothes, and soon made himself more presentable. Then he spent an hour or so strolling round the West End.

There were quite a number of officers and men about in khaki, but otherwise it looked little different from when he had last seen it. After an almost complete stoppage of business, trade had begun to recover, and many of the shops had printed slogans in their windows carrying the words 'Business as Usual'.

In a few brief bulletins the public had been informed that the B.E.F. was in contact with the Germans and had inflicted heavy losses upon them; but not one in ten thousand had the vaguest idea what was happening in France, so the well-dressed, well-fed crowds showed no sign of depression. On the contrary, there seemed a new buoyancy and cheerfulness about them. Kitchener, so the Duke learned, had been made War Minister, and no appointment could have given greater confidence to the nation. On every hoarding there were pictures of him with a pointing finger, and the legend under it 'Your country needs YOU'. He had called for a million volunteers, and from boys of fifteen to elderly men who were dyeing their white hair black in order to be taken, Britons from every city, town and village, and from every country in the world were flocking to the colours.

In a somewhat more cheerful frame of mind the Duke returned to

Carlton House Terrace, but Sir Pellinore did not get back by six o'clock, nor seven, nor eight: so at half past eight de Richleau sat down to a solitary dinner. It was nearly ten before his host joined him, and said abruptly:

"Sorry to have left you on your own. Had the hell of an afternoon. To start with I couldn't get hold of anyone I wanted. No good goin' to little people on a thing like this. Sir Bindon was at a meetin' of the Committee of Imperial Defence that didn't break up till five. He's very grateful to you, and inclined to be optimistic. He says the withdrawal of those six Corps might still make all the difference. But Kitchener poured cold water on me. He's very under the weather these days, and who can blame him? He confirmed though that, since the 26th, German troop trains have been leavin' Belgium for the Russian front. The size of the transfer surprised him, and he'll pass the information on with the latest M.I. reports. But he feels that it's up to the French, and doubts their ability to do anything. Felt I must let 'Mr. Marlborough' know, so I barged in on him at dinner. He took a very different view. He said, 'Now is the hour! This secret intelligence is the one thing which might stiffen the backs of the French and save the situation. We've got to *make* them dig their toes in'. So you and I are off to France first thing tomorrow morning."

"What!" exclaimed the Duke.

Sir Pellinore nodded. "Yes. Unofficial mission, of course. But somebody's got to talk to 'papa' Joffre, and hammer what this means into his thick head."

"I quite see that; but I'm afraid that I can't possibly go with you."

"Oh, yes you will!" Sir Pellinore's chin jutted out belligerently. "You're the feller who knows the facts. They're much too down in the mouth to take any notice of mere hearsay. But when they learn that you had it straight from the horse's mouth—actually heard old von Moltke give the order—they'll believe it. Then with any luck they'll get their peckers up."

"I see that, too," replied de Richleau unhappily. "But you have evidently forgotten that I was exiled from France. Directly I tell them my name, they will arrest me."

"Oh, no they won't! They'll not dare to lay a finger on you. I've thought of that snag already. You're coming with me dressed as a British Brigadier-General."

De Richleau laughed. "Well! That is quite a promotion from an Austrian Colonel."

"I'd give you a higher rank if I didn't feel that would be overdoin' it," grinned the baronet. "But we want to impress these fellers as much as we can. They'll take a lot from a soldier that they wouldn't from a civilian. If they think we think enough of you to have made you a Brigadier, they'll take what you have to say about the stuff you picked up in Germany pretty seriously."

"All right, then. I'm taking it for granted that you will protect me from the wrath of the British Army if it hears about this. But what about uniform?"

"Don't worry about that. Hundreds of young chaps are being granted temporary commissions overnight now. The shops are full of ready-made tunics and breeches. My man will measure you. Then I'll telephone Sir Woodman Burbridge. Old friend of mine. He'll send one of his people down to Harrods before the store opens to-morrow. They'll get you everything you want up here by nine o'clock. That'll be plenty of time. We're leavin' on the ten-thirty for Dover. Make a list out, and don't forget to put on it a couple of rows of medal ribbons. The more the merrier!"

So, at ten-thirty next morning, a very tall grey-haired gentleman with a fine cavalry moustache, and a slim, dark-haired Brigadier-General left Charing Cross. Overnight the Admiralty had made all arrangements for them, so they were met at Dover by a young R.N.R. officer, who took them along the harbour and on board a destroyer that was acting as a fast ferry several times a day, to run staff officers to and fro across the channel.

They landed at Calais well before two; but were held up there for a while, as the Admiralty was short of cars and a special arrangement had to be made for them to be provided with a military car and driver. But by two-thirty they were on their way to Bar le Duc, in the department of the Meuse, where *Grand Quartier Général* was established.

Owing to the invasion they could not cross northern France via Arras, Laon and St. Menehould, but had to go round by Paris; and even the direct route to the capital was now unsafe, as the Germans were in Amiens: so that meant an additional detour down the coast to Abbeville and then by way of Beauvais. At a rough calculation they reckoned that they had to cover some three hundred miles. That meant there was no possibility of their reaching G.Q.G. that night; but they hoped to do so in the early hours of the morning.

For the first forty miles of the journey, all went well. But then they began to run into columns of refugees, the awkward, undisciplined straggling of which slowed their pace and sometimes forced them to halt for several minutes at a time. Abbeville was choked with the transport of these poor people who, for the past fortnight, had been forced to flee in ever increasing numbers before the advancing Germans. Here and there were carriages and primitive, high-wheeled autos; but the bulk of the jam consisted of farm waggons, traps, handcarts and perambulators, all piled high with pathetic household goods, and generally topped by mattresses, on which were perched shrivelled old crones clutching the youngest children of the families.

It took an hour for the car to nose its way through the town, and twenty miles beyond it the straggling bands of refugees began to be interspersed with columns of marching troops. The men looked dispirited and weary. Their scarlet trousers and long blue coats were now a mockery under a heavy coating of fine grey dust; and their equipment was pathetic. Much of their transport consisted of commandeered farm wagons, the horses that drew them were sorry nags, and quite frequently the dirty, half-rotten harness was tied together by pieces of string. De Richleau knew that they must be reserve troops, collected from anywhere and everywhere, which were being pushed up to join the army that General Maunoury had endeavoured to assemble round Amiens: but by comparison with the smart turn-out of the reserve formations he had seen while on his train journey through Germany, they made a very poor impression.

The car did not get them to Beauvais until seven o'clock, and from there on to Paris the congestion of the roads was far worse, so it was after ten when they entered the capital.

Their eight hours of crawling and constant enforced halts had proved very tiring, so they felt that they were entitled to a good supper, and directed the car to the Ritz. The restaurant was crammed with officers and women in evening dress; and although there was a suggestion of strain in the atmosphere, its occupants did not seem unduly depressed.

As Sir Pellinore and the Duke had not eaten since lunching in the destroyer on the way over, they had hearty appetites, and the good food, washed down with a plentiful supply of champagne, soon banished their fatigue. When coffee was being served to them a tall, thin man came up to their table. He was immaculately dressed, had a dark, pointed beard, wore the rosette of the Légion d'Honneur in his buttonhole, and was about the same age as Sir Pellinore; who introduced him as the Marquis de St. Eloi, and asked him to join them in a brandy.

The Marquis accepted with a graceful bow, gave the Duke, whom he evidently knew by name, a quick look of interest, and sat down.

For a few minutes they talked of the general situation. It showed no improvement. Compiègne, Soissons, Rheims and Châlons had fallen; the Germans were now over the Aisne in great strength, and their flying columns of Uhlans were said to have reached the Marne.

Sir Pellinore glanced round at the expensively dressed crowd and remarked: "I wonder more people aren't quittin' Paris. They'll get locked up here if they're not careful."

With a shrug of his elegant shoulders, the Marquis replied: "Many people are: but not the *haute monde*. They are confident that there will be no siege. Paris will be declared an open city."

"Are you certain of that?" asked the Duke quickly.

"Yes. Our War Minister, M. Messimy, wished to hold it. When the retreat began, he ordered G.Q.G. to return an army of at least three Corps from the front for the defence of the capital. General Joffre was very loath to part with any of the formations he was hoping to employ in a new offensive, so he delegated the task to General Maunoury, who was forming a new Army in the neighbourhood of Amiens. But Messimy has since been sacked as a scapegoat for the failure of our offensive in Lorraine. So Joffre had been freed from that obligation. He wishes both to keep his forces in the open field and to spare Paris the horror of a bombardment, so he will let the Germans march through it."

Sir Pellinore grunted and the Duke's mouth suddenly took a hard, angry line; but both forbore to comment. Ten minutes later, when the Marquis had left them, de Richleau asked:

"Do you think that fellow really knows Joffre's intentions?"

"I've not a doubt of it," Sir Pellinore replied glumly. "He's a banker, with whom I do quite a bit of business. Member of the *Comité des Forges*, too. Republic or not, France has never ceased to be run by the *Cent Familles*. That gang have a finger in every pie. France couldn't carry on for a month without their millions. He knows what he is talking about all right. Shouldn't be surprised if Joffre hasn't had his orders from them. They won't want their houses in the Bois destroyed. They'd rather pay up an indemnity, as they did in 1870; though it will prove a whacking big one this time."

By half past eleven they were on their way again. Bar-le-Duc lay a hundred and forty miles due east of Paris, and they had hoped to get there in the small hours; but it now looked as if they would be lucky if they reached it before dawn.

The coming of night had not halted the streams of refugees: they were more numerous than they had been to the north of Paris, and there was much more military transport on the road. Hour after hour they crawled on, through Coulommiers, Sézanne and Fère-Champenoise. From the latter place the road lay parallel to the advance of the Germans and, at most, only twenty miles from their cavalry screen. They knew that if an enemy spearhead had made a thrust in that direction during the day, there was an unpleasant possibility of their running into a troop of Uhlans; but to have gone by way of Troyes and Chaumont would have meant another big detour, so, in view of the urgency of their mission, they had decided to chance getting through on the shorter route.

The anxiety they felt at the proximity of the enemy kept them very much on the alert. De Richleau took over from the driver and they agreed that, at the first sign of trouble, they would abandon the car and take to the fields. That did not prove necessary, but when they reached Vitry they were warned by Military Police that German patrols had been located north of the town. In common prudence they turned down a by-road leading south. It soon became a winding lane and forked three times in less than two miles; then they found themselves heading west. Passing troops were fewer in these by-ways, and none of whom they asked the way had ever before been in the district; so after several more false casts they were angrily compelled to admit that they were hopelessly lost.

It was now about five-thirty, that chill pre-dawn hour when vitality is at its lowest. All three of them were dog-tired, so they decided to snatch a short sleep in the car and go on again when full daylight came. At half past seven they roused up, drove for a few miles through a maze of lanes towards a church steeple, and found the church to be that of the township of Joinville. From it, Bar-le-Duc lay thirty miles to the north, so they did not reach their destination till a little before ten. Then, to their fury, they learned that General Joffre had shifted his headquarters two days before to St. Dizier.

After breakfast and a wash at an inn crowded with soldiers, they started for St. Dizier, a town some twenty miles away, to which they must have passed quite close in the early hours of the morning. But when they reached it, they were told that General Joffre had been there only a day and shifted his quarters again the previous night.

To add to their frustration, no one could tell them where he had gone; but, rightly assuming that he was moving backwards in conformity with the enemy advance, they continued on the road south-eastwards. During the middle of the day and the early hours of the afternoon, they tried several townships in vain, but at four-thirty they at last ran him to earth at Bar-sur-Aube.

He had taken over the Mairie of the little town as another temporary H.Q. and everything was still at sixes and sevens. It was ludicrously small for a *Grand Quartier Général* and its facilities were totally inadequate to the requirements of a C.-in-C. controlling eight Armies. But so, apparently, was his staff; it consisted of only half a dozen officers, a few orderlies, the chauffeurs of four large dusty cars and some motor-cycle dispatch riders.

Sir Pellinore and the Duke were asked to wait in a wash-room and, after kicking their heels there for over an hour, were eventually taken to see Joffre's Director of Operations, a Colonel de Grandmaison, who occupied a small room in which even a telephone had not yet been installed.

In execrable French, Sir Pellinore stated quite unscrupulously that he represented both the Secretary of State for War and the First Lord of the Admiralty. Then, having produced his diplomatic *laissez-passer*, he asked bluntly: "*Comment va la bataille?*"

"The battle," said Colonel de Grandmaison, "develops itself. The Commander-in-Chief has every confidence."

"Confidence in what?" inquired the Baronet, his slightly protuberant blue eyes taking on their belligerent look.

"In ultimate victory," came the bland reply. "The enemy has made a great penetration into France. We learn that he is now across the Marne in strength at both Epernay and Château Thierry; but his front is now one vast bulge, and both his flanks are exposed. In due course we shall close upon him. *Voila!*"

"Good!" said Sir Pellinore, a trifle more cordially. "When?"

The Colonel shrugged. "*Au moment juste!* The moment psychological, for which our great C.-in-C. has been waiting."

"I trust that he will not wait too long," put in the Duke. "The situation appears to be extremely precarious. With the Germans across the Marne, you have not much time to waste if you mean to try to save Paris."

"It may prove advisable to declare Paris an open city; but the capital is in no immediate danger of either attack or investment. For the past twenty-four hours news has been coming in that von Kluck's army, contrary to our expectations, is not advancing on Paris, or to the west of the city. Instead, it has taken a south-easterly direction. By doing so it has exposed its right flank to General Maunoury, whose Army is situated just north of Paris."

"The Devil!" exclaimed de Richleau. "Can the Germans possibly have made such a blunder! If they have, now is the time. By attacking their flank, General Maunoury should be able to turn it and throw the whole of their right wing into confusion. If, at the same time, you halt your retreat and fling in everything you've got here in the south, there is a real chance of smashing the enemy. And I think it better than you have had any opportunity to realize."

The Duke then went on to describe his activities in Germany and report the ordering by von Moltke of six Corps to the East Prussian front. For ten minutes he spoke of the original Schlieffen Plan, pointing out how, instead of strictly adhering to it, von Moltke had allocated only six-sevenths instead of seven-eighths of the German forces to the West, and that, owing to over-confidence in victory, the withdrawal of the six Corps had further reduced the six-sevenths to five-sixths.

Colonel de Grandmaison listened with intent interest. After congratulating the Duke on his escape and the news he brought, he said:

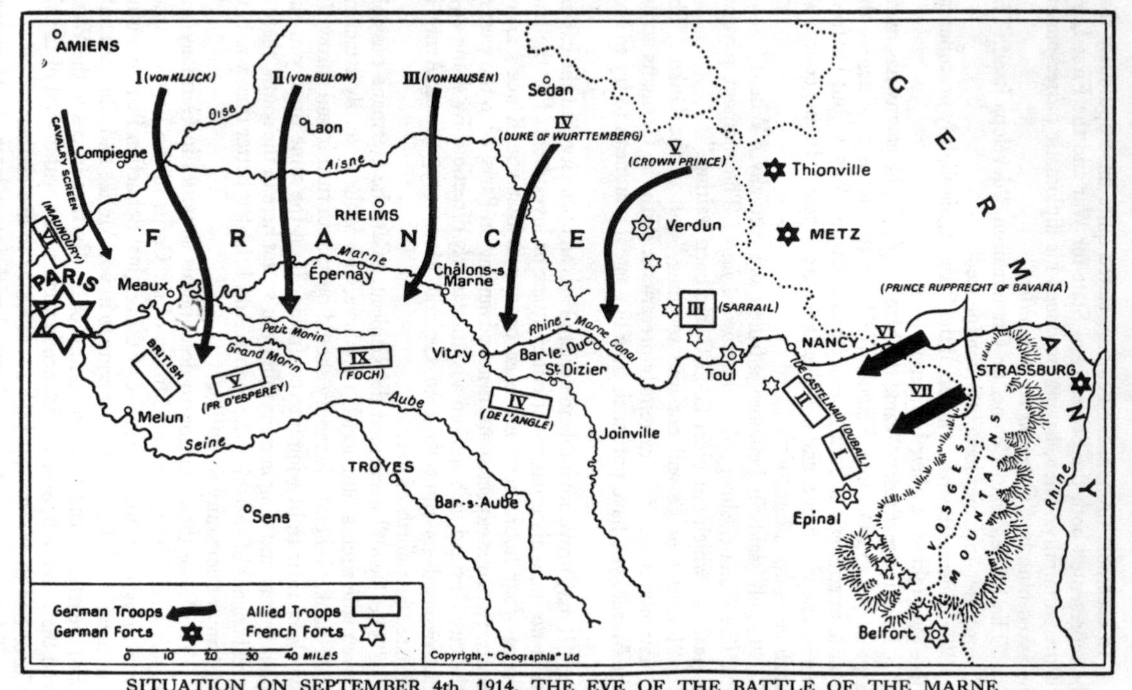

SITUATION ON SEPTEMBER 4th, 1914, THE EVE OF THE BATTLE OF THE MARNE

"This ties up with our intelligence reports. For some days past troop trains have been leaving Belgium for the East. It is reported, too, that there are no German troops west of the line Senlis-Paris, so Maunoury's attack should have a good chance of clearing the country south of the Marne, and containing the enemy to the north of it."

"*South* of the Marne," de Richleau said in a puzzled voice. "But little is to be gained by lopping off the heads of the enemy columns. Surely *north* of the Marne is the right place to strike? It is von Kluck's centre and rear at which the blow should be aimed, with the object of throwing his whole army into confusion and cutting his communications."

"Ah! But we must act with some caution," the Colonel replied. "Maunoury's Army is of no great strength, and it would be wrong to ask too much of it. General Joffre has sanctioned this attack only because his old colleague, General Galliéni, who is now Military Governor of Paris, pressed him so strongly to agree to it. He would have much preferred to wait a little until he feels it time to launch all his Armies in a general counter-offensive."

Sir Pellinore had been following the conversation with some difficulty, but he had gathered the gist of it, and suddenly cut in:

"What's this? D'you mean to say that you're goin' to let this chance slip? Here you've got the Huns walking sideways-on to you and all you mean to do is to let Maunoury have a smack at their advance guards. You're crazy! Plumb crazy! You ought to be issuing orders now for every man on your entire front to turn and fight."

De Grandmaison stiffened. "That," he said coldly, "is a matter for the Commander-in-Chief. The Armies that have been fighting for the past fortnight are now near exhaustion. His view is that we should give them time to recover, and wait until they have been strongly reinforced before returning to the attack."

"Reinforced from where?" asked Sir Pellinore.

"From Verdun. We intend to give up the fortress, so as to make available for field operations the great body of men who form its garrison."

"*Give up Verdun!*" De Richleau rose slowly to his feet. He went white to the lips: his grey eyes were blazing. Suddenly he leaned forward and crashed his fist down on the table.

"*Surrender Verdun!* Shade of St. Louis! I wonder that the ghosts of the Marshals of France do not rise up and strike you dead! Do the glories of Rocroy, Austerlitz and Jena mean nothing to you? How dare you even contemplate such a step and still call yourself a Frenchman!"

The other two had also risen. Sir Pellinore took the outraged Duke's arm, and said in English: "Steady the Buffs! Don't want this feller forcin' some stupid duel on you."

"I'll meet him and shoot him any time he wishes," snarled de Richleau.

De Grandmaison was trembling with anger, and burst out: "You are protected by your uniform. But I shall report your disgraceful behaviour to Sir John French. Now, leave my office before I forget myself."

As they left the building, Sir Pellinore said philosophically, "Well, that's scotched any hope we had of gettin' a decent dinner off these fellers. That chap was 'papa' Joffre's blue-eyed boy, you know. Not surprisin' is it, that with stiff-wallahs like him about, they're in such a howlin' mess?"

"He ought to be shot!" muttered the Duke savagely. "He ought to be shot! Just think of it! To give up Verdun and let the Germans through the only part of the line that's holding!"

"Yes, quite shockin'," agreed the Baronet with unusual mildness. "To think, too, that the Germans have counted their chickens before they are hatched, and that we can't take advantage of it. Evidently old von Kluck thinks the Allies are as good as in the bag already, or he'd never risk marchin' his crop-heads across the front of our army. Still, it's the last round that counts. Sooner or later we'll knock the stuffin' out of the Huns. British Empire is unbeatable."

It was now six o'clock, so they decided not to return to Paris until the morning, and set about finding accommodation for the night. That proved easier than they expected, as General Joffre appeared to have only his operations staff with him, and apparently did not bother to keep in close touch with the heads of all the organization departments necessary to the maintenance and manipulation of a vast army. At a pleasant inn they got rooms for themselves and their driver, shaved, had a brush up, and came down to dinner.

But it was a far from happy meal, as it lay heavily on both their minds that their mission had proved an utter failure. Colonel de Grandmaison had obviously registered the transfer of the six German Corps, but only as an interesting piece of information; and one that made no significant difference to the immediate situation, as he had no intention of advising his C.-in-C. to engage in a new battle.

Sir Pellinore suggested that next day they should look in at H.Q., B.E.F. on their way back to Paris, and, having agreed to start at nine o'clock in the morning, they retired unhappily to bed.

They were, however, unable to start at nine, as their driver reported that four hundred miles over the bad French roads had broken one of the back springs of the Crossley; but he added that he had been "parley-vooing with a French garage hand who seemed a sensible cove" and he thought that the car could be ready for the road again by about one o'clock. In consequence, they had an early lunch in Bar-sur-Aube, and started soon after one for Melun, where the British G.H.Q. was situated.

The roads were as congested as on the day before and the car was considerably delayed in getting through both Troyes and Sens, so it was not until after five that they reached Melun. General French's Headquarters were in a pleasant château just outside the town, and for the travellers it was a tonic to see the good order and discipline that reigned there.

De Richleau was not the type of soldier who believed that weary troops should be made to polish buttons when they might be called on to fight or march again at dawn next morning, but he did believe that proper pride in routine turn out increased a man's respect for himself and his service, and that there was no excuse for anyone at a rear headquarters to appear ill-shaven or slovenly. Here, both officers and men were as spick and span as they would have been at Aldershot. On the drive in front of the house the chauffeurs were whistling as they busily polished the metal work of the staff cars, and some stocky bow-legged orderlies were walking half a dozen beautifully groomed horses up and down.

Sir Pellinore's inquiry elicited the fact that Sir John French had not yet returned from a day's tour of his front line units, and that his Chief of Staff, Sir Archibald Murray, had just left to visit Sir Douglas Haig at Ist Corps Headquarters. But Sir Archibald's deputy was in, and the Duke was delighted when he found this to be the brilliant strategist he had met at the Carlton Club, General Sir Henry Wilson.

Sir Henry cocked an eyebrow when he saw de Richleau dressed as a Brigadier-General, and the Duke, much embarrassed for once, said quickly that at least he was entitled to the decorations he was wearing. Sir Pellinore added that they had been "doin' a bit of Comic Opera stuff in an attempt to ginger-up the French"; which the tall Irishman thought a huge joke and, roaring with laughter, took them into the Mess. As he was providing them both with whisky and soda, Sir Pellinore asked:

"Well! How's the contemptible little Army gettin' along?"

"Oh, not too badly," replied the General. "Naturally the men hate retreating, but they've given a pretty good account of themselves. They did all they were asked, and more, in spite of the fact that they were up against six times their numbers. In the first week we took a nasty hammering, but the 4th Div. has joined us since, and several drafts, so on balance I'm inclined to think we're in even better shape than when we started."

"I wish to God that could be said of the French," remarked the Duke.

"So do I," agreed Sir Henry. "Their best troops showed tremendous *élan*, but the bulk of their Army hasn't stood up to the Huns as well as we expected."

"The Admiralty always told you they wouldn't," said Sir Pellinore, unkindly. "Still, it's not the men—it's 'papa' Joffre and his Young Turks that are to blame for the mess we're in. We've just come from G.Q.G. and it has to be seen to be believed. One horse and a boy. Joffre's the horse, and they're both chewin' the cud in a *pissoir*."

"What had they to say for themselves?"

"Oh, that the battle is arranging itself. They're helping, too. Goin' to declare Paris an open city and surrender Verdun."

The General swung round. "You can't mean that?"

"If you don't believe me, ask de Richleau. When he heard it, I'd have given anybody ten to one that he'd either have an apoplectic fit or kill that feller Grandmaison on the spot."

"Archie Murray was right then, in his decision this afternoon."

"If it was to get you fellers down to Le Havre and back to England, home and beauty in the *Brighton Belle*, he probably was."

"No. We had Galliéni here. Just before Messimy was sacked, he made the old boy Governor of Paris. It was a thundering good appointment, as he has both brains and guts. The trouble is that, although he was Joffre's boss when they were in Madagascar together, he is now in quite a subordinate position to the C.-in-C., and has only a very limited sphere of action. His reconnaissances report that there are no Huns at all west of Paris, and yesterday our aviators confirmed that."

Sir Pellinore nodded vigorously. "So they told us at G.Q.G. Von Kluck is wide open. It needs only a kick in the ribs from Maunoury's lot to fold up the German flank and land the whole German right in the devil of a mess."

"That's Galliéni's view. But 'papa' Joffre will give him permission to attack only south of the Marne, not north of it. So I'm afraid it won't do much good. He came here to ask us to join in, and attack von Kluck from the south; but we turned him down."

"Why?"

"For one thing, because he hasn't a shadow of authority to launch a counter-offensive on his own. For another, because, now that we are in better shape, Sir John wrote to Joffre the day before yesterday offering to stand and fight again. But G.Q.G. replied that they thought it better not to for the time being. We can't afford to be left with our right wing in the air; so we must continue to conform to the general retirement."

"Do you realize, though," put in the Duke, "that, not only is von Kluck's flank open, but he has nothing behind him? The two German Corps allocated to invest Namur, which should now be following him up, have been sent to the East Prussian front. And four others with them."

Sir Henry gave him a sharp glance. "Are you certain of that? What leads you to suppose so?"

De Richleau told his story as briefly as possible. The General showed a sudden excitement and, when he had done, asked:

"Does Galliéni know this?"

"Not as far as I know. We told de Grandmaison at G.Q.G., but he didn't seem to think it could make much difference now."

Sir Henry gulped down the rest of his drink. "Come on," he said. "We must go to Paris. This may be just the lever Galliéni needs to force Joffre's hand."

Two minutes later the three of them were in the car. Again long columns of troops and streams of refugees held them up infuriatingly; so it took them the best part of two hours to cover the twenty-five miles to the capital. But by seven o'clock they arrived at the Invalides, and at a quarter past were with Galliéni.

The Governor was a tall, thin, grey-haired man, with a heavy moustache, very big ears, and slender, nervous hands. A pair of steel-rimmed pince-nez waggled insecurely on his rather fleshy nose. He heard what they had to say, asked de Richleau a few shrewd questions, then stood up and began to pace the room agitatedly, muttering to himself: "So von Kluck has nothing behind him. Von Kluck has nothing behind him. Nothing behind him. Nothing behind him."

After a few moments he suddenly turned, snatched up the telephone on his desk, and asked to be put through to G.Q.G.

While a line was being cleared for him, Sir Pellinore coughed and said in his appalling French: "We were at G.Q.G. yesterday, *mon Général*. They told us there that Paris is to be declared an open city, and that Verdun is to be surrendered. Can nothing be done to reverse these terrible decisions?"

Galliéni took off his pince-nez, and they waggled between his fingers with the strength of his emotion. "It shall not be!" he cried. "As long as I am Governor of Paris we shall hold it to the last man. And Verdun will not surrender! I have spoken on the telephone with General Sarrail, who commands there. He declared to me that his honour would never permit him to obey such an order."

"*Bon pour vous!*" exclaimed Sir Pellinore. "*Et bon pour Général Sarrail. Le vieux ésprit de France, eh! Jeanne d'Arc encore!*"

The call came through. An incredible conversation ensued. By every means known to the voluble and emotional French, the Governor strove to stir the sluggish brain of his phlegmatic C.-in-C. at the other end of the line. For twenty minutes he shouted, and at times almost wept, into the telephone. He spoke of the honour of France, of the glory of her Generals, of the bravery of her soldiers. He pleaded, threatened, argued. He said that the blood of the dead on the fields of Lorraine cried aloud for vengeance. Those who had sent them to die must not betray them. He talked of the old days in Madagascar when Joffre had served under him; of comradeship and loyalty; of death rather than dishonour.

At last his spate of words began to cease for brief intervals and, instead, between pauses, he uttered staccato exclamations. Then he put down the receiver. His face was pale but triumphant as he turned to his visitors and cried:

"It is decided! I am permitted to attack *north* of the Marne. The retreat is halted. *Voila!* The whole army of France turns about and faces her enemies. Maunoury flings himself on von Kluck to-morrow, the 5th. General battle is to be given at dawn on the 6th."

Sir Henry Wilson jumped to his feet, seized the astonished Frenchman in his arms, kissed him on both cheeks, then swung him round in a dance—just as he was to do four years later, when a Field Marshal, with Premier Clemenceau at Versailles in the hour of final victory. Sir Pellinore shouted, "Bravo!" clapped his hands and gave de Richleau a slap on the back that nearly knocked him over.

When their excitement had subsided a little, the Governor said: "This chance will never come again. If our blow against von Kluck's flank fails, we shall have lost the war. Maunoury needs every ounce of support we can give him. I shall strip Paris of her garrison and send it to the front. And it must go to-night. I will commandeer all the 'buses and taxi-cabs in Paris to transport it. The men must be in the line by dawn to-morrow. Every man capable of bearing a rifle will be needed. Every man! *Messieurs*, I thank you from the bottom of my heart. But not a moment must be lost, and I have much to do. You will excuse me now."

As they left his quiet room Joseph Simon Galliéni was already giving his first orders for the opening move of the battle that was to have more far-reaching consequences than any since Waterloo—a battle that would never have been fought but for his tenacity, courage and indomitable spirit.

When they got outside, the Duke said to Sir Henry: "You heard what he said. Can you sign me on as a Tommy and get me a rifle?"

The General laughed. "No; but I can make a better use of you than that. You talk French like a native, and you're one of the comparatively few people who know what is really happening. You'll be invaluable to us as a liaison officer between B.E.F. and old Galliéni. For that sort of work it's just as well that you should continue dressed as a Brigadier. I'll put that right with General French when we get back."

"And what about me?" boomed Sir Pellinore. "Don't think you're goin' to leave me out of this. I may not speak this French lingo over well; but I'm a darn' good shot, and it's not all that long ago they gave me a V.C."

After considering for a moment, Sir Henry said: "All right. Come back with us to G.H.Q. We're quite well off for riflemen; but we could use you in our Intelligence room. There are plenty of younger men there who are worrying themselves sick to have a cut at the Hun; and they are trained in modern tactics. We need them with the troops, so it would be a real help if you relieved one of them."

So they had a quick dinner in Paris, then returned to Melun. The British Expeditionary Force was still retreating, and it could not be stopped simply on a conversation between Sir Henry Wilson and General Galliéni. But the retreat was slowed up, and in the early hours of the morning a dispatch rider arrived with a request from General Joffre that the B.E.F. should halt, turn about, and prepare to advance in a north-easterly direction on the 6th.

For those who knew the inner picture, the days that followed were stupendously exciting. Maunoury's attack caught von Kluck by surprise, and on the following day his spearheads were brought to a halt by the strong resistance of the B.E.F. One of his five Army Corps had been shattered by Maunoury's first onrush, so he was compelled to turn sideways, then right round, which placed him facing north-west instead of south-east. But in the meantime von Below's Army, on his left, continued to push south-eastwards, so a great gap thirty miles wide opened between them. Into the gap poured the British and Franchet D'Esperey's 5th Army, while Foch's 9th Army took the weight of von Below's continued attempts to advance. Meanwhile, the four French Armies on the right of the line prevented all attempts of the other five German Armies to break through, and gradually forced them backwards.

It was a battle of giants, but of tired giants. Both armies were near exhaustion even before it started: the Germans from their month-long advance, the French from many casualties and the depression that is inseparable from a prolonged retreat. Just a little more weight on either side would have given the victory to whichever had it. As things were, neither was any longer capable of rushing to the assault, but both held their ground firmly, pressing on the other. For a time everything hung in the balance, and all depended on through which of the closely locked armies a sudden conviction would first run that it must give way because it could stand the strain no longer.

De Richleau's work took him frequently to Paris, and it was on Monday the 8th—the critical day of the battle—that at about six o'clock in the evening he went into the Ritz for a drink before returning to Melun. As he walked through the lounge, and past a table at which three smartly dressed women were sitting, he heard one of them suddenly exclaim:

"Armand! *Mon Dieu!* Can it possibly be you?"

Pausing he found himself facing a beautifully corseted lady with fine brown eyes, whose flawless complexion belied her forty years.

"Why! Madeleine!" He smiled as he bent to kiss the plump, heavily ringed hand she extended. "How truly delightful to see you again."

"But you! Back in Paris after all these years!" With a fingertip she touched one of the scarlet tabs on his khaki tunic. "And as a British General, too! This is a story that I cannot wait one moment to hear. You must tell it to me over an *apéritif*."

Turning, she gave the two women who were with her a charming smile and said: "*Mesdames*, it is not every day that one meets again a friend of one's youth. I feel sure you will forgive me." Then she stood up and the Duke, after bowing to her friends, took her through to the ladies' side of the bar.

She was several years older than himself, and had already been married to the Marquis de Frontignac when he had first known her. But that had not prevented her from teaching him many pleasant things that a young man should know; and their love affair had lasted considerably longer than most of his youthful peccadilloes. They had parted as friends and, although they had not met for many years, still retained a deep affection for one another.

Over their drinks he gave her a suitable account of himself, and for half an hour or so they revived happy memories of the good times they had had together. Then, on a sudden inspiration, she said:

"Armand! I have an idea. You can do me a great kindness, and I am sure you will not refuse. I have never been blessed with children, so, now that I am no longer young, I devote myself to charity. You must lunch with me one day soon, and that will enable me to raise a lot of money."

In his anomalous position, to re-enter French society was the very last thing he wanted, but she swiftly overruled his protests.

"Be silent please. I will take no denial. You have already told me that as a liaison officer you have to come to Paris every day; so you cannot plead the war to get out of it. Listen now! You are a most romantic figure. Everyone who matters knows how you barely escaped from France with your life. And now you come back to us as a gallant soldier of our Allies. I know a score of wealthy women who would give their eyes to meet you. I shall give a big luncheon party, and afterwards they will give generous cheques to my charity for the privilege of having done so."

Loath as he was to agree, he felt that he could not possibly refuse such a request from so old and intimate a friend; so they arranged that he should lunch at her house in the Parc Morceau on the coming Friday.

Next day, the 9th of September, *and the fortieth day* from the German order for mobilization, there came the first indications of the turning of the tide. The Germans, now fully extended, fighting at a great distance from their bases, without reinforcements to call upon, and in desperate fear that their right wing would be completely rolled up, had had enough. Slowly at first, then with increasing speed, they began to retire across the Marne and fall back on the Aisne. By the 10th, along the whole front dog-tired French and British troops were staggering forward.

If only von Moltke had retained the two Corps allocated to the investment of Namur, they could have filled the fatal gap between the Armies of von Kluck and von Below. And four other German Corps had been withdrawn for the Russian front. Had those 350,000 men still been in the west, the French could not conceivably have borne their weight. Inevitably the French army would have been borne back, collapsed, and forced to surrender. Had Joffre not thrown away 300,000 men in his senseless assault on the great German fortress line in Lorraine, things would have gone the other way. The exhausted Germans would not merely have been halted and compelled to retire, but routed, and suffered so severe a defeat that the war might have ended by Germany asking in September, 1914, for an armistice.

As it was, another four years' dogged, unending slaughter, had to be endured before the Kaiser's mailed fist was finally shattered. But the Germans never again reached the Marne. Paris was saved, and new heart for future ordeals put into the French army. Hour by hour tidings came in that one enemy division after another was giving way; and as de Richleau received the news he felt more than ever that, however hideous the deed he had done upon the train, he was absolved from blame.

On the 11th he gracefully fulfilled the rôle of guest of honour at the Marquise de Frontignac's lunch. About thirty people were present, the great majority being middle-aged, heavily bejewelled women. As he was introduced to them, few of their names meant anything to him, but he realized that they were the wives of wealthy men and had social ambitions. In every great capital there were many of their kind who, for the privilege of lunching with a Marquise and meeting a Duke with an ancient name and romantic background, would willingly give big sums to charity. He was pleased that he had come, as he felt certain that the draw of his presence would enable his *chère* Madeleine to make a good haul.

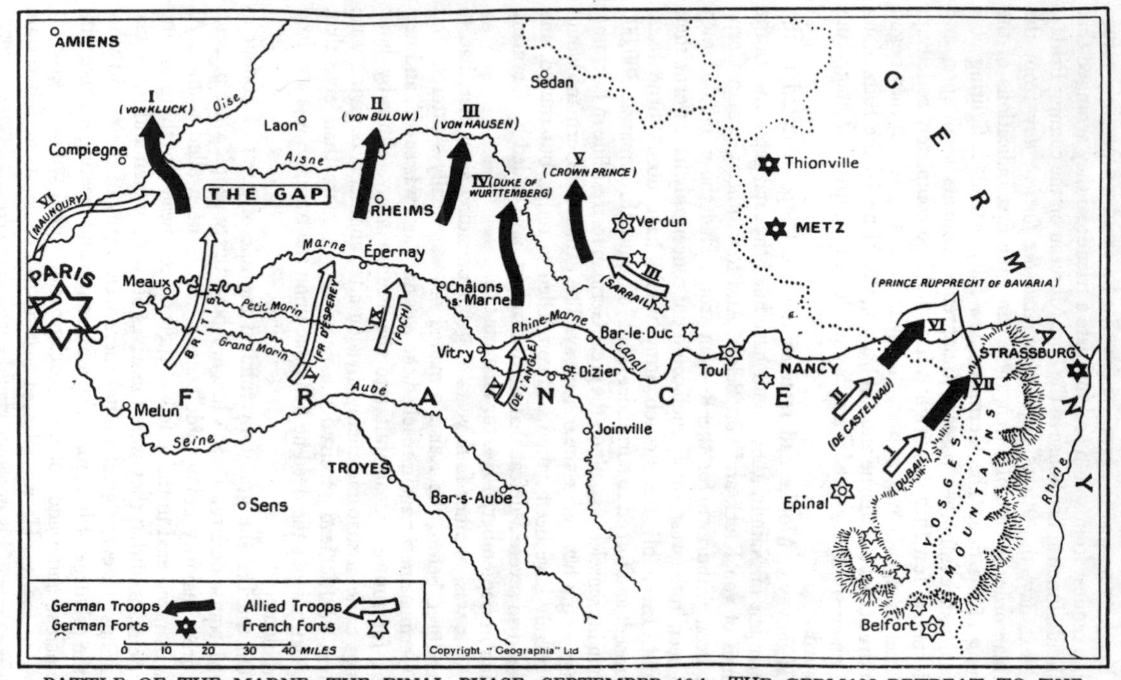

BATTLE OF THE MARNE. THE FINAL PHASE, SEPTEMBER 10th, THE GERMAN RETREAT TO THE AISNE

After the meal they adjourned to the Marquise's *salon*. An elderly tabby-cat man, of the type who always seems to stage manage such affairs, called for silence. The Marquise produced some notes and studied them for a moment through her lorgnette. Then she addressed the company:

"My dear friends, I have a confession to make. I feel I have got you here to-day under false pretences. Perhaps that was very naughty of me; but I wanted to speak to you about the charity that means so much to me. Now, please don't be angry. I know how generously you are all giving to the new war charities for our poor, brave wounded. But we should not forget our other obligations. Both in peace and war more people are killed by disease than by bullets. Alas, we cannot stop the bullets of our wicked enemy; but we can help to save lives threatened by disease. Most of you know of the great work in which I am so deeply interested. It is the checking of that greatest of all scourges—Tuberculosis. I want your help—your generous help—to stamp this awful plague out once and for all from our dear France. And I wish to remind you of one thing. I do not appeal to you now only to help to protect the poor. This terrible disease is so contagious that every day it menaces your own dear ones. A consumptive nursemaid may easily give it to your children. No one of us is too rich, too far removed from the slums, of too high station, for our homes not to be threatened by it.

"Let me give you an example. Many of you will recall the beautiful young Archduchess, Ilona Theresa of Austria, who stayed in Paris for a short time this spring, on her way to England. She was then a lovely, healthy girl, full of the joy of life. In the summer she contracted tuberculosis. She became subject to a galloping consumption. Only yesterday I saw the great Swiss specialist, Dr. Bruckner, who has been attending her. He tells me that now he cannot give her more than three weeks to live——"

CHAPTER XXVIII

ACROSS THE RHINE

Two afternoons later, de Richleau was standing in the fringe of a pine wood on the west bank of the Upper Rhine. With the same pair of powerful Zeiss glasses that, eighteen afternoons earlier, he had used to study the German-Dutch frontier, he now scrutinized that between Switzerland and Austria. He had felt then that his life depended on his getting out of the territories controlled by the Central Empires: he felt now that something worth more than his life depended on getting into them again.

Madeleine de Frontignac's innocent disclosure about Ilona had struck him like a thunderbolt. He had known for a long time that her illness was more serious than she admitted, and latterly that it was a matter for considerable anxiety: but he had not thought for one moment that she was in any danger of death. Yet the Marquise's report had not been based on idle gossip. She had received it from Dr. Bruckner.

Her terrible words had temporarily paralysed de Richleau's brain. He felt sure that his social instincts had carried him through the last half hour of the party, and that he had said the appropriate things to her and her guests before leaving; but he could remember practically nothing about that. His mind had become obsessed with the thought that, if Ilona had only a few weeks to live, he must get to her at the earliest possible moment.

He had had neither compunction nor difficulty in terminating the work he had been given on the fateful evening of September the 4th. Returning at once to Melun, he had told Sir Pellinore the facts. The Baronet had agreed that his commitment was an entirely voluntary one, and that he was free to go whenever he wished. After an earnest expression of his sympathy, he added:

"Battle's won now, anyway. Sir John's movin' his H.Q. forward to-morrow. So I'm goin' home myself. Thunderin' glad to have had the chance to lend a hand here. Experience I'll never forget. But many more urgent things than drawin' lines on maps with coloured pencils waitin' my attention in London."

Sir Henry Wilson had proved equally amenable. To him the Duke simply said that he wished to be relieved of his duties on account of private affairs that needed immediate attention.

"I'm sorry you're leaving us," the General said. "But you know the position as well as I do. The Huns are digging in on the Aisne, and the French haven't another kick left in them; so there is bound to be a stalemate now for several weeks. It may even be the spring before either side has recovered sufficiently to launch another full scale offensive. You've been a big help to us in the past week, but it is no longer necessary for us to keep in such constant touch with General Galliéni. How long do you think it will take you to arrange these affairs of yours?"

"About a month," de Richleau had informed him glumly.

"Well, when you're through, if you care to come back to us, we'd be glad to have you. I'm afraid I can't promise you the rank of Brigadier-General. But hundreds of people are being given temporary commissions now, and experts of all kinds are being granted field rank at once to enable them to be used to the best advantage. I should have no difficulty in getting you made a G.S.O.I., and with your ability you would soon be stepped up to full Colonel."

If anything could have pleased the Duke, the thought that he could now take up a post in which he could use his military knowledge would have done so. But for him the future was filled with nightmare uncertainties. Nevertheless, he thanked Sir Henry with all the cordiality he could muster, and promised to report for duty as soon as his affairs were settled.

Next morning, Sir Pellinore saw the British Ambassador for him and secured him a permit to enter Switzerland. He bought himself a civilian outfit, packed his uniform into a suitcase and parked it at the Ritz. After lunch they parted with regret and affection; Sir Pellinore to return to England, de Richleau to seek a way of reaching Ilona's deathbed, so that he might give her the comfort of his presence when she died.

Early on Saturday, the 13th, he had arrived at St. Gall, near the south-east corner of Lake Constance. There, he bought a large scale map and hired a car to drive him the fifteen miles through the Appenzell to the village of Alstätten. In the village he had paid off his hired car and lunched; then gone out on his reconnaissance.

Alstätten lay on a slope of the mountain range he had just crossed. To the east of it spread the low ground of the Rhine valley, which was there some eight miles wide; then on the Austrian side the ground rose steeply again to the mountains of the Vorarlberg. About four miles below him lay the village of Kriesseren; a mile beyond it wound the river, and two miles beyond that another village which he knew must be Hohenembs. For a few moments he searched the heights above it intently, knowing that the Imperial villa would be somewhere upon them. On one spur he could see a little irregular patch which he thought might be it.

Having mastered the general lie of the land from his vantage point, he returned to Alstätten, and took a local 'bus down into Kriesseren. There was a little hotel there with a vine-covered terrace overlooking the river. From it he could now see the patch with his naked eye and confirmed his belief that it was a large châlet.

At that hour in the afternoon the terrace was deserted, and having ordered himself a Kirschwasser he got into conversation with the waitress. She was a daughter of the proprietor, and lamented that the war had ruined the summer tourist trade of Switzerland. Few foreigners were coming there now, apart from invalids, and they were no good to a little hotel lying on low ground near the river.

After a while he pointed to the châlet, remarking on its lovely situation, and asked if she knew who owned it.

"The Emperor of Austria," she replied. "It is occupied now by an Austrian Princess. I forget her name, but she is said to be very beautiful. She came there for her health soon after the war started, but they say she is in a bad way and unlikely to recover."

He winced, looked quickly away, and said: "In spite of the war, you still get news then of what goes on over there across the river?"

"Oh yes," she nodded. "We are not at war with Austria, God be thanked; so trade continues. But they are very careful now who they let in and out, because of spies and deserters."

After finishing his drink, the Duke walked down to the bank of the river. The Rhine was not very broad there, so he knew that he could easily swim it, but, obviously, it would be preferable if he could get a boat to take him over. As it was not a war zone, there were no defences, but he felt certain that, even in peace time, occasional night patrols would be on the look-out for people endeavouring to enter Austria clandestinely.

Britain was the only country in Europe which had continued to allow the products of other countrys' cheap labour to be dumped without limit or tax upon her. All the others protected their principal industries by duties; so, although travellers had been permitted to pass freely from one to another, all European frontiers had customs guards stationed along them to prevent illegal imports.

This had resulted in the creation of a vast international smuggling organization, and the gradual building up of a complete system of underground communications. De Richleau knew that on the frontiers of all countries still at peace the smugglers' operations would have continued to function, and he felt that if he could get in touch with the local Rhine smugglers they would easily be able to put him across.

Strolling back to the village, he began to make a round of the few peasant drinking dens that it contained. At the first he tried, a sour-faced woman brought him his drink and regarded him with quick suspicion when he endeavoured to get her to talk about smuggling; but at the second he was luckier. Two fairly prosperous looking men were drinking there, and readily accepted his offer that they should join him in another round. They were not very communicative on the subject of smuggling, but admitted that it went on in the neighbourhood. After a while he took the bull by the horns, said that he wanted to get across the river that night and, under the table, showed them a handful of French gold.

The chances that a police spy would possess so much foreign money were remote, so the sight of it allayed their suspicions. They discussed the matter between themselves in *patois* for a few minutes, then told de Richleau that for twenty *louis d'or* his crossing could be arranged. It was decided that he should dine at the little hotel and remain there till it closed, then return to the drinking den, and when the moon was down someone would take him across.

Everything went without a hitch. The moon did not set till three, but it was a night of drifting cloud with few stars, and soon after four o'clock he was put ashore at a derelict landing stage on the Austrian bank.

A few hundred yards inland he came upon a tin-roofed shed. It lay at the bottom of the garden of a house in the village of Albach, which was nearer to the river than Hohenembs and about three miles from it. There he sat down to hide until the village was astir. Soon after seven, he left the shed, skirted the north of the village, and reached the road. An hour's walk up a series of gradual slopes and across the railway line brought him to Hohenembs.

It was quite a small place, with only one inn and half a dozen shops; but one of them was a barber's. Although it was a Sunday morning, like most hairdresser's on the Continent, it had opened for a few hours to smarten up its patrons before they went to Mass; so he went into it and had himself shaved. Then he went to the inn for breakfast.

Only one table in the little coffee room was occupied. At it sat two Austrian officers: a Major with a large fluffed-out red moustache and prawn-like eyebrows, and a dark little Captain. With them were two young women whose smart clothes suggested Vienna. De Richleau soon decided that the officers were probably stationed in the locality and had imported two good-looking *demi-mondaines* to amuse them over the week-end. Not wishing to embarrass the party by appearing to be listening to their conversation, he asked the elderly waiter to bring him a paper, and the old boy shuffled back with the previous day's *Innsbrucker Zeitung*. Propping it up against the coffee pot, the Duke glanced through its principal news items, while eating a ham omelette he had ordered.

The Austrian communiqué admitted that the German invasion of France had been brought to a halt, but stated that the check was merely temporary, and that their invincible allies would soon be in Paris. The big news came from East Prussia, and they were now able to give a full account of a second great German victory there.

Between August 28th and 31st, during the battle of Tannenberg, the Germans had killed or taken prisoner three and a half out of the five Corps of which General Samsonov's Army had consisted: but the Hindenburg-Ludendorff-Hoffmann combination had not been content to rest upon its laurels. From September 1st they had begun to re-deploy their forces against Rennenkampf; who, on learning of his colleague's defeat, began to withdraw his troops, and ordered them to entrench themselves along the Insterberg Line—a position of great strength, as its right flank was protected by the Baltic and its left by the northern end of the Masurian Lakes.

By that time the first two of the Army Corps dispatched by von Moltke had arrived from the Western Front; so Hindenburg had six Corps to dispose of. Four had been directed north to make a frontal attack on the Insterberg Line: von François was to bring his Corps and all the cavalry right round the southern end of the lake chain, and von Mackensen to push his Corps through the Lötzen gap in its centre.

The brilliant and indefatigable von François had been given charge of the whole outflanking movement, and by September the 4th he was already thrusting into Russian-held territory south and east of the lakes. By the 9th the rest of the army was in position and general battle was joined. The German assault failed to break the Insterberg Line, and von Mackensen found himself unable to force his way out of the Lötzen gap, as the Russians had its exit held too strongly. But in the past four days von François had worked his way right round behind them. Falling upon the four divisions opposed to von Mackensen, he cut them to pieces, thus opening the way for his colleague. Then the two Corps Commanders had hurled their troops north-eastwards against the flank of the main Russian Army. But Rennenkampf had had enough. He had given orders for a general retirement during the night, leaving two of his divisions to protect his retreat by a desperate rearguard action on the 10th. Both of them had stood with great gallantry, but been wiped out. That day Hindenburg had driven the last Russian from German soil, and his whole army was in full pursuit of the flying Rennenkampf. The paper de Richleau was reading concluded its account with the statement that the Germans had captured many thousands of prisoners, and vast quantities of booty, as the spoils of victory; and that the pursuit of the Russians was still continuing.

It was clear to the Duke that there was nothing more to be hoped for on the East Prussian front for a considerable time to come. Both General Jilinski's Armies had been decisively defeated, and he would be hard put to it to re-form the remnants of his fifteen Army Corps on the line of the Nieman. But this Russian disaster, serious as it was, had not the awful finality which would have crowned a similar German victory in France. Russia had territory to give—hundreds of miles of it—before any of her principal cities would be menaced; and her Siberian Army should now be arriving to fill the gaps in her torn front. Besides, on her southern front she had been more than holding her own against the Austrians.

As de Richleau re-folded the paper to read the latest reports on von Hötzendorf's doings, he heard a motor car drive up outside. He had caught enough of the conversation of the group near him to gather that they were about to set out for a Sunday picnic. Out of the corner of his eye he saw a soldier-servant enter the room, and heard him report to the Major that the baskets had been put in the car. The two officers and their girls stood up and, laughing together, went out into the passage.

There was not much in the paper about the Austrian Army's recent activities; but the Duke thought the brief communiqué significant. After announcing that the stalemate on the Serbian front continued with only sporadic fighting, it added that General von Hötzendorf had made a strategic withdrawal from Lemberg. As de Richleau knew well, the little Austrian C.-in-C. was the last man to make strategic withdrawals unless positively forced to it; so it looked as if von Hötzendorf must now be in a pretty bad way.

De Richleau was not seriously thinking about the war. More than half his mind was occupied with the thought that within an hour or so now he would be with his beloved Ilona. His vague speculations about von Hötzendorf having got into serious difficulties were engendered only by the fact of having the newspaper there in front of him. He had just stretched out his hand for a plum, with which to round off his breakfast before starting for the châlet, when the two officers re-entered the room followed by the orderly.

As the Duke looked up his glance chanced to fall on the orderly's face. Like so many men with nondescript features, when put into uniform he looked like thousands of other soldiers, and entirely lacking in any marked individuality. De Richleau had scarcely noticed him when he had come into the room a few minutes earlier; now he found himself staring full at the man across the Major's shoulder. His face was white and excited. It was also suddenly and horribly familiar. Instinctively the Duke half rose to his feet.

At the same instant the officers drew their pistols and the Major snapped, "Put your hands up!"

* * * * *

Less than an hour later the Duke was locked in a prison cell. For the rest of the day—the day that had started so well, with only a walk up a hillside separating him from Ilona—he was left to brood over his misfortune. For it, no blame attached to himself. He had been guilty of no stupid oversights like those which had betrayed him in Holland. His detection had come about through a piece of sheer bad luck. But that was immaterial. The fact remained that he had been caught; and not merely caught entering the country illegally, but definitely identified.

As he sat on the wooden bench with his hands clasped between his knees, seeking a ray of hope where there was none, he knew what that meant. Within twenty-four hours he would be handed over to the K.S., and that would be the end of him.

While in Serbia, Austria and Germany, he had skated on thin ice for days on end, several times deliberately prolonging periods of peril which might have landed him in the same situation as he was in at present; and he had got away. But that was little consolation now. However marvellous the long run of luck he had enjoyed in places where at any moment he might have run up against someone who knew the truth about him, it was a bitter pill that here, in a tiny village where he had every reason to consider himself free from any risk of recognition, a man who could denounce him as a spy and murderer should have come upon the scene.

He had fallen a victim to one of those strange strokes of fate which appear to occur only through blind coincidence; yet, all the same, so often have a subtle connecting link with an evil action done in the past. The soldier-servant who had recognized him was the peace-time valet of the late Baron Lanzelin Ungash-Wallersee.

The Duke had left him three weeks ago on the platform of the railway junction outside Berlin, with his dead master's body and baggage, and had never expected to set eyes on him again. But the explanation of his appearance in Hohenembs was quite simple. The Major with the fierce red moustache and prawn-like eyebrows was a Count Zelltin, and Lanzi's nephew. The depôt of his regiment was at Dornbirn, a small town about seven miles from Hohenembs; and, on hearing of his uncle's death, he had applied for this admirable personal servant to be transferred to him.

In spite of de Richleau's civilian clothes, the soldier had recognized him at once, but had had the sense to wait to tell his officers, until they came out to their car, that the Duke was a British spy, about whom he had been questioned at great length by the German police. Then, all three of them had returned to the coffee room fully prepared to overcome the Duke by force, or shoot him if need be. But he had been taken entirely by surprise. Before he had a chance to get at a weapon they had him covered, and threatened to kill him there and then if he moved. The ex-valet had searched him and removed the two pistols he was carrying. The picnic had been postponed, and the two glamorous young women left round-eyed with excitement, while their swains ran the prisoner into Dornbirn. They had taken him to the barracks, at which, as the regiment was on active service, Count Zelltin was the Commandant. There, the Duke had been put in one of the defaulters' cells, placed under double guard, and left to contemplate his impending fate.

He had as yet no idea how much the K.S. knew about him; but, as nearly three weeks had elapsed since he had escaped from Germany, it was a fair assumption that by now Nicolai and Ronge between them would have completed a dossier containing all there was to know. Even if there remained a blank in it here and there, it was certain that they would have collected enough evidence to have him shot on at least one charge if not several.

His thoughts naturally turned to Ilona as his one possible life line. As a prisoner awaiting trial he considered it unlikely that he would be allowed to communicate with her, or anyone else, by letter; and as his money and belongings had been taken from him, he had no means of bribing one of his guards to carry a message to Hohenembs. But, as soon as he had had time to think matters over, he decided that it would be not only futile, but wrong, to attempt either.

She had herself confirmed what Major Ronge had said in Vienna: that although a member of the Imperial Family she had no official status. So obviously she had no power to make the Commandant release a prisoner about to be charged with serious crimes; and it was equally clear that she was in no position to help him break prison.

Had he felt that there was the remotest chance that she would be able to save him, he would have strained his wits to the utmost in seeking some way of getting in touch with her; but, since she was powerless to do so, to involve her at all would be both cowardly and wicked. The burden she had to bear was great enough already, without his adding to it. The thought of his trial and execution would immensely increase the suffering of her last days, and to inflict that upon her when she could do nothing to assist him was unthinkable.

He had wanted so much to give her the small consolation of their love ending on a high romantic note, and to prove how deeply he loved her by risking death himself to see her again before she died. But now a last meeting was to be denied them, he could only hope that she would remain in ignorance of his plight until, if fate proved adamant, a firing squad had removed all possibility of her torturing herself with vain prayers for his release.

On Monday he was again kept in solitary confinement, and no one came to interrogate him. His guards were evidently under orders not to enter into conversation; as, when they brought him his food, they simply thrust it into his cell and ignored his attempts to get them to talk. However, at mid-day he asked if he could have something to read, and one of them brought him a Bible, a few other books, and a newspaper.

From the latter he saw that the cat was out of the bag about von Hötzendorf. The communiqué gave the situation in carefully guarded phrases, so as not to cause alarm; but certain place names were mentioned, and it was obvious to the Duke that a disaster had overtaken the Austrian Armies on the Russian Front, of such magnitude that it could no longer entirely be concealed.

Apparently von Hötzendorf had suffered from genuine ill-fortune in his great offensive to the north and east. After initial encouraging successes during the latter part of August, early in September he had all but encircled and destroyed an entire Russian Army; but false reconnaissance reports on the critical day had caused both wings of his enveloping force to believe they were about to be attacked in rear: both had faced about, and thus given the Russians just time to slip away before the jaws of the pincers closed upon them. Meanwhile it emerged that the bulk of General Ivanov's Southern Army Group was concentrated against much weaker Austrian forces farther south. Von Hötzendorf had shown great courage in holding on there till the last possible moment, and sending everything he could spare north to the front that promised him a brilliant victory; and, even when it became apparent that ill luck had robbed him of it, he had re-deployed his forces in a series of brilliant moves that might yet have spelled disaster to the Russians. But the enemy's weight had proved too much for him. After a final effort on the 9th, involving a whole day of battle from one end of his two hundred miles long front to the other, he had, on the 11th, ordered a general withdrawal to behind the line of the river San.

That much was clear from the communiqué. What it did not reveal was that, with a determination unequalled by any other Commander-in-Chief, von Hötzendorf had kept the great majority of his troops marching and fighting for twenty consecutive days. Had he had better luck and better material at his disposal he might well have achieved victories comparable with those of Hindenburg. As it was, he gave up only because what was left of his forces was in no condition to continue the struggle an hour longer. They had suffered appalling losses, many of his Army Corps having been reduced to less than the normal strength of a Division. In three weeks he had lost 600,000 men. The remnants of his four Armies were dead beat. They no longer had the strength to carry out the movements ordered by their Commanders, and thousands of them were dropping in their tracks from exhaustion. As the Russian pressure increased, the whole front had collapsed. For the past four days the Austrians had been streaming back in hopeless dejection and inextricable confusion; and many days were to pass yet before they could be finally halted and re-formed on the line of the Carpathians, nearly a hundred miles to the rear of the area in which they had sustained their terrible defeat.

So ended the last and longest of the opening battles of the great war; and as de Richleau laid down the paper he knew that the final outcome had now been decided. On four fronts the great Armies had clashed and fought themselves to a standstill. The carnage had been unbelievably appalling. In a little over three weeks not less than 2,000,000 men had been killed, captured or seriously wounded. Battles of such magnitude could never take place simultaneously on several fronts again. The manpower of the nations did not permit it. Either the war-mongers had learnt their ghastly lesson and there would be peace by Christmas or, if an evil pride kept them obdurate, a new kind of war must emerge. In it, from time to time great offensives might be launched with appalling losses to the attacker, but in the main the combatants must be reduced to endeavouring to wear one another down. And in such a contest the Central Powers must prove the weaker.

In a prolonged struggle the effects of the Allies' blockade would gradually become apparent. Cut off from the outer world by mighty Fleets that they could have no hope of defeating, Germany and Austria would be deprived of all but a trickle of many of the commodities vital to their war economy. Now that the Austrian bolt was shot, Russia would be able to concentrate her efforts against East Prussia. The rickety Dual Monarchy might be able to maintain armies in the field, but Germany would have to shoulder the main burden, and wage a desperate, long-drawn-out war on two fronts. Her only real hope had lain in putting France out of the war by a swift overwhelming victory, so that she had both hands free to assist Austria against Russia. That hope had been the key to everything—and it was gone.

The Duke smiled at the thought that he had been instrumental in influencing the German High Command into taking a decision that had robbed Germany of victory in the West. It was not much consolation to him now; but he felt that it would be a comforting thought on which to die.

Any lingering hopes he had of being able to escape the final penalty were dissipated on the Tuesday afternoon. At half past five he was taken from his cell to an office on the ground floor of the barracks. The Commandant was there, and with him was Major Ronge.

It was soon clear that, from the moment of his leaving Vienna to that of his having been released from prison in Maastricht, the broad outline of his activities was fully known. Ronge did most of the talking, while the Count eyed the prisoner with a malevolent stare. Not much was said about the deaths on the train, but the fiery-moustached Commandant made it abundantly clear that he believed de Richleau to be responsible for his uncle's murder. To all specific charges the Duke replied only with a shrug, and a statement that he reserved his defence; as, although it was futile to argue, he saw no reason why he should make a gratuitous admission of anything.

They questioned him with great persistence as to why, having succeeded in escaping, he should have given himself up as a hostage to fortune by re-crossing the Rhine into enemy territory; but they got no satisfaction from him.

At length Count Zeltin informed him that he would be tried by court martial on the following afternoon at three o'clock, and that in the morning a Prisoner's Friend would be sent to help him to prepare any defence he cared to put before the court. Then he was taken back to his cell.

Next morning a pink-faced Lieutenant, who was limping from a wound received on the Serbian front, arrived and offered his services as an advocate. Obviously he did not like the task for which he had been detailed, but he courteously endeavoured to hide his distaste, and produced all the materials requisite for making copious notes. De Richleau swiftly relieved him of his embarrassment by saying that he would prefer to conduct his own defence.

At three o'clock punctually, he was marched from his cell between soldiers with fixed bayonets to a large cheerless room. On the wall opposite the door hung a picture of the aged Emperor, in his white Field Marshal's tunic, gold braid and ribbons. At a table beneath it the court was already sitting. It consisted of Major Count Zeltin as President, an elderly, red-faced Captain who looked like an ex-Quartermaster sergeant, and a monocled Lieutenant. There were two side tables. At one sat another Captain; a dark little man wearing gold spectacles, who was acting as Prosecutor and, opposite him, at the other, the pink-faced Prisoner's Friend; the presence of the latter, whether he uttered or not, being required by the court as a formality which technically guaranteed the prisoner a fair trial.

As the Duke had often sat on courts martial himself, he knew well that in war time such trials were rarely conducted with the scrupulous fairness usual in the administration of civil justice. The members of such courts were not qualified to go deeply into legal technicalities, nor expected to give time to examining the finer points of evidence. In a spy case they were usually pre-disposed against the prisoner, and it was accepted that spies should be given short shrift in war time; so unless the accused had ample means of proving his innocence he had little chance of an acquittal.

In view of the blackness of the case against him, and the fact that Lanzi's nephew was President of the court, de Richleau felt that he had none at all; but he was most strongly in favour of the admirable dictum that 'while there is life there is hope'; so he was determined to do his utmost to procure a postponement of sentence; for, if he could gain a week or two, or even a few days, there was always the possibility that he might manage to escape.

In consequence, at the very opening of the proceedings, he challenged the court's right to try him at all. He pointed out that in the Austrian Army he held the rank of Colonel, and therefore could not be tried by officers of lesser rank.

The President was obviously somewhat shaken by this, and called over the Prosecutor, with whom he held a whispered conversation. He then ruled that as the rank given had been an honorary one, it did not carry any seniority for the purpose of a trial such as the present.

A long list of charges was read out, to all of which the Duke pleaded not guilty.

The Prosecutor asked baldly why he should attempt to waste the court's time by denying the obvious; but at that the Prisoner's Friend intervened, and said that the accused had a right to assert his innocence.

With a grim smile the Prosecutor produced a sheaf of affidavits, and started to read out one that had been made by Colonel Nicolai.

As soon as he had finished, the Duke said that he wished to cross-examine this witness; but the President replied that in time of war it was not practicable to bring officers engaged on important duties many hundreds of miles to testify in person, therefore the court was prepared to accept sworn statements as evidence.

The next statement read out was by Herr Steinhauer. There followed those of the Sergeant-Conductor of the train; Colonel Tappen; the garage proprietor in Aix-la-Chapelle from whom de Richleau had hired the car he had abandoned near the frontier; and a score more by orderlies and other people. It was clear to the Duke that the material from which the Prosecutor was reading must be the dossier of the case compiled by Colonel Nicolai, and that Ronge had had it forwarded from Germany during the past two days. When the reading was finished, he said:

"I submit to the court that all this is irrevelant because it is not supported by the personal appearance of the witnesses. Even if those statements are accurate about a certain person, it does not follow that the person referred to is myself."

"I am fortunately in a position to satisfy the court upon that," replied the Prosecutor; and he called his first witness, *Soldat* Johan Weber, Lanzi's ex-valet.

Soldat Weber definitely identified the accused as the officer who had accompanied Colonel Baron Ungash-Wallersee from Przemysl to Wartenburg and, with Major Tauber, on the train from Wartenburg to Berlin. Prompted by questions from the Prosecutor, he recounted the whole story as he knew it, and his testimony occupied nearly three quarters of an hour.

De Richleau knew that it was futile to attempt to shake him, but at least he had the satisfaction of learning that the manner in which Lanzi and Tauber had met their deaths was still in doubt. Obviously everyone believed that he had killed them, but his efforts to destroy any evidence against himself had been so successful that the German police had failed to make out a prima facie case against him.

He stoutly maintained that *Soldat* Weber's testimony proved nothing at all, except that he had accompanied Baron Ungash-Wallersee from Przemsyl to Berlin, and there was nothing criminal about that.

Major Ronge was then called. It was the first time that the Duke had seen the fat Secret Service Chief in uniform, but he proved a no less shrewd and formidable antagonist on that account. He recounted what was known of de Richleau's activities in Serbia, told the story of his arrest, and release owing to the intervention of Her Imperial Highness the Archduchess Ilona Theresa, and of his obtaining an appointment on General von Hötzendorf's operations' staff under false pretences.

In cross examination the Duke forced him to make the following admissions: that there was no proof of his having committed any act of espionage while in Belgrade, or in Vienna: that he had been about to leave Austria before war was declared, whereas a spy would normally have gone into hiding there with the object of continuing to learn all he could: that he had been prevented from leaving by arbitrary arrest: and that the Archduchess had procured his release because there was not a shread of evidence to support any charge against him. But the two things he could not disprove were that he had deceived General von Hötzendorf concerning his nationality, and had left Vienna clandestinely when he had been warned by the police that, as an enemy alien, he must remain there.

When called on to make his defence, de Richleau took the line that he was an entirely innocent British subject who, merely on suspicion, had been detained in Austria contrary to his will. He pointed out that no charge had been preferred against him of communicating Austria's military secrets to the enemy while on von Hötzendorf's staff: that the crimes imputed to him while in Germany were based solely on the written evidence of witnesses whom he had not been given an opportunity to cross-examine; that he had been denied the opportunity to call witnesses, such as the Hungarian Minister-President, Count Tisza, to testify to his character and conduct while in Vienna: and, finally, that, having been illegally prevented from returning to his own country before the outbreak of war, no blame could be attached to him for having done so at the first opportunity.

The case had looked so black against him to start with that he now felt things might have gone far worse. No evidence at all had been forthcoming about the deaths of Lanzi and Tauber, and he had raised issues which he was certain would have caused a civil court to adjourn the hearing until more conclusive proof of his guilt could be brought. With new hope he saw, too, that he had succeeded in arousing doubts in two members of the court. The monocled Lieutenant was regarding him quite sympathetically, and the elderly Captain with grave, rather kindly interest. But Lanzi's nephew continued to stare at him with black hostility and, brushing up his fierce red moustache, called on the Prosecutor to make his final speech.

Adjusting his gold spectacles, the dark little Captain proceeded in a quiet unemotional voice to go over the ground again. He did not contest the fact that the accused had been on the point of leaving Vienna before the war broke out, but drew attention to his having left his attempt to do so to the very last moment. That, he suggested, was because the accused had wanted to secure the latest possible information on the Dual Monarchy's intentions before returning to London; and there could be no doubt that his many contacts in high places had given him access to information, both diplomatic and military, which could be of very great value indeed to the enemy. Therefore the K.S. had had the best possible grounds for preventing him from leaving.

He then dealt with de Richleau's activities after being released from prison, and showed that although actual proof of espionage might be considered scanty, the circumstantial evidence against him was overwhelming. The statements of Colonel Nicolai and Herr Steinhauer about his attack upon them could not be brushed aside; and it was known to them that the accused had been in communication with the British Committee of Imperial Defence the previous spring. Having escaped to Holland, he had, only a few days ago, returned to Austria in secret, and refused to give any reason for having done so. He had lied his way on to General von Hötzendorf's staff, and given General von Moltke misleading information. How, therefore, could there be the least doubt that while posing as an Austrian officer he had been guilty of acts which called for the extreme penalty?

When he had finished the Duke was marched into an adjoining room to await the decision of the court. He knew the drill only too well, so could imagine what was happening. Military law ordained that the Lieutenant, as the junior member of the court, should first be asked his opinion. The Captain would give his next, and finally the President would give his. If there was any disagreement they would discuss the pros and cons of the matter. Unless both the juniors were strongly opposed to the President, as the senior and more experienced officer, his opinion nearly always proved decisive—and the President was Lanzi's nephew.

With that in mind, and the damning speech of the Prosecutor still ringing in his ears, de Richleau's hopes fell again to zero. He was not kept long in doubt. Barely three minutes had elapsed before he was sent for and marched back into the court room. He had been found guilty of falsely representing himself as an Austrian subject, with intent to learn military secrets; of having entered the country illegally; and of acts deliberately calculated to damage the military operations of the Central Powers. The President then passed sentence of death upon him.

In spite of the fact that he had been prepared for it, when the sentence was actually delivered, it came as a shock. Something inside himself had continued to argue up to the very last moment, against the logic of his brain, that he would not be called on to pay the extreme penalty. Yet he knew that for them to have sentenced him to a long term of imprisonment in a fortress would have been to evade the issue; either they must find him innocent, and acquit him of all but the minor charge of having re-entered the country illegally, or guilty; and if the latter, guilty of crimes which could not possibly be paid for by less than death. The blood drained from his face for a moment, then he bowed to his judges, faced about, and with his chin held high walked between his guards back to his cell.

As they led him into it, he found that his Prisoner's Friend had followed him. The young man had never seen a death sentence passed before, and his pink cheeks had gone quite pale. In a low voice he said: "I—I'm sorry I was of so little use to you."

De Richleau managed a smile. "Please don't worry. As you knew nothing of the facts of my case you could not possibly have done better for me than I did for myself."

"Is there anything I can do to make things easier for you?" asked the Lieutenant.

"Perhaps. When will it be?"

"To-morrow morning. At the usual hour for—for these things. Soon after dawn."

"I trust that I am to be shot?"

"Yes. As a soldier you are entitled to that."

"Good! I should greatly resent the indignity of being hanged. Now, this is what you can do for me. See that the squad make a neat job of it by aiming for my heart. For God's sake don't have any youngsters or recruits among them. Detail some tough old sweats, and tell them beforehand that I have given you the money that was taken from me when I was searched, to distribute among them as a reward for ensuring me a quick, clean death."

The Lieutenant's eyes goggled and he looked as if he were about to be sick; but he stammered, "Yes. I—I promise to arrange it like that. Is there anything else?"

"Only that I should like to write some letters and make my will; and I would be grateful if you would take charge of them. If you can let me have some paper now, and come back at about eight o'clock, I'll have them ready."

When the Lieutenant had fetched the writing materials and gone, the Duke suppressed a tremor of excitement and sat down to write to Ilona.

His trial had introduced an entirely new element into his outlook and, he felt, provided him with legal grounds which entitled him to seek her help. It had disclosed the fact that the German police were unable to bring home against him the killings on the train, and that but for minor matters all the evidence against him was circumstantial. He was convinced that, had he been tried by a civil court, he would have been granted the right of appeal. Ilona might have no official status, but her prestige was immense, and it was a part of her functions as a royalty, to receive and consider petitions from people who felt that the authorities had dealt unjustly with them. Only the Emperor had the right to pardon, but a message from her to the Commandant would, the Duke felt sure, result in a postponement of his execution.

He was still greatly distressed at the thought of bringing such a worry on her, but considered that justified by the fact that where she could have done nothing for him before she could now do much. In his extremity he reasoned that, if she could get him a retrial in Vienna, there was a fair hope of his securing an acquittal on all major charges; and that if there appeared the least doubt about his guilt, many of his influential friends there would endeavour to save him, particularly Count Tisza. The Count would realize that it was his having delayed to the last moment the rescinding of the parole he had exacted that had resulted in the present situation. As Minister-President, even in the worst event, he could secure a remission of sentence to a term of imprisonment in a fortress. With all this in mind, de Richleau had swiftly reached the conclusion that only a quixotic fool would have refrained from appealing to Ilona now he could arm her with a legal pretext as the means of saving his life.

First he wrote the formal petition, giving full particulars of the trial, pointing out that he had been condemned on written evidence, and praying Her Imperial Highness' gracious intervention. It was a carefully worded document that she could quote to the Commandant as her justification for intervening, and, later, forward to the proper authorities. Then he covered many sheets, in which he expressed all that he felt, in case she should be unable to do anything for him. He wrote glowingly of the hours they had spent together; of his undying love for her; and ended by saying that if he must die to-morrow his only regret would be that he had not first held her in his arms again.

By the time he had finished it was getting on for eight. As he stuck down the envelope of his letter he took considerable comfort from the thought that, if Ilona could do nothing, she had at least been spared the agony of awaiting his trial. All would be over within a few hours of her receiving it, and as she was so soon to die herself she might gain comfort from the thought that within a little time they would be together once more. But he knew that she would move heaven and earth to save him, and felt confident now that she would succeed.

On the Lieutenant's arrival, de Richleau greeted him with a calm but serious air, and said: "I want you to have this letter sent by dispatch rider to Her Imperial Highness the Archduchess Ilona Theresa, at Hohenembs. I cannot too strongly impress upon you its urgency and importance. I was greatly averse to involving Her Imperial Highness in this affair as long as I expected an acquittal. But now my life depends upon it."

The Lieutenant looked at him in blank surprise, then exclaimed, "I'm sorry! Terribly sorry. But what you ask is quite impossible. It is strictly against orders for prisoners to send letters to anyone."

When the Duke had contemplated writing to Ilona soon after his arrest, he had thought it probable that he might come up against prison regulations, and have to think out some way of circumventing them. But now that he had been tried and condemned he could hardly credit that he was to be denied the small privilege of dispatching a letter. In swift consternation he began to plead and argue.

"I'm sorry," repeated the Lieutenant. "It is more than my commission is worth to go against orders in a case like this. Of course, I will take charge of any letters you care to leave with me, and do my best to see that they reach their destination. But I cannot possibly send this letter off now without the Commandant's permission."

"Then ask it at once," replied the Duke tersely. "And should he refuse this simple request, I demand to be brought before him."

"I'm afraid I can't do that either," said the Lieutenant unhappily. "You see, he has gone out to dinner somewhere in the town with Major Ronge; but where, I don't know."

Seeing that nothing could be done for the moment, de Richleau restrained his anger and fresh anxiety as well as he could. "All right," he nodded. "But be good enough to ask him to see me the moment he returns. I can rely on you to do that, can't I?"

"Certainly! I've no idea when he will be back; but I promise you I'll hang about for him and let him know of your request immediately he comes in." With an apologetic glance the Lieutenant withdrew, and the cell door was locked behind him.

More agitated now than at any time since he had been in prison, the Duke began to pace up and down the few feet of floor that lay between the door and the wall opposite it, which was blank except for a small barred window set high up near the ceiling. A few minutes earlier he had been next to positive that, now no really damning evidence had been brought against him at his trial, Ilona could save him. But, unless he could get his letter to her, he would die with her still in ignorance of the facts.

Even if the Commandant did not return until the early hours of the morning, there would still be time to get the letter to Hohenembs and for her to telephone the barracks. But would the Commandant agree to send the letter? That was the awful doubt that now haunted the Duke.

At one moment he felt that no human being could be so stony-hearted as to refuse a condemned man a request that might secure his reprieve: at the next he recalled that Count Zelltin was Lanzi's nephew, and had good cause to wish to see his prisoner shot.

In an agony of anxiety de Richleau strode to and fro for what seemed an interminable time. His hands were sweating and his dark hair was damp on his forehead. Now, more than ever before, he realized how good life could be, and how desperately he wanted to live. And for him life or death now hung upon the decision of a man who had every reason to be bitterly antagonistic to him.

At length, with a great effort, he pulled himself together and sat down again at the small table. In case—just in case—the worst happened, there were still things that he ought to do. Forcing himself to concentrate, he wrote his last will and testament; then started on letters to numerous friends. In each he said that he had had the misfortune to be caught in Austria, tried and condemned to death for espionage. He no longer felt any shame at admitting that he had acted as a spy. On the contrary, he now derived a curious pride in doing so. He added that he was much consoled by the thought that he had been of some service to the Allied cause; then sent all good wishes, and endeavoured to end his letters on as light a note as possible.

It was nearly eleven o'clock when Count Zelltin entered the cell, accompanied by Major Ronge. The Duke was still writing. He at once stood up and produced his letter for Ilona, with the request that it should be sent off by hand immediately.

The Commandant replied with a shrug: "I see no particular hurry about this. It will be taken care of with those others you are writing, and duly forwarded to-morrow morning."

De Richleau's mouth was dry. He swallowed, and said: "*Herr Graf*, I have a particular reason for wishing it to go to-night. As you are aware, I am an honorary Colonel in Her Imperial Highness's regiment. She has always been extremely gracious to me, and has even honoured me with her personal friendship. Even if she is in no position to alleviate my case, I feel certain that, if informed of it, she will give me the benefit of her prayers at the hour of my execution."

For a moment Count Zelltin played with one tip of his fluffed-out ginger moustache, then he said: "It is against regulations in such a case as yours for any letters to be sent till after execution. But I find it hard to refuse a last request from a man who has been condemned to death. All right; give it——"

"One moment, *Herr Graf!*" Ronge intervened swiftly, catching the Commandant's arm as he extended his hand for the letter. "If you take my advice, you'll think again before you allow this fellow to communicate with Her Imperial Highness. He is a special protégé of hers. If she learns that he is to be shot, she will create a fine to-do. She will demand that his execution shall be postponed until further inquiries have been made. And you will be faced with the choice of letting her have her way or risking the trouble she can make for you in Vienna."

Still the Commandant seemed to hesitate, and for several seconds the three of them stood there in so tense a silence that one could have heard the ticking of a watch. Then de Richleau began to plead; but Ronge cut him short, and exclaimed to the Commandant:

"You must not send it! I tell you it would be a crazy thing to do! This man has earned death a dozen times over! He is one of the most dangerous devils I have ever had to deal with. You can't possibly wish to give him this chance to prolong his life!"

Count Zelltin turned to the Secret Service Chief with a sigh, and muttered: "Well, you know more about these things than I do. Perhaps you're right." Then he glanced at de Richleau, made him a formal bow, and said, "I regret, but I cannot see my way to send your letter."

De Richleau felt a sudden shiver start to run through him, but he suppressed it. Drawing himself up like a French aristocrat about to be taken to the guillotine, he shrugged, made an airy gesture with his hand, and replied:

"Very well, then. In that case I will get a few hours' sleep. At three o'clock be good enough to send me a priest."

* * * * *

It was six o'clock in the morning. Dawn had already come an hour ago, and Ilona had woken with it. Since she had been at Hohenembs the doctors had made her spend a great deal of her time in bed; and even during the periods when her temperature remained normal they made her lie down for a nap in the afternoons; so she had acquired the habit of waking early.

During those early morning hours she rarely read. She allowed her thoughts to drift, and they ranged over many things. Down there on the Swiss frontier she was far removed from all the battle fronts; but she thought a lot about them and the misery they were bringing to the women of her country.

To begin with, like nearly every young person, she had felt a certain glamour and excitement at the coming of war. Her conviction that the Serbs were a barbarous race of murderers, who deserved severe chastisement, was still unshaken. She had not a shadow of doubt that the Dual Monarchy's cause was just, and that but for the unscrupulous ambitions of other countries the war would never have spread. Yet she had soon been given cause to rue it, for it had robbed her of her lover—the only lover she had ever had in her life. And she realized now that she was only one of millions of women to whom the war had brought the agony of separation.

Only the day before she had had a letter from her cousin, the Archduke Charles, who had become the Heir Apparent on Franz Ferdinand's death. He was a young man of mild and kindly disposition; and he wrote from his headquarters on the Russian front that every day the war filled him with greater horror. He said that the troops who had started out so gaily were now gaunt with fatigue and terror; that often they had to be driven to the attack by their officers threatening to shoot them from behind; and that even regiments which had fought with great bravery to begin with now broke and fled at the dread cry 'The Cossacks are coming!' But that they could not be blamed for that, as of the great host that had marched against the Czar one man out of every three would never return to his wife or sweetheart.

Ilona would have given her life to stop it, but she realized the futility of such a thought. She could only be thankful that, temporarily at least, she had saved one couple from the fate that had already overtaken so many. At the end of August, although Dr. Bruckner had not actually told her that her case was hopeless, she had known that he considered it so, and she had used that as a lever to make Adam Grünne abandon his intention of leaving for the front. He and Sárolta had then been on their honeymoon, and, now that they were married, were qualified to become the Master and Mistress of her Household. With great tact she had persuaded the Aulendorfs to return to Vienna, so that she could appoint the Count and Countess Grünne in their place, and thus protect Sárolta for a while from premature widowhood.

They had taken over their new duties on the previous Saturday, and she had awaited their arrival with hardly bearable impatience; not only because she was naturally eager to see these dear friends again, but because in her letter to Adam she had asked him to see Major Ronge on his way through Vienna, and find out anything that was known about de Richleau since his disappearance.

The K.S. Chief had a grim tale to tell and had shown Adam all the data on the case that he had received from Colonel Nicolai. Adam had been greatly worried, and at first considered suppressing the worst accusations in the account he gave Ilona. But Sárolta had said it was better that she should be told the whole truth by a friend, as she might otherwise learn it bluntly and brutally from someone else later; so together they had given her as gently as they could the story of her lover's desperate acts after leaving Vienna.

Ilona had taken it much better than Adam expected. She had been quick to seize upon the fact that de Richleau had committed no crime against Austria, and to point out that, even if he were guilty of all the charges laid against him, whatever he had done had been done in the service of his country. She glowed with pride at the thought of his daring and resource, and the way that he had fooled the Germans, whom they all detested. Above all, she was overjoyed to know that he had succeeded in getting away.

Over the week-end they had talked of little else; and privately Adam admitted to Sárolta that she had been right in urging him to conceal nothing. It was clear that Ilona did not care if the Duke had committed every crime in the calendar: she thought of him only as her man, and was animated by a new gaiety and happiness from the knowledge that he was safe and free.

Now, as she lay in bed, she was thinking of him, and wondering what he was doing. Had he become an officer of the British Army? Even if he had, he might be able to get leave and come to Switzerland. If so, she could easily cross the frontier and meet him there. Her doctor was urging her to move there as it was. How marvellous it would be if they could be together again—even for a few days.

A room on the ground floor had been turned into a bedroom for her, so that she could go straight out to sit in the sunshine on the small terrace, without the fatigue of going up and down stairs. Her curtains had not yet been drawn back and the room was still in semi-darkness; but outside it was full daylight.

Suddenly the shrilling of the front door bell cut across her thoughts. She wondered who it could possibly be at such an early hour in the morning. It shrilled again, and again—impatiently, urgently. Then there came footsteps in the hall, followed by the faint sound of voices in hurried argument.

After a few minutes there was a knock on her door, and at her call to enter, one of the housemaids looked in. The girl was not yet fully dressed, and said with a flustered air:

"I am sorry to disturb Your Highness, but there is a priest here. He insists on seeing you, and won't take no for an answer."

"A priest!" exclaimed Ilona. "What does he want?"

"He has brought a letter. He says he must give it you personally, and that he promised to deliver it at once. He says it's from a Count Königstein."

In an instant Ilona was out of bed. Her long, curling chestnut hair was loose and unbrushed, but she shook it back from her head, hastily pulled a satin dressing-gown over her nightdress, and cried:

"Show him in! Show him in at once!"

As the maid disappeared, Ilona pulled back the curtains of the window, and the early morning sunlight came streaming in. At the joyous thought of a letter from her lover, her heart was pounding as though it would burst through her breast. The blood had rushed to her cheeks; her blue eyes were shining. Turning, she glimpsed the black-robed figure in the still darkened hall just outside the doorway. Stretching out her hand, she gasped excitedly:

"Bless you for coming, Father! Give it me! Please give it me!"

The priest stepped across the threshold, quickly closed the door behind him, and only then took off his big shovel-brimmed hat.

She took one pace forward, staggered and nearly fell. With a little moan of almost unbearable ecstasy, she held out her arms.

The man in priest's clothing caught her to him. It was de Richleau.

* * * * *

Side by side, his arm about her, they sat upon her crumpled bed. He had told her how he had been caught, and of his trial, and was just beginning the story of his doings after he had left Vienna, when she clapped a soft hand over his mouth.

"Enough! Enough! Adam found out for me from Major Ronge about all the awful things you've done, or that are imputed to you. The truth could not be worse than what they told me. But I've forgotten it already; and I refuse to hear another word about it."

He kissed her hand and sighed with relief. "You forgive me then?"

"Of course. Nothing matters except that you have come back to me."

"I had to commit another crime this morning to do so," he confessed. "To get these clothes I had to lay hands on a priest."

"Oh Armand! That was sacrilege!" Her eyes widened in sudden horror. "You—you did not——"

"No. I put him only to a slight inconvenience. When Count Zelltin refused to send my letter to you, I realized that in a priest lay the one chance I had left. I hoped to make him my messenger, but had also to provide against failing in that. I asked them to send him to me at three o'clock. That left ample time for him to take a letter to you; but at that hour, if he refused, everyone except the guard would be asleep. Although I pleaded with him very hard, he did refuse. He said he could not break the regulations. I asked him then if he remembered the words 'Render unto Caesar the things that are Caesar's, and unto God the things that are God's'."

Ilona gave her lover a puzzled look. "Why did you ask him that?"

"That was just what he asked," smiled the Duke. "My reply was, 'Because mercy is a thing of God's, and it should lie in the hearts of all true priests. Since you refuse it me, I must take the things that are Caesar's—the outward show by which you pass yourself off as a priest.' As I spoke I moved round behind him. Under my coat I had been holding a small hand towel. I whipped it over his face and tied it firmly to stifle his cries, pulled off his soutane, tied his hands and feet, stuffed my handkerchief into his mouth as a gag, put him in the cot with his face to the wall, pulled the sheets up over his back, put on the things I had taken from him, and rapped on the door for the guard to let me out. As I passed him I murmured a blessing, and raised the priest's hat to the level of my face to hide it from him for a moment before putting the hat on. Then I walked off down the corridor with bent shoulders and my hands clasped behind my back, as though in deep thought. It was still dark outside, but I didn't dare take a chance with another guard on the main gate of the barracks, so I came out over the wall of the Commandant's garden."

Ilona kissed him, and murmured with a smile: "You are the most thrilling man. And that horrid priest deserved it. How dare he refuse a condemned man's last request. I have my own chaplain living in the house, and he is a darling. I am sure he will absolve you from what you did, before you go. But, Armand, you should never have come here."

"I had to see you, beloved."

"Oh, my love! I know! But you shouldn't have. You should never have allowed that to weigh against your life. You should have swum the river while darkness lasted. You would have been safe then. Now it is daylight; you have thrown away that chance, and are in mortal peril again."

Her lovely face now filled with alarm, she hurried on: "We must hide you, and provide you with different clothes. Uncle Otto used to come here quite often, and there is a whole wardrobe of his things upstairs. I am sure they would fit you. We'll hide you in the cellar for the day, then you must get across the river to-night."

De Richleau shook his head. "I fear they'll not give me much chance to do that. I hadn't the time to make a detour and climb the mountain, so I had to come through the village to get here. It was daylight then, and a dozen people saw me. They are certain to have remarked the presence of a strange priest in a small place like Hohenembs. To start with, Ronge will probably assume that I got across the river; but he's too much of a born bloodhound to take that for granted, and he knows I regard you as my protectress. As soon as he has made inquiries along the river bank, he will come out to Hohenembs. Someone who saw me come up here will give him the good news. He will ask you to surrender me, and if you say I have left he won't believe you. He'll picket the river to-night and put a ring of troops round the châlet, and keep them there till he gets me. I wouldn't have a hope of getting through."

The tears started to her eyes. "Oh, Armand, you were mad to come! It will kill me if they re-arrest you. What are we going to do?"

"I've still got a life line left," he smiled, and produced his letter to her from his pocket. "This, my sweet Princess, is a petition to you. It gives particulars of my court martial, and on reading them I think any lawyer would agree that I have been condemned on insufficient evidence. It humbly begs you to request Count Zelltin to stay the execution of the sentence until further investigations have been made. You can do that, can't you?"

"Yes. Yes, I can do that; but I have no authority in legal matters. I cannot force him to. He may refuse."

"I hardly think he is likely to do that. No officer would deliberately go out of his way to offend a member of the Imperial Family."

"But if he agrees: to what will it lead?"

"To my re-trial in Vienna."

"How can that benefit you?"

"It will give me time. I may get a chance to escape again. At a second trial I might be acquitted on the capital charges, and get off with only a spell of prison for having crossed the frontier illegally."

"No!" she shuddered. "No! The risk is too great. From what Adam said, the case is terribly black against you. There are those two Germans that you hit on the head and left half-dead in East Prussia. You can't possibly escape conviction for that. And they will never forgive you. Even if I asked the Emperor for a pardon for you, he couldn't grant it in a case like this. We are terribly dependent on Germany now, and dare not give offence to the German Ambassador. A re-trial could only lead to your being condemned again, and—and shot."

De Richleau knew that she was right. He had hatched his scheme when in dire extremity, with the object of securing a postponement of his sentence. It could still serve for that, but no more. He felt now that his other thoughts about Count Tisza coming to his rescue had been only wishful thinking.

Ilona threw a bare arm round his neck. "Your idea of a petition is no good, darling. It means that I should have to give you up to them when they come for you. Once Ronge has got you back into his clutches he will make very certain that you do not escape again. You are free now, and you must stay free. That is your only chance. How long do you think it will be before they come here?"

"They *might* arrive at any moment. My escape will have been discovered soon after five, when they went to my cell to get me. But I think it unlikely that they will come straight here. It is much more probable that Ronge and Count Zelltin have sent out all the men they can muster to make inquiries, and are sitting in the middle of the spider's web, waiting for reports to come in. Sooner or later one of their men will telephone that I was seen in Hohenembs, then they will jump in a car and drive out to question you. But that may not happen for an hour or two yet."

"I must get you more time, somehow." Ilona beat a fist desperately on her knee. "If only they can be put off from coming for a few hours, you could get away into the mountains before they put a cordon of troops round the house."

For a moment they sat deep in thought; then she exclaimed, "I have it! I will telephone them myself. I will say that you tried to break in on me, and that my people seized you—and that when we found out who you were Adam had you locked up in the cellar. I'll say that he had already told me all Ronge had told him about you, and I was horrified to think that you should have expected me to protect you. So I want them to come out here and take you back to prison. But not until half past ten; as I want to hear more about your case from them, and my doctor does not allow me to get up till then."

De Richleau smiled. "My own, you are a wonder. It is barely half past six yet, so if I can get away by seven your plan will give me three and a half hours' clear start."

She stood up, shaking back her long chestnut curls again. "We must not lose a moment. I'll telephone at once, before they have a chance to learn that you were seen in Hohenembs. Then I'll wake Adam and Sárolta. He'll get you Uncle Otto's clothes and provide you with a map of the district. Sárolta can have some food got ready for you while I dress. And I'll send for my chaplain to absolve you for having laid hands on that horrid priest."

As she made a move towards the door he checked her. "Even if it costs me my life, I must snatch a few moments to hold you in my arms."

She abandoned herself to his embrace, and they clung desperately together. Then she burst into tears and cried, "Oh, my dear one, my dear one! Why didn't you cross the river when you had the chance? Why did you have to come here and risk your life again?"

"For the same reason that I left France and crossed the Rhine on Saturday night. You look so beautiful that I can't believe it's true. But I had to see you again before—before——"

She jerked her face away from his and stared into his eyes. "What do you mean, Armand? Tell me what you mean?"

"I was in Paris," he faltered. "I went to a lunch in aid of a tuberculosis charity. A friend of mine who was running it cited your case as an example of how swiftly the disease can strike down a young and healthy woman. She had seen Bruckner only a few days before, and he had told her that—that you had only—not long to live."

"Bruckner!" Ilona exclaimed. Then she gave a queer laugh. "What Bruckner said isn't true, darling. It isn't true! I've a new doctor now—another Swiss, named Kutz, has been attending me since the beginning of the month. He has been working for years on a wonderful serum. I shall never be strong. I won't live to be an old woman. I've let things go too far. But he swears that he can check the disease. I'm not going to die, darling! I'm not going to die. He has promised me at least a few more years of life."

De Richleau was near to tears as he murmured, "Oh, my heart! How I thank God for this!"

Ilona kissed him again, violently upon the mouth. Then she sighed. "If only you can get away, we may be happy yet. This morning, just before you arrived, I was making marvellous plans. Dr. Kutz wants me to take a châlet in Switzerland near his clinic. If I went there you could come to see me. Even if you are a soldier, you could spend your leaves with me."

He nodded, his grey eyes shining. "Yes! Yes! I asked for a month before I left Paris. If only I can get over the river to-night, you could join me in St. Gall to-morrow. I've got to get away now! I've got to!"

"But you said it was certain that Ronge would have all the men he can get out picketing the river to-night."

"True! I fear he will. Then, much as I shall grudge them, perhaps I had better wait for a few nights before making the attempt to cross."

"You can't live for long alone in the mountains; and if you go to one of the farms the people might betray you."

"If you can get me a good start I'll manage somehow. The very fact of having seen you again, and hearing your wonderful news, will give me fresh courage and endurance."

Ilona stood away from him, put her hands on his shoulders, and looked deep into his eyes. "Is it really true, Armand, that you came back to Austria and risked your life only to see me?"

"Of course!" he replied, his devil's eyebrows going up in surprise. "Why else should I do so? I could not let you die without making the attempt to reach your bedside."

"Oh, but I love you for that," she whispered. "And how much I want to prove to you that I am worthy of the love you've shown me. Perhaps I can. I mean to try."

He smiled. "You have no need to prove your love for me. I have never doubted it. And if they get me, somewhere up there in the mountains, I beg you not to grieve too much. Think only of the happy times we have had together, and how infinitely poorer we would have been without them."

* * * * *

At half past ten, Ilona received Count Zelltin and Major Ronge in a small sitting-room. As they bowed before her, they endeavoured to hide their astonishment. She was now fully dressed, but very strangely for such an hour in the morning. Both her costume and her manner suggested that she was about to go to a fancy dress dance as Ophelia in the mad act of *Hamlet*.

Her chestnut hair still rippled freely down her back, but on top of her head blazed a diamond tiara. Beneath it her full red mouth made a splash of violent colour in her dead-white face. She was wearing a ball dress of oyster satin with a short train. Across her breast ran the broad ribbon of the order of Maria Theresa, and with nervous fingers she kept tugging at its ends. Her blue eyes sparkled with a hectic, unnatural light.

They knew that she had been very ill, and as she waved them to chairs, they wondered uneasily if her illness had affected her brain. When she began to address them in short, excited, sentences, they felt it must be so. Smiling brightly at them, she said:

"Do you like my dress? I hope you do. I so rarely get a chance these days to put on nice clothes for anyone. I hardly ever have visitors. And this is quite an occasion. First the escaped prisoner, then yourselves. He saw me in my night things. Wasn't that shocking? But I owe you an apology, gentlemen. I ought to have received you earlier, to tell you all about him. It's been such a busy morning, though. And such an exciting one! I have been ill, you know. They say excitement is bad for me. But I like it! You see, on top of everything else, I am going on a journey. That's terribly exciting, isn't it? After lunch to-day I'm going to Switzerland. I expect to remain there for the duration of the war. In fact I shall probably never come back. The doctors say that I shall never again be strong enough to resume my royal duties. I can't honestly say that I am sorry about that. Dressing up like this now and then is fun; but not dressing up day after day to talk with a fixed grin to endless people one has never seen before, and never wants to see again. In Switzerland I think I shall buy a *dirndl* costume and go about like a gay little peasant girl. I am sure it will do me a lot of good to be there. As I am no longer strong enough to be of any use to my own country, I might just as well live in one where my health will be better. Don't you agree? Yes, I can see you do."

They both politely bowed their acquiescence, and Major Ronge thought to himself: 'She is either mad or foxing. Probably the latter. She has dressed up to lend colour to this crazy nonsense, and is simply talking against time to give her pet Colonel a better chance to get away.'

Ilona continued to play nervously with her sash, but she knew that etiquette forbade them to interrupt her, and went on jerkily:

"How surprised you must have been when you found your prisoner gone this morning. And the poor priest all tied up in his bed. What a wicked man Count Königstein must be to have done all these terrible things. We thought he was a nihilist at first until we recognized him: then it came out how he had got hold of his priest's clothes. I am terribly proud to have caught such a slippery customer after he had managed to get away from such clever people as yourselves. He gave us very little trouble, though, and after a time seemed quite resigned. But what a fool he must be to have come here instead of swimming the river while he had the chance. He wanted me to get him a new trial in Vienna, you know. I wouldn't hear of it. I felt that he should get what he deserved."

Major Ronge regarded her with a tolerant smile. He guessed that she meant another chance to escape. But he was not worried. Count Zelltin had had his troops out in the mountains for the past three hours. If, as he suspected now, she had provided the prisoner with a change of clothes and sent him off soon after she had telephoned, he would not get very far. There were many hours of daylight yet, and they would have him back in gaol again before the evening.

"Of course," remarked Ilona. "There are fools, and *fools*, aren't there? He may not have neglected his chance to get away across the Rhine this morning because he is a born fool, but because he was fool enough to risk his life for a few moments with the woman he loves. I wonder if you had thought of that?"

Count Zelltin continued to look blank and to fidget uncomfortably, but Major Ronge permitted himself a slight smile. He had certainly thought of that; and he was sure too that he was witnessing the spectacle of a desperate woman fighting for time to give the man she loved a chance to escape from death. He did not think, though, that she could keep it up for very much longer; and he was right.

Ilona stood up, and said: "I expect you would like to see my prisoner. Come with me, and I will take you to him."

As they followed her from the room, the K.S. Chief hid a grin. He could guess what was going to happen now. She would take them to the cellar, unlock the door, and they would find it empty. Probably the bars of a small window in it would have been forced aside, and she would exclaim with pretended astonishment at the clever prisoner having got away again.

But she did not take them to the cellar. Instead, she led them to a door that opened into the largest room in the châlet. Outside it, she turned, and said with an excited laugh:

"I expect you are wondering why I am wearing my hair loose? But, as I told you, I am leaving Austria. I had it done that way this morning to symbolize my new freedom." Then she opened the door and they followed her into the room.

In it were a dozen people: Sárolta and Marie Nopsca, both, like Ilona, in evening dress; Adam Grünne and an elderly man who was Ilona's new equerry, both in full dress uniform; her secretary, her chaplain, her reader, nurses and servants. On a table at one end of the room a cold buffet was spread and in ice-buckets there were several magnums of champagne. All those present held a glass of wine in their hands. Near the table stood de Richleau, dressed in tails and a white tie.

Ilona led Count Zelltin and Major Ronge up to him. As her eyes met his, her nervousness disappeared. With her sweetest smile, she said to them:

"Gentlemen. Here is my prisoner. He came here because of his great love for me. And I love him so much that I could not bear to let him go. At half past two this afternoon I am taking him to Switzerland. I hope that you will join us in a glass of wine to wish us luck on our journey; and to console yourselves for the thought that in the four hours before we leave it would be quite impossible for you get a document from Vienna empowering you to stop us."

She paused for a moment, laughed with the splendid gaiety of youth that has broken all the bonds of care, and cried:

"I need hardly remind you that no member of the Imperial family can be arrested without a signed order from the Emperor. And half an hour ago my chaplain enabled me to increase the family circle."

Taking de Richleau's arm, she added: "It is my pleasure, gentlemen, to present you to my husband."

This book, designed by
William B. Taylor
is a production of
Edito-Service S.A., Geneva

Printed in France